Overheard at dinner in the Faculty Club—

"Speaking of Cadet Pruett, Jonathan, he couldn't get his mind off you today after soccer practice."

"Well, he is my aide. I guess he knows which side his stripes are buttered on. What was on Christopher's mind besides slide tackles and tomorrow's game?"

"Magic," RJ answered: "Witchcraft, covens in Main Barracks—that sort of thing . . ."

Advance Praise for *Rough Magicke*

"*Rough Magicke* is a compelling work of fantasy. John William Houghton has created a memorable character in Coke-swilling Annandale Military Academy Chaplain Jonathan Mears. Houghton knows his stuff, bringing the reader inside academic and religious traditions wonderful and strange. Intellectual and literary, *Rough Magicke* juxtaposes the arcane and the sacred while providing a glimpse of the divine. It's *Dead Poets Society* with a dash of *Harry Potter* and *The Name of the Rose*. *Rough Magicke* is worth checking out if you have the tiniest Shakespearean bone in your body."
—Mike Brotherton, *Star Dragon* (Tor Books, 2003)
and *Spider Star* (coming in 2006)

"*Rough Magicke* is *Goodbye, Mr. Chips* meets *The Father Brown Mysteries*, with the welcome and in fact sorely needed addition of witchcraft, telepathy, quicksand and magic rings."
—Mark O'Donnell, *Getting Over Homer* (Knopf, 1996)
and Broadway's *Hairspray*

"An occult thriller, scary, learned, and charitable in the true tradition of Charles Williams and his fellow Inklings."
—T. A. Shippey,
J. R. R. Tolkien: Author of the Century (Houghton Mifflin, 2001)
and *The Road to Middle-Earth* (Houghton Mifflin, 2003);
editor, *The Oxford Book of Fantasy Stories* (1994)

D1712954

Rough Magicke

But this rough Magicke

I heere abiure:

Rough Magicke

a novel by

John William Houghton

For Kathy,
A learned colleague and
an esteemed friend—

John W. Houghton
The Hill
25 January '08

Unlimited Publishing
Bloomington, Indiana

Unlimited Publishing LLC
Bloomington, Indiana
http://www.unlimitedpublishing.com

Book and cover design by Charles King. Copyright © 2005 by Unlimited Publishing LLC. The design for this book was created with Adobe® InDesign®, using the Adobe Caslon® and Adobe Garamond® typefaces. The book design incorporates one or more typefaces specifically licensed by and customized for the exclusive use of Unlimited Publishing LLC.

This is a work of fiction. All characters, products, corporations, institutions, and/or entities of any kind in this book are either the product of the author's imagination or, if real, used fictitiously without any intent to describe their actual characteristics.

Excerpt from "Little Gidding" in *Four Quartets*, copyright 1942 by T. S. Eliot and renewed 1970 by Esme Valerie Eliot, reprinted by permission of Harcourt, Inc.

Excerpt from "Among School Children," reprinted with the permission of Scribner, an imprint of Simon & Schuster Adult Publishing Group, from *The Collected Works of W. B. Yeats, Volume I: The Poems, Revised*, edited by Richard J. Finneran. Copyright © 1928 by the Macmillan Company; copyright renewed © 1956 by Georgie Yeats.

Excerpt from Revelation in the Revised Standard Version of the Bible, copyright 1952 (2nd edition, 1971) by the Division of Christian Education of the National Council of Churches of Christ in the United States of America. Used by permission. All rights reserved.

Library of Congress Control Number: 2005922296

First Edition

Copies of this fine book and many others are available to order at:
www.UnlimitedPublishing.com/authors

ISBN 1-58832-125-8 Hardback
ISBN 1-58832-124-X Paperback

Unlimited Publishing LLC
Bloomington, Indiana

For Dan, obviously,

and for my godchildren,

Caroline, Tristan, Rachel, and Emily.

Part I: The Constitution of Silence

Chapter 1: Friday, October 23

"MORNING, HOLINESS," a voice shouted from behind me as I entered the Humanities Building. "Where's your Coke?"

I didn't have to turn around to recognize the cadet who'd called: "Good morning, Keeks," I answered. "It's in my pocket. Aren't you going to be late for Mr. Acker's class?"

Climbing the marble steps two at a time, in accord with an academy tradition that had been old twenty years before, when I wore Annandale's blue and gray, Chris Pruett, the Regimental Aide to the Chaplain, soon caught up with me. "Aren't you going to be late for yours, sir?" The bell rang.

"Apparently. But I no longer have to answer to the Commandant of Cadets, and the class won't start without me."

"True, sir, but Mr. Acker hasn't sent anyone to the Commandant for twenty years."

"Twenty-five, I'll bet," I said as we came to my classroom door. "But that doesn't mean I can't write you up myself. Now put it in gear!"

"Yes, sir. See you at the soccer game." He saluted, more or less, and ambled down the hall to Jack Acker's room.

Reflecting on the absolute authority enjoyed by the faculty of a military academy, I opened the door to my own classroom, a generous rectangle, but crowded with twenty student desks arranged in a rough circle, my inevitably cluttered workspace, two mismatched bookcases of the some-assembly-required variety, a metal cabinet of AV equipment and a hall tree my father had once had in the breezeway of our home. With my seniority at AMA, I had a corner room—Jack could have had it, but preferred to have more wall space—with blackboards on one wall and a bulletin board, adorned with an old *National Geographic* map of "Shakespeare's England," on the other. One set of windows looked west to the Auditorium, the other south, over a parking lot and the Annandale Inn, to the lake that had enchanted my pioneer ancestors more than a hundred and thirty years before. Alumnus and native son, teacher and priest, I was as much in my element as one could hope to be. Tom Adams, the section marcher, called my Third Classmen—sophomores, in the civilian world—to attention.

"Sir," he reported, "the class is formed. One man absent."

I tried to look a little more military than Chris had done when I returned Adams's salute, but between reaching for my M.A. gown and trying to remember where I'd stopped in my lecture on the witches in *Macbeth* the day

3

before, I'm not sure I was very successful. A quick glance over the fifteen boys standing beside their desks didn't reveal the absentee; but my poor memory for faces is notorious. "Very good, Mr. Adams. Whom are we missing?"

"Mr. Brandon, sir."

"Oh, Larry? Where's he?"

"He's in court, sir."

"In *court*?"

"Yes, sir. They said he's getting a divorce from his parents, sir."

So much for keeping the chaplain up to date on counseling problems, I thought to myself. " 'Emancipation' is the word, I think, Tom, not 'divorce.' But we can look it up during vocabulary drill. Give the class 'Seats,' please."

It was an uneventful day, to tell the truth, until eighth (and last) period, my second daily section of First Classmen. While some schools offer their seniors a variety of elective English courses, in preparation for college, my department has always felt that the graduating class needs some common experience. Consequently, First Class English is a course in Modernism, and we were discussing *The Sound and the Fury*, concentrating on Faulkner's use of motifs to give unity to the novel: it was a subject I had found more stimulating before I discovered that it is covered in one of the most popular cribs for the book. But some things are too important to let drop, even if they are soiled in the marketplace. Annandale, after all, has long prided itself on having both more Medal of Honor winners and more Rhodes Scholars than any other prep school in the country of equivalent age, and the boys usually rise to the challenge of a demanding curriculum. On this particular day, though, it was obvious that about half the class had used the crib notes, and I finally sent the lot of them away, telling them to come back next week with the book read. They had the decency to look embarrassed as they filed out.

Two of the kids hung around—Rob English, a silver striper (that is, an aviation cadet—we have infantry, artillery, and cavalry as well, and a naval program in the summers) who was the first from his squadron to have been made Regimental Commander, and Richard Platt, in the red-striped trousers of the artillery battalion, where he was personnel officer, the cadet with general responsibility for the morale and *esprit de corps* in his unit.

"What's wrong, guys?" I asked, taking a last sip from the Coke—my fourth of the day—which I had been nursing all period. "Are you the only innocents in this mass of perdition?"

"Not that innocent, sir," Platt answered. "I've read the notes, too. But I never would have picked up the business about honeysuckle blossoms, gasoline and camphor if you hadn't explained it."

"Thanks, Dickey. I'm glad there's still some use for me. And that motif of odors is a favorite example of mine, because most people *will* use some repeated *picture*, and I have such a rotten visual imagination. In any case, since you've made your confession, why don't you try that assignment on Dilsey for your penance? The extra credit couldn't hurt."

"Well, sir, that's true," he said, running a hand through his dark brown hair and allowing himself an embarrassed if non-committal smile.

"Actually, Father," Rob said, "confession is more in the line of what we wanted to talk to you about. You know, more the biretta than the mortar board."

"Oh, I see," I responded, trying now to read their faces for some hint of what was up. Rob was so fair that he could probably have gotten by without shaving for two or three days in a row—though that wasn't the sort of attitude that had made him the highest ranking cadet in the corps. His jaw was square, his eyes (just on a level with my own) an unrevealing blue. I realized, irrelevantly, how infrequently one saw his eyes: he managed to wear his pilot's sunglasses almost constantly, just the way some of the troopers gave the impression of sleeping in their boots and spurs. Dickey (or rather, Richard, as he'd reminded me often enough), who'd gone over to shut the classroom door, had brown eyes that seemed huge even from halfway across the room: they somehow counterbalanced his considerable nose, a feature which gave him, from some angles, the look of a rather startled rainbow trout. In this case, though, it was more than being startled: *whatever they want to talk about*, I thought, *this boy is scared.*

I gestured toward the stole that hung—a bit informally, I have to admit—with my M.A. hood on the coat rack near the door. "Do we need . . . ?"

Rob shook his head. "No, Father. It's not actually us. Something's come up in B Battery. Dic—Richard, I mean, talked to me about it at DRC, and I said we should see you before we went to PE." (DRC—Dinner Roll Call, that is to say, lunch—falls between fourth and fifth periods: so the two had wasted no time in coming to see me.)

Speaking of Phys Ed, I thought, *I have to go watch Keeks in that soccer game this afternoon. But it won't start until four.* "What about the Battery? Did you talk to the Unit Commander or the Counselor? Or the Battalion Commander, for that matter?"

"Well, sir," Platt said, by now sitting on the edge of a desk in the front row, "as you'll see, it's not the sort of thing we want to have a lot of people in on. That is the point of having a personnel officer, after all, isn't it?"

"Touché. I've just been obsessed with Standard Operating Procedure today, I guess. Well, come on: out with it."

"Right, Father. You may want to sit down for this, though: it'll take a while. Richard'd better tell you how it started."

I sat in the armchair beside my desk while Richard took a deep breath and began: "Okay. There are these two kids on my hall, a third class plebe named Rhys Kirkfleet and a third class sergeant, Tom Adams."

"I don't know Kirkfleet, but Adams is the section marcher in my first period class. In fact, his father had Rob's job my first class year. His given name is Geoffrey, after one of our classmates who died in a house fire."

"Uh, yes, sir. Well, as I was saying, Adams has always been a little odd—sort of a New Age type, playing with crystals and hypnotism and that kind of stuff. By itself, that's just been kind of a standing joke. But now Kirkfleet has gotten into the act, and it seems like he's making more of it, somehow. They're having these little sessions in Adams's room on Friday and Saturday nights, and that has me worried."

"Why? What harm can they do with a couple of crystals and a Ouija board?"

"That's not it, exactly, sir. Somehow, Kirkfleet is making it all into a religious ritual, and it all seems to be, well, queerly convincing, at least to the younger cadets. They're really beginning to draw people into this, and that's what I'm actually worried about."

"You make it sound like some sort of proselytizing—a Great Awakening, or mountain snake-handling: do we really need to be worried about that?"

Dickey looked puzzled, but Rob had followed my sloppy reasoning. "No, Father. When Richard said Kirkfleet had added religious ritual, he didn't mean *Christian* ritual. It isn't that they've lost any of Adams's spooky stuff: they've made it worse, almost sort of perverse. You mentioned the Great Awakening, but this is more like Judge Hathorne than Jonathan Edwards. These two kids are starting a coven, 'right here in River City.' "

"Oh, you've got to be kidding," I said—hoping, actually, that they were. "Witchcraft in Main Barracks? Aleister Crowley and Gerald Gardner right here? It's ridiculous—I don't believe it!"

I sounded too vehement: they both jumped to their feet. "We don't believe *in* it either, Father," Rob said, "but you'd better believe that it's happening!"

"Sir, they're doing something strange, something abnormal, that's sucking in a bunch of kids from my battalion. I don't know if it's witchcraft, but I know it's wrong. And those kids are my responsibility. Sir."

Richard's tone was, I suppose, what I deserved for answering their problems out of a sense of my own; it nonetheless provoked a certain degree of asperity in my response: "Yes, Captain, your responsibility, and your Commander's, and mine, before God. So what should we do with this burden of ours?"

"You're scheduled to be Barracks Inspector in Main tomorrow night, Father. Are you still going to be on, or have you traded off?"

"No, Rob, I haven't. I suppose I should have, to work on my sermon, but then I can usually get some writing done on Saturdays, what with everyone being off at the movies."

"Everyone who isn't in Room 319 of Main Barracks, sir. That's what Rob is getting at."

"Exactly, Father. If Adams and Kirkfleet are having another one of their sessions—"

" 'Esbats,' I imagine."

"Right, esbats. If they're doing it, we can try to join in, and then if you came by on your next inspection tour, you could look in to see what was going on, and have two reliable witnesses to start off with."

"And all of that without your having to send a report through channels. It's an idea with some attractiveness."

Dickey's smile was distinctly untroutlike: "You mean, you don't have a better idea, right, sir?"

"Right as usual, Richard. I'll see you two tomorrow night, then, in Room 319. Dismissed."

I noticed their salutes were getting a bit sloppy, too.

———

BETWEEN WATCHING KEEKS in the game (he's a good player, really, quick, with a good sense of position on the pitch, but he could write a book about how to trip people without getting caught) and facilitating the Jewish Services (the Commandant, Col. Somerset, wants an adult there, but I can't help thinking it is at the very least silly for a *goyishe* priest to lead the Shabbos worship), I didn't get home until fairly late.

My house is the place my brother Dan and I grew up in, in the part of Annandale my family reserved for itself when they were laying out the town. Between them, town and gown surround the north end of Lake Annandale, including Glenarm's Bay, which protrudes into AMA's campus, providing a sizable harbor for the summer naval school's use. From School Street, just west of my house, to the monument on the far side of the Academy that marks the pioneers' first campsite in the area is exactly three miles, spanning three sections of land. (In all the states of the old Northwest Territory, the pioneer surveyors marked the land they were stealing from the Native Americans off into 'congressional townships' of 36 square miles, numbered as sections 1 through 36 in an unrelenting imposition of Cartesian order on the wilderness.) The Academy and the bay take up the two eastern sections of the three, 17 and 18; the boundary between the town and the Academy is Pershing Road (Black Jack visited the school once, after WWI), which runs north and south along the section line between 16 and 17. Thus from my house, at Mears Street and Academy Road, to the Wabash Gate, where Academy ends at Pershing, is just nine-tenths of a mile, a distance Dan and I measured pace by pace for years—my father was a great believer in walking (or, admittedly, bicycling) uphill to school in the snow—until I got my license, about halfway through my sophomore year.

It's not a big house—only two bedrooms, so that Dan and I shared bunk beds until I left for Harvard in the fall of '70. But there was enough room for me and Dad when he invited me to move off-campus after Mother died, in my second year on the faculty. And when his own health required him to move to Happy Villa, the nursing home just across Great-Aunt Irene's cornfield to the north of us, there was plenty of space for me by myself.

I hadn't had supper at school, so my first step on getting home was to put a cheese lasagna dinner in the microwave. Then I sat down at the kitchen table to go through the mail. I don't get much correspondence at home: back in the days when everyone lived on campus, the local post office developed the practice of automatically delivering all faculty mail, both personal and business, to the Academy branch, but as a native son, I'd established a pattern of getting mail at 609 Mears Street long before I started work at AMA. Most of what came to that address, though, was junk mail or stuff intended for Dad. I was a bit surprised, then, to find a real letter in the box—until I saw that it was from Fr. Mathis, the Rector of Christ Church in Withougan, the county seat. For most people, it would have been more natural either to phone me at school or to send a letter to me there—or even, for the up-to-date, an e-mail. Herbert Mathis, however, had a private fixation on the fact that Annandale—both the town and the Academy—fell within his parish. If I, or some other Anglican priest, had not been the Chaplain, there would have been Mass in the Chapel only when Herb drove down to preside, probably on a weekday evening. The faculty, townsfolk and lake people who came to Sunday Mass at the Chapel would, according to canon law, have had to go to Christ Church instead, though I imagine a fair number would in fact have gone to the monastic services at All Angels' Abbey on the east side of the lake, or simply attended whatever services happened to be offered at the Academy. In any case, from the time of his arrival at Christ Church and discovery that the Bishop had explicitly authorized the locals to come to the Chapel, he has affected (always politely) to ignore my connection with

AMA, communicating with me as a brother priest who just happens to live in a neighboring town.

"My dear Jonathan," his handwritten note began, "I write to you privately, but in your capacity as President of the Standing Committee of the Diocese of Michigan City"—Standing Committee, I should explain, is sort of like the Senate of an Anglican diocese, elected by the annual diocesan convention partly as a group to advise the Bishop and partly as a separate power center to carry on relations with other dioceses during the year—"to bring to your attention certain concerns I have developed about the nomination of Fr. Donald Newman to be Bishop of Delaware." (In our church, each diocese elects its own bishop, but it has to get the consent of a majority of the other bishops and of the other Standing Committees, or else of both houses of the triennial General Convention. Some objections are usually lodged whenever there's an election, but it's almost unheard-of for a nominee actually to be rejected.) "Fr. Newman's election, I am sure, will attract organized opposition; for that matter, I have already received a request to join a letter writing campaign against him. The fact is, I do not think he should be a bishop; I do not think he should be a priest. My opposition does not, however, come from the same principles I understand to lie behind this movement: I have other information about the nominee. This information, however, is not of a sort which one would necessarily wish to have widely publicized. I wonder whether we might meet one day this week to discuss the matter. Given the demands of your own schedule, I could arrange to visit you on campus if it would be more convenient for you. With every good wish, Faithfully, Herbert+"

Coming from Herb, the offer to appear on campus was roughly the equivalent of alarms going off in a bank. I even thought for a moment about phoning him yet that evening, but reminded myself that nothing irreversible was likely to happen overnight. I had my lasagna and spent what was left of the evening working on a sermon for Sunday.

Chapter 2: Saturday, October 24

I SLEPT IN a bit on Saturday morning, but made it over to campus in time to visit the boys in the Infirmary and still be in my office in the Chapel by 10:30, which seemed a reasonable time to phone Herb. As I cleared away a small pile of memos to make room for a Coke can, I noticed that Luke Faber—Larry Brandon's company counselor—*had* sent me a note about Brandon's problems with his parents (or, rather, with his mother and stepfather).

"Christ Church rectory, Fr. Mathis speaking."

"Hi, Herb, it's Jonathan. I got your letter and thought I should call."

"That's kind of you, Jonathan. I've been worrying over this for some time, and even now I'm not entirely clear in my mind about it."

"It all seems quite mysterious. Is there a confidentiality issue involved?"

"No, not in any strict sense, though one might be able to develop some sort of an argument if one had the time."

"I see. Well, would it be convenient for me to come up some time today and talk about it?"

"I'd prefer that to talking over the phone, certainly. Perhaps if you were to come up this morning we could chat here and then I could buy you lunch somewhere."

"That's the best offer I've had all morning. I have to grade some essays this afternoon, but it doesn't sound as though we'll talk forever about this."

"Oh, no, not at all. We'll not take any time away from your students."

"Excellent. I'll fool around here and get organized, so I should be there by a quarter after or so."

"Wonderful. I'll see you then."

⁓

I'VE ALWAYS LIKED to take the little back country roads from Annandale to Withougan—I know most of them pretty well, and they mostly run along the section lines in any case, so there's not much chance of getting lost. I like the sense of being in touch with my native countryside, and I've also found that I can make pretty good time, unless I happen to get caught by a train on the old Nickel Plate Line. It was ten after eleven when I knocked on the half-open door of Herb's study, in the parish house next to the church.

"Father, it's good to see you," he said. "Do come in, have a seat. You'll see I can offer you a little hospitality—" he gestured to a glass of ice and can of Coke standing on a silver tray on a butler's table beside one of the chairs (our bishop's wife once described the decor of the room as "Early English Vicar," and I have to admit I had never seen a Coke presented to look quite so much like sherry).

"Why, thank you," I answered, taking my seat. "This is very thoughtful of you."

"Think nothing of it. I appreciate your coming to cater to my conscience."

"I'm happy to do it. What's the story?"

"In its briefest form, Jonathan, it's simply this: I have reason to believe that Donald Newman is not a Christian."

"Do you mean that he's a heretic, or are you thinking in charismatic terms, that he's never had spirit-baptism?"

"Neither, Father. Though I do think his opinions are heretical and I see nothing in him of the work of the Spirit, I mean that he may never have received the Sacrament of Holy Baptism itself."

This was startling news. The Anglican Church believes that baptism with water in the name of the Holy Trinity is the foundation of Christian life. Indeed, in its more bureaucratic moments, the Church tries to keep track of the baptisms of all its members, to the degree that every parish priest, if he or she has kept the records up to date, can look up the date and place and presiding minister for the baptism of every person in the parish. It's information that a candidate for ordination has to provide about as often as taxpayers give their social security number.

"That would mean he'd given misleading statements . . ."

"It would mean he's been falsely celebrating Mass for years, solemnizing invalid marriages, and for that matter performing invalid baptisms of who knows how many other people."

"Well, Herbert, presumably the sacraments he celebrated would be valid—at least for anyone who didn't know that he was a fake."

"Yes, yes, of course they would. But you'll agree that's no excuse from his side of the matter."

"It certainly wouldn't be. But we should go back a bit. What brings you to this suspicion? And what's the potential confidentiality issue you mentioned?"

"Those are, of course, connected points. I think you're familiar from your own divinity school days with the undergraduate Secret Societies at Yale." Herb, like me, had attended Cloyne Divinity School in New Haven, Connecticut: his older brother had studied at the city's other, more prominent, educational institution before he enlisted and earned his Medal of Honor the hard way at Khe Sanh in February of '68, during the Tet offensive.

"In general I am, yes. I mean, I know they're like our Harvard final clubs: fraternities for the Ivy League upper crust."

"Precisely so. And you know, then, that they take that secrecy very seriously."

"Sure. The story is that members of one of them will actually get up and leave the room if they hear the name of the club mentioned."

"I've seen it happen, in fact. Now, apparently, some of these societies initiate their new members by requiring them to do or say embarrassing things—or to confess such things in their pasts. Aside from the intrinsic titillation, the shared information provides something for the other members to hold over the heads of anyone who might seem likely to leave the fold."

"Right, I imagine they also play strip poker."

"I don't know, Jonathan. I imagine they think they can distinguish between the obscene and the merely vulgar."

"No doubt. But I interrupted you."

"Yes, well. We can take it, then, that these statements are given under expectation of strict confidentiality, although there may be some element of compulsion involved as well, either in the peer pressure to take part or in the desire to join the prestigious group in the first place."

"Granted, though to talk of confidentiality may be taking fraternity pranks a bit too seriously."

"Perhaps. But still, given that premise, if a person who had heard such a statement were to repeat it, one might argue that the expectation of confidentiality passed to the hearer, even though that hearer had not been a party to the original agreement, and even though the teller had in fact violated that agreement."

"I suppose so, ethically, though I'm not too happy with the idea that a person can create an obligation in another person by violating that obligation himself."

"I see the problem, but it does seem to me the inevitable conclusion. Let me pose another hypothetical example. In clinical situations, instructors and students often present cases they've seen, suppressing the identifying personal information to protect the client's confidentiality."

"Of course they do. And given the way this is going, I might also point out that that personal information does sometimes leak out. I think the names of a number of Freud's patients are known, for example."

"True enough. But, again, the presentation of the anonymous case presumably creates an obligation of confidentiality in the audience."

"I'm not sure I see what you're getting at. Surely these things are quasi-public—they're often published, for that matter."

"Yes, of course. But if someone in the audience recognized the case, he'd be obligated not to say so."

"Fair enough, I suppose."

"And if the hypothetical case involved the confessional, the case would be all the stronger."

"If it involved the confessional, the person who told the story in the first place should be defrocked. The sacramental seal is absolute."

"I agree. And if a hypothetical someone in the audience for a particular case thought it might be derived from a confession, though the presenter didn't say so . . ."

"I'd say the person should err on the side of caution, unless he had some way of finding out for sure what was going on."

"I'm inclined to think so, too. In which case I may already have said too much."

"I certainly trust your discretion, Herbert. I'm sure you wouldn't have said anything if you hadn't thought all these matters through already. But if you feel the whole matter should be placed under the seal, of course I'll treat it that way."

"I'm obviously of two minds about it, Jonathan. On one level, I wanted to speak to you precisely so that you would say something; on the other . . . Why don't I go ahead, and we'll just assume confidentiality for now."

"Very well. What's the story?"

"Did you have occasion to study with Eric Noel Thaxted in your time at Cloyne?"

"Eric the Red? No, I avoided him—a bit too liberal, even for my taste."

"And all the more so for mine. But, as it turned out, I had to take his historical theology course one year, because no one else was offering one, and I remember that when we were discussing the Donatist heresy, someone in the class objected that all this stuff was hopelessly out of date and that no pastor in a real church today would have to worry about whether someone had been validly baptized. Fr. Thaxted said that that was not, in fact, true, and that he himself could remember a case from not all that long ago, even, of a young man who had come to him because he was dubious about his own baptism. He went on to say that he'd told the young man that it made no difference, so long as he was 'firmly grounded on the foundation of emergent Being,' or words to that effect, which was simply disastrous advice, so far as I can tell. But the significant element is that someone had talked to him about baptism, relatively recently."

"But he wasn't a parish priest, surely."

"Not at that point in his career, no. He'd been in a parish right out of seminary, but that would have been back in the late forties. Of course, on my basic assumption, one of our fellow seminarians might have spoken to him; but it seems to me that someone who had been asked about the details of his own baptism as often as even a first-year would be past being merely dubious. One would have had plenty of opportunity to consider the matter, at the very least. An undergraduate, on the other hand, might actually be dubious. And Thaxted was chaplain to one of the undergraduate colleges for a couple of decades."

"So the likelihood is that an undergraduate asked him the question. Fair enough. That would have been the occasion for the confession we were discussing, I suppose."

"Yes, that's what I was thinking."

"Well, it's cautious of you, which is what I just suggested, but it seems to me that there are several reasons why the conversation might not be confidential. In the first place, if the student had not in fact been baptized, there would by definition have been no sacramental confession, though I admit there might have been a canonical expectation of confidentiality. Secondly, the conversation as you report it doesn't require the context of confession. Again, admittedly, anything can come up in confession, as we both know, but at least the issue itself wouldn't be cause for a confession, either in a technical sense or in the mind of anyone who wasn't surprisingly scrupulous. And then, thirdly, it is Eric Thaxted you're talking about, who must be the most unlikely clergyman to have heard a confession one can imagine. When he wasn't being so modernist he hardly even believed in God, he was adamantly Protestant. Surely he would have seen confession as a matter to be settled between the Penitent and the Foundation of Emergent Being themselves."

"Granting all of that, we are still dealing only with probabilities."

"Which make notoriously difficult ethical cases, I agree. But I take it there's another shoe to drop."

"Yes, right. This is, actually, the earlier of the two episodes, but it didn't seem significant until one had heard Fr. Thaxted's anecdote. My brother, Vincent, visited me once at college in the fall of 1967—he was home between tours of duty, I think—and we talked about New Haven, because I was looking at Cloyne for divinity school. Even as, or perhaps especially as, a Yale dropout, he felt obliged to give me the lowdown on New Haven and the university, and he mentioned to me that he'd been invited to join Lambda Theta, one of the secret societies, as a sophomore, not long before he enlisted. Apparently, he actually went through the whole pledging process, whatever they call it, then quit in disgust because it all seemed silly compared to the war."

"And I take it that disgust showed itself in tales out of school about this invitation."

"Among other things, yes. I don't need to go through the whole sordid business, but one of Vincent's larger points was that he couldn't imagine taking one's theological education in so irreligious a place as New Haven. Not only was the university infested with atheists and agnostics, there were even weird new religions claiming equal status with Christianity—not within Cloyne, presumably, but within the university. It was discussion of those—the first pioneers of what I suppose we today would call the New Age movement—that led Vincent by easy stages to comment on one of his Lambda Theta pledge-classmates. This was a young man whose initial sexual experience came, at a surprisingly young age, as a sort of confirmation arranged by his church. It was, apparently, a reconstructionist Christianity—the faith as it should have been, had it been designed by anthropologists. Confirmation, you see, was a rite of passage, and so, with a certain kind of logic, they substituted a more anthropologically sound ritual."

"I see. And for communion?"

"I'm afraid that, like some ancient heretics, they consumed various bodily fluids. I infer that they balked at cannibalism."

"That's comforting. What about baptism—I assume that's where we're heading?"

"Exactly so. In the case of baptism, at least as Vincent reported it, they turned to texts from Revelation, literally washing the initiate in the blood of a lamb."

"Rather like the old cult of Mithras. Whereas valid baptism requires water and the name of the Trinity."

"Indeed it does. Though might one not argue that blood is mostly water?"

"One might argue that, yes, but then so is strawberry gelatin. I think the outward sign of the sacrament has to be recognizable as the outward sign, or it can't function as a sign at all. But presumably this tale intersects with the Thaxted story to triangulate on Donald Newman."

"No, not without one other fact, which is simply that when we were introduced several years ago at a conference Newman himself told me that he and my brother had been pledges in the same secret society, though of course they'd been in different colleges."

"Even so, might there not have been more than one person in the same situation?"

"Well, yes, but that's part of my point. Newman assumed that I would know that he and Vincent couldn't have been in the same college. Do you happen to know how many residential colleges there are at Yale?"

"Around a dozen?"

"Thirteen, in fact. Now in the Greek arithmetic system, in what we call Ionic numerals, the letters also stand for numbers."

"As they do in Hebrew."

"Precisely. Now Vincent and Newman were, as I said, pledged to ΛΘ as sophomores. And the two letters, ΛΘ, as it happens, express in Ionic numerals the number thirty-nine, which is three times thirteen, as if to indicate the society's membership includes three people from each of the thirteen colleges—presumably a sophomore, a junior and a senior."

"Well, I certainly defer to your knowledge of Greek arithmetic. But why wouldn't Lambda Theta refer to a Greek motto, like most fraternity names?"

"I suppose it might do that, as well. But the societies generally pride themselves on not being like mere fraternities, and Lambda Theta is in fact the only society with a Greek name."

"And I take it you've established that Newman was an undergraduate in the college of which Thaxted was the chaplain." He nodded emphatically. "I see. So then Newman would be the representative of his college in your brother's sophomore pledge class at Lambda Theta, and also the person who told Eric Thaxted he had doubts about his baptism—assuming that Lambda Theta indeed has only one member per year per college, and that Thaxted was telling the anecdote about one of his undergraduate flock. But even so, Newman may have been properly baptized since then—how would Thaxted know whether or not the person followed his advice?"

"How indeed? I think the whole matter bears looking into, but I don't feel as though what I've been saying is definitive. The question is how, or whether, one could urge such an investigation under the conditions of confidentiality we have been discussing."

"I understand. And taking it all together I'm not sure that it does add up to a violation of confidentiality, always assuming that we dignify secret societies with the idea of confidentiality in the first place. Again, I recognize the need for caution in these questions of probability—but you're not saying that you know something as a result of violating a confidence, just that several para-confidential remarks from other people have made you suspicious of something. Why not just take this up with the Bishop?"

"Partly, Jonathan, because I have noticed the Yale diploma hanging on the Bishop's wall, and strongly suspect he would have belonged to a secret society in his own day; and partly because it is not the Bishop, but you, who are a close friend of Archbishop Williams. If some sort of discreet inquiries were to be made, it would be best that they came from that quarter."

"I agree. Would you like me to pass on the whole story to New York myself, or do you just need an introduction?"

"I'd be just as happy if you'd handle the whole affair, I think."

"Very well, then. I'll see to it first thing on Monday."

"Thank you very much, Father. Now I hope you're ready for lunch."

———

BETWEEN EATING, napping, and grading a set of execrable third class papers on irony in the "Prologue" to the *Canterbury Tales*, the time before my BI duty passed quickly, with little chance for reflection on the various questions Rob and Richard had raised. I ate SRC in the Mess Hall (the suppers had not improved in a quarter century), where I discussed faculty politics with the deputy commandant and Richard Davies, the history department chair, and was in the Battery B counselor's office—mine for the evening—by seven.

The L shaped Main Barracks is the oldest one on the Annandale campus, having been put up after the fire of 1887 destroyed the old wooden Lodge. It runs roughly east and west, with the short leg, the "Annex," at the west end, reaching north toward the Mess Hall. The halls on each of Main's four stories are uniformly floored in red clay squares, with uniform lime green ceramic tile on the walls to a height of four feet, and uniform cream-painted plaster above that. Dropped acoustical ceilings had been installed since my own cadet days, along with fluorescent overhead lights that gave the institutional decor an antiseptic gleam. BI's spend a lot of time counting: counting kids, out of duty, and things, out of boredom; I had served as BI often enough to know the layout of my two floors by heart. Four rooms on either side of the east end of the long leg of the L, then, on the south side, the two doors of the counselor's office (on the third floor) and the intern's apartment (on the fourth)—the only doors without windows in them—and the latrine and the staircase on the north; then four more uniform maple veneered doors on the north side and six on the south, including #19, the corner room. Around the corner, two rooms on each side, another bath and staircase, and the commissioned officers' room, #24. All the rooms are doubles, except for #21, a single because of the stair, and #24, which is a quad—47 boys to a floor, 94 in my bailiwick on the top half of the barrack, including those on leave, in the infirmary, or otherwise absent. "Otherwise," on a Saturday evening, includes attendance at the weekly movies in the Auditorium. At five after seven there were still twenty kids in the barrack; half an hour later I saw only six, one of them the orderly on duty at his little desk outside my office. Neither Adams nor Kirkfleet (he apparently lived in 321) was in his room either time. When I made my third tour, however, I found a towel blocking the window of Adams's door from the inside: a clear enough violation of the regulations, which do not encourage privacy. I opened the door and went into the darkened room, flipping the uniformly placed light switch as I did so. Rob called the room to attention and reported to me, with a very correct salute.

Seven cadets had crowded into the two-man room, all of them—even Richard and Rob—as naked as jaybirds: "skyclad," I assumed they would call it. Nudity, I knew, was part of the Gardnerian heritage of witchcraft, but however well it might be suited to Magick, it made their current military posture look a bit silly. The freckle-faced Kirkfleet I was able to pick out by elimination, since I knew all the others: besides English, Platt, and Adams, they were Jefferson Mills, the B Battery Personnel Officer, a Staff Sergeant who was engaged in a perpetual contest with the Commandant to see how long he could go between haircuts, and Mike Leone and Miguel Perez, third classmen from Troop A, whose predictable boots and spurs could be seen in the pile of uniforms tossed on the bottom bunk. There were fluorescent-marker drawings of pentagrams, the witches' five-pointed star, attached to the four walls, and a white chalk circle had been drawn on the floor. In its center were a red candle and a school letter opener in the shape of a miniature saber.

"At ease," I said. "What's going on here, Mr. Adams?"

"It's an esbat, sort of a séance, sir," he answered.

"Names are merely the consequences of things, Thomas. What are you doing, specifically? You're out of uniform, this towel is a violation, those odd little drawings are over the two-posters-per-room limit, and I imagine the Commandant would take a dim view of drawing on the floor. How does it all add up?"

"It comes from Wicca, sir," he said, "a nature religion. That's why it's best to dress, well, naturally. And the pentacles on the wall and the circle help us to concentrate—someone said they're like a pot to hold in the energy we create, until we're ready to release it."

"Release it for what?"

"Different things, sir. It depends on what people need."

"I see. How about this evening? Mike, what are you after?"

"Do you really have to know, sir? It's kind of embarrassing."

"Michael, you're sitting there on the floor stark naked: it's a bit late for embarrassment, isn't it?"

"Yes, sir. Well, I'm running for Student Senate, and I thought, what the hell, it couldn't hurt."

"What the hell. Quite. And you, Mr. Mills?"

"I'm partly here out of curiosity, sir. But I'm battery personnel officer, and most people who've had this job have been made lieutenants by Christmas."

"True enough. And you, Colonel English? Hoping to be a General by Halloween, perhaps?"

"Sir, no, sir."

"No 'sir sandwiches,' Mr. English. You of all people should know better." This was laying it on a bit thick, especially in front of junior cadets, but it was true—he did know better, and he would have braced any plebe who'd used the stereotyped but unmilitary expression.

"Yes, sir," he resumed. "Captain Platt and I were really just here out of curiosity, Father Mears."

"Uh-huh. Miguel?"

"My sister, sir." She was, I knew, a good deal older than he, and trying, under various hardships, to raise his three nephews by herself. They'd shown up in the intercessions at Mass more than once.

"And you, Mr. Kirkfleet. What's your cause?"

"I'm just the facilitator, Chaplain. But, sir," he said, throwing my comment about names back at me in its original Latin form, "if you really think *nomina sunt consequentia rerum*, shouldn't you stay around to see the *res ipsissima?*" (Which, being interpreted, is "the thing in its truest self"—"the real thing," I suppose one might say.)

So the kid thinks he's a Latinist, eh? We'll see about that, I thought. "*Immo vero, care discipule. Sed non nunc: brevi tempore, officiis meis completis, revenibo. Amicite. Accipisne?*" If I had imagined this antique way of saying "Indeed, dear student. But not now: in a minute, when I have my duties finished, I'll be back. Get dressed. Do you understand?" was going to put Kirkfleet in his place, I was mistaken. He followed me without missing a word (though everyone else but Rob English—who was in the AP Latin class—looked at us as if we had just stepped out of a UFO), and answered without missing a beat.

"*Comprehendo, Reverende Pater. Vesticepes nos vestiemus*," he said, meaning "I understand, reverend father. We youths will get ourselves dressed."

"*Bene. Festina, adulescentule*," I replied, that is, "Very well. Hurry up, youngster." *If you can alliterate in Latin, young man*, I thought, *we'll see how you do with Latin puns. You call yourself "vesticeps", that is, a boy with his first beard, but "adulescentulus" is both a recruit—a plebe, as we say here—and a noticeably beardless young man.* Whether he got the point or not, Kirkfleet didn't react, and I turned to English: "*Roberte, nonne accipis?*"

"Yes, Father, I understand. All the lads will be dressed when you get back."

As I went on with my rounds, I couldn't get Kirkfleet out of my mind: not just because the little twit wouldn't be one-upped in Latin conversation, but because his face seemed familiar. Though, if anyone had challenged me, I would have had to admit that, after sixteen years, they'd all begun to look alike. For that matter, if challenged, I'd have had to confess that my curiosity about Kirkfleet was mostly a way of keeping my mind off the anxiety with which I awaited the demonstration in room 319.

The boys were dressed when I returned, and sat down in what were obviously assigned places when I put them at ease.

"Chaplain," Tom said, "If you would sit between Miguel and Mike, we can resume."

"No, wait. Don't we have to recast the circle, Adams?" Jeff asked, the brass chevrons on his collar glinting in the candle light.

"Not if Father Mears opens a gate, comes in, and closes it after him," said Mike.

"But we've all left and returned without making gates, as far as that goes," Miguel added.

"Excuse me, gentlemen, but I don't think I'd better actually join your circle. So you can decide this without considering me."

"Thank you, Chaplain," Tom said. "I think maybe Mr. Mills is right, though: we've all broken the circle."

Kirkfleet answered him, with something as much like exasperation as a plebe was likely to get away with in addressing someone of such lofty station as a sergeant. "We can go on. We've never grounded the power from that first session, so it's like we never stopped. But let's get on with it."

As I was still standing next to the door, he asked me to turn off the overhead lights: "*Fiant tenebrae, Reverende Pater*," parodying Genesis: "Let there be darkness."

I answered him with a Biblical quotation of my own: "*Lux lucet in tenebris et tenebrae eam non comprehenderunt*, Mr. Kirkfleet. 'The Light shines in the darkness and the darkness does not overcome it': At least that's what St. John's gospel says. But you shall have your darkness for the moment, and we'll see what it can overcome." Talking Latin makes me verbose (as does talking English, some of the kids would say).

I hit the switch and sat down in one of the room's two standard issue chairs, between Richard and the door. Kirkfleet was in the center of the circle, facing east, staring into the candle flame. Tom sat at the west point, with Richard, Miguel, Mike, Rob and Jeff clockwise from him.

"I think we'd gotten to the meditation, Rhys," Tom said.

"Right," the boy said, and he changed his voice: it's a trick, sort of the opposite of a falsetto, that the younger ones pick up during plebe week, when they want to call step like the officers; but Kirkfleet was using it to particular effect. And now it was not only his freckles but his voice that seemed familiar to me. "Think about your breathing. Attend to the way the breath comes in and goes out, in and out, in an endless circle, an unbroken cycle. Breathe deeply and feel how the cycle of breath reaches to the base of your spine, breathe, and feel how it touches the crown of your head. Feel how the cycle of breath has tied you to the world, how your breath joins heaven and earth as your crown is in the clouds while you sit upon the earth. Breathe in and touch the sky, breathe out and touch the earth. Picture the cycle of which you are a part. Picture the cycle that is you and the earth and the sky, your breath and the spirit of life. Your breath is spirit and that spirit is a living thing. See it now as a living thing, see it as a beautiful green and gold snake, a snake that curls around, so beautiful, so alive, as alive as your breath, and this beautiful huge snake is rippling with the power and glistening in the light like gold and emeralds, and the strange thing is that this beautiful glistening snake is holding on to its own tail, it's making a huge green and gold pulsing circle, and it shimmers, the light moves around it in a circle just as your breath moves from the earth to the sky through you, moves through the universe through you and we're all breathing at the same time, and the light glimmers on each snake at the same time, now at the top, where the head joins the tail, and now running down the side and now at the bottom, and lingering there for a second and now running up the other side and back to the top and now you're all going to join hands and all six snakes are going to join themselves head to tail in an even bigger circle, and you'll pass the spirit around the circle, pass the breathing from one to the next, pass it on like a wave, so this side is breathing out as that side is breathing in, and you can see the light following the breath, following the spirit, around the circle of snakes, glowing on their golden bellies as the pulse of power goes around and now it's one great cycle of breathing, one spirit, one breath in all of you that makes the circle, that links the east and south and west and north, and the snakes have all become one snake, one giant serpent that circles around the whole world, and the power pulses around it with every breath the circle takes, and the gleam of light moves around it, the spirit, the breath moves around the world, around the universe, holding order in and chaos out and the spirit is strong, it is power, the golden serpent, the snake that encircles the world, is changing now, it's changing into a circle of gold, a ring, and the light of power still flashes around it—it's a ring of power, the power that life generates, the power that generates life, and you are part of it, part of the ring of power, and you can control it, you can shape the world that lies within the ring, you can raise power in the circle, in the world in the center of the ring: look! there's light in the center of the world, light that reflects, light that is reflected by, the pulsing light that runs around the ring of power and now a spiral starts out from that center, it circles around in step with the spirit, in step with the breathing and it picks up everything as it spirals and grows, it is power for everything, spiraling, power in everything, growing, growing, power for Geoffrey who is dead, power for lieutenant's stripes, power for wisdom, power for office, power to help a mother, power for understanding, and back to the beginning but stronger now, larger and faster, Geoffrey, stripes, wisdom, office, mother, understanding, Geoff, stripes, wise, office, mom, understand, Geoff, stripe, wise, job, mom, see, Geoff rank wise job mom see, Geoff rank wise job mom see, Geoff rank wise job mom see, Geoffrankwisejobmomsee, Geoffrankwisejobmomsee, GO!"

He almost screamed the last word, stretching his body as taut as if a current were running through him, and then dropping to the floor. They all slumped over, drained, and it was a minute before Tom spoke again: "Okay, let's ground and open the circle."

"Do not," Kirkfleet said. "There is something more: *Look!*" And there beside him, between the ridiculous toy saber and the blood red candle, lay a golden ring, an Annandale Military Academy First Classman's ring, the distinctive design that senior classes at the Academy have worn for nearly a century, each one presented to a rising senior by his patron in the graduating class at midnight on the last day of his junior year. He picked it up and held it out to me: "*Suscipe, Reverende Pater,*" he said—receive this. Without thinking, I stood, took a step toward him, and reached over Richard to take it. As my hand crossed the line of their circle, there was suddenly a cylinder of yellow brilliance from floor to ceiling, and both the ring Kirkfleet held and the one on my finger glowed with a pulsing golden light. I took the second ring, and even as I was stepping back, Thomas said, "Ground!" and recited the rhyme to open the circle. I turned on the lights without even looking away from Kirkfleet for a second: nor did he break eye contact with me, staring as if he had never seen me until that very moment.

"Gentlemen," I said, "I think it's time you were all getting back to your rooms. I'd like to see the three first classmen in the office immediately. Dismissed."

As I stepped through the door, Kirkfleet was still staring at my back. "Chaplain," he said, in his natural voice, "give us your blessing."

I turned, and he was kneeling. *It couldn't hurt*, I thought.

"Very well," I said. "The Lord be with you."

"And also with you."

"Let us pray. Visit this place, O Lord, and drive far from it all snares and deceits of the enemy; let your holy angels dwell with us to preserve us in peace; and let your blessing be upon us always, through Jesus Christ our Lord."

"Amen."

"May the peace of God which passes all understanding keep your hearts and minds in the knowledge and love of God and of his Son Jesus Christ our Lord: and the blessing of God Almighty, Father, Son, and Holy Spirit, be upon you and remain with you always." Rhys stood and turned away from me and the others: it hardly needed my years in schools to know that the boy was crying, but perhaps it was experience that suggested he should be left to it without interference from me.

I made a quick circuit of the halls on my way back to the office, and thus found Rob, Dickey, and Jeff waiting for me at the orderly desk. They looked a bit pale, though that may have been the effect of the hall lighting.

"Come on in, gentlemen. Have a seat. Here, Rob, take this one from the desk." (I had the time to wonder how Major Chadwick conducted business with only three chairs in his office.) "Jefferson, I don't know what Rob and Richard may have told you, but the fact is that my presence at this evening's ceremonies was not entirely accidental."

Slouching in a regulation straight-backed chair, he grinned, a curious sort of half-smile. "Oh, no, sir, I didn't think it was. Kirkfleet has been saying for the last couple of weeks that you'd be at one of the esbats before Samhain, I mean, before Halloween."

I sat down on the edge of the desk. "He has, has he? Well, we'll have to come back to that part. Rob's plan was for me to see the session myself and have two unimpeachable witnesses to whatever, uh, curious things might be going on. Remind me I have a couple of background questions on that score, too. In any case, as a first classman, your observations carry more weight than an underclassman's might. It looks as though we should be able to answer two questions: What went on here this evening? and Is this evening a typical one?"

"Excuse me, sir," Richard said, "I can see this is going to be very logical and detailed, but can't we just this once jump into the middle of things? What in the *hell* happened in there?"

"That's it, Father. Let's start with the good stuff. Where did that light show come from, Jeff?"

"Damned if I know, Rob. This is only the third time I've gone, but there's never been anything like that before. No one's even *said* anything about such a spectacle, for that matter. I guess it's part of the power of the mystic circle that we haven't seen before."

"Was that the only thing that was different, Jeff?"

"I think so, Chaplain. I don't remember any other changes."

"Oh, come on, Jeff. Dickey and I were just faking, to begin with, then the whole business was interrupted for about twenty minutes, and after that everyone was dressed. There's a whole bunch of differences."

"Well, sure, but none of those things should make the magic work *better*—if they have any effect, it should be to scuttle the whole business."

"He's right, Rob," Dickey said. "Usually they say magic only works if you believe, but even though the two of us were sitting there being pretty much uncooperative, something certainly happened. I think I know something else that was different though: it seemed to me like Adams was ready to close the show when Kirkfleet brought on the main attraction."

"I think that's right. Always before, we've grounded right at the end of the meditation. I mean, after all, the way the kid does it, you want to roll back onto your pillow and have a smoke afterwards."

All three of the boys smiled, and Dickey said, "Isn't that the truth? And all that business about big shiny pulsing snakes joining together. I think D. H. Lawrence writes the kid's dialogue."

"Read the crib notes on him too, huh, Richard?" Rob asked ironically. "Look, Jeff, what about the ring: has he ever produced an artifact before?"

"Not that I know of. That looked like a real Annandale first class ring, too."

"Yeah, guys. Too bad we didn't get a closer look at it, huh? It'd be neat to see it even now, wouldn't it?"

"Okay, Richard," I said, rising to the bait. "I *can* take a hint. I just wanted to hear what you all had to say before I put in my two cents' worth. Let me ask Jeff a question first, though: Is Kirkfleet's meditation always the same?"

"No, sir, Chaplain. He does something different every week: it always ends up in a spiral, though."

"Yes, I can see that it would. But the snakes-in-a-ring business was new tonight?"

"Yes, sir, completely."

"That's what I thought: tailor-made for the occasion. Okay, then, here's the ring." I handed it to Rob, who was the nearest of the three.

He read the date and initials from the bezel of the ring.

" 'LHE 1970:' that's your class, isn't it, Father?" I nodded, and he asked: "Who's LHE?"

"Go ahead and look at the ring, first. I'll tell you in a minute."

"Seems like the real thing to me, Father. What do you guys think?" He tossed it to Jeff, who held it so he and Dickey could look at it together. Richard took off his own ring for comparison.

"They sure look the same, sir: though this one is a different color of gold from mine. But I bet it's one of the standard shades."

"There's no way to tell, airhead. It's twenty-some years older than ours."

"Oh, right. It's in awfully good shape, though. Our rings aren't even six months old and they've already got some scratches—this could pass for brand new."

"You can't tell though, guys: it could be a replacement. People do buy new ones, don't they, Father?"

"Surely, Rob. After all, they do get lost or worn out. I ran mine through a leaf grinder once by accident: my little brother and I had to sort through half a ton of mulch in the bed of my dad's pickup before I got it back. In any case, though, you're all satisfied that it's an authentic first class ring?"

They nodded agreement.

"Okay, then. Jeff, who is LHE?"

"How should I know, Chaplain?"

"Now who's an airhead?" Dickey asked. "He wants you to look inside it, dummy."

"Oh, right. Oh, wow. Chaplain, there's no name in this ring, just a design."

"I know; I looked at it on my way back to the office. Go ahead and show it to the guys."

Richard glanced, and gulped, and passed it back to Rob, who said: "Let me guess before I look. There's a snake engraved on the inside, right? A snake holding its own tail?"

"Very nearly right, Colonel English: it's two snakes making one circle. And now for the grand prize: there are supposed to be only two rings with that engraving on the inside. Can you tell us where either one of the legitimate ones is?"

"Surely, Father," he said, still holding the artifact. And taking my right hand, he kissed my own ring. As he did so, a pale golden light played across his face.

"I'm not the Pope, Rob, regardless of what Keeks calls me, and there's no need to kiss my ring. But you're right: until this evening, I thought the only two rings with this engraving belonged to me and my brother Dan. Now here's a third one."

"Who's LHE, Chaplain? Do you really know?"

"The only LHE in my class was Louie Evans—Llewellyn Hyw Evans, Staff Sergeant, Battery A. He did his best to make me miserable for every day of the six years we spent together here. If I could have shot one person in my class, it would have been Louie. Unless, of course, I could have thought of something more painful and humiliating."

"Why would he have his ring made like that, sir?"

"To get my attention, Richard. To provoke me. You're right, by the way—it is a new ring; I've seen his original, and it didn't have that design. So he's spent a fair piece of money on this stunt."

"What's his connection with Kirkfleet, Chaplain? And why is the pattern in your ring so damn important?"

"I'll have to check Kirkfleet's database entry tomorrow to be sure of an answer for the first question, and the answer to the second would take a lot more time than we have this evening. Look: I'll have Pruett take tomorrow afternoon's Christian Athletes meeting, and we can talk about this in my office right after DRC, okay? I can give you the whole story then. Till then, keep this as quiet as you can."

"Not even a hint for us, Chaplain?"

"Come on, Father, you can't keep us in suspense all night."

"They're right, sir, come on."

"Oh, very well. The fact is, it isn't the design that's important, but my family—or, rather, the design is important because it's a sign of my family, a kind of Mears heraldry. Or a mark of Cain."

"What do you mean, Father?"

"I mean that magic comes naturally to me, Robert: it runs in my family. I'm a witch. Dismissed."

This time they hardly bothered to salute at all.

Chapter 3: Sunday, October 25

THE ANNANDALE MEMORIAL CHAPEL, "built in the Tudor Gothic tradition as a Memorial to the Gold Star Sons of Annandale who served their country in the World Wars, Korea, and Vietnam," as the guide-book says, stands about six minutes' walk from the center of campus, on a low hill looking out over the retreat parade ground toward the Naval Building and the lake. My oak paneled office-cum-sacristy, at the east end of the north aisle, not only looks nicer than the company counselors', but also has room for half a dozen cushy red leather armchairs and a couch well-suited to my penchant for afternoon naps (a habit which is almost unaffected by my constant consumption of caffeine). Altogether a better setting for a long story than Main 309.

Full Garrison Mounted Parade—with horses, trucks, howitzers, and an aviation fly-over—comes at high noon on Sundays, between Chapel and DRC. At 1300, the boys sat in my office in their West-Point-style full dress uniforms: that meant that they had come straight from the meal without going back to their barracks to change. With six years of service stripes and his staff sergeant's chevrons, Jeff looked rather impressive: though the brown hair beginning to curl over his collar at the back gave the gray uniform a distinctly Civil War flavor, reminding me that his middle name was Davis. Richard's rank allowed him to add a red sash, a saber, and, on his shako, a black eagle plume: all of which was suitably imposing, but nothing compared to Rob's Senior Captain's uniform. The silver aviation officer's sash was in itself a good deal flashier than Richard's artillery red, but Rob added as many decorations as an eastern European field marshal, along with the ivory-and-jewel-hilted Major General J. R. Nicholson, III, Memorial Sword ("presented each year to that officer, who shall, in the opinion of the Professor of Military Science and the Commandant of Cadets, exemplify the ideals of leadership, service, and manliness to which General Nicholson devoted his life") and an exceptionally large white eagle plume.

"I'm glad you're here, gentlemen—looks as though you were so eager to hear my story that you didn't take time to change."

"Uh, sir, correct me if I'm wrong, but aren't you still in your cassock, cincture and pectoral cross? Is that usual, or are we filming a remake of *Going My Way?*"

"Why do I put up with you, Richard? Tell you what—I'll unhook my collar if you'll unhook yours."

"You're on, Father," Rob said. "Go for it, guys. And let's get on with the story." He took the couch—rank hath its privileges—and the rest of us distributed ourselves comfortably in the chairs.

"Let me start back in, uh, '68, I guess it was, when I was a third classman in the Band and the big fashion in civilian clothes was Edwardian—tie pins, vests, and watch chains, that sort of thing. Like some cadets even today (ahem), I worried more about how I'd look in mufti than about the appearance of my uniform, and I wanted a pocket watch and chain something fierce. My dad—you know Dan and I were day students—had an old watch he was willing to give me, but there was no chain for it. Then my mother got to thinking that she'd seen something like that in my Dad's grandfather's things: this was a man who'd died not long after the Second World War, only the second American generation of the family—his father, my great-great-grandfather, was born in southern Indiana in 1818. In any case, we went up into the attic and looked through a trunk that apparently hadn't been opened in twenty years, and before long she had sorted out a jewel box from among the clothes, cigar boxes full of arrowheads, and so on. Of course, we looked inside right away, and you could see the chain easily: it stood out from the other trinkets, 'cause it hadn't tarnished at all—we knew it must be almost pure gold. So we stuffed everything else back into the trunk: except for the arrowheads, which we thought Danny would like. We got everything downstairs and told Dad what we'd done, and I went to our bedroom to put the arrowheads on Danny's desk and see how my new chain looked with a watch on the end. As I was doing that, naturally, I looked more closely at the pattern of the thing—and that was when I saw that every link in the chain was a pair of worms ouroboros."

"Worms ouroboros, sir?" Richard asked.

"He means the snakes biting each other's tail, airhead," Jeff answered. "It's the Wiccan name for it."

"Thanks, Jeff. Who died and made you the *Oxford English Dictionary*?"

"At ease, gentlemen. Father Mears is trying to tell the story, remember."

"Thank you, Rob. As I was saying, at the time I didn't know the Worm Ouroboros had to do with witchcraft—though I had read the fantasy novel which has that title, the book doesn't really have anything to do with human witchcraft. The chain did look awfully peculiar, though, and I wanted to find out more about it. Somehow, I didn't think it was good idea to start off by asking my parents, who had never seemed the mysterious heirloom type.

"Luckily, however, there was a bigger heirloom than this one still around in those days: my great-great-grandfather's Homestead house, that used to stand on the hill across the road from the Twin Sisters Restaurant north of town."

"You mean that place where there's like a barn and some sheds and then just a chimney where the house used to be?"

"Right, Jeff. I thought that I might be able to find out more about great-grandfather's peculiar taste in jewelry by looking through his father's house. So I waited till Danny got home, and swore him to secrecy, and we started planning to go out and play detective at the Homestead on Saturday, after we got home from General Inspection. My cousin Rafe, from over in Wolf Creek, owned the farm—no one had lived in the house since his mother died—and he had never raised a fuss about our poking around the grounds: though I confess I had never asked him if we could go in the house."

"Wouldn't it have been locked, Father?"

"Sure, Rob, but I'd paid close attention to the urban guerrilla warfare lectures in Military Science class, and no nineteenth-century lock was likely to keep me out for long."

"Did you just take your brother along for moral support, sir?"

"Well, that and to carry the crowbar and yardstick. Besides, any great detective needs a sidekick."

"Preferably one who's not quite as bright as the detective, right, sir?"

"He *is* still my brother, Mr. Platt. But I guess you're probably right about what I was thinking at the time, and I am the elder. In any case, with my shiny new driver's license, I borrowed Dad's car and we got out there about one o'clock.

"It was a Greek revival house, or as near as they could get in Indiana in the 1860s: a pillared front porch at the east end of a two-story box with symmetrically placed windows and matching walnut trees on either side of the front walk. I parked by the well shed in back of the house, and we ended up using Danny's Quartermaster Store charge card to open the back door."

"I knew he'd come in handy!"

"Jesus, Dickey," Rob said, "would you just let the man talk?"

"As I was saying, Dan got us inside. The first floor had a hall running through to the front porch, with a kitchen and a dining room on one side and two parlors on the other—of course, they were all empty by then—Rafe had auctioned off the furniture after his mother passed away. Danny wanted to search those rooms first, but they looked pretty ordinary, not exactly the places you'd expect to find a worm ouroboros. I'd heard my Great-Great-Aunt Chloe (who was actually younger than her nephew my grandfather) talk about the Grange having met in one room of the house, and, figuring that such a great hall would have been the strangest part of a farm building, I wanted to start our investigations there. None of these first floor rooms was big enough for a meeting. So we went upstairs, where there were four bedrooms at the back, and, all across the front, a huge brightly lit space that obviously had to be the old Grange meeting room, with doors that opened out on to the balcony of the front porch.

"Well, measuring and tapping on the walls and such didn't turn up any hidden rooms or secret doors. Finally, the only things left were the ceiling, which we couldn't reach without a step-ladder, and the floor, which was covered with "Leave It to Beaver" era linoleum. So we pulled some tacks (I tried not to think what Rafe might say, much less Mom and Dad), and pretty soon we were ready to roll up the linoleum. It was a little stiff, but not old enough to be brittle, and between us, we managed it fairly well. And there in the floor, inlaid in a different color of wood, we saw a great circle, in the form of two snakes devouring each other's tail.

"From where we were standing, next to the roll of linoleum, we could see that there were things written on the floor at the compass points, but the lettering was too small for us to read. I left Dan to keep the flooring rolled up while I read the inscriptions. As it happened, the south point was the closest one, so I went to it first. It was in Latin, with some words that weren't in my vocabulary, but I could see it started off in the general neighborhood of 'your holy archangel Gabriel' and ended up three paragraphs later with 'through Jesus Christ our Lord, Amen.' I ran to the other points, and sure enough, each one of them was a prayer about an archangel. Danny, of course, was pestering me to know what I'd discovered, and I was too excited to stop and tell him. The center of the room had an even longer message, with different parts apparently addressed to the different persons of the Trinity. 'Come on, Jon-jon,' Dan said. 'What is it?'

" 'Come here and see,' I answered. 'The linoleum won't any more than unroll.' In fact, it did unroll a bit, but we hardly noticed: because when Danny stepped inside the circle, all the designs on the floor began to glow—it was a pale blue shimmer in the bright afternoon light, but you could tell it would have been a lot brighter in the dark. And suddenly it felt as though someone were there, watching us. It wasn't threatening, exactly, but we were still scared shi—scared out of our wits."

"Doesn't he recover nicely," Richard whispered, earning twin hushes from his colleagues.

"What did you do, Father?"

"I think we both wanted to run for it, but we couldn't leave everything torn up like that. So we unrolled the flooring and tacked it back down. As soon as we stepped out of the circle, of course, the light went out, but we didn't stick around to find out all the permutations: just hustled out the way we'd come in and broke the speed limit getting home. Of course, the limit *is* only 20 miles an hour, but I did get us home in a hurry.

"I didn't want to tell the folks we'd broken into the Homestead, much less what had happened there: but I did want to know more, and so did Danny.

We sort of divided our tasks—Danny began to really investigate the family genealogy (Wabana county genealogies make the ones in Yoknapatawpha county look straightforward), and I did some discreet study of magic. Of course, at that age, neither one of us was a great scholar—but we kept up the work for several years, and kept each other posted on what we were finding out. It became our private, secret project. That's why we had the worms engraved in our rings.

"The house burned down over Memorial Day weekend in '75, though, and that seemed to sap Danny's interest in the project. I don't think we've really talked about it since. By then, he'd done some respectable work, and had traced the Mears family back to the 1600s in Hampshire, England."

"Isn't that where Gerald Gardner claimed to have joined a coven?" Jeff asked.

"Right, though not in our part of the county. Eventually, I added to what Dan had done, and traced the family directly back to the thirteenth century. You wouldn't believe the files I've got at home."

"And your own side of the project, Chaplain?"

"I didn't discover all that much until after college, actually—Danny was having all the luck at that point. I did find out about a cousin who could dowse for water, and my mother's father, who was some sort of a faith healer. But even those things were really sort of sidelines to Danny's work. The Academy library, of course, has only a couple of books on witchcraft and magic, and then in college, I was honestly too busy to get into the Houghton rare books library more than once or twice, though I could probably have answered a lot more questions there than I did. The house burning down, though, had the opposite effect on me from Dan: I got a lot *more* interested when I saw the resources beginning to slip away. 1974-1975 was my first year at Cloyne Divinity School, of course, and the Neo-pagan revival was just beginning, so that fall—fall of '75, I mean—I took an independent study course in Witchcraft as a Contemporary Religious Phenomenon. I read piles of Aleister Crowley, and Margaret Murray, and Gerald Gardner—the last of whom was an ex-nudist who is pretty clearly one of Kirkfleet's sources. Which reminds me, Jeff, I was going to ask you yesterday: have Kirkfleet and Adams conducted any sort of initiation as part of these rituals?"

"Not that I know of, Chaplain. At least, they've never said anything about it around me."

"Well, let's hope not. Some of the modern traditions I have been hearing about lately wouldn't go over very well.

"Anyway, my research for the paper made it pretty clear that all this modern witchcraft was just made up out of whole cloth: it all started long after the homestead house was built. So I had to look farther and think harder to make sense of what Dan and I had seen. I finally concluded that there are three possibilities when something happens that seems supernatural: one, it's really natural, but we don't understand it; two, God Godself has done something directly; three, angelic power has done something."

"So psychics," Jeff said, "would fall into the first category: human powers we don't understand yet."

"Right."

"And when you say Mass, or Moses parts the Red Sea, or whatever, it's God acting directly, and the human beings are just following orders."

"Right, Rob."

"But, sir, now we've got your third category left, and black magic and white magic both to be accounted for."

"Right, Richard. But it works. The general category is human powers getting angels to do what they want. There are two kinds of angels, good and bad, which gives you white and black magic; for that matter, Dante says there may be some angels who tried to remain neutral between God and Satan. And there are also impersonal angels, parts of creation that strike us as forces rather than persons."

"But, Father, that arrangement makes it sound like the person who's using the magic doesn't make a difference."

"I didn't mean for it to: of course a person would be morally responsible for the use of his psychic powers just as much as any other ability; and on the other hand, when God chooses to use someone, the person's moral character really doesn't make a difference. But in the other cases, I do think that there's a difference of attitude."

"What kind of attitude do you mean, sir?"

"I mean that most people who try to manipulate any of my three categories seem to be after power themselves—sometimes with good motives, sometimes with bad, but you don't see a lot of people who are into the disinterested public service side of magic. They may want power to do evil or to do good, but they want power."

"Don't you have power as a priest, Chaplain?"

"Not me personally, no, Jeff. The power in the sacraments belongs to the Church, and that belongs to God. It's not really about having power so much as it is about giving up power. What we're doing in there is making the remembrance of Almighty God's death on a Roman gallows: the difference between magic and the mass is the difference between Rhys Kirkfleet standing in the center of the circle of power and Jesus Christ hanging helpless on the cross."

"Speaking of Kirkfleet, Father, you wanted to be reminded about looking something up in his record."

"Right, Rob. In fact, I've already done that. But let me deal with two other points, first. One is that, in '75, while I was working on the project, I was home for Thanksgiving. By that time, I knew that Neo-pagan witches, at least, usually keep a written record, at least of their history and more formal rituals. Now it's 'rather dubious,' as one of my seminary professors used to say, to assume that modern Wiccans have really preserved ancient traditions: but I thought that I might as well look for a written record, what they call a 'Book of Shadows.' After all, the family had thought enough of their circle ritual to work it into the floor. There hadn't been any sort of book in the Homestead when Danny and I went there, unless it had been magically concealed; nor was there anything like a grimoire in my parents' attic. A phone call to a Wolf Creek retirement home confirmed that cousin Rafe's widow had sold the few things he'd saved from his mother's auction—though she didn't remember that there had been any old books among them. The only choice was to start asking all my relatives: sort of a bizarre parody of looking for an old family Bible. I started at the top, with Great-Great-Aunt Chloe—97 years old, she was still living by herself (except for about a dozen cats) in a house she'd designed. And, as it turned out, she knew about a big old book with some kind of strange writing in it."

"Knew what about it, sir?"

"Well, she didn't know what it said, of course—she couldn't read it. But she knew that she had given it to Danny when he and his friend came to visit, on Decoration Day that past spring."

"When's Decoration Day?" Jeff and Richard asked in chorus.

"It's the old name for Memorial Day," Rob said. "Has it occurred to you that maybe you're *both* airheads?

"Father," he went on, "can I guess the way this turns out? Was LHE the friend your brother took with him to see your aunt?"

"We've never talked about it, but after last night's episode, I'm betting that's who it was."

"And if it isn't confidential, can you tell me whether Rhys Kirkfleet's mother is remarried?"

"That can't be confidential, it's a matter of public record. Mr. Kirkfleet is her second husband: they've been married for about five years."

"So Rhys, if he's a third-classman, about sixteen years old, must be the son of her first husband, later adopted by her second husband?"

"Clearly, O Socrates."

"And that first husband, who gave the boy a Welsh name like 'Rhys' and suggested that he come to Annandale Military Academy, was your brother's friend, your worst enemy from school, Llewellyn Hyw Evans, Class of 1970."

"Nothing could be clearer, Socrates. In fact, my guess is that Louie Evans is even picking up the tab for Rhys to come here, despite Mr. Kirkfleet's having adopted the boy."

"Uh, sir," Richard said, "I don't know whether two people can be paranoid together, but aren't you and Rob suggesting that Mr. Evans is spending all that money, and making his son a cult figure, just to—what did you say yesterday, sir, to provoke you?"

"That's almost it, Richard," Rob answered, "but not quite—remember, the special effects yesterday evening all started when Father was in the circle along with the rest of us. And we know that Father doesn't usually put on these light shows by himself; so when there was magic last night, if it didn't come just from Father Mears, then the other agent must have been either Mr. Evans's ring or his son—or possibly both. In any one of the three cases, we must conclude that Mr. Evans is a witch, and thus that he did not *make* his son a cult leader, except by *making* him in the first place."

"Which suggests," Jeff answered, "that if Mr. Evans and the Chaplain are both witches, then maybe the one really is out to get the other. The extra first class ring seems to support that view of things."

Richard leaned back in his chair and laughed. "This is so fucking *strange*. I'm sorry for the language, sir, but, I mean, I'm sitting here, in the Chaplain's office, in the Memorial Chapel, at a hot shot prep school, and we're adding up who's a witch like people casting a production of *The Crucible*."

"Richard," I answered, "I don't know what to tell you. I don't know what to say to any of you: if I'm right about Louie's involvement in this thing, you're all being used to get at me, and, maybe, Danny. And if I'm wrong, I'm dragging you all into an elaborate paranoia of my own. Either way, it's the old story of kids caught in the middle of the adults' games: and you shouldn't be stuck there."

Rob stood up and walked over to stand behind Richard's chair. "Excuse me for saying so, sir, but that is both the stupidest and the most insulting thing I have ever heard you say. What do you think all this crap on the uniform means? Do you think we're wearing this stuff just because we want to look like Patton and Montgomery in fancy dress? My grandfather was a general, and my uncle and father are both colonels. If I just wanted to play dress-up with uniforms, I could have stayed at home in the den. When I took this job and let them put all these stripes on my sleeve and this sword into my hand, I put *myself* into the middle of a thousand kids, a hundred and fifty faculty and staff, and more parents than I care to count. The same thing's true of Richard in his battalion and Jeff in his battery. Now the system may be wrong to offer that kind of responsibility to a high school senior, but I took it on consciously and eagerly, and I think the system works. It made me, and whatever else that ring on your hand may signify, it sure as hell means the system made you too. You talked a good game about responsibility on Friday: now let's see you stick with it on Sunday. Sir."

There followed a short pause while I stopped blushing. "Do you guys all feel that way?" I asked.

"Yes, sir. I knew what I was doing when I took a commission."

"Damn right, Chaplain. Besides, I was going to meetings before you and Rob and Dickey got into it, and nobody forced me to be there. So let's just get on with this. I have a specific question."

"Shoot."

"It's this: what's Evans's motive?"

"My guess is that the answer to that is, or was, in Aunt Chloe's book. I think I may have seen some Evanses mentioned way back in family records; but it's an awfully common name. And it has always looked to me as though the Mearses came to this country two hundred years ago in the attempt to escape from something. That's all I know without doing some new research."

"Thank you, Father," Rob said, in his best take-charge tone: whether born or made, he *was* a leader. "That would seem to give us about as much of the basic information as we're likely to get. So the question is, what shall we do about it all? We need to think about goals, strategy and tactics. Could we use that marker board, Father? Thanks. And Richard, do you mind taking notes? Thanks. Oh, and, uh, are there any Cokes in the refrigerator, sir?"

"Sure. Everybody want one?" They all nodded, and I walked over to the door of the walk-in safe behind my desk—part of the sacristy furnishings, it held the vestments, altar plate, and a small refrigerator for bread and my Coke supply (I think the first chaplain, a Methodist, used it for grape juice). More recently, the safe had also become the home of the mysterious LHE ring.

"Okay, goals first," Rob said. "What do we want to achieve? Let's brainstorm. Jeff?"

"Find the book."

"I want to get the séances out of my battalion, out of the corps," Richard said.

"Stop Mr. Evans from using Kirkfleet."

"And Adams and Perez and Leone and all the rest of them," I added from across the room.

"Find out how it works."

"End the feud, or whatever it is."

"Anything else?" Rob asked. "Go ahead, Richard."

"I think we need to act quickly, before they get any other kids in on this."

"Fine. Is that it? Okay, if I can take that marker, it looks to me like these fall into three groups: first, we've got Jeff's research questions, finding the book and finding out how the magic works. Second, we have the adult issues, stopping Mr. Evans's manipulation of Rhys and ending the feud. And third, we have the specifically regimental issues: stopping the sessions; counseling the participants; and preventing the spread of this business, presumably by acting quickly. Does everyone agree with that organization?"

"Yeah," Jeff said, "that makes sense, but I'm not sure you can actually divide the task up that way. The Chaplain probably can't settle the feud without reading the book, and I bet Richard won't see the last of the esbats until Evans is out of the picture or Kirkfleet is expelled. It all ties together."

"Exactly. Which answers one of Father's possible objections, that the first two categories are none of our business." (I had returned and was handing him a soda.) "Thank you, Father."

"First, I have to sit here in my office and be dressed down by a teenager, now people are explaining why I'm wrong before I even get a chance to talk. God, I love teaching! Here, have a Coke, Richard."

"It's okay, sir. It's just a sign of affection. Rob never talks that way to Lieutenant Brennan. Of course, Lieutenant Brennan combines the insight of Charles I with the breeding of Attilla the Hun, but he serves to make the point."

"I'm always enlightened by your comparisons, Richard."

"Think nothing of it, sir. It's a free service."

Rob was anxious to get back to the point: "If you're quite through with the vaudeville act, gentlemen, let's go ahead, shall we? I think I've named things in cause and effect order. We certainly can't stop Rhys without doing something about his father, and ending the feud is the best, if not the only, way to do that. I'm not sure, though, that we need the book to end the feud."

"Well, clearly, I could quit and move away. As I've said, if it really is a feud, we've been running from the Evanses for two hundred years."

Rob frowned. "You're a slow learner, Father. Granted that your leaving would solve our problem here, would it stop Mr. Evans from using Rhys to get at you? No. Would Rhys inherit the next generation of the feud? Yes, almost certainly. And is Rhys Kirkfleet part of your cure of souls?"

"Yes, of course. He's even Anglican, for that matter. So I can't run away because I'm my enemy's keeper. Fine. The only other choices are to talk him out of it—"

"Which means," Jeff interjected, "that you need the history part of the book to know what you're talking about."

"Probably. Or I can stand and fight."

"Which means a magical duel, for which you would need to learn the spells in the magic part of the book."

"Again, probably, Jeff, but not necessarily. I can assure you, though, that this priest is not going to engage in a duel arcane. I prefer to keep all of my magic in there under that little red lamp; and besides, I come from a long line of pacifists: I won't fight with any weapon, magic or not, not even to save myself or my family."

Rob looked out the window with a sort of grim smile that suited his uniform better than his years. "Well, Father, I think that settles the question of strategy. Given your principles, you can only put an end to the Evans family's abuse of power by some sort of submission to it that will transform the whole feud. Which brings us to tactics. What can we specifically do about this, and on what schedule?"

"Well, I can call Danny and try to get the book from him. But it's been almost twenty years, and he's never said anything about it: so let's not count on it."

"Still, it has to be looked into. Thank you, Father. Assuming we do get it, the next step is for you to try to talk Mr. Evans out of this. If that works, there's an end on it: the only thing left will be the counseling of the cadets involved. If it doesn't work, which is my guess, then we come to a confrontation, in which case we use the book to look for a win-by-losing solution to the magical duel."

"Preferably one that saves the Chaplain, I think," Jeff said.

"Yeah," Richard agreed, "That'd be nice. I'd hate to have to find another straight man."

"Right, Dickey," said Rob. "And since we end up in the same place but worse without the book, I think that keeping him around is what we have to focus on. What can we do to guarantee that this duel will turn out the way we want? I assume Father would have the choice of weapons."

"Not weapons, but rituals," Jeff interjected. "Magic is the weapon."

"You know, Mr. Mills, I'm beginning to think I'm not the only one who's read through the Library's magic collection," I said. Jeff shrugged noncommittally.

"In any case," I went on, "as I understand it, if I accept a challenge from him, I get to choose the ritual for casting the circle, though he—or his champion—can assist. Logically, I should use my grandfather's circle spell, which had the benefit of being explicitly Christian. That much I can do, even without the book, because I reconstructed the words from other sources while I was at Cloyne. And the whole thing is just a detailed version of what we call a 'Procession with Stations,' so I have no religious compunctions about using it. For that matter, I ought logically not only to use the family ritual but also the family house, if it were still standing. This sort of thing is very territorial."

"Why not do it right here, Chaplain? The Chapel is at least as much your space as the house would have been."

"No, Jeff. Even if everything I might do is appropriate to a church, that's no sign that Evans might not commit some desecration. Besides, the Chapel belongs to the school, not to the Mearses: and not to the diocese, either—even under canon law, I'm not in formal possession of the church."

"What about the ruins of the house, sir? Is it safe to go out there? Is there anything left of it?"

"Not really, after so long," I said, fingering my pectoral cross. "But I do have this cross: it's made out of nails that I took from the ashes. It might be enough. Certainly, the place is safe enough, as far as that goes. Good idea, Richard. But I don't know what I could actually do inside such a circle to follow Rob's strategy. The magic books I've read have a rather different ethos, as you might expect, and I don't think it would get us anywhere to cast the circle and then sit down to sing Vespers."

"Father, did you say Kirkfleet was an Anglican?"

"That's what it says in the computer, Rob."

"Well, Tom Adams described Rhys as a Wiccan. I wonder if he's actually been converted to Neo-paganism."

Jeff Mills leaned forward in his chair: "He can't very well be a convert: he's not exactly a Christian in the first place. At least, he said last week that he'd never been baptized."

"That could be part of the routine," Richard suggested.

I got up and went over to my file cabinet. "It's easy enough to check," I said, "I've got a more detailed religious record for all the Anglicans whose parents bothered to fill one out. See, here they are. And the Kirkfleets, being nice cooperative types, have filled in all the little blanks.

"Oh-ho, isn't this interesting: he's a catechumen. I've never seen one in the flesh. You're right, Jeff, he's not baptized: but he's been given formal instruction to prepare him for it. That's the theoretical norm, but you almost never see it done. I should look into that."

That was the moment, I guess, at which Jeff thought of A Plan. "Suppose he still wanted to be baptized, Chaplain. Could it be done?"

"Surely, Jeff, all it takes is water. It'd be best to wait until a major feast, though, like Easter or Pentecost."

Rob thought for a moment and picked up my prayer book from the corner of the desk. "Yeah, here's the list: the feasts or vigils of Easter, Pentecost, the Baptism of Christ, and All Saints' Day—that's a week from today."

"True enough, fearless leader. Dickey and I could certainly keep the lid on for that long. What are your plans for Halloween, Chaplain Mears?"

"You've got to be kidding!" I exclaimed. "I can't use the sacraments of the Church to carry out my private vendetta. That's inconceivable!"

"Of course it is, Father. But you can carry out the sacraments of the Church at the appropriate time, even if you know that someone else means to interfere because he has a vendetta against you. The early church went on meeting in the catacombs, and Becket went to Vespers with the king's men at the door."

"Only in the books, Rob! The real Becket was dragged into the cathedral by his monks—by three young ones, I imagine." I sighed. "I'll have to think about it, Rob, and talk to the boy. But it doesn't sound right."

"That's okay, Father. We'll think of something."

"Right," I answered, and, sitting down at my desk, rested my head on my hands. "I won't make the mistake of saying again that you all shouldn't be involved in this, but at least let me say I'm grateful that you take your duty so seriously. Thanks."

"You're welcome, sir," Richard said. "But remember Lieutenant Brennan: duty's important, but so are respect and affection."

This time it was my turn to stare at the carpet. "Thanks, Richard," I said.

Rob brought them to attention and reported their departure.

I returned his salute with a vague wave of the hand.

———

I CALLED DANNY that night, after eleven. As usual, I had to let the phone ring about a dozen times. I've never been able to visualize things, to see what's not actually there in front of me, but, sitting in the living room of the house in which the two of us had grown up, even I could almost picture my brother. Always thinner, slighter of build, than I, he has been the taller brother since he was about fourteen. His thick brown hair is about the same shade as mine was before it faded and thinned to its present sparse clerical gray. His thick-lashed eyes are deep brown: I remember how, when we were young, he looked like one of those self-consciously "touching" baby animals in popular art, the ones whose dark eyes seem the size of dinner plates. I guess, for that matter, that his dark brown gaze remained attractive after childhood: at least, it was, not the only, but the most immediately observable, explanation for the lengthy romantic career that had preceded his marriage (at All Saints' Chapel in Sewanee, the day after his and Susan's graduation) and followed his divorce.

"Hello?"

"Hi, little brother. How's it going?"

"Pretty good. You?"

"Oh, I'm fine. Can't afford to be anything else."

"And Dad?"

"I haven't been over to the home since Thursday, but I'm sure he's okay. There's no real change from one day to the next, and he doesn't really know anyone anymore anyway. Just sits there in his old blue bathrobe and stares into space. Is Caroline okay?"

"Oh, sure. She's with Susan this weekend. What's new?"

"Not much. It's something old I'm calling about, actually—an old book."

"Still after my Swedish Erotic Movie Catalog, huh?"

"You've had it for twenty years that I know of, Dan. I doubt if there are any pages that haven't been worn through yet."

"Well, there are one or two that are more to your taste than mine, Jonathan. Seriously, though, what's the book?"

"Thomas Mears's Book of Shadows: the old family grimoire you got from Aunt Chloe on Memorial Day of 1975."

"That's pretty specific."

"There are more efficient ways of insulting me than pretending I'm stupid. Don't dodge the question."

"I can't talk about it, Jon. I'm sorry, but I can't."

"This isn't the Arson Squad, little brother. It's me. The one in the top bunk. The one you could talk to about Santa Claus. The one you could talk to about buying Trojans. The one you could talk to when Susan left."

"Arson, huh? Sounds like you don't need to learn anything from me, anyway."

"Just about the book. Look, let me make this easy. I'll tell you what I think happened. You stop me if I'm wrong. Memorial Day of '75 was Alumni Weekend at the Academy: my class's fifth reunion. You were already home from college for the summer. Sometime over the weekend, Louie Evans, who was back for the weekend, talked to you about magic. He seemed to know you were a witch; in fact, he knew a lot more about it than we did. And he didn't seem to see anything wrong with it. He suggested there must be family records around somewhere. One way or another, you ruled out the Homestead itself: that made Aunt Chloe the obvious place to start, since she was the eldest and lived closer than Rafe. She gave you the book with no arguments. The two of you took it to the Homestead, rolled up the linoleum, and stepped into the circle with the book. Something happened. And by the time the dust settled, the house was burned and your interest in the project was gone. And now Louie's son is here at the Academy starting a coven in Main Barracks, and giving me a first class ring with Louie's initials on the outside and our worms on the inside."

"You know a lot, Jon. But you've got to *listen* to me. You may be a witch, you may be my brother: but you're also an English teacher. I said, I *can't* talk to you about it."

"Okay, can't, not won't! Dammit, Danny, what's stopping you?"

"Not what, who."

"You mean someone's there?"

"No, I'm here all alone in my little log cabin in the woods. I was just sitting here having a little drink and watching a little fire burn in my fireplace. I wonder how many of our witch ancestors were burned at the stake? It must be a horrible death, burning alive."

"I'm sure it is: but none of our ancestors were burned. They hanged witches in England. Listen, Danny, I think I'm catching on. I'm here in the living room at home, and while we talk I'm walking over to our fireplace, making sure that the damper is open and the glass doors are shut, and I'm picking up that portrait from the mantle, the double one with you and me that we gave the folks on their twenty-fifth anniversary. And now I'm slipping into the kitchen to grab the fire extinguisher just in case. You follow me, right?"

"Sure. I could do all that with my eyes closed. In fact I've got my copy of that double picture right here in front of me, off of my own mantle."

"Good. You're one step ahead of me. Now I want you to look at the picture, see how we're standing with our arms across each other's shoulders. You can just barely see my ring next to your ear, and the way you're gesturing with your right hand puts your ring almost in the middle of the picture. Got all that?"

"Sure."

"Okay. Good. Now, I want you to picture me sitting here in the room, looking at the photo, just the same way you are. You know how I am about imagining things, so you have to have this crystal clear for both of us. You can see the picture, see my right hand holding it, see the ring on that hand."

"Got it. I'm holding the picture the same way. You don't have to imagine anything—it looks just the same here as what you're seeing."

"Excellent. That's just what I had hoped. Now concentrate on the rings, I want you to picture a light, a golden light, around them."

"Okay, a golden light: I've got that." I could see that he did: there was a very real light shining around my own ring. "Perfect, Dan. Now, do you remember the bedtime prayer we used to say together, the one about Matthew, Mark, Luke, and John? Without losing track of the light, we're going to say that rhyme together now, okay? Except we'll say 'chair' instead of 'bed' and 'sit' instead of 'lie.' And you picture the light expanding, until it makes kind of a dome over each of us. Ready, here we go:

Matthew, Mark, Luke and John
Bless the chair that I sit on.
Head and foot and either hand
Angels from the starry band
Keep me safe in Jesus' light
From all the perils of the night. Amen."

The startled gasp at the other end of the line confirmed that the same opalescent globe of golden light that had sprung up around me had also enfolded my brother.

"Congratulations, Dan," I said. " I think we've just set up the first long distance magic defense in the history of witchcraft. Now listen: before you say anything, understand that any force directed against this circle, if it isn't simply reflected back whence it came, will be channeled from that end to this, and from this out to the place I have prepared for it. That's safe, because Louie needs me alive for some reason—if my assassination were enough to satisfy him, I'd have been dead long ago. Now quickly, what's the story?"

"You've got the right idea, except that Louie had talked to me long before he came back for the reunion: he was the national president of my fraternity, and he came south for my chapter's induction ceremonies. We thought it was an honor at the time, and I scored a lot of points with the group for knowing the Grand Supreme President from school, and for having such a long talk with him during the initiation. I didn't tell you about that at first because it was a part of the fraternity secrets. At the '75 reunion, after we had the book, we went to the house just like you said: the pages were covered with some sort of gibberish, and Louie thought that they might change to something readable inside the circle—which would be why the circle spell is written on the floor rather than in the book. But when we got there, we couldn't even make the circle light up, though Louie tried a bunch of things, including reading all the Latin prayers written on the floor. That was when he finally lost his temper. He ordered me to come outside with him, and then he threw the book in through the back window, said a couple of words, and the whole place was on fire. That was when he promised that if I ever said anything about it, I'd burn just like the house. And he showed me myself burning in the middle of the fire. Oh, Jonathan, it was horrible—I could smell it, like meat cooking, and see the bones beginning to show through as the flesh blackened and sizzled and shrank away . . ."

As he spoke, I could smell it, too, and was glad, for a change, that he had inherited my share of the talent for visualization. "No, Danny. Don't! It's a lie. It never happened, and it's not going to happen." Cradling the phone against my shoulder, I pointed at the fireplace: "Remember, anything aimed at you is aimed at me and beyond me to the place prepared. You just think about the light from our rings, okay? Anything else, you just hand it on to me." The golden globe around me wavered like something seen through the turbulent air over a brazier. I was beginning to feel hot, and the whiff had become a stench. "Danny, stop thinking about it! Think about the rings, think about our circle: leave everything else to me, okay? Dan?"

"Okay," he said dully.

When I was about eleven, we were in our bedroom, and I was trying to repair an old radio of grandmother's—well, actually, I was playing with it, I guess—and thought I was safe because I had the switch turned off. It wasn't unplugged, though, and, predictably, I got my screwdriver across a live wire. If Danny hadn't shoved me away back then, I suppose Louie Evans might have been saved a great deal of trouble. Sitting in my living room, I felt, as soon as Danny spoke, that same electrical shock, that burning paralysis, in my hand. The light almost vanished: but the room was darkened by far more than the absence of that glow would explain. A jet of darkness, like a photographic negative of a rocket blast, leapt from my hand to the fireplace, an anti-coruscation of consuming energy as hot as the black shadow around the heart of a flame. It only lasted a moment, but that was long enough, not merely to leave my arm numb for days, but also to burn a hole through the glass of the fireplace door.

As our own light sprang back up, Danny cried: "Jon-jon! Are you still there? Are you okay?"

"Yes, yes, I'm here, Danny, it's okay."

"Jonathan, I can't keep this up, I'm sorry. I feel so tired."

"That's fine. I'm a little the worse for wear, myself. Listen. I've got to see you. Can you come up here for the weekend? It would really help if you could be here for something I'm doing on Halloween. I need you."

"Okay, sure. I can have my hired hand look after the horses for a couple of days. I'll have to bring Caroline, though. We'll come up right after work on Friday—what's that, the thirtieth?"

"Yes, that's it. That'll be fine. I'll look forward to it. Let's go to bed. And say, little brother?"

"Yes?"

"About that catalog: page 73 was always my favorite."

"There's a surprise. My brother: I love him."

"You too, kid. God bless."

Chapter 4: Monday, October 26

IN FACT, I did not get around to making Herb's phone call as quickly as I'd intended to: as often happens, events at school presented me with new priorities. The Registrar always gives me the first two periods free, and (when I manage to keep to my schedule) I use the time to make my daily visit to the Infirmary. Sick Call is five minutes after Reveille—0635—so by two hours later the admissions-and-discharge cycle has usually settled down. As I hadn't been in on Saturday, there was a substantially different patient population than the one I'd last seen. Seriously ill cadets, of course, we send on to the regional hospital, so long-term inmates only accumulate when we get hit with an epidemic of flu or measles. I stopped at the nurse's station on the second floor to get an update from Betty Simcox, the head day nurse, who could probably have taken retirement a decade ago and has an entirely too capacious memory for the misdeeds of one's youth.

"Morning, Mrs. Simcox. What's new?"

"Morning, Chaplain. Not much, really, though there's a trooper named Shaw in room five who's either rediscovered your brother's trick with a thermometer and a desk lamp or spiked a temp of 113."

"Should we be grateful that he can walk as far as the desk?"

"In the sense that his mobility avoids the need for bed pans, yes. He's in for a legitimate gastro-intestinal upset of some sort, but I think he wants to stretch it out into a Halloween vacation."

"I'll speak to him. What else?"

"There's Calbee, a plebe from Charley Company, in the isolation room. He's in a bad situation psychologically, but you're not going to have time to help him much."

"How's that?"

"Apparently his platoon leader and company personnel officer brought him in last night after he drank some sort of detergent out of the janitor's closet; so of course we went right into our poison control protocol. According to what I read on his chart, he did it on a dare, rather than a suicide attempt, but we still wanted to keep an eye on him and notify his parents. So the night staff tried calling both of them—they're divorced, which doesn't surprise me—and neither one could be bothered to pick up the phone. We finally got hold of an uncle—the mother's brother—about one A.M. our time. In any case, Dr. Spaht was ready to discharge him this morning after Sick Call, and the brat

44

grabbed the keys to the drug cabinet off the desk in the reception area and tried to hide them by stuffing them down his pants."

"Tried, you say."

"Yes, dropped them right through. Apparently he's not used to wearing boxer shorts. So Colonel Somerset will be arranging his transport home ASAP, if they can find a family member to take him in."

"Great. He must feel loved."

"I bet he does. Besides those two, you have roommates Gilbert and Burnet, from the aviation squadron, also plebes, who now presumably *do* know what poison ivy looks like and why the Bird Sanctuary is off limits, in three, and, in four, with a splendid view of the Chapel, Oren Abrams, whom you know."

"What's wrong with Oren? I saw him at services on Friday, and he seemed fine."

"Yes, he would have been. He didn't actually come in to Sick Call, for that matter. You know the Regimental Sergeant Major and the staff sergeants from each battalion come in to supervise the sick kids and to write out the infirmary reports—"

"Couldn't that be done on computers by now?"

"Yes, we're hoping to have laptops for them by next year. As I was saying, though, Oren was here doing his job, and wincing a little bit when he put his arm on the desk to write. So Dr. Spaht noticed and insisted on having a look at it. He apparently burned his arm while checking the engine of his jeep after Parade yesterday."

"Serious?"

"Not really, but since the boy wasn't taking care of it, Dr. Spaht did want to keep him here overnight just to keep an eye on it. I do wish you'd talk to him, Jonathan, and possibly to Sergeant-Major Chuff, as well."

"You're suspicious."

"Yes, I am. The boy's a second classman, and he came here when he was in junior high. In his fifth year, he ought to be able to poke around under a hood without burning himself."

"Surely, even experienced mechanics have accidents."

"Of course. And I only agreed to being suspicious, not persuaded. But I think it's worth trying to find out more."

"Roger that. I'll keep you posted if I find out anything. If he's staying overnight, does he have his prayer things, do you know?"

"Yes, he mentioned them to Dr. Spaht, so one of the other boys got them from his room after Sick Call, took them to Main Guard, and had an orderly bring them over. Doctor says he's to be careful about wrapping the straps around his left arm."

"Very good. Well, I'd better get to it."

"Good luck. And let me know if you want me to have a look at that arm *you're* favoring. I swear, you're as bad as your brother."

Most of the visits were, as usual, brief. Poison ivy only calls for so much spiritual counsel, and while I did talk with the GIU boy, Lt. Brennan, the deputy commandant, had arrived to hustle the would-be drug thief off to the airport by the time I got to the isolation room.

Oren was sitting up in pajamas and a bathrobe, staring out the window, when I knocked at his door, but he jumped up dutifully when I came in. Even in his stocking feet, he was over six feet tall, with carrot-red hair, which he wore more closely cropped than most, and wire-rimmed glasses.

"As you were, Oren. How's the arm?'

He sat back down in the chair, and I perched on the end of his bed. "Oh, it's okay, Chaplain." He shook his head in irritation. "Dr. Spaht is just being overcautious—probably thinks I can't keep myself clean."

"You do seem to have joined the uniform-impaired."

"C'mon, sir, there has to be some trade-off for being stuck in here all day."

"I daresay. So what did you do to your arm, anyway?"

"Oh, Sergeant Major Chuff likes for us to check over the vehicles when we get back to the Armory, that's all. I'd propped up the hood and brushed against the exhaust manifold when I went to pull out the dipstick."

"That's easy enough to happen, I suppose. Oren, what rank are you this year?"

"Battalion staff sergeant, sir."

"Which is why you were riding in a jeep instead of a deuce-and-a-half like the common folks. Do you get to wrap and carry?"

"Yes, sir. Artillery red sash, sword, and NCO belt—the whole outfit. Mother says it doesn't go very well with my hair, but she's taken lots of pictures, anyway."

"They're like that. I always sort of wanted to be an officer when I was in the Band, just for the extra stuff on the uniform. But my roommate was our platoon leader, and it did always seem to take forever to get him dressed up to wrap and carry—lots of little pins and things."

"I know what you mean, sir. Of course, I suppose officers take longer, with the sash across the shoulder instead of just around the waist, but either way it's kind of a nuisance."

"That's always been my impression. So do you want to tell me again how you burned your arm? On your honor?" I tossed him my ring.

He flinched, but caught it. No adult with two functioning neurons to rub together invokes the AMA Honor Code any more often than he has to, particularly not when actually questioning a kid. We all know—most of us know, at any rate—it's best not to present them with needless moral dilemmas, and they often feel torn between their senses of honor and of duty to their friends. But few of my colleagues can invoke the Code with a reminder that they grew up with it themselves: the ring was a challenge, and Oren rose to it. "If the cadet had been wearing a full dress uniform coat, sir, the cadet could not have burned his arm, whereas if the cadet had taken the time to remove his sword, NCO belt, half-sash and uniform coat, the engine might have cooled off enough that the cadet would perhaps have not burned himself."

He reached behind him to the desk and picked up the blue velvet bag in which I knew he kept his siddur, tallis and tefillin (the daily prayer book and the shawl and phylacteries that one wears while praying, in accordance with Deuteronomy). Handing it to me, he went on, "The cadet invites the former cadet to see for himself, sir."

Despite Oren's formality, this response was, in the technicalities of the Code, an evasion, as I had asked him a direct question; but I took the bag and laid its contents out on the bedspread. Even though I didn't have a detailed sense of how the various pieces were supposed to look, it was clear that all of them had been tampered with. The blue and white shawl had been repeatedly slashed; the small containers on the tefillin, which were supposed to hold passages from the Torah on tiny scrolls, had been ripped open; and someone had tried to rip apart the prayer book, though with only limited success. I picked it up and opened the dangling cover gingerly. Inside the back cover—presumably the front cover to vandals unaccustomed to Hebrew books—someone had scrawled a swastika and a pointed message: "Next time we'll show you how to really burn a Jew."

"This happened after the arm, I guess?"

"Yes, sir—or maybe at about the same time."

"Which was when, exactly?"

"Sometime late last night, sir. Jim Lanier, my roommate, woke up and thought he smelled something burning, and he saw that his clock radio was off. Well, people throw the circuit breakers all the time, and since the box is right outside our door, he got up to reset it, and see what else might be up. As soon as he stepped out into the hallway, someone—a couple of guys, I guess—dropped a blanket over him and dragged him outside."

"As an NCO in A Battery, you're in a corner room on the first floor of Main Barracks, next to an outside door."

"Yes, sir. I guess that must have made enough noise to start waking me up. But the first thing I knew was a bunch of guys stuffing something in my mouth, dragging me out of bed, bundling me into a blanket, and hauling me off down to the shower room—"

"The only room on your floor with no windows."

"Yes, sir. Anyway, that's where they stretched me out on the floor; and one of them tried to burn my arm with something."

"Tried to? I thought you were really injured."

"Yes, sir, but I have the impression they meant to do more, or worse. The guy with the whatever-it-was—one of those traveling irons, maybe—just didn't have the balls to really do more than touch me with it. I mean, I wasn't exactly cooperating with all of this, and I think when he actually saw real live moving flesh he chickened out. At least, I heard something drop on the floor, and then several of them were muttering, swearing at each other. Of course, they didn't want me to recognize their voices, or anyone to hear us. At any rate, before the guy could try again, I heard the door open, and some guy whose voice I didn't recognize said flat out, 'Come on, let's go!' Jim and I figured that must have been one of the ones who'd grabbed him. Anyway, they all took off, and as I got my head out of the blanket, all I saw was a bunch of sweatsuits headed out the door."

"How many, do you think?"

"I figure there were nine in all, sir. I'll tell you more about that in a minute. But, after I was loose, I went back to the room—which was the first time I knew Jim was gone. So then I put on my own sweatsuit and some shoes and started out to look for him. He could have been inside or out, of course, and I just had to pretty much make a guess at random and start looking. So I went outside, and kind of followed the walk around the lake side of East Barracks, trying to keep out of the streetlights, and from the east end of the walk, where it splits to go up in front of Sally Port or down to the Naval Building, I could see the flag poles."

"Of course."

"Well, they'd put duct tape over Jim's mouth, tied him to the flagpole, and taken his boxers. Apparently, they were going to leave him there for main guard to find at Reveille."

"Mr. Lanier is the Regimental Sergeant-Major, isn't he?"

"Yes, sir, and I know it's traditional to paint the Sergeant-Major's ass green and hang him over the balcony of Haddam Hall—" (Haddam Hall is a club house for the first class, and the Regimental Sergeant Major is the highest ranking cadet of the second class) "—but that's on Saint Patrick's day, and it's not even Halloween yet."

"And it's not fair to grab the target when he doesn't have a sporting chance to escape, either. But still, you must have wondered whether or not the whole thing was a prank."

"Yes, sir. That was why we didn't say anything—or partly. The other thing was that we'd both heard people talk about the Nine."

"*Nine for mortal men doomed to die*," I thought to myself, but it seemed unlikely that the two of them had heard gossip about Tolkien's ringwraiths. "The nine what?"

"The Nine, sir. The secret society that enforces Annandale traditions. Like making sure that Jews don't get one of these—"

"Don't toss it—I'm a terrible catch."

He handed me the ring. "Anyway, I thought it might be them, though Jim wasn't so sure. But after seeing my things, I'd say it's pretty clear I'm right."

"Oh, nonsense. This is some bunch of two-bit anti-Semites who've been watching *Lords of Discipline*. I doubt if they've even got brains enough to read the book. There's no such tradition at Annandale."

"It's a secret tradition, sir. The whole point is that no one is supposed to know about it."

"Oren, I've been on this campus summer or winter or both almost every year since the Eisenhower administration, and my little brother overlapped with a lot of that time. It's hard for me to believe that there's a secret society at work here that I've never heard of, much less one that's transparently plagiarized from a popular film."

"You didn't know about that witch kid up on the third floor of Main."

News does travel fast, I reflected. "It took me eight weeks to find out; that's not the same as thirty years or more. Besides, it's not as though the academy has a *secret* history of anti-Semitism. One of the admissions deans used to mark potential folders 'NSJ,' for 'Name Sounds Jewish.' And a Jewish alumnus from the fifties—who did receive his first class ring, by the way—wrote in his memoirs about asking someone to pass the bread at one of the old sit-down regimental meals, and getting a piece with a swastika marked on it in ketchup."

"You have an odd way of cheering a person up, sir."

"I'm not trying to cheer you up, I just want you to think clearly. There may be a gang of nine kids who attacked you and Lanier, but there's no secret tradition behind it."

"Okay, sir, supposing you're right, and this isn't a tradition. What do you think we should do?"

"I think you should follow doctor's orders and stay right here until he's convinced you won't be too macho to take care of your arm. Meanwhile, I'm going to find those nine Nazis and get them kicked out of my school. Before they do start a tradition."

"Is this the part where I'm supposed to say I don't want to cause any more trouble?"

"I suppose it's traditional. But I intend to make sure there won't be any more."

"Well, go for it, sir. But do you think we need to worry about Jim? I mean, if they thought he ratted on them, they might do something else to him."

"Not before Taps, I imagine. I'll make sure someone keeps an eye on him, but with any luck we can have the whole affair wrapped up by then."

"Tomorrow would be okay, sir. Maybe by then Dr. Spaht will have let me out and I can be in for the kill."

"I think we'll probably just send them home, Oren. May I take the evidence with me, please? I'll take good care of your things."

"Of course, sir. Good luck."

I repacked the bag, gave Betty an update, and marched myself straight to the Commandant's office in Sally Port, where, for the first time in my life, I actually swept past a secretary (or past the secretary's desk, at least—I'd glimpsed her at the coffee-maker as I came in) and burst into a room. Inside, I found Rob and Richard already closeted with Colonel Somerset.

"Excuse me for interrupting, Colonel, gentlemen. I have something of an emergency."

"That may have to wait for Mr. English's emergency, Chaplain. It appears that something strange is going on in the Artillery Battalion. Have a seat."

Richard shot me a cautioning glance and Rob said, helpfully, "Something we just heard about at BRC, Father."

"The Lanier and Abrams episode?" I offered.

"Good work, sir. Rob's going to have to watch out or you'll be taking his job."

"I'm sure the Chaplain appreciates your confidence, Mr. Platt. Was this same emergency you were concerned about, Father Mears?" (The Colonel is of that educational school which holds that students ought not to be aware that faculty have given names.)

"Yes, Colonel. At least, I suppose it is, though when I came in, I thought Messrs. English and Platt must be here for something else—I just now heard about this myself."

"Very well, then, Father, why don't we combine these discussions? Let me summarize what we'd heard before you came in. I had a report from the Security Officer on duty last night that as he was proceeding along the Lake Walk from the Memorial Building to the Naval Building in the normal course of his business, at about 0245 hours, he swept the searchlight of his vehicle across the fronts of Main and East Barracks, and observed a cadet in Athletic Uniform B"—a sweatsuit—"running across the gap between the buildings. As he would have had no opportunity to turn and pursue the cadet until he reached the water fountain where Pershing Walk intersects with the Lake Walk, and knowing the difficulty of finding one cadet in the whole barrack, he made a note of the incident and went on. Meanwhile, as I was reading the report this morning before I went up to eat, Mr. English was noticing that his Regimental Sergeant Major was late for the formation. When Cadet Lanier arrived, he explained that he had been delayed in returning from his usual duties at Sick Call because he had to deliver the Artillery Battalion Infirmary Reports on behalf of his roommate, Cadet Abrams, whom Dr. Spaht had unexpectedly confined to the Infirmary. Mr. Platt, who was sitting at the Commander's table, confirmed that he had seen Mr. Lanier distributing the paperwork as the Artillery Battalion formed up. Having for some reason *not* connected with the usual performance of his own duties been awake and looking out his third floor window at about 0300 hours—"

"I'd just gotten back from the bathroom, Colonel!"

"Very well, Mr. Platt. I will admit that cadets working on 'all-nighters' usually do so with the curtains closed. In any case, Mr. Platt commented at breakfast that if one of Mr. Lanier and Mr. Abrams had caught cold, he would have expected it to be Mr. Lanier, Mr. Lanier having been out of uniform when Mr. Platt saw him returning to barracks. Mr. Lanier, being duly embarrassed, explained that he thought he had been the victim of a prank, and was disinclined to give anyone the satisfaction of seeing that they'd provoked him to a response. Mr. Abrams, however, he reported, was afraid that Mr. Lanier's kidnapping had been the result of some secret society called 'The Nine.' Mr. English, quite rightly concerned to nip any potential wave of hazing in the bud, took note of Mr. Lanier's narrative, reported to me at the faculty tables under the mezzanine as he was leaving the Dining Hall, and requested the meeting in which you find us engaged. Does that square with what you've come to say?"

"It does in part, Colonel, though I believe Mr. Lanier must have omitted a few details out of consideration for Mr. Abrams. Here's the final version of the story as Abrams told it to me at the Infirmary just now."

When I finished Oren's version of the story, I passed around the shawl and prayer book. As Colonel Somerset read the message, I could watch the contours of his face change—his jaw set into a different, harder, line, and his brows tightened. However stern he thought it best to appear in dealing with our teenaged charges from one day to the next, in that moment he revealed the young officer who'd spent his own nineteenth Christmas with McAuliffe in Bastogne and earned the purple and white ribbon on his chest in the process of killing a Nazi no older than the *ersatz* Hitler youth in our midst. He closed the book carefully and held the shredded cloth gently in his hands. "Now Rob, Richard, Jonathan," he said, "you three boys listen to me. *I was there.* The 101st and the 103rd went into Landsberg at the end of April of '45, with Patch's Seventh Army. It was about two weeks after the

President died. Landsberg was one of the subcamps of Dachau, where they brought Jews back from Auschwitz to get more work out of them. I saw that gas chamber disguised as a shower. I saw the ovens. Once the camps were liberated, Ike made sure as many of the troops under his command as he could manage were marched through them. We left the dead unburied for weeks, naked corpses they hadn't had chance to burn. He wanted to make sure—as sure as he could—that these things would not be forgotten. Not a man I know ever forgot them, as long as he lived. And as the Lord God of Israel is my witness, they will not be forgotten here." He folded the tallis and laid it on the desk before he continued.

"Mr. English. If Lanier and Abrams were seen going back into Main, I wouldn't be surprised to hear that some of the perpetrators of this assault were also spotted coming or going. Use your command structure and see what you can find out—be discreet, but make it clear that we're not trying to crack down on the usual bunch of people eating popcorn and playing poker."

"Yes, sir."

"Mr. Platt. You see if anyone else has heard about this group of nine. You may want to concentrate on the second class. Again, your watchword is discretion. You want to trace the rumor, not spread it."

"Yes, sir."

"Chaplain, if you would, I'd like you to keep your ears open, too. Your main task, though, will probably be to keep an eye on the victims here."

"Of course, Colonel. May I suggest that you may also want to contact my cousin Kenny, who owns the video rental place on Academy Road? He'd probably be able to tell you whether a cadet rented that movie lately. Of course, it won't help if someone brought it from home, but it's worth a try."

"Good idea, Chaplain. And I'll check with the library, too, just in case someone *has* been reading the book. Is there anything else for the good of the order?"

"No, sir," the boys answered together.

"Actually, Colonel," I said, "there is an entirely different matter in the Artillery that Mr. English and Mr. Platt have been looking into for me. There doesn't seem to be anything disciplinary involved, but I'll send you a heads-up if anything comes of it."

"Anything I can do to help, Chaplain. Now if any of you have third period class, you'd better get going. Dismissed, gentlemen. Father, thank you for coming by."

I had a chance to talk with the boys on the way out. "That was the least I've heard from the two of you since we read *Age of Innocence*."

"Come on, sir, it was summer reading," Richard said. "Picture Edith Wharton in a bathing suit."

"Actually, she was a fine figure of a young woman. And she once wrote half a dozen pages of a porn novel just to prove she could do it."

"Strangely enough, Father, I believe you. It's true, though, the Colonel does have a sobering effect, even when he's just putting on his usual act, much less when he's really serious. And I think now that I've never really seen him serious before. It wouldn't surprise me if he had the whole thing unraveled by lunch."

"Let's hope so, Rob. I'll see you guys eighth period."

"Not today, sir," Richard replied. "Monday's our drop day. But we'll be in touch."

I WENT STRAIGHT to the Dining Hall after my fourth period class. Lt. Brennan, having apparently seen to the departure of young Calbee, was supervising the formation, and as Col. Somerset was not at the faculty tables, I concluded that he hadn't yet wrapped up his investigation. Luke Faber, George Chadwick and several of the other unit counselors were sitting together, somewhat apart from the other faculty. I went to sit with them, and had hardly put my tray down before George accosted me.

"So, now, Jonathan. We understand that you're the expert on this scandalous business in the Artillery Battalion."

"That depends on the scandal, Major. To whom have you been speaking?"

"The Commandant. Or, at least, he has been speaking to us. We've just come from the weekly counselors' meeting, and he is very much exercised over this assault on young Abrams."

"I know what you mean. Was the collective wisdom able to make any progress?"

"Not too much," Luke said. "We mostly got our marching orders."

"We did agree, though," George added, "that some attention should be paid to the question of why Abrams—why this particular Jew, that is—should have been singled out as the first victim."

"My company commander is Jewish," one of the troop counselors commented, "and we heard this morning that one of the aviation units has a boy who has an Israeli flag hanging on his wall. So Abrams is neither the highest ranking nor the most obvious Jew in the corps."

"Not to mention," George added, "that we have Catholics, African-Americans, Orientals, and, presumably, the less-visible minority, and yet this group of nine chooses to begin with a Jew."

"Mightn't here be some other factor at work?" I asked.

"That's my theory," Dean Alexander, counselor of Aviation B, volunteered. "It seems to me that we have to look at the physical situation. I mean, here we have boys on the first floor, next to an outside door, at the intersection of several campus walkways, and with the nearest resident faculty member on the next floor halfway down the building. It's a target of opportunity."

"Or, rather, an opportune target," George said.

"I suppose," I offered, "someone could just have it in for one of the two—or both of them, for that matter. The rest could just be window dressing."

"Yes, the Colonel thought of that himself," Dean said. "Tom Logan—" the A Battery counselor "—is looking into it right now."

"Easier said than done," George added sympathetically.

"What angle is the Colonel himself pursuing?" I asked.

"I think he's working on the chronology," Luke answered. "He mentioned two specific times to us, but apparently he's wondering exactly how there was time to do everything that happened. As for myself, if you'll all excuse me, I think I'm going to take a cup of coffee over and sit with my unit and see if I hear anything."

This idea gained wide acceptance, and I finished my dessert in splendid isolation.

⸺

I SPENT SEVENTH PERIOD actually preparing for my Tuesday classes— another of those regular parts of my schedule which I occasionally have the discipline to observe. Monday was, as Richard had reminded me, the drop day for my eighth period section. Each of our classes meets only four days a week, but someone decided a long time ago that it would be too simple if we just met Monday through Thursday. So first period lower school classes take Tuesday off, while middle-schoolers have their first period drop day on Wednesday, and about two thirds of the upper-schoolers who aren't taking history drop first period on Monday: it's a completely arbitrary system which persistently confuses even the oldest hands on the faculty. So of course we're irrevocably attached to it. I used the free time to phone Marcia Kirkfleet. It was a substantially more relaxed conversation than the one I'd had the night before.

I found out that Louie had opposed having Rhys baptized as an infant; the marriage had fallen apart (as far as I could tell) when Rhys was about six. Marcia said that she and Louie remained on good terms, though something about the tone of her remarks made it sound to me as though Louie might have been an abusive husband—then again, I was not eager to see the best in him. In any case, after the divorce, Marcia had thought it just as well to wait until Rhys had reached years of discretion. He'd been prepared for baptism with the expectation of having the ceremony at Pentecost, at the end of his ninth grade year.

That was when Louie had offered not only to pay for Rhys's education at the Academy but also to take him on a summer vacation to the ancestral homeland in Wales: a trip which would leave, as it happened, just before Pentecost. I could understand how, despite whatever unspoken mistrust of Louie she might have entertained, this would have struck Marcia and her second husband (Gerard, his name was) as too good an opportunity to pass up. So Rhys had remained unbaptized, and had come back from Wales to follow his father to Annandale.

Marcia was eager for me to talk with Rhys about rescheduling his christening, and had no objection to doing it on Halloween, even after I explained—without, I admit, mentioning Louie by name—that the revival of All Saints' Vigils reflected a deliberate effort by the Church to reclaim the night from the Neo-pagans. I did point out that Louie and I had been enemies since our days at the Academy, and that he might therefore have particular objection to my administering the sacrament. Marcia made it very clear that she and Jerry were Rhys' legal parents, that Louie had no rights over the boy whatsoever. Not even Louie, she thought, would explicitly make Rhys's being baptized a reason to cut off the money for his schooling. I wasn't all that sure that I agreed with her.

I turned to the next item on my mental list, calling the archbishop about Donald Newman. By then, it was almost 3:30, 4:30 in New York, where the city slickers were still observing Daylight Saving Time (we don't mess with God's clocks in Indiana), and I decided it was unlikely that Axton Williams would still be in the archiepiscopal offices. Thinking I should touch base with the Colonel before going home, I gathered up my papers, tossed them into the back seat of my car, and walked through the Athletic Center as a shortcut on my way to Sally Port. I was about half way down the main hall, between the Natatorium and the Performance Gym, when a cadet in Athletic Uniform A—shorts and a T-shirt—hailed me and came over to introduce himself.

"Chaplain Mears! Good afternoon, sir. I'm Jim Lanier. I was just coming to see you." He was about 5'5", stocky rather than heavy, with thick dishwater blond hair and a firm handshake that accorded well with his weightlifter's physique.

"I'm pleased to meet you, Jim. You've sort of been in the news today."

"Yes, sir. That's what I wanted to talk to you about. May I walk with you? We might be more private outside," he added quietly.

"Of course. I was just on my way to the Commandant's office, in fact."

"Very good, sir." Once we were outside, he continued, still rather quietly, "Chaplain, I'm worried that so many people keep hearing my name—our names, I mean—in this investigation. When I spoke to Colonel Somerset at DRC, he explained to me that there wasn't any tradition about the Nine, but there are still a bunch of guys out there somewhere who already broke into my room once, and if they think I ratted them out, they'll be after me more today than they were yesterday."

"And this time they might treat you the way they treated Oren."

"Yes, sir, or worse if they had the chance. So, since the Colonel told me to talk to you if I had any other concerns, I was coming to ask you if maybe you could arrange for me to stay in the Infirmary with Oren for a night or two, until this is cleared up."

"Every cadet should feel safe in his room, Jim. You should all feel safe anyplace on campus, for that matter. I'm sure we can arrange for you to stay in the Infirmary. In fact, I'll ask the Commandant right now. Would you like to come in and wait? I'll make excuses for your uniform."

"No, sir, that's okay. I'm going to go lift for a while."

"Okay. I imagine you'll be just fine, but you might stay in places where there are lots of people around—and make sure your battery orderly desk knows where to find you."

"Yes, sir, I will. Thanks again, sir."

He turned back toward the gym, and I went through the arch of Sally Port and into the Commandant's office, where I waited to be properly announced. The Colonel was talking with Tom Logan when I came in.

"Hello, Jonathan. Thanks for stopping by. Tom and I were just trying to make sense of all this. English and Platt gave me preliminary reports during eighth period, and the two of us have talked to a number of youngsters over the course of the day."

"What did Rob and Richard find out?"

"In general, what any of us already knew: first, there are an awful lot of kids out of bed after Taps, and, second, rumors got through the corps like grease through a goose. Specifically, though, it looks as though most of them do get to sleep by 0230 or so. English got a few names of random individuals who just happened to be seen up and about last night. He's also shown some initiative in getting names of late-night regulars, as he calls them, to ask whether they saw or heard anything. Of the first group, he's talked to three already, and doesn't think any of those were out of their barracks. Two more live in the new quad, and we agree that's quite a long way for someone to travel in the middle of the night. The outside engineer, by the way, was checking the machine room in the new library at 0250, and walked across from there to Verdun. He wasn't outside very long, but does say he didn't notice any cadets on campus.

"As for tracking down references to the Nine, though it's probably a job for some sort of professional, young Mr. Platt has been chipping away at it. Many of the cadets who said they've heard of the group told him they didn't remember who mentioned it to them. Several told him they'd heard about it from Abrams or Lanier."

"That's not much help," I observed, "though it does lead to the question of whom *they* heard it from."

"Neither one remembers," Tom said. "You'd think they didn't care."

"Well, they probably didn't when they heard it. But Jim seems to be taking it seriously now. He just stopped me to ask if we could put him up in the Infirmary overnight. I told him it could be arranged."

"Of course it can," the Colonel said, "if you still think it's a good idea after you hear what we've just been saying."

"All right, you've got my attention. What's your secret?"

"Harry's been trying to work out the schedule for all of this," Tom said. "The coming and going parts work out fine, but it's hard to see when Abrams's religious equipment was meddled with."

"Couldn't someone have been doing that in his room while others had him in the showers and the rest were pantsing Lanier?" I asked.

"Yes," the Colonel answered, "though the more the force was divided the harder it is to account for Lanier and Abrams being overpowered. Neither one of them is a weakling."

"Harry's right about that," Tom added. "They both spend a lot of time lifting weights. Beyond that issue, though, there are other problems. For instance, Harry wondered how they knew where to find these things to begin with, though I had to tell him that Oren generally keeps them on his bookshelves, where anyone might have seen them at one time or another and made a mental note for later. Another problem is that Oren told you this morning and me this afternoon that the assailants grabbed Jim as he was going out to turn on the circuit breaker, and the lights were still out when he got back to his room. So how did the vandal see to write in Oren's prayer book? And I'll remind you that the security guard did not report seeing any lights on on the lake side of Main Barracks—if he had, he'd have had a place to go to look for the kid he saw running into the building. I suppose a kid *might* have held a flashlight in one hand and written in the book with the other, but I'm dubious."

"Well, then, someone must have done the vandalism later, as Oren suggested. Sometime between Sick Call and whenever the things were taken to Main Guard."

"Someone who could go in and out of the room at a time when the halls are full of kids going to the showers, the call boy announcing the time remaining until BRC, and another plebe sweeping the hall to prepare for inspection."

"I'll admit it's difficult, Tom, but it is a corner room. Someone might slip in and out. Or maybe one of the assailants is in A Battery—" They both looked at me, waiting. "Or . . . maybe Lanier was in on it from the start. He could go into his own room without being noticed, if anyone could, and we know he was late for BRC."

"And he was the one who brought the things to Main Guard," the Colonel added. "I checked with the Officer of the Day."

"Not damning," I said, "but admittedly suspicious. Is that the whole case against him?"

"Mostly. But as his counselor, I did notice one thing in the story as we finally heard it. Oren says that when he went to look for Jim, he snuck along the lake side of East Barracks, where there are a lot of shrubs and not too many streetlights. But everyone agrees that when they came back from the flagpoles, they ran right through Sally Port, past the potentially sleeping Officer of the Day, and across the Plaza, where there are no bushes, plenty of lights, and windows from three different barracks, including Dickey Platt's, who could be number one on English's list of notorious night owls."

"Is it any shorter?"

"Maybe by a foot or two. The thing is, though, I wouldn't have been surprised to hear that Jim had streaked Sally Port in broad daylight, never mind at three in the morning. He's one of those kids who treat the whole barracks like a locker room, to the point where it annoys the other cadets. I heard the XO tell him the other day that he might try wearing his towel on the way to and from the shower, instead of carrying it on his shoulder."

"So the whole 'attack' on Lanier sounds to you like something he himself might have planned."

"Absolutely, Jon. I'm sure he picked the way back to barracks, and I don't think he'd have minded being discovered at Reveille, either."

"Still, this behavior might at best be reason for some counseling: it doesn't count as evidence."

"No, it doesn't," the Colonel said. "And that's the frustrating part of a lot of these affairs—unless the boy speaks up, you don't have the kind of evidence you'd like to have, and the parents often end up feeling their darling hasn't gotten a fair shake. So I am reluctant to take any action against Mr. Lanier until we find out more than we know now. Which brings us back to your question, Jonathan, of where to put him up for the night. If he is one of the assailants, do we really want to put him in the same room as Abrams?"

"Well, he can hardly do anything with a nurse right there on the floor—and I think Abrams could probably take him in a fair fight."

"Yes, Jon, but he must have some reason for wanting to stay in the Infirmary—presumably he's not actually afraid of this group, if he's really part of it."

"Not necessarily, Tom. He did say he was afraid they'd think he'd ratted them out, which would make just as much sense, or more, if he'd been one of them."

"Or," the Colonel added, "he could just be keeping up the appearance of being a victim. Even if our hypothesis is right, he doesn't have any reason to think we're on to him, so he'd naturally go on with his act."

"So does he go or not?" Tom asked.

"On the whole, I'd say he should—if we're worried about him and Oren, we can always have Betty put them in different rooms."

"Thank you, Jonathan, I agree. Unless Tom has an actual objection, I'll see to it."

"No, no, I don't object at all. I'll bet you'll have Abrams eager to get out about the same time you put Lanier in—not out of fear, I mean, but just because he'll be bored and itching for a fight."

"Fair enough. I may go over and speak to him myself. Gentlemen, thank you both."

It was as good as a dismissal, and, having agreed that Tom would speak to Lanier, I made my way back to my car and so home, where I had a short nap.

———

THAT EVENING, I went to the *de facto* Faculty Club—one of the town's three taverns (there are also seventeen restaurants, or roughly one for every hundred residents)—for supper, and ended up sitting with my two lay eucharistic ministers, RJ Esther (a colleague from the English department) and Brad Peniston (a French instructor) in their usual booth near the back door of the pub. I ordered the fried chicken special and a large Coke.

"Good Lord, Jonathan, how much of that stuff do you drink in a day?" RJ asked, pouring the rest of a bottle of his own favorite, Bass ale, into his glass.

"He must have missed the divinity school lectures on why Anglicans drink sherry, heh, heh, heh," Brad said. Somehow, he's never gotten the hang of laughing and thus resorts to pronouncing a number of standard transcriptions of laughter: it's a disconcerting effect, like meeting a dog that actually says, "bow-wow."

"What did you do to your arm, Jonathan?" RJ asked. "You've been holding it funny all day."

"Oh, I strained it doing some stuff around the house last night. It'll be better in a day or two, I'm sure. You two guys go ahead and eat—don't wait on me. How was soccer practice?" RJ and Brad were two-thirds of the varsity-JV soccer coaching staff: the other man, the head coach, was a former Olympic player who worked full time for the Athletic Department.

"Same as usual, run two laps and scrimmage for an hour and a half," Brad answered. "And this with a game tomorrow!"

RJ shook his head. "The trouble is, Henry knows how to play the game so well, but he can't explain anything. So we just go out and screw around: what a waste!"

"But we learned not to argue with Henry after we tried to play your buddy Keeks at center half instead of striker," Brad added.

"That lasted for the first how many minutes of the West Lafayette game?" I asked.

"Oh, I don't remember. However long it took Henry to get back from parking the bus and start chewing us out, ha, ha, ha."

"Speaking of Cadet Pruett, Jonathan, he couldn't get his mind off you today in the locker-room."

"Well, he is my aide. I guess he knows which side his stripes are buttered on. What was on Christopher's mind besides slide tackles and tomorrow's game?"

"Magic," RJ answered: "Witchcraft, covens in Main Barracks—that sort of thing. Said you spent all afternoon yesterday talking to English about it."

"Did he give any indication of where he came up with this idea?"

"Well, he didn't use footnotes, but I gather you asked him to take the Christian Athletes meeting yesterday?"

"True enough, I did."

"And while he was setting up the meditation chapel for the meeting, he saw English, Platt, and Mills going into your office. Chaplain, Regimental Commander, Artillery Battalion Personnel Officer, and B Battery Personnel Officer: so Keeks started asking around about what might be going on in red-stripe land in the spiritual crisis line."

"And he was announcing this to all and sundry in the locker room?" I asked. "Good God Almighty, they're worse than a bunch of old women."

The waitress brought out my chicken basket just then, and I took a moment to put ketchup on my fries, set the little paper cup of cole slaw on the table, and position the "Finger Bowl in a Bag" envelope next to the extra napkins. My colleagues, recognizing a dramatic pause when they saw one, waited patiently. "So it's true?" Brad asked when I had finished saying grace.

"Oh, sort of. Look: I am concerned about all this, but it's more complicated than you might think—Brad, are you going to use that straw? Thanks.—and I did have some hope of figuring out a solution that would avoid sensationalization—though flat-out disbelief will remain a strong possibility. I spoke this afternoon to the mother of one of the ring-leaders, Rhys Kirkfleet, and she and I were pretty well agreed about what to do: so I am making progress."

"Kirkfleet, huh?" RJ said. "He's in my fourth period French class."

"No," I answered, "You're thinking of the wrong kid. This one's a Latinist."

"Jonathan, I refuse to believe that we have two cadets named Rhys anything, much less two Rhys Kirkfleets. This is a little brown-headed kid with freckles. Besides, I'm sure that my Kirkfleet is in B Battery, and not even Lieutenant Brennan would assign two kids with the same name to the same unit. What made you think he takes Latin?"

"The fact that he carried on a conversation with me in that language on Saturday night."

"That's a damn sight better than he's ever done in French. He's a nice kid, but he's no Charles Berlitz. Ha."

"It has occurred to me, Brad, that you may not be entirely unconscious of how obnoxious that little laughing habit is. I'm telling you, though, this kid is fluent in Latin: if you didn't say otherwise, I'd swear he had a real gift for language."

"Perhaps," RJ drawled sarcastically, "the two of you are ignoring the possibility of the boy's being possessed."

"That's more likely than you think," I answered. "Anyway, it is something else for me to consider. Look, guys, I think this is one of those things that could cause a lot of trouble if it got blown out of proportion. I'm going to wrap it up by Halloween, if I can, and I'll probably need your liturgical help then. In between times, I'd appreciate anything you could do to help keep the whole affair quiet.

"Now, did anyone see what I did with my finger-bowl?"

Chapter 5: Tuesday, October 27

CONSCIOUS OF MY DUTY to Herb and the larger church, I called the Archbishop as soon as I got into my office on Tuesday. While there is a toll-free number for the church headquarters—1-800-VIA-MEDIA, in honor of the Anglican claim to be the "middle way" between Rome and the Protestant churches—I thought the occasion warranted using Axton's direct line.

"Hello, Axton, it's Jonathan Mears."

"My dear Jonathan! Good morning! How good to hear from you. What's new in the Midwest?"

"Oh, we're getting along, thanks. Still pretty much the same as you'd remember from a childhood in Chicago. And you're managing in the big city?"

"Tolerably well, I think, no more time than I actually spend here. Did I once think I'd be able to trot across the street and do research at Columbia?"

"I remember you saying something of the kind, yes. Not the way it's turned out, I guess?"

"Not quite, no. I have the feeling there are parts of the cathedral I haven't seen yet, much less the rest of Manhattan."

"It *is* the largest Gothic cathedral in the world."

"Two thirds Gothic, one third Romanesque. And it does look as though we'll finally see it finished in my episcopate, thanks be to God."

"Amen."

"So, Jonathan, what can I do for you? Not that I mind just chatting, but you would have called me at home if you hadn't had something in mind."

"So I should. It's Donald Newman, I'm afraid. I've been spoken to as President of our Standing Committee."

"Oh, goodness. Well, I'm sitting down. Tell me the worst."

I repeated everything from Herb's conversation that seemed safe from his concerns about confidentiality.

"Let me see if I have the bottom line here straight," Axton said. "Don Newman may never have been properly baptized; if he wasn't, he has probably consciously decided not to be, in defiance of heaven only knows how many canons and the indisputable tradition of the church; and the catch is that the suspicion arises from the overlapping of a set of variously confidential statements and one or two moderately solid inferences."

"That's pretty much it, yes."

"You know, I could have been a professor at some nice little Midwestern liberal arts school."

"You could have been a professor of labor law at Harvard or Yale, for that matter. But instead you've got a neat hat and a rent-free apartment in Chelsea Square. Axton, is there anything to be done about this? It does seem improbable, but on the other hand, if it's true, you certainly don't want Newman to be consecrated a bishop."

"Indeed, I do not. Why don't I just call him and ask? If he doesn't think the question is important, he'll probably not mind telling me the answer."

"Unless he figures *you* think it's important, and tells you what you want to hear. After all, on my informant's theory of the case, Newman's virtually done that every time anyone asked him about his baptism."

"Virtually, but not quite. Still, I could ask Eric the Red, too."

"Is he still alive? He must be over eighty."

"Eighty-one, I think. But yes, he's still alive, and a priest of my diocese, assisting at a parish in the Village. He's still a well-known character out here."

"It sounds like a plan. Let me know if you find out anything."

"I'll let you know, either way. If I find out anything, I'll let the whole church know."

With that obligation discharged, I went on to the Infirmary. Betty met me in the first floor hallway.

"Looks like you get a little more time to grade papers today, Chaplain. We're fresh out of patients."

"Cured them all, did you?"

"All the ones that were sick, anyway."

"And what about the one who wasn't sick?"

"Abrams convinced Dr. Spaht that he was capable of taking care of his dressing without further supervision, and he and Lanier left before Sick Call was even over."

"Did they indeed? Well, I don't know what else I expected. Keep up the good work!"

"You, too, Jonathan. See you tomorrow."

Given the unexpected free time, I felt as though I should bite the bullet and call Louie Evans, just to see if whatever ancient grudge he was nursing could be settled by conversation. As it turned out, I needn't have bothered: I ended up leaving two messages with his secretary and a third on his machine at home, but he hadn't deigned to answer any of them by the time I left for class.

I HOPED TO SEE the Colonel or Tom Logan at DRC, but neither of them showed up, so I kept Rob and Richard after class with the somewhat contradictory purposes of finding out what they'd heard about Lanier and warning them to squelch any rumors they might hear about Rhys.

The second of these points appearing to be the simpler, I dealt with it first. When I brought up the first issue, however, both boys looked solemn. Rob said, "Richard, why don't you go ahead to athletics and I'll catch up with you." I could hardly argue, and Platt hurried out of the room.

"Now, then, Father, how much do you want to know?"

"That doesn't sound promising. Has there been some new offense here?"

"No, Father, I don't think so. Possibly an Honor Offense, but I think it was more like a ruse of war."

"I see. Well, you might as well tell me all about it."

"Yes, sir. Yesterday evening after SRC, I was over in Haddam Hall, and I noticed that there were a lot of my commanders there, so I called a sort of informal meeting of the Cadet Club."

The Cadet Club consists of the cadet captains—the unit, battalion, and regimental commanders—meeting as a sort of interfraternity council to manage the social aspects of Annandale life—sponsoring dances, decorating the campus for homecoming and other such not-particularly-military activities. The problem is, of course, that it's not always easy for the boys to decide whether a particular issue is military or social—and sometimes they don't care to.

"The Colonel did tell you to use your commanders. So what happened?"

"I gave the guys an outline of what I'd heard about Lanier and Abrams, as a kind of background to why I'd been asking for information about the nightlife in their units. So we tried to figure out exactly what had happened, and it began to look to us as though Lanier had been in on the whole thing. That business with the flagpole sounded really fishy to the people who live with him—Mike York, his battery commander, says they've actually had to tell him to put some clothes on when he's walking around barracks, and he's apparently been looking forward to Saint Patrick's Day ever since the promotion list came out last June. And then the explanation he gave about being late for BRC didn't really account for all his time once we went back and started looking at all the details."

"Did you report all this to the Commandant?"

"No, sir. It struck me as likely, but still just an implication."

"Inference."

"Yes, sir, inference. In any case, Blair Turley, from Troop A, said that as a Jew he felt he should do more than sit around and talk about this. Someone else asked if he had a plan. He didn't, but Mike said as long as we were playing detective maybe we should take our example from Sherlock Holmes."

"No cocaine, I hope."

"Hardly, Father. Though I have seen pictures of the Cadet Club room from 1970 in which several members seem to be smoking something odd."

"I was only a sergeant, Mr. English."

"And photo editor of the yearbook, sir. In any case, what York was referring to was 'The Five Orange Pips.'"

"Which has something to do with the Klan."

"Yes, sir. From what Mike told us, the Klan threatens people in the story by sending them five orange seeds in an envelope—a warning to leave town or be killed. Then, at the end, when Holmes has figured everything out, he notifies the police—but he also sends the orange pips himself to the Klansmen. So what Michael suggested was sending Lanier a letter from the *real*, so to speak, secret society, giving him a deadline to go tell the Colonel the truth."

"This was the 'ruse of war' you mentioned?" He nodded. "What did the letter say?"

"'There is no Nine. There will always be the Twelve. Talk to the Commandant by 0700.' At least, that was what they were talking about. And for the five orange pips, they were going to stamp it with twelve first class rings dipped in blood."

"Gruesome touch. Couldn't they just use sealing wax?"

"The thought was that blood would smear more than wax, so he'd get the general impression without seeing specific initials."

"Nothing if not thorough, our lads. I take it from your commendable use of the subjunctive that you don't actually know that they carried out this plan."

"No, Father, it's just an inference. In fact, I told the guys that I thought it was a bad idea—and no nudge-nudge wink-wink stuff about it, either. If one person terrorizes another one, that's no excuse to terrorize him. But it was a social gathering, and I don't usually think it's a good idea to give orders unless you're fairly sure they will be obeyed. So I don't know for a fact that such a letter was written or delivered. If you tell me, though, that Lanier scooted out of the Infirmary ASAP this morning and that the Colonel has been busy all day, I have my theory about what happened."

"Very good, Rob. Thanks for your help. Have I made you late for anything?"

"No, Father. You're going to miss Chris's soccer game if you don't get a move on, though."

"Yes, and I have to stop by my office, too. I'll see you tomorrow."

"Sure thing, sir. Bye."

———

IT WAS GETTING ON for four o'clock when I walked into the office. There were no messages, from Axton or from Louie. I could easily believe that the Archbishop had had other problems than mine to deal with over the course of the day, but, having still not heard from Evans, I did begin to conclude that I'd go ahead and speak to Rhys on Wednesday.

By the time I had straightened up my desk, locked the sacristy, and walked over to the soccer pitch, I'd missed the kickoff. I was in time, though, to see the first goal of the game: a winger from the Wolf Creek team lured our keeper to the far left of the goal, then lofted the ball to a striker at the right side, who jumped out of the crowd of defenders like an NBA player among pigmies and headed the ball in. I took a seat on the team bench next to Brad. "That looked pretty impressive," I said.

"All it takes is practice. In fact, I know a drill on that very play—Hey, ref, you're missing a good game!—but we come out and scrimmage instead." He jumped up: "Position, Keith! Play your position!"

The first half of the game was touch and go: Wolf Creek scored another two goals through well-drilled teamwork, while we got two points for sheer individual brilliance—one when Keith, the center fullback, vastly out of position, made a spectacular breakaway run, and one when Chris, with his usual sense of geometry, intercepted a Wolf Creek fullback's forward pass and rifled it past the goalie, who thought he still had a defense on that side. As usual, a few of the fans came down at halftime to chat with the players on the outer edges of the huddle while Henry gave what passed for a pep talk. In order to get the games over before dark, our league takes the shortest possible breaks, and before long, our side were giving a convincing demonstration of how to bungle a kickoff play.

"That isn't good, is it, sir?" asked one of the cadets who had been standing behind me, as he stepped over the bench to sit down. ("Team bench" is a somewhat loose concept in our league.)

"It stinks, to tell the truth," I said, turning to see who it was. "Oh, hello, Rhys. You're not usually a soccer fan, are you?"

"No, sir, not too much. Actually, someone told me I might find you here. I wanted to talk to you."

"Well, as far as that goes, I wanted to see you, too. Shouldn't we go someplace more private?"

"No, this is okay, I guess. Sir, my mother says you called her about arranging for my baptism."

"Yes, I did, yesterday. Are you still interested?"

"Yes, sir. I'd do it right now if we could. Can we really do it as soon as Saturday, sir?"

"We could, certainly, especially since you've already been through the catechumenate. I know I suggested that to your mother, but I'm a bit surprised to find that you are in such a hurry. What's the story?"

Action on the pitch caught his attention for a moment: "Look, sir, Brandon has a breakaway!" We jumped to our feet to watch our newly-emancipated right wing race half the length of the pitch and kick the ball past the outstretched arms of the diving goalie—and, unfortunately, past the goal post as well.

When we sat back down, I moved to the farthest end of the bench for some semblance of privacy. *I don't quite understand,* I said to myself, *why people keep dodging my questions this week.*

Taking a place beside me, Rhys brushed against my arm. "Are you cold?" I asked: "You're trembling!"

"I'm scared, sir. My father—" he looked as if he were about to cry, and I gave him my handkerchief.

"If you're that upset, we'd better go to my office," I whispered.

"No! Sir, it's safer here, it's like, he can't pay such close attention when I'm in a crowd."

"You mean he's reading your mind?"

"Almost, sir. It's worse when I'm around you, because you're what he's interested in—or your family, I guess I should say. But here at the game, the other people, and the interruptions, it feels like they distract him, somehow. Sometimes, though, he makes me feel like my head's a sort of cabinet: he just opens it up whenever he wants and takes out or puts in whatever he likes. Whatever the good of our family requires."

"And that's what you're afraid of—the way he's poking around in your mind to get at me?"

"No, sir, not really, sir. I'm mostly afraid of what he said you'd have to do to me. I don't want to be burned, sir." The crowd cheered at some successful defensive move—probably Keith, I thought, someplace in the back of my mind. "I know you wouldn't mean to hurt me, sir—I know you'll say that you wouldn't burn anyone—he never means to hurt anyone—but when—well, sometimes things have to happen for the sake of our family, it sort of takes over. Like what had to happen with the puppy Mother got me when I was five. There's just no choice. That's why I want you to baptize me as soon as you can."

I was still trying to avoid drawing attention to us, or I would have grabbed him. "Rhys, you've got to believe me," I whispered fiercely. "I would never hurt you, I'd never hurt anyone, that way. Nothing could make me. But baptism will not absolutely protect you from being hurt that way. That's how I hurt this arm, when your father attacked my brother and me."

"I know baptism isn't some kind of shield, sir. But if I am going to die, I don't want to die without it."

This time I did take his arm. "Rhys, you are not going to be killed—at least, not that way, and certainly not by me. Get that straight, to begin with. Second, remember that as a catechumen, you already count as 'inside the church'—if anything should happen to you, God forbid, before you are baptized—whenever that happens—you would go to your grave just as much a Christian as one who had been baptized. Third, understand that I will baptize you whenever you like, if it comes to that: I don't want you to think your receiving the sacrament somehow depends on this tenuous scheme to end a family feud."

"I understand, sir, but I at least want to think about the Saturday idea: after all, it's my family feud as much as it is yours. What are we talking about doing?"

It was a question which demanded a specific answer, though I wasn't sure at first that I could put it in sophomore terms. "The suggestion is that performing your baptism on Halloween, in the ruins of what used to be my family's homestead, with some additional elements of magical ritual (ones that won't conflict at all with the sacramental rite), might somehow put your father in a position to end this whole business. It wouldn't be a duel, which is what I think he wants, and it wouldn't keep you out of it, which is what I want. And it might not prove anything at all—I'm not sure why it should. Or your father could be right—the extra rituals might somehow compel me against my will, make me some kind of a puppet that would try to burn you the way he tried to burn my brother and me last Sunday night. But I don't believe the magic has been thought of which could compel me to take a life."

The activity was all still at the far end of the pitch: our defense was apparently holding up, but we hadn't scored.

When Rhys answered, it was so quietly that I could hardly hear him. "Please, sir, let's try it. I don't know what else anyone could do. We can use whatever rituals you think would help. Please, though, let's take the chance."

"Okay, Rhys. We'll do it somehow. Listen, there's a special blessing for catechumens—you may know it from before—why don't you come to Mass tomorrow night, and we'll do that as part of your spiritual preparation for Saturday. Now let's look like we're watching a soccer game."

Otter made a spectacular dive to stop a shot from Wolf Creek's best striker, then booted the ball almost to midfield, where the center half got control and passed it on to Brandon at right wing. Larry ran it up the sideline as far as he dared, then crossed to Keeks, who feinted to the right but in fact passed the ball backwards to the center, who shot and scored the tying point. It was more teamwork than our side had displayed all season.

"Do they break ties, sir?" Rhys asked, as the cheering died down.

"In league games like this one they do. There's an overtime with two five-minute halves, then a shootout: up to five penalty shots from each team's best forwards against the other team's best goalie."

As we entered the last minutes of play, overtime seemed a real possibility; then a referee saw Keeks making one of his discreet trips, gave him a yellow card warning, and awarded Wolf Creek a direct kick. Sensing how little time remained, the whole Wolf Creek team, even the goal minder, came up for what seemed likely to be the last play of the game. I think people on both sides assumed Henry was about to replace Keeks if he had a chance to do so without slowing the game disastrously. Indeed, in some leagues he'd have been required to do so. The increasing dimness of the late October afternoon may have had something to do with it as well: but in any case, the Wolf Creek defense, thirsty for blood, ran past Chris (who was standing dejectedly at mid-field) as though he were a disembodied spirit. Our keeper grabbed the Wolf Creek kick out of the air and, before anyone had quite registered what was happening, kicked it back to Keeks, who trapped it, turned, and ran for his life toward the Wolf Creek goal, easily outdistancing their startled goalie, who had been standing more beside him than behind him. With no one to stop him, Chris scored the winning goal just seconds before the final horn sounded. On the way back to the locker room, Rhys drifted off with a couple of other plebes from the bleachers, and I had a brief conversation with Chris about the importance of avoiding rumors: albeit after I congratulated him for the winning play.

———

I HADN'T MUCH MORE than redded up my dinner dishes when the phone rang.

"Hi, Jon. It's Richard Davies calling."

"Hello, Richard. What's up? Nothing wrong in the History Department, I hope."

"No, not at all. I'm actually calling as faculty advisor to the Honor Council. Could you come to a meeting first thing tomorrow morning?"

"Of course I can. How early is 'first thing'?"

"Could you manage a quarter to eight, in my classroom?"

"It'll be a bit of a strain, but I'll be there. I hope this won't be one of those marathon sessions—we have our chapel staff meeting at 8:30 on Wednesdays."

"I hope to be done by then, certainly. They just need you as a witness to one conversation."

"This would be the Lanier case, I suppose: we certainly didn't talk for very long."

"Lanier and Abrams both, as I understand it."

"Well, Abrams admittedly didn't quite tell me the whole truth, though I'd say it was mostly a technical violation. I guess that's for the kids to decide."

"I suppose so. I'll see you at quarter to eight tomorrow morning, then. Have a good evening."

"You too, Richard. God bless."

I couldn't help thinking, as I sat in the living room that night grading *Macbeth* quizzes, that Llewellyn had an unnatural interest in people being burned. I could set aside the idea that he might be bound by modern Neo-pagan ethics, which stress ideas like "Whatever you send out returns threefold," since Louie's magic—and, presumably, mine—long antedated the modern "revival" of witchcraft. Beyond ethical questions, however, the vivid fear of burning which he had instilled in my brother and in his own son—not to mention the eldritch flame he had unleashed against us—seemed somehow obsessive; he invoked more horror than ought to have been necessary to secure either Danny's silence or Rhys's cooperation. Such an emphasis suggested that the real reason for the motif lay in something other than its immediate uses. Danny, I remembered, had spoken as though he thought death by burning were punishment for witchcraft in England, something I had certainly never told him: it was possible that he had picked it up from popular culture, but equally possible that he had heard it from Louie; and Louie, in turn, might have picked it up somewhere—or have learned it as a part of his family's tradition. If the popular misconception were the source, the fact shed little light on Louie's obsession; if, on the other hand, the Evanses had a tradition about burning, and particularly if it had some reference to the Mearses, Louie's pyromania might simply be one aspect of his mad desire to destroy us. Where could the Mearses and the Evanses have met around an *auto-da-fé*? Earlier in their relationship, obviously, rather than later; and, if there really was a burning in England, no earlier than the notorious statute *de Haeretico Comburendo*, which Parliament passed to allow the execution of the Lollard heretics in the fifteenth century. Realizing that I might have found a clue that would allow me to reconstruct part of the lost Book of Shadows, I set aside my homework papers to get out my genealogical files and the *Lightning-Maximilian* volume of *The* Encyclopedia (I had long ago talked the school into letting me take home an old classroom set of the Britannica, so I can practice what I preach when my students work on research papers).

I soon discovered that the first burning in England was actually illegal; the Archbishop of Canterbury was so anxious to be rid of one William Sawtrey that he had the man executed while the statute *de Haeretico* was still being debated in Parliament. The final passage of the act followed quickly, however, and made it clear that Archbishop Arundel intended to show no mercy on those who refused to abandon the teachings of John Wycliff. That severity, I knew, led after about ten years to the failed rebellion of Sir John Oldcastle (the model for Shakespeare's Falstaff), who had finally been taken and hanged above a slow fire in 1417. But Sawtrey and Oldcastle were twenty or thirty years later than Wycliff. Where were the Lollards in the interim? Scattered here and there around the country, apparently: but particularly, the encyclopedia pointed out, in Wales. Given the Welsh origins of the Evanses, this much seemed relevant to my quest. Possibly, one of Louie's ancestors had been burned—not as a witch, but as a Lollard: certainly not before Sawtrey died in 1401, and probably not much after 1430, when, according to the article, persecutions died down.

Of course, even with the copious files Dan and I had accumulated, I hardly had at home the records of the various ecclesiastical courts which condemned Lollards, nor did I have specific genealogical charts for Louie's family. I couldn't even be sure when the first Evanses showed up in Hampshire. At best, my papers might show the first official interaction of the families: a Mears witnessing an Evans will, an Evans making an inventory of a Mears estate, or something of that sort. Still, barring a quick trip to Britain, such records were the best place for me to turn.

After a bit of digging—though less than would have been required if I hadn't typed up abstracts of most of the documents back in the eighties—I tentatively decided that the earliest Evans I could find was David, of Titchfield, who was left ten pounds in the 1433 will of Thomas Mears of Durley. I took out my photocopy of Thomas's will to look for more details. David Evans, I discovered, was "the baseborn son of my daughter Gladys Mears." For a moment, I thought Gladys must have had a romantic interlude with one of the Evanses: though, legally, baseborn children couldn't take their fathers' surnames—which made David Evans hard to explain.

But Gladys, with her own Welsh name, was not one of Thomas's children, as the next clause made clear by leaving the residue of the estate to "William and Edward the sonnes of my late son Ralph and the said Gladys his relict, the said Gladys to be custodian of their portion until they shall reach their majority." Gladys, then, was Thomas's daughter-in-law, so her maiden name could hardly have been Mears—which explained David Evans: he was surnamed not after his father, but rather, as custom required, after his mother, Gladys Evans. That moved the quest back one generation. But how had a Welshwoman with an illegitimate child come to marry a Hampshire farmer, and what connection could she have with someone burned as a Lollard? Chronology suggested a brother, father, or possibly a nephew: but I couldn't get much farther than that on pure logic.

I looked in the will for more information on the Mears side of the marriage. Besides the residue bequest to William and Edward and the ten pounds to David, there were fifteen pound provisions to Alyss and Marjerie, Thomas's daughters, a lamb to each of various godchildren, and token amounts to three executors: "John Aubrey, my brother [-in-law, we would say today], Rich. Appleford, my sister's son, and James Mears, my cousin." The will began, in standard fashion, with instructions for burial, then a bequest to the Church—or, rather, bequests—in this case, there were 12 pence for the poor men's box at St. Peter's Church and twenty pounds to the Abbey of St. Mary and St. John the Evangelist in Titchfield.

That caught my eye: twenty pounds was a remarkable amount for a farmer to give away. For that matter, it was more money than Thomas had given to either of his daughters. The whole inventory of his household added up only to about 175 pounds, so (even allowing for a fair amount of cash around the house that might not show up in an inventory), the twenty pounds came to something between a ninth and a tenth of the whole estate. In fact, I realized that David and the Abbey had come out as well as the two daughters taken together: as I ruminated over the figures, that mathematical evenness began to look, well, odd. Ralph, as represented by his sons William and Edward, had two-thirds of his father's estate, about one hundred twenty pounds; the remaining third had been divided in half, into two sixths, worth thirty pounds each, one of which was shared equally between the daughters, the other split two to one between the Abbey and David. What could explain all this subdivision? I had a hunch, but without a record of births, I couldn't confirm it directly.

Even though I knew the document didn't mention any Evanses, I turned to one of the few earlier wills I had, that of Thomas's older brother, another Ralph, who died in 1406. And there I found what I was looking for: bequests of three pence each to "Ralph, Marjory, Alyss, and Thomas, the sonnes and daughters of my brother Thomas of Durley and his wife Alyss." So Thomas had had *four* children, which made it look suspiciously as though the Abbey and David Evans had split the portion of Thomas, Jr.—perhaps because he was a member of one and the father of the other.

I took out my history of the Abbey and its order, the Premonstratensians, or Canons of St. Norbert. The early fourteen hundreds had been fairly quiet there, marked only by the occasional royal or episcopal visit, or by the election of a new Abbot, such as that of then-Prior Richard Aubrey in 1420. But, I reflected, *John* Aubrey, the witness to the will, had been the brother of Thomas Mears's wife, Alyss—so it looked as though Thomas, Jr., might have had an uncle highly placed in the Abbey which I already thought he might have joined.

As I was closing the book, I glanced at the frontispiece, a sort of genealogical chart of the other abbeys of the Premonstratensian order, and how they were related. Titchfield was a "daughter" (as they put it) of Hales-Owen and a grand-daughter of Welbeck. Among Welbeck's other daughters was Tally; that is, Talyllychau, the only Premonstratensian house in Wales. I looked up Tally in the index. The article on the Abbey was quite brief, but did reveal that in 1410 it had secured a decree of some sort that said any official who wanted to look into its affairs would have to come to Wales to do so, rather than summon the abbot of Tally to come into England. We also knew that in 1414 the Abbot of Welbeck had surrendered his special parental jurisdiction over Tally. On that occasion, under the rules, there would have been an official inspection by representatives of two other abbots—and the two nearest houses were Halesowen and Titchfield.

It was likely, then, that Richard Aubrey, Prior of Titchfield, had been in Wales in 1414 for the official Visitation of Talyllychau. That was my first proposition. I knew, too, that David Evans was at least eighteen by the time Thomas died in 1433, since he, unlike his half-brothers, had not been given a custodian. That meant he had been born in 1415 or before—my second proposition. A look forward in my abstracts revealed that Gladys, according to her tombstone, had died in 1452 at the age of 55: thus, if she would have been unlikely to have had children before her fifteenth birthday, her eldest son David must have been born after 1412—proposition three. It began to look a lot as though Fr. Prior Richard had been accompanied to Talyllychau by a nephew who behaved in a rather unmonastic (or, more precisely, un-canon-like) way with a young Welsh Lollardess and was accompanied or pursued into Hampshire by the prospective mother of his child—a woman who eventually married the canon nephew's elder brother. And someone in her family had been burned as a Lollard heretic, which could only have happened in England: what could have brought that someone out of his Welsh sanctuary, if he hadn't pursued her immediately (which he apparently hadn't done: it was difficult to imagine a pregnant woman making her way from Wales to Hampshire without being overtaken by someone who was really trying to catch up with her)?

Possibly a Lollard crisis would have suggested the chance to set free two birds with one adventure: for a brief time in 1417, one might have planned to rescue Sir John Oldcastle from the gallows and to recover a kinswoman from the Saxons. But Sir John had been burned promptly, within a month of his capture: it was unlikely that a rescue operation could have been conceived and put in train before his demise would have made the project pointless (a result which was precisely what the government intended in getting rid of him quickly). So however mixed the original intentions may have been, eventually the sole goal would have been the recovery of Gladys from her farm in Hampshire. But with child and husband, the lady didn't want to leave. And somehow the rescuer himself is seized—Titchfield was a small enough town for a stranger to be conspicuous—and is tried, condemned, and eventually, like Oldcastle himself, hanged for a rebel and burned as a heretic at the Buttercross in the center of the county town, Winchester, say sometime in 1418: a traumatic enough sight for a three-year-old David hanging onto his mother's skirts.

One last look at the wills gave me the only further insight I could get into the shaping of David Evans. In his word-of-mouth will, taken down in his last illness in 1430, Ralph Mears referred quite clearly to his three sons, *including* David. Three years later, David was denounced as a bastard by his grandfather and sent packing with his bequest of ten pounds, whereas he might have expected twelve times as much. And someplace in the midst of this he found out he was a witch, like the uncle he'd seen burned in Winchester.

I was beginning to see what sort of a family history Llewellyn Evans might have received from his ancestors.

Chapter 6: Wednesday, October 28

I PAID THE PRICE, the next day, of having stayed up so late (when I finally went to bed, it was about three in the morning, and my study was littered with enough books and photocopies to look like a setting for the first scene of *Doctor Faustus*). My early departure for school served to remind me of the foolishness of imitating Dickey Platt's study habits at more than twice his age.

My testimony at the Honor Council meeting went pretty much according to the customary script. I waited for a few minutes in the History Department office, presumably while another witness I saw standing in the hall was being questioned. At about five minutes till, Dr. Davies came to call me into the meeting. Following long-established custom, Dickey, whose office made him President of the Council, opened by reminding me that all the proceedings of the council are confidential. After I had told my story, he asked me to wait around in case any further questions should come up: so I went back to the office and had a cup of coffee with a couple of my history colleagues. Time wore on a bit, and I was about to phone Charley DiRosa, the organist, to say I'd be late for the staff meeting, when the good doctor came back into the office.

"Jonathan, you're going to get a formal apology. Will you be in your office later today?"

"I can be. I'm free second and seventh periods, and I have a sixth class study hall to supervise during fourth."

"Hmmm. The Commandant and the Superintendent have to hear the sentence and sign off on it. Why don't I take your study hall? I think I can cope with thirteen-year-olds for one period."

"I find a whip and chair are usually enough—rarely any need to use the pistol."

"Didn't Captain Breve call them 'little monsters' when you were a cadet?"

" 'Little beasties,' as I remember. And some things don't change."

"Forewarned is forearmed. Thanks for your help, Jonathan."

"Don't mention it. I'm glad to support the system."

—————

ALLOWING FOR MY pronounced disposition to yawn at inappropriate moments, the rest of the morning passed uneventfully, though I did let the third classmen go a couple of minutes early so that I could be sure of getting to my office on time for my fourth period appointment. At a few minutes after eleven, there was a knock on the door.

"Enter," I said, trying to sit up straighter in my chair.

Blair Turley opened the door. He was wearing his Dress A blouse, with cavalry yellow sash and saber, to indicate he was the cadet Officer of the Day. Standing on the threshold, he saluted, properly. "Sir, Cadet Major Turley, E. B., reports to the Chaplain."

"At ease, Mr. Turley, and come in." I was about to ask what I could do for him, but once he stepped aside I saw that there were two boys standing behind him. After a moment's recalibration, I realized that they were Lanier and Abrams in civilian clothes.

"Thank you, sir. If I may, I'll wait outside."

"Of course, Mr. Turley. Oren, Jon, have a seat." Blair shut the door firmly behind him as the other boys sat uneasily on the sofa.

"Well, guys, I guess I can see what the council decided."

"Yes, sir," Jim said. "The Superintendent called our parents while we were still in his office. We both have flights out of South Bend this afternoon."

"Well. He takes all this pretty seriously. I guess that I'm a little surprised, though, Oren, that there was this much fallout just from not giving me a direct answer."

"Yeah, well, I guess that's what we're here for," he answered. "I was supposed to come and talk to you and tell you what happened."

"What do you mean?"

He squirmed nervously, and glanced at Jim. "The whole thing was a fake, Reverend Mears. Nobody came to our room. Jim burned my arm earlier in the evening, then we snuck out and I tied him to the flagpole. The rent-a-cop saw me going back into Main, so I put something about that into the story we had worked out. Then I went back out and 'found' Jim, and brought him back through the Plaza, where there would be a good chance of Platt or somebody seeing us."

"I see. And you two started the story about the Nine?"

"Yeah. It made the story better, and depending on how everything worked out, Jim could have ended up controlling the group if it actually started."

"It seemed like a great prank," Jim interjected. "We never expected York and the others to prank us."

"That was why I saw him waiting for the Honor Council this morning?"

"Oh, sure," he answered. "It wouldn't be honorable not to explain how we were tricked."

"I suppose not. What about the vandalism to Oren's things?"

"Oh, we did that Saturday afternoon when we were planning the whole thing."

"That surprises me, Oren. I always see you at services."

"Services are a required formation, just like Chapel. Someone's being either place doesn't tell you what he believes."

"So what do you believe?"

"I don't believe in anything, and neither does Jim."

"Religion is just superstition, like magic," Lanier added.

"Jim's right. Scientifically, there's no difference between Shabbos prayers and the little kid in Battery B who thinks he's a witch."

"Exactly, sir. Science proves religion is nonsense. There's nothing to believe in but yourself."

"What science are you thinking of, precisely?" I asked.

"The Big Bang, for instance. That proves you can't believe in Genesis."

"How so, Oren?"

"According to science, the universe goes back millions of years, or maybe it just keeps bouncing back and forth for ever. According to the Torah, ha Shem created the world about 5700 years ago."

"I notice that you said 'ha Shem' instead of 'God'—so you're still not taking the name of the Lord your God in vain."

"Just a superstitious habit. Are you trying to change the subject?"

"No, it was just an observation. Have you ever heard of Moses Maimonides?"

"The Rambam, right? He was a medieval rabbi, wasn't he?"

"Yes, he was. Supposed to have been the most insightful teacher since the first Moses. And the most recent science of his day was the philosophy of Aristotle, which was just being rediscovered. Now Aristotle says that universe extends back infinitely in time, so that there was never a beginning. Yet the first word of the Torah is 'in the beginning.' So do you know what Maimonides did about the contradiction?"

"Trashed Aristotle, I suppose."

"No. He said that if science contradicts the obvious meaning of scripture, then we must be reading the scripture wrong. After all, he says, Torah also says God brought Israel out of Egypt with a strong right arm, but no one thinks God actually has a right arm."

"So this Jewish guy says the Bible means whatever he wants it to mean."

"Not quite, and not just him, Jim. St. Augustine of Hippo said about eight hundred years before Maimonides that if Christians expect to be believed when they talk about real miracles, like the Resurrection, they shouldn't make the Bible contradict common sense when they talk about everyday things."

"Still," Jim said, "if the Bible can mean whatever someone says, it's not going to persuade me to believe anything."

"I didn't say it can mean 'whatever'; what I'm saying is that its meaning isn't tied to some particular science, especially not the science of the time when it was written. But no, it's not going to persuade you, and I'm not either, particularly not between now and lunchtime. But I don't think the Bible is particularly written for the purpose of persuasion, either. You'll believe or nor believe, five minutes or five months or fifty years from now, because of your experiences—which I, unlike you at the moment, am persuaded to see as God at work in you."

"Everything turns out for the best," Oren said, "and God's in his heaven and this is the best of all possible worlds. Isn't that the same crap religions have always said?"

"In fact, no, there have been religions that said other things. The old Vikings believed that evil would win in the last battle. But I'm not saying either thing. What I am saying is that I accept the experience of Israel, even through their generations of slavery, that the God of Israel remains sovereign over his creation. And I accept the experience of the Church, that that same God by taking on the form of a slave, by becoming subject to evil and death, and by overcoming them, showed that sovereignty yet more powerfully."

"So evil is okay because God plays by the same rules," Jim objected.

"No, evil is evil and yet the evidence of God's sovereign promise is that he plays by the rules."

"I don't think there is such a thing as evil," Oren said. "It's all just what you think, or what society tells you. Anyway, we were supposed to come and tell you what happened. We've done that, so can we go?"

"Of course. But I do have to say one other thing. What we've been talking about is perfectly sound theology, something people can debate calmly or even have passionate feelings about. And pranks, unlike your Nine, really are an old Annandale tradition. Destroying religious items, though, would make a psychologist sit up and take notice. And burning somebody with an iron, or agreeing to be burned, would be a danger sign, too."

"It was just a joke, Reverend Mears. Don't take everything so seriously."

"I'm not trying to take *it* seriously, Oren, I'm trying to take *you* seriously, both of you. And there's not much I can do to do that but try to warn you to take yourselves seriously. It sounds to me as though each of you is mad about something, though you might not even know what. That's bad psychological technique, by the way—you're not supposed to just confront a client with a conclusion. But we haven't got the time. Maybe it really was all a joke; I hope so. If it wasn't, though, it may have been serious indeed. So all I can do is urge you to pay attention to yourselves."

"Is that it, sir?"

"Yes, Jim, that's it. Good luck to you both. I suppose Mr. Turley will be waiting outside."

I waited a few minutes after they left to give them a decent head start, and then left for the Dining Hall myself.

<hr />

THERE WAS A Faculty Executive Committee meeting scheduled for 4:15. By the end of eighth period, at 3:05, I was actually weary, and dragged back to my office to take a nap. As I opened the door, I could see the pulsing light on the phone that indicated I had a voice mail message. With Dad's health as tenuous as it was, I always felt a chill when I found the malevolent little orange lamp flashing at me. This time, thankfully, it was another, safer, message, though not one I could ignore. With a reluctant glance at the couch, I dutifully called the Bishop's office in Michigan City. Mrs. Equitone, one of those indispensable secretaries who know the entire history of the organization, connected me with only the briefest of greetings: every cleric in the diocese recognized this as the early warning sign of the Bishop's displeasure.

"Jonathan," he began, "I had a call this afternoon from the Bishop of Western Pennsylvania."

"Yes, sir?"

"It seems he had a call from Donald Newman wanting to know why the President of my Standing Committee had decided to sabotage his election."

"I appreciate Fr. Newman's highly developed sense of professional courtesy."

"And he yours, I take it. This was some sort of question that he could have just been asked, but instead the Archbishop's office launches a virtual whispering campaign?"

"The precise accusation was that he had on several solemn occasions given a false answer to the question. And so far as I know the Archbishop's intention was to contact, in person, precisely two people, one of whom was Fr. Newman. Did Bishop Rodin happen to say how Fr. Newman knew the Archbishop was looking into this, if no one did speak to him directly?"

"No, I was led to believe someone who was contacted notified him."

"Testimony either to a highly developed sense of honesty or to a scrupulous attention to confidentiality all the way around. As I am perfectly confident that the Archbishop would not have mentioned my name, I think Fr. Newman must have been doing a good deal of reflection about which of the Archbishop's friends might have passed on the request."

"I imagine so."

"Now Axton has, in fact, a lot of close friends, of whom not a few are on Standing Committees and many, I should think, are bishops. Or am I wrong?"

"No, you're quite right. Axton's probably the most popular archbishop we've had in a decade. Quite a feat for someone who started as an attorney."

"So then Fr. Newman must have had a way of narrowing down the list to just Michigan City—unless he has a whole team of patrons phoning dioceses all across the country."

"Possible, I suppose, but unlikely."

"I think so, too. But the alternative is that Newman worked forward, so to speak, from the episode that gave rise to the question, decided that only a few people could have known about it, whether at first or second hand, and then cross-checked that against his mental list of friends of the Archbishop to look for associations, if not for identities."

"Strictly logical. But then why complain about the Archbishop's friend rather than the actual informant?"

"Because explicit acknowledgment of the informant might reinforce the informant's claim."

"I don't follow."

"I mean, it could be that the only linkage that would allow Newman to identify the informant also proves that Newman must be who the informant thought he was."

"Oh, right. But then he might have been better off saying nothing."

"He might frequently have been better off saying nothing, throughout his career. But you know as well as I do that his instinct has always been to attack."

"Discretion is certainly not his middle name. I have noticed, by the way, Jonathan, that you've managed to avoid giving any specific details."

"As I am obliged to. If you'd like, though, I'd be happy to explain to the Bishop of Western Pennsylvania in words of one syllable that there's a good reason why canon law prevents him from sticking his croziered-and-mitered nose into the affairs of his own Standing Committee, much less that of another diocese."

"Oh, no, thank you, Father, that will be all right. I do have to get along with these people at meetings, after all."

"Better you than me, Bishop. If I do hear anything I can tell you, of course, I'll call you right away."

"Thank you, Jon. God bless you."

"Amen."

THERE DIDN'T SEEM to be much point in trying to get to sleep, no more time than I had left, so I headed back down to the quadrangle for the FEC. We met for an hour and a half, to discuss starting a food cooperative "just to sell staples, cheese and flour and that sort of thing." By the time we had decided to refer that idea to a committee, it was 5:40 and I had twenty minutes to get back to the Chapel and prepare for the Eucharist.

It was the Feast of Sts. Simon and Jude, and Christopher had everything in the sacristy and side chapel ready by the time I got there. He'd even put the service book with the special prayers for the Catechumens at my chair in the sanctuary. That particular bit of foresight, however, meant that I didn't have a way of looking over the order before the service began. So when I called Rhys forward—he came up with Tom Adams, whom he had asked to be his sponsor—I was reading the liturgy cold, seeing it for the first time since I left Cloyne. As Rhys knelt, I picked a collect at random from among those provided, only to find myself saying "Come, O Holy Spirit, come; come as the wind and cleanse, come as the fire and burn . . ." Between the language of the prayer and the effects my jewelry had lately been providing, I was glad we had been taught at Cloyne that only bishops could wear rings while saying Mass.

Chapter 7: Thursday, October 29

AFTER STOPPING by the nursing home to look in on Father, I spent most of Wednesday evening—before a very early personal Taps—looking into a suitable liturgy for the baptism of a witch catechumen by a witch priest on Halloween. I hadn't expected the subject to be covered in detail in any of the standard reference works, but I did find, somewhat to my surprise, an order for a Vigil of All Hallows' Eve, different from the vigil for All Saints', to be used with a procession to a graveyard and including such lessons as the Witch of Endor and the War of Michael and Satan.

My first class on Thursday morning wasn't until eleven. I usually use the time after my infirmary visit to get to work on my sermon for Sunday, and I did in fact read over the lessons again—"Let us now praise famous men," from Ecclesiastes, the vast crowd of saints, from Revelation, and the Beatitudes—but they are familiar texts, and while I couldn't say I could preach about them in my sleep, the fact is that Rhys's baptism did a better job of holding my attention.

Using the order for All Hallows Eve and the circle-spell I'd developed while I was at Cloyne, I eventually produced a vigil that began with a Paschal Candle ritual and went on through an elaborate procession, the ancient hymn "Phos Hilaron," a selection of the All Hallows lessons and canticles, Baptism itself, and the Holy Eucharist. What with thurifer, crucifer and acolytes, the whole thing seemed to require a cast only slightly smaller than that of *Aïda*: but there was sure to be no shortage of cadets interested in being off-campus at midnight, especially on Halloween. Though I felt some responsibility to the Commandant not to take the whole Corps with me, and a good deal more to the kids not to expose them to Louie's magic, I was also reluctant to conduct a private baptism, particularly in a case where there already several rather unusual aspects to the ceremony. It was the question I'd faced when the idea first came up on Sunday, and I wrestled with the ethical issue again as I walked to my classroom.

Having "done" Faulkner, after a fashion, I wanted to move my First Classmen on to T. S. Eliot. I wrote my senior honors thesis on Eliot, and I suppose I spend more time on him in class than most people would—I start with "The Love Song of J. Alfred Prufrock," which is more or less standard, and press on to *The Waste Land*, which is about as far as high school kids usually go; but I also like to at least expose the classes to Eliot's later, more obviously religious work, particularly the *Four Quartets*.

Eliot, being Eliot—being, frankly, a snot-nosed Harvard intellectual (and yes, it takes one to know one)—starts "Prufrock" with a longish quotation from Dante's *Inferno*, one he offers to his readers in the original Italian. So I find that teaching the poem requires a short course in Dante, at least enough so the boys can understand that the opening quotation is only the most obvious connection between Eliot's poem and the older one.

Stuart Cook, one of the kids in my fourth period class, took exception to Dante's picture of the underworld. "I thought Revelation says all the damned will burn in Hell, Chaplain." It was only the second or third time he'd talked in class since August, and if I hadn't been looking right at him when he spoke, I wouldn't have been sure whose voice I was hearing.

"It certainly does at some places, Stu," I answered, "though Dante could point to other biblical passages with other images, like 'outer darkness.' And, technically, he only claims to be describing Hell as it is now, between the death of the individual evildoer and the resurrection of the dead at the Last Judgment. God *could* have other plans for those souls they've reunited with their bodies. Though I have to say he doesn't usually write as if he thought there were going to be great changes; and what he says about suicides probably suggests that he does think the interim Hell reflects the final one.

"The main thing for him is this idea of the *contrapasso*, what we might call making the punishment fit the crime. Essentially, each of the souls is frozen in whatever it chose instead of God."

"Sin." Stuart didn't like to waste words.

"Yes, though 'sin' can also refer to the whole human state of being cut off from God. The idea is, souls who denied the Resurrection wait for it, ironically, in burning tombs; souls who started schisms are split apart; flatterers are up to their noses in sewage; and in the particular case that Eliot quotes, people who gave evil advice are in tongues of flame, since it was their tongues that characterized their sin. He's thinking like the Native Americans in cowboy movies who say 'white man speak with forked tongue.' "

"And Pentecost."

"Right. By giving bad advice, these people are sort of opposite to the Apostles, upon whom tongues of flame appeared when the Holy Spirit came to them on Pentecost." I paused, and when there was no further comment, went on: "In Dante's big picture, it's important that these are the first people in Hell who don't want to be remembered back in the land of the living. Their lives are so horrible that they just want to be forgotten, and that's probably the point of overlap with Eliot's Prufrock character, though he does in fact picture himself as a counselor from time to time. He compares himself to Polonius, for example, a character you'll remember from reading *Hamlet* last year." They were beginning to shift nervously in their seats, and, as usual, some had even closed their books by the time the bell interrupted me. "But that will have to wait for tomorrow. Dismissed."

Brad and RJ were sitting by themselves at one of the faculty tables when I got to lunch, and I soon joined them.

"Witches and Nazis, heh, heh," Brad said. "You are having a busy week."

"Well, at least the Nazis were fake," I answered. "And as far as the other, how busy are you two likely to be during the day on Saturday?"

"I've been keeping my social calendar open since you spoke to us," RJ said, and Brad nodded in agreement. "What's the plan?"

"As I told you, I've been hoping to avoid making a sensation. Or maybe at this point I should say, a bigger sensation. Anyway, the plan is to take Rhys out to my old family farmhouse Saturday night and baptize him."

"Why not just do it in the Chapel?"

"Well, RJ, that's the complicated part." As no one seemed to be threatening to sit down near us, I gave them an outline of the whole Mears-Evans affair. To their credit, they managed to keep shoveling in their meals pretty steadily, pausing only during the most sensational moments.

"So basically you think the boy's the bait in a magical trap, and you're not only believing this, but proposing to walk right into it."

"In fact, Brad, he's proposing that we should believe it and walk right into it with him."

"Good point. I stand corrected. Still, I can believe any number of impossible things before BRC. And it's not as though I have anything else planned for Saturday."

"No more do I. So I guess we go."

"Thank you both, gentlemen. I do appreciate it. Now the problem I've been fretting about again this morning is the kids. Rhys, obviously, has to be there, and Rob and Dickey and Jeff will insist that it's part of their duty to attend. Rhys has asked Tom Adams to be his sponsor. That's pretty much the limit of the kids who are directly involved. It would make life easier for me to have Keeks there, and, again, it's arguably his duty. I'm wondering, though, about the other kids involved in the esbats in the first place—this might give them some sort of closure. And I suppose Rhys might just want to invite his friends to his baptism in the ordinary way."

Brad pushed a last bit of steamed broccoli idly around his plate with his fork. "What exactly are you worried about, Jon? Is there some real danger to the kids, or is it just a question, as you said, of sensationalism?"

"Well, the second, I guess. I really think Louie's only interested in attacking me, and I guess it's hard for me to believe that anyone would want to harm innocent teenaged bystanders."

"But, Jonathan," RJ said, "on your own account of things, he's already hurt all the kids involved in these séances. Not physically, maybe, but really, nonetheless."

"I agree, Jon. It seems to me you're being naïve, at best. You could probably throw a baked potato from here and hit half-a-dozen innocent kids whose parents wanted to harm them. Even physically, in some cases."

"You're right, of course, Brad. Though I have to say that from Louie's point of view there wouldn't be anything harmful in an esbat—he presumably takes it seriously, somehow, possibly even as a religion. On the other hand, he's certainly terrorized Rhys—you might not be able to make a case for actual abuse, though I think you could come awfully close. And he scared the hell out of my brother a long time ago."

"And yet you don't think he'd harm an innocent bystander."

"Okay, I'm an idiot. Should I just call in Rob English and say, 'This has gotten too serious, we're taking it out of your hands'?"

"He does understand that we're the adults, doesn't he?"

"Of course he does, Brad," RJ said. "But if we give him some adult responsibilities, we can't complain about him not instinctively drawing the line where we want him to."

"And for what it's worth, he is an adult; I mean, he's eighteen and some change."

"Right, Jonathan. But that isn't where I was going, exactly. I wanted to ask you whether there were anything you could do to protect any hypothetical kids who might be involved in this exercise."

"Yes, I think so. Really, that's the point of all the elaborate ritual stuff I was talking about. But if you ask me whether these are *reasonable* precautions, I have to say I don't have any way of telling. The whole business is unreasonable in the first place."

"Okay, Jon. You don't know whether these defenses are reasonable," Brad said. "Would you say they represent the state of the art? Would your interesting ancestors have trusted them?"

"I think they did trust them, yes. And on the one occasion when we had to rely on them lately, they worked."

"Then that seems to me a decent basis for proceeding with the kids who've actually involved themselves in this already, either from the esbats or from their offices. But I wouldn't bring in any new, unrelated, cadets, even if Kirkfleet does want the support of his friends."

"So you're accepting Jon's idea that the kids who've been participating in this would benefit from seeing it brought to a close."

"It seems reasonable to me, Brad. Then again, I'm not the chaplain."

"But I am, and I suppose I'd better get back to it. Thanks for the help, guys. I'll keep you posted on the details, but figure on working on the project Saturday during the day."

We stuck our trays in the rack just ahead of the usual rush of kids who'd suddenly remembered that they had a 12:40 class, as, indeed, did I.

I talked with the sophomores about Lady Macbeth's sleepwalking scene, and it seemed that the period was over before I knew it. I just barely remembered to give them a writing assignment for the next Monday. Rob and Richard's class made somewhat heavy going of the Dante lecture, but we got through it somehow, and I headed back to my office about half-past three.

Since my path took me right by Main Barracks, I decided to stop in and see if I could find Rhys to talk with him about his guest list. He wasn't in his room, so I left a note on his desk. The miniature saber I had last seen at Saturday's esbat was lying out—apparently Rhys had stopped to collect his mail on the way back from his last class—and I idly picked it up, half expecting it to activate the golden light of my ring. When it did not, I drew the little blade—it was about eight inches long, and something less than a quarter of an inch from the cutting edge to the back. I saw that, unlike the usual model as sold in the souvenir section of the Quartermaster's store, it had engraving on the blade—D.O.M. to L.H.E. 1972, went one side, while the other had a Greek phrase that I knew to be the motto of Dan's fraternity. Presumably, the thing dated back to Dan's initiation, which had been so honored by Louie's deigning to visit. At least, I thought, if Dan had fallen into bad company during his college years, he'd preserved enough sense of good manners to have an appropriate gift for the visiting dignitary. I suppose he would also have had clean underwear if he'd been hit by a truck.

There were no voice mail messages waiting for me this time, and I thought about just going home, but decided it would be easier for Rhys to get hold of me if I stayed at school for Retreat Parade and SRC. So I had the pleasure of an uninterrupted nap, and was actually sitting at my desk reading e-mail when, as the chimes rang half-past four, there was a knock at the door.

"Enter," I said, and to my surpass Herb Mathis came through the door. I jumped up to greet him.

"Father! I'm sorry, I was expecting a cadet. Please, have a seat. I'm afraid I can't offer you any sherry, but if you'd care for a Coke, I might be able to scare up a proper glass."

"Thank you, Father, I'm sure," he said, sitting down wearily in one of the armchairs. "A can of soda would be fine."

I took two from the fridge and sat down on the couch. "What brings you down to Annandale?"

"You would not believe it, Jonathan, but I have been on the telephone almost all day."

"Over the Donald Newman affair, I take it."

"Indeed. And let me say to begin with that I have no doubts at all about your discretion, or that of the Archbishop. It's obvious that Newman has somehow figured out that I was the source of these inquiries. And that seems to me a virtual admission that I was right in the first place."

"The same idea had occurred to me," I said, and gave him a summary of my conversation with the Bishop.

"Apparently there's some sense of decorum at work," he replied. "I haven't heard from any bishops, myself, but there have been an assortment of priests and at least one cathedral dean."

"What, precisely, are they asking? It's not as though they could threaten a person . . ."

"A couple have tried, certainly. Not threatening one's health or safety, of course, but making clear suggestions that if one ever wanted to move to a parish outside Wabana County, one might play by the rules."

"Does one, in fact, want to move to such a parish?"

"In fact, one has purchased a space in one's parish columbarium. I didn't say they were effective threats."

"What would be involved in playing by the rules?"

"Letting a diocese choose its bishop without 'external interference,' apparently. The mere fact that a conservative diocese like Michigan City might disagree with the theology of a liberal diocese on the east coast doesn't constitute a reason to prevent that diocese from choosing a similarly enlightened bishop."

"I suppose it doesn't, until enlightenment passes on into heresy. But you haven't said anything about baptism."

"No, curiously enough, it never came up."

"It strikes *me* as curious—non-ironically, I mean—that no one has called *me*. Why single out you and the Bishop?"

"I imagine they think you're incorruptible—you don't work for the Church, you live on land which, as you always say, your family stole from the Indians, and you show no signs of ambition commensurate with your well-documented talents."

"Thank you, I'm sure."

"I didn't mean to compliment, Jonathan, or to insult. But from Donald Newman's point of view, you're presumably beyond direct influence."

"I suppose so. And I am only one friend of the Archbishop, and one vote on the Standing Committee, whereas you and the Bishop are individual players, so to speak. I take it from the way you've reported these events that you didn't drive down to tell me to phone Axton and call off the dogs."

"No, I did not. Until you said so just now, I didn't know that you hadn't been harassed, and I came down to lodge a personal appeal for you to stay the course."

"That's easy enough: I can go on doing nothing in particular fairly well, I think."

He laughed with clerical politeness. "You are a *bit* unfair to yourself, Jonathan. Besides, if the Bishop and I have been hearing all of this, it's at least possible the Archbishop has been the recipient of a certain level of response as well. If you were to have a call from New York, you might have to do more than 'stand and wait,' as Milton said."

"Well, 'Barkus is willin',' as Dickens said." A beep from my computer interrupted our literary exchange.

"Is that the sound that means you have mail?"

"Yes. I left it open when you came in—but not to worry, it'll keep."

"Oh, no, no worry at all. I'm just curious—it's a whole new world to me. What do you have to do to retrieve the message?"

"It's quite easy—step over here behind the desk and I'll show you."

A moment or two later, we were reading together a news bulletin, dated for release on Friday, from the national church offices. The Standing Committee of the Diocese of Delaware, it advised, had, in consultation with the office of the Archbishop, determined to withdraw its request for consents to the election of the Reverend Donald Newman until such time as the consents might be obtained from the General Convention of the Church. Bishop Bays, the incumbent, would remain in office until his scheduled retirement on the First Sunday in Advent, after which time the Standing Committee would become the Ecclesiastical Authority of the diocese. Father Newman had graciously agreed to the Standing Committee's request to serve the diocese as Canon Administrator until the General Convention.

It was an outrageous plan, enough to leave both of us sputtering. The provision to have General Convention give consent to an election was meant to save time and money when the new bishop had been elected within a few months of the convention's triennial meeting—but it was nearly two years until the next scheduled session, and Delaware had, in any case, already begun the usual approval process.

"Good grief, Jonathan," Herb said, as he found his way back to a chair. "Surely that violates the canons. I mean, they're saying in effect that they don't think they can get the votes, so they're just going to hire him anyway."

"No 'in effect' about it, that's exactly what they're doing, and I'm sure it's uncanonical. I suppose the argument would be that they could rescind the whole election now, and re-elect Newman a few months before the next convention. But I don't even think that's up to a Standing Committee—you'd have to call the Diocesan Convention back into session to cancel the election. At least, you would in this diocese."

"What's going on, then?"

"Politics, presumably. They're thinking that some conservative diocese will have elected a bishop by the next convention, and they can trade votes for votes—which someone in New York must have at least suggested: they wouldn't try this if they weren't sure they were going to be allowed to get away with it. And it isn't as though there were some court that could step in. I suppose Newman could object to being put on ice, but that's probably why he gets the new job."

"A carefully arranged compromise, then."

"Very carefully arranged, as if by a master negotiator. I'd say the only question was whether your contribution pushed the whole thing over the edge, or something like this was in the works all along."

"Do you think you'll ever find out?"

"Eventually, perhaps. But I do get the feeling I shouldn't ask right now. I don't know whether you noticed the return address line of that e-mail, but it didn't come directly from the Archbishop's office: it was sent by some functionary a good ways down the organizational chart."

"So there are subtleties to this form of communication, too."

"Apparently so, though I wouldn't have thought it."

"And I don't suppose you could phone the Archbishop at this time of day, in any case," he said wistfully.

"No, it's a bit late, I guess. Maybe I'll hear something tomorrow. Or if I disabuse myself of the impression that I'm supposed to lay low, I may call."

"Of course. Well, I suppose I should head back to Withougan."

"It's almost time for Retreat Parade—you might as well stay and see the show. It's not the same as the Sunday spectacular, but it's still impressive. And I do owe you a meal, if you can stay for supper."

"Thank you, Jonathan, perhaps I shall. Didn't you say you were waiting to see a student, though?"

"Yes, in a general sort of a way, but by now he's probably forming up for parade. If I catch him and make an appointment, we should be fine."

⸺

I HAD NO TROUBLE finding the Rhys in formation before the parade, and arranged to come by his room at the beginning of the evening study period. After retreat, I carted Herbert off to a nice dinner in the Bayview Room. By half-past seven, I had brought him back to his own car and was once again climbing the stairs to the third floor of Main. I met Rhys on the second landing.

"Chaplain! I was just on my way down to meet you. Good to see that you can still double time up the stairs, sir!"

"Cheeky brat!" I puffed. "You're supposed to be marching in the halls, anyway, aren't you, rather than chatting with passing strangers?"

"Sir, yes, s—I mean, yes, sir. But long-lost cousins aren't actually strangers, are they?" He grinned.

"Perhaps not, but alumni are still alumni. Wipe that smile off your face and let's go. I suppose you've signed out to the Library?"

"Yes, sir. I thought we could talk on the way, or in one of the study rooms when we got there."

"Sounds like a plan."

We took the walk toward the old library, officially the Memorial Building, on the lake side of West and South. It would have been pitch dark in my day, or nearly so, with only a few widely-spaced streetlights. Now, it was a brightly-lit pathway: so I could see clearly when, in the middle of some idle prefatory chit-chat about the day's events, the boy's face twisted—or, rather, froze—and he began to laugh. It was that deeper voice I'd heard on Saturday night, and now I realized that it was less natural to him than I'd thought: not ventriloquism, but not something under his control, either. At this distance, it seems melodramatic to call it an evil laugh, but just then I had no doubt of the malice behind it. Without really thinking about what I was doing, I put my hand on his head, knocking off his uniform cap, and commanded: "In the Name of Jesus Christ, be gone!" There was a flash of welcome golden light, and the episode was over as suddenly as it had begun, leaving only the shaking boy behind as evidence of what had happened. Picking up the cap, I steered Rhys back to his room, told the Barracks Inspector I was giving him permission to lie in his bed even though it was study period, and gave the orderly change and orders to bring us sodas from the vending machine in the company lounge.

When Rhys seemed to have calmed down a bit, I asked: "Was that your father?"

"I guess so, sir. It's never been like that before. I mean, he pokes around all the time in my head, but this only happens in the esbats, once we've made the circle of power, and I've never thought it was just him, I mean, I thought there was some greater power behind it all, or something. I'm sorry, I just don't know . . ."

"That's all right, Rhys. I suspect there may well have been a greater power at work in all of this. And a priest isn't supposed to deal with powers like that by a blast from his magic ring, either. I don't know how much sense I can make of it, but I'm not sure either of us is in good enough shape to try to figure it all out now. Listen, little cousin. I want to go over the names of the cadets who are coming to your baptism on Saturday, because I have to take care of the paperwork tomorrow. Then I want to arrange for someone to keep an eye on you for the rest of the night. I'll see if I can find Mr. Platt, since he apparently doesn't need much sleep."

Rhys gave me the names of the boys who were already involved, for better or worse: apparently the attendance had not been restricted to the group I'd seen on Saturday evening. We ended up with Jeff Mills, from the First Class, and one second classman, Willie Hawkes, the B Battery First Sergeant, who'd once had a pizza delivered to himself in my British Lit class. Adams, Leone and Perez represented the Third Class, and there were two fourth classmen whom I knew only as names: D'Angelo and Clay. With Rob, Richard, Keeks, Brad, RJ, Danny, Caroline, and me, we made a group of sixteen: or three more than a witches' coven. But I was just as happy not to be doing everything according to Wiccan precedent.

I gave Rhys my blessing, and admonished him to say his prayers before he went to bed. Then I tracked down Richard, who had signed out to Haddam Hall. As an alumnus, I needed no invitation to enter the sacred precincts, and I soon had the Personnel Officer in a discreet corner of the second floor library. I told him about the most recent event and gave him directions to stay with Rhys for the rest of the night: "You can sit up in his room, or move him down to your quad—whatever you think best."

"Don't worry, sir. I'll manage something—every now and then we have to keep tabs on a kid who's being hazed, so there's a precedent. Is there something I'm supposed to do if anything happens? Could Rhys be hurt?"

"He could, certainly, but I doubt it. He might very well be scared, though, even if nothing else happens, and that's what I'm mostly concerned about. If anything actually out of the ordinary happens, call me at home right away, and send for any adult help you can get, even Lieutenant Brennan. And here, for what it's worth, trade rings with me for tonight. And say your prayers."

We managed the switch of jewelry, though we had to wear the rings on odd fingers to make them fit, and I went home to a fitful sleep.

Chapter 8: Friday, October 30

WITH CONSIDERABLE EFFORT, I made it to school not long after Reveille. Rhys had spent the night on a mattress on the floor in the officer's quad, where he had apparently gotten the indulgent attention that might have been lavished on a foundling puppy in other circumstances; indeed, he seemed quite proud of himself for having hung out with the big kids, though he wouldn't have put it that way. I retrieved my ring from Richard and had breakfast in the Dining Hall, where the Friday abstinence gave me an excuse to turn down the proffered Creamed Chipped Beef on Toast (universally known as SOS, by way of abbreviation for 'Shit on a Shingle').

Back in my office after visiting the Infirmary, I drafted the Special Order for the Commandant in such a way as to give some of the boys two separate leaves—one for the core group, right after DRC on Saturday, for us to go out and get the place cleared up and ready, then another, general, one at ten-thirty—half an hour after Taps—for the service itself. I also requisitioned the Building and Grounds' department's huge tent top, and reserved the school vans to haul everyone back and forth: it wasn't really too far to march, but I didn't see why the kids should have to walk when they could ride. And I ordered the Mess Hall's classic box lunches to have along in case we worked through SRC, which was at five-fifteen on Saturdays. In the afternoon I went to watch another soccer game: we played Withougan High and lost, 1-0.

Danny and Caroline pulled into my driveway about half-past eight that evening—they had made pretty good time, given that Danny always works in his office until after five. I was in the bathroom when they arrived, but Danny (who had after all grown up in the house just as much as I) let himself in through the breezeway door, which had never been locked since the breezeway and garage were built in '62. I walked into the living room to find Caroline inspecting the family rogue's gallery on the mantle. She was tall for an almost-fifteen-year-old; her red-blond hair hung below her shoulders. She heard me step on the squeaky sill of the doorway into the hall, and came running to hug me.

"Uncle Jon!" she cried, "Daddy won't tell me what's going on!"

"And a cordial good evening and welcome to you too, my darling niece and god-daughter," I answered.

"I'm being rude again, aren't I? I'm sorry. But we don't *ever* just throw things in the pickup and drive off for the weekend. And Daddy has been *so* mysterious. Is something wrong with Grandpa?"

"No, dear, nothing like that, though he's no better. It's something to do with the Academy. I'll explain it all later. Where is my baby brother?"

"In the kitchen, I think," she said.

"Well, if you're willing to let me loose, O best beloved, I'd like to go say hello."

"Oh, all right. But you're not getting away." With Caroline sticking right by my side, I went into the kitchen, where my brother's hindquarters protruded from the refrigerator.

"Excuse me, sir," I said, "Am I to understand that you are responsible for this?"

"At least fifty percent," he answered, without changing his posture. "Don't you keep *any* food in the house anymore? Human beings weren't meant to live on tofu and yogurt."

"I thought we could go down to the Corner Tavern."

"Do they still make pork tenderloin sandwiches?"

"By hand. But I was thinking of the 'bar shrimp basket,' myself."

"I thought the Lakeshore was the place to go for baskets," Caroline objected.

"Hush, dear one," I answered. "Children should be seen and not heard. Your father and I are discussing adult questions here."

"Well, why don't the two of you stop discussing and let's go eat."

"Once again, Dan, your amazing daughter has penetrated to the existential heart of the matter. Why not, indeed? Which leaves only the minor technical question of who will drive."

"Well, my big pickup truck is blocking your tiny little car, Reverend Brother: so that answers your second question. If you are willing to let my daughter go, we could probably leave right now."

"Let her go!" I exclaimed. "She's the one who's holding on to me." She did release me, then: but I was free only to be clasped in an even more suffocating embrace by her father.

"Careful," I whispered, "I hurt my arm somehow last Sunday."

"That's what you get for being your brother's keeper," he replied.

Over dinner at the Corner, a malted (Dan insisted) at the drug store for dessert, and tea and Laphroaig (my favorite single malt whisky) at home in the living room, I recounted the recent events with Rhys Kirkfleet and my reconstruction of the fifteenth century history of our family. Caroline listened quietly for the most part, asking only a few questions, unlike her father, who constantly pressed for more details. It wasn't until I had reached the end of the tale that she asked, "Does this mean I'm a witch, too?"

Dan looked at me, with the full effect of those magnetic eyes, as he had when he waited for me to tell him of Mother's death, hoping that by their force he could somehow change what he knew I was bound to say. "Only your uncle would know for sure, dear," he said quietly.

"I'm not sure, either. But I imagine you are. It seems to be a dominant trait; after all, if it weren't, it would have died out by now."

"What can we do to find out, Uncle Jon?"

"Well, the family talent seems to run to light, whatever that's worth. I'm a little hesitant to experiment, though, with Louie Evans breathing down our necks, as it were."

"Did Grandpa and Grandma teach you the prayer you talked about before?"

"Yes, of course," I answered.

"And did you say it every night—that particular prayer, I mean?"

"Yes, Jon and I both did. What does that have to do with anything, princess?"

"Well, Uncle Jon has said all this about magic being in our family for five hundred years, and yet you talk as though Grandma and Grandpa never used magic at all. Maybe they just didn't know about it, but just a second ago you really wanted to protect me from all this—couldn't it be that they wanted to protect you all, too? And that the only thing they taught you was the one thing that could only help, the one thing that could never go wrong, and the one thing you wouldn't even recognize as magic? I mean, maybe it wasn't an accident that Uncle Jon thought of that prayer when he wanted something to protect you. They just concealed the visible part of the magic, somehow."

"Child, you are too wise by half. I'm sure you're right. In fact, it wouldn't surprise me to find out that there's some sort of concealed magical protection around the whole house—potentially, at least. Do you remember the prayer?"

"Yes. Daddy taught it to me when I was little, too."

"But I apparently didn't know what I was doing. What are you thinking of, Jonathan?"

"Are we about ready to retire? I've made up the bed in Mom and Dad's room for Caroline, and the attic room . . ."

"Is for me. At least you've gotten rid of the bunk bed in our room. In any case, I'm certainly ready to call it a day."

"Me, too, Uncle Jon."

"Okay, then. Why don't we just kneel right here and Caroline can start our evening prayers with Matthew and company. And Dan, you and I will try to be supportive without actually doing anything ourselves."

We knelt and joined hands, and Caroline recited the childish prayer, just as her father and I had recited it thousands of times before. But this time—whether it was happening for the first time, or, rather, as I am inclined to think, we were seeing for the first time what had always happened, a dome of Lady-blue light surrounded us—not simply covering us, as had been the case with the golden light when Danny and I worked such magic over the telephone, but expanding outward until it reached, and then passed into, the walls themselves. There, it seemed (I say seemed, for one could see nothing), it remained—a barrier against assault, and perhaps even a tripstring to summon, if need be, those mighty ones for whose protection she had prayed: or some such lesser powers as might have reason to defend our house and our home.

"That seems to answer that question," Danny muttered.

"Indeed," I said. "The Lord be with you."

"And also with you," they answered.

"Let us pray. Almighty God, from whom all fatherhood in heaven and earth is named, behold and bless our family gathered here, and all those whom we love now absent from us: defend them from all dangers of soul and body, and grant that both they and we, drawing nearer to you, may be bound together by your love, in the communion of your saints and the fellowship of your Holy Spirit."

"Amen," they answered.

I went on: "I ask your prayers for Rhys David, who is about to be baptized."

"And for Grandfather, who is dying."

"And for Susan."

I waited a moment for further intercessions, then led the *Our Father*. When I gave the Benediction, I looked like the man with the burning hand in *Julius Caesar*.

Chapter 9: Saturday, October 31

I WOKE UP to the unaccustomed smell of someone cooking breakfast. Tossing an AMA regulation robe over my pyjamas, I padded out to the kitchen to find Danny at the stove.

"Whatcha cookin', baby brother?"

"Mostly things I brought up with me from Bean Blossom, to tell you the truth. Thank God you *did* have some eggs in the ice box."

"We try to cooperate with the needs of our guests. What's the menu?"

"Scrambled eggs, buckwheat pancakes, venison sausage, biscuits and gravy. Coffee, if I can ever figure out where you've taken to hiding it."

"Over here in the freezer—it keeps better. I'll get it."

"Thank you. And, if your tastes haven't yet matured, I suppose I could whip up some Maypo."

"That's okay, I can live without it this once. I used the last of it for a Sunday supper a couple of weeks ago, anyway. Is my god-child still asleep?"

"Her? Hardly. She's out running. Should be back by the time breakfast is ready, though. Why don't you get the coffee out for me and then see if you can get dressed and shaved in less than forty-five minutes."

I tossed the frigid coffee can at him—irritatingly, he caught it with no trouble—and went to dress. I made it back in just over half an hour—admittedly, what was left of my hair was still damp, but I *was* technically dressed and ready to eat.

The three of us breakfasted gloriously, read the morning papers, and drove to the nursing home to see Dad. The nurses had him sitting up, still in the old blue chenille bathrobe he refused to relinquish, but he seemed no more conscious of us than usual. We all spoke to him, held his hand, kissed him, but the same vacant stare and mumble continued. I had brought the oil for the sick along, as I often did, thankful that my office at least gave me something to do for him. That day, on an impulse, I asked Dan and Caroline to join me in laying hands on him as I anointed him. There were no spectacular luminescent effects, but I think they were reassured by joining me in the ritual.

We met Brad, RJ, and eight of the boys at the Chapel, and loaded one van with an assortment of candlestands, the thurible and incense-boat, a wooden processional cross, the holy water vat and sprinkler, the verger's wand, two dozen folding chairs, and the portable altar Father Franklin had made back in the sixties. We had a sort of bucket brigade running from Dan in the safe to Keeks in the van, but I packed the huge shell we used for a baptismal font by hand.

Eventually, we had left only the silver ewer and the communion vessels, which Danny suggested would be more secure if left in the safe until the last minute. Dan had also, with more foresight than I was bringing to bear on the situation, put three rakes and the lawn mower from our garage into the back of the pickup. He began to seem almost as eager for the ceremony as Rhys and I were. After stopping by the Mess Hall to claim the box lunches, our little cortege proceeded west and north to the Homestead.

Predictably, the kids, used to the relative if spacious confinement of the campus, took off in every direction as soon as we had pulled up in the tall grass at the end of the rutted dirt driveway: some ran to the barn, some toward the basement that was all that remained of the house, some toward the assortment of weathered sheds that held the rusted remains of 30-years-unused discs, harrows and plows.

Rob and Dickey were on the way to the well-house (made of the remains of the original log cabin) when I called after them: "Mr. English! Will you kindly organize this detail!"

"Sir," Rob said, stopping as briefly as possible, "Cadet Colonel English, R.M., respectfully suggests to the Chaplain that in the case of a religious project Cadet Captain Pruett, C.S., Regimental Aide to the Chaplain, is the responsible officer."

"Gotcha," Danny whispered in my ear.

"Wipe that smile off your face," I said, with deliberately indefinite pronoun reference, and then shouted "Pruett" at the top of my lungs—somewhat superfluously, as he was standing about six feet behind me on the other side of the van. Amidst the general amusement of my brother and colleagues, I asked him to assemble the troops—which, to give him credit, he did with some expedition. Before long, Willie was supervising one detail of three as they policed the basement by hand, picking up old nails, half-melted pieces of glass, and other fragments of a home; behind them, Mike and Miguel raked, while RJ followed up with the mower.

Brad, Keeks, Rhys, Danny and Caroline were waiting to help me move the assorted liturgical bric-a-brac I had accumulated for the occasion.

"Chaplain," Rhys said, holding the shell carefully in his hands, "Do we have to use this for a font?"

"Well, no, but I'm not sure what we could use instead of it. Did you have something in mind?"

"Actually, sir, I did. We were down in the barnyard just now, and there's this big thing, like a long narrow bathtub, or one of those old-fashioned stone coffins—"

"A sarcophagus."

"Yes, sir. It's about three feet deep. It looks like it would be perfect, sir, and I think there are enough of us here to move it up the hill and lower it down into the basement."

"Rhys," I said, smiling, "that's a cattle trough, something for cows to drink out of. I don't really think it would be appropriate for a Christian baptism."

Keeks answered me: "That's true, sir, but then again a place for cows to eat out of wouldn't be appropriate for a Christian nativity, either."

"Ouch," I said. "Well, if I don't know the Bible, I at least know how to choose good assistants. Okay, so there *isn't* any theological reason not to be baptized in a cattle trough. But there are some practical difficulties: water, first of all—though I suppose we could divert the old artesian well, if the main valve isn't rusted shut—and if you really want to be immersed instead of having water poured over your head, I don't have one of those weighted-hem modesty gowns they make for the purpose. You'd have to wear a swimsuit or gym shorts or something."

He persisted: "But isn't it traditional to wear nothing at all?"

Hmph, I thought, *still stuck on that "skyclad" nonsense.* "Surely," I answered, "but the tradition died out several centuries ago. Besides, there will be a young lady present: that sort of thing would hardly be appropriate."

"Uncle Jonathan!" the young lady in question objected.

I turned to Dan for support, but he was at least as much a liberal as his daughter: "It'll be okay, Jonathan: don't worry about it."

"All right, I can tell when I'm beaten. I'll have to rewrite a bit of the liturgy, though, and bring an alb for Rhys to wear once he's been baptized. And we'll need a lot more oil: there's an extra anointing involved, as I remember. We'll have one greasy Christian on our hands."

"I could bring my own towel," Rhys added helpfully.

"Okay, fine. We'll do it. Dan, can you, Brad, Caroline, and Rhys work on moving things so the trough will be inside the circle? Keeks and I will deal with the rest of this stuff once there's a place cleared for it."

"Right," Dan said. "But despite what Rhys says, moving is going to be a real project. I imagine the thing weighs a ton. We'll have to use the winch on my truck, and maybe make some kind of a sled. It'll be like building Stonehenge. And then we'll have to see if there's enough of that tin gutter stuff in good shape to reach from the well house to the basement. I guess we could always get some more from the farm supply store, if we had to: though it might look funny in Jonathan's financial records." They wandered off to the barnyard debating strategies among themselves.

By five thirty, after two trips to the farm supply store for some sort of plastic pipe that had apparently replaced tin in barnyard plumbing, the debris had been cleared from the basement, the weeds had been mowed, and a reasonable, if somewhat odd, facsimile of a baptistery and sanctuary had been installed, all under the just-in-case protection of the vast maroon and white canvas. After rehearsing the elaborate ritual, we ate our sack lunches in the space we'd created, which was dim even then: by eleven o'clock, I could tell, it would be as black as the inside of a cave. Or a tomb.

We took the kids back to school, giving them strict instructions to get some sleep. Brad and RJ headed to the "faculty club" for a nightcap. While Dan and Caroline went to buy a large bottle of olive oil at the Park 'n' Buy on their way home to nap, I stayed in my office to rework the liturgy and run off copies of the revised version. When I had stapled about twenty copies (it's always good, I find, to have a few extras around), I stretched out on the couch for a nap myself. Keeks, who had a key of his own, awakened me as he let himself in at about a quarter to ten. We prepared the communion vessels and packed them into a large cardboard carton along with the altar linens, the oil of chrism (blessed by the Bishop at his last visitation) and a silver box full of ashes (made from the fronds we'd used at the previous Palm Sunday). With Christopher saying the responses, I blessed about a gallon of holy water in a large jug, and placed that alongside the other items in what was beginning to look like a peculiarly ecclesiastical picnic basket. By that time, the rest of the crowd had arrived, and we were ready to go. That same compulsion that makes people check to be sure they've turned off the water led me to take one last look around the safe as I closed it. Though I didn't see anything I had planned to take along still on the shelves, I couldn't escape the feeling that I *was* forgetting something.

Getting everyone vested in the darkness out at the Homestead turned out to be more of a challenge than I had expected, but Brad thought to turn the cars around so we could use their headlights, and eventually we were ready. Mike, with his previous experience as an acolyte in the Roman Church, was thurifer, Miguel would be Crucifer, and D'Angelo and Clay would accompany him with "torches," the candles-on-poles traditionally borne by acolytes. In accordance with the unique ritual requirements of the evening, there were three extra acolytes devoted to carrying things: Rob, with his sword; Richard, with the box of ashes, and Jeff with the aspersorium and aspergillum—the holy water vat and sprinkler. Dan was Verger, Brad and RJ were resplendent in albs and white brocade tunicles as Subdeacons, with RJ carrying the great Paschal Candle, and Keeks was Master of Ceremonies, responsible for having the rest of us in the right places at the right times.

After making one final check of the improvised water pipe and turning off the headlights, we picked our way down the old stone steps into the basement to stand at a small table between the altar and the cattle-trough-cum-font, which had been installed almost at the center of the space. Straightening my cope for what seemed to be the hundredth time—perhaps I have poor posture, but the heavy satin-lined liturgical cape always wants to slip off my shoulders—and taking a deep breath to calm myself, I launched into the only part of the ritual that I had had to commit to memory (I still remember an old priest at Cloyne who told me, "Never trust your memory, lad. Read the missal. I trusted my memory once and married two people with the words 'Those whom God hath joyfully loined together let man not put asunder.' ")

"Light and Peace in Jesus Christ our Lord," I sang, and everyone responded on cue, "*Thanks be to God.*"

I went on to the short lesson and the Collect for All Saints' Day: "Then the angel showed me the river of the water of life, bright as crystal, flowing from the throne of God and of the Lamb through the middle of the city . . . There shall no more be anything accursed, but the throne of God and the Lamb shall be in it, and his servants shall worship him; they shall see his face, and his name shall be upon their foreheads. And night shall be no more; they need no light of lamp or sun, for the Lord God will be their light, and they shall reign for ever and ever.

"Lord Christ, your saints have been the lights of the world in every generation: Grant that we who follow in their footsteps may be made worthy to enter with them into that heavenly country where you live and reign for ever and ever. Amen."

In an abbreviated version of the great liturgy of Easter, Mike struck sparks into the brazier on the table with flint and steel (being a Boy Scout is an important background for a thurifer), and I blessed the new fire. Then Brad used a taper to transfer the fire to the Paschal Candle, singing just one verse from the *Exsultet*, the ancient hymn with which such candles are dedicated on Easter Eve. With the Paschal Candle burning, Mike put the charcoal from the brazier into the thurible, while D'Angelo and Clay took flame from the Candle to light their torches and the two small candlesticks on the table. The five flames cast peculiarly overlapping shadows, but there was enough light for me to read the lengthy anthology of blessings prescribed for the various substances and objects involved in the liturgy.

Holy water we already had, so we dealt first with the ashes, which Richard brought forward for me to pray over: "Almighty God, you have created us out of the dust of the earth: Grant that these ashes may be to us a sign of our mortality and penitence, that we may remember that it is only by your gracious gift that we are given everlasting life; through Jesus Christ our Savior. Amen." By then, Mike had the smoke-pot ready, and putting a conservative spoonful of incense onto the charcoal (it was likely to get pretty thick under the tent), I said the appropriate blessing, took the thurible, and censed the ashes—getting rather more smoke in Richard's face than he would have liked. At Chris's signal, Jeff came up with the holy water, which I sprinkled sparingly on the ashes, to avoid making too much of a muddy mess of them. Richard returned to his place, and we went on to prayers over the objects, beginning with Robert and the sword.

I chanted the versicle, "Strap your sword upon your thigh, O mighty warrior:"

And the people responded: *"Ride out and conquer for the sake of justice."*

"Almighty God, your word is sharper than any two-edged sword, piercing to the division of soul and spirit, of joints and marrow, and discerning the thoughts and intentions of the heart: Bless this sword, that he who bears it may do so with discernment to see, and intention to preserve, true equity and justice, to your glory and the defense of the gospel of your son our Savior Jesus Christ."

"Amen."

Then we blessed Dan and the Verge similarly, each item getting the full treatment of prayers, incense and holy water. When all of these preliminaries were finished, Keeks shepherded us into a procession which would go around the cellar, beginning at the font and making the first of five stops— "stations," as liturgists call them—at the easternmost point of the space, directly behind the altar. I said the versicle, "Let us go forth in Peace," the people answered *"In the Name of Christ, Amen,"* and we were off, the thurifer and subdeacons leading us with smoke and fire, Miguel following them with the cross and his own escort of torches.

An unlit candle in a huge free-standing brass holder had been placed at each station. When we arrived at the one in the East, Brad lit it from RJ's Paschal Candle, as he would each of the others, and Rob traced a five-pointed star on the wall behind it with his sword, the lines he marked glowing a faint but discernible red. I had rather more than half-expected something of the sort, and so was able to maintain an appearance of calm: but there were some definitely audible gasps from around the room. I chanted the first of three prayers, in the same general pattern as the blessings: "Holy Michael Archangel, defend us in the day of battle:"

"That we perish not in the dreadful judgment."

"O everlasting God, you have ordained and constituted the services of Angels and men in a wonderful order: mercifully grant that as your holy angel Michael always does you service in heaven, standing at the right side of the altar of incense and fighting with all his Angels against the dragon, so, at your direction, he may succor and defend us on earth, through Jesus Christ our Lord, who lives and reigns with you in the unity of the Holy Spirit, one God, now and forever.

"*Amen*," the congregation answered, and Mike censed the spot on the wall.

Dan stepped up to the wall and marked a six-pointed star, the Shield of David and Seal of Solomon, on the same space, his verge leaving a green trail behind it. People took this better than they had Rob's similar exhibition, and I went on to the second versicle: "God created mankind in his own image:"

"*Male and female created he them.*"

"Lord God, even while you placed cherubim and a flaming sword to bar the way into Eden and the Tree of Life, you clothed Adam and Eve in garments you made for them, and promised that the seed of Eve would crush the serpent's head: grant that we, their mortal sons and daughters, confessing Jesus to be the Christ who has destroyed the serpent's power, may know his cross to be our Tree of Life, and come at length to reign with him in Paradise."

"*Amen.*"

Then it was Richard's turn: feeling about for a relatively dry part of the little silver box, he scattered a fistful of ashes on the spot.

Holding the processional cross horizontally, Miguel marked a cross of blue light on the wall with its foot. "The glorious company of the Apostles praise you," I sang.

"*The noble army of Martyrs praise you.*"

"Almighty God, you instruct your church through the witness of your apostle and evangelist Matthew, who left his job as a tax-collector for the sake of the Gospel: grant, we pray, that we, being defended through his intercession, may, following his example, readily obey the calling of our Lord and Savior Jesus Christ, who lives and reigns with you and the Holy Spirit, one God, now and forever."

"*Amen.*"

At which point Jeff gave the spot a healthy sprinkling of holy water, and the procession reformed to move to the south, where we repeated the ritual, invoking now Gabriel, Abraham and Sarah, and Mark, with the same sequence of red pentagram, green Star of David, and blue cross. Then we did it all yet again, in the west, citing Raphael, David and Bathsheba, and St. Luke.

By the time we got to the Station at the North, the old cellar had taken on a strange quality of light similar to what I imagine the showrooms of a neon lamp manufacturer must look like. Here we remembered the Archangel Uriel—I had hesitated over him, back at Cloyne, because he appears only in the Second Book of Esdras (where he mostly asks riddles), but finally decided to keep him—Mary and Joseph, and St. John.

From there, we returned to the Font at the center of the cellar, where I had yet another triad of collects to recite, while we circled the font itself. RJ put the Paschal Candle in its stand beside the little table, and he, Brad, and I took places behind it.

"Almighty God," I chanted, as Mike, with the incense, and Rob, his sword still unsheathed, walked around the great stone box, "Father of Lights and Source of Being, you are throned upon the cherubim and the seraphim continually sing your praises; make this place part of your heavenly sanctuary, so that we may, with all your angelic host, sing the eternal hymn, Holy, Holy, Holy, Lord God Almighty, heaven and earth are full of your glory: Glory be to you, O Lord most high."

"Amen."

And as Mike and Rob came back to the place where they had begun, the four red stars expanded and joined into a red dome over our heads.

Richard and Dan set out with ashes and the verge as I sang the second prayer of this set: "O Jesus Christ, our Lord and God, Son of Adam, Son of Abraham, Son of David, and Son of Mary: having made us of the dust of the earth, you became human that we might become divine; preserve in us the new life to which we have been raised in Baptism, and nourish us with your most precious Body and Blood, that we may finally join with all our holy mothers and fathers in the joy of your eternal kingdom."

"Amen."

And the red dome was overlaid with green.

Miguel and Jeff began their circuit of the trough with the Cross and holy water. "O Holy Spirit, by your power the Apostles and Evangelists proclaimed the Gospel to all the world: speak in us and through us, that we may worthily confess that Jesus Christ is Lord to the glory of God the Father."

"Amen."

Blue light joined the red and green to make a brilliant white, and we sang *Phos Hilaron,* the evening hymn:

> *O Gracious Light,*
> *pure brightness of the everliving Father in heaven,*
> *O Jesus Christ, holy and blessed!*
> *Now as we come to the setting of the sun,*
> *and our eyes behold the vesper light,*
> *we sing your praises, O God: Father, Son, and Holy Spirit.*
> *You are worthy at all times to be praised by happy voices,*
> *O Son of God, O Giver of life,*
> *and to be glorified through all the worlds.*

When the hymn was over, we went to our seats, where I said the opening prayer for the vigil, and we sat for the first of six lessons, each of which would be followed by a Psalm or Canticle. Tom Adams read the Call of Abraham, from the twelfth chapter of Genesis, and, after the Psalm, Keeks read the story of the Witch of Endor calling the prophet Samuel up from the dead. Caroline read Ezekiel's vision of the Valley of Dry Bones, and Mike took the fourth lesson, the story of his patron saint's war in heaven, from Revelation.

I led a Canticle. Then Brad chanted the Epistle, from Paul's letter to the Church at Rome: "Do you not know, that all of us who were baptized into Jesus Christ were baptized into his death? Therefore we are buried with him by baptism into death: so that as Christ was raised from the dead by the glory of the Father, even so we should walk in newness of life. For it we have been joined together in likeness of his death, we shall also be joined in the likeness of his resurrection: knowing this, that our old human nature is crucified with him, so that the body of sin might be destroyed, that henceforth we should not be slaves to sin. For one who has died is freed from sin. Now, if we are dead with Christ, we believe that we shall also live with him: knowing that Christ, being raised from the dead, will not die again: death has no more dominion over him. For in that he died, he died unto sin once: but in that he lives, he lives unto God. So reckon yourselves also to be dead indeed unto sin, but alive unto God through Jesus Christ our Lord."

As the congregation sang "Alleluia," RJ, escorted by the torch-bearers and thurifer, came to me with the gospel book. Avoiding the table and the font, we processed right out into the midst of the little congregation, where I censed the book and sang the account of the Resurrection and the Great Commission to go into all lands and baptize, from the Gospel of Matthew. After the Gospel, I kissed the book and handed it back to RJ; he and the various servers escorted it back to a place of honor, but I stopped at the font, and preached a homily on the lessons, especially on the linkage of baptism with death and resurrection. I didn't talk long, and Keeks soon had us arranged for the Baptism proper.

I said, "The candidate for Holy Baptism will now be presented," and Dan, still acting as Verger, went out to bring forward Rhys and his young sponsor.

"I present Rhys David to receive the sacrament of baptism," Tom said.

"Rhys David," I asked, "do you desire to be baptized?"

"I do," he answered, confidently enough.

"Let the candidate be anointed with the oil of exorcism," I said.

A crowd of servers gathered around Rhys, partly to help him out of his uniform and partly, I have to admit, for the ancient liturgical purpose of obscuring my niece's view.

When he had stripped, Rob and Brad, in their plain albs (having laid aside their brocade for the moment), fairly doused him with olive oil, pouring it over him as though he were a pig being prepared for a Fourth of July contest—and getting a fair amount on themselves while they were at it. Keeks had, with his usual forethought, brought along a bowl of lemon slices, and the subdeacons used these and some towels to get the oil off their hands while I proceeded with the next step of the liturgy.

"The candidate will face the west," I said, and when Rhys, still screened by acolytes, had turned toward the congregation, I went on:

"Do you renounce Satan and all the spiritual forces of wickedness which rebel against God?"

"I renounce them."

"Do you renounce the evil powers of this world which corrupt and destroy the creatures of God?"

"I renounce them."

"Do you renounce all sinful desires that draw you from the love of God?"

"I renounce them."

"Turn to the east. Do you turn to Jesus Christ and accept him as your Savior?"

"I do."

"Do you put your whole trust in his grace and love?"

"I do."

"Do you promise to follow and obey him as your Lord?"

"I do."

Addressing the whole gathering, I went on: "Will you who witness these vows do all in your power to support this person in his life in Christ?"

"*We will*," they responded.

"Let us pray for this person who is to receive the sacrament of new birth," I said. While Brad and RJ led the people in a short series of prayers, I took off my cope, and Dan opened the valve he'd installed on our end of the water pipe. The artesian well was obviously as strong as it had ever been, and a jet of water fell noisily into the stone box of the cattle trough.

When Brad and RJ had finished, I said the thanksgiving over the water, a prayer which rehearses almost every significant mention of that element in the whole Bible, beginning with the Spirit of God moving over it at the beginning of creation and the crossing of the Red Sea, and ending with the Great Commission I had read in the Gospel lesson. By the time I had made the concluding sign of the cross on the surface of the water, a fair amount had run into the font: Rhys David would be well and truly baptized, and might even get some of his oil washed off. Assisted by the screen of acolytes, he climbed into the trough and stood near the jet of cold water. He was shivering again, but this time the October air was a sufficient explanation. Miguel held a book so that Rhys could read the responses.

"Let us join with this person who is committing his life to Christ and renew our own baptismal covenant," I said. "Do you believe in God the Father?"

"*I believe in God the Father almighty, creator of heaven and earth.*"

"Rhys David, I baptize you in the Name of God the Father," I went on, and tipped him backward and down under the running water.

"Do you believe in Jesus Christ the Son of God?"

"*I believe in Jesus Christ, his only Son, our Lord. He was conceived by the power of the Holy Spirit and born of the Virgin Mary. He suffered under Pontius Pilate, was crucified, died and was buried. He descended to the dead. On the third day he rose again. He ascended into heaven, and is seated at the right hand of the Father. He will come again to judge the living and the dead.*"

"Rhys David, I baptize you in the Name of God the Son."

Again, I pushed him under the stream, and, noticing that he was still pretty greasy, held him there a bit longer. He came up sputtering.

"Do you believe in God the Holy Spirit?"

"*I believe in the Holy Spirit, the Holy Catholic Church, the communion of saints, the forgiveness of sins, the resurrection of the body, and the life everlasting.*"

"Rhys David, I baptize you in the Name of God the Holy Spirit." This time I was a bit more restrained in the actual immersion, and the world's newest Christian came out of the water of his new birth none the worse for wear. Keeks handed me the consecrated chrism, and, dipping my thumb in it, I made the sign of the cross on Rhys's brow, adding a new layer of oil to the old: "Rhys David, you are sealed by the Holy Spirit in Baptism and marked as Christ's own for ever."

"*Amen,*" everyone answered.

The acolytes helped Rhys out of the tub and dried him off while Danny shut off the water. Having dressed Rhys as discreetly as possible in his underwear and an alb, they deposited him in front of me without further escort. I said the final prayer over the newly baptized, and then presented Rhys to the congregation: "Let us welcome our newest brother in Christ."

"*We receive you into the household of God. Confess the faith of Christ crucified, proclaim his resurrection, and share with us in his eternal priesthood.*"

"The peace of the Lord be always with you," I said, expecting the usual response: and indeed, people began to answer, "*And also with you.*" But from the group of acolytes and ministers behind me—distinctly from there, and not from Rhys, who was standing beside me, still dripping a bit of oil from the lobe of his left ear—came a response in that voice I'd heard through him. It was a shouted Latin tag: "*Vade prius reconciliare fratri tuo!*"

Calm, I knew, was of central importance: I restrained myself from turning around. I recognized the line from the Sermon on the Mount, "Go, first be reconciled to your brother," and answered with the next verse, an exhortation to agree with one's adversary quickly, for fear of prison: "*Esto consentiens adversario tuo cito, ne in carcerem mittaris.*" Only then did I turn to look behind me.

In the *Inferno*, I had told my students, Dante describes the souls of those who have given false counsel as being encased in tongues of flame, spirits more sensed than seen within their glowing cloaks; now I saw what the poet had described. If the magic Louie had unleashed against us on Sunday had been a torrent of dark fire, then what I saw at this moment was a single giant tongue of black flame burning—or un-burning, in some awful parody of light—at just the spot where Danny had been standing; somewhere in its center I could see the form of my brother, my adversary.

Something gave way, collapsed inside me, and in that moment the figure raised the verge, now, rather, a wand. I knew nothing about how to defend myself, but instinctively threw up my hands, like someone warding off a projectile, and shouted "No," simply out of fear. Apparently, it was enough: a wall of light, of a piece with the dome, sprang up between us, dividing Danny's part of the cellar from mine. I could feel the flame pounding on my shield for a moment, but then the attack stopped as quickly as it had come, and the wall vanished as well.

"*Bene, Jonathan. Alteras vias habemus.*"

" 'We have other ways'?" I translated sarcastically. "No wonder you stick to Latin: in English you'd sound like a grade B movie villain. Speak English, Louie. *Anglice sermone, Llewellyn: conjuro te!*"

"I shall, but you would do well not to confuse my free choice with your conjuration. It is I who am sovereign here: this is my hour."

"God alone is sovereign, Llewellyn, and this is his holy ground," I answered. "But it is my circle and my home which you destroyed. This is the center of my family."

"Which of them will help you now? This one who is wholly mine? The girl-child, more ignorant even than yourself? Or perhaps that soul which wanders even now, lost and gibbering on the fringes of the darkness which will claim it in good time?"

" 'If God be with us, who can stand against us?' What help do I need when your magic has already failed you?" I asked.

He laughed. "Failed? Hardly. My methods, perhaps, but not my power, which indeed you have yet to taste. Observe."

He—Dan—the un-Dan—waved the wand over the congregation and servers, who were still too shocked to have responded in the moments we had been talking. About half of them fell unconscious to the ground: the other half, except for Rhys and Caroline, were suddenly fixed on the figure in the flame, their attention riveted unswervingly on that coruscating darkness. "Seize them," he said, sounding more B-movie than ever.

D'Angelo and Clay grabbed Caroline—not without a good deal of effort—while Jeff and Tom went for Rhys himself, and Mike and Miguel wrestled me to the ground. The cinctures of the several people who were vested in albs provided more than enough rope with which to tie up the three of us, and soon we were bound back to back around the Paschal Candle's heavy brass stand. Throughout the process, none of the entranced crew said a word: they might as well have been some sort of sophisticated marionettes.

"Louie," I said—for some reason, they hadn't gagged us—"this is ridiculous. Whatever happened between the Mearses and the Evanses was five hundred years ago. It's not worth all this: it wasn't worth murder and sacrilege even then, much less now."

"How strange," the voice from the flame answered. "It seems it was only yesterday. And 'whatever it was'—religion or patriotism or love of his sister—seemed worth dying for to Gryffydd Evans then. Wasn't it murder, wasn't it sacrilege against the temple of the Holy Ghost, when he was hanged and burnt at Buttercross in Winchester?"

"Whatever it was, it was at least the law—king's justice and church's justice, however much we would regret them."

"Mears justice in the court it was, and Mears justice in the Church as well. And English justice, all of it. Gryffydd was as good as dead the minute they laid hands on him."

"And will killing your son make it any more just?"

"Abraham was willing to sacrifice Isaac and it was counted to him as righteousness. A child's life is the father's to give or take away, for the good of the family."

"Then Gryffydd Evans had no right to take his nephew away from the boy's father."

"But every right to take his sister. But quibble me no quibbles, priest—this is the moment of my triumph, and I'll not be distracted from it by any of your nonsense about fathers and sons."

I had been staring into the blackness, more or less of necessity, since I was tied up facing that direction (though I could move my head around). Our hands and arms were less mobile, but both of the kids had been wiggling and twisting their wrists—a process in which the still oily Rhys had something of an advantage—and at some point in the middle of this speech each of them succeeded in grasping one of my hands—I assume they had each other's hand as well. As they did so, I heard a voice, Caroline's voice somehow blended with Rhys's: "*Open the dome. For just a second. Open it. Now!*"

It seemed a distraction from the real issue, and I was by no means sure how to do it; but I turned my thoughts for the moment to opening our circle, finding as I did so that the image of a door to which I had the key suddenly appeared in my mind, like a prompt for an actor who has forgotten his lines. I put the key in the lock and turned it.

Whether because of that, or something the flame had said, or some momentary inattention on its part to the several magical tasks it had in hand—or perhaps some combination of all these, there was suddenly a kind of spark, a sort of unelectric lightning bolt, flashing from someplace outside the cellar to the three nails of my pectoral cross. Even seen against the glowing background of our futile defenses, it must have been intolerably bright: for me, it was blinding. While my pupils were still adjusting to it, I heard yet another new voice—or rather, one long-familiar but long-unheard, chanting:

"By your oath with which you bound yourself
To the circles of this world
By your life with which you bartered
To gain mere deathlessness
By your name with which we named you
And by our common blood
I summon you, command you and conjure you,
To come among us, to appear before us,
to confront us in this circle,
In your own form, in your own shape,
in the semblance you retain,
And not as any other creature,
neither your children nor my own.
David Mears, I call you by name:
stand now and answer!"

As the chant ended, my vision cleared, and I saw, among the unconscious bodies and the liturgical impedimenta, a man in a blue robe, standing with his back to me. On the ground in front of him lay Dan; and beyond him stood a thing, a shriveled, wizened, mummified man, old beyond imagination, but still alive, as much a prisoner of immortality as the ancient Sibyl of Cumae whom Eliot quotes at the beginning of *The Waste Land*. David Mears, the man in blue had called this undead thing: Mears, rather than Evans. It was then, could only be, the son of Thomas Mears and Gladys Evans that stood there, having pursued his vengeance for five hundred years and half way around the world.

With one last greasy wriggle, Rhys freed his hands from the ropes and, in a moment, had his bare feet loose as well. The crowd of automata around us stood motionless, the mind that controlled them being preoccupied with the challenger who had called it by name. Shaking off his ropes, Rhys ran, the only moving figure in a waxworks tableau, straight toward his ancient forefather.

Neither of the magicians seemed to notice him, whether because they thought him insignificant or because each hoped to distract the other, I could not then tell. The man in blue had gone on after his chant: "For five centuries you have pursued us, and because we would only shield ourselves from you, and preferred to flee you when we could, you thought us cowards. You prided yourself, once, on your faith, and now you have left it so far behind that you muddle even the bits of scripture you quote to your purpose.

"You would cite Abraham, and yet you have thought me a fool, because I gave my children only the most unconscious of defenses, left them open to your worst attacks, risked all there is of my family to lure you here."

"Fool indeed have I thought you, and fool you are: look here!" He gestured at Rhys running toward him: but even as he did so, the boy stopped and knelt beside Dan. I couldn't see what he was doing at first, but then he stood, and a gold ring glinted in his hand. "Now you see my strength, coward: see how he comes to me of his own free will.

"Take it, Rhys," he continued. "Put it on, join me as we destroy these enemies. Together we can share the vengeance that nourishes freedom."

"Would you have freedom, indeed, grandfather?" he asked. "Then someone must set you free." And he tossed the ring to the man in blue. Almost as soon as he did so, the black fire raged out at him: but he was already wrapped in a cloak of blue that seemed to glow only brighter for every increment of the power directed against it.

"LHE," the nearer of the sorcerers read, "Llewellyn Hyw Evans: and yet within it we find the worms ouroboros, sign of the Mears family for centuries even before you were born, ancient as you are. And it's fine Welsh gold, I'm sure, for all the fine English words inscribed upon it. This is truly a token of your life, my many-times-great-uncle, as well as a tool of your enchantments. Here we see Mears and Evans linked forever."

"Linked only till you die, Henry Lawrence Mears, and your sons and granddaughter with you. Which shall be now, now as you hold that token of my power, now even as you stand here in the ruins of your house, now even as your spirit lingers in the ruins of your mind and body. Die, die, die!"

For a third time he raised his black fire, and it seemed all the stronger for the frenzy with which he directed it against us. The wall which had divided the dome before sprang up again between us, but it was no longer a flawless division: the thinnest pencil of roiling blackness pierced through it to the ring, one part of the ancient sorcerer's magic drawn to another as like calls to like. I expected my father to raise for himself and us that same blue shield with which he had protected Rhys David: but he did not. As the stream of dark fire ate away at the white wall like a jet of water eroding and undermining a great dam, constantly growing in size and force, and, I knew, constantly burning him, sapping his strength, he began a second chant, in something of the same vein as the first.

> "By the life your mother gave me,
> by our common flesh and blood,
> I call you:
> By the Art my fathers gave you,
> by my worms upon your ring,
> I call you:
> By the sleep our parents bought us,
> by the trump to which we'll wake,
> I call you:
> Come to me, cleave to me, be joined to me.
> Son of Adam, I welcome you:
> master of magic, I claim you as brother:
> brother of my fathers, I embrace you as kin:
> So shall we be bound, so shall we be tied,
> so shall we be enfolded,
> in the constitution of silence,
> in the symbols you have chosen,
> Now, David Mears,
> in a symbol perfected in death."

As he sang this final allusive phrase, a worm of blue twined itself, almost too fast to see, around the black jet that was still playing on him: it passed the wall, and then suddenly the wall was gone, and I could see the ancient creature at the other end of the room, wrapped in blue coils and drawn toward us. My distant uncle David struggled, and poured even more power into his attack, trying now to expand it beyond the limits set by the sapphire spiral that was wrapped about it. Yet almost as fast as it had moved toward him, the blue returned to its source, drawing the withered figure with it, until the sorcerer was standing in the same place as my father, and all the energies of their two magics were released in a flash which did not merely blind but also bypassed the eyes to numb the mind directly, to stun us who saw it at every level from immediate revulsion to profoundest grief. And in that explosion vanished Rhys's blue shield and the mental bondage of the ensorcelled cadets and the stupor of the others, and even the warlocks themselves: though I knew of a certainty that even then the nurses at the home would be trying to call me, to let me know what they had long expected.

Rhys went to the place where Father had stood, and felt for something in the grass. Rob and Dickey untied Caroline and me, and we ran to Dan, who looked gray and drained. As I knelt behind him, holding him up in my arms, he stiffened with a spasm of nausea, and was sick all over the grass. Yet I knew it was a passing effect: and as I looked at Rhys and Caroline kneeling side by side at his feet, their hands unconsciously intertwined, I remembered the rest of the lines from Eliot's poem that my father had cited in his chant, the last words I would hear from him, and those unlooked-for:

> "These men, and those who opposed them
> And those whom they opposed
> Accept the constitution of silence
> And are folded in a single party.
> Whatever we inherit from the fortunate
> We have taken from the defeated
> What they had to leave us—a symbol:
> A symbol perfected in death.
> And all shall be well and
> All manner of thing shall be well
> By the purification of the motive
> In the ground of our beseeching."

And the light of the Paschal Candle picked out a glint of gold on the fourth finger of Rhys's right hand.

Part II: Rough Magicke

Introduction

HAVING DESCRIBED the confrontation at my cousin Rhys's baptism, I should probably say at the beginning of this second memoir that the episode had, so far as I could tell, no ill effects on the cadets who had been briefly involved. Indeed, it appeared to provide in some degree the closure we had hoped it might, though it did not do so without causing more of a public sensation than I would have liked. Of course, any sort of fuss violates my Anglican sense that things ought to be done "decently and in order" (as one of our fundamental documents phrases it), all the more so when much of the fuss is focused on me. Thankfully, the boys involved—even Chris Pruett, I have to admit—maintained some sense of decorum about what had taken place. The fact that there had been a double hoax earlier in the same week worked together with a widespread (though not, admittedly, universal) skepticism about magic in general to produce what is, I suspect, the usual state of affairs, that people believed pretty much what they wanted to.

Louie Evans illustrated the same point in an opposite sense. His body was found in his basement in a ritual magic circle, amidst a host of occult paraphernalia from wax dolls to slaughtered neighborhood pets. He had furnished the room with a small library of guides to the dark side of the New Age, from Aleister Crowley's *Book of Lies* down to the most recent Satanic scriptures. Even I was, and am, inclined to think that most of this stuff was window dressing, whether for his own benefit or that of others; but, again, whether people thought he was merely insane or one of Satan's advance guard was pretty much a matter of what they wanted to believe. What was less ambiguous was his will, which left Rhys a rich lad, if he would resume the surname "Evans." His mother and stepfather left the decision up to him, and after some serious consideration, he decided to do so. "After all," he told me, "I'm keeping the ring."

As for the long-term victims of the case—Rhys himself and my brother, Dan—I have to say that on the surface they, too, seemed to recover right away, or almost so. I hadn't known Rhys well enough before the incident to have a basis for comparison, but I couldn't remember life without Danny, and I did see in him after the affair some greater hesitation than I had known in our earlier years.

That hesitation was one factor in the way the four of us—Rhys, Caroline, Danny and I—dealt with our magical heritage. For me, there was the individual element of my inability to visualize things—visualization being, so far as I can tell, a major part of most magical processes. Danny didn't, and doesn't, share that disability, though the two of us have it in common that we cannot communicate with each other telepathically, the way Rhys and Caroline can. These differences I attribute to some hereditary variation of talent, of the same order as Caroline having no portion of Danny's beautiful singing voice.

Beyond that element of nature, however, our situation owed a great deal to nurture. My father's plan to keep us ignorant of magic while providing us with unconscious protection, all in order to use us as bait for the Evanses, the other branch of our family—that plan had not, presumably, anticipated that Louie Evans would at one stroke destroy both of the repositories of our family's traditions. It's likely, too, that he'd never expected the process to take as long as it did, in which case he may perhaps have meant to teach us something himself. Whatever his intentions, however, the effect was that we lacked both the knowledge and the skills for using such talents as we had.

There are, of course, even in ordinary shopping mall chain book stores these days shelves full of texts on ritual magic, of every flavor from the feminist to the sort of Satanist books Louie displayed, while New Age booksellers carry yet more esoteric collections. None of these, however—at least none that I have seen—reflects the combination of magic with strict Christian orthodoxy which my family had apparently practiced. Knowing that they had had some sort of ritual for creating a magic circle, and that it involved a cycle of prayers, I was able to make something of the sort out of the church tradition of a procession with stations. Similarly, knowing that they had put some sort of magical shields around their houses, I could adapt the Church's rite for blessing a home. On the other hand, none of the ceremonies I had developed managed to reproduce the blue light Danny and I first saw in the old house. Moreover, what other things such magic as ours might be able to do—and I by no means accepted the vast array of claims made in all those books—I had no way of knowing, and thought it dangerous to guess. Given his experience, Dan was, at the time, yet more reluctant than I to experiment: though it was a reluctance he did eventually overcome.

All that being said, after Father's funeral, Danny and I sat down—accompanied by Rhys and Caroline—to piece together our scraps of magical knowledge and map out the dimensions of our arcane power. When we finished, we still couldn't have started a fight for love or money, but from all the various hints and guesses, we succeeded in assembling a considerable range of defenses. In particular, we were able to take full advantage of the shields of golden light which, we eventually concluded, Father had tied to our rings when we had the Worms engraved in them: by the time we were through tinkering, each ring (including the one Louie had made) was not only a shield, to be triggered by the presence of hostile magic or activated by a conscious decision, but also an alarm to summon the other three people—and though Caroline didn't have a ring, the bond between her and Rhys was already so close that it was almost impossible to contact one without getting the other as well. Any attack on one of us would now be answered by all four: answered in action, at least, if not in words. We also—even I—learned some degree of control over the rings, enough to make the golden light appear at will (useful mostly as a parlor trick, I suppose) and to expand, modestly, the area it covered—not enough to protect a house, but better than, say, trying to cast a circle around one's automobile.

I suppose, reading back over this, that I've made our efforts to deal with our curious situation sound more or less desultory—as perhaps in all honesty they were. But I must point out that these preparations seemed, on the face of it, to be like locking the barn door after the cows had gone; the chances were slim that we had a second five hundred year old cousin out there plotting revenge. But in July, a year and a half after Rhys's baptism, a different threat arose to put our new defenses to the test.

Chapter 1: Monday, July 4

"YOU KNOW, JONATHAN," the Bishop said, as I slammed shut the breech of the howitzer and attached the firing cord, "you rather remind me of Leonidas K. Polk."

Entertaining official visitors has never been my strong suit, and having had to meet this one so early in the morning had done nothing to make me less irascible. The lake and the playing fields had been scenically veiled with a light fog at dawn, but the first rays of the fierce summer sun had already burned that scrim away, as if to say that nature saw no reason to exert itself in wishing me a nice day. I studied my pocket watch and listened for the first notes of Reveille, keeping the cord taut with my right hand.

"Well, let's see," I answered, "to begin with, his middle initial wasn't actually 'k.' He was a bishop, whereas I'm a priest. He was a Confederate general, whereas I come from a long line of Union pacifists. And as far as I know, he wasn't a witch. Other than that, I suppose the comparison has some merit.

"Remember not to look at the muzzle until after you hear the shot—sometimes the gun doesn't fire the first time I pull the cord. Fire in the hole!"

As the second hand reached the top of its inset dial, I looked up and saw a glint of light from the base of the flagpole, where the corporal of the guard was waiting to hoist the flag and Matt Heath, the Regimental Bugler, was lifting his coronet to his lips. I pulled the lanyard.

Nothing happened, and I pulled again. The never-quite-familiar roar of the blank shell shook us even as it drowned out the opening notes of the bugle call.

Beyond the flagpole, I knew, in the hallways of the Academy's crenellated brick barracks, prosaic electric buzzers were sounding to insure that the Midshipmen and Aviation Cadets would awaken to another sweltering day at summer camp; farther to the east, between the Tudor Gothic of the Chapel and the Great-Gate-of-Kiev sprawl of the Riding Hall, someone would be walking through the tent encampment with an air horn, rousting out the Troopers. The sound of the horn wouldn't quite carry to where we were standing at the lakeshore: but in my office the week before, vesting for an early Mass, I'd heard someone attempting a compressed air version of the galloping theme from von Suppé's "Light Cavalry Overture:" honk honk HONK honk-honk, honk honk HONK honk-honk, honk honk HONK honk honkity honk-honk. It had sounded, at the time, like the mating scene from a lost ballet of "Goose Lake."

The Bishop cleared his throat as the lake breeze blew the gunsmoke back at us. I opened the breech to extract the spent cartridge, and he resumed the thread of his conversation. "There's no reason to be so testy, Jonathan. I was just thinking of his combination of the military and the ecclesiastical."

"Oh, I don't really mean to sound upset, Ted. And I suppose you're right in sensing that there's a strong debt to Confederate Romanticism in the whole institution of a military academy, including the office of Chaplain. Annandale's first successful Superintendent was a Confederate Colonel, as far as that goes. I never did think much of General Polk, though: it isn't just that he took the southern side in the war—I do happen to think that was a deplorable cause, but I can't see laying down the crozier and miter to pick up a saber even in defense of a good cause. After all, even Bishop Odo of Bayeux had the decency to carry a mace rather than a sword at the Battle of Hastings, so he wouldn't be guilty of shedding blood on his half-brother's behalf."

"Excuse me for interrupting, Jonathan, but have I mentioned to you before this that you seem to have a mental block against the use of examples taken from modern history?"

"You may have a point, at that. Though modern examples on this subject are a bit sparse, one way or the other. Could you help me put this cover back over the barrel? Thanks. I mean, you have, what, half a dozen bishops who are still the titular heads of military academies, and then there's the Suffragan Bishop for the Armed Forces. I suppose a certain number of priests are officers in the reserves, but how many of them happen to get elected bishops, even after they've retired from the service?"

"Well, a couple, I think. But one that we know of, the Abbot of All Angels'."

We walked back toward Sally Port, center of the school's military life, where I would put the shell and the firing cord back in the ammo safe in the Guard Room. Bishop Parker, at 64, was half again my age, but set a pace I found it hard to keep up with. I was inclined to ascribe this to his having longer legs than I—at 6'5" without miter, he was nine inches taller than I am. In the photo of him that hangs over my desk here, in what was once his office, he shows an Old-Man-in-the-Mountain face beneath a thick shock of white hair worn rather long, partly to conceal a tiny hearing aid in the right ear. Though everyone knew he had contact lenses, he's wearing half-rim glasses in the picture, partly to make up for not having bifocals and largely for effect. The white band of his clerical collar, startling against his florid complexion and his scarlet shirt, is hard pressed to fit in the small space his short neck allows between ear and shoulder. He still has the triangular torso of the rower he was at Yale, still looks like one who jogs every morning in a purple warm-up suit and swims frequently in purple trunks. The photo fairly screams "*in corpore sano*," and I imagine the wall of books in the background was meant to emphasize the "*mens sana*" end of the schoolboy motto, though it was a point about which extended acquaintance with the Bishop had left me somewhat dubious. (John Harvard's dubiousness about Eli Yale, I'll grant you, but still. . . .)

"You mean that Colonel Bishop Father Abbot Trout is still your official diocesan thorn in the flesh? I thought the old boy had settled down to writing his memoirs or something. He must be pushing eighty, surely."

"In fact, Jonathan, he'll be eighty three weeks from today, on the 25th. At which point he'll no longer be eligible for re-election to the Abbacy."

"He's been serving on some sort of limited term, I take it?"

"One five-year term, starting when he was sixty-six, and three year terms since then. He's always been unanimously approved, of course, but I sense in him a kind of Coriolanus—not terribly pleased to have to submit himself to these democratic proceedings. He would hold on till he dropped if dear old Bishop Cockburn hadn't insisted on having a retirement clause, among other things, in the Rule before he approved the foundation. Trout has had a most exotic career, though: packed a lot of living into those eighty years. . . . My Lord, look at all those shells! Are you expecting an invasion?"

"Not really." I explained while I used the contents of a jar of cold-cream (which nestled in a most unmilitary manner amongst the ammunition) to get the grease and powder stains off my hands before closing the safe. "Sergeant-Major Chuff restocks the safe on Tuesday mornings, so there should only be enough for today. One for recall from drill, one for retreat at parade this afternoon, and thirteen for the salute to the colonies tonight before the fireworks. Oh, and these three over here are for use if there's a tornado warning. So there must be eighteen altogether. About half a second's worth at the Battle of the Somme, if you insist on having a modern example."

"Noted. Do you have to fire all these?"

"No, thank goodness. One a day is my limit. Sergeant-Major will bring three more howitzers down from the Armory and supervise firing all four guns tonight; and as for the rest of the day, my duties as Officer-in-Charge will end when I pass these keys on to Brad Peniston—you know him, he's one of my two lay readers—which I intend to do as soon as I get to the Mess Hall."

"Let's go, then. How often do you pull this duty, anyway?"

"Oh, I'm not on the roster, actually. RJ Esther—my other lay reader—wanted to go away for the long weekend, but he had OC duty today. So he switched with Brad. But then Brad was invited to a party at a cottage over on the east shore for Sunday night, and didn't want to be back at Taps to relieve yesterday's OC, Lieutenant Brennan. And I'm not sure he was looking forward to getting up at 5 A.M. after a night on the town, either. So I took Brad's place from Taps through BRC—Breakfast Roll Call, that is. I do know how to do the job, if only from having been here forever. But ordinarily we separate religion and the military enough that I don't have to fool with this particular charade."

"Quite so. Which brings us back to Fr. Abbot Trout."

"You do have Trout on the brain today, don't you? I thought your letter said you wanted to take advantage of a break in your schedule to see what a day in the chaplaincy was like."

"I am seeing, aren't I? I mean, I've already had a long drive just to get here, when I could be over at Syracuse, sound asleep."

"Strapping on your water skis for an early morning zip around Lake Wawasee, if I know you. Does all that exercise really do any good?"

We had come to the bottom of the broad granite staircase that leads up to the south-eastern doors of the Mess Hall: a pair of midshipmen on some sort of detached duty were running up the stairs two at a time, obeying ancient Annandale tradition. "I'll race you to the top," the Bishop answered, starting off without waiting for me to accept. It was, thankfully, one of the traditions I had never abandoned (though I had given up Brasso and spit-shined shoes the moment we tossed our caps into the air at graduation), and I managed to catch up just at the top of the steps; we reached for the door handles simultaneously, and if I was a bit out of breath, I couldn't help thinking that the Bishop was, too.

The Pritchett Memorial Dining Center, as it is officially known—almost everything at Annandale has been renamed to honor some benefactor over the years—was built in 1917 to permit the whole corps of cadets to be served a sit-down meal simultaneously; cafeteria service had been installed late in the 40s, and redone in a particularly inconvenient way in the 80s; but with its cadet gray marble walls and white tile floor, the vast space, spanned by an unsupported ceiling with stained glass skylights, retained a certain dignity. We walked past rows of empty tables to the serving line.

"Now, as I was saying, the Abbot's tenure will expire in a bit more than a fortnight; the community will have to elect a successor; and since I am the Episcopal Visitor, I will have to supervise the elections, either in person or through a Vicar. They're voting a week from today—the feast of St. Benedict, of course—and I want you to come along as a scrutator of the voting."

"But Bishop," I said, handing him a cafeteria tray, "wouldn't it make more sense for one of the canons to go? You may have noticed that I have a full-time job."

"I was aware of the fact, yes. But the Superintendent says that he will be glad to spare you for a day or two. I spoke to him Saturday, and he owes me a few favors. Is there skim milk for this cereal somewhere?"

"Yes, just around the corner there—these lines were designed by an architect, not an efficiency expert. Have I missed something, by the way, or did we just skip over the question of why you want me in particular to do this?"

He took a glass of milk and two of orange juice. "Not deliberately, at least. There are several reasons, but I suppose the first thing that occurred to me was that you're the only priest in the diocese with a monastic affiliation: in fact, you're specifically a Benedictine, and All Angels' is supposed to be following a Benedictine rule. Then there's the fact that you're in your second term as President of the Standing Committee of the diocese. And the place is just across the lake from here. So you seem like a natural."

We threaded past the empty salad bar and walked toward the faculty tables under the mezzanine on the east side of the room. "But Ted, I'm only an associate of St. Thomas's Abbey—that's hardly the same a being a resident monk under vows and all. I don't suppose I've spent more than two weeks out of my whole life actually living at St. Tom's. Nor do I think there's anything in the diocesan canons that would put All Angels' under the jurisdiction of the Standing Committee as long as we have a sitting bishop. And as far as proximity is concerned, All Angels' might as well be on the other side of the moon as the other side of the lake. I haven't been in the Abbey Church twice in the last twenty years. I don't even shop at their little fruit stand, for that matter. More to the point, all you actually need is someone to count ballots, so my credentials have nothing to do with the case."

" 'Tra-la, have nothing to do with the case,' " he sang as we came to the table. "Isn't that from *Mikado*? Well, as I said, there are other considerations." We sat down and arranged our trays, and he said grace; then, reaching into the pocket of his seersucker jacket, he pulled out an envelope, which he laid on my tray. "This came after I'd already arranged to visit you, but it seems best suited to face-to-face discussions." He began to dissect his grapefruit while I looked at the letter.

It had been postmarked in an Ohio city from which we've always drawn quite a few students; I didn't recognize the handwriting or the return address, and the sender's name wasn't given, only the initials JDM. Those are my own initials, of course: but that information in itself wasn't enough to ring a bell. When, unfolding the letter, I saw that it was written on stationery from Haddam Hall, the Annandale First Classmen's Club, something fell into place, and I didn't need to look at the bottom of the page to realize that the author was Jefferson Davis Mills, who was now presumably enjoying a well-earned vacation after his first year of college. Why he should be writing to the Bishop was not so easy to guess.

"Dear Bishop Parker," the letter began, "You don't know me, though I've seen you a few times when you came to Annandale to preach in Chapel while I was a cadet there. I'm writing to you on behalf of my cousin Lee, who is Brother Alfred at All Angels' Abbey in Annandale. I know that he wants me to write to you, because he is in danger and hopes that you can help. He can't get a message out to you directly, or he would have done it already, but he really needs your help. He feels like it's really important for you not to say anything about his problem, especially not to anyone at the monastery. Please keep this letter confidential, too. I can't explain all this to you exactly, but you've got to believe me when I tell you I know about Alfred's problem. Alfred didn't want me to tell anyone about this but you, but I think it would be safe, if you think so, to tell Chaplain Mears at Annandale. I'd contact him myself if Alfred didn't insist that I write just to you. If you ask the Chaplain about how I used to use the library, he should be able to explain some of this to you, parts that I can't. Thank you for reading this. I hope that you can help Alfred as soon as possible.

Sincerely,

Jefferson Davis Mills."

"We didn't make a great prose stylist out of him, did we?" I remarked.

"No, but apparently he's quite a reader. What's the story about him and the library? Did he color in the books or something?"

"No, no, nothing like that. I'm sure it's his choice of books he's referring to. He was one of the kids who helped me look into the Rhys Evans business year before last, and at the time I noticed he showed more familiarity with some of the finer points of, ummm, arcane knowledge than I would have expected. So I made some remark about how I apparently wasn't the only one who'd ever read through the library's collection of books on magic. He never denied it, either; in fact, now that I think about it, of the three kids who really helped me figure out that business, he was the only one who had actually been involved in the magic rituals before we began investigating them." I poked meditatively at my omelet. "What he wants me to tell you, Bishop, is that he's communicating with his cousin by magic. Which probably means the cousin uses magic, too. Which might mean that there are some rather odd things going on at All Angels' after all."

"So if you were me," he said, toying with his amethyst signet, "you would take this letter seriously?"

"If you were me," I said, and held up the ring I wore on my right hand, engraved with the symbol of my own family's witchly heritage, "wouldn't you?"

At that point, Brad came in, looking not too much the worse for wear. I gave him the keys to the guard room and reintroduced him to the Bishop. Having finished breakfast with diocesan small talk, and visited the lone camper who was spending the glorious Fourth in the infirmary, the Bishop and I resumed the thread of our conversation sitting in the already welcome coolness of my office-cum-sacristy in the chapel building. I was sipping a Coke taken from the supply I kept in the refrigerator in my vestment closet; he had a mug full of instant decaffeinated coffee that he'd cajoled out of the infirmary dietitian.

"I take it, then, Jonathan, that you have no further objections to accompanying me to All Angels'."

"Now that I've read the letter? No, I can't object. But I can't say I'm excited about it, either. I know we've been over this territory before, Bishop, but the whole business of magic leaves me very uneasy. I've seen for myself that it offers plenty of opportunity for malice, if not out and out evil; and I'm not at all sure that it offers equal opportunity to do good. Moreover, you have to remember that I've never had any training in the use of magic. I was educated in priestcraft, not witchcraft. I have the heritage, but I don't actually know how to do anything with it."

"I thought young Mr. Mills wasn't the only one who had read through the magic textbooks."

"How would you have liked to have had to say your first mass solely on the basis of textbook knowledge, without ever even having seen it done?"

"I wouldn't have liked it, of course: but I could have done it if I'd had to. So could you, I imagine. There are bound to be rituals in any system which aren't used often enough for people to know them well. That's true for the Masons and the Knights of Columbus as well as for warlocks and priests. I've read that when Queen Victoria died, there was no one alive who remembered how to do a coronation; but they managed to make Edward king anyhow."

"But neither the King nor Archbishop Temple was in mortal danger if he happened to put the crown on backwards—which he did."

"True enough. But I've heard you preach on duty to these kids more than once, Jonathan. Wouldn't you yourself be compelled by your own principles to say that if there had been mortal danger, it would precisely have been their duty as King and Archbishop to face it?"

"I suppose—but that's a duty based on their offices, not on their natures. Being a witch may be a talent of some sort, so I suppose you could argue that it has to be used responsibly: but that's not the same as having a responsibility to use it."

"I rather think there's a parable that demolishes that argument, Jon, but let me just proceed on your premise for a moment. It's official duty which you see as eliminating the possibility of inaction, right? The private citizen may choose to watch the war from his den, but the general has a responsibility to act. And you're implying that your office as priest doesn't carry a responsibility to get involved in magical affairs."

"Not in itself, no. I don't know what I'd argue if it were made a matter of ecclesiastical obedience, but that's hardly the same sort of duty you were talking about."

He leaned forward out of the depths of my red leather armchair, staring at me intently with only a flicker of the smile of one who has just sprung a trap. "Very well, then, Jonathan. Having in mind your concept of office and duty, and your well-demonstrated piety and devotion, and your unique knowledge, I intend officially to appoint you to be exorcist for the Diocese of Michigan City."

"Jesus H. Christ," I said, jumping to my feet in such agitation that I knocked over the Coke can. "Ted, how can you possibly sit there and say something like that! You don't need an exorcist. There's probably not another diocese in the country that has one. Why do you have to try to manipulate me just because I'm a witch?"

He stood up, towering over me, and grabbed my shoulders in his hands. "Jon. I could say 'Yes: exactly: because you are who you are.' But the real answer is what you've already told me: I have to take your Jefferson Mills seriously. Don't you?"

I wilted, and steering me to a place on the couch beside his chair, he resumed his seat. "Yes, Bishop. I do take it seriously. Just as you say."

"And?"

"And I'm afraid."

"So am I, Jonathan. Help me."

"I will, if I can; but I don't know if I can. May I think about it and let you know next week?"

"I shall take that as a tentative yes. But do think about it, and pray about it, Jonathan, as shall I. As for now, I'd better be leaving." He stood to go.

"The day's not half gone yet; are you leaving already?"

"I think I'd better. I've told you what I came to say, and given you something to think about. And I have seen part of your day. And I do want to get some skiing in today. If you should have a great deal of spare time, by the way, you might want to look up the curious career of Bishop Trout: I'd be interested to hear your opinion.

"Unless I hear otherwise by Wednesday, I'll send you a note about our schedule for All Angels'. And call me if you get any insights into the place from reading about the Abbot."

After reading the Bishop's letter, I wanted to check up on something about Jeff Mills at the Alumni Association: but the school's administrative offices were closed for the holidays, as usual—a circumstance which annually made us wonder, down at the tavern, why we needed the administration in the first place. Having made some futile inquiries about Jeff with my office computer terminal, I used the rest of the morning to lay out the Chapel Bulletin for Sunday, did some preliminary reading on my sermon in the afternoon, and generally tried to avoid both the Bishop's question and Jeff's cousin's problem.

That evening, as we were lining up for the faculty processional for the Formal Opening of Summer School (another of our customary ironies, as the camps had by then been in session for almost two weeks), General Delmar, the Superintendent of the Academy, stopped me.

"Excuse me, Padre, I hate to put you on the spot when you're trying to think of an invocation and all, but I have sort of a technical religious question."

"It's your dime, General. Ask away."

"What's an Interdict?"

"It was the medieval device of the Pope excommunicating a whole country as a way of getting the prince to comply with some decree. Why in the world do you ask?"

"Well, Padre, I'll tell you. Your Bishop Parker called me last Saturday to say he was offering me a carrot and stick deal to get you off of work—I wasn't sure what the Interdict was, so I decided to give you the day off and take him up on the offer of eighteen holes and dinner at his country club in Michigan City: that was the carrot end of the deal."

"You probably made the wiser choice, General. Just don't let him talk you into playing for the after-game refreshments—I don't think he's bought a drink for himself in the ten years he's belonged to that club—and he's not a teetotaler."

"Roger, Padre. Say, this Abbot across the lake that you're going to retire: isn't he the same Colonel Kurt Trout I heard about in Vietnam?"

"I imagine he is, General. I know he was in the Army. But he must have been nearly sixty during Vietnam."

"Oh, sure. Colonel Trout hadn't been on active duty since Korea, but people still talk about him out East of Suez. Escaped from the North Koreans and ran his own private war for sixth months. Sort of a small scale MacArthur. If it is him, you might just want to stay on his good side. From what we used to hear, he was the meanest sombitch in this man's army—closest we ever came to having a Colonel Kurtz, like that Brando character in the movie. I'm not sure tying a rope around the middle does much to change a man like that."

"I'll remember that. For what it's worth, though, sir, it's the friars who wear ropes."

At that point Colonel Somerset, who, as Commandant, marshaled all our military ceremonies, came by to shepherd me to my proper place in line, and the band launched into the "Colonel Bogey" march, the theme from *Bridge on the River Kwai*—it's one of the Superintendent's favorites, but it struck me as a bit too British for the occasion.

As always, the PA system made mush out of my prayer, and reduced the reading of Mr. Jefferson's Declaration to an assortment of buzzes and whistles. But Sergeant-Major's thirteen cannon shot came off without a hitch, the fireworks were splendid, and we recessed to "American Patrol." All in all, it was a satisfyingly patriotic evening.

Chapter 2: Tuesday, July 5

THE NEXT MORNING, I stopped by the Alumni Office on my way back to the Mail Room—I don't get all that much actual mail, but even in the age of the electronic office, it's a slow day at Annandale that doesn't bring at least four memos. My cousin Patty is the Deputy Director of the Alumni Association; that is to say, she stays on campus and runs the office while the Director is out shaking hands, making speeches and, generally, raising money. Patty and I have been teasing each other ever since we got into a fight over the last piece of one of Great Aunt Eva's cheesecakes at a family gathering back when we were both kids. Of course, she hadn't been quite so lissomely attractive at nine or ten as she was to become later when my brother Dan had occasionally reflected that we were only *second* cousins, and once removed at that.

"Harvesting the Orders of the Day, Jon?" she asked as I walked into her office.

"Lord, yes," I said, waving the latest sheaf, "but they're not just growing, they're breeding."

"Perhaps you should circulate a memo prohibiting procreating memos. What can I do for you?"

"Well, it's about a memo, actually. Have you circulated one yet that lists the alums who're coming in for Homecoming?"

"Not yet, no. We had Monday off, you know."

"Yes, the rest of us noticed. I checked the Alumni Data Base myself, but I didn't find anything."

"No, you wouldn't find it in ADB. This isn't permanent information; it's in a word processing file somewhere. Was there anyone in particular you were wondering about?"

"Yes, actually; I'm curious about Jeff Mills: he's winter school class of '93."

"Let me see if he's in the computer," she said, and turned to her keyboard. " '93 would be the other end of the file. Doesn't look like it, Jonathan. Let me just double check by his name. Do you happen to know his middle initial?"

"Yes. It's 'D' as in dog."

"Good. Oh, yes, here he is, Jefferson Davis Mills. The winter school classes are listed separately from the summer, that's all. There's quite a little crowd of '93's at that."

"Really? How many?"

"Let's see . . . Looks like a dozen. Shall I copy a list to your mailbox?"

"Please. And print one out for me, too, would you?"

"Happy to. Speaking of homecomings, are we having a family reunion again this summer?"

"Sure. Same as always, down at the old Vandalia Depot on the Sunday closest to my birthday."

"When's that?" she asked, handing me the printout. "I always forget."

"Look it up in the computer," I taunted, as I ducked around the corner, out of range of the rubber bands she'd been known to shoot with disturbing accuracy. I needn't have bothered, however; the keyboard was an equally powerful weapon, and she already had it in her hands. I hadn't taken more than four steps down the hall when I heard her call after me: "Durwood? Your middle name is Durwood?" As her laughter echoed in the tiled hallway, I realized I'd made a tactical mistake that might pursue me through many reunions yet to come.

I read over the list on my way to the Infirmary, stopping by the Canteen *en route* to buy a Coke. Most of the boys listed had been in my classes at one time or another, of course, so the names were familiar—but I was mostly looking to see whether the two or three I thought of as Jeff's gang were coming back. Summer homecoming—always the second weekend in July—is really meant for summer school alumni, and its schedule of sailing races, golf matches, tennis tournaments and polo games reflects the country club atmosphere of our summer operation; but the same activities make the weekend attractive to any alumnus, winter or summer, who can afford the time to travel to Annandale for the fun. Meals are free at the Dining Hall, and a lot of the summer people rent out their cottages pretty reasonably for four or five days to individuals or small groups, often throwing in the use of their boats. It's a tempting opportunity for the college crowd, who generally seem to have fairly flexible schedules.

Between these kids and the older summer alumni, who come back to see the school, play a bit, and write big checks, the town becomes even more of an *ersatz* Cape Cod than it is on the Fourth. The townspeople long ago decided that there was no point in fighting this development, and determined to work it to their advantage. The second weekend in July is thus the occasion for the Annandale Lake Regatta and the Volunteer Fire Department Corn Roast, while neighboring villages offer the Wolf Creek Round Barn Festival, the Aunt Bertha Strawberry Social (named after a neighboring town's founder's mad first wife), and the Menominee Indian Encampment. It's a busy, if rather eclectic, time of year.

Jeff, I discovered, would be spending it at the Martin cottage, along with Stuart Cook, Rob English, and Richard Platt.

From Stuart—an almost painfully quiet kid from Company C who'd actively avoided getting even the Sergeantcy that is the usual consolation prize for a First Classman of no military skill whatsoever—to Rob, who had been the first aviation cadet ever promoted to be Cadet Colonel, Senior Captain and Regimental Commander, was a wide range by the Academy's standards—that is to say, by those of the adults who run the school. That the four had developed, particularly over their First Class year, a close friendship was another of the many reminders that the school we operate subsists in an overwhelmingly adolescent society of which we are only marginal and uninformed members, with little direct influence and even less real power (short of removing someone altogether). Having been Midshipman, Cadet, and Instructor at Annandale, I can attest that the cautious buzz of activity in the barracks at 1 A.M.—long after the faculty are asleep in their beds—is a more authentic (and thus more influential) sociological datum than the flawlessly aligned columns at a Sunday garrison parade.

I'd finished the Coke by the time I arrived at the Infirmary, where the invalid population was, thankfully, still relatively low. We have twenty-eight beds in semi-private rooms upstairs, and in case of an epidemic, the nurses could put another two dozen or so in wards in the basement: but on this Tuesday, there were only six patients, and the traffic in the halls indicated that not all of them were particularly sick. Feeling some sort of responsibility to deal with the bedfast first, I dodged between three of the elementary-aged campers (Indian Scouts, we call them officially) who seemed to be trying to club each other with maces they'd made by stuffing something into the toe of one of their knee-length uniform socks—presumably the other sock, since the impact of these weapons was even more bloodless than Odo of Bayeux might have hoped. Behind them, but already ahead of me, Mrs. Simcox, the head day nurse, was coming out of one of the rooms with a towel in her hand and fire in her eyes. Thinking to buy the brats a few seconds' head start, I called out to her, "Morning, Mrs. S."

"Morning, Chaplain," she said, as the three dashed for their beds. "I see you're giving aid and comfort to the enemy again."

"It goes with the job, I guess. 'He came to set the captives free,' and so on."

"Right, Jonathan. Well, if you get along so well with the little ones, I hope we can expect to see you back here in about ten days."

"Come on, Betty: I'm here every day—what's the secret?"

"Well, those three have been in and out of the nurse's office over at the Scouts' camp for the last two days, complaining of this and that, and today their problem finally came to the surface."

"That is to say?"

"Chickenpox. My guess is they've been at school long enough to expose all 700 of the Scouts, and I'm betting we see a lot more cases before the summer's over. We may need some extra hands around the place."

After seeing the way three of them behaved, I could imagine the building with twenty or thirty ten-year olds running riot. "Well, gee," I answered, "thanks for the invitation, but I've made an appointment to have root canal work that week, and I'd just hate to miss it for the sake of lazing about in the company of a building full of contagious ankle-biters."

"That's fine, Fr. Mears," she replied. "You go right ahead and have your fun. But don't think we won't remember the next time you need an injection!" She grinned menacingly and walked off to her station.

The other three patients included a Trooper who'd collapsed from the heat at the Field Day track meet on Monday afternoon—he was watching a videotape in one of the air-conditioned rooms and drinking a large cup of Gatorade (a situation which struck me as being, on the whole, preferable to mucking about in the stables in 100 degree weather); one of the little campers with a sore stomach that probably wasn't, Betty had said Monday, appendicitis; and Larry Brandon, who, having plenty of money and no home to go to, was one of the thirty or so kids who come to Annandale, as I did in my own day, both summer and winter. It was his first class year in Naval School, and he would be a first classman at the Academy the coming fall, as well. He was sitting up in bed and reading (from a book whose cover I recognized), oblivious to the commotion outside his door. Larry wasn't all that tall, and being confined to bed deprived him of one of his most characteristic traits, his bantam way of standing on his toes, as if always ready for a fight.

"Isn't it a bit early to be studying for senior English?" I asked as I went in the door.

"Oh, hi, sir. No, sir, not really. I mean, yes, sir, it is early, but I figure I'm better off for reading ahead."

"Well, you display commendable industry. Tell me what you're in here for, and then maybe we can have a look at your poetry. What ails you?"

"It's my hip, sir. I was running the last leg of the 4×100, you see, sir, and as I was coming around the turn there by the Riding Hall, just past the scoreboard, I felt something right along this bone here, sir, and all of a sudden I was lying on the track."

"Did it hurt much?"

"Like someone was burning my balls off with a blowtorch, sir. I was screaming and yelling and of course they stopped the meet and the security guy drove his car out on to the track, and Dr. Davies, my counselor, had been standing there at the turn, and he came running over as soon as I dropped. It took him and the cop and one of the track coaches to put me in the back of the car and bring me over here, sir."

"Is there a diagnosis?"

"Well, I wasn't bleeding, so that ruled out my guess that someone had sewn razor blades into my jockstrap. They took X-rays and stuff last night, and I'm going to South Bend to see the specialist this afternoon, sir. But Dr. Spaht says he thinks this tendon or ligament or whatever it is here got so tight after I hurt it last fall in soccer that when I tried to run on it yesterday it actually pulled off a little piece of the hip bone. Can we talk about the poem now, sir?"

"One last question—will they put you in a cast?"

"No, sir, just crutches, I think. My girlfriend is coming up for the Homecoming dance, and I wouldn't want to have my, uh, hips in a cast when she was here."

"No, I suppose not. I knew we should never have stopped putting saltpeter in the mashed potatoes."

"Potatoes! We always thought it was the chipped beef."

"That'd be silly: I mean, nobody eats the SOS in the first place. You could put botulin in it and never see the effect. In any case, what are you reading?"

"It's this poem by Yeats, sir," he said, taking a stab at pronouncing the name.

"Actually, it rhymes more with 'hates' than 'Keats,'" I said. "Which poem is it?"

"'Among School Children', sir."

"'O body swayed to music, O brightening glance, / How can we know the dancer from the dance?'"

"Yes, sir, that's the one. But I'm still stuck close to the beginning."

"Well, it takes some study, even for someone as bright as you. Have you read the notes in your edition?"

"No, sir. You told us the poem should stand by itself, didn't you, sir?"

"Hoist with my own petard. All right, the fact is that you do have enough information in the poem itself to go on, though we won't have the time to go through the whole poem that way this morning. Why don't you read the first stanza?"

"'I walk through the long schoolroom questioning;
A kind old nun in a white hood replies;
The children learn to cipher and to sing,
To study reading-books and history,
To cut and sew, be neat in everything
In the best modern way—the children's eyes
In momentary wonder stare upon
A sixty-year-old smiling public man.'"

"Nice reading; you've got a good voice for it. Now, what's the setting of the poem?"

"A school, sir."

"Okay. Does the narrator know his way around?"

"No, sir, an old nun is showing him around."

"Fine. So he's a visitor. Is he just looking around, being a tourist?"

"I don't think so, sir, it says he's 'questioning'—that's different from just asking questions. It's like a lawyer and a witness, or a philosopher."

"Fair enough: You'll want to bear the second part of that in mind for later. So you've got a visitor asking some sort of legal inquiries at a school run by the Roman Church. What's he doing there?"

"I guess he's making some sort of an inspection, sir. He says he's a 'public man.'"

"Good work. Now if you'll look at the notes you'll find that the poem was written after Yeats had been elected a member of the Irish Senate, and as a Senator he was asked to visit schools. So, like Plato's slave, you knew the answers all along."

"Thank you, sir, that's a big help. But I see what you mean about time. It's a fairly long poem and that's just a few lines."

"Well, it is summer: we have some time to spend. This is the best we can do for right now, though. I have to look in on the chickenpox epidemic. Why don't you see what you can dig out of the poem while you're laid up, using the notes just this once, and then come by my office when you're out of here."

"Okay, sir, but it is puzzling. I mean, look here at the next verse. What does 'Ledaean' mean?"

"That you can solve for yourself. Back up a bit and read his 'Leda and the Swan'."

"Okay, sir, I will. Sir, I know I've been joking around, but would you pray for me at your service, if it's okay, I mean? I'm a Presbyterian."

"Of course I will, Larry. Even for a Presbyterian. In fact, why don't we pray right now?"

"Okay, sir, I guess."

So I put my hands on his head and began the familiar ritual from the Prayer Book. In all the years I've been doing this with kids, though, I've yet to find a graceful liturgical way of ending the visit: so, after the final collect, we shook hands and I left Larry to continue his struggle with the Irish poet.

Betty had by this time convinced the three little combatants to stay in their rooms, and while they didn't seem to be in grave need of spiritual counsel when I stopped by, I felt obliged to stay long enough to say one or two words about making life easier for the nurses. I ended up promising to call their counselor and ask him to bring them more comic books from the cabin's common collection.

Returning to my office, I decided to do a little of the research the Bishop had suggested: there would be time to do some reading before lunch. I grabbed a Coke from the refrigerator in my closet and took the *National Church Directory* off the shelf to look for more information about the Abbey. The directory is a biennial listing of the official organizations and ordained ministers of the Anglican Church. It wouldn't tell me much about Br. Alfred, whose title suggested he was not ordained, but I could at least expect to find the institution described in a more organized way than I was able to do from my own few assorted impressions of it.

I guess I'd always thought that the Order began at the time it appeared in my little world, when the monks bought the long-vacant Voreis place in 1965. I was still a Methodist in those days, and I remember the grown-ups at church being puzzled, maybe even uneasy, at the idea of having such a Papistical enterprise in the neighborhood. There were a convent and a high school seminary in Wolf Creek, about twelve miles away—but the Roman Church operated them, and I suppose now that that made them less threatening to my elders and betters than the dubious idea of a group of Protestant monks. We kids were mostly disappointed at the loss of what we'd been thinking of as the local haunted house. Our story—a rundown version of historical facts—was that an Indian prince named Pakashak had killed his father, and that the old chief had been buried where the Voreis farm was, while the son, when he eventually died, was buried at Long Point on the opposite side of the lake. So when there was a full moon, you would see Pakashak paddling his canoe across the lake to apologize to his father. When I was in Cub Scouts, our den mothers even arranged for us to have an overnight in the old place: and arranged for two of our fathers to come in in Native American costumes and phosphorescent makeup and scare the bejesus out of us.

It turned out, in fact, that the Order of All Angels had begun far more exotically on September 30, 1963—the day after the Feast of St. Michael and All Angels—in Kuching, Sarawak—part of what is now Indonesia. James Trout (Colonel Kurt had taken the new name on becoming a monk) was apparently the only head it had ever had—first as founder, then Prior, then Abbot. From its earliest days, the order had been an enclosed Benedictine house—that is to say, its members had sworn the ancient Benedictine vows of stability, obedience, and review of morals, rather than the more common poverty, chastity and obedience, and the community was intended to be, as much as possible, shut off from contact with, though not from concern for, the outside world. The abbot, prior and five other life-professed members of the order—its permanent and full-fledged core—made up less than half the total community, joined, at the time of printing, by two men in annual vows, three novices, and three postulants. There was nothing to indicate how many or which of the seven older men might have come from what was now Indonesia, though clearly no one would have spent thirty-one years as a novice. The Right Reverend Bishop James Trout was duly listed as Abbot, with the Very Reverend Alcuin Shaw as Prior. There were presumably other officers as well—Cellarer, Sacristan, and so on—but they would be subject to reassignment every year by the Abbot. The Abbey mailing address and telephone number ended the entry.

I turned to the biography section to find out more about the Prior and Abbot. Fr. Shaw reported that he was a Briton, having been born in 1938 at York—which accounted for his name in religion, St. Alcuin the Deacon being one of that city's favorite sons—and baptized Cedric Cuthbert. After earning his degree at a red brick university, he said, he had taken a place with an import company. In 1962, he'd been ordained deacon and priest in something called the Independent Episcopal Church of South East Asia (the IECSEA, as I decided then and there to call it); the next year he joined the OAA, and he'd come to the US with the order in '65, being received into the Anglican Church as a priest in the next year. The community had elected him Prior in 1973, and he'd held the post ever since. He was the author of several learned articles on Native American spirituality: I copied out the titles for future reference.

The Abbot's bio was, as the Bishop had hinted it would be, wildly exotic. He was a native of Carmel, Indiana, which suggested he was related to the grocery-store-magnate Trouts of Indianapolis who had a row of summer cottages on the east shore of Lake Annandale. His parents had christened him Kurt Wilhelm, a pair of names which must have made childhood interesting for a boy who was only a bit over four years old on Armistice Day. He'd earned an A.B. at Longstreet Military College in 1936, and a B.D. from St. Luke's School of Theology three years later. Ordained a deacon in June of 1939, and a priest in January of 1940, he had served as Vicar of St. David's Church, Clermont—about 20 miles south of Annandale. In September of 1940, though, he had left St. David's to enlist as an infantry lieutenant. Apparently, he'd been a good officer, earning a series of temporary promotions to Lieutenant Colonel, and remaining a Captain when the war ended.

He hadn't come home after VJ day, but had instead taken a place in an Anglican Church on Okinawa for two years, following that with a similar job in Manila. His tenure there had ended with the outbreak of the Korean War when, true to the Polk tradition, he had returned to active duty.

The directory didn't go into details, but it was presumably at this point that the stories the Superintendent had heard fitted in. After the truce,

Trout had resumed his collar, but not as an Anglican: he was Rector of St. Saviour's Church, Kuching, in the IECSEA, and it was there that he had been consecrated by bishops from the Philippine Independent Church to be the IECSEA Bishop of Sarawak, the job from which he'd resigned on founding the Order of All Angels.

I reflected, as I tilted my head back to get the last drops of Coke out of the can, that, taken together with the Superintendent's hints about a renegade officer fighting his own war, all of this made a varied, if somewhat perplexing, portrait. I decided to consider it over lunch—which was not much different from putting it out of my mind entirely, as the rest of my day was filled up with the ordinary parts of my job.

My afternoon nap was shortened by a frantic phone call from the elementary camp athletic director—the man who was supposed to referee a tournament soccer game between two unit teams had canceled at the last minute; could I possibly, somehow, be persuaded to come over and fill in? Though I coached the game for years, I've never cared for officiating, and there was nothing appealing about the prospect of doing so in heat so intense that I, if I had been in charge, would have canceled the game and sent everyone into the lake. But I've also taught at Annandale long enough to know that you can never tell when you may need to be able to call in a few favors: so I agreed. This involved a trip home to get my clothes and cleats, my usual off-season search to find out where I had put my whistle at the end of the last season so that I could be sure to find it, and a frustrating afternoon watching a bunch of little kids run around after a soccer ball as if their coaches had never mentioned the concept of position to them. Both teams made goals, but the score had less to do with the players' skill than with the fact that the pitch ran distinctly uphill from one goal mouth to the other.

I got home, showered and changed, and was just getting ready to make myself some supper when a note I'd stuck to the refrigerator door reminded me that I had Barracks Inspector duty at school that night. I grabbed a copy of Yeats to read over during the evening, and hopped back in the car to drive off to SRC in the Dining Hall and three hours of monitoring the conduct of the aviation cadets on the top two floors of Main Barrack. Most of the cadets were out of their rooms, watching interunit basketball games, and I spent the evening puzzling by turns about Yeats's mystical philosophy and about why a boy from a good Hoosier family would first stay in the Far East to start a monastery and then move the whole operation back to the figurative, if not literal, banks of the Wabash. Having made little progress on either front, I got home about 11:30 and went straight to bed, where I slept the sleep of the just.

Chapter 3: Wednesday, July 6

WHEN I LEFT for work at 8:30 the next morning, it was already 85 degrees. I put the air conditioner on overdrive as I entered my office. At nine on Wednesdays, I have a staff meeting with the chapel musicians to go over the services for the coming Sunday and plan ahead for the one after that. Janice Sterling, the Choirmaster, and Charley DiRosa, the Organist for the upper camps, work at Annandale year round, and we have things down to a fairly efficient process; but Rebecca Young, choir director of the elementary age camp, is only with us for the summers, and comes from a public school music department background, rather than an ecclesiastical one. As a result, we never seem really to understand one another until the summer is almost over, and our meetings tend to drag on. The chapel bells were ringing 11:00 by the time I got to the Infirmary. Larry had been issued crutches that morning and sent on his way, happily unburdened by a cast; the Trooper was back in the saddle; little Tommy Fulson had been transferred to the county hospital for observation of his non-appendicitis, and what the nurses had begun referring to as the "Plague Ward" was ankle deep in comic books.

As I walked on down the hall after looking in on the chickenpox patients, I couldn't help hearing *La Marseillaise* floating out from behind a partially closed door. Knocking, I stuck my head inside to find Luke Faber, who spends the summers as the adult commander of one of the Indian Scout divisions and an instructor in Indian dancing, propped up in bed and watching the VCR, his left foot and ankle completely immobilized in a cast.

"Aren't you about a week early for Bastille Day?" I asked. For some arcane reason, the Indian Lore staff have been celebrating Bastille Day every summer for the last fifteen years, usually in the immediate neighborhood of an assortment of alcoholic beverages.

"Oh, hi, Jonathan. Actually, I'm watching *Casablanca* again. But Major Furlong and the staff are planning the usual party for next Thursday night. I'm sure you'd be welcome."

"No, thanks. I don't think I'd better. Beer and I just don't agree, and drinking single malt Scotch in a tipi to honor the French revolution sounds a bit far-fetched, even to me. What did you do to your ankle?"

He ran both hands through his thick blond hair and blushed. "I broke it."

"What's so embarrassing about breaking an ankle?" I asked. "Did you catch your foot in the rail down at the Lakeview Tavern?"

"No, nothing that much fun. You know that big hill in the Cub area?"

"The one next to y'all's dining hall?"

"Exactly. Well, at the top of that hill, there's a fire hydrant, next to the trail that runs between the cabins, and what with it being so hot yesterday, we decided to cool the kids off a bit."

"You were hosing them down, right, and tripped over the hose?"

"No. Worse. We rolled a strip of heavy gauge plastic down the hill and ran the hose on it to make a water slide. And before long, the kids wanted us to go down the hill, too. Of course, it was all a muddy mess by then, but I figured, what the hell, I'm as hot as the kids are. So I took a seat on the plastic and pushed off. And it was kind of fun, actually—like riding down a log flume into a hog wallow. But then I stood up—or started to—and slipped and fell right back into the middle of the mud, with this leg twisted underneath me."

"So you broke your ankle by acting like an eight-year-old?"

"Well," Luke laughed, "at least it got me out of the heat. And I had a chance to chat with Larry Brandon, who stopped in to see me and said you were giving him a head start for the fall."

"A little bit of one, perhaps. But to his credit, he was studying on his own when I first looked in on him. Is he going to be an officer in your company next fall?"

"I didn't promote him on the June make order, but I expect he'll be a lieutenant of some kind, at least. He's basically a good kid, but living in that screwy family has left some issues that it will take him a while to outgrow. I was pleased that he was able to get himself emancipated."

"Doesn't it make it a bit odd to have a cadet in your company who's legally an adult and paying his own tuition?"

"Somewhat, yes. Which is one reason I haven't promoted him yet. But he'll come around in time."

Having ascertained that there was nothing in particular he needed, I prayed briefly with Luke and left him with my usual ritual handshake. As I was crossing the street on my way back to the Chapel, the carillon struck the half hour.

I hurried inside, and saw that RJ Esther, back from his vacation, had begun setting up the altar for the noon mass. In my office, I added the new invalids to the prayer list, and we chatted about the weekend while we vested. The service itself went just as usual: RJ led the intercessions, Brad and Chris Gregson, one of the first classmen in his company, read the lessons, and there were about half a dozen other kids, all of them midshipmen, in the congregation. But when I turned to RJ to give him Communion, the chalice in my left hand and a host in my right, there was someone standing between us, so close he was almost on top of me. He opened his mouth to say something, looking straight into my eyes, and even reaching up as if he were about to receive the sacrament. I instinctively held it out to him: and then he was gone, and there was nothing in his place.

I do not mean that things were suddenly back to normal, with RJ standing about two feet away from me, and empty air between us. Not at all. For only the blink of an eye, the mysterious visitor was gone and I stared into absolute nothingness. It seemed like a rip that would inevitably spread, as though the whole world would suddenly discover that its being was the unsupported walk of a cartoon character who's wandered off a cliff and not yet realized that there's nothing to hold him up. The sequence of events was so fast that I didn't even have time to pull back my hand—I would have reached right into the abyss if it hadn't vanished—or, rather, if actuality hadn't returned—just as I was about to touch it with the outstretched host.

With his left hand, RJ took the bread from me, using his right to steady the chalice until he could relieve me of it as well. After he had taken a sip of wine, he set the chalice down on the altar, stepped closer to me, and whispered, "Jon, you look terrible. Go sit down and let us take care of this." He pushed me discreetly toward the sedilla and gestured for Brad—who was just coming to the rail, so suddenly had it all happened—to come up and take the paten. The two of them distributed communion, and RJ concluded the service as quickly as decency permitted, if not rather faster; I followed him out to the office the short way, through the door between the sanctuary and the choir. I had no more than sat down behind my desk—still in my chasuble—when Brad, followed by the whole congregation, burst into the room, all of them demanding at once to know what was wrong.

"I'm fine, really," I said. "I just felt dizzy for a second, and Mr. Esther here is a bit overprotective."

"You just don't know how to deal with heat, is all," RJ replied. "If you insist on trying to carry on with things as usual—track meets and all—you at least need to have the sense to quit before you drop."

"And common sense has never been Jonathan's strong point, heh, heh," Brad added.

"Well, whatever my shortcomings along that line, I'm in no danger from the heat in here. Thank you all for being so concerned, but I really am okay. If we all stand around here and talk, you're going to miss your lunch. The Mess Hall stops serving for DRC at one, doesn't it?"

"We like to think of it as 'two bells,' in the Naval School, Chaplain," Gregson said, helpfully.

"Whatever you call it, it's only five minutes from now. So thank you all very much and I'll see you tomorrow. Now scoot. Dismissed. *Ite, missa est.*" I stood and waved them toward the door. Soon, only RJ, Brad, and I were left.

Opening the door to the safe, I took out several vestment hangers, handing one to RJ for his alb. "You know, I really am all right," I said.

Brad had sprawled himself on the sofa I keep for my afternoon naps. "You certainly look okay now. But when I passed you as you were sitting down in there, you looked greener than that chasuble. What happened?"

I hung up my cassock and took three Cokes out of the refrigerator, handing one to each of my colleagues before I plopped down in an armchair directly in front of my air conditioner. "I'm not sure I know," I said, and described what I had seen.

"What did this guy look like, Jon?" Brad asked.

"A guy, I don't know. He was only there for a second, and I couldn't describe you if you weren't lying there in front of me."

"The famous Mears lack of visual imagination," RJ observed. "I bet you remember the facts, though, even if you can't put them together into a picture. What color was his hair?"

"Dark, I guess—I don't remember seeing it."

"You mean he was bald?"

"No, more covered up, somehow."

Brad sat up: "Wearing a hat?"

"No, not that either. I guess it was a hood of some kind. Definitely dark, though, brown or black. I'd remember if it was white, like an amice."

RJ tried another tack—"You said you saw his mouth open as though he were saying something. Was he wearing a beard or a mustache?"

"Yes, both, and they were red, I think."

"Very good. Now, if you could see his mouth and beard, was the hood pulled back far enough for you to see his eyes?"

"Yeah, but I couldn't swear to the color."

"That wasn't what I was going to ask. Remember that I was looking right at you—I didn't see anything, after all—and you didn't seem to glance up or down. What I wanted to ask was, were you looking right into his eyes, as you seemed to be?"

"I guess I was, yes. So we must have been the same height, eh?"

"Precisely, Watson."

"So," Brad said, "he saw someone about 5'8" with a red beard and mustache wearing a shallow dark-colored hood, who looked like he wanted communion. Aren't ghosts supposed to howl or bleed or something? This character doesn't sound very frightening."

"It wasn't him that scared me, but what came after. In theology class, we used to talk about two different kinds of nothingness; the first kind is *me on*, the non-being of something that could be, but isn't. Monday's fireworks are *me on*, like tomorrow's sunrise. But a four-sided triangle, or a flying pig, is *ouk on*, the non-being of something that could never be at all."

"Like a good meal in the mess hall, heh, heh, heh."

"Exactly. So, since it's now after one, we've missed *ouk on*, absolutely nothing. Really, though, the idea is that *ouk on* is the absence of creation—it's the non-stuff in the non-place and the non-time where God isn't doing anything at all. And that's what I was looking at. It was like the last second in a falling dream, the one just before you hit the ground, when it's rushing toward you a million miles an hour, and you can't close your eyes, and you know you have to wake up, or else you'll—"

Now it was RJ's turn to blanch. "Stop right there," he said. "Some of us have perfectly fine visual imaginations, thank you very much."

"And some of us are a little bit afraid of heights, heh, heh."

"Not funny, Mr. Peniston. And for that matter I seem to remember an incident when we took those kids to Mammoth Cave, when the rangers turned off all the lights . . ."

"Fair enough, RJ. Forget that I ever said anything. But seriously, Jon, if I followed what you said, you can't see this *ouk on*. I mean, it can't be there to be seen, right?"

"No, you're quite right, it can't. But this was as close as I'd want to get, I'm sure of it."

"All of this metaphysical speculation is well and good for the What Happened angle," RJ said, "but we've dropped Who, and we don't seem to be getting on toward Why and How."

"You think this was someone actually doing something, and not just Jonathan imagining things."

"Of course I do. Jonathan couldn't just imagine something like that, even if you paid him. We may be improving his visual memory with our little exercises, but making images up is just not in him. If I watched him drink a fifth of Rebel Yell and he started talking about pink elephants, I'd call the zoo. So if he saw this, it's because somebody showed it to him."

"Or somebodies," I added, tossing my empty can toward the wastebasket at the end of the couch. "I can't help feeling the blackness cut off the guy in the hood." The can missed.

"Which could mean," said Brad, picking it up and putting it in the basket, "that the hooded man had a message for you that someone didn't want you to hear."

Suddenly, things fell into place. "A message or a request," I said. "I think I know who it is now, but if I'm right, I can't tell you—not yet, anyway. Why don't we drive into town and get a bite to eat? I think it's coney-dog day at the root beer stand."

This was not the most subtle maneuver I've ever used to avoid an issue, and they flashed each other "Is he going to get away with this?" glances, then shrugged. "Fine, Jon," Brad said, "but we'd better clear the altar before we go."

"Quite right," I answered, "I'd forgotten all about it."

"Oh, you'd have remembered soon enough," RJ said as he opened the door. "You left your First Class Ring lying next to the corporal, and none of you alums can go very long without one."

Especially not me, I thought, as I hurried past him to retrieve it.

———

BRAD DROPPED ME OFF beside my car in the Chapel parking lot about three-quarters of an hour later. I'd been toying with the idea of calling the Bishop right away to report what had happened; but I eventually decided not to contact him until I'd found a few objective facts to confirm my suspicions. I had yet to read any of the Prior's articles, which might give me some indirect insight into his character; nor had I been to visit the Abbey itself, from which, I was quite certain, the noonday apparitions had come. I decided to drive over and see what could be found out by casual observation.

Our Lake Annandale has the leaf shape of Native American flint scraper, relatively broad at the north end, but first widening and then tapering almost to a point at the south; the overall length is two miles, the greatest breadth about one and a half. Annandale Military Academy grasps this Stone Age tool at the north end, thrusting it between the Town, on the west shore, and the Summer People, on the east. The most fashionable bit of the East Shore lies along a stretch of bluffs just south of the Academy's property line. Thus, as I drove uphill from the Indian Scout camp and past the Academy golf course, I quickly entered a Gatsbian never-land of Victorian gingerbread houses, sporty Mercedes convertibles, and discreetly placed security systems. One of the largest of these "cottages"—the fourth house after our Southeast Gate—was the old Martin place, where Jeff and the gang would be staying for the weekend. In my childhood, it had still been called "The House of a Thousand Candles," on the theory that Meredith Nicholson had written the novel of that name while visiting the place. At one point, the set of four houses had been owned by the Trout family of Indianapolis: they were respected merchants in the state capital, but had the reputation in town for being even more eccentric than the usual cottage crowd. One of the cousins had become a successful novelist, a development which was widely taken as confirmation of the popular opinion. These were the people to whom I now assumed the Abbot was somehow related. In my own salad days—the summer before I was a second classman at the Academy—the Martin house had been the site of that swimming party at which my classmate Robert Adams—later to be Tom Adams's father—had almost drowned Geoff Davidson: after which they'd been the best of friends until Davidson was killed in a fire, back in '76.

Farther south, the land slopes back down to water level, and the smaller houses crowd closer together, while the Aubenaubee Association golf course on the east side of the road gives way to a large apple orchard. At just the point where one would expect the road to curve west, following the narrowing lakeshore, it makes a ninety-degree turn to the left and dashes off to the east, some engineer having decided that this was the ideal point at which to resume the mile square road grid which overlays all the land of the old Northwest Territory. In the northeast corner made by that turn lies the Abbey of All Angels.

From where I pulled the car over, almost opposite the entrance drive, the Abbey didn't look much different from the farm it had once been. The drive ran uphill a bit to the house and barn, which were set back something more than a couple of hundred yards from the road. A rail fence surrounded the property and followed the drive up to the buildings. A sign on the south side of the drive said:

Abbey Farm
Strawberries – Blueberries
Apples – Cider
Chestnuts
Christmas Trees
Follow drive to parking lot.

About the same distance, or a little farther, up the lane, on the north side, a large stone cross marked the site of the Abbey cemetery. The old house sat, square and sober, somewhat off center from the end of the drive—its three stories and attic, all covered in white clapboard, made it look like a large sugar cube someone had decorated with a roof and porch. Balanced against it, and partly concealed from my view by trees, was the great red bulk of the barn, topped now with a cross rather than a weathervane. Following a local tradition, the barn was round, rather than square; it had been converted into a very dramatic church, reminiscent of the Templars' chapels in England, on its lower level; the upper level was the monks' chapter room, which I had never seen.

Thinking of the nothingness that had confronted me earlier, I wondered briefly whether it was either wise or safe to drive in. *Well*, I thought, *nothing ventured*, and, slipping the car into gear, I turned into the drive. *I should at least be able to get some strawberries*, I reasoned. The further I drove, though, the more I had that feeling we all sometimes get of an unseen presence—the feeling that someone is watching you, even stalking you, from just beyond the limit of your peripheral vision. In my experience, this is a feeling we're most likely to associate with a strange or deserted place, or especially with a darkened room. I remember, in fact, that when I was a third classman, I got myself and a bunch of my friends into a near-panic by asking them to imagine what it would be like to flip on a light in a dark room, whirl around, and discover that the source of the feeling was the crucified Jesus, standing there face to face with you, gaunt, sunken-eyed and hollow-cheeked, the blood still dripping from his brow, his palms, his side, running down through the dust on his face to clot in his already matted beard. . . . I made it a fairly sanguinary account (which goes to show that you don't need to be able to visualize in order to describe), and it was gratifyingly effective even on me, not to mention on my companions. I happened to see the then-chaplain, Father Franklin, the next morning, and told him about what I'd done. "You forget, Mr. Mears," he said, "that the point of the Incarnation was precisely not to be terrifying. What one might rather fear would be the appearance of Christ in glory. Go read the sixth chapter of Isaiah!" (We Annandale chaplains have a long tradition of pomposity.)

Unlike that pious ghost story of my misspent youth, the feeling I had in the lane at All Angels' was not my doing, and was not so easily dismissed. Even though I was driving my own car in broad daylight, it became so strong that it left me actually nauseated. Despite the feeling, I would have gone through with my little reconnaissance mission if I hadn't noticed, as I turned the wheel to the left to pull into one of the space marked off in the center of the parking lot, that my ring was glowing, giving off a light too bright to be confused with the summer sunbeams glancing off the yellow gold.

I pulled straight through the parking place and headed back to my office.

What was that all about? came the combined telepathic voice of my niece and my nephew-to-be.

Just a warning, I thought back. *I'll try to be more careful.*

Danny/Daddy says to call him and let him know what you're up to.

I'll phone this evening, I answered.

Back at my desk, I unlimbered my computer terminal, and discovered, after a certain amount of poking around, that while our library did not subscribe to the esoteric journals in which the prior's articles had appeared, I could have the pieces transmitted to the school overnight, where they would be copied to my account or printed out for me in the library's electronic media room. As usual, I chose both options—in the world of computers, I feel safer wearing a belt with my suspenders. I thought about getting back to work on my sermons for Sunday—I have one morning prayer service for the Scouts and another for the high-school aged boys, plus the Sunday Mass, and I try to make my remarks appropriate to the different age levels, so there's a fair amount of preparation involved. In fact, I got as far as digging out the citations for the lessons again: Zechariah 9: 9-12, Romans 7:21-8:6, and Matthew 11:25-30; but somehow, before I could look up the commentaries on the readings, it occurred to me that I hadn't yet had my nap, and the more I reflected on it, the more I thought I was entitled to one. I plopped myself onto the couch, trusting, as usual, that the inevitable afternoon phone call would awaken me before I spent too much of the day in sleep.

In the event, someone knocking at the door that awakened me, and a good deal sooner than I had intended, at that. It was Larry Brandon, on crutches, with a fat book clutched in his left hand.

"Hey, sir," he said. "Wanna teach me some English? It's rec period, and I won't be much good to the company soccer team like this."

"Sure, Larry," I answered. "Come on in out of the heat."

He swung in and lowered himself into the armchair nearest the door. "It must be hard to navigate with that book in your hand," I said, dropping back onto the couch.

"It's not too bad with just the one, sir. I don't think I could do two, though—one or the other would always be slipping. This is the complete Yeats, though, and I thought I had better bring a copy."

"Good idea, actually. I either left mine in the car or else it's lying on the table in the breezeway at home—one or the other. In any case, we'll use yours. Are you still working on 'Among School Children'?"

"Yes, sir. It does make more sense to me than when I started, at least. The business you did with me about him being in a school gave me more of an idea of how to go at it: it's like we have to walk through the long poem questioning, the same way he walks through the schoolroom."

"That's good, Larry; I hadn't thought of that. What part of the poem are you working on right now?"

"Well, sir, it seems to me that the main thing that he thinks of when he sees these kids is how old he's getting, and how surprised his mother would be at how he's turned out."

"That's true enough, though I'm not sure I'd say it's the main point: I may have set you off on the wrong track when I emphasized that Yeats was a senator. Try a different angle. When he looks at the kids, he thinks of someone else, doesn't he? Read the second stanza again."

" 'I dream of a Ledaean body bent
Above a sinking fire, a tale that she
Told of a harsh reproof, or trivial event
That changed some childish day to tragedy—
Told, and it seemed that our two natures blent
Into a sphere from youthful sympathy,
Or else to alter Plato's parable,
Into the yolk and the white of the one shell.'

And I know now that Ledaean means having to do with Leda, who was the mother of Helen of Troy; so this body must look like Helen or her mother. Which is a roundabout way of saying she's really pretty."

"Exactly. She's Yeats's girlfriend, in fact, and he remembers how she told him once a story about her childhood. Then he gives us a metaphor for the kind of loving feeling he has for her. Wasn't there part of Plato's *Symposium* in your writing text for last year, the legend about why people fall in love?"

"Right. People were originally big balls with two heads, and four legs and so on, and we're always looking for our missing halves. But he makes it like yolk and white, instead of two halves. That way it fits with Ledaean, too, doesn't it? I mean, wasn't she raped by a swan, and all her babies were hatched out of eggs?"

"Very good. You've paid more attention over the years than I gave you credit for. Would you like a Coke?"

"Sure, sir, if you have enough, I mean."

"There's always enough," I answered. "I get a wholesale discount, you know." I noticed that he didn't laugh. When I'd handed him a can and opened one for myself, I sat back down on the edge of my desk. "What comes after the union of souls part?"

"First he wonders whether his girlfriend looked like these girls when she was their age, and he pictures her as a child; then he thinks about what she looks like now, and he even reminisces that he used to look pretty studly himself. That's when he comes to the part about what his mother would think of him now."

"Which is where you came in. Exactly."

"Right, sir. Anyway, after that he gets back to mothers and contrasts their images of their children with nuns' images of saints or God or whatever."

"Contrasts?"

"Well, compares and contrasts. They're all heartbreakers, all images are, I mean, not all nuns and mothers."

"Right—whether the images come from romance, or religion, or family relations."

"Nice alliteration, sir."

"Thanks. Now, how about the last part: he turns to the images themselves in the bit we were just talking about. What does he have to say to them?"

"That still confuses me, sir. I can see that he says we can't distinguish the dancer from the dance, or the flower from the tree; *and* he says that work shouldn't pit mind against body. It's the connection that bothers me."

"And bothers him, too, as far as that goes. What does he remember about that moment with his girlfriend in the second stanza?"

"How much they were drawn together, I guess—their feeling of unity."

"Okay, then you have those Greek philosophers we skipped over—all of them were thinking about the connection between the thing and its idea, between appearance and reality or between reality and the ideal. And when he turns to the ideals themselves, he really goes back to that moment remembered in stanza two."

"And tells them that it's the unity that's important. Of course! The dancer and the dance, the mind and the body, the idea and the reality are all—I mean, each pair of them is, only one thing. To try to know them as two things is like trying to know the yolk and white as separate parts instead of one egg—if you make the separation, there isn't an egg anymore."

"From Leda and the Swan to Humpty Dumpty."

"Yes, sir. Exactly. Before you could tell which part of Helen was human and which part was Olympian, you'd have to divide her into pieces that all of Menelaus's horses and men couldn't put back together again."

"I think it was Hector who tamed horses, but that's certainly the idea, Larry."

"Well, I'm embarrassed—I should have figured it out quicker."

"More quickly. Why do you say that?"

"It's the kind of thing my grandmother always says. I could even see her saying that line about the dancer, now that I think about it."

"Is she a poet?"

"No, not really. She's an Indian, Miami and Potawatomi."

"You're kidding."

"No, really, she is. I'm one-quarter Native American. She was born down around Peru [Indiana, I knew he meant, since he pronounced it PEE-roo, in our Hoosier fashion] and says there was still real prejudice against Indians when she was growing up."

"When would that have been?"

"Oh, I don't know. I guess she's almost ninety. It must have been around the First World War."

"Wow. Has she been able to pass on Native American traditions to you?"

"A lot of them, I guess," he said, and made a furtive glance at his wrist watch, as though the carillon, less than two hundred feet away from us in the tower, had not been chiming every quarter hour during our whole conversation.

"Sir, it's almost time to get ready for retreat parade: I have to change into my middy and stuff and form up with the Sick Squad at Sally Port. It'll take me awhile."

"Oh, right. Of course," I answered, responding to my cue. "You really had better get going, I guess. Dismissed."

Standing carefully, he juggled his crutches and the Yeats into some semblance of a salute and galumphed out my door and down the aisle. *Well*, I thought to myself as I picked up the reference books I'd need to work on the sermons at home, *I wonder what nerve we touched on there?*

Chapter 4: Thursday, July 7

THE BELLS THAT marked off the time of my conversation with Larry had also ticked away the last hours in which I might have called the diocesan office to tell Bishop Parker I could not honor his request that I become the diocese's exorcist. It was, I suppose, an insightful move for the Bishop to have said he would take my silence as agreement: at least, it took advantage of my desire to say and think as little about the subject as possible. Honestly, though, I'd have to admit, if I were pressed, that I had agreed in my heart to do what he asked on Monday—I'd stalled for time only in the hope of finding some way out of the dilemma with which he'd confronted me.

I called Danny as soon as I got home, and told him as much of what had happened as I could without betraying Jeff's confidences. As I've said, our earlier experience had left him more cautious than I remembered, but there wasn't much he could say that hadn't already occurred to me: that I should stay away from the Abbey and keep an eye out for trouble from the Abbot. Rhys, he told me, was visiting him (or, more accurately, Caroline) in Bean Blossom.

"Jon, it's almost eerie—they're so completely linked by this telepathy business that it's as if they're already married, or more than married. I mean, they don't even talk out loud unless I'm there."

"Well, in a sense, I suppose they are linked. But 'marriage is a sacrament ordained by God,' as the Prayer Book says. I mean, I look forward to marrying Caroline and Rhys, but I'd just as soon put it off until they're quite a bit older."

"It also says that 'a sacrament is the outward and visible sign of an inward and spiritual grace,' doesn't it? What I'm getting at is that they have the inward grace so strongly that they don't seem to be worried about the outward signs. Not as much worried about them as we were at their age. Besides, they're not that young anymore—they'll both be eighteen before long."

"Fair enough. They do seem to be made for each other. I suppose it's a natural result of their family backgrounds."

"Or more cynically, it's the result of selective breeding."

"Either way, I'm glad of it. Listen, I don't know how this business with the Abbey is going to work out, but I'd appreciate it if you three could be more on the alert than usual for the next few days. If I need help, I'll probably need it in a big hurry."

"Sure thing, Jon. I can take off work and we can come up there, if you need me to."

"No, don't waste your vacation time. With the kids' talents, I don't think it's necessary for you to be here physically."

"Very well. We'll be ready at a moment's notice. Don't worry about it."

"Great. That'll be one load off my mind, anyway. Well, I suppose I'd better at least pretend to get some work done. Give my love to the kids."

"Of course. And you try to stay out of trouble."

"Easier said than done; but I will try. Bye."

―――

I WORKED ON my sermons fairly diligently for the rest of the evening. Though I know all about Calvin's emphasis on those parts of the Bible which say that God knows every sparrow that dies and has counted every hair of your head, I can't say that I've ever been inclined to see God as arranging each little incident of life, like whether your toast burns or you run out of dental floss. I have to admit, though, that I'm made a little suspicious by coincidences like the Bishop's having asked me, a witch, to be an exorcist the week before a Sunday when the Gospel is the passage where people accuse Jesus of casting out demons by the power of Satan, and he replies that in that case the kingdom of hell is in real trouble, divided against itself—language Mr. Lincoln borrowed when he said that the union couldn't survive half slave and half free. Looking at that as the Gospel gave me plenty to think about, but not necessarily a lot I wanted to put into a sermon for the kids. By Thursday morning, though, I'd made a fair beginning toward something by using the Prince of Peace images of the lesson from Zechariah and St. Paul's ideas about Christ ending the power of sin by submitting to it. I worked most of the morning in the office to develop full-fledged drafts, and by the time I left for the Infirmary, I had a couple of sermons I could have used without further polishing if I'd had to.

The chicken-pox population continued to increase, but Tommy, at least, was headed back to his cabin: the county hospital had found nothing wrong, his temperature and white blood count had gone down, and they'd shipped him back to us. When I saw him, he was sitting happily in the nurse's office, eating a Popsicle and waiting for someone to take him back to the Scout area. The new arrivals from upper camps consisted of a yellow-tinged midshipman whose embarrassed description of his symptoms accorded well with Betty's diagnosis of an infected prostate, a second middy who'd cut his foot open in water skiing class, and an aviation cadet who'd thrown up twice during the night—Betty reported that his roommate, who'd brought him in, had told her the boy was supposed to solo that day.

Luke was still in his room, though he had progressed from *Casablanca* to *Ferris Bueller's Day Off*, which he seemed to be reciting from memory about one beat ahead of the actors. "Hi, Jonathan," he said, switching off the sound with his remote control.

"Hi, Luke. Don't let me interrupt your film."

"Oh, it's okay. I've seen it before. How's by you?"

"Oh, okay, I guess. Say, do you know much about Native American spirituality? It's connected with dancing and so on, isn't it?"

"Oh, yes, certainly. But of course what we teach the kids is really just the external part, the dancing itself, divorced from the spiritual side of it: which is a white man's way of looking at it in the first place. What I mean is, they learn something about the cultures and how the different dances fit into them, but we don't generally aim for them to have the religious or spiritual experience a Native American might have. So I can't say that I know much about the spiritual side—it's a big topic, in the first place, and I've never needed to really get inside it, if you see what I mean. Why do you ask? Something you've been reading?"

"Something I'm about to read, actually: I've ordered some articles on the subject written by an Anglican monk, and I'm curious to know whether he's talking through his hood, so to speak. Could you look over a couple and tell me what you think? It'd have to be done fairly quickly."

"Sure, I'll be happy to do what I can: I'm not going to be dancing myself for awhile."

"Great. I'll look you up tomorrow. Good luck tonight."

"Thanks, I'll need it."

It was 11:50 when I left the Infirmary, and the first companies march in to DRC promptly at noon: so I went straight to the Mess Hall, to avoid an endless wait in line. Lunch featured some sort of elaborate "sandwich" with a special sauce—the sort of messy concoction that makes nonsense of the noble earl's original idea. I have to admit, though, that they tasted good, and I ended up having two of the gooey things while carrying on a pointless conversation of the well-it-certainly-has-been-a-hot-one variety with Richard Davies (the day's Officer in Charge), Sergeant-Major Chuff and one of the more Neanderthal ice-hockey instructors (who was, in my opinion, in no position at all to complain, having one of the only jobs in school that required him to spend eight hours a day in a refrigerated room).

Taking a last Coke with me from the fountain in the serving line, I walked back to the office, trying to generate as little heat as possible. I washed the last bits of sauce off my hands in the sacristy sink, reflecting as I dried them on a towel that today I should be able to get in a nice full nap.

I dozed off quickly, as I usually do, and was soon, unusually, dreaming: not that I don't know dreams are a normal part of all our sleep, but I hardly ever remember what I have dreamt. On this occasion, however, the memory stuck with me quite clearly. I was shut up in a dark place—I felt as though I could touch both walls if I stuck out my arms—and it was oppressively hot, so much so that when I awoke I was drenched with sweat, though my air conditioner was running as fiercely as ever. The main "sensation" which accompanied this dream, though, so far escapes my description that I'm hesitant even to use so general a word as that for it. It was as though I were a victim of dual personality caught in the very moment of transition, a Stevensonian monster caught in the instant of being both Jekyll and Hyde, and thus somehow neither of them. Moreover, I/we were simultaneously in my office as well as in the tiny prison: the prisoner was dreaming me at the same time I dreamt him. It was the very image of perfect knowledge, of complete and utter communion between two persons, even more than "the yolk and white of one egg." And yet I did not in fact know anything more than I already had, did not think any thoughts but my own. Indeed, it seemed as though the dreamer, my other self, were not thinking at all, as though perception were the only higher brain function still at work in him. Perception, and whatever level, whatever reptilian limbus or primatial cortex it is that can feel—did feel—an absolute (I might almost say, unreasoning: but it was precisely my own remaining bubble of reason which made the deluge the more intolerable), a radical and essential, fear of annihilation. It was a night-terror of being ground down and obliterated, the horror of an extinction so utter that whether one lived or died was irrelevant. I would say it was hair-raising, or gut-wrenching, or paralyzing, but the fact is that this was a threat pressed down so directly on my-his-our being that the kinesthetic world—even the sense of terrible, suffocating heat—was insignificant.

This time, it *was* the phone that awakened me: Mrs. Hardwicke from the Library, calling to let me know that my articles were collated and stapled and I could come to get them anytime. I thanked her, perhaps a bit more hastily than I might have otherwise, and punched in the Bishop's 800 number as soon as she was off the line.

The WATS line rings directly into the bishop's office, and when Mrs. Equitone was away from her desk, he often answered it himself; but I was surprised when the Archdeacon picked up.

"Hi, Carl. This is Jonathan. Where's Himself?"

"Well, it's 2:15," he answered, in the tone of an old TV curfew warning. "Do you know where your Superintendent is?"

"Aha! Today is the famous golf game, I suppose."

"Insight is your strong suit, isn't it? Seriously though, the Bishop did say you might call. I gather he half-expected you might phone him yesterday to turn down some job connected with the Abbey visitation?"

"Right. I think I'm committed to that now, though."

"That would be my impression, yes. May I say, by the way, that it entirely escapes me why the two of you didn't just join the CIA in the first place if you intended to be so secretive about this whatever-it-is?"

"I suppose it might. Actually, I didn't realize the Bishop was treating this as such a high security business until you said so just now, but I suppose the reason is that the job grew out of a specific case he was asked to keep confidential, rather than out of the Abbey election itself. Does that help, at all?"

"It does make some sense of things, thanks. How's the weather down there?"

"Hotter than hell, in my professional opinion. I don't know how the kids are surviving it, frankly. They swim a lot, I guess, and we have a lot of movies in the auditorium, which is air-conditioned. And one of the faculty was telling me the other day that they've been setting up a waterslide for the elementary aged kids. We're getting by, but I wouldn't go much farther than that."

"And your Coke supply is holding up?"

"Just. I have it trucked in, you know, the way Herb Mathis buys sherry. Is the big lake giving you folks any relief?"

"Some, I guess. Of course, in the city we don't have to get outside much. It strikes me as a bit warm for golf, though."

"Me, too, if the truth be known. But I guess they're big boys and can take care of themselves."

"Even if they can't, there's about as much chance of influencing them as a bandersnatch. Do you want to leave a message, by the way?"

"Well, yes. Have the Bishop call me as soon as he can: I should be in the Chapel office, or the Academy Operator can ring my beeper. Tell him I've done some of the research he suggested, and have some urgent new experience to bring to bear on the case."

" 'New experience,' right. I'll make sure he sees it. Have a good afternoon, Jon."

"You too, Carl. Bye."

I was by now quite sure that my truncated vision of Tuesday afternoon and the nightmare of confinement that Bess Hardwicke had interrupted were both somehow communications from Jeff's cousin Alfred; and it struck me as suspicious, at best, that the magical defenses I focused through my ring should have reacted to a screen around the Abbey when I drove over there. It was tempting to conclude that the same person had interrupted Tuesday's episode, placed the screen around the Abbey, and subdued Brother Alfred into physical immobility and psychical stupor. That Alfred should nonetheless have been able to draw me into such a union suggested that the novice had extraordinary powers; but, by the same token, it seemed likely that such an exercise of power must certainly have attracted further attention from the brother's jailer. Absent the Bishop's directions, though, I had no canonical or legal right even to enter the Abbey; and without any real magical training, I knew of no way to meet Alfred's captor on his own grounds, even if I had been his equal in raw power.

I could, at least, pray; and, locking the office door behind me, I stopped in the nave to do just that before I left for the library to pick up my copies of Fr. Prior's essays. I noticed, as I knelt down in a pew, that it seemed to be getting cloudy outside; by the time I'd finished my devotions, the clerestory windows were dark with the threat of a Midwestern thunderstorm, and I ducked back into the office for my raincoat and umbrella.

Before I was even halfway across campus, the storm broke: the sailboats still on the lake abandoned all hope of tacking back to the pier and headed for the nearest point of land downwind; athletic classes hurried into the gym (that is, the Wayne Memorial Athletic Center); and the surprisingly large number of kids who always seem simply to be wandering around school ducked into the doorways of various barracks. In a matter of seconds, I was the only person still walking about on campus.

I trotted along quite comfortably, smug at having had the foresight to bring the proper equipment. My self-satisfied reverie came to an abrupt halt when, with a flash and crack that would have left the Sergeant-Major as green as his uniform with envy, a bolt of lightning struck one of the ancient sycamore trees in the First Classmen's Garden, no more than ten or twenty feet from me, tearing the heavy trunk in a spiral, as if a giant had tried to twist it out of the ground. I could smell the ozone from where I was standing, almost as soon as I saw the event which produced it.

It's a misleading part of my later legend around the school that some aviation cadets who observed this event from the windows of Verdun Barracks saw me turn after the lightning stroke and continue calmly on my way. It wasn't actually that I was all that nonchalant—it's just that I didn't think, given my sedentary nature and lack of co-ordination, that running for shelter was likely to get me there much faster than my usual brisk walk. Really, there didn't seem to be much else to do. Unconscious of the clouds of accumulating myth I was trailing behind me, I came to the entrance—the barbican, almost—of the castellated old Library Building, climbed the front steps, saluted the memorial to the Gold Star Men of Annandale, and pushed open the heavy oaken door.

Miss Percy, who was on duty at the circulation desk, sent me on to the computer laboratory in the basement of the new Library: another god-awful architectural disaster of the 1980s, all slick and sterile and impotently contemptuous of the Neo-Norman keep next to which it grovels. A tunnel connected the satisfying gloom of the old dungeon to the cool fluorescent glow of the new basement, so I was able to get to the computer room without making a second trip into the storm. The articles made quite a pile of paper, taken together, and, rather than carry them first to the lounge, on the second floor of the old Library, and then back to the Chapel, I sat down at one of the high-tech carrels to read through some of the essays while I gave the storm a chance to blow over.

"It must necessarily seem strange," Fr. Shaw wrote in the first article ("Sweat Lodges and Jesuits: Notes toward the Recovery of a Spiritual Creole"), "if not, indeed, presumptuous, that an Anglican priest, born in Yorkshire, ordained in the Orient, and living in an enclosed Benedictine community in the wilds of Indiana, should write upon the vision of spiritual development, one might almost have said, the articulated sequence of spiritual disciplines, practiced amongst most of the Native Americans of the former Northwest Territories, that is to say, the Algonquin tribes of the present states of Ohio, Indiana, Michigan, Illinois and Wisconsin. It is nonetheless the case that these disciplines (and they are a not inconsiderable family) have proven (insofar as they can be recovered and reconstructed, not only from archeological evidences and the observations of the European—which is to say, in the specific area with which we are concerned, the British—settlers, but also from testimonies of the heroic French priests, who, in the company of the explorers and the *coureurs de bois*, were the first Christian religious to encounter and, in some rare cases, enter into dialogue with, the various Native American religious traditions represented in the area) to be both practicable and edifying when used by the author and members of his community over the course of the last several years."

He went on like that for quite a while. If it hadn't been for the storm, I would have been tempted to take the whole pile of offprints with me and use them as sleep aids in the office. As it was, I plowed on through the piece, not reading with great attention to detail, and wishing from time to time that I had a raven to send out to check on the weather. Fr. Prior had, in brief—or rather, at some length—reconstructed a whole course of exercises—fastings, meditations, saunas, and whatnot—which he felt the Native Americans in our neck of the woods had used for spiritual training before people like my great-great-grandfather arrived and sent them off on the Trail of Tears. That much of his essay was outside my field, and I couldn't judge how reliable his anthropological work was. The other two steps he took, though, left me a bit dubious. First, he noted that there were similarities between the Native American spiritual techniques and those of Christian mystics. Now that isn't all that surprising: after all, there are only so many out-of-the-ordinary things a human being can do—you either pray or keep silent, fast or feast, shave your head or let your hair grow, and so on. From this coincidence he concluded that Christians could take over the external parts of the program. Then, on the basis of some equally coincidental resemblances between Christian belief and the theology of the Native Americans, he deduced that the intended, and achieved, end of the Native American exercises was the same as the end sought by Christian mystics, so that one could not only use these techniques in place of traditional Christian ones, but could even supplement traditional Christian doctrine with Native American insights. And finally, he concluded that all these things that could be done had in fact been done by some of the early Christian missionaries. Now it's not that I don't think Christian theology can't gain greater self-understanding from study of non-Christian thought (look at what Thomas Aquinas got out of Aristotle); but seeing our heritage in a new light is different from decking it out with new bits borrowed from whatever faiths the theologian happens to find attractive, as if neither that religion or one's own had any integrity. Fr. Prior seemed to be a confirmed member of the "decorative bits" school of thought.

Moreover, his essay made it clear that some of the monks at All Angel's were actually working through a program like the one he had reconstructed; we were left to our own opinions as to whether the community had also put into effect its Prior's ideas for supplementing the Deposit of the Faith.

I was spared from reading another of Fr. Prior's exercises by the intrusion of Chris Gregson, the midshipman Officer of the Day, decked out, despite the heat and the storm, in full uniform with leggings, saber and hat (carefully worn indoors, to reflect the fact that he was officially "under arms"). He was wet, red-faced, and out of breath, but managed to bring himself to attention and salute: "Sir, Midshipman Gregson, J.C., First Class, reports to Chaplain Mears."

"At ease, Mr. Gregson. What have I done now?"

"Nothing, sir. But Dr. Davies has the Guard running all over campus looking for you. You had an emergency phone call, and no one knew where to find you, and apparently your beeper isn't working—"

"I suppose not. This room is probably a Faraday cage: the inside of a closed conductor, so that no radio signals can get in."

"Whatever you say, sir. But would you please come with me to a phone so you can make this call?"

"Surely; just let me grab my papers here. Do you have the number, or do I need to check back with Dr. Davies?"

"No, sir. I have it right here. It's an 800 number, sir." He handed me a slip of paper as we left the room.

"Oh, right. This is just my bishop returning a call. It's not really an emergency, quite, but I asked him to call me as soon as he could. I don't know what Dr. Davies is so excited about."

"He seemed more worried than excited, sir. Isn't that the way out of the tunnel, sir?"

"You're a Lieutenant Commander, Mr. Gregson: you know rank has its privileges. This is a faculty shortcut to the postern."

"Postern, sir? Like a castle?"

"Well, the back door. It goes out through the office, so I can use the librarians' phone." This was something of a bluff, as the basement door to the back stairway is locked about as often as I forget my grand-master key, and I might have ended up looking sillier than usual; but it seemed that I had been living right. "Watch your head," I warned, "this does take us back into the old Library."

"My kind of dungeon, sir," he said, patting his saber. "Clerics in front and fighters in the rear."

Clerics and magic users, I thought to myself, as we climbed through the gloom of the circular staircase. "Do you enjoy role-playing games, Mr. Gregson?"

"Yes, sir. But I don't play them any more. My parents read somewhere about a kid in Utah who played one of those games and ended up getting possessed by a demon. I told them that was silly, but they made me get rid of my stuff, even my crystal twenty-sided dice. I still think they're wrong, though. Nobody could take all that supernatural stuff seriously, anyway, and I . . ."

I had opened the office door at the top of the stairs, letting in a flood of light, just as Gregson came around the last twist of the spiral, and I think he just then remembered to whom he was speaking—for some version of the story about Rhys had surely passed from winter to summer school long ago, making its rounds in the Corps.

"And you what, Mr. Gregson?"

"I guess I'm just going to have to live with it, is all, sir."

"Nice recovery, kid. Come on out of there: the phone's right over here."

Beneath its vaulted ceiling, the office had the usual clutter of books received, books bound for rebinding, CD's, computer disks, and coffee mugs; all the librarians themselves were seemingly out in the stacks or at the circulation desk. I dropped the pile of papers in the first open place I could find; Gregson followed me like a puppy. "Did Dr. Davies tell you to watch me call, or may I dismiss you to get on with your duty?"

"I'm supposed to wait around in case you need me, sir."

"Very well. Have a seat on the edge of the desk, there. I've got dibs on this chair."

"It's okay, sir, I'll stand," he said, gesturing toward his saber hilt.

"You mean you can't sit down because you're under arms? That seems a bit exaggerated."

"No, sir. I can sit down—or, I mean, I may sit down. But with the saber on, I can't. I always seem to trip over it when I try to stand back up."

"That happened to me once, too, when I was a middy. I was sitting on a bench outside Sally Port, and the Superintendent came up—full Air Force summer uniform with three stars—and when I went to stand up, my saber chain caught in the slats of the bench . . ."

"Sir, the phone call?"

"Right, the phone. Maybe Dr. Davies is right and I do need a keeper." I pressed the Bishop's number, and Carl answered on the first ring.

"Hi, Carl, it's me again."

"Jonathan! Finally! Listen, this is quite serious. Are you sitting down?"

I hadn't, yet; but I did. Carl was not given to exaggeration.

"Okay, Carl. Go ahead."

"Jonathan, the Bishop was killed this afternoon."

"Oh, my God! Ted killed? Murdered, you mean? Did someone take a shot at him?"

"No, no, nothing like that—just an accident. He and your Superintendent were still on the golf course this afternoon when a thunderstorm came up. They started for shelter, but before they could get there, the Bishop was struck by lightning."

"Were they both hurt?"

"No, I don't think the General was really even dazed, though they're keeping him here at St. Luke's awhile for observation. He started CPR on the Bishop right away, of course, but apparently it didn't make any difference. They had the full treatment—paramedics and electrical resuscitation and all—but he was d.o.a. at the hospital. Severe burns, they said, on top of everything else."

"May his soul and the souls of all the faithful departed . . . Have you told his wife?"

"Yes. She was over at Syracuse at Villa Maria. Canon Gabriel walked over from the retreat center to tell her, and the two of them are on their way up here now."

"That's fine. Alexandra's very good with people at times like this. Jeez. This is incredible. Carl, do I have to call a meeting of the Standing Committee or anything?"

"Not right away, Jonathan, no, though that is why I wanted to phone you immediately. Next week will be soon enough. Your committee became the ecclesiastical authority of the diocese at the time of his death, but he wasn't planning any official work that can't wait. You'll have to make arrangements for a retired bishop, or one of the neighbors, to come in and do confirmations and the other episcopal acts, but there's no great hurry. Summer is the off season for all that."

"True enough. The Anglican church tends to run on a nine-month calendar, I think, with a long summer vacation. But I do know one thing he was planning to do, soon."

"Oh, yes, of course, your secret mission to All Angels' Abbey. I suppose you're still bound by confidentiality?"

"Well, yes, I guess. But I'm probably going to need your help. You did say that the Bishop expected to hear from me yesterday?"

"Yes, and he assumed when he didn't that you'd agreed to do whatever it was that he wanted you to do in the first place."

"That's what I thought. Now, when he was down here, he said he was going to send me a letter with the logistical details. I wonder if he did that yesterday afternoon or this morning, say."

"If he did, it's probably in the mail already. I don't see anything lying on his desk to be signed. Is it important to have it right now?"

"Well, yes. It has a certain bearing on what we do about Monday."

"Okay. Let me see if there's a copy in his word processor. Hold on for a second—I'm going to put you on the speaker phone. Just a second."

I turned to the O.D. "Look, Mr. Gregson, this may involve something confidential. If you must stay, could you wait out there in the stacks? It's the door right next to where we come in. I'll call for you if I need anything."

"Aye aye, sir." He went out and shut the oaken door behind him.

"What did you say about stacks?"

"Nothing, Carl. I was talking one of the kids. The Officer in Charge sent him with the message for me to call you, and now he won't leave."

"Oh, of course, I should have thought of that."

"I beg your pardon?"

"Your persistent young friend is probably my fault. I asked them to make sure that someone was with you when you called me back. I sort of expected an adult, but I suppose those are in short supply down there."

"Well, yes, and I suppose Richard thought I might need to send a message back to him, or something. Anyway, have you found the letter?"

"Yes, it's coming up now. Written yesterday morning, actually, so he must not have been too worried that you'd back out. There's the usual I-enjoyed-the-visit stuff, then he thanks you for agreeing to be the exorcist—*exorcist*, Jonathan?"

"That's the part I was wondering about. But read on. It probably gets worse."

"Doesn't seem to: he just says you're supposed to be there at 5:30 Sunday afternoon and he'll pick you up at your house at 5:10."

"Sunday? I thought it was supposed to be Monday."

"Right. He says he knows that will come as a surprise, but the Prior called him yesterday morning to talk about Monday's schedule, and mentioned that they have a Solemn Profession planned for Sunday. So the Bishop offered to come in and hear the vows, and the Prior couldn't very well say no."

"No. But why did the Bishop want him to say yes?"

"He says you'll see the point of this when he tells you that the one who is going to be professed is Brother Alfred."

"That does clear it up, yes."

"For you it does."

"Well, all right. This is the condensed version. Brother Alfred is the cousin of one of my former students. He—Alfred, I mean—used magic to tell the cousin to tell the Bishop that he—Alfred—was in some kind of trouble at the monastery. The cousin suggested that the Bishop ask me for my advice. And I think Alfred has tried to communicate with me, as well. And I know for a fact that there is some sort of a magical screen around the Abbey."

"Oh, I see. I suppose I can deal with that."

"Liberal of you. Now, look, here's the thing. The letter nails it down that the Bishop was taking all this pretty seriously, and meant to do something about it. Do these things—the profession and election, I mean—require a Bishop, or the Standing Committee, or what?"

"Not the whole committee, certainly. You're not talking about any decisions, so I'm sure the President can stand in for the whole group when it's just a matter of carrying out policies. I know that that canon is in there, because I wrote it myself. I'll have to call you back about the rest of it, though; I'm supposed to meet the Canon and Mrs. Parker at the hospital."

"Okay, Carl. I'll be sure to stay in touch this time. Give Mrs. Parker my sympathy, and of course I'll be whatever help I can."

"Fine, Jonathan. Good-bye."

"Bye."

———

I GOT UP and let Chris back into the office. "Thank you for waiting, Mr. Gregson. The telephone call was about a death, and my friend wasn't sure how I'd react to the shock, so to speak. If you don't mind sticking around for another second, though, I may need you for a messenger."

"That's what we're here for, sir."

"It's a little bit after five—I mean, after two bells: would Mr. Peniston be in his office right now?"

"No, sir, not since the rain has stopped. He runs in the cross-country meet every Thursday—the whole company does, for group spirit, you know."

"Well, that answers that question. Would you please catch him at the finish line, and tell him I need to see him this evening for supper at my house at, oh, say, 6:30."

" 'The Chaplain presents his compliments to Mr. Peniston and would Mr. Peniston kindly join him for dinner at the Chaplain's quarters at one bell in the second dog watch.' Aye-aye, sir."

"I love it when you talk like that. You don't happen to know Mr. Esther's daily schedule equally well, do you?"

"No, sir, but I wouldn't be surprised if he was at the race, too. Not running, I mean, but watching. Shall I give him the same message if I see him, sir?"

"Yes, please. I'll try phoning him, but he doesn't usually remember to carry his beeper. Tell them both that it's urgent."

"Aye aye, sir."

"Very well, Mr. Gregson. Dismissed."

He snapped off a salute and left through the door into the stacks, which would bring him out into the Great Hall near the circulation desk. I gathered up my papers, umbrella, and raincoat, and started back to the Chapel, where I'd left my car; I could call RJ from home.

Our house was perhaps a bit small for a family of four when my brother Danny and I were growing up there, but it's quite large enough for me now that I live there by myself. There are, as a result, some problems around the house that I've never gotten around to fixing; one of those is that, even though my father built a two-and-a-half-car garage, he only had a single car driveway laid down. Moreover, since he sort of expected people to come into the house from the drive via the breezeway, he never put in a walk between the front door and the street. Thus the blue Ford with Ohio plates parked in my drive when I got home meant that I would have to park in the street and slosh through the wet grass to the front door to get in. Annandale is a small town, and, like any native, I don't much mind people just walking into the house when I'm not home: if I did, I'd lock the doors; but I hate parking in the street, particularly when it's been raining. Not, of course, that there's much traffic on out little one-block-long avenue: our house is the only one that faces it, though I do have some neighbors to the north, on Academy road. I pulled up next to the mailbox—we have one of the huge old rural route kind, big enough to hold a youngish elephant—checked the contents (two bills and three advertisements) and slammed the door shut. After making the driest progress I could across the lawn, I slammed the porch door, just for good measure, and I might have slammed the front door, too, depending on whom I'd found inside. I didn't, though: I dropped my armload of impedimenta onto the couch, instead. It made an equally nice noise, and could be read as expressing surprise as easily as irritation.

"Hi, Chaplain Mears," Jeff Mills said, standing as I came through the door. "The house was unlocked, and you always told us we should make ourselves at home. Besides, I had to use the toilet."

"Call me old-fashioned, Jefferson, but I do prefer to get the greetings out of the way before we move into the apologies. Come here." We hugged, and as I released him, he embraced me again, this time with his head at my left shoulder instead of my right.

"What was that all about?" I asked, as he let me go.

"Oh, just one of Richard's ideas. He says the balance is important. It's some kind of pre-psych thing." He sat back down in Dad's armchair. "Chaplain, I'm worried about Alfred."

"With good reason, from all the evidence I've seen. How'd you know the Bishop had talked to me?" I straightened up the pile of Fr. Prior's papers and took a seat on the couch.

"I guessed, mostly. But what else could he have done?"

"Not much, I guess. You haven't been keeping tabs on him magically, then?"

"No, nor on you either."

"You couldn't keep track of me that way if you tried: my brother Danny and I have taken a few more defensive measures since the Evans business."

"I couldn't follow you while you're in this house or wearing that ring, no, sir. But I understand you take it off fairly often. Were you going to say I should have been keeping track of him?"

"Someone should have—you, me, or his guardian angel. He was struck by lightning on the golf course this afternoon and killed."

He shook his head. "Wow. That's awful. That could be a disaster. It reminds me, though, did you ever see this movie with Bill Murray . . ."

"Yes, when it came out, in fact, which was well before you were old enough to be admitted to the theater. I'll tell you something that wasn't in the film, though: I just missed getting hit myself today, not more than a few minutes away from the time the Bishop played his last hole. One of those big sycamores in the First Class Garden took the slug that was meant for me."

"Then you think—"

"I didn't then, of course; I figured it was my own damn fault for walking through the storm. But when I heard about the Bishop it put a different light on things. Let's not get into all this now, though; I mean to have Mr. Esther and Mr. Peniston over here to talk about this, and with you here, it'll be even better. You can stay for dinner, can't you?"

"Well, sir, the cottage we're staying in isn't rented until Friday, so I don't really have a place."

"Fine. You're probably safer here, anyway. Let me call Esther, then we'll get you put in the guest bedroom, and I'll start some supper. Do you have luggage in your car?"

"Yes, sir."

"Great. Go get it. And move your car off the paved part of my driveway, while you're at it!"

"Sir, yes, sir!" he said, in fake military style, and saluted mockingly as he went out.

I served gazpacho for supper: the heat had lasted so long that I'd fairly well exhausted my repertoire of cooling foods. The events of the day, and what had led up to them, made a somewhat surprising account, even for my three rather experienced guests, but it didn't interfere with anyone's appetite, and we made good progress toward dessert, which, at that point in a Hoosier summer, is predictable.

"Not bad, Jonathan," said RJ (who had in fact been watching the cross-country meet) as he ladled the last of my strawberries over a second shortcake biscuit. "Pass the whipped cream, please."

I handed it to him. "Thank you. I do enjoy cooking when I get the chance."

"I'm quite sure you do. What I meant, however, was that your summary of what's happened around here wasn't bad."

"This is one of those 'heads you win, tails I lose' situations, isn't it?"

"Somebody has to keep you on your rhetorical toes. The soup was good, though, now that you mention it."

"It really was, Jon, first rate. And the berries were good, too. I've never seen them flambéed like that before."

"Sort of strawberries jubilee, eh, Chaplain?"

"That is what it amounts to, really. Look, Jeff, now that I've brought everyone up to date on this end of things, we should hear about what's gone on with you. Shall we retire to the drawing room, then? Be careful of the step up."

When we had disposed ourselves in the recliner, the rocker, the settee, and the couch, the room being somewhat darkened, despite the long summer evening, because the porch to the east and the dining room to the south cut it off from direct light, Jeff began his tale.

"Jackson Lee Davis is my first cousin: his dad is my mother's brother, and our moms were college roommates. He's about four years older than I am, and his folks live over in Bryan, so we visited back and forth a lot when we were small. But it was, gosh, I must have been eight one summer when our parents thought it would be a good deal to send us off to spend the summer at my grandparents' farm. I thought at the time that they wanted us to see what farm life was like; it happens all the time in children's books. It wasn't a lot of work for us, I guess, when I look back on it, because our grandfather hadn't been that well for a couple of years—in fact, he died that next spring—and he had one of those deals where the neighboring farmer did most of the field work. Gramps had a couple of horses, some pigs, and a few chickens to take care of, more to have something to do than anything else—the crops were what brought in the money.

"One afternoon, we went for a walk along the country road, Lee and I, and Grandpa's dog went with us—it was a little gray poodle named Magda, who I gather was one of the Gabor sisters.

"We walked out along the little country road to the state highway, about half a mile away. We intended to turn north on the highway, and walk up to the section road, and then cut down the back lane and come back to the house. We weren't doing anything in particular, just walking along chucking stones into the drainage ditch and talking about whatever little kids talk about—some Tom Sawyer crap or other. When we got to the corner, though, we realized that the mutt was going to be a problem. She wasn't on a leash or anything, and she felt like she had to wander off to sniff at whatever happened to catch her attention. That was okay on the section road, but on the highway there was just enough traffic that we might have ended up going home with Eva pancakes."

"Magda, you mean," Brad added helpfully.

"Right. So we decided to cut across the soybean field back to the house. That was fine with the dog, because she fit under the bean bushes. But for a couple of kids, it was about like cutting through a short rain forest. So about halfway across, we were getting a little bit on the tired side, and pretty hot, on top of it. And just then we come to this like, little valley, where the drainage ditch ran through the center of the field. The valley must have been about two and a half, maybe three feet deep, and maybe six feet across, with a stretch of sand on both sides of the water.

"Well, you know how little kids are around water anyhow, and in our condition, this looked like an oasis. So I climbed right over the edge, or, really, I sort of jumped, no more of a drop than it was, and Lee was maybe a step or so behind me. And as soon as I landed, of course, I knew there was something wrong, and I yelled, and Lee stopped in his tracks, which was a good thing, because it was quicksand, you see, and I was in it up over my knees as soon as I hit. So then Lee laid down on his belly and reached over and grabbed my hand. He could reach me easy enough, but he wasn't strong enough to pull me back out.

"Well, so, I couldn't think of how I was going to get out, and I kept screaming, and it was a good thing my pants were already wet with the mud or I'd have been really embarrassed, and he kept telling me to calm down and he was going to send for help."

"This is where Magda comes in, right?" RJ asked. "Like Lassie and Rin Tin Tin?"

"That stupid mutt? No, sir. She just bounced around and made little yipping noises. But Lee closed his eyes for a second, and his lips moved a little bit. It even felt like he was losing his grip for a second, and I held onto him tighter than ever, and then he opened them again—his eyes, I mean—and said, 'Grandpa's on his way with a rope. Just hang on.' And sure enough, he was there pretty quick, though it didn't seem fast at the time, and with a horse on one end of the rope and me on the other, it was pretty easy to pop me out of the bog."

"So that was your first experience of that kind of thing?"

"Yes, sir, Mr. Esther. And my last, I hope. It's like being caught in gelatin. Hungry gelatin."

"I meant, of Lee's magic. Do you know what he actually did?"

"Yes, sir, though I'm not sure it was magic. Basically, he just talked to him, was all. But that was just the first step. We ended up spending the whole summer getting lessons in that kind of thing from Grandfather. That was what my mother and his dad had sent us there for, of course; neither one of them had any talent at all, and Grandpa had convinced them they'd never know whether we did unless they let us live with him for awhile."

"But," Brad interrupted, "if he knew he could talk to your grandfather, Lee must have already developed these talents without any lessons."

"He didn't know, until he tried. All he knew he could do was hear people from a distance. But it struck me as a fine time for him to try the experiment, when I got a chance to look back on it."

"What did you actually learn to do?" I asked.

"Professional curiosity, huh, Jon, heh heh?"

"Not really, Brad. Magic is strictly my hobby, for the moment, at least. I have a pastoral interest in Jeff's talents, is all."

"Lee's, you mean, Chaplain. He and I didn't turn out the same at all."

"How so?" RJ asked.

"Just plain ability, in the first place, sir. He's like a virtuoso, a first string varsity player, and I'm just a bench warmer. But beyond that, Lee can hear and speak at a distance, which is what we were just saying, I guess. And it sounds to me like you've also seen that he can actually appear where he isn't, or make himself look different to you, or just keep you from noticing him all together."

"He makes himself invisible?"

"Yes, sir, Mr. Peniston. It's not perfect, though, 'cause he can't keep your eyes from seeing him, he just keeps your brain from knowing that it sees him. It's a weird feeling. You know how some of these modern statues are really realistic, like a wax museum only more so, and there's kind of a creepy feeling from something looking so human but not being alive? This is kind of the opposite of that: you feel like there's something alive there, but you can't see it. He did it with Magda once and she really freaked out."

"Really? I'm surprised you can do the trick with animals."

"Well, at least he can, sir. Course, it works better with higher animals, I guess, but I think that's how he seems to be able to know what's going on far away, like where you left your axe in the woods or something—he borrows the senses of the animals around there, and patches them together with his own reasoning."

"So he can read minds, too?" I asked.

"A little bit, Chaplain. It's easy for him to intercept the senses, and emotions aren't too hard to read, but if you're thinking out a whole thesis of some sort, that would be hard, unless you were like making it into words, talking to yourself. And besides, for the one who's doing the mind-reading, I think it's always a little bit like the feeling that you had when you were asleep today. You don't have the other person's thoughts or feelings or sensations out there in front of you like things to look at, exactly: mostly, you plug yourself in, deeper or not so deep, and think or feel or sense them yourself, just as if they were your own. It's like thinking two things at once, but both things tend to feel like they belong to you."

"What happened during my nap, then? I certainly wasn't trying to read *his* mind."

"No, sir. But if it's possible to share someone else's mind, it's also possible to share yours with them. That's what he was doing, I'm sure."

"Share by force, you mean. It's thought control!"

"Oh, come on, RJ. Do I *look* thought-controlled?"

"No, sir, but Mr. Esther is partly right. He was forcing his thinking, or rather his feeling, on you, while it lasted. That's not the same as changing your own thoughts, of course, but he can do that too, a little bit, I think. He can block thoughts—that's easiest; he can blend your thoughts and his, which is harder; but to create a new feeling or whatever in you is hardest of all. Hypnosis would be easier."

"Is there any limit on the distance?" Brad asked.

"There may be some, I guess. We've never tried to find one. Lee talks like there may not even be a limit on time—as though you could mind read back into the past. But I'd be afraid to try that even if I could."

"And your grandpapa taught you all this?"

"Yes, sir; or coached us, really, I guess. It's more a talent than knowledge, you see."

"What about you, Jeff? What did he coach you in?"

"Well, Chaplain, I can talk and listen, that's about the extent of it in that direction. And he used to call me the family exorcist, 'cause he said I could control Maxwell's Demon."

"Which demon?" RJ asked.

"Maxwell's," I said. "It's not a real demon. Jeff's grandfather must have studied some physics before he went into farming. James Clerk Maxwell observed that temperature is a measurement of how fast a molecule is moving: so if you divided a room, say, into two halves with a partition that had a molecule-sized door in it, and then opened and closed the door in such a way that only fast molecules could go through from north to south, and only slow ones from south to north, eventually, the south end would be hot from all the fast molecules, and the north would be cold because of having the slow ones. Maxwell's Demon is the little guy who would have the job of opening and closing the door fast enough to make the sorting work."

"Thank you. What did your grandpapa mean by that, Jefferson?"

"Just that my talent seems to run in that direction, Mr. Esther: to boil water, or freeze it, make a room cold or hot, and so on."

"What about fire?" Brad asked.

"That too, sir; but it's a lot harder. Depends on how easily something burns, of course. And I can meddle a little bit with electronic equipment: I can run my computer without touching the keyboard—that part's something I thought up myself."

"Have you ever tried your hand at lightning?" I asked.

"Like the storms this afternoon? No, sir. That would be quite a bit beyond my scale, sir, even if I were Lee, if you see what I mean."

"I think I do, actually. Look, Jeff, I hate to keep you talking all night, but we still need to hear your version of what's happened over the last week or so. Shall we stop for a minute, and I'll get some Cokes out of the fridge, then you can tell us about it?"

I went out into the kitchen and got the Cokes ready, reflecting as I struggled with a recalcitrant ice cube tray that I might equally well have served warm soda and let Jeff cool it off for us. Returning to the living room, I set down the tray of drinks on the coffee table, and hit the wall switch behind the couch to turn on the ceiling light. When Brad returned from the bathroom, Jeff took up the story again.

"As far as I know, Lee didn't make much use of his talents while we were growing up, though we both knew right away when Grandpa died. I never did mine, either, but they were the reason I was so interested in magic while I was here at the Academy. Lee became fascinated with religion when he was in high school—my aunt and uncle were pretty much unreligious, and I understand they had a fit when he decided to enter a monastery instead of going to college."

"That would have been about five years ago, then?" Brad asked.

"Yes, sir. And he seemed to like it fine. I think he always felt guilty about his talents, like there was something sinful about them, you know, and he really wanted to get into the monastic stuff as a way of making up for it."

"Then they shouldn't have let him in," I said. "That's a route that never got anybody anywhere. You can do penance for your thoughts and your actions, but not for what you are. How many 'Hail Mary's' should I assign a person for having brown eyes instead of blue?"

"Yes, sir, Chaplain. I think they did tell him that eventually. I know the Fr. Prior told him he would someday be able to use his talents for the good of the Abbey, just like singing or writing or cooking. And he said the point of all the disciplines was just a kind of first step, to get the monk's mind clear and ready for the real progress, the real developments. But those were secrets, that only the life-professed monks knew; the Abbot himself taught them all that in the chapter meetings, the Prior said."

"Alfred hadn't been to chapter meetings himself?"

"No, sir. The life-professed are the only ones who go to those. The other monks hardly ever even see the Abbot, according to Alfred."

"Sounds like Shangri-la," I said, unable to resist the temptation to literary allusion.

"Like what we read when we were fourth classmen. That's what I told him, too, sir. Anyway, the thing that made him contact me happened last month. He's eligible to make his permanent vows this year, which is supposed to be a mutual decision between him and the senior members; but he didn't feel like he was ready, and wanted to stay in his annual vows a while longer. So the Abbot himself started having little pep-talks with Alfred, really stressing how the Abbey needed him, you know, till he began to feel like they were more interested in his talents than in him—which made him that much more unwilling, of course. So then one day he went to the Abbot's office for another one of these talks, and he felt like maybe there was something strange, but it wasn't till they'd talked a little bit that he realized someone had started to try the mind-control business on him. Well, the first thing Grandfather did was to drill us until it was an instant reflex kind of thing to shield ourselves from that sort of outside force, which Alfred did, before he even stopped to think about it. And for just a second, less than the blink of an eye, he said, the Abbot looked really, really old and sick: "half-dead," he said. And at the same time, he saw that the Prior was in the room too; and when his attention started to turn that way, it was suddenly, like, where he saw the Prior there was nothing there, like that absolute nothing, the *ouk on*, that the Chaplain described to us just now. Then the whole business stopped, and it was back to normal, or as close to normal as it had been in the first place, and the Abbot was still talking, still in the middle of a word, almost. So Alfred went on like nothing had happened, for the rest of the meeting; but he contacted me that night, as soon as he could be alone where he thought he could be safe."

"Where could he go?" RJ asked.

"He'd go to the Chapel, apparently, where they have the communion bread, the reserved sacrament. There's a place to pray there, he says, right in front of the safe they keep it in—"

"The aumbry?" I suggested. "The tabernacle?"

"Aumbry, he said. Anyway, he'd talk to me from there while he was saying extra prayers after their last service of the day. He talked to me every night, from then on until Wednesday night, yesterday. He never saw anything like it again, and I couldn't persuade him to just break and run, because he was really into sticking by his own vows. I suppose he means obedience; chastity and poverty don't seem to have much to do with it."

"No," I said. "As a Benedictine, his vows would be stability, obedience, and review of morals. You could read stability as meaning you have to stay put in your house and try to fix what's wrong with it. A Benedictine with a certain attitude toward his vows could never just run away from his problems."

"That's certainly the way he was thinking, Chaplain. He can be really idealistic, more committed to ideas than to people, even—or at least, more than to himself."

" 'Both nuns and brothers worship images,' " I said.

"It's 'nuns and mothers,' Jonathan," RJ corrected, as one English teacher to another.

"But then it's not so relevant."

Jeff shook his head: "I'm not sure it's relevant either way, but I'm probably better off not knowing. Anyway, when I didn't hear from him yesterday, I thought I should come running. They've been leaning on him pretty hard, and I thought they might have gotten desperate."

"I bet they were," RJ said. "According to what Jonathan's already told us, that was the day the Bishop insisted on coming to the life profession Alfred hadn't even agreed to go through with. And it was that noon that Alfred tried to contact Jonathan—"

"Which he can only do when Jon isn't wearing his ring. So he may have been trying for quite awhile, and not just from their chapel."

"Exactly, Brad. And wherever he was, he gave himself away, and the Abbot clamped down on him."

"Clamped down is right," I said. "If what I felt this afternoon reflects what's really happening to Alfred, the Abbot must have turned back to his Colonel Kurtz days. Putting someone out to roast is a technique for brainwashing the old fashioned way."

"Tiger cages, you mean, sir. We studied them in ROTC class."

"Right. All of which makes it sound to me like a matter for the Sheriff's Department."

"Ha, ha, ha. I can picture the two of you trying to get a writ of *habeas corpus* with your nightmare as probable cause; you couldn't cite Jeff's little bulletins, since they'd be hearsay—or thinksay, rather. You'd have about as much chance of proving that the Bishop was murdered by a tame lightning storm."

"They can't very well just leave him there to be tortured, can they, Brad?"

"No, hardly. But going to the police won't get us anywhere. It seems to me that the simplest idea might be the best. If Jeff went over there tomorrow and asked to see his cousin, wouldn't they have to produce him?"

I shook my head. "They certainly wouldn't. If he were really going to make his life profession, he'd go on retreat beforehand. I'd expect only three days, where this would be four, but with their sweat-lodges and whatnot, they'd have a reasonable explanation for him being in seclusion for a week."

"But, Jon, he can't really be in any physical danger, can he? Whatever they want him for, they'll surely have to have him in one piece and functional."

"I suppose you're right," RJ said, "but I'm not sure how far we might answer for his mental condition by Monday."

"That's certainly the risk," I answered. "It's funny that you should say Monday, though."

"I just meant, the morning after."

"Right. But doesn't it strike you that they're moving heaven and earth to get Alfred into life vows on Sunday?"

"Certainly," Brad said. "But that could be just because the Abbot is retiring: they want to get Alfred in under the wire."

"That doesn't make sense, sir. They'll have another Abbot right away, never mind by next year. There's no sign Alfred was going to leave the monastery—he just wanted to wait; and if anyone was going to object to

172 — John William Houghton

him joining because of his talents, they could certainly do that any year. Is there something he can do as a life member that he couldn't otherwise? I mean, there must be some privileges, but which ones would actually make a difference as soon as Monday?"

"Will it give him a vote in the election?" RJ asked.

"No. The Bishop told me the whole community votes. It's not like they have campaigns or anything, of course. From what I've read about these things in novels, everyone gets a ballot with all the eligible names, and then you mark off the one you want to vote for, and cross through your own—"

"I've got it, sir! That's gotta be it—it really is like Shangri-la."

"What do you mean?"

"Just think for a second, Chaplain. Who's eligible to be Abbot?"

Then I understood: "Of course! Only the life-professed. They want Alfred to be the next Abbot. But why?"

"I think they've made that pretty clear," RJ said. "Somehow, they figure you can't be Abbot of All Angels without these talents that Alfred and Bishop Trout seem to share. The question is, what are they doing that requires a Prior whose nature seems to be absolute nothingness or an Abbot who can make himself look younger when he's got one foot in the grave?"

"Nothing good," Brad replied, "or they wouldn't use torture to get one."

"Whatever it is, I doubt if they're going to tell us. One doesn't disappear for the sake of the publicity."

"No, Chaplain, but if you're fond of publicity anyway, you may leave hints. Have you read the rest of this Prior's articles?"

"No, just the one I told you about. Do you think he might have let something slip in one of them?"

"Possibly, sir. Especially if we have an idea of what we're looking for."

"Well, regardless of what you are looking for, I'd suggest you look for it tomorrow—in fact, another ten minutes and it'll be tomorrow. And Brad and I have to be at school at Reveille, or at least in time for BRC."

"Oh, yes, of course," I said. "We have been running on, and I can sleep a good deal later than you honest working types. And, Jeff, of course, you're welcome to sleep as late as you like. Would you all like to say Compline, as long as we're all here in one place?"

We prayed that ancient monastic bed-time service, and my colleagues left for their apartments. I made up the bed in the guestroom for Jeff—some years ago, I replaced the bunk beds Danny and I used in our childhood with a twin bed for myself, setting aside my parents' room as better suited to visitors—and was soon asleep myself. Jeff said later that he'd stayed up quite a while reading a couple of Fr. Prior's articles.

Chapter 5: Friday, July 8

I WAS UP and out of the house before Jeff awoke. I left him a note on the coffee table with instructions about where to find the coffee, cereal, and so forth, and how to turn on the dishwasher. I took along several of Fr. Prior's articles, including the one I'd already read, in order to get Luke's opinion of the Native American side of them. A night's reflection had led me to the potentially uncharitable conclusion that the Christian content could be neatly summed up by the single word, "heresy."

The heat outside was as terrible as it had been at any point in the last unrelenting week, and I wondered how wise it really was to trust Alfred's safety to the rather theoretical proposition that the Abbot couldn't afford to have him seriously damaged. There was no arguing, though, with the observation that I had no evidence on which to call in the police, or even to support a formal canonical investigation.

Carl called not long after I'd gotten to the office, while I was still reading through the first two memoranda from the Commandant to have been zapped to my electronic mailbox that day.

"Hi, Jonathan," he said, after Mrs. Equitone had put him on the line. "I've got a fair amount of information for you here."

"That's to be expected, I guess. Shoot."

"Okay, here goes. First, there's the funeral. It's a long stretch, but Mrs. Parker wants to wait until Tuesday for the service. That's the first day the former Archbishop can get back—he's visiting in Lambeth—and he and the Bishop were such close friends—roommates in seminary, I guess—that she wanted to have him do the actual funeral, rather than have a private service right away, and a public Requiem Mass a bit later, which was what I suggested in the first place."

"There should be quite a crowd of visitors—he was well liked, as Willie Loman used to say."

"Yes, and the delay will leave time for people to fly in, as far as that goes. Of course, we'll have your friend the present Archbishop, and I'm sure we'll have every bishop in the province, and then a bunch of people with Sewanee or Old Blue connections: possibly even that new president of Yale. We're talking about a 10:30 service here, and then the Guild will serve some luncheon afterwards."

"That doesn't leave much time to get to the cemetery and back."

"No, but that's another of the little surprises. It turns out he'd arranged a long time ago with the Dean to be buried right here in the Cathedral, in the crypt."

"The crypt! My lord, we haven't put anyone in there since Bishop Ethelbert, back in the 1870s—does anyone even know how to get into it?"

"Apparently Dean Philips does. He says it was 1867, by the way. Prides himself on the thoroughness of their records, you know."

"All too well. So is there anything in particular I'm to do at the funeral mass?"

"Sandi Gabriel is still working on details—she's going to be the MC—but I was thinking you and the rural deans might concelebrate with the former Archbishop, and Dean Philips and I will be chaplains to him and to Archbishop Williams. We'll have it all worked out before everyone gets here, anyway."

"Right-oh. Now what do you know about the Abbey?"

"Well, I think you're in good shape to intervene there, if that's what you're up to. On the one hand, as I said, we've got a canon that lets the President of the Standing Committee deputize for the Bishop in cases of vacancy, and it turns out the Abbey's charter has a provision to allow the Bishop to exercise his responsibilities as Visitor through a Vicar. That's what we call the St. Teresa's clause here in the office. After the hospital, you know."

"Oh, right. Back in the 70s they wanted to move out of Gary to the suburbs, and Bishop Cockburn was an *ex officio* trustee, and said they were founded to work in the inner city. So they started calling meetings of the Board when he couldn't come—"

"Generally on Sunday mornings."

"Right. And they wouldn't let him send a proxy, and then they tried to dump him on the grounds that he missed too many meetings. So they went ahead and moved, and he sued for, what—two and a half million?"

"Three. Which is why we have the St. Teresa's health care endowment today; exactly. In any case, you'd have to look long and hard to find an organization in the diocese today that can insist on having the Bishop appear in person to perform a purely administrative duty. Certainly not All Angels', the way I read it. I'd say you should be there on Sunday as scheduled to receive this life profession."

"That's good, I guess. I don't know how enthusiastic I am about all this, but it looks now like there's a lot going on over there, and none of it any good."

"Nothing you've told me about, certainly. Do you want me to call the Abbot and let him know whom he should expect?"

"Not right away, no. I want to have lightning rods installed on my house first. He's already had one crack at me this week. Seriously, though: I would like to wait as long as we can—I think hearing this might tend to force his hand, and I don't want to do so prematurely. Could you possibly wait until tomorrow?—I know you don't usually come into the office on Saturday."

"No, though I hardly need to be in the office just to call Abbot Trout. In any case, though, I will be here. We've got all sorts of messages coming and going about the funeral, and I have to coordinate with Dean Philips and the hotel and so-on. How about if I call the Abbey just before I leave for lunch? That ought to be between 12.30 and 1: will that buy you enough time?"

"That'll be great. Thanks, Carl."

"You're welcome, Jonathan. Good luck."

WHEN I GOT to the Infirmary, Luke was sitting up in a chair reading a horror novel. "Don't tell me you've finally sated your taste for films," I said as I walked into his room.

"No, hardly. But I'd pretty well exhausted the nurses' tape library, and they really wanted the tube so they could set it up in the chicken-pox ward. Apparently, too, the Indian Lore Department made a big contribution to the epidemic: the little fellow who started it all takes two hours of dancing and two hours of crafts out of our five class periods a day, so we were one of his prime places for meeting people. Not that the nurses actually made me feel responsible or anything, but I do like to be part of the solution rather than part of the problem. It must be a zoo down there."

"Worse, I think. In zoos the animals are kept at a safe distance from visitors. These little monkeys think of anyone who wanders in as fair game for the latest shenanigan, whatever it is. If I get hit with one more of those stuffed sock things, I'm going to be sorely tempted to recall a text from Samuel Butler."

"I know what you mean; but we do really have to spare the rod, even if it does spoil the child. These are all loaners, after all."

"Oh, I know. But when I was their age, the counselors used to make us stand at attention out on the porch, under the light, if we talked after Taps. The mosquitoes would get so thick you wondered if you were working for Walter Reed."

"Not when you were nine, you didn't. You may have been precocious, but I'm not going to believe you knew the history of Yellow Fever when you were in fourth grade. Are those the articles you wanted me to read?"

"A couple of them, yes. There turned out to be a fair pile, and I'm farming them out. Jeff Mills is looking over a few—he was winter school class of '93, if you remember him."

"Of course I do—you're the one with the visualization problem. He was in B Battery, a lieutenant; about six feet tall, brown hair that was always about half an inch longer than regulation; grew up in Ohio someplace. I don't remember his mother's maiden name, but then I never had him in class."

"It's Davis: old southern family. Anyway, he's read one of these, and I've looked over the other, so we're asking you for a second opinion—or, rather, for an expert opinion, since neither one of us knows beans about the Native American angle."

"Well, I'll do what I can for you. You know, though, speaking of Winter School, someone you might ask for a horse's mouth kind of an opinion is Larry Brandon. His family, or what's left of it, is very much involved in Native American traditions, even religious ones. He's talked about it some with me."

"I did know he had a Native American background, but he seemed awfully skittish about letting me in on anything."

He paused a moment, reflecting. "Well," he said at last, "I think I can see that. He's awfully religious, as far as I can tell, and I wouldn't be surprised if he doesn't feel a pretty strong tension between his grandmother's traditions and his own brand of Christianity. Talking to someone in a dog-collar might highlight the problem."

"I suppose it might, at that. And he does seem to be very self-consciously Presbyterian. But I wish he'd said something, all the same. He's not likely to find another chaplain with more reason to understand a tension between family traditions and Christianity."

Luke hesitated, as if he were thinking about saying more; but he finally answered, "Not among palefaces, anyway. Well, who knows? Maybe this sudden research interest of yours will give you the opportunity to open up the whole business with him. Do keep me posted, though, as far as you can—it'll be a help to me in the winter to know where you've already gone."

"Sure, Luke. Anything that's not in confidence, of course."

"Great. Now then: have you picked up your paycheck yet?"

"Good Lord, no. I'd forgotten all about it. I guess this is the second Friday of the month, at that. I'll try to get it and deposit it before the noon mass."

"Just what I was hoping. In that case, would you run an errand for me on your way downtown?"

"Sure. Name it."

"Take my keys here, stop by my apartment, and bring me back some videos. I figure I should be able to get my machine back in the evenings, once the rugrats are in bed."

He looked too pitiful to be laughed at, though it seemed to me there was a hint of a smile underneath. "Aye aye, sir," I said. "I'll have them here for you before the afternoon is out."

"After your nap will be fine," he said, as I went out the door.

⸻

Typically, each of my errands took longer than I'd expected it would: the person in front of me at the bank, for example, was apparently trying to buy traveler's checks in zloty denominations and pay for them in Micronesian trade goods—at least, that's the only reason I can imagine for holding up the line so long. And with my own second cousin once removed the President of the Bank, at that. With my luck running in such a direction, I wasn't surprised, as I came into the Chapel—not late, exactly, but without much time to spare—to see both Brad and RJ sitting in the choir stalls with the rest of the congregation for Mass; ordinarily, one or the other of them would have been doing the set-up work, putting things in place for the service. I hurried a bit faster, unwilling actually to run, anticipating that I'd have to arrange things myself. *Probably both forgot their keys*, I thought, as I fished for my own to open the door of the office-sacristy.

The door was, however, unlocked. Inside, I found Chris Pruett, vested as an acolyte and carrying the cruets of wine and water. "Afternoon, your Holiness," he said: "I see you haven't gotten any more punctual over the year."

I shook my head. "Keeks, Keeks, what am I going to do with you? If I had a dollar for every time you were late for class in four years at the Academy—"

"You'd still only have about two minutes to get into your chasuble," he laughed. "Let me put these things out and I'll be back to help."

Chris had laid out white vestments, even though the usual color for the day would have been green: evidently, someone had told him of the Bishop's death, and he'd correctly anticipated I would want to say a Requiem. That kind of prediction was typical of him. I've found that there's something about working with an acolyte who's gotten used to your own little habits that is, I imagine, what it must be like to have a skilled valet: or possibly it's like the relation between a surgeon and the rest of a crack operating team. There's a kind of concentration on the task at hand, a focussing, that you can only reach when someone is there to make sure that exactly what you need is precisely where you expect to find it at just the moment you want. I don't mean, of course, that presiding over the Eucharistic community with the help of someone like Keeks is so trivial as Bertie Wooster getting dressed with the aid of the inimitable Jeeves, but the freedom from distraction must be the same in both cases.

It was an uneventful Mass. "It is good to have you back," I said to Chris, as we exchanged the Peace.

"And good to be back," he answered. "Especially here."

At Communion, RJ came up to distribute the cup; we communicated the usual assortment of faculty, cadets, troopers and midshipmen, and I had turned back to the altar, thinking we were finished, when he whispered, "What about the Brandon kid?"

"What about him?"

"He's sitting down in the front pew in the nave. But I saw when he came in that he started to come up into the choir, then he had second thoughts about trying to come up the chancel steps on crutches without a handrail. So he probably thinks he couldn't make it up for communion."

"Okay. Better safe than sorry, at least. Bring the cup and we'll go down and see."

I rather think even Larry didn't know whether he'd really come to Mass simply to watch or to communicate; but once RJ and I were standing in front of him with the Sacrament, he decided, put his hands out for the bread as he had seen the others do, and took a somewhat startled sip of the wine. It occurred to me as RJ and I were returning to the altar that he'd probably been expecting grape juice.

Though there was quite a little crowd in the sacristy after the service, Larry wasn't among them; I made a mental note to myself to look him up before the day was out. As usual, the dubious lure of lunch in the Mess Hall eventually called away all the campers and RJ, leaving Chris, Brad, and me in the room.

"What do you think, Keeks?" Brad asked: "Has he changed much in the course of a year?"

"Not so much, I guess," Chris answered. "I suppose I've changed more, though it's easy enough to get back in the groove with a celebrant with habits you really kind of don't have to stop and think about. It's funny, though, how you notice little things: the Chaplain always used to take off his First Class Ring when he was about to wash his hands at the lavabo, at the end of the offertory, and he'd put it on the altar about two inches to the right of the corporal—same place, same distance, every time. And today he didn't."

Brad glanced at me, and I shrugged my shoulders: "It's hard to keep a secret from someone who knows you that well, I guess.

"I've been having some, uh, unusual experiences lately," I continued, "and they mostly seem to happen when I'm not wearing my ring: at Mass on Wednesday, for example. So I thought I'd better wear it today to avoid another unedifying incident."

"More magic, huh? Gee, Holiness, we do need to talk."

"I suppose so. But this particular thing isn't really mine to keep secret or explain. So I can't tell you much about it right now."

"I'd like to catch up with you, too, Chris," Brad said. "But I have to hit the Mess Hall myself, so I can cover a 'Review of Beginning French' class this afternoon. Are you going to be around all weekend?"

"*Oui, monsieur.* I'm staying over on the East Shore with the rest of the guys from my class."

"Great. Then I'm sure I'll see you before the weekend is out. *A bientôt, messieurs,*" he said, as he went to the door.

"Later, dude," we answered in improbable chorus, and Keeks immediately cried, "Jinx! You have to buy me a Coke!"

"That's easy enough," I said, laughing. "But wouldn't you prefer to have it with some lunch?"

"Only if I buy the lunch," he answered.

"It's a deal," I said, and we shook on it.

———

CHRIS DIDN'T BRING the subject of magic up again over lunch—I imagine he didn't think it an appropriate topic for discussion in a booth at the Olde Towne Cafe. We did talk about his year at school, the rigors of the pre-med program which he'd already encountered, and those which likely lay ahead of him. He talked, too, about the parish church he'd been attending, and about his new girlfriend—not necessarily in that order. He was right, too: he had changed a lot—or, rather, grown, developed more fully hints that had already been present four years before in the round-faced tow-headed fourth-class plebe whom I remembered more clearly than he did. I'm not sure whether, in listening to him, I showed—or even whether it is possible to show to one in his position—how much of the reward, the delight, even, of my own work comes from seeing just such growth. Sometimes I have a real sympathy with the Christmas tree farmer out west of town: he, too, has to wait years for his crop to ripen, and even then rarely sees it in its glory.

On the way back to the Chapel, I said to Chris: "You know, I really like this car. It seems to me as though everything is either automatic or plush or both. I can't help thinking, though, that one of the things this Homecoming lets you young winter alums do is show off how big a car you've gotten during your first year at school."

"You're probably right," he said, and smiled. "But let's skip the Freudian analysis. In any case, there's no real competition this year. English has it nailed down."

"Oh, really? That suits the Regimental Commander, I guess. What's he driving?"

"Nothing. That's the key. He flew in this morning in his own plane."

"Wow. That is a trump card, isn't it? You've already seen him, then?"

"Just for a second. He and Jeff Mills were leaving the cottage as I came in—Jeff had met him at the airfield, and they'd brought his stuff over—Rob's the one who signed for the house, so he had the keys, which is why he came in so early—dropped it off, and they were going back to the field."

"Really? What for?"

"Rob was going to take Jeff up in the plane: he wanted to show it off, and Jeff said he wanted to see the lake and stuff from the air. Rob asked me to come along, but it was after 11, and I wanted to be sure that I had time to surprise you."

"You certainly did that," I said, as we pulled up next to my own aging Plymouth, and I got out. "Listen, it is good to see you again, Keeks. I may come over to the cottage this evening, or maybe I'll see you guys at my place: the whole lake becomes kind of one large party before the weekend is over."

"Right," he said. "I gotcha. Later, dude." As he drove off to the cottage, and I opened my own car to get Luke's tapes out from the back seat, I reflected that I could probably name one local landmark Jeff Mills wanted to put under aerial observation.

At the Infirmary, Sally Brownlee told me, as I passed the nurses' station, that Luke was taking a nap. Medical advice to the contrary notwithstanding, I couldn't pass up the revenge of waking him from what I hoped had been particularly pleasant dreams.

"Hoist with your own petard, sleepyhead," I said, after a few knocks on the open door had brought him back to consciousness.

"I'm convalescing. I'm supposed to get lots of rest. What's your excuse for being awake at this ungodly hour?"

"Haven't had a chance to sleep, actually. Chris Pruett took me out to lunch after the noon Mass."

"Pruett? The world's sneakiest soccer player? How was his first season with the big boys?"

"College seems to be doing him good: I'm not sure he's playing on a team, though. He's in one of those intensive pre-med programs that run right into medical school; they apparently keep him busy."

"I can see how they would. Did you find the tapes?"

"Easily," I said, setting the bag of them down on his bedside table. "Have you read the articles?"

"Why do you think I was asleep? Jonathan, the man may not know anything about Native Americans, but he deserves some kind of a prize for being the most—what's the word I want?"

"Turgid," I suggested. "Prolix, verbose, obfuscatory, long-winded . . ."

" 'Turgid' is it. The most turgid writer since the nineteenth century; there's a kind of empty pomposity about these things that makes you want to shoot something."

"I agree completely. But what about your opinion as an ethnologist? I can judge the literary style myself."

" 'Ethnologist,' huh? Fancy name for teaching a bunch of twelve-year olds the canoe step.

"The first of these," he went on, picking up the copies, "is fairly general—talks about parallels between Native American and European ascetical practices, and suggests that Christians can benefit by taking over the practices and the theology to boot."

"Right. That's the one I've read: I'd file it under 'heresy' or 'syncretism,' I think."

"That's your specialty. As far as I can tell, there's nothing terribly wrong with what he says about the Native American side of it, descriptively, though I'm not sure a Miami or a Sioux would look on a sweat lodge, say, as an ascetical practice. I think the idea is more purification than mortification, if you see the distinction. And that brings me to the second article."

"That's the one on the medicine lodge?"

"Right: '*Mede-Wewin*: The Great Medicine Lodge as a Model for Initiation,' he calls it. His main argument is the same, that this Native American practice can be used by Christians for the equivalent purpose. Specifically, he wants to match the four stages of the medicine lodge to four stages in the monastery—"

"Postulant, Novice, Annual, and Life—"

"Right. Now, again, his description of the rituals themselves sounds about right to me, though it's pretty general—the kind of stuff you could get out of any good reference book. And, for that matter, there's a long history of reading European culture into the medicine lodge—the fourth degree involves a cross, and when Pere Marquette saw that, he was sure the Indians were naturally Christian. And that was nearly four hundred years ago. People even tried to tie the lodge in with the Masons, because of the four steps, you see; I imagine that's why European scholars usually call them 'degrees' and 'lodges,' for that matter."

"But four hundred years of thinking something doesn't make it right."

"Well, no. Though the lodge doesn't go all that far back into indigenous history, and there may really be some European bits worked into it. What I was going to say, though, is that your Prior seems to me to have found two new angles of misunderstanding. One of them fits in with the sweat lodge problem—in fact, sweat lodges are part of the medicine lodge ritual. I pointed out the mortification issue there; here, he talks about getting a totem animal, a spirit guide, which is, I guess you could say, the climax of each degree of the lodge. He says—I thought I had it marked—oh here: He says, 'One may, without entirely unjustifiable peril of overgeneralization, observe, if only after the fashion of an *obiter dictum*, that the great majority of the Native American mystical techniques, whether in the medicine lodge or the peyote ceremony, aim at the acquisition of a spiritual guide which can, after the same fashion as the more impersonal force usually, but not always, experienced by the European mystic, develop in the soul that innate ability to separate the spirit body from, and eventually discard altogether, the corporeal body which is the final stage of the mystical journey, the glorious fulfillment which lies beyond the novice's initial enlightenment and the adept's unifying vision.' "

"Ye gods! That whirring noise I hear must be Julian of Norwich rolling in her grave!"

"Her or Hiawatha, one or the other. I can tell you, 'without entirely unjustifiable peril of overgeneralization,' that that passage makes absolutely no sense at all in the terms of any Native American culture I've ever heard of. They simply do not have this idea of opposing soul to body. Spiritual body would mean to them the soul and body taken as a whole, not the soul separated from the flesh. And that's especially true in rituals like dancing."

" 'O body swayed to music, O brightening glance / How can we know the dancer from the dance?' "

"That's the idea, certainly. Who wrote that? Eliot?"

"No, but you're close. It was Yeats. Now, look here: you're a good Catholic. You know perfectly well that this business of disembodied souls is supposed to be only a temporary consequence of sin and death. As far as I know, the Church still believes in the resurrection of the body, not the discarding of it."

"It may now, but it won't for long if this Prior has anything to say about it. He actually tackles this point. Doesn't St. Paul say something about the 'spiritual body'?"

"Well, yes, but more in the way you just said the Native American would understand it: Jesus may walk through walls, but St. Thomas can still put his fingers into the wounds."

"The Prior advises that that passage is not to be taken literally."

"Oh, garbage! There's no point in arguing with you, though—you agree with me. What's his other misunderstanding: you said there were two?"

"Yes. This one's not quite so clear; I see the point in general, but I don't know enough history to pick up the actual allusion. Here it is in his own deathless prose. He's talking about the Masonic parallels, and that sort of thing, and he says: 'It has frequently been observed by historians, ethnologists, and ritual anthropologists alike, that it is a possibility not entirely to be excluded from consideration, that the *mede wewin*, with its incarnationalist mythos and cruciform symbols, along with its system of degrees, may reflect some European influence on Native American culture, the more so given some, admittedly inconclusive, evidence that the lodge had its beginnings among the easternmost Algonquin tribes and spread westward not so very many years before the penetration of the upper Midwest by the Jesuit missionaries. What has not been, it seems to the present author, so thoroughly considered, is the question of which specific elements of European society may have given rise to the observed influences: that Freemasonry was either imparted to, or observed by, Native Americans at the time of the earliest European contacts is a fantasy which can, perhaps, be summarily dismissed, especially in the light of the overwhelming role of Roman Catholics, and particularly Roman religious, in North American exploration. Few of these Jesuits, we may be allowed to conclude, will have been Freemasons. On the other hand, the very mention of the Society of Jesus necessarily reminds us of that period, beginning as early as 1760 and continuing at least until 1814, in which that Company of Ignatius survived, despite Papal and Royal suppression across the continent of Europe, in the persons of a few devoted souls in Russia; that a religious order could endure, in the face of the developed powers of modern centralized states, for some fifty years, will perhaps lend credence to the suggestion put forward by certain learned persons with access to unique sources, that other, older, religious orders, having fallen under the no less cruel but at least less thorough tyranny of states and church not yet so fully centralized, may have survived suppression more quietly, and for a substantially greater period of time, than the Jesuits; such authorities, with whom the present writer is strongly inclined to agree, would hold that the European elements of the *mede wewin*, including its basic structure, were derived from contact, possibly through Spanish rather than French channels (though the latter would be, *prima facie*, the more expected), with Christian religious traditions which had by then been undercover for nearly three hundred years in the hemisphere of their birth; and that thus, in the Great Medicine Lodge, we have access (however fragmentary) to an otherwise lost—or perhaps, even after so many years, still hidden—mystical and devotional heritage of the

Christian church. If so, it would seem to be incumbent upon us to recover and, insofar as it may be possible, reconstruct, that heritage.' "

"Hogwash! Pure, unadulterated, tripe!"

"I gather you see what he's driving at."

"I certainly do, and it is the most ludicrous thing I've ever heard."

"To wit?"

"Templars, Luke, Templars! He thinks this whole thing was started by the Knights Templar!"

"Weren't they all burned at the stake as heretics or sodomites or something?"

"A number of them were, including Jacques de Molay, who was their Grand Master. But that was back in the time of Philip Augustus of France, in the 1300s, I think."

"Well, he says three hundred years."

"Fine. So he can do elementary subtraction. That doesn't make it likely that a monastic and knightly order could go on for, what, ten generations in secret like that, much less that there would just happen to members of that secret order in the earliest European trips to America."

"I can't really argue with you: it sounds ridiculous to me, too. But he seems to be citing that as an ulterior motive for copying the medicine lodge in a monastery. It sounds like All Angels' might be set up to imitate the Templars, at least as the Prior and his mysterious sources understand them."

"It does explain the house, at least."

"Hmm?"

"The farm house they turned into their monastery: or rather, the barn that goes with it. They made the barn into their chapel, you see: and that would certainly fit the Templar pattern."

"Worshipping in a barn, you mean?"

"No, it's the architecture I'm thinking of. You know the Round Barn Festival they have, down at Wolf Creek?"

"Sure. It's one of those tacky little fairs they have around this time of year to sponge off the homecoming alumni. Fire trucks in a parade, a Round Barn Queen, tractor pulls, and that sort of thing."

"I'll have you know I competed in tractor pulls when I was a kid—and won, too. The secret is adding quite a bit of extra weight right over your back axle. What I was getting at, though, was the barns: they're round, you see, and—"

"I had grasped that point, actually."

"And, as I was saying, most of them are within a mile or two of Wolf Creek. There's only one of them in this township, the old Voreis farm."

"The Voreis farm being the one the monks bought, I take it. I have *seen* the place, Jon."

"Of course. I don't mean to plod. But the thing is, the Templars' distinguishing tradition, architecturally, anyway, was that they built round barns—round chapels, I mean—in their monasteries."

"Aha! That's pretty interesting, at that. And you know, the property is a Native American site, too, a burial ground."

"Pakashak's father, right?"

"No, I know that's the story, but if you look back far enough, the early accounts seem to suggest he was buried separately from his people, farther up the shoreline: maybe even on campus, though a lot of that side of the school is filled-in land, and I doubt the site was that far north. In any case, though, the main tribal burial area was down near the bend in the road, where the Abbey is."

"Fascinating. I've read accounts of his murder over in Sumner's Tavern, but I never saw anything about his burial, much less the usual site."

"There's nothing about any of it in the county histories, strangely enough; but you can piece some of the facts together from early letters and journals. But before that research, if I were you, I'd read up on the Templars, and have another talk with our friend Larry, too. Show him that second article, or see if you can find one that deals with the *wabeno* and *ceseko*."

"*Wabeno* and *ceseko*. Right. Larry would be able to say something about them in particular?"

"I'm pretty sure he would be able to; I'm not sure he would. But I think it might be good for him to. It's worth a try, at least. Tell him you've talked with me."

"Okay. I meant to talk to him today, anyway. When are you getting out of here?"

"Tomorrow morning, after Dr. Spaht makes his rounds, unless he finds something wrong. I'm going to have to use a golf cart to get around over there in camp, though: I can just see me breaking something else trying to get up and down those hills on crutches. I could end up back here in the Infirmary, like Phineas in *A Separate Peace*."

"God forbid: he dies when they try to set the second fracture. You should stay as far away from here as you can."

"I have no intention of coming back, thank you," he smiled.

"Good. I'll come by camp tomorrow if I don't see you here."

"Okay, Jon. Don't work too hard."

"No danger of that," I said. "G'bye."

IN ANY SCHOOL, I think, the faculty who get to know the students best are generally the ones who go to things: the ones who turn out for plays, athletic contests, dances, and the like. It's all the more true in boarding school, where such activities are among the few parts of the student sub-culture open to adults: most of what the kids do among themselves, whether good or bad, takes place only when adults aren't around. In the winter, I'm particularly likely to go to soccer games and wrestling and track meets—things I've either competed in (however ineptly) or coached—and, of course, basketball games, a basic constituent of life in Indiana. The summer schedule has an almost relentless variety of intramural athletic activities, both in the upper schools and in the Scout Camp. The height of this competition for the Naval School, however, is the weekly crew race, where two crews of midshipmen from each company—one lightweight, or "chippy," and one heavyweight—compete with the other crews of their same weight class to row a mile-long course from somewhere off Long Point to the buoys that mark the mouth of Annandale's harbor in Aubenaubee Bay. While we have, in the winter, regulation crew shells of the sort the Bishop had rowed at Yale, these summer races use naval launches: it's a lumbering, ponderous business as a result, rather like dinosaur racing might have been. Not that the crews don't get up a good speed, but the effect is always surprising, like seeing great whales plunging through the waves, rather than delicate insects skimming over the surface (amazing how Yeats gets inside one's head).

All of which is only to say: on a Friday afternoon in July, especially on Homecoming weekend, the place to be at Annandale is the crew races; there, if anywhere, I would find Larry Brandon. I went from the Infirmary back to my office to look for an article on the topics Luke had mentioned—and, admittedly, to grab a few Cokes out of the fridge and stick them into one of those insulated carrying bags that let you keep sodas cool. By the time I found "*Wabeno*: Brightest and Best of the Sons of the Morning," it was getting a bit close to starting time, but the Naval Building and pier are due south across the Retreat Parade Ground from the Chapel; packing the article with the Cokes, I cut across the much-trodden grass and made it to the pier in plenty of time.

Larry was easy to find: the chippy crews race first, and he was standing with his company's heavy crew outside the casemate where the oars are stored.

"Hey, sir," he said. "Did you come to watch us lose?"

"That's quite an attitude," I said. "Why don't you expect to win?"

"Ordinarily we would, sir, but I'm not rowing today, so what hope is there?"

"You are a cocky little bastard, aren't you?" I said.

"Yeah, right, Brandon," said one of his crewmates, and faked a punch to his stomach. Larry leaned back to miss the blow, then brandished one of his crutches: "You wouldn't pick on a cripple, now, would you, Carlos?"

"Yeah, yeah, I know—your life's so rough. Can't walk, can't get a date, can't stand it we're gonna win without you, and you gonna watch us from the pier!" They both laughed, but it seemed to me Larry *was* disappointed not to be going out with them.

"I think I can fix one of those problems, Larry," I said. "Why don't you come out with me in the Commander's boat?"

He looked dubious. "Do you think we could, sir? There's a lot of alumni and stuff around today, VIP's and all."

"I'm a past President of the Alumni Association myself, as far as that goes. Hold these Cokes for me and I'll see what I can do."

I hadn't yet seen Terry Crespin (whose strictly Annandale rank of "Commander" merely reflected his job as head of the actual naval instruction program) in the crowd around the building, so I walked quickly out the pier to see if he was already at his boat. The dock is one of few places at Annandale where running is officially discouraged. Terry, it turned out, was on his way back into shore, and I met him a little bit past the first finger pier.

"Hi, Jon. You coming out today?"

"Yes, please. Do you have room for one more, too? There's a midshipman I need to have a private chat with."

"I don't know—haven't you got a building of your own for that?" he asked in mock exasperation. "Besides, I've got some stuck-up alumnus and his wife on the Whaler already. There's room, but I'd have to send them to ride on the pontoon boat with the lower classes if you want any privacy."

"Who is this albatross, ancient mariner?"

"Damned if I know. Some geek from Connecticut. Bright red hair, what's left of it, and a Yale golf cap."

"Thad Moulson," I said. "He was two years ahead of me in Indian Scout camp, and then he was Commander of the First Battalion my plebe year in Naval School. He was a geek twenty-five years ago, too. Tell you what I'll do: I'll go get him off your boat, and you can have one of the Cokes I brought with me into the bargain."

"I should have thought of it: send a Harvard man to chase off a Yalie, same way you'd buy a snake to keep your house free of rats."

"There wouldn't be rats in the first place if our Princeton tigers weren't such pussycats. Where's your boat?"

"In the first cradle after the third finger pier. Where's your midshipman?"

"He's guarding the Cokes, back at the casemate. You can bring him and them back out with you."

"Okay. Who'm I looking for?"

"Larry Brandon. Sort of a short kid, first classman, goes to winter school . . ."

"Oh, yeah. The boy who ditched his parents. Always walks on the balls of his feet. Company Two took him off their heavy crew today with a medical excuse."

"That's him. He screwed up his hip in the field day track meet, but he's just on crutches, and seems pretty mobile. I'm sure he could swim to shore if we were shipwrecked."

Terry smiled. "You know the drill as well as I do," he said, and quoted, as if he'd been asked by an inspecting officer, a passage from the Standard Operating Procedures that midshipmen had been required to memorize even in my day. " 'All of our boats float, even when full of water,' sir, 'and in case of an accident,' sir, 'I will stay with my boat,' sir."

" 'And I will never go on the water without my Personal Flotation Device,' sir," I concluded. "I'll bear it in mind. Meet you out at the boat."

I took a certain mildly criminal pleasure in pulling rank on Thad, to whom the passing years had been less than kind. Actually, I trumped him three times: as Chaplain with a pastoral problem to be solved, as a faculty member with a handicapped student to be helped, and as a past president of the Alumni Association in contrast to his own place as one of twenty-seven vice-presidents. By the time Terry returned, carrying the cooler of Cokes, with Larry right behind him (moving a lot less cautiously than I would have used crutches on a pier), I was in undisputed possession of the Boston Whaler. Terry helped Larry into the boat, got in himself, and we were soon off to Long Point.

"What were you looking for me for, sir?" Larry asked, over the whine of the motor, as we bounced across the waves on the main part of the lake.

"Did I say I was?"

"No, but if you hadn't been, you'd have come straight to the boat. What's up?"

"A couple of things. First off, I wanted to tell you I was glad to see you at the Eucharist. You're always welcome to come."

"Thanks. You kind of caught me by surprise, at the end there, but it was pretty neat. Do you always dress up in that white poncho thing you were wearing?"

"A chasuble, we call it. No, not always, but usually I do. It really is a poncho, an old imperial Roman overcoat, basically. They come in several colors. All the vestments boil down to being what a well-dressed man wore for a night out on the town in the fourth century."

"Right. So you have church the way some of these orchestras give concerts on the original antique instruments."

"I hadn't quite thought of it that way, but there's some truth to the comparison, I guess; except that we never completely stopped using the old instruments in the first place."

"Fair enough, sir. What was the other thing you wanted? You said there were two."

"Yes, there are. But this one's—I can't say, more important, but more complicated, at least, and I can't tell you all about it. But this is the main thing, the part that I need your help with: I've asked Mr. Faber today to read over a couple of articles—academic articles, I mean, from professional journals."

"I know the kind you mean, sir."

"Good. Well, after he read two of them, he specifically suggested that I ask you for your ideas about another one."

"It's about Indians, huh?"

"Well, yes. It's in the cooler there with the Cokes: you can have a look at it."

He didn't say anything, but unzipped the insulated pack where it lay in the well of the boat and took out the Prior's essay. He glanced at the paper, and had hardly read more than the title when he looked back at me, his face at once pale with fright and at the same time suddenly marshaled, put into a definite order like a gaggle of teenage boys turned at the First Petty Officer's command into a company of midshipmen. "Mr. Faber told you to have me read this one in particular, sir?"

"More or less, yes. He told me to see if the author had written one with that word in the title; he seemed to think that was something you'd be interested in."

"Did he tell you what it means?"

"No, just mentioned that and *ceseko*. Why?"

He reached across the boat and took my right hand, not as if to shake it, but holding it flat, examining it. "It won't bite," I said, following his glance. "It's not really a weapon, whatever the stories may be around campus. It's just that the snakes on the inside are my family's symbol, and since my visual imagination is so poor, the ring makes a handy focus for the little bit of magical self-defense that my brother and I know how to do."

Oh, I understand, sir, he said—and I could hear him perfectly, the slap of hull against wave and the growl of motor fading into the background—*It's like the snakes are your totem, your clan animal. But ours is the morning star.* Wabeno *is the Indian word for witch.*

That explains everything, I thought back at him.

A lot, maybe, sir; not everything. But maybe the rest really can be explained; I never thought so until today.

Till now?

Not so much as at noon. The way you came to me with the bread and wine when I wasn't ready, didn't expect it. But it was reassuring, not scary: not like when the General comes to inspect your room before you've cleaned it up—which is what I've always expected.

I remembered my own conversation with Fr. Franklin. *He didn't give his Body and Blood to terrify anyone*, I thought in response. *And I'm afraid our souls are rooms he inspected long ago: when he comes, all he wants is for us to get out of the way so he can clean things up.*

Terry interrupted our silent conversation—or else Larry let it drop when the Commander spoke: "I know you're having trouble finding a date, Brandon, but you're not going to discover one by reading the Chaplain's palms. Maybe you should advertise."

Larry was instantly all kid again. "Judas Priest, Commander! Why don't they just put my sex life on TV—'Brandon stood up, details at ten.'" Terry laughed sympathetically.

"No need for television," I said. "Everyone seems to know the details but me. What's the story?"

"Oh, it's no big deal, sir. The girl who was gonna come up here for the weekend can't come, is all, and I just heard about it back in barracks before we came down to the races."

"When I picked you up back at casemate three, Carlos Sanchez was saying something about ripping the telephone off the wall."

"Well, yeah, Commander, but he exaggerates, even if he is my roommate. I think I did throw the telephone directory out the window, though."

"Did you break it?" Terry asked.

"With an Annandale telephone directory," I said mockingly, "all twenty-five pages of it? Besides, who'd have the windows closed, in this heat?"

"Right, sir, it was open. Though I may have made a hole in the screen, if that's what the Commander meant. Anyway, though, that's the story. Her parents basically didn't want to let her drive up this far by herself, and she didn't have any other way of coming. She wanted to just get in her car and come anyway, but I told her to stay home; they'd probably send her off to a convent if she ran away from home to come see me."

"Good advice, Romeo. I'm sure you're better off waiting a couple of weeks, and being able to see her with her parents' approval. Romance seems to be safer when you take it in small steps, anyway."

" 'They stumble that run fast.' Good advice, Friar Lawrence," he answered. "At least it'll give me time to read your essay this weekend."

"The sooner the better. I have to know by Sunday at the absolute latest. Call me right away, or get me on the beeper if you can't find me when you've finished."

"Aye-aye, sir," he said.

"Are you guys going to watch the race or not?" Terry asked, as we pulled up next to the starting line.

Other than the heat, it was a good afternoon for crew races, actually, and these were the first official ones of the summer, the previous Friday's having been just for practice. Brad's chippy crew—Company One—won their weight class by less than a boat length. The Company Two crew had put on a remarkable burst of speed—or, rather, several short bursts in a row with almost no time to recover between them—to pass the Company Four boat not far from the finish line and draw up beside Company One (which had itself overtaken Four around the halfway point). But the Company Two coxswain had started the push just a little bit too late, and so they had to settle for second place. Larry was upset, but not crushed. "It's the overall points that count," he said. "If they don't finish in the same order next race, we can still win for the day. Besides, last year our chippy coxswain couldn't even steer a straight line."

"We used to tell ours to aim right for the Chapel," I answered, "but I'll refrain from giving you a symbolic exposition."

"It's still what we tell them, sir; but our coxswain last year was an atheist. I think he steered poorly just to express his religious opinions."

"Was he the same one who didn't want to use the front door of the library because saluting the Gold Star men implied a belief in personal immortality?"

"That's him, sir," he laughed. "What he actually said was that he didn't believe in saluting ghosts."

Larry's heavy crew, as Carlos had suggested they would, won handily, though their jerky start and one or two instances of catching a crab early in the race both reflected that the crew weren't completely adjusted to rowing with the replacement oarsman. In the end, Company Four was second, Three third, and One came in last: so Larry's company were the overall winners. He wasn't quite sure whether to be happy at this successful start to the season or disappointed that it had been accomplished without him: but when we pulled back into the mooring and he got out on to the pier, he was quickly swept up into a gang of jubilant kids from Company Two, and the last I saw of him that afternoon, he was being carried off the pier, just like his crewmates who'd done the actual work. Someone had his crutches and was waving them about like a pair of bizarre pom-poms, as if the whole thing were a parade at Lourdes. But the rolled up copy of Fr. Prior's article was still clutched firmly in Larry's hand.

By the time I got back to the Chapel, gathered up the things I thought I might want at home, and drove back to the house, it was about six o'clock. Jeff, as Keeks had said, had taken his things to the cottage. Since there are Jewish faculty members on the staff in the summer who are willing to lead the Sabbath services, I can start my summer weekends with a leisure I rarely have in the winter, when I'm required to be both priest and rabbi. I toyed with the idea of going out for dinner—the tavern's breaded shrimp basket is one of my Friday favorites. But I realized that with the Festival and Homecoming, the two blocks of the city of Annandale's downtown entertainment district would be hopelessly crowded; even though the tavern *per se* doesn't draw a great number of alumni, the townsfolk displaced to it by gangs of strangers in the other local restaurants would have made it yet another sardine tin. I ended up making myself a savory I found once in a British cookery book: kippers and avocado slices on toast points with Welsh Rabbit as a sauce. It tastes better than it sounds, though I suppose that's not saying much. I made a pitcher of iced tea, for the sake of variety, and was enjoying a second glass of it while I read the funnies from the South Bend paper, when the phone rang and my beeper went off at almost the same time. I pushed the mute button on the pager and picked up the phone: "Good evening."

"Oh, good, Holiness, you're home—"

"Yes, I'm here, Keeks. Listen, can you hold on a second while I check the number on my beeper here—I got a message just as you called."

"That's okay, sir. It's just Stu." He shouted—Annandale does, at least, build strong voices—apparently turning away from the phone handset: "Hey, Richard, tell Stu it's okay, I've got him at home!" And then, resuming a more conversational, but definitely agitated tone: "Stu was calling you at school on his car phone while I tried your house. How fast can you come over here to the cottage?"

"Pretty quick, I guess—ten minutes or so, depending on the traffic. There'll be alumni all over East Shore Drive."

"Yeah, well, screw them. There's something wrong with Jeff, and I think you'd better look at him right away."

"All right, I'm on my way. Have you called the EMTs?"

"I don't think that'd help much, sir: it's not exactly medical. You'll see when you get here."

I drove like crazy to the cottage: not all that fast, I suppose, but the highest speed limit in town (as I've said elsewhere) is only 20 mph. I passed one of the town cops *en route,* just before I entered the Academy's private roads: he told me later he'd have pulled me over if he hadn't recognized the car. He said he'd poked along behind me so often around town, always driving about five miles under the speed limit, that he figured if I was speeding, I must have an emergency on my hands. He radioed ahead to his colleagues, and as I came out of the Academy's south east gate, Jim Box (my sixth grade teacher, now in his retirement the Lake Shore Patrol officer who usually waits on a side road off East Shore Drive to snag delinquent visitors) was ready for me, pulling out on to the road ahead of me with lights flashing and sirens blaring, accelerating like a teenager at a stop light that's just turned green. He was obviously determined to give me an escort, just like in the movies, and couldn't have known I had less than a quarter mile further to go before turning off into the cottage's gravel driveway. By the time he'd noticed, turned around, and followed me up the drive, I was out of the car and inside the house. One of the kids—Richard, I guess it must have been—ended up telling him what was going on: or as much as he thought the police ought to know.

Keeks and Richard greeted me hastily at the door, and Keeks hustled me upstairs to one of the old house's countless bedrooms; Stuart and Rob were inside, Stu standing at the foot of one of the twin beds, and Rob kneeling beside it. Jeff lay on the bed, apparently asleep, in cut-off jeans and a short-sleeved sport shirt.

"What's the story?" I asked.

"Hi, Father," Rob answered, looking up: "I'm glad you're here. He's been like this since we got back from our flight: he said he felt groggy in the plane, and I drove his car back from the field. We got here, and he said he was going to come up and take a nap, that he'd been up most of the night at your house."

"That's true enough."

"Right. So I went on with the afternoon—we swam and played some tennis, and whatnot. When everyone was showering and getting ready for dinner, I noticed he still hadn't gotten up. That meant he'd been napping for over five hours."

"A little out of the ordinary, I guess, but I've had it happen before, especially when I was really tired."

"Exactly, Father. So I didn't think anything of it; but then when we were finally downstairs trying to decide what to do about food, and Chris excused himself to come up here to the toilet, I asked him to wake up Jeff so he could come along to dinner. He can tell you the story from there."

"Well, sir, I knocked, and there was no answer, so I stuck my head in and called Jeff's name, and he still didn't wake up; so then I came in, to shake him a little bit, the way you do when you want to wake someone; he still didn't stir, but that was when I recognized the chain around his neck."

"Excuse me?"

"The chain, Father. Come here and look."

I didn't recognize the chain myself, actually; but when Rob opened Jeff's shirt, I saw why Keeks, always the observant acolyte, had found it significant: it was mine, the chain on which I wear—on which Jeff was wearing—my cross of nails. I wore the cross (unlike my ring) only occasionally, and did not depend on it for defense; but the nails still had woven in them the elaborate and powerful magics with which my great-great-grandfather had surrounded his house when he built it in the 1860s. I instinctively reached out to touch the cross; and though the skin on which it lay was warm, even feverish, the hand-wrought nails were as cold as a pump handle in a February freeze, so cold I was half-surprised they had not marked Jeff's chest with a cross the way young cows are branded with a cryogenic iron. I jerked my hand back, and Stuart said, "You see why we called."

I nodded. "Has there been any change at all?"

"Not much that we've seen, sir," Keeks said. "He's beginning to show the 'Hippocratic facies,' which is a traditional sign of prolonged fever. And indirectly, we think he must have been even more feverish earlier: see how damp the pillow is here, and how his hair's stuck down on his forehead."

"Yes, I see what you mean. Have you checked his actual temperature?"

Richard had come into the room in time to hear the question. "Give us a little credit, sir. The hard part was finding a thermometer in a rented house."

"But you did."

"Yes, one of the electronic kind with the little disposable probe. While Keeks and Stu were calling you, it was still over 101."

"Well, the sweating could indicate it's going been going down, which is what you'd expect from a natural fever in the evening, a flu virus or something. He doesn't feel that hot now. Is there really any connection between the fever and the cross? Have you tried taking it off him?"

"No, Father," Rob said, and Chris added, "you see, Holiness, it seemed like if he was so hot with something that cold lying on him, he might really be roasting if we took it off."

"That could be; but it's easy enough to put it back on him if that's what happens. I'm going to try it and see."

Kneeling beside the narrow cot, I lifted Jeff's head off the pillow with one hand and grasped the chain with the other, intending to take it off him without fiddling with the jeweler's clasp. Doing so was like bridging an electrical circuit; I felt like a channel, waves of heat flowing from Jeff through me to the cross. And at the same time I remembered feeling that heat myself, in my nightmarish joining to Jeff's cousin. I could almost, I think, have been drawn back into such a union, had the desperate mind at the other end not already been so precisely matched to a spirit far more akin to it than mine. As it was, simply being an element in the circuit seemed likely to make short work of me: but whatever good the cross may have been doing for Jeff until then, the magic with which the nails had been imbued at their first use was meant for the defense of my family before that of its friends and guests. With one great blinding burst of the blue light I associated with my twice-great-grandfather's spells, the cross dissolved into thin air, breaking the circuit within which I had been trapped, and leaving behind only the red mark of the nails in my palm to show how desperate my unwilling grasp had been.

Rhys and Caroline were in my mind instantaneously. *We all saw that flash, even Daddy. What in the world is going on?*

It's okay, I thought back. *Just one more thing for me to explain. None of you three actually did anything just then, did you?*

No. Are you sure you're okay?

Yes, really. I'll be fine, and I will explain everything later. I'll try to avoid further surprises.

Let's hope so. Take care of yourself.

As I slipped back into normal consciousness, Rob, his own hand wrapped in a fold of the bedspread, was pulling my hand away from Jeff's. "We don't need two people in stasis, Father," he said.

"No, hardly. But I would have been number three if it hadn't been for the ancestral defenses there. Is everyone all right?"

"Yes, fine, except for you," Rob said, and the others nodded.

"I'll keep for a minute or two, anyway; but I guess that's all the help we're going to get from that old cross. At least I know what Jeff's up to, though. What time is it now?"

"8:13, sir."

"Good, that's almost sundown. He should cool off from now on; but that may not be enough to bring him back. He's tied himself into a mental connection with his cousin, and I'm not sure he'll be able to get out."

"Can't you help him, sir?"

"I don't know how, Richard. I can't just wave my hands and say the magic spell: there may be one, but I don't know it."

"That's probably just as well," Keeks said darkly. "I think we've all seen enough magic to last us. We'd be better off praying."

"That, at least, we can do. Not that I know any prayers that are right on target, either, but adaptability is one of the great advantages devotion has over the exercise of power. It would help to have my Prayer Book, though: let me run down and get it out of the car."

Richard smiled: "No need; I saw you didn't have one when you came in, and I thought you might want it, so I grabbed this one out of Chris's stuff when I came upstairs."

"You are on an efficiency kick today, aren't you?" I asked as he handed me the book, one of the compact pocket size versions I usually give kids for their confirmations. The fact that the gilt edging had been worn away on the pages devoted to evening prayer suggested that Christopher did not simply carry the book around for show. I turned to the Order for the Sick. "I think a couple of parts of this service for healing would be appropriate," I said, "is someone willing to start us off by reading Psalm 91?"

"Okay," said Stuart. I handed him the book, open to the right page, and listened in some surprise as he read the passage. His voice was still quiet, understated: but he gave the ancient hymn a suitable authority, as well. "He who dwells in the shelter of the Most High, abides under the shadow of the Almighty . . . Because he is bound to me in love, therefore will I deliver him . . . I am with him in trouble; I will rescue him and bring him to honor."

"Thank you, Stuart. Now we have to improvise a little bit. Can we all stand close enough here to put a hand on Jeff's head?"

We could, as it turned out, and as we did I adapted one of the prayers from the service: "Jefferson, we lay our hands upon you in the name of the Father and of the Son and of the Holy Spirit, beseeching our Lord Jesus Christ to sustain both you and Alfred with his presence, and to give you both the peace for which he died and rose again. Amen." Then we said the Lord's Prayer, and I concluded with the blessing, just as it appears in the prayer book: "The Almighty Lord, who is a strong tower to all who put their trust in him, to whom all things in heaven and on earth and under the earth bow and obey: be now and evermore your defense, and make you know and feel that the only Name under heaven given for health and salvation is the Name of the Lord Jesus Christ. Amen."

That is the point at which I always revert to my anticlimactic handshake when I'm visiting people in the infirmary. For once, I didn't need it: the change in Jeff was instant and obvious—his tense muscles relaxed, he began to take slow deep breaths rather than quick shallow ones.

"Call him," Stuart said, and when I said his name again, Jeff opened his eyes and tried to sit up. Chris pushed him back to the pillow.

"Just a minute; you don't need to get up yet. Do you feel okay?"

"I'll live, I guess. But now I really am tired, and hungry to boot . . . And thirsty, yes, please, thank you, Richard," he added, as Platt pantomimed drinking, then left to get something suitable. "Thank you, Chaplain. Lee is so desperate for something to hold on to, and they're pushing down on him so hard, it's like he's zonked out on drugs—you know what it felt like—and I couldn't get loose. It's like breaking free from a drowning man."

"Is he actually drugged then, do you think?" I asked.

"Maybe a little, but not mostly. Not unless they've found a drug that gets shaken when you remind it that all things in heaven and earth and below the earth must obey Jesus. That was the part that rattled whatever it is—Alfred was himself again long enough to let me go, to push me away, even; but now that I am loose, I haven't got any way of knowing what shape he's in."

He'd raised himself up on one elbow while saying this, and when Richard returned with a huge mug of Gatorade, he sat up on the edge of the bed to drink it.

"You are going to explain all this, aren't you, sir?" Richard asked.

"Yes, indeed; before the night is out. But I imagine Jeff really is hungry—"

"Damn right I am."

"So you might want to get some food into him first. Maybe we should order something delivered."

Richard shook his head and laughed. "I don't see why you keep expecting us to be disorganized, sir! After all, we spent five or six years apiece—"

One of the other young alumni cut him off, shouting up from downstairs: "Did you guys up there order pizza? The delivery boy is here."

"Be right there," Richard yelled back, then said to us, grinning: "I'll meet you all in the kitchen as soon as Jeff's up to coming down. You see, sir, we did learn about planning an operation. Come on, Stu, you can help me set stuff up."

They left quietly, and it was only a couple of minutes later when Jeff pronounced himself ready, with a little support from Rob, to head down to dinner; meanwhile, Chris marched me off to the bathroom to put some gauze on my hand. It was a very professional job.

After having praised my kipper supper, I'd like to be able to say that I wasn't hungry for pizza; and perhaps I wasn't: but that didn't stop me from eating again with the kids—or rather, as they had shown more than once while they were still perhaps kids, the young men. Rob was still the most GI of the five, his light blond hair cut short and the pilot's mirrored sunglasses that he'd made part of his uniform still dangling from his left shirt pocket. Richard had gotten taller over the year, so that he was now almost caught up with Stuart, who'd been by far the tallest of the gang while they were cadets. College had mellowed Richard a bit, too: not that he's ever been hard-edged, even as an officer, but he seemed to have aged in the way some foods taste better when they've been left to sit over night—as he grew up, the elements were becoming more mixed in him.

Stu had grown a beard and mustache that were, as far as I can remember, a lighter shade of brown than his thickly curled hair. And whatever other effect college might have had on him, it hadn't made him at all less taciturn than he'd been as a cadet—the story ran that once, when the school's rock band were practicing on the balcony of Haddam Hall, Stuart (who was the drummer) said "Smoke" with so little inflection that the bass guitarist had handed Stu a cigarette before he realized the message meant his amplifier was on fire.

They'd ordered plenty of pizza for the six of us, though the several other parties floating in and out of the huge old house suggested to me that any leftovers would be gone before morning. Jeff was ravenous, and hadn't gotten much of the background to his story out between mouthfuls of double-cheese-with-everything-but-anchovies and bantering questions from the others when the kitchen door swung open and three more were added to our party.

"Wow, man, 'za," Larry Brandon said, while RJ told Brad: "I should have bet you he'd be stuffin' his face."

A brief melee of greetings ensued, revealing, among other things, that Richard really had developed the two-fold hug with which Jeff had credited him, and that nine people, one of them more or less on crutches, were too many to socialize even in a fairly spacious kitchen. With Rob—who stood to pay the bill if the rugs had to be cleaned—carrying the remaining pizza carefully on a platter, we adjourned to the study, in the north-west corner of the first floor, where Nicholson is supposed to have written his novel, looking out over the lake from the big bay window.

"Doesn't this school have Taps anymore, Mr. Brandon?" I asked as we walked through the house.

"Not till eleven tonight and eleven-thirty tomorrow, sir. Besides, Mr. Esther and Mr. Peniston fixed it up with Dr. Davies."

"I was in my office in barracks, Jon, when *mon ami* here hobbled in to ask if he could use the outside line on my phone to call you. He said you'd told him to call you as soon as he finished reading some article, so I figured it must have something to do with Brother Alfred and his Prior; when Larry couldn't get you at home, I was pretty sure you'd be over here, from what you'd said this afternoon. RJ and I were coming over anyway, so I got hold of Richard and told him to expect Larry back when he saw him."

"It'll be the latest I've stayed up legally in three years at camp," Larry said. "Though there was that night with the toilet paper rolls in the rigging of the *Admiral Nelson* last summer."

"About which none of us need to know anything, Mr. Brandon. Take a seat, and don't brag about your still when you're drinking with the sheriff."

Rob had taken a place on the window seat, whether he instinctively noticed that it would command the room, or it seemed to us to do so because he took it. He pulled the light summer curtains closed behind him.

"Okay," he said. "It's 2130, and it looks to me like we have a very long evening ahead of us, just to figure out what's going on. So let's get this show on the road. Jeff, I gather you've told some parts of your adventure to most of the people here, but no one knows the whole history. So you'd better start at the beginning again, and anyone who's heard some part before can keep himself busy eating pizza."

After summarizing the childhood reminiscences he'd shared with Brad, RJ, and me the night before, Jeff recounted what had happened from the time of Br. Alfred's mysterious interview with the Prior, weaving in my parts of the story as he came to them. The clarity of his presentation suggested the considerable energy he must have spent Thursday night in sorting through and organizing the whole affair.

When Jeff had come to the end of his summary of two of Fr. Prior's articles, Larry broke in: "That nonsense is where I come into the picture. You guys wouldn't believe some of what this character says in the article I read this afternoon."

"*Credo quia impossibile est*," Stuart quoted from Tertullian, but Rob, who was a more than competent Latinist, was determined to suppress the banter that often slowed down their discussions.

"Stu, you could believe four impossible things before breakfast, and probably never tell anyone about them—so let's not get distracted now, either. Larry, I want to hold off on your report for a minute, until Jeff has finished with what happened to him this afternoon. Then if Father Mears has anything to add, we'll take that, and then we'll come back to you for this most recent article. There's no sense getting you back in time for Taps the one time you have a legal excuse for missing it. Go ahead, Jeff."

"Well, I got up this morning fairly late, I guess, though I hadn't actually slept very long: but I was going to be just about in time to keep my appointment to pick up Rob. The more I thought about the situation, the more I thought maybe I could do something to help Lee; I mean, if his talent had been tailor made to help me when we were kids, mine sounded pretty well suited to the kind of 'sweat lodge' he seemed to be in now. But I had no more sense of Lee's mind at the Chaplain's house than I'd had in Ohio. So it seemed like a good idea to get even closer: but I wasn't sure that it was very safe to just drive into the Abbey. From what the Chaplain had said, the people there had already killed the Bishop, and had tried to kill him, and they were brainwashing Lee—one more crime wouldn't have been all that big a deal. But of course I knew Rob would have the plane, and I thought a quick fly-over might put me close enough to get through to Lee and yet be unexpected enough, and fast enough, to get us out again before something horrible might happen to the plane. So I gathered my things together, and started to come over here, to meet Rob like I'd told him I would: and as I was going through the Chaplain's living room, I saw his cross lying there on the coffee table where he'd put it with his Prayer Book after we said Compline last night. And I remembered how it had been a kind of talisman for him during the Rhys Evans business, and I thought, *Well, why not give it a try? It couldn't do any harm.* So I put it around my neck under my shirt and headed off to pick up Rob."

"You might have told me what you were up to," Rob observed.

"Well, when I first called and offered to meet you, I didn't know what was going on—that was Thursday morning, remember; and this morning, I still didn't have the idea that this was going to turn into a committee project; and I guess maybe I was in kind of a hurry to get it over with, too. In any case, I'm sorry.

"Anyway, after we came by and opened the cottage and let Keeks in, we went straight back to the field, and took off; and when we flew over the Abbey, I was able to reach out and feel Lee's mind, just barely—but it was enough to let me know where he was: not map co-ordinates, I mean, but to feel where he was, so I could do my shtick and try to cool him off.

"The cooling off part wasn't hard, except for the scale of it; I mean, it was really hot out there today, and trying to keep someone cool was like trying to eat a truck full of gelatin—every bite is easy, but they do add up after awhile. The trouble, though, wasn't in that; but like I said to some of you before, I couldn't get that close, mentally, to Lee without him noticing—I guess that's not quite the word for it, because he was almost unconscious—but anyway, without having an effect on him; and he was trying to grab at me—"

"Like a drowning man, you said."

"Right, Richard, exactly—and at first I could hold him at arm's length, sort of, though it took almost everything I had: but even in his condition, he's a lot stronger than I am, and by the time Rob helped me upstairs, I was just about gone, drawn into his own world, like the Chaplain, but worse, I think, because the two of us—Lee and I, I mean—are a closer fit in the first place. It'd be easy for us to become kind of mental Siamese twins—which is really what happened, I guess, until your prayers gave Lee a little elbow room, which he used to get rid of me entirely—absolutely shut out. And that's where we are right now."

"Great. Thank you, Jeff, that was about as easy to follow as I think it could be. Now, Father, what about you? Anything to add?"

"Not much, Rob. Jeff's told you what happened to me, and he's described two of the Prior's articles, one of which I read myself and both of which I showed to Luke Faber, who says they're just a hundred and eighty degrees from what he understands Native American culture was like: and I can attest that they have only a superficial resemblance to Christianity, as well. At Luke's suggestion, I gave one of the articles none of the rest of us had read to Mr. Midshipman Brandon, here, this afternoon. I get the impression he's read it already."

"You're damn right I have, sir—excuse me, but it's awful. Mr. Faber is right, too. This *wabeno* article is completely off base. Your Prior wants to drag these Indian practices into Christianity, as you saw in the sweat lodges piece. He says he's already talked about using the medicine lodge for a pattern for how Christian monks can find a spiritual guide and all that; and now in this article he talks about the particular kinds of spiritual guides that he thinks certain Indians had, or have, and how Christians can have the same ones. The one category he talks about are the *ceseko*: I guess you'd say they're shamans, or something like that. They're fortunetellers and jugglers and can heal people and so on. The animal you tend to think about in connection with them is the turtle, because it's the messenger, the link between them and the Great Spirit. So he wants to Christianize that, I guess, by making the turtle into an angel—Gabriel, I guess he must mean—because of the role of being a messenger."

"So," Chris asked, "he's saying that this monk can learn to meditate, then have the beatific vision, then get a spiritual guide like a totem animal to show him how to separate the soul from the body, then get an angel to give him kind of a hot line to God."

"That's how I'd put it together, Mr. Pruett, yes, sir. The mystic becomes a prophet."

"You're not a plebe anymore, Larry," Rob said, "and we're certainly not First Classmen. Go ahead and call us by name."

"Okay, Rob. The thing is, though, that he puts the *wabeno* as yet another layer on top of everything Chris just said. In the Indian tradition, they are more powerful than the *ceseko*: they can control the weather, or handle hot coals, or turn into animals, or magically protect or harm someone. So the Prior makes this into the next stage: after you're a mystic and a prophet, you can become an actual miracle worker, like St. Gregory Thautamark—"

"Thaumaturge," Stuart corrected, "the Miracle Worker."

"Right. That guy. Or anyone who does wonders, I suppose."

"If that last stage depended on Gabriel or some such," Brad said, "this one sounds like it'd have to use to use the Holy Spirit himself. What's the totem animal, the dove?"

"No," I said, "that wouldn't work out systematically. If he were going to drag in the Spirit, he would have needed it at the other level, too: it's the Spirit who speaks through the prophets, and . . ." Rob glanced at me, and I caught myself before we faculty drifted off in the way he was preventing his peers from doing. "But maybe he's inconsistent. Larry can tell us."

"Actually, I can't, sir. I mean, he never explicitly says what the analogous Christian power is to the patron of the *wabeno* in the Indian version. But I think that's related to something else he never says, that in the Indian world, the *wabeno* is basically evil. It's a malevolent kind of magician, one that has something bad in mind even when it does something immediately helpful. None of that shows up in the essay."

"Well, I can see where it wouldn't," Brad said. "It does shoot the bottom out of the analogy, doesn't it: I mean, a miracle worker and a witch—forgive the expression, Jon, you know what I mean—are more opposite than alike. But what's that got to do with the patron saint of the *wabeno*?"

" 'Patron saint' may not be the best word choice, sir. The totem power of the *wabeno*, according to some traditions, is the sun, which is the power that created the world; but most of the traditions, and the Prior here, say it's not the sun, but the morning star."

" 'How far have you fallen, O Morning Star, O Son of the Dawn,' " Chris said. "I see the connection."

"I don't," said Richard.

"Keeks quoted a modern translation," Stuart said. " 'Morning Star' is *phosphoros* in the Septuagint."

"Which is the Greek translation of the Old Testament," I said, when I saw that Stuart had no intention of continuing. "*Phos-phoros* means 'light-bearer,' the way 'Christoforos' . . ."

"Means 'Christ-bearer.' "

"Exactly, Christopher," I said. "You should know. This *Phosphoros* gets translated literally in the Latin version of Revelation, though the rest of the passage comes out a little differently, so that it runs: 'How have you fallen from heaven, you who rise in the morning.' Then the Latin treats the translation of *Phosphoros* as the name of the one who rises in the morning."

"But what's the translation?" Richard insisted.

"Lucifer," Larry said. "Satan is the Morning Star that fell from heaven."

"It must be one hell of a monastery," Brad observed.

"It's one hell of a life, sir," Larry said.

"What do you mean, Larry?" RJ asked.

For answer, Brandon stood up—an action he managed to invest with more drama than I'd have expected from one his height or in his orthopedic condition—grabbed the loose bottom of his middy blouse, and his T-shirt with it, and pulled both off over his head, stepping out of his shoes as he did so. In another second or two, he'd slipped off pants, shorts and socks, and stood in the center of the room stark naked except for the beaded leather pouch tied around his chest with long rawhide thongs so that it hung between his solar plexus and his navel. He crossed his arms, and bowed toward RJ; and in the instant that he began to draw himself back up again, there crouched in his place a huge timber wolf—not simply another member of the pack, nor even an alpha-male, but as it were the father of all canids: Fenris wolf, or the wolf that sat at the feet of Zeus, or the dog that walked beside Adam in the garden, as next best thing to a help meet for him. We had hardly had time to see this, much less to have been as terrified as we ought, before the great hound was replaced—with perhaps a flicker of Larry in the middle—by an owl, the prince of owls; then a rattle-snake and a grizzly bear followed at the same tachistoscopic pace, ending in a bald eagle made on the scale of a condor, or (almost it seemed in that room) a roc out of the Arabian Nights. I said an eagle, but thunderbird would have been more precise: for it opened its mouth as if to give its cry, and as it did so, there were a flash of light and a clap of thunder outside, a single pillar of electricity I could see through the curtained bay window, stretching from the front lawn to the sky. Someone finally had time to say "Holy shit!" But before the light and sound outside had faded, there was again only a rather short teenaged boy facing his teacher: unsteady on his feet, but master enough of himself to say, "I mean, sir, that the morning star is my totem: I am *wabeno.*" Beyond that, though, his strength did not run, and he would have fallen from exhaustion had Jeff and Richard not sprung up to catch him: he did begin to weep, from terror or from shame, as those two put him back in a chair, and the rest of us crowded around him, speechless now in our astonishment.

Richard knelt beside the chair, his arm around Brandon's shoulders, repeating "It's all right, Larry, it's okay," like a father comforting a son awakened by some night terror.

In a minute or two—I couldn't say how long, exactly—he was calmer, much of his composure regained.

"It's okay, Larry," Jeff said. "Look." He closed his eyes and cooled the room momentarily to about sixty degrees. "Does that make me a spawn of Satan? Chaplain, do the light thing."

I held up my ring to focus my attention, and for a moment willed the protective magic in which I had been continually surrounding us to appear as a sphere of yellow light.

"Look at that, dammit!" Jeff went on. "Does that mean he's in league with the devil?"

"It's different," Larry insisted. "Two different things, from different places: and this thing comes from the devil. That's what my mother said, that's what the preacher said, that's what you guys said yourselves—the morning star—Lucifer—that's who I made the bargain with when I inherited this medicine bag. My great-great-grandfather was never even half a Christian."

Keeks had been on the fringe of the small knot of people around Brandon's chair, and hadn't said anything for some time; but now he wormed his way in, so that he could look Larry square in the face. "That may be what your mother thinks, or your minister, or this Prior, or even Satan himself, for all I know. But the Bible has more than that to say, even about this *phosphoros* business. Almost the last thing Jesus says in Revelation is "*I* am the son and offspring of David: *I* am the bright and morning star." I'm still not sure I approve of any of this magic, but you can't just quote one verse out of the Bible as a reason to put yourself down."

"Thanks, Keeks," Rob said. "Now maybe if we're going to have a theological discussion Larry here would like to find himself a couple of fig-leaves before we go on. And I think I'm feeling the consequences of too much iced tea and Coke, as well. Let's break and meet back here in five minutes. There are two bathrooms upstairs, everyone, one on each floor, and there's a washroom on this floor whose location I'll release as soon as I'm back from it. People in the other parties may be talking about the lightning, but I don't need to remind you we know nothing about it besides that it happened. Fall out!"

It was nearly a quarter after eleven by the time we reassembled, so Larry at least had his wish to stay up after Taps. When we sat down again, he took a chair between Jeff and me. "Might as well have all the witches in one place," he announced.

"Have to find some first," Stu said as Rob was calling us back to order.

"What did you say, Stuart?" he asked, when everyone had quieted down.

"I said, I don't think any of them is a witch, not if that means anything to do with Lucifer or the Goddess, or whatever. Jeff's just psychic, to begin with. Chaplain Mears says prayers, and everyone's surprised when they work. Larry's a nudist. Big deal."

"But that's just it," Larry said. "The power comes from the medicine bag and the totem. And even if Chris is right about the morning star—"

"He is," I interjected.

"Even so, the bag itself is evil. Being naked is just part of how you have to use it, and I guess I don't really think that's evil, but the story is the bag requires a death. The price of the magic is a murder, almost a sacrifice to the power you use."

"But you just used it, didn't you?"

"Yes, sir, Mr. Peniston."

"And you haven't killed anyone here lately?" RJ asked.

"No, sir. But I think you can do the magic on credit, so to speak. I'm not sure that the price comes before the power."

"No, I can see where you wouldn't be. And there's plenty of literature about death being the price of something; even Jonathan's father's death might fit that pattern. So I don't want to just toss out what's concerning you, Larry, and I don't want to sound like this Prior of ours, either. But it still seems to me as though, if you read this morning star business Christopher's way, with the star as Christ and all, won't you be tempted to see the death a little differently? Jonathan can correct me if I'm wrong, but I do think Christians believe in one sacrifice, don't we?"

" 'He stretched out his arms upon the cross, and offered himself in obedience to your will, a perfect sacrifice for the whole world,' " I quoted. "Yes, as far as I know that's still in the Prayer Book."

"You said it today at Communion," Larry said. "But are you putting all this together to say Christ died so I can do magic?"

"Well, no," I answered. "I guess Mr. Esther is saying that Christ is the one who has the magic, and you have a share in it."

"So scratch nudists," Stuart said. "That just leaves psychics and people who pray."

"Fair enough, Stu; but we've got to move on. Now, if we have wandered a little bit off the point, I still think we've answered some questions: we've not only established Larry's credentials for saying the Prior's article on *wabeno* is as misleading as everything else he's written, but we've also established what must lie behind it: in the Abbot, if not in him. Someone is using very great supernatural powers at All Angels. It can't be powers that come from God or the good angels, because tiger cages aren't a direct part of the divine plan, as far as I care to know, and *ouk on*, absolute non-being, is the opposite of God. So we must be dealing with either human psychic powers, or the agency of devils; or possibly both. I'm not sure how we can tell the difference."

"Maybe not from effects," Jeff said, "but I think maybe from style. The Chaplain and Lee both talked about this nothingness, and it sounds to me from their description more like something that's almost not there at all than something that's, say, camouflaged or concealed. I don't think a person could do that, give that tone of not-being."

"But a fallen angel certainly could, " I said. "Trying to be without God amounts to trying not to be at all."

"Interesting," Rob said. "That may be the reason they're so anxious to make Jeff's cousin their new abbot. If they could combine a fallen angel's power with Alfred's psychic ability, the combination might be more powerful than either piece taken separately."

"Which raises the question of what they're after anyway," Brad added. "I find it hard to believe that the Abbot signed a contract with Satan that included a clause offering retirement to his childhood vacation spot."

"Maybe they just like to sit around being evil," Richard said.

"The Prior seems to be doing his best to spread Satanic heresy," Chris observed. "That should count for something."

"It would count for more if he weren't so boring."

"Right, Larry," Brad said. "And it hardly takes the whole monastic setup to pull off a heresy. All a person would need is an apartment in LA and access to desktop publishing."

"Whatever the original reason for the Abbey was," Jeff said, "it couldn't have involved Lee. Not unless they could predict the future, too."

"Let's hope not," Rob said, "or this discussion will be pretty much pointless. Were you going to say something, Stu?"

"It's either the place or something in it. Look at the Indians and the pioneers. It's like C. S. Lewis said: Neutral magic's getting harder every day, and the Abbot and his buddies want to control as many objects and sites as they can."

"Satan can't win by getting more power on his side," I objected.

"Satan has already lost," Chris said. "If he understood that, he'd understand about power, too. But he doesn't, obviously."

Rob brought us back to business. "We seem to be starting to wander again. But I'd say the question before the house is even more pointed now: how do we keep them from making Brother Alfred into a pawn of Satan?"

"Well, they can't make him, can they? Faustus is tricked by Mephistopheles, not brainwashed."

"Are you teaching Brit Lit next fall, Mr. Esther?" Rob asked. "You're taking on sort of a Renaissance tone tonight."

"Renaissance or not," I said, "he's right. When it comes down to it, they'll have to get, and keep, his willing consent, however deceptively. But what's their deception going to be?"

"From what he told me, they must have started out to make him think this was all for the good—putting his talents to the use of the Church, and all. But they've pretty well blown that. What else would they try?"

"I've got an idea, Jeff," Richard said. "They might still do to him what's been done to Larry here: convince him that he's already one of them—that his talent's evil anyway, so he has nothing to lose. I think that's always the easiest kind of temptation—the one that works on us most easily, I mean: the one that says I'm already so guilty, I might as well go farther."

" 'I am in blood,' " RJ said, " 'stepp'd in so far, that, should I wade no more, returning were as tedious as go o'er.' "

"*Macbeth*," I said, "Act III, scene iv. Still the Renaissance, RJ, but at least you're branching out to other playwrights. Richard could be right, though—specifically, I mean: I'm sure he's right in general. The only angle of attack we have, though, the only window of opportunity, will be Sunday at the ceremony—they're certainly not going to let us in to talk with him before then. So what can any of us say to him in the middle of the ritual?"

Keeks asked: "What if he's already agreed to something by then, Holiness?"

"That'd be more difficult, psychologically, I guess, but it's not technically significant. A bargain with the devil isn't an enforceable contract; you can back out any time. Even Faustus . . ."

Stuart interrupted my own plunge into the Renaissance drama. "Light," he said, and Brad, who was sitting next to him, nearest the door, reached up and turned the dimmer switch to full power. But even after he'd done so, the warning yellow glow around my ring was clearly visible, and I felt the reinforcement of our shield by the rest of my family.

Jeff sprang up and turned toward me. "I bet it's Lee, sir."

"That's what they want us to think," Keeks said. "Keep the shield up, sir."

"That's fine," Jeff answered. "I could easily be wrong. There's no reason everyone should risk it. But I'm just going to step outside and see if it's not him."

He headed for the door, but Robert stopped him. "No, Jeff, wait. I think we ought to take the chance; with everyone observing, someone might see what someone else didn't." He glanced around the room, and the other young men nodded their agreement. "Father, let him in," he said.

I looked to Brad and RJ for adult opinions, and they too nodded. *I'm going solo for a minute here*, I thought to Rhys and Caroline. I might have done as Rob asked by visualizing some sort of switch or lever to be thrown, or key to be turned; but given my lack of visual imagination, I simply took off my ring and put it in my pocket.

Immediately, he was standing there, in the center of the room, face to face with Jeff, habited and bearded, clearly the same person I'd seen at Mass.

"Hey, Jeff," he said. "Looks like quite a party."

"Hey, Alfred. It's all for you."

"I'll remember that the next time I tell you a secret. Listen, Jefferson, I've only got a second. I talked to Fr. Abbot tonight, and everything's going to be all right. It's the Prior who's behind all this—ordeals and initiations and everything. But Fr. Abbot can't do anything about it without my help, after I'm life professed. So I'm going to stick it out till Sunday evening."

"Are you okay?"

"Yeah, I'm fine. The Prior was pretty surprised when he came to let me out this evening, though—I was a little bit more like Shadrach, Meshach and Abednego than he'd expected. You'll have to show me how to do that Maxwell's Devil trick myself. Look: I'm supposed to be in silence until Sunday. You have a good reunion, and don't worry about me." He turned around, as if he were surveying the rest of us, and nodded slightly to me. "Thank you for your prayers," he said. "Thank you all for your concern. And, Jeff, remember—when we can talk, teach me Maxwell's Devil." With that, he was gone.

Larry's transformations had stunned us into silence; now, everyone jumped up and started to talk at once, and it took even Rob a minute to restore some kind of order. When he had done so, it was Keeks who spoke first. "I'm sorry, Jeff, you were obviously right."

"Not that obviously," Larry said. "It can't be that much harder to turn into a monk than, say, a monkey."

I grabbed his hand before he could reach for his middy again. "That's okay, we'll take your word for it," I said. "What do you think, Jeff?"

"Oh, it was him, all right. I'm sure I'd know an impostor. But I'm not so sure about what he had to say. I don't see how this Abbot could ever convince him that he's a good guy. From what you've said, the nothingness that broke off him talking to you is the same as the nothingness he saw in the office in the first place, and he certainly didn't trust that. I don't believe a word he said."

"You could believe one word," Brad said. "I'm just a humble language teacher, but it seems to me that *un démon n'est point un diable*. Weren't all you folks who passed physics talking about 'Maxwell's Demon?'"

Rob and Keeks and Richard and I nodded, and Jeff answered, "That's what Lee said—he wants me to teach him the Maxwell's Demon trick; he even repeated it."

"No, what he repeated was *Maxwell's Devil*. You're so used to hearing the phrase the right way that you unconsciously corrected it. It's all Greek to me, but that made it easy for me to see it wasn't the same Greek. Didn't anyone else notice?"

RJ shook his head. "I couldn't swear to it one way or the other," and Larry added, "Me neither." But when all eyes turned to Stuart, he said, "Definitely 'devil'; and I did pass physics." He leaned back in his chair and began to whistle *Ein' Feste Burg*, with a relevance which was not apparent to me until, two weeks later, singing the hymn in church, I realized what line he'd been thinking of: "And though this world with devils filled / Should threaten to undo us / We will not fear, for God hath willed / His strength to triumph through us."

Jeff sat back down. "That just goes to prove what I was saying, then. We can't take Lee's speech at face value. If he's trying to stress the word 'devil,' he must have figured things out the same way we have. He knows there's something Satanic going on there, and wants our help."

"Not necessarily," said Brad. "The trouble with that kind of message is that you can never be sure how to distribute the negative. He might mean that he doesn't believe the Abbot or the Prior for a minute, but wants you to stay away for your own good; or he may mean that he needs reinforcements right away; or he may just mean that the whole message was made up by the Abbot himself, so we should ignore it."

"True enough, sir," Richard said. "I understand that they had that problem with pictures of POWs in Vietnam when the Americans would try to slip some message past their captors. If it was subtle enough to get by, you usually couldn't tell what it meant."

"But at least you could tell they were alive and kicking," Rob replied. "I don't think this episode can change any of our basic thinking, but it does back up the idea that they want Br. Alfred in a condition to give his 'free' consent on Sunday. We've sketched in a plan to take advantage of that, but we haven't decided who will actually do what. Maybe someone has a good idea, but if not, I'm about ready to suggest we recess for the night."

"I do have one idea," I said. "Before we get into any of the rest of these elaborate plans, I do think I'm going to go back out to the Homestead tomorrow morning whilst you young folks are recreating and see if I can't find myself some more of those nails."

"Do you mind if I come along?" Jeff asked. "I feel a certain professional interest at this point."

"Sounds fine to me. Are you going to spend the night here?"

"Yeah, I think so. I realize that there are no defenses, but I don't think I'm really a target at this point. Why don't I come by your house first thing tomorrow morning and pick you up?"

"As long as it's not too early. Will 9:30 still give you time to play later?"
"Sure."

I had another idea, actually: that same one I'd had before more than once over the course of the last couple of years, that there was no reason for these young men to be involved in my problems, whether with Rhys Evans or with the Abbot and Prior of All Angels'; I was on the brink of saying so again when Larry pressed a note into my hand, scribbled on the back of the yellow form that was his official permission to be off campus. The slip, which (as it seemed to me) he passed on with an adept secrecy acquired from months of practice under the eyes of the faculty who supervised our study halls, read "Put ring on, don't get caught."

"Getting back to the plan," Richard said, "I can't help feeling that we'd be better off if we stuck together . . ."

As he went on talking, I slipped my hand, as inconspicuously as I could, into my pocket, and put my ring back onto my finger, thus triggering myself (as, I reflected, I ought to have done some time before) to the reconstitution of my defenses. Much to my surprise, that wasn't easy to do: despite the care Danny and I had spent on perfecting the voluntary aspect of our protection, there was a kind of pause, like the dead time between taking a phone off the hook and hearing a dial tone; then everything was back to normal. But before the defenses took effect, as my habit or reflex or prepared response was still kicking in, I was conscious of a struggle, as if the four of us were fighting against a strong wind or swimming upstream against a current. And when the struggle ended, and my family's magic once more enfolded us, I could not have said that we had succeeded because our strength was the greater; if anything, I felt as though something had let us win. I glanced at Larry to see if he were going to say anything, and it seemed to me for a moment as if he might: but when, as Richard finished, he spoke, it was to pursue the main line of the argument.

"Richard's right. You always hate to divide your forces."

"Sure, Larry," Keeks said. "Except when you can put one group in a position to support the other. What we need is prayer warriors."

People looked a bit puzzled by the oxymoron. "You're slipping into jargon, Chris," Rob said.

"It's an idea from a group I belong to at college. We try to train people to be evangelists, you see, with a combination of lectures and discussions and stuff. But the gimmick is that the lecturers are just other students, and sometimes a speaker can be kind of intimidated when he gets up to talk about religion to a whole room full of people. So each speaker has a 'prayer warrior'—another student in the organization who goes to the chapel and prays for the speaker while the talk is going on. It really helps when you know there's someone there praying especially for you."

"What are you suggesting then, Keeks?"

"Basically the same thing, Mr. Peniston. The Chaplain should take a few people with him to the Abbey on Sunday, and the rest of us should be in the Chapel praying. If this magic works the way we've been saying, that should do as much good as anything else, probably more."

"That's a good idea, Chris," Rob said. "But I don't want to divide our forces, even for support, if we can't communicate. There's no reason to have field artillery or air cover if the guys on the line can't call for help."

"I couldn't agree more," I added. "It's the best tactics to leave one magic user with the clerics, so to speak. And I think there's a natural candidate, too—the Superintendent would not be likely to look kindly upon my taking another student off to be in the middle of a magical fight. One Rhys Evans episode is enough to last him, I'm sure. So Larry had better stay on campus in the Chapel on his knees."

"Pity he won't be able to show off that physique, though," Stuart said.

Larry blushed as everyone laughed, but Jeff responded: "I'm not so sure. Not about Brandon's taste in clothes, I mean, but about who should go with the Chaplain. It's not my special talent by a long shot, but still, of the three of us, I'm the one who comes closest to just being a walkie-talkie—unless you think you're going to have to refrigerate the monastery. And if Lee really was meaning that I should stay away, we'll be cooperating."

"And besides," Larry said, "as long as I'm the one paying my bills, I'd like to see the Superintendent keep me at camp."

"I thought your estate had a trustee, Mr. Brandon."

"Well, yes, sir, Mr. Peniston. But you know what I mean: it isn't like my parents are going to complain, or my grandparents are going to show up on his doorstep."

"Still, you can understand that we don't want to have you get hurt."

"Sure, sir, but if those guys can kill your Bishop on a golf course in Michigan City, and almost take out the Chaplain here while he's walking across campus, magic ring and all, I'm not going to be much safer in the Academy's chapel than in the Abbey's."

"Once again," I said, "I should have thought ahead before I got a kid involved in such a mess."

"You didn't get me involved, sir, you asked for my opinion. I got myself involved. It's not your fault that I'm *wabeno* and this Prior has a thing about Native Americans."

"You're right, Larry," Rob said, "but you'll never convince him of that. I should know—I've tried. In any case, it's all water under the bridge now. We just have to go ahead.

"Father, I know I've been acting like I'm still the Regimental Commander, but I do know, too, that you're going to be the real point man here. And we all know anyone here would be happy to go with you on Sunday. The only question is who do you want to take?" RJ and I both grinned, and he went on: "Well, all right, *whom*?"

I thought for a moment more before I answered. "I suppose it would make sense to have Keeks stay with the prayer warriors, since they were his idea: but this is partly a liturgical business, and he proved a long time ago that he's the perfect acolyte; so I'd like him to come along. And, assuming he can get another permit, I'll take along Mr. Brandon, though it's against my better judgment."

"Oh, Dr. Davies will give him a permit if he wants," Brad said. "I suppose he's right that no one is in a position to complain. But I would like to bring him back in no worse condition than he's gotten himself into already."

"Right. I'll do my best. Then I think one more person should do it—and not really knowing for sure what we'll find, I'd like to have Stuart come along. I think his combination of out of the way knowledge and common sense might come in handy."

"I don't know, Chaplain," he said. "Maybe I should stay. You're the expert on out of the way knowledge—"

"If not in common sense."

"Right, Keeks. But I was going to say, if Chaplain thinks arcane knowledge is important, we should have one specialist with each group, me here, him at the Abbey. And common sense is supposed to be common, isn't it?"

"Supposed to be, yes," RJ said, "but one has one's doubts. Still, I imagine it's a little late now to worry ourselves about introducing that particular element into the equation. I'd be just as glad to have you in the Chapel with us as anybody else, Stuart: but I can't say whom I'd pick to finish up Jonathan's foursome."

"Dickey," Stuart said. "You've got a liturgist and a magician: might as well have a shrink to round it out."

"Or square it off," Ron replied. "Father, Richard, is Stuart's suggestion okay with the two of you?"

I nodded, and Richard said, "Sure, of course."

"Fine. Then our two parties are Fr. Mears, Brandon, Platt, and Pruett, to go to All Angels', and Mr. Esther, Mr. Peniston, Cook, Mills, and myself to stay in the Chapel. Has anyone got anything else for the good of the cause, or may we adjourn?" There were no objections.

"Very well, then. Let's plan on getting together right after Mass on Sunday, unless you hear otherwise. And until then, let's see if we can enjoy the weekend. Dismissed."

"Or, as we used to say," Jeff added, "party on, dudes."

Chapter 6: Saturday, July 9.

I WOULD HAVE PREFERRED to sleep late on Saturday morning. Not that staying up itself bothers me. My natural day, I think, would probably run until about one-thirty or two in the morning, but I wouldn't get up until nine or ten. It was in fact getting on for two by the time we all cleaned up the last of the pizzas and Coke and made our good-byes, and I got home and was ready for bed. But I had my appointment to go out to the old Homestead with Jeff, and I wanted to call Danny. And, before leaving, I'd taken Brandon aside and arranged to see him early Saturday afternoon for an explanation of his secretive note. So I got up early—relatively early, anyway—to call down to my baby brother.

"I hope you don't mind my cooking breakfast while we talk," he said, after the usual greetings.

"No, not at all. I just wish I could have some."

"You're always welcome to come down. Maybe you need a break."

"That or a hideout. Things aren't getting any easier up here. The Bishop's dead and I'm fairly sure the Abbot killed him—and I'm in charge of the diocese in some vague and general sort of a way. Meanwhile, it turns out one of Rhys's classmates is a Native American witch who's personally offended by the Prior. And I almost got caught in some kind of psychic thing with Jefferson Mills and his cousin, but my cross of nails blew up and got me out of it. That's the part you all saw last night."

"You *have* been busy. Do you really want to come down here? Or we can still come up."

"No, thanks. Aside from work, I have to be around to cover my new diocesan duties. It looks like I am going to have to face off with the Abbot on his own turf, but you can be as much help to me from down there as you would by actually being here."

"If that's how you want to play it, we'll be ready to help. What's the plan?"

I described the arrangements we'd made the previous night, and Dan promised that he and the kids would be waiting when I went to the Abbey on Sunday afternoon.

"First thing this morning, though, I'm going to go back out to the Homestead with Jeff Mills and look for some more nails to replace my cross."

"That sounds like a wise precaution: it may not be easy, though. We cleaned up a lot of that stuff for Rhys's baptism."

"Right. But we're bound to find something."

"Very good. Well, be careful anyway. I don't want you to follow your Bishop into oblivion."

"Bad theology, Danny—at least, I hope he's not in oblivion. But I appreciate the sentiment. Give the kids my love."

"Will do. Bye."

After I got off the phone, I said my prayers, toasted myself an English muffin, and sat down at the dining room table to read the funnies with my breakfast. Jeff picked me up promptly. I was ready to go, but he'd hopped out of his car and rung the doorbell before I had a chance to put down the paper and go outside.

"Mind if I come in for a minute?" he asked, almost pushing into the living room.

"No, of course not. It's the plain door at the end of the hall, you know."

"Right. I didn't actually need the head, but now that you mention it that's a good idea. Can you see that church parking lot from the window?"

"The Lutheran church lot? I guess so; you might have to stand in the bathtub to get the best angle. Why?"

"It'll sound strange after everything else, but I think I'm being followed."

"By Lutherans?"

"No, and not by demons either: at least not on great flapping bat wings. But I'd just about swear that the car that pulled into the parking lot over there has been behind me ever since I pulled out onto East Shore Drive. So I want to see if I can get a better look at it."

Sure enough, as we peered out from between the bathroom blinds, we could see a plain gray late model car sitting on the gravel lot: it didn't seem to be going anyplace, but neither did it seem particularly menacing.

"Well," I said, "if this is another representative of the Abbot, it looks like they're trying to revive more old-fashioned methods. What do you want to do?"

"Not much we can do, I guess, just go on about our business. It might really be a Lutheran, after all. But keep your eyes on the rear-view mirror for me, just to be on the safe side."

"Roger that," I said. "Let's go."

The car did, in fact, follow us; at least, it eased out of the church parking lot when we were a couple of blocks down Academy Road, and turned north on State Road 17 not far behind us. We didn't have far to go, of course—you could probably see the Homestead from my house, if the low hill the Lutheran church stands on weren't in the way—and once we turned up the lane to where the old house had stood, there wasn't any way for someone to follow us and maintain even the pretense of innocent purpose. The car went on past the driveway toward the county seat—or at least to the nearest section line crossroad.

My cousins had put the fields out to rent, so our way up the drive was lined with corn; otherwise, the place looked much as it had when I'd been there last, though yet more run down and overgrown. There were sandburs everywhere as we got out of the car at the end of the lane, and little white clovers were growing through the cracks of the old concrete walk.

"Do you suppose any one place is better than another, sir?" Jeff asked.

"No, not really," I answered. "There used to be nails and broken pieces of glass all over here. Most stuff collapsed into the basement, of course, but that's also where the fire was hottest and where we did the most cleaning up for Rhys's baptism. So I'd guess the odds are about even all around."

"Then let's go on downstairs; I'd like to nose around down there, anyway."

We picked our way down the old stone stairs. The water trough we'd used as Rhys's font incongruously dominated the space.

"The weeds are pretty thick here, too," Jeff said.

"Yes, I guess we'll just have to root around. I suppose you don't have a shovel in your trunk."

"No, 'fraid not. Nor a metal detector."

"Well, then, I guess it's hands and knees. Be careful of glass, though."

"Right."

We grubbed around in silence for awhile, but Jeff located a first nail fairly quickly. It was covered with rust, of course, but seemed fairly solid at the core. It was a bit longer before it occurred to me that raking and cleaning for the baptism had probably resulted in a pile of debris. Getting up, I began to look along the foundations, and soon found a pile of gleanings scraped together in the northwest corner.

"Jeff, look over here," I called, kneeling down to poke through the heap.

"Good thinking, Chaplain," he said as he came over and saw what I'd found. "Not much archeological value, of course, as a disturbed site, but handy for treasure hunters. Do you see any more nails?"

"Not yet, but there should be plenty. I should have thought of this in the first place."

He squatted beside me. "Do you mind getting some other scrap metal along with your nails?"

"No, I guess it'd be easier to sort things out than to dig around. Do you have a psychic magnet up your sleeve?"

"Not exactly, but I may be able to sort metal from dirt. Let's see."

He put one hand on either side of the pile, about six inches away, palms facing inward, and furrowed his brow. There were none of the spectacular effects I'd been accustomed to associate with magic: but in a matter of moments, there were two piles where there had been one.

"Nice work, Jeff," I said. "Did you ever try that system to get nightcrawlers?"

"No, sir. I think it would be easier to just pop the fish right out of the water. What have we got?"

"Part of a hinge. A couple of these spikes, really too big for jewelry, but I think I may take them along anyway. And there are certainly enough of these smaller nails for me and for the rest of the family, to boot. And, as you said, a pile of scraps—those little things are roofing nails, modern, of course, and various modern screws—I don't know what all these are for, actually."

"Yeah, well, Annandale needs shop classes. What about these little pyramid dealies?" He nudged two of them out of the pile with a forefinger, and I picked one up. It was about a quarter of an inch on a side at the base, and made a rather flat pyramid; there was a short point in the center of the base.

"It looks as if it's hand-forged," I said.

"Some kind of upholstery nail, maybe."

"Possibly: but there hadn't been any furniture in the house for years when it burned."

"*At the time when it burned.* Does that suggest something to you?"

"Yes, it does, now that you mention it. Bookbindings: big solid bookbindings from the Middle Ages, with ornamental nails all over them."

"Why don't you see if you can get in touch with your brother, sir?"

I had already thought to do so: which was in itself enough to convene a family council.

Hi, everyone. I'm out at the Homestead with Jeff Mills. We were looking for some more nails, and he came across something interesting. It's a little pyramid shaped nail—

No need to describe it, Uncle Jon: we can see what you see, and we'll pass it on to Dad.

Charming. Everyone can use my visual imagination except me. Well, then, if we all know what I'm thinking of, we can skip the twenty questions phase of this. Has Dan seen the thing before?

He says it doesn't ring a bell.

Ask him to picture it on a bookbinding.

"Right," he says. "That's from the Book of Shadows." He says don't go trying any experiments by yourself.

Oh, I don't intend to. I've got enough to keep me busy for the next few days. I'll talk to you all tomorrow.

Right, bye.

Jeff said, "Welcome back. I don't suppose you heard a car just now?"

"No, but that doesn't mean much. Let's go up and see."

"Right. Make sure you've got your souvenirs."

We climbed out of the cellar to see a county sheriff's car pulled up behind Jeff's. The deputy got out as we walked toward him: he looked to be about seventeen.

"Is one of you gentlemen Jefferson Davis Mills?"

"Yes, he is. What's the story, officer?"

"Well, Reverend, we had a phone call up to Withougan that reported trespassers out here, so the sheriff figured I'd better check it out. What's the interest here for folks from Ohio?"

"You're being misled by that license plate check, Deputy. Mr. Mills is from Ohio, but I'm a local boy."

"I see, Reverend. And what did you say your name was?"

"Jonathan Mears, Deputy. I'm the Chaplain over there at Annandale, and this is my family farm."

"I suppose you gentlemen have some ID?"

As we reached for our wallets, it did momentarily occur to me that if I only knew how to take advantage of them, the odd bits of ironmongery in my pocket would be better evidence of my identity than any driver's license.

"That's good," the deputy said. "These seem to be in order. Now, Reverend Mears, did you say you owned this place?"

"No, I didn't; my cousins over in Wolf Creek own it. What I said was that it's my family farm—this was our homestead."

"That's going to take a little while to check up," he said dubiously, as if he were contemplating a title search.

"Look, officer," Jeff said, "why would anyone call all the way to the sheriff's department in the county seat instead of phoning the cops in town?"

"Well, we're outside the town limits here . . ."

"Yes, by a couple of hundred yards: it's fourteen miles or more to Withougan. The point is, anyone from Annandale would know the Chaplain, and know he belongs here. Why don't you radio the Lake Patrol and ask Officer Box about the Chaplain and the farm?"

The deputy thought about it for a moment. "All right," he said. "You gentlemen just wait here."

"So do you think this is just an interested neighbor at work?" Jeff whispered when the deputy was out of earshot.

"Hardly. I guess the Abbot's technique of the day is harassment. Maybe he can only do the lightning trick once a week."

"Or he just likes variety. Are you any good as a pitcher?"

"No, why?"

218 — John William Houghton

"Well, I have picked up several odd little pieces of concrete here, from the basement wall, and while you were talking with the deputy, it occurred to me to wonder if a person could chuck one of them and hit—don't turn your head and look—that crow that has been sitting so attentively on the fence post over there."

"I couldn't chuck one and hit what's left of the broad side of that barn over there; but you might be able to."

"I'm pretty sure of it, in fact. Here goes." He turned and whipped the concrete all in one rapid motion—it hit the bird with a blue flash, as it was still extending its wings, and then there was nothing there.

"It's a little late for fireworks, Mr. Mills," the Deputy said as he came back.

"Just one last cherry bomb, Officer. Nothing to worry about."

"It'd better be the last one. They're not even legal in this state."

"Well, Reverend Mears, Officer Box gave me quite an earful, starting with when you were a third grader and recited the Gettysburg Address for the American History class he used to teach: but it all seemed to boil down to 'get back to Withougan and stop bothering the natives,' with something in the middle about 'pioneer families' and 'law abiding citizens.' So I guess I'll be going. Sorry for any inconvenience."

"That's quite all right, Deputy. I'm glad you're taking your job so seriously. God bless you."

"Thank you, Reverend. I guess I'll see you around." He returned to his car with some semblance of dignity and drove dustily off down the lane.

"Well," Jeff said as we got into his own car, "I may not have killed it, but I bet I did some serious damage."

"I bet you did, too, if there was really anything there to hit. I'm not so sure that it was a great idea, though. I'm going to wire three of these nails together as soon as I get home. Do you want me to make a cross for you, too?"

"It might be a good idea, at that. I can always just wear it on a thong of some kind."

It was just as well that Larry and I had settled on the afternoon: as it was, I didn't get to school until a little after eleven, and I had to hustle to visit the infirmary before lunch. The influx of chicken pox victims had apparently slowed down, but the epidemic had filled up most of the beds in the basement ward: not that any given sufferer seemed to spend very much time in bed, despite the nurses' best efforts. From what I could tell, talking to the boys, most of the cast for the evening's scheduled Indian dancing pageant had been laid up, leaving me to wonder what Luke and his colleagues were going to do for replacements. The show must go on in any case, of course; but on a weekend when the campus was thick with alumni whose wallets we hoped to prise open, it was all the more important to have the whole program working up to the standard of perfection ascribed to it by nostalgic memories.

I had a fairly quick lunch in the Dining Hall: none of the young winter alumni were there, whether because they were not up yet, or because they were out making up for the recreation time they had lost on Friday. The flotilla of ski boats on the lake made a constant roaring background to every conversation and, it seemed, almost to thought itself: I could well imagine that, despite the day's being another in the apparently unending series of "scorchers," the golf course and the tennis courts were thronged with people playing, and waiting to play, on the sites of their fondly remembered adolescent triumphs. Though I have worked as a coach for a long time, I was an entirely undistinguished student athlete myself, both summer and winter: so I can easily resist this particular temptation. On the other hand, I have always been eager to contribute when the student literary magazine, *Tenth Muse*, invites submissions from alumni and faculty. So perhaps I shouldn't sneer.

Saturday's DRC was the first time I'd eaten at the faculty table since the Bishop's death, and, as I might have expected, the incident was a hot topic of conversation: the more so since the Superintendent, who had apparently been released from the hospital on Friday afternoon, had just returned to work that morning. People had questions for me about the funeral, or expressed their condolences, but only one of them, a young naval ensign, remarked that he'd heard from a kid that I'd had a close call myself. Being only a summer faculty member—really not much more than a sailing instructor in a white uniform—the ensign apparently did not have reason to consider that lightning striking, or failing to strike, me might have an unmeteorological explanation. Or, more likely, he'd heard stories, but, like most people, dismissed them out of hand. In my experience, being a witch would attract a good deal more attention if it were not for the fact that people think of magic as a pointless medieval superstition; one could say much the same about religion and being a Christian.

In any case, I escaped from lunch without any unfortunate connections having been drawn between my situation and the Bishop's, at least so far as I could tell. Larry was due in the office a little after one, and I spent the brief interim making sure the altar flowers, bulletins, and other paraphernalia were in their places for the Sunday services. Given the way the summer military system works, with a new temporary promotion order every week, there's no way for me to have a permanent aide for the summer of the sort that Keeks had been in the winter. So I have to check these mechanical points myself.

The chimes were just starting to ring the quarter hour when Larry arrived; I was surprised—on medical, if not on psychological, grounds—to see that he had given up his crutches. "Hey, Larry, how're you doing?" I asked, as he came through the open door of the office.

"Well, sir, I'm not up to full speed yet, but I'm getting there. I bet you I get a dance with someone tonight, even if I don't have a date."

"It wouldn't surprise me at all," I said. "Have a seat, and let's hear what you didn't want to talk about last night."

"Sure thing, sir. Just let me get the door." He shut it with an oaken boom that echoed in the nave; then he sat down carefully on the sofa. I waited. "Well?"

"Right, sir, I was just thinking where to start. You remember when I was doing the shape changing thing, and I got to the eagle, last night I mean?"

"Is it the sort of thing you'd forget so quickly?"

"No, sir, I guess not. Well, the thing is, I didn't have anything to do with the lightning right there at the end."

"Do you mean that you didn't consciously cause it, or that you're sure you didn't do it at all?"

"Well, I guess I'm not positive, but I'm pretty sure it wasn't me. It certainly wasn't conscious."

"Okay. Go ahead. Do you think this was another visit from Father Prior?"

"I'm not so sure about that. All I really know about him is his writing, after all. But I don't think it was him: I mean, I don't think it was an effort to attack us—I didn't feel like I had to defend myself, or anything. It seemed to me like the lightning hit right where it was supposed to. Anyway, the feeling I had after that didn't seem to be like what you people were talking about—it wasn't that kind of nothingness that everyone mentioned. If anything, it seemed familiar—too, I don't know, too intimate, rather than being almost not there at all. What about you, though, sir? You've been up against both of them: did it seem like the same thing to you?"

"Not really, now that you put it that way. But what other choices are there? If it was the 'morning star' in either one of the senses we were talking about last night, I think we'd have known we were dealing with something a lot more powerful than what we had on our hands."

"Yes, sir, of course. But there's another possibility—or, at least, I don't know enough to say there's this specific thing that may have happened, exactly, but at least there's an element we should consider: Did you see where the lightning did strike?"

"Generally, yes. It was in the front lawn, just about straight out from the bay window. Why?"

"Well, it was dark, of course, but a couple of times Coach McNeil has had us run around the lake, for distance training."

"Distance is right: it must be getting on for ten miles."

"I suppose it's eight, anyway, sir. But the thing is, I've run past the lake side of that cottage in the day time when we were doing this practice, and there's a little hump in the middle of the front lawn—it doesn't run smooth straight to the edge of the bluff. And I think that bump was the place the lightning struck."

"Well, shouldn't lightning strike the highest place around?"

"Natural lightning, I suppose, yes, sir. But even if we weren't both sure this was unnatural, with the house and the trees around, this little hillock wasn't anybody's version of the highest point in the neighborhood. I think that lightning struck a grave."

"The grave of Pakashak."

"Well, not him, sir, but his father. The son is the one buried over on Long Point."

"Quite right: I'm sorry. But I don't know the Native American version of the story, in any case, only the pioneers' stories. Do you have any insight into what actually happened?"

"I know what my grandmother's grandmother told her about it: and Pah-koo-shuk, as they called him, was her brother."

"The *Oresteia* as told by Electra, eh?"

"He was older than she was, actually, but I suppose you're right if you mean that I heard the family version. You hear stories that the old chief drank too much, or that the elders didn't trust his dealings with Colonel Tipton, the Indian agent. And there may be some truth to both those things, I guess—liquor didn't do anyone any good in that generation, I think. And I do suppose he may have had a drink or two before he died—it's true it happened in Sumner's Tavern, like the white man's story says—but that was because he knew what was coming—at least, that would explain it, if you ask me. You see, he wasn't just the chief, he was *wabeno*, and he knew he was getting old. But if he had just died and left the medicine bag to his son, he was afraid the son wouldn't be able to use it right away, until he paid the price: and the old man felt like the tribe needed a magician around."

"Being caught between my English witch ancestors moving in, on the one hand, and the US Army supporting them, on the other—I'd say there was a definite crisis at the time, taken from his point of view."

"Exactly. So rather than die and leave the bag to his son, he gave Pah-koo-shuk the bag first . . ."

"And volunteered to be the sacrifice so his son would have full powers right away. I suppose I might take a drink under the circumstances myself. Is this the grandfather you said was only half-Christian?"

"Yes, sir: you see what I meant."

"I guess. He does seem to have gotten the sacrifice part right, at least. Laying down one's life for one's friends . . . But if the whole thing was pre-arranged, why does the story say that, uh, Pah-koo-shuk keeps paddling across to seek his forgiveness? Or is that just in the white man's version?"

"No, that's Indian, all right. You can tell from what I've said that the old chief was working against the tradition for the *wabeno*—he'd used his powers to defend his people, not for his personal malice, and now he was going to die so his son could do the same. But with the old chief out of the way, Pah-koo-shuk turned out to be the traditional *wabeno* type—used the power only to cause trouble, set himself up as a tyrant. People were glad when he died of something he caught from the white folks, because the elders wanted to get rid of him, but no one was sure they'd just be able to come after him with a tomahawk or whatever and live to tell about it. But they were never sure that a *wabeno* was really dead, which is why neither the father nor the son is buried with the rest of the band. And the business of Pah-koo-shuk paddling across the lake shows how they thought the old man looked at the way his son had used the power that he gave him."

"I see. And is that the same medicine bundle you have today?"

"Yes, sir. When Pah-koo-shuk was just about gone anyway with whatever it was he had caught—I've heard everything from chickenpox to syphilis—Great-Great-Grandmother brought her son in to put the tyrant out of his misery. By the time Great-Grandfather died, nobody quite believed anymore—this must have been during the Korean war, or something around then—and he just left the bag to my grandmother. And as far as I know, she never tried to use it—just studied everything and left it to me."

"Why not to your mother?"

"Her? Take something Indian? You must be kidding. She wanted to be pure white so bad I think she'd've bought a statue of General Custer for the living room if she'd been able to afford one. And that so-called stepfather of mine only encourages her: he wouldn't want any of the guys at the country club to know he was married to a squaw. At least my real dad had wanted me to learn about both sides of the family, the Indian and the Scots. If it hadn't been for him, Mom probably wouldn't even have let me speak to Grandmother, much less visit her house."

"That's kind of complicated: it sounds like you went through the emancipation business more so you could stay with your family than so you could get out of it."

He thought for a minute: "Yes, sir, I guess that's true, though I never looked at it that way at the time. I just wanted to get away from living with those two: if you want to call it living. At least, the way Dad had things fixed, Dumbo and the Bride of Frankenstein couldn't touch the money he left me. Not that number two was around then, of course. But Dad was careful about money."

"You did say he was half Scots."

"Yes, sir, right: of course. Anyway, I was glad enough to be out of there. But still, like you said, I guess I have kind of stood up for the Native American side, in a way."

"But at the same time, you didn't want the *wabeno* part. Kind of like having your cake and not eating it, either."

"I guess so, sir. Until yesterday, anyway. But maybe I'm starting to see it differently. That reminds me, though: have you seen these posters the scout camp people have been putting up this morning about a pow-wow?"

I hadn't, and was about to say so when someone knocked at the door: I moved to get up and answer, but Larry said, "It's okay, sir, I can get it."

I'm not sure how quickly I would have recognized the person Larry admitted, if he hadn't introduced himself; the complex layers of his accent might have jogged my memory of one of our very infrequent meetings. He stood, I guess, somewhat less tall than Larry—even allowing for Brandon's habit of standing on the balls of his feet—and was dressed in plain black summer weight clericals whose cut I did recognize (more from the experience of enviously studying their catalogue than from any expertise in religious haberdashery) as the products of England's premier church outfitters. Poverty is not, of course, explicitly a Benedictine vow: one of the professors when I was in seminary was a Benedictine who not only smoked, but used an ivory cigarette holder.

"Father Mears," my guest said, "I'm Alcuin Shaw. I'm terribly sorry to interrupt—I should have realized that you might be counseling one of your naval cadets. I'm sure I don't envy you having to juggle your work with the lads here and the press of diocesan business as well. I came right over after the Archdeacon rang us up, you see: I do hope you can spare me a few minutes of your valuable time."

"Of course I can, Father Prior. I can speak with this lad later today, I'm sure." I glanced at Larry, who was showing no inclination to leave—other than, perhaps, the fact that he had not yet let go of the door handle. It occurred to me that perhaps it was just as well that Father Prior not know his name: some kinds of magic revolved around such fine points as that. "I'll catch you at the meet, son—you're not running, I hope."

"No, sir, I'm not. Look for me at the high jump pit." He didn't move.

"Very good, midshipman. You may go. Don't worry about reporting out."

Larry's fascination at the presence of our enemy had not, at least, made him incapable of recognizing an order when he heard one.

"Aye aye, sir," he said, and saluted.

"Dismissed." I returned his salute, and he closed the door behind him.

"Please have a seat, Father Prior. May I offer you a Coke? I'm afraid we're fresh out of Pimm's."

He favored me with a razor thin smile as he took a place on the sofa. He sat almost on the edge, as a plebe does in the dining hall when first classmen put a butter knife between his spine and the back of his chair. There's no danger in the butter knife, of course: though there may be some in the first classmen if you let the cutlery slip out of place. "A Coca-Cola will be fine, thank you, Father," he answered. As I got two sodas out of the refrigerator, he went on: "Your young friend is a persistent sort, isn't he?"

"Remarkably so, Father. He was laid up in bed with a bad hip only at the beginning of the week—but he was determined to be up and about for the dance this evening."

"Amazing, Father. To work with youth must give you great satisfaction; one hopes for great things from the Church of the Future."

"Most of them have been baptized, Father: I've come to think of them as the Church of Today. You were saying, though, that Father Carlson had called."

"Oh, yes, indeed, Father. I must say I hadn't quite anticipated how much responsibility had devolved upon you with the passing of dear Bishop Parker. Even between now and the funeral there must be countless details you have to oversee."

"True enough. But Father Carlson, Canon Gabriel and the Dean are seeing to most such things."

"Quite expertly, I'm sure, Father. But we—Father Abbot and I, that is—certainly would not wish to see All Angels' add in any way to your burdens at a time so characterized by bereavement and by these many administrative preoccupations. And, I must say, honestly, that Bishop Parker had himself, perhaps, impressed us as being somewhat overextended—spread a bit thin, you know. But *de mortuis nil nisi bonum.* In any case, though, we wouldn't wish to seem to insist on your distracting yourself from other more important affairs simply for the Abbey's sake."

"No more than I should wish to give the impression that the contemplative life was anything other than central to the diocese as a worshipping community."

"An attitude that we certainly appreciate, and, I feel safe in saying, hope to reciprocate. What we would like to propose, Father, is simply this—that you not trouble yourself with Brother Alfred's life profession, which is after all the sort of thing we're set up to deal with internally in any case—and then that we simply postpone this affair of an Abbatial election until some more convenient time, after the funeral, or perhaps even after the new bishop is elected. I'm sure you see that to do so would provide a much greater measure of continuity than for us to have a new Abbot learning the ropes without being able to turn to the Bishop as an external impartial observer, as well as our diocesan Father-in-God, as dear Bishop Cockburn always used to say."

Having finally delivered himself of this proposal, he sank back into the chair—if "sank" can be used of so rigidly postured a motion—and allowed himself a sip of the Coke. It was the sort of proposition which is traditionally met with "What kind of an idiot do you take me for?" On the other hand, it certainly might work to our advantage that they should think me some kind of an idiot: so I didn't indulge myself in making a snappy answer.

"That's very kind of you, Father Prior, really, very considerate. I'm not sure that it's necessary, though. I'd been looking forward to the life profession, actually, as it's not the sort of thing one sees or takes part in very often. And as for the election, I thought I'd understood Bishop Parker to say that Monday was just about the last day canonically possible."

"I suppose, Father, that it may be, strictly speaking, but certainly we wouldn't wish to become narrowly legalistic at such a time as this. 'The Sabbath was made for man,' you know. One would imagine that you, or the Standing Committee, would have the authority to allow an exemption from the strict terms of the Charter, if asked to do so by the Abbot and Chapter."

"Perhaps we might, though I'm inclined to doubt it. But as you say, any sort of policy decision, rather than mere carrying out of existing plans, would require a meeting of the Standing Committee—which we don't expect to have until after the funeral—so there isn't actually any legal way for me to change things." I couldn't resist rubbing it in a little bit: "The Bishop, of course, could have made that kind of decision by himself, but I don't have the same freedom of action. I'm afraid it seems as though my hands are tied."

He edged back to the front of his perch. "Am I to understand, then, Father, that you propose to pursue this whole schedule as Bishop Parker originally planned it?"

"It really would seem best to carry on. All in the best tradition of the service, after all. Will it be early enough if we get to the Abbey about one-thirty?"

"We, Father? Excuse me, but Father Carlson hadn't mentioned any of the other members of the Committee."

"No, I'm sorry. I was referring to an acolyte I'd like to bring along. I know it's an affectation, but he was my aide-de-camp, so to speak, during his time here at the Academy, and I've gotten used to working with him. He keeps me on the liturgical straight and narrow, you see. Just have your master of ceremonies plan on my Aide assisting me the way I would have stuck with the Bishop if I'd come as his Chaplain. It'll be a great help for me."

"Very well, then, Chaplain," he said, and stood as if to go. "I'm sure that under the circumstances whatever time you and this *young man* of yours choose to arrive will be equally convenient. Thank you very much for the—what is the Americanism?—oh, yes, for the 'soda-pop.' Good day."

At that point I really had had enough. "You must excuse me for not getting up to see you to the door, Father Prior, but you seem to be getting so much pleasure out of being condescending, and I know that that is easier to do when one possesses the temporary illusion of being the taller: or the more important."

He froze, looking almost apoplectic, and I added: "Very well, Father Shaw. You may go."

The Chapel is a relatively long building, and it is a credit to the Prior's histrionic ability that, having once determined to storm out of the office, he succeeded in continuing to storm the whole 238 feet to the front doors. It was, in its petty way, a fairly impressive gesture.

I WONDERED, as I walked past the Riding Hall toward the track and my meeting with Larry, what the Abbot and Prior had been up to all day—perhaps they had taken me for some sort of fool: either the sort who wielded magical defenses, but could not draw the connection between a lightning-riven sycamore and the Bishop's death; or perhaps, rather, the sort of fool who would happily take advantage of the opportunity to abdicate responsibility. What they would not have anticipated, I reminded myself, was that I was, instead, the kind of idiot who was cowardly enough to avoid responsibility in the first place, but too stubborn, or too legalistic, to let it go after I'd accepted it.

Arriving at the high jump pit, I found that Luke Faber had, in fact, obtained a golf cart: at least, one was parked next to the pit, where he was ensconced in a lawn chair under a beach umbrella. The same black market in possible favors that led me to officiate at the occasional Scout Camp soccer game had persuaded him, with less caution, to agree to be the impartial high jump official for all of the weekly upper camp track meets the summer before; inevitably, so prolonged a volunteer commitment had not escaped the eye of the camp director, and the job had duly been added to Luke's contractual duties for succeeding years. Annandale's nearest approximation to the real armed services is probably to be found, not on the parade ground, but in the ingenious way the bureaucracy arranges that no good deed go unpunished.

I had apparently arrived between heats—the kids at the jump were taking practice runs, and Luke was checking over the entry form on his clipboard. "Hi, Luke," I said. "Must be fun to do this twice in one week."

"Right, Jonathan. I don't see you volunteering to come out here and get baked." He grinned. "Besides, I didn't have to work over here on Monday—it was just Field Day, and didn't count for the medal or the all-round trophy: so they didn't need an outside judge. I think Dr. Davies was the official."

"I didn't think I'd seen you. In fact, I didn't expect to see you here this afternoon—Larry Brandon said the Indian Lore department had something special on for this evening, and I sort of figured you'd be out at the Council Ring helping to get ready."

"There's not much to get ready; that's the point, in fact. We had too many kids sick to put on the show we'd planned for this week, so Major Furlong came up with this idea of having an Alumni Pow-Wow."

"By which he meant?"

"That we're just going to set the Council Ring up with the drum, and some lights, and have some kilts and moccasins ready out back, and hope that we have some alumni who'll be willing to come out and dance, sort of for old time's sake."

The loudspeaker crackled out some unintelligible message about field events and the 100 meter dash, and Luke went on: "Excuse me for a minute while I get this started, Jonathan.

"Okay, gentlemen, that's first call for the Senior division. We have Aaron first, then Adams, then Austin Barrett: you know the alphabet. You can take one official trial run before they start counting, and you get three attempts at each height.

"That should hold 'em for a minute. Before we get carried away on our recent tradition, I promised to tell you that Mr. Brandon has gone off to the concession stand, and will be back here ASAP."

"Right, thank you. But what if you give a dance and nobody comes?"

"Well, then, Mr. Darcy, it wouldn't be very much like a dance, would it?"

"I don't think that's Darcy's line: but when did you start reading Jane Austen?"

"Never, willingly: but there's a great movie with Lord Olivier. His *Pride and Prejudice* is almost as good as the *Wuthering Heights*, where he plays Heathcliff—you know, 'I wondered how anyone could imagine unquiet slumbers for the sleepers in that still ground.' "

" 'For the sleepers in that quiet earth,' is what the narrator says. I know the story fairly well: it's on the tenth grade reading list, so I've been doing it at least once a day during April for the last ten years. What were you saying about the dance, though?"

"Oh, right. Well, Furlong has stacked the deck a bit. Most of the dance instructor staff are alumni, of course, and there are several people back visiting who were in the Master Dancer Society, our honor organization. Furlong talked to some of them yesterday, and got their names on his dance card, so to speak, before they put up the ads. So we've got enough commitments to make a decent night even if no one crawls out of the woodwork. And then there's Larry."

He glanced over his shoulder, away from the jumpers and toward the concession stand across the football field. "Here he comes now.

"Don't hurry or anything, Brandon," he shouted.

"Sorry, sir," Larry said as he came up to us. "They didn't have anything but Diet Decaf when I went over there, and I had to wait to get you Classic. Here it is, though." He handed over a liter bottle of Coke and some change, and Luke, thanking him, turned his attention to young Mr. Aaron's first real jump.

"Hi, Chaplain. How did it go?"

"All right, I guess, Larry: I'm not sure. I insulted him as he was leaving, so maybe I shouldn't stand out under the open sky like this. He interrupted you, though."

"Actually, sir, I interrupted myself. We were talking about the Native American thing, and that reminded me of the Alumni Pow-Wow posters."

"Mr. Faber was just telling me about that idea."

"Good. You see, what I decided while I was talking to you is that I want to go dance in it tonight."

"But you didn't go to Scout camp, did you?"

"No, but I learned a couple of Potawatomi steps and dances from my grandmother and some of her friends. One was an old guy she knew who said I was learning to dance like a girl: he showed me some fancy stuff. Besides, I've been to a couple of Council Fires, enough to see how things are worked out there. Mr. Faber said it would be okay with Major Furlong."

"I said I *thought* it would be all right," Luke said, without looking away from the jumpers. "I'll talk to him at SRC."

"Yes, sir. Thank you, sir. That's what I meant, sir. Anyway, Chaplain, I know it's kind of a crazy idea, but I'm getting into it, just from thinking about it."

"It doesn't strike me as crazy, Larry; if you want to dance, go ahead and dance. It might do you good. I wouldn't answer to what it will do for your hip problem, though."

"Probably nothing good. But maybe body can be bruised just a little bit to pleasure soul: 'No pain, no gain.'"

"That may be: but it's still the first step down the slippery slope toward Fr. Prior. Watch yourself."

"Oh, he'll watch himself, all right," said Luke. "Did I tell you about the three extra mirrors he put in his room in winter school?"

"Just pay attention to the jumpers, sir. I think that last guy took an extra step."

"Right, Eagle-eye. At least I didn't mention the 8×10 color glossies and the Mr. October poster."

"Mr. October?" I asked.

"It was a present from a girl I used to date, Chaplain. Like those deals where they put your picture on the cover of *Time* or something."

"I understand completely, Larry," I said. "And we won't ask where she got the original photo." He grinned, and I motioned him out of earshot from the small group of athletes and spectators who were beginning to gather around Paul's chair in order to read the score sheet over his shoulder. "I gather you had more to say about your grandfather."

"Well, yes, sir. You can see what I was getting at. Maybe the Indians were right, and he's not gone, not completely, anyway. Can you have souls without bodies, or vice-versa?"

"Vice-versa, certainly. We call them corpses." He glared at me. "But I guess you mean besides that. Well, one theory has it that we don't have rational souls right away at the moment of conception: so you might say that the baby in early stages is a living body without a rational soul. Then Dante, at least—I don't think any theologian ever said this—shows a character in Hell who was still alive on earth, with the explanation that his soul has already been carried off and a demon inhabits his body: that would be a body without a human soul, at least. As to souls without bodies, you just about have to say something along those lines if you want to have a picture of something going on between death and resurrection; but from Saint Paul on, everyone says that situation is abnormal, just like Yeats and your grandmother do."

"Well: if a demon could be joined to a human body in the place of a soul, could a human soul be joined to one of those elemental forces we were talking about yesterday, instead of to a body?"

"Not instead of a body, no. An elemental force would be just as much an incorporeal spirit as the soul itself is. But that does suggest something, though. Saint Augustine seems to think that the soul is eternal because, and when, it looks at God, who is truly eternal in Godself. The Fall is being distracted from the vision of God to look at lesser, changing things. Now the elemental forces of the universe aren't eternal—I mean, they don't exist outside of time and space, the way that God does. But they are, what should I say, *sempiternal*—"

"You mean, they last as long as the universe does—through all time, rather than outside all time."

"Yes. That's what I was driving at, exactly. So perhaps a soul could focus its vision, so to speak, on an elemental force—"

"And end up waiting for the Resurrection trapped in the world, contemplating that force, rather than outside it, contemplating God."

"Precisely. It wouldn't be Hell, exactly, because it isn't contemplating Satan or some fallen angel, but it's still focussed on a lesser good than God. I don't believe I've ever heard anyone propose such a thing, but I think it's a consistent hypothesis."

"Well, sir, consistent or not, something woke up at that cottage last night. It wasn't just a hypothesis that was watching us."

"No, hardly. Which reminds me—have you had that same feeling any time since last night?"

"Not after you put your ring on, no, sir. But by the time I was apart from you, we were away from the house—I figured whatever it was was tied to that specific place. And then, too, I took off my medicine bag when I got back to barracks, which could have something to do with it. Unless you've been keeping us all covered with the ring?"

"No; not that I wouldn't like to, but my brother and niece and cousin and I haven't been able to figure out yet how to make the ring's protection work away from one of the four of us. It's on the to-do list."

"Could you sort of expand it, like a bubble-dome over the whole campus, or whatever?"

"You would think so, but even together the four of us can only blow the bubble so big. That's where I think Stuart tries to make everything too simple: if it was just a matter of prayer and angels, I can't see why there should be any particular limits. My guess is that it's like grace—divine and human action going on at the same time, but on different levels. So the human abilities make a sort of limit for the whole business."

"I think I understand. Does that mean I won't have to take theology class this winter?"

"No, but it might mean you'll be able to follow the lectures, which is more than a lot of people do. You know, though, now that I think about it, if the—oh, call it the presence—felt benign to you (you said it was familiar, or some such word), you might want to think about wearing your medicine bag for the next couple of days. It may not have been pure coincidence that the Prior came by my office while you were talking to me. You'll have to judge for yourself which risk is the greater."

"Okay, sir. I'll think about it. Are you going to come see the pow-wow?"

"I intend to, yes. I've seen most of the regular repertoire over the course of the last thirty years—they don't write new shows all that often, you know. But this pow-wow will certainly be different. Are you going to stay here for all the senior jumpers?"

"Not necessarily, no, sir. Why?"

"Well, I'm going to stay and work the crowd a bit, but I thought I'd start off by visiting the concession stand. You want to walk over with me and I'll buy you a Coke of your very own?"

"Sure thing, sir. But then I'd better go practice my double-action step."

The track meet lasted till about four o'clock: they run two divisions—senior and junior—of every event, and since each unit—five naval companies, two troops, and two aviation flights—can have two entries in each event in each division, the track events sometimes have to be run in several heats. Depending on your view of track and field, it's either "somewhat time-consuming" or "about as exciting as watching paint dry." I tend toward the paint-drying end of the spectrum, myself, but the length of the proceedings gave me a chance to chat with a couple of homesickness cases, and check up with the trooper who was to read the lessons for the upper camps service the next morning. The track is at the farthest edge of the Main Campus, and I thought it would be easy enough to stroll on to the Indian Scout Camp to see to my last errand, the lector for the Scouts' service: but by the time I had walked on across the road, made inquiries about the boy's whereabouts, left a message with his counselor, and walked back to my office, it was time to go to the alumni barbecue at the Superintendent's house. I decided to drive.

———

THERE WASN'T a receiving line: with so many alumni, and their wives and children, the barbecue wasn't even a social function, really, despite the pose of having it at Annandale's answer to Buckingham Palace. More than anything else, it was an exercise in discreet crowd control, all managed from behind the scenes by Cousin Patty. Food and drink were arranged around the grounds with an attention to tactical advantage worthy of the General's distinguished former career. Relying on considerable previous experience, I made my way, smiling and shaking hands, to the screen porch, where the bar was set up, out of the way of the younger guests. I'd just received my drink when the boss caught up with me.

"That looks more like a gin and tonic than a Coke, Padre!"

"Yes, sir, General. But everyone needs a change now and then, particularly when you're paying for the liquor. It's good to see you up and about, sir."

"It's good to be here, or anywhere, for that matter. I can't tell you how sorry I am about Bishop Parker. He was a good man, even if he was beating me. I'm sure you'll miss him particularly."

"Thank you, sir, I'm sure I will."

"I understand from Reverend Carlson that you're the man in charge until they have an election."

"Well, more or less, yes, sir. I'm the president of a committee that's in charge, actually. But it won't interfere with my work."

"No, that isn't what I was getting at." He leaned a bit closer, near enough that I could have counted the silver bullion threads in his epaulets. "Listen, Padre, you remember what I told you. I heard about that near miss of yours. Maybe there's no connection, but east of Suez they used to say that Colonel Trout's enemies had a way of having accidents—I never heard about the weather turning on anyone, but there were stories about people being attacked by animals, or problems with jeeps or planes or guns. If Trout thinks you're worth getting rid of, he won't stop trying because of one mistake. I know how you dog-collar folks are about confidence, so I'm not asking any questions: but I want you to be careful."

"Roger that, sir. I'll take no chances."

"That'd be the first time. Good luck, Jonathan. Enjoy the party." We shook hands, then he wandered off in search of alumni with deeper pockets and fatter checkbooks than my own, while I left the porch and worked through the crowd to the nearest food line.

I met up with Stuart at the potato salad. "Taking a pass on the salad, Stu?" I asked, as I reached for the spoon.

"Mayonnaise," he said, shaking his head.

"Good point. Maybe I'll have some of this nice vinegar cole slaw, instead. Is the rest of the gang here?"

"Lake side."

I followed him round to the south front of the house, away from most of the crowd, where his classmates had commandeered several benches that overlooked Glenarm Walk and the bay. Sixty years ago, when it was common for graduates to marry within a year or so after commencement, it was traditional to bring one's date for the final ball to this stretch of the walk and propose by offering her a miniature copy of one's First Class Ring. In my own day, a row of shrubs had been allowed to grow up in front of the mansion, making the walk an ideal place to go smoke things of which the unsuspecting Superintendent of that period would not have approved. Someone must have caught on eventually, though, for by the time I returned as a faculty member, the bushes had been removed, and the walk was used simply as a way into town. With the shrubbery gone, the view was spectacular, almost straight along the axis of the lake from the only high point on the north shore. Though Annandale's fleet was tied up for the night, sailors and skiers from the summer cottages wove a pattern of bright colors across the sparkling lake.

Either Stuart was a straggler or else he'd gone back for seconds: for the rest of the group were already eating dessert. "Hi, Holiness," Keeks said, and stood up. "Have a seat."

"Thanks, Chris. How's it going with you guys?"

"Pretty good, Chaplain," Jeff answered. "I think between us we've played every sport but ice hockey and Frisbee golf: and of course we didn't get started until almost noon."

"Speak for yourself, Jeff," Rob answered. "I didn't bring pads or a stick, but I rented some skates and took a couple of laps around the ice. It was someplace between tennis and water-skiing, while Richard and Stuart were swimming."

"Did you guys sail, too?"

"For a while, yes, sir. Richard's quite a skipper." This provoked a round of laughter from the rest of the crew.

"I'm a perfectly good skipper, thank you. That idiot in the ski-boat almost caused the accident. You see, sir, I had talked the Commander into letting us take out the Class A scow. I've sailed big boats like that up in Michigan, so he let us have it, if I'd answer for the crew. Most of the guys here know enough to handle a line, at least, so I vouched for them, and we were out on the lake by about one o'clock, when the kids were getting ready for the track meet.

"We were making a great run on a port tack, holding a north-easterly course, coming back from Long Point, when a power boat overtook me from the port quarter and then cut right across my bow. If it had been just him, my only problem would have been cutting across his wake: but he was towing a skier, and we were heading straight for the rope. The skier was someplace upwind of me, so I was afraid to come about for fear of hitting the person or the rope. I yelled to the guys to prepare to jibe, and put my helm to windward. The boom slammed across, of course, and it's a wonder that it didn't decapitate anyone: but we missed the tow line and the skier, which was the important part. Anyway, after that I decided it was too crowded to sail a boat that big, and we headed back in."

"What about you, Chaplain?"

"Nothing so exciting, I'm afraid. Jeff must have told you about this morning. After he and I got back, I mostly ran errands; though I had an interesting visit this afternoon from the Prior of All Angels'."

"Stands to reason," RJ said, "he's scoping out the enemy. What'd he have to say, Father?"

I summarized our conversation.

"Well, Chaplain, I don't know how much that really helps us with Lee, but at least it gibes with what we figured. It's a sign we're on the right track."

"I think so too, Jeff," I answered. "I should tell you all, too, that General Delmar just warned me about the Abbot, again: if any of you needed to be reminded to be careful until this is settled."

"Hardly, Father. Jeff's been wearing your new cross all day. There is one question, though, that's been puzzling all of us."

"Shoot."

"What was the note about that Brandon passed to you last night?"

I laughed. "I thought he was being really careful."

"Not him," Stuart said, "you."

"Looks like you've been a cop a little bit too long, Chaplain—you're losing your criminal skills."

"Oh, well," I answered. " 'When a felon's not engaged in his employment, he is just the same as any honest man.' "

"*Pirates of Penzance*," Richard said. "But what about the note?"

"I don't think I'd better say, guys. He seems to want to keep it personal, so I'd better let him tell everyone in his own good time. I imagine it will all be made clear tomorrow afternoon. But I'd been meaning to ask if any of you were planning on going to the Council Fire this evening."

"I don't think so, Father," Rob answered, and the others shook their heads in agreement. "I suppose we can if there's some particular reason to."

"No, not really. They're having a kind of amateur night, I guess, and young Mr. Brandon'll be dancing, so I thought I'd go watch. Just so we have an idea of where everyone is as the day goes on. I'll be a little late for the Ball, but I'll catch up with you guys before the Officers' Figure. There's no way I'd miss the chance to stand around a hot gym in a suit and swill strawberry punch while I watch a mob of people dance to music I don't understand. I do it two or three times a year, just like having my teeth cleaned."

"The punch is a highlight," Keeks said ruefully. "But everyone who's anyone will be there."

"Yeah, Chris," Jeff said. "Too bad you can't take that hot car onto the dance floor."

" 's okay," Pruett answered. "I can park in front of the door.

"Anyway, Holiness, we've got places to go and people to see. We'll catch you at the punch bowl, eh?"

"Sure thing, gentlemen. Drive carefully."

I went home after supper to check my mail (which contained nothing of more interest than a postcard reminder of the family reunion) and to change clothes. Dressing for the evening was a small puzzle: the Ball was technically formal for the Corps, though suits had been an acceptable alternative to adult formal wear for as long as I could remember. Council Fires, on the other hand, called more for mosquito repellent than for sartorial display. I eventually compromised on a khaki suit and short-sleeved clericals, figuring I could leave the suit coat in my car during the Pow-Wow. I stopped by the drugstore for a can of bug spray on my way over to the Council Ring, and pulled into the cinder parking lot with plenty of time to spare.

The Council Ring is set well back in the small wood on the north side of campus. The school's story is that it was a real meeting place for Pakashak's band, but I'm not sure I believe that any more than I do the official claim that the site was chosen for the Indian Scout camp by the Prince of Wales on a visit to the United States in the 1890s—"Let your young Indians dance in the steps of the old ones," he is supposed to have said, though campers and faculty alike long ago corrupted this to "Let greenbacks replace redskins." In any case, one reaches it from the parking lot by way of a twisting cinder path lit (a bit superfluously in the long summer evening) by torches, and guarded at each turn by Scouts in impressive Native American costume. Having stood at such corners myself at their age, I knew that these were the Scouts who had been enrolled in dance class but proved too inept to learn even the simplest of the steps. A separate path leads to the camp, by way of an underpass at State Road 10: the main body of the Scouts were waiting there, out of sight in the shadow of the trees, for the signal to enter the ring and take their seats.

The Ring itself is actually a horseshoe of wooden bleachers, with seating for about 1000 campers, parents and guests; the center of the U, spread with fine sand, is the dance space, and across the open northern end, at a distance of some six or eight feet from the ends of the bleachers, is a cliff face modeled in concrete, suitable for use as a stage set in a variety of productions. Behind it are dressing rooms, storage spaces, electrical control boards, and the like. On this particular night, the cliff was essentially unadorned, and a single white spot shone on the great medicine drum at its base, stage left. It wasn't yet too dark to see that wood had been laid for a fire at a symmetrical point on the right. I took an aisle seat in the lower bank of bleachers.

Philip Cicero, one of the younger members of the Indian staff, came out costumed in a breech clout, moccasins, a roach of deer hair, and the umber body paint the department bought by the barrel in order to give the sons of the Europeans the hue of those whom their forefathers had dispossessed.

Blond campers wore black wigs as well: but Philip's sable ponytail seemed at casual inspection, from my distance, to be his own. He began a simple slow beating of the drum, like the tolling of a church bell before mass, which he kept up while the campers filed in from the woods and stood at their places, as silently as could be expected from boys of their age; when he saw that all the units were present, he concluded his drumming with a rapid *accelerando* to an almost maddened tempo, ending with a single reverberating stroke, at which signal the boys sat down.

Philip stood with arms crossed on his chest while Alden Furlong, in a full ceremonial outfit made of some white leather, with a hawk as his headdress, came around the rock from stage right. He carried a lighted calumet—a hint, for those in the know, that there would not be any campers in the dance: state law and general opinion agreed that we shouldn't offer tobacco to the boys, and the usual Council Fire featured dummy pipes. Some scrupulous souls objected even to the pretended depiction of smoking, but Major Furlong had insisted that he be allowed at least that much authenticity. Solemnly, and without speaking, he came to the center of the ring and presented the calumet to the four compass points, rather as I would have invoked the saints and angels in setting up a circle of magical defenses. *Still*, I reminded myself, *it is only an act*. For when he had finished, he gestured toward the fire, and it burst into flame with a phosphoric flash whose very brilliance suggested an electro-chemical stage effect rather than the intervention of an elemental force. Native American magic, unlike the sacraments of the Church, was apparently not efficacious *ex opere operato*, simply by performing the actions.

Once he was sure the fire had caught, Alden turned back to the audience and explained the reason behind, and format for, the evening's performance, working in some educational remarks on the effect European diseases had had on the real Native Americans. There was also an element of bribery in the remarks: he told the boys (with what accuracy, I cannot say) that Native Americans honored guests at their pow-wows by inviting them to drum for the dancers. Particularly attentive members of the evening's audience, he hinted, could be similarly honored.

The first few dances were interesting enough—some older alumni in a southwestern Kachina operation; then about half a dozen younger fellows, former members of the Master Dancer Society, doing a hunting dance that involved one poor devil wearing a buffalo costume that must have been hotter than blazes. At various points in these two performances, campers were in fact brought down to drum—even Bernie Stromfeld, the Indian Camp director, was rewarded with a stint in the percussion section. The third dance acted out a legend of the thunderbird, and when the dancers came out in eagle costume, I thought at first one must be Larry: but they all moved with too much agility (as it seemed to me then) to be the boy who'd been on crutches the day before.

By the time the eagle dancers had finished, it was quite dark, or would have been but for the fire and stage lighting. The spotlight on the drum was dimmed, and Captain Cicero slipped away from his post. The kids began to murmur a bit in expectation of something special, a show-stopping finale.

Someone tapped me on the shoulder, and I turned to see Philip crouching beside me, the effect of his body paint somewhat spoiled at close quarters by blue eyes and bits of undyed white skin around the eyelids. "Chaplain Mears," he whispered, "they've asked for you to help drum in the last dance. Please come with me."

I followed him back up the aisle and out of the ring; as we walked toward the stage left wings, he said, "This is going to be the hoop dance: it starts off with the plain toe-heel rhythm—ba bum, ba bum, ba bum—which we're supposed to take a bit slower than usual; then after each jump, we usually switch to the double action, which is basically just what its name suggests, the other rhythm doubled. Just keep the same time I do, and we'll be fine. If the dancer wants to speed up or slow down, he'll give me a signal. If you get confused, just lift the drumstick up and down gently, so that you look busy."

We slipped back into the darkened ring, and took our places at the medicine drum; looking through the firelight, I could see the shape of the dancer waiting in the wings at stage right; his stature, and his balls of the feet stance (along with my having been asked to drum) convinced me that it was Larry. Philip glanced off-stage, got a hand signal from Major Furlong, and began to drum the slow toe-heel step; I joined in. Larry came into the ring, wearing only a breech clout and his medicine bag; he carried in his right hand a hoop—perhaps some three feet in diameter—wrapped in strips of cloth all around its circumference except for a few inches on either side of the place where he held it. There were, I knew, a more and a less dangerous way of doing this dance, and the darkened oval suggested what an odor of kerosene confirmed, that Larry had chosen to make his premiere in the more hazardous form. I hoped that his grandmother's friend had been a good teacher.

After bowing to each of the compass points, Larry took the hoop to the fire and held it in the flames: almost instantly, it ignited, and he held in his hand a ring of brilliant light. The dance began now in earnest—he made a circuit of the ring, still at a relatively slow pace, with much bending and twisting of his body, and brandishing of the hoop as near as he dared to the front row. Every few paces, he would hold the hoop about waist high, rather as if he were carrying a flaming piece of luggage, and then swing it, first away from and then toward his body, jumping into and out of the circle of fire before its pendulum motion carried it back away from his side. I noticed that he did this always from the right side, perhaps so that his stronger right hand could offer optimal control of the hoop, but also, I suspected (despite his apparent recovery), so that he could push off for the little hop with his unhurt left leg.

When he had completed the circle in this way (and even at a slowed pace, it went quite quickly), he returned to the center and offered the hoop to each of the compass points, as Alden Furlong had the calumet. At the north, he grinned at us and nodded slightly, like a king greeting an archbishop; I missed a stroke or two as Captain Cicero picked up the tempo. Larry turned on to the east, and, holding the hoop with both hands now, he turned it so that it stood up before him, as though he were looking through a fiery port hole. He danced in place for a couple of steps, then spun the hoop down like a jump rope, putting his whole body through the ring feet first and pulling the hoop on around over his head. As soon as he was clear, we shifted to the double action, and he danced wildly at this higher speed—it was, like the military double-time, really only about half again as fast as the basic rhythm, but he whirled like a dervish: until he halted facing the south, where we switched back to the toe-heel rhythm, and he repeated the jump-rope step. The whole process had two more iterations, and when Larry finished his last burst of double action in the center of the ring, Philip whispered "Once more and he's done."

Brandon lifted the hoop as he had before, took the same sort of timing steps, but this time twirled the hoop up and backwards, toward his head: it was obvious that his co-ordination would have to be perfect if he were to lift his feet at just the right time to step out of the hoop as it swept toward his heels from behind. He made it, perfectly, even graciously, and we began a triumphant double-action. After only a second or two of this, though, Larry gave a great screaming cry, like an eagle's, and Philip stopped, apparently taking this as the final cue. Less well prepared, I slipped in an extra beat. But then, when I did try to stop, I found that I could not; indeed, I speeded up until the double-action was well and truly doubled. Cicero would have stopped me, I'm sure, if he hadn't been too stunned by what Larry was doing.

Back in the center of the ring, he'd reverted to the forward jump rope, doing it not once, but repeatedly, at the pace of the double action, spinning the hoop about himself more and more rapidly as I increased the tempo, until he seemed to be dancing in the heart of a torus of fire—so strong was the effect of persistence of vision in the contrast of the dark night and the flaming hoop that even Larry's figure seemed to blur and dissolve.

" 'Shining light and enfolding dark,' " I thought, remembering Alfred's earlier reference to Shadrach, Meshach and Abednego—though the full appropriateness of the quotation eluded me at the time. The dance went on, in a blur of flames and feet, until suddenly the kerosene was exhausted, the spinning put out the last wisp of flame, I gave the drum one last beat, and (before our eyes, which had been fixed on the fire, could readjust to the darkness) Larry had run out of the circle, pursued at length by wild cheers and applause.

I followed after him, and found him in the locker room back stage, being received by the other dancers and the staff with roughly equal proportions of amazement at his performance, awe at his daring, and irritation at the risks he had taken. I hung back outside the door as the others were leaving, and overheard Alden Furlong talking to Luke Faber:

"You might have given me a little better idea of what to expect!"

"What was there to expect?" Luke answered. "Just a few days ago, the two of us were getting physical therapy together, and being fitted for crutches. You didn't see me out there doing the hoop dance, did you?"

When the two of them were out of earshot, I went in and sat down on a bench beside Larry. "That was pretty impressive work for a cripple," I said.

He looked pale in the fluorescent light. "You said I was a cocky little bastard, didn't you?" he answered, fiddling with the sweat-dampened thong that tied on his heirloom.

"Cocky yes, super-human, no. That would have been a pretty astounding exhibition, even for someone in good shape."

He removed the bag, laying it carefully on the bench, and sniffed meditatively at an armpit. "I stink like a dead tennis shoe," he said. "Is that superhuman?" With the bag gone, I could see that his heart was racing, the pulse still visible in the center of his chest.

"I suppose not; but you needn't take everything quite so literally." He didn't answer, but stood up and slipped out of the breech-cloth, reaching to wrap himself in the towel hanging from his locker door.

"What's gotten into you all of a sudden?" I asked, already suspecting the answer (for no common force could have made me into a puppet drummer without even alerting my family).

He turned, and started to walk to the shower, still without responding. I saw that he was not only limping again, but trembling: it was enough to confirm my suspicions. "Larry, what are you so scared of?"

He slumped down on the bench across from me. "Didn't you see?"

"See what?"

"Grandfather—he was dancing beside me in the fire."

"I only saw a blur."

"Maybe. But he was there, I know it. It wasn't just my imagination: there was another presence there, someone beside me. It was almost like he was doing the dance, just pulling me along with him."

"It's been a good week for that sort of thing. Listen, Larry—did this presence actually seem menacing, or was it 'familiar' like it was before?"

"Like before: but it was scary to feel like I was losing control."

"I had that feeling, too: I didn't just instinctively know to drum so fast, you know. It must make you afraid of what you might do if this presence took over control completely." He nodded. "But if this presence is what you seem to feel that it is, we should be cautious, but we don't need to talk ourselves into being frightened—nothing bad has happened so far." He took a deep breath and tensed his muscles, willing himself into self-control.

"Okay, sir," he said, exhaling. "Maybe you're right."

"I know I am. Now go take that shower, and I'll give you a ride back to main campus so you can get ready for the ball. You not only stink, you need a shave."

"I don't know," he said, as he walked to the showers, "it must be my white side coming out."

Even after taking a moment to drop Larry off at Logansport Gate, I got to the ball in plenty of time to have my fill of strawberry punch. Dress uniforms had changed a bit since my day, and the music had become yet louder and more incomprehensible to the adult ear—probably just as well, as I imagine I'd react to their lyrics about the way the commandant in my day did to Jim Morrison's "Girl we couldn't get much higher." For all of that, though, the general effect was the same—some campers whose girlfriends from home had come to Annandale were dancing, some alumni and their wives were doing their best to match old steps with new rhythms, and the vast majority of people milled about the two levels of the recreation building and watched the happy few. I dutifully milled, as well; exchanging wry smiles with other faculty and polite greetings with Thad and the other alumni. From the balcony, I saw Larry come into the ball: or, rather more precisely, I saw him, having arrived, cut in on another midshipman's dance. There was still some hesitancy in his moves, but he seemed to be recovering, even without ancestral help.

It was getting on for ten o'clock when it occurred to me that the band would probably take a break before Officers' Figure, the military version of a promenade or Roger-de-Coverly which invariably begins at 10:30 at Annandale balls. The temporary pause in the music would release the thirsty dancers from the floor, and we had been known to run out of punch at such points, particularly on such a sweltering night. I began working my way through the observers around me and down the stairs which led to the main floor and the refreshment table. I'd gotten about as far as the landing between the floors when a wave of nausea swept over me—it was like smoking your first cigar while being hung over and simultaneously suffering from a severe attack of the 'flu, all during a bout of sea-sickness. I just about fell down the lower flight of stairs, and would certainly have given the General's cole-slaw a wide distribution if the feeling had lasted any more than a split-second. My immediate suspicion that this feeling was unnatural was confirmed when, as I reached the foot of the staircase, I saw Keeks and Richard rushing a pasty-faced Jeff through the lobby.

Richard saw me, and called out: "It's his cousin, sir. We're going to the Abbey in Chris's car. Get the rest of the team and come on." Before I had time to object, they were out the door, and seconds later, they were off.

I went into the main room, looking first for Rob and Stuart in the crowd. Making my way as quickly as I could, I worked around the outside of the gym; about half way through the circuit, I broke into a space from which the mass of people had drawn back. Larry was sitting on the floor in the middle of the clearing, with RJ, Brad, and Richard Davies kneeling around him. A short distance away was the partially digested evidence that his resistance had been a bit lower than my own.

"It's the Abbey," I said as I knelt beside them. "Three of the kids have already taken off for there. It looks like our plan has been pre-empted."

"What are you talking about this time, Jonathan?" Richard asked.

"I'll explain it all later," I said.

"It does knock things into a cocked hat, Jonathan," RJ said. "Brad and I have to be with our kids for at least another hour, and we ought to stay in barracks awhile after Taps, too."

"I know. You can't very well be chaperones and prayer warriors at the same time, though I'd appreciate anything you might find time to say to the Boss. One of you might keep an eye on our young friend here, too."

"No, Chaplain, I'm coming along," Larry said.

I shook my head. "We've been through all this, Larry. It's better for you to stay here. We haven't got time to argue."

"A lot's changed since then, sir. And you can't keep me here, anyway. Not without a real strong cage."

"I suppose not. All right."

"Doctor Davies, can you spare this self-possessed young man for another evening? It's a dangerous project, but I guess he's taking responsibility for his own actions."

"Yes, sir, I am. I don't want to break the regs or withdraw, either one: but you all are not *in loco parentis* for me, and I intend to go, sir."

"Okay, Larry," the counselor said. "I can't stop you, even if I don't know quite what's going on. But at least be careful. I'll mark you 'On Leave' on the Taps report."

"Great, sir, thanks." He stood up—maybe a bit queasily—and said "Come on, let's get moving. Who are we still waiting for?"

"English and Cook," I said, standing myself. "Have you seen them?"

"They were talking over by the door of the squash courts when I saw them last, sir. Let me go on around that way, and you head back the other way, and we'll meet at the door to the lobby."

"Great. Let's not waste any more time." I went back the way I'd come, and didn't see either of the young alumni: but I hadn't been waiting in the lobby for more than a minute or so when Rob and Stuart came sprinting out, with Larry right behind them.

"D'you have your car here, Father?" Rob asked, as we went through the door.

"Right across the street," I answered. "There's some advantage to having a reserved parking space."

"Then let's go, Batman. Too bad you don't drive a convertible."

We made good time getting to the Abbey: either Officer Box was becoming complacent, or, more likely, he was preoccupied with keeping peace (or at least relative quiet) in the various rented cottages, most of which were by now brightly lit vessels floating in seas of gin and oceans of beer. Not all of the alumni are satisfied with strawberry punch.

I pulled into the drive of the Abbey, and almost rear-ended Chris's car. We jumped out, and ran up to the BMW, where the other three were standing by the right front fender.

"I'm glad you waited," I said.

"It's not on purpose, sir," Jeff said; "We can't get any farther. You can't see anything, but there might as well be a wall around the place."

"D'you think it's psychic, Jeff?" Rob asked.

"No, not so far as I can tell. Seems to me more like it's in the Chaplain's department. It certainly makes this cross light up." He held it in his hand as he took a step or two up the lane, and he was suddenly enveloped in blue light, which vanished again as he stepped back.

"Not a good sign," I said. "My ring reacted to that magic the other day, but I wasn't wearing my cross. If they both react now, I'd assume it indicates a stronger force than the ring's defense can meet by itself." Taking my own cross out of my coat pocket—I hadn't had it on at the dance—I walked up the lane myself. I did not feel the same sense of another presence I had on my earlier trip, but both the cross and my ring did indeed glow. *This could be it, gang,* I thought to Dan and the kids. *It looks like we're going to have to force our way in, if I can figure out how.*

Whatever help you need, Uncle Jon, we're here: but battering rams aren't quite in our line.

Nor mine. I resumed my normal conversation. "I guess it's a good thing we made that trip to the Homestead. We've got a substantial magic defense here, and I don't know anything about breaking through one. Remember, I've never learned any of the fancy stuff, never even seen it done."

"David Mears," Stuart said.

"That's right, Chaplain. How did he break through your father's shield at the baptism?"

"Danny and I think it was because there was already something of his inside the shield, the ring that Louie had had made. Unfortunately, I didn't think to leave my hankie behind when I visited here the other day."

"No, Father," Rob said. "But what about that cross of yours—not as a family heirloom, I mean, but just as a cross? Those guys must have a cross someplace inside, even if they're just pretending to be an Abbey."

"Of course they do, airhead," Richard said. "There's one on top of the barn you can see from here."

"There's one where they've got Lee, too," Jefferson said.

"Very well then, if we're going to do ritual magic, we've got the material and the agent: what about the ritual?"

"You're representing the Bishop, Father. Isn't there something a bishop says when he enters a church?"

" 'Peace be to this house and all who enter here.' That's not very much to the point."

"No, Holiness. Rob's thinking of Psalm 118, 'Open to me the gates.' They use it for an anthem."

"Of course, so they do. Well, let's see what happens." Walking back to the edge of the defensive screen, I began with an exchange all the boys knew:

"The Lord be with you."

"And also with you."

"Let us give thanks to the Lord our God."

"It is right to give God thanks and praise."

"We adore you, O Christ, and we bless you," I went on, though only Keeks knew the rest of the responses.

"Because by your holy cross you have redeemed the world," he said.

"Open for me the gates of righteousness."

"I will enter them and offer thanks to the Lord."

"Peace be to this house and all who enter here," I concluded, making the sign of the cross: "In the name of the Father and of the Son and of the Holy Spirit." Suddenly, it was as if a searchlight shone on us from the barn roof, an almost blinding glare.

"That tears it," Richard said. "They've seen us."

"Not hardly," Jeff answered. "If they had a light that big up there we'd have seen it when we flew over."

"It's not the first time a star has stood over a stable," Keeks said. "Try the shield again."

I thrust my arm forward into the light: it met no resistance. "Good call, Keeks," I said.

"Let's move out," Rob ordered. "Form a squad in two teams. Brandon, Cook, Chaplain, go with Platt as Bravo; Pruett and Mills, come with me: we're Alpha. We'll go first."

In this "Onward Christian Soldiers" manner, we rushed to the barn, leapfrogging the teams up the lane. Having seen no one along the way, we burst through the door into the narthex, just outside the church proper. There were only a few lights on, but they sufficed to show that the large room was empty.

"Maybe they're in the old farm house," Larry said. "We could check."

"No, let's follow the light while we can," Keeks countered. "What's upstairs?"

"The chapter house," I said: "And it's apparently some kind of secret: only the life members go to the meetings there."

"There's a staircase over there," Richard said, and Rob nodded:

"Okay, let's try it. Stick together, everyone. Team leaders in front."

The double doors on the landing at the top of the stairs were a different matter from the front door, not so easily disposed of. They had been locked from the inside.

"How fast can you burn them, Jeff?" Rob asked.

"Not much faster than they'd burn naturally, I'm afraid. Can you do anything, Chaplain?"

"No, it doesn't feel to me as though there's a shield here. Maybe Jeff can jigger the lock, or Larry can change into something that can crawl under the door."

Larry pulled off his shirt as he answered. "I don't see any light under it, sir—unless I change to a slime mold, we're out of luck on that score." But he went on with his divesture.

"And I'm trying, Chaplain," Jeff added, "but I can't quite visualize the pins in the lock to move them—it's like something is blocking my view."

"Break it," Stuart said. "There are seven of us."

"It's worth a try, I guess," Rob said. "Right shoulders, everybody, on three—and be ready for trouble if we break through—this won't be subtle."

With Larry still in his boxers, we backed up as far as we could—only about five steps—and smashed against the doors *en masse*; they held the first time, but on a second try the hinges gave way, and we burst into the chapter room. Despite Rob's cautions, we were not immediately attacked, and as soon as we had a chance to take in our surroundings, the reason was obvious: everyone in the room was sitting inside a great ritual magic circle, of the sort that one dare not leave without either making a gate or else releasing the energy of the circle itself.

The room was capacious, not much changed from its original character as a barn, though the walls had been paneled. The light from candles in sconces on the walls and in candlesticks on the floor at the compass points of the circle didn't reach to the high spaces of the roof, but showed clearly enough that five men—presumably the life-professed monks of All Angels'—were sitting on cushions roughly along the inner perimeter of the intricate band of ritual symbols drawn with chalk on the floor. Near the eastern end sat Fr. Shaw and Br. Alfred; between them, on a kind of dais of cushions, was the man I took to be Colonel Bishop Abbot Trout. In front of him, on the floor, lay a nearly life-sized crucifix, realistically painted; its face had been mashed in and the limbs broken, in the fashion of Japanese *ebumi*—the requirement that suspected Christians stomp on a sacred picture. The desecration had been so thorough as to detract from its own purpose: it emphasized the triviality, that this broken thing was only a painted wooden image.

Behind the Abbot, though, was the thing that dominated the room—a great rectangular altar (seemingly carved from a single piece of black stone), upon which sat a huge, hideously painted statue: the body of a human being, obscene in its tumescent hermaphroditism, sitting cross-legged, hands on hips, was combined with vast bat wings and the head of a goat with fiery yellow eyes.

"Baphomet," Stuart said; "Up shields, Father," said Rob.

We made a small enough group that I'd actually been covering us all with the ring's defense since we started up the lane, but now I let the protective dome light up, enough to make the limits clear while allowing us to see out; the ritual circle flared up as if to match, setting a red cylinder of light in the midst of the room, from floor to ceiling. The monks themselves seemed as immobile as their idol, but I knew that ritual magic could be done without twitching a muscle, if things were properly arranged beforehand. In fact, no sooner had the cylinder been raised than the first attack came: not this time with any pretense of natural phenomena, but as twin black lightning bolts of supernatural non-energy, two raging streams of anti-force, any infinitesimal portion of which would have passed as the negative image of the biggest blast from the biggest thunderstorm of a Kansas summer. The blue light from our crosses sprang up to meet the initial onslaught, joining the yellow from the rings, but the adversary didn't vary his attack, didn't try to shift or catch me off guard: he simply, mindlessly, pressed on as he had begun. This was to be no parrying of spells and chants, but a straightforward matter of brute force. As the unrelenting attack went on—after only a matter of instants, really—I began to feel that I was slipping under the burden: or rather, that all my strength was being sucked out of me.

Are you ready for help now? asked Caroline and Rhys in their combined telepathic voice, and even before I heard them in my mind, I felt the conscious diversion to my defense of the full powers of my brother, niece and cousin.

If it's convenient, I responded.

It's no fun just playing defense. How long do we have to keep this up? they asked.

Defense is our specialty, I'm afraid. But this won't last long—just till I think of what to do next.

Think fast.

The warning was not idle. I didn't think all of the monks in the circle were actually joined in the attack on us, but I could tell that, however many were, even all four of us defenders and the older magic of the Homestead were only just holding out.

"What do you guys see on the altar?" Jeff asked.

"Some kind of a statue," Rob answered.

"That's what I thought," said Jeff. "It's an illusion. There's an old guy lying there. He looks like he's death warmed over—they've got IV's in him, and oxygen. It's like a granite hospital bed. I'm sure it's their Abbot: it must have been him I hit with that chip of concrete at the farm this morning."

"There can't be two of him," Richard objected. "Who's that sitting on the pile of cushions?"

"That's the thing, everybody. There isn't anybody sitting on the cushions next to Lee—they're empty. The Abbot we saw there was only an illusion, like the statue. Look, maybe I can show you. Let me see if . . ."

As he spoke, the chapter room went pitch black and deadly still around me. I called out to the others, but heard nothing: I was deaf and blind. Instinctively, I put my hands up to feel about for the others; as I was doing so, someone else's hand poked me in the ribs. Evidently, more than one of us had been affected. I grabbed on to the intrusive arm, but before I could try to identify its owner, I heard Jeff speaking in my mind.

Damn. There's nothing wrong with you, guys: just stand still and stop bumping into each other. It's only another illusion, but I think Lee is helping them now.

Yes, Rob, he went on, answering a question I had not heard, *I can see. I can protect myself, but I can't help the rest of you. They're all standing up and clapping and stomping their feet. And the Prior is stripping off his habit, and there's something he's got in a cloth sack. Oh, gross. It's a skull—looks like it's painted red. Now he's starting to dance with it.*

I thought back at him: *Tell Larry to go for it.*

He already is, Chaplain. He's dancing too, some step I've never seen. Robert says, isn't there a way to get over the top of that cylinder?

There might be, but remember we only know self-defense, not how to attack.

Rhys and Caroline added their advice: *But when your father conjured against David, he didn't use any special ritual, he just called him by name.*

It's worth a try, I answered. *Did you catch that, Jeff?*

Yes, sir. They're talking so all of us can hear.

They like to be useful. It was odd to speak into a vacuum, to chant without hearing one's own voice: but I did the best I could.

"I conjure you, Kurt Wilhelm, by the Blood
Of Christ which washed you clean from sin;
I conjure you, O Deacon, by the Name
Of Jesus who was servant to the world;
I conjure you, O Priest, by that same Blood
And Body which your hands have lifted up;
I conjure you, O Bishop, by the tongues
Of apostolic flame he gave through you;
I conjure you, James, Abbot, by his grace
Through whom we cry out 'Abba' to our God.
Now, Christian, Deacon, Priest and Bishop, Monk
And Abbot, cease to menace me and these
Who come with me, and all those in your care:
I order it in Jesus' holy name."

The vacuum of evil that sucked at us weakened perceptibly at the name of Christ, but did not stop; and when my chant had ended, the attack resumed the unimaginative force it had had before. The enemy had no sense of variety.

It didn't seem to help, Jeff thought. *They've stopped the clapping, and the Prior's changing now.*

Rhys added, *At least it sounded impressive.*

A new mental voice, both ancient and young. entered the conversation: *He changes to a bear. We see them all, not with the eyes, but with the heart, as we speak to you. We see the great darkness on the altar stone. He has defiled our graves for his medicine, but we see him and he does not know us.*

Was that Larry? I thought.

Jeff answered: *I thought so, but Richard says it sounded to him like a "compound ghost." Whoever it was, the monks are opening a gate in the circle. . . .*

Tell Richard I'm glad someone paid attention in my T.S. Eliot lectures, I answered. *Compound ghost is right—it must be Larry and his grandfather.*

Sounds good to me. In that case, they just changed into a bear, too: but it's huge, prehistoric. The other one, the Prior, came out of the circle, and now they're fighting . . . Stuart says, "Darkness on the altar?"

Rhys and Caroline suggested, *Maybe the person you conjured isn't there.*

But I see him, Jeff objected. *Now they've changed to wolves. Larry still seems to have the upper hand, though. There's blood all over. Chris says, "Can the Abbot be possessed?"*

It was a good suggestion. *He surely can,* I thought. *That might explain it all. Tell Chris I need a prayer warrior, right now. I'm going to try something you're not supposed to ad lib.*

You've got five of us, sir. Do what you have to do.

Eight, my family corrected.

Larry and the Prior are changing so fast I can't tell what's what, Jeff reported, *but the monks are just sitting again.*

Okay, here goes. I took a deep, if unheard, breath, and began an *ad hoc* exorcism with familiar lines from the monastic office: "Our help is in the name of the Lord, who has made Heaven and Earth."

As I made the sign of the cross, I remembered a passage of scripture my spiritual director had required me to memorize once when I was in seminary: he'd thought I needed to be reminded of the virtue of humility (as I did), but it seemed relevant now.

"Christ became obedient unto death, even death upon the cross. Wherefore God has also highly exalted him, and given him a name which is above every name, that at the Name of Jesus, every knee should bow of things in heaven, and things in earth, and things under the earth: and that every tongue should confess that Jesus Christ is Lord to the glory of God the Father."

I went on with a prayer made up, in the usual Anglican way, of snippets of other prayers I'd used over the years: "Lord Jesus Christ, you saw Satan fall like a star from Heaven: by your death you destroyed death, and by your rising from the grave, you broke the kingdom of Satan: now by the mystery of your holy cross show us that you are that king whose power is made perfect in weakness, and defend us from every power of evil. We ask it in your name, to which every power in heaven and on earth and beneath the earth must bend the knee. Amen.

"The Lord Jesus Christ gave his disciples authority over unclean spirits, to cast them out: therefore, whatsoever spirit you may be, by Christ's authority committed unto me and his holy Church I command you to depart hence and return to that place prepared for you from before the foundation of the world, never again to tempt any human being. In the Name of Jesus Christ, I order you, be gone.

"Non sit draco mihi dux: Sit crux sancta mihi lux."

My God, the light, Jeff thought.

The last, Latinate, part of this impromptu liturgy had been tossed in as an afterthought, being nothing more than the Latin rhyme inscribed on the back of my St. Benedict medal, "Don't let the devil be my leader: let the holy cross be my light." It must have been all right to include it, though: for as Jeff spoke, the by-now-familiar stream of black lightnings ceased, for an instant, and our senses were restored. The candles had been extinguished during the course of our two struggles, and the luminance of our own protective dome was the sole source of light in the room. But I got only a stroboscopic glimpse of the monks rushing together to the fragmentary remains of their black altar before there was a renewed flash and crash of lightning and the darkness descended a second time.

But this time there was no attack: the lightning had been a single stroke, and not aimed at us: at least, it did not strike against our shields.

What's happening, Jeff? I thought.

That was the wabeno *battle: it's over, but I can't tell who won. The one who got hit evaporated, and the other one is still a bird. Look, guys, this isn't the same illusion as before that's affecting you. Now, I think I can—Wait, though: the eagle is changing. It is Larry: I think he's in bad shape, though. Oh, hell. Wait a second.*

Not much more time than that actually elapsed before our hearing and sight returned, apparently to stay. The candles were even relit.

"What'd you do?" Rob demanded, as Richard and Chris ran to help Brandon, and Stuart wandered toward the ritual circle, his apparent aimlessness matched by that of the small swarm of monks which buzzed around the altar.

"I got us a truce," Jeff answered. "This second blindness was just Lee by himself; I could tell right away. So I lit the candles as a kind of reminder that I could do some damage of my own in that line. So now he's waiting to talk to us."

"Great," Rob said. "So what's wrong with the other monks?"

"I imagine the Abbot had them under some kind of control," I answered.

"And Cousin Lee isn't turning them loose till he's sure he won't need them. Smart move, I guess."

"Smart enough," I said. "Well, gentlemen, let's go parley."

Should we go now, too, Uncle Jon?

No, stick with me for a minute, if you can, I replied. *It's only a truce.*

"You two guys go ahead, Father," Rob said. "I should go back and help check on Larry."

Jeff and I walked to the edge of the circle, where Stuart was already standing, and Brother Alfred came to meet us. In comparison with my vague memories of the image he had projected of himself, he seemed haggard, his nerves drawn tight, as if over a knife edge. I noticed that he could hardly keep his eyes on us, but kept glancing off to the side, as if he might still have been being watched.

"You needn't be frightened," I said. "Whatever it was that had taken possession of your Abbot is gone now, I think."

"I have no doubt," he said, in a heavily sarcastic voice, "and I notice that Jeff's friend has scuffed the Prior's true name out, there on the floor, so there's no chance of bringing it back even if you wanted to." He shivered, though the room had in fact grown warmer in the brief time we had been there.

"You asked for help, Brother," I said. "What can we do to help you?"

His eyes, when they crossed with mine now, were memorable even for one with my poor visual recollection: they were dilated—shocky, I suppose an EMT might have said—to me they seemed almost despairing, numbed, like the blank eyes that stare back from photographs of the survivors of Bataan and Corregidor. "Nothing," he said, and added dully, "no one can help me now." His earlier edge of sarcasm was gone: it had been his one remaining weapon, and now that it had been expended, there was nothing left in its place.

Jeff scowled. "It's over, Lee: you said so yourself. The good guys have won. You're free to go. So why go on taking their side now?"

The monk shook his head slowly, heavily: "Not just theirs: it's mine now, too." He seemed so exhausted that I was surprised he could stand; when he did start to wobble, I reached out to steady him, and he jerked away.

"Go on," I said. "Tell us more about it."

He seemed to draw on some resource of strength simply to speak to us. "I thought I could trick them—pretend to go along with the Prior and Abbot, then fix everything from the center out. But they knew everything. Once I agreed, there was no way out. They kept me from turning back until it was too late."

"That's what we felt, isn't it?" Jeff asked. "What did they do to you?"

"Don't ask," his cousin sighed. "It doesn't matter any more."

Given the Prior's interest in the mythology of the Knights Templar, and Alfred's reaction to my touch, I could guess at the reception that he'd met with. But Jeff persisted: "Lee, it's all right. You can show me."

He did show him, then—and he must have put the whole experience into one simultaneous moment of psychic revelation, without any attenuation of his own horror and shame. One could not have expected anything else, I suppose—but even so it was brutal, a telepathic blow that brought Jeff to his knees. As I helped him stand back up, there were tears in his eyes. "My God," he murmured. "Now I understand."

The monk shook his head a second time.

"No," I said. "That wasn't it, was it? Not what they did to you, but what you did, afterwards. That would be the part that went too far." I looked toward the center of the circle, and saw that Stuart was staring fixedly down at the mutilated crucifix I'd noted earlier.

"Jeff, come and help me carry this," he said, when he realized we were watching him; and the two of them laboriously brought the cross back to the place where Brother Alfred and I were standing, lifting it no more than they had to—almost, indeed, dragging it. The broken limbs dangled wildly from their nails, but now they glittered in the candlelight: I thought once again of *Macbeth*, this time of the place where the hypocritical murderer describes King Duncan's body as a relic, "his silver skin laced with his golden blood."

Alfred stared at the precious object in amazement. "It was wood," he said. "We did horrible things—I can't say: but I know it was wood, not gold like this."

"Maybe it was an illusion," Jeff suggested.

Alfred reached out to touch the modeled metal body, as if he weren't quite convinced that this might not be the illusion: but he said, "No, it was real. I would have known. They wanted me to know that what we did was real. But this, this wasn't here, not like this." He poked at a golden arm, and it swung in a massive pendulum's arc.

"It must have been changed when you zapped the Abbot, sir," Jeff said. "Or at least what was left of him."

Whatever the exact moment of the change, it suggested to me a way of getting Brother Alfred to snap out of the fog of despair he was in. "I suppose you're right; in any case, though, I think it makes a point. Look here." I held out my own cross. "See, Brother: three long iron nails from my homestead house, hand-forged by some forgotten smith, and none too neatly, with a rough edged chisel point. These three date back a century or so, but Roman nails in an impoverished province would be even worse. Think of that ragged chisel point ripping through sun-browned skin, tearing flesh and tendons, probing, scraping against bones until it finds a space within the joint, along a nerve, and rages through to reappear and tie the wrist down to the hard dry wood. And think of this repeated twice again, before the strain of lifting and the jolt as the crossbar slips into its place on the post. Then imagine hanging there in the hot spring sun, each breath an agony of tearing nerves and muscles, each drop of blood and sweat a reminder of the thirst that almost seems to be a fire inside. Add all that to the flogging and the thorns, the spitting and the calls, the mockery and desertion and shame. Such an agony and despair that death itself could be welcome as a release from torment. Then see that wounded head lifted up again, the eyes straining to see through the bloody mist of pain, the Word that shapes the universe laboring with cracked lips and swollen tongue to make words from the feeble breaths of lungs already nearly drowned. Before those eyes, Brother, eyes that even now can pierce into your soul, you know that this business here tonight amounts to nothing; when those eyes are fixed upon us, we know that we consented to the trials and condemnation, we shouted for Barabbas, we lined the streets to jeer, we cast the dice and hammered in the nails. The God who makes us came among us as one of us, and we declared it good that he should die in agony. Not Caiaphas or Pilate, Brother, but you and I. And you have the gift, Brother, you can see and hear him even now—you can look back into those eyes, you can hear the whispered voice even now: and you know what it will say."

It was, I admit, an impassioned speech: but not even my teenaged experience of frightening myself and my friends had prepared me for the effects of this passion, which seemed to strike Alfred with the same sort of brutal force he had turned against his cousin moments before. He didn't collapse, as Jefferson had: rather, more disturbingly, he stood, staring into an unfocussed distance, like someone who'd been shot and not yet realized he was dead. On the far side of the circle, his zombie-like brothers snapped to the same rigid attention as he. The only motion among the lot of them was that of the tears that began to run down their cheeks.

"Alethos houtos ho anthropos huios theou en," Alfred said.

Stuart's Greek was better than mine—at least when it came to hearing the language spoken—and it was he who recognized the scriptural quotation: " 'Truly, this man was the son of God.' That's John."

"No, it's Mark," I said. "It fits with what I was saying: but why Greek?"

Jeff was hesitant—almost more in awe of what we were seeing than of what had already happened. "I think because you've made him *see* it, sir. You know I said we'd wondered if we couldn't look back in time—and now you've done it. They're really watching Jesus die—and they're fixated on it."

"Are you sure?"

"No, sir, I couldn't be, not without looking into David's mind myself: and I've already been nearly trapped that way once this week."

"If we don't bring them back," Stuart suggested, "they may be trapped, too."

"It looks to me like they're pretty well fixated, as Jeff says: I don't know how we could get them out, without breaking into the vision. And I'm sure you're right, Jeff, that it's too easy for you to get caught up in Alfred's stream of consciousness. But I'd be less susceptible. Can you, so to speak, pry open a crack in what he's seeing, and let me in through it? Maybe I can sort of get his attention the way you dream about a bell and wake up to find your alarm is going off."

"I couldn't do it ordinarily, sir, but maybe by concentrating so hard on the one thing, Lee will actually be kind of distracted. Besides, if he puts up a fight, that could be enough to distract him from distraction, so to speak. It's worth a try. But I think I could do better if we were all touching. Here."

Stepping closer, he took the bandaged hand in which I still held my cross, wrapped his cousin's unresisting fingers around it, and held both together in his own. For a moment, I could look at him and see that this wrestling with the stronger currents of Alfred's mind was costing him more effort than I would have imagined; but in the next instant, I was within the vision myself.

The setting was not, as we had thought it was, or as it perhaps had been, Calvary, but rather indoors, in a dimly lit room: the Upper Room, I assumed, where the Galilean disciples had gathered behind locked doors for fear of the Judeans. It was a sensible next scene, if Alfred's inner time machine was running at fast forward through the gospel history. I could pick out Alfred's face among the crowd in the shadows.

I hadn't thought, really, about what to say. But my mere appearance in the vision was enough to get their attention, just as I had thought it might be. That preconception on my part initially kept me from realizing that they were not reacting to me as a twentieth century intrusion on their vision of the first. But when I looked down at my feet, it was clear to me that, as the alarm clock appears in the dream in the guise of a bell, so I too had been given a place within the context of Alfred's vision; as a demon had appeared in the guise of the Prior, so now I too had, appallingly, taken on the guise of another. But, however disturbing my transformation, it at least meant that I knew my lines. "*Shalom aleichem*, peace be with you," I said, stretching out my wounded hands for them to see the imprint of the nails.

———

I HADN'T REALIZED that Danny and the kids would follow me into the monks' vision, but they did so, and when the crisis was past, they let me hear about it.

Daddy says, He doesn't think the Council of Ephesus allowed for four human personalities in Jesus.

Well, tell him they didn't allow for smart-aleck little brothers, either. And anyway, he means the Council of Chalcedon—Ephesus was about something else entirely.

Whatever. He says, How about if we come up and see you guys, now that the work's all done?

I'd love it. But get some sleep first.

You can depend on it. We'll see you this afternoon.

The Easter image of forgiveness—followed in St. John's Gospel by a commission to the Apostles to be agents of forgiveness—had in fact been enough to break through Alfred's single-minded absorption in the vision to which I had led him, and more, to do what I had originally intended—that is, to break through his equally single-minded absorption in his own sin and unworthiness. Such an obsession with what one has done wrong seems as if it should be only a step away from true contrition: but it's a step in the wrong direction, and its presence in Brother Alfred was the most insidious legacy the Abbot and Prior had left behind at All Angels.

Their other legacies, though less dangerous, required more labor to correct. Brother Alfred was, when the vision ended, still somewhat weakened by his ordeal—but a good deal spunkier than he had been at first. When he restored the other brothers to the full use of their faculties, they, too, seemed alert enough. Even so, with their help, it took a good deal of time to put everything into a presentable state. The chapter room had to be cleaned, eventually, and the ritual circle completely eradicated. But first there was the matter of the body.

The mortal remains of Colonel the Right Reverend James Trout, Bishop and Abbot, lay, as I have said, on the ruins of the altar he had made to his strange god—if, I reflected in a more Dantean moment, his soul had not been lost long before, and that body become the dwelling of whatever demon controlled it at the end. The brothers freed the corpse from the collapsed tangle of hospital tubes and wires, and as they stretched it out on the floor, we all saw the aged body Jeff had told us about. One of the monks glanced at me questioningly, and when I nodded, he began a prayer used at the time of death: "Deliver your servant James, O Sovereign Lord Christ, from all evil, and set him free from every bond. . . ."

As he prayed, the body changed again—not, so far as I could tell, into the appearance of the Abbot that had been projected to the world, but more subtly, into one no less aged, but less ravaged—it was the difference between a house that has been aggressively restored, one that has been deliberately wrecked, and one that has simply gotten old. I looked at Brother Alfred, but he shook his head; Jeff, who was standing beside me at that point, said, "No, sir, it's not an illusion this time—it's a change, for real."

When I finally left them behind to arrange things and turned my own attention to Larry, he was standing and talking with the other young men.

"Are you okay?" I asked, putting a hand on his shoulder and adding the mental question, *Is your grandfather still there?*

"Yes, sir, I'm fine. I could use another shower, though." *Not now,* he thought back, *but he's not exactly gone, either. Keep an eye on that skull for me.*

"We do have to get him cleaned off, sir," Richard said: which was true enough—Larry had a lot of cuts and scratches, particularly on his back, and several of them looked nasty—he was almost covered with blood.

"And we might be thinking about how to explain this to the coroner," Rob added.

"What am I supposed to say?" Larry asked. " 'I did a little war dance, and my grandfather and I turned into a bunch of animals, and then there was this lightning bolt that finished everything off.' I don't think that would sell very well."

"Insanity defense," Stuart murmured.

"Or else you'd have to call an elemental spirit into the courtroom to testify, like in Gilbert and Sullivan," Jeff added.

"*Iolanthe,*" I said, unwilling to let any allusion go unattributed. "I think Larry's right, though: no judge would believe him even if he changed into a wolf right there in the courtroom. The legal system isn't designed to deal with magic."

"But who's guilty, anyway?" Keeks asked. "The Prior attacked us, not the other way around, so it's self-defense, isn't it?"

"Not to mention that he had probably already killed the Bishop," Richard added.

"And was probably not human anyway," Stuart added.

"True enough," Rob said. "Besides, knowing what we do, could we say whether it was Larry or his grandfather that did this?"

"Or even the magic itself," Jeff suggested: "I mean, the power behind the magic. It seems to have a life of its own."

"Can you change yourself into a chestnut tree, Larry?" I asked. I thought at first he wasn't going to get the joke, but then he said, or chanted, " 'O chestnut tree, great rooted blossomer / How can we tell the blossom from the bole?' "

" 'O body swayed to music, O brightening glance, / How can we know the dancer from the dance?' " It was Brother Alfred who concluded the quotation: while we were talking, he had come across the room to where we stood.

"We cannot know, can we?" he went on. "Isn't that the point? Surely there's no legal question, whatever moral puzzles you're left with. There's no body, after all. All we can say about the Prior is that he's vanished."

"Rather literally," Stuart said.

"But still," Alfred answered, "you couldn't swear to more than that." He smiled. "You didn't really see it, after all."

"I did," Larry objected. "But I suppose you'll say that's not admissible."

"Not if the witness was a bear at the time, no," Rob said. "If that's the end of that, Father, shouldn't we be heading out of here and letting the brothers tend to business?"

"Before you go, Father," Alfred said, "what's left of the community thought you should take these." He handed me a key ring. "With the Abbot and Prior gone, you seem to be our only authority."

"Very well. Did you discuss the question of the election just now, as well?"

"Yes, Father. If we can, we'd like to move it up to tomorrow afternoon. Maybe that's too soon, but you know what it says in the Rule: 'they live in a community and desire to have an Abbot over them.' "

"Quite right, too," Rob said. "Any community needs to have someone in charge."

"There is still Jesus," Chris answered.

"But he seems to run most of his franchises through local managers," the monk observed. "What do you think, Father Mears?"

I weighed the keys in my hand, thinking of how I'd begun the week by setting out what was and wasn't my responsibility. "Well. You said it might be too soon. I suppose that, if you mean you and the other brothers won't have recovered from all this by tomorrow afternoon, you're obviously right. You know as well as I do that there's a long distance between absolution from our sins and removal of the sinful patterns of our common life. So it's certainly too soon to elect an abbot who would be able to lead you all out of this because he had already gotten beyond it himself. On that score, Chris is right: there's only one Captain of our Salvation, only one who was tempted in every way as we are but did not sin.

"The other side of the affair, though, is that everything I just said would be true of any abbot, anywhere—people don't hold the office on the basis of their own moral perfection. The sacraments have their effect by the doing of them, not because of our moral character. Any abbot, bishop or priest is bound to be caught up in the whole web of sin, just like any other Christian. The question is how grace and penitence are at work in the person: and you brothers may have a head start on that score.

"I think it would be best for you to have your elections. I'll bring the keys back with me tomorrow afternoon."

"That's great, Father, thank you.

"Mister Brandon," he continued, "would you rather clean up here, before you go back to campus? We have showers, of course, and a little sort of infirmary."

Larry nodded his head: "I suppose that would be better."

"That, and you'll be away from school a little longer," Jeff added, and everyone laughed. The sound echoed lightly in the great round room.

Chapter 7: Sunday, July 10

IT WAS A BUSY DAY—would have been a busy day, indeed, even without the complications of All Angels'. Visiting alumni meant that all three services were more crowded than usual, and that Mass took a good deal more time simply because of the greater number of communicants—though with RJ and Brad both administering chalices, things didn't drag on too long. Then there was the annual alumni business meeting and luncheon, somewhere in the middle of which Danny and the kids arrived (a bit earlier than I'd expected, but Rhys had helped with the driving, and I think used more than a radar detector to insure that it was safe to speed—though when I asked, he said it was because they had come up State Road 23 through Logansport instead of taking Route 31 with its notorious Kokomo bypass). Then our whole party from the night before went back to the Abbey—where, after I presided at another Mass, to ask divine guidance in the election, Br. Alfred (who had been duly elected and professed, however despicable the other ceremonies that were added on) was elected Abbot on the first ballot, to no one's particular surprise. He asked for some time to pray about it before accepting, and he and I walked for a while in the cloister garden: but when the time came he accepted, and I returned the keys of the house to him. The other formalities of his blessing and installation, we all agreed, should be postponed until after the funerals of the Abbot and the Bishop. But some modest sort of celebration seemed to be called for, and Rob invited the crew of us back to the cottage to take pot luck of whatever refreshments might be left in the refrigerator. Abbot Alfred seemed unperturbed by the prospect of inaugurating his reign with two-day-old snack foods, and his community (who were, as I later discovered, looking for a chance to throw together a party of their own) were happy to have him out from underfoot for a while. He took a few minutes to gather up some things he wanted to bring along, and to change out of his habit, then we all drove back to the cottage.

It was about 4 o'clock, I guess, by the time we were all seated on the deck with Cokes and iced tea and a strange assortment of leftover junk foods. "Might as well use it up," Richard had said as we brought out the remains of an antipasto tray and a deli package of cole slaw. "Whatever's left tomorrow we'll just have to throw out."

"Or up," Stuart answered, as he peered into a container of three-day-old onion dip.

"You certainly picked a nice cottage," the new Abbot said, looking back across the lawn toward the house. "It's good to see it in person."

"That really was you, then?"

"Oh, it was me, all right, Chris. As I said, I'd gotten the crazy idea that I could face down the two of them by myself."

"If there were two," Stu said.

"What do you mean?"

"The way the Prior vanished just when the Abbot died—that's fishy."

"Well, he certainly wasn't an illusion—I would have seen through that. And he opened doors and things. I've seen him eat and drink in the refectory, for that matter."

"He put up a hell of a fight for a figment of my imagination, too," Larry added. "My back's still sore."

"It will be for a while," Keeks said. "You've got some nice gashes there. You'll want to be careful not to get them infected. I wouldn't go swimming for a couple of days, to begin with . . ."

"If you can stop practicing pre-medicine without a license, Chris," Jeff said, "I want to hear the rest of Stuart's theory."

"Well, look—suppose we say the Abbot—"

"I think you mean 'former Abbot,' " Rob corrected.

"Right. Him. Suppose he was possessed—so much that there was hardly anything left of the human soul. Suppose the demon could only do truly human things through a human puppet. That accounts for why he wanted Brother Alfred—"

"All of which we figured," Jeff said.

"But we didn't figure on a familiar." Several people opened their mouths to respond, but Stuart pressed on, before they had a chance to correct him. "I know, the legends all say that witches were the ones who had familiars; but we know that isn't true—look at the Chaplain, and his family. And familiars are supposed to be in animal shapes—but there's no reason why they couldn't be human."

"Mephistopheles has a human form in *Faustus*," RJ noted. "I suppose you could even call him a familiar."

"But even if all this is true in general," Jeff said, "what makes you think it applies to the Prior, besides the time he vanished?"

"Well, first, what we've heard about his interest in getting people 'spirit guides.' Then the fight. I don't think he was a real *wabeno*, or he wouldn't have been able to fight with Larry."

"The old *wabeno* fought with each other," Larry said. "That's what grandmother said, anyway."

"They may have," Stuart conceded. "But not with their elemental magic—not with the same spirits involved on both sides."

"Like the Chaplain's sermon this morning," Keeks said. "If Satan's house is divided against itself, how can it stand?"

"That's exactly what I mean. 'Impersonal forces of nature' is fine, but you can't have the same force going both ways."

"I guess not," Larry said with a shrug. "I admit he seemed to run through the same changes I did, mostly, after the first switch."

"Which probably wasn't the best strategy."

"Right, Rob," Keeks said. "If he was a demon posing as human, though, I wonder how he lived in a monastery all this time. How could he say Mass, or even take communion?"

"The time Abbot Alfred appeared during Mass at Chapel, the Host seemed to scare off whoever it was that blocked him out," I observed.

"I think that was him," Alfred said. "He never said Mass at the Abbey—his name was never on the roster. I'll admit it was odd, but it was just one of those we've-always-done-it-this-way routines. And of course all the other celebrants were life-professed, too, so they could have known not to give him communion, even if he pretended to take it."

"There's something else, too," Brad said. "At least if I followed what everyone reported about last night. We've all seen that Mr. Midshipman Brandon had two preconditions to the use of his *wabeno* powers—the one being that he has to work *au naturel*, and the other that he has to wear his medicine bag. But from your descriptions, the Prior didn't follow the second of those rules, just the first one. That could be another sign that he was faking it."

"There was that skull he carried," Jeff said. "Wouldn't that serve the same purpose?"

Larry looked dubious. "There's supposed to be more to it than just a bone or something."

"Maybe he had other things in that sack," Richard suggested. "Can I get you something else to drink, Abbot?"

Alfred had gotten out of his lawn chair and was walking back toward the landward side of the deck. "Oh, no, thanks," he said, as he returned with the brown paper grocery sack he'd brought from the Abbey. Reaching inside, he brought out the Prior's cloth sack—made of purple velvet, I noted, now that I could see it for myself—and removed from it the red skull, which he set temporarily on the deck in front of him. "I thought we might end up wanting this," he said. "But as far as I can tell, the bag itself is empty. And it was certainly never designed to be worn." He passed the sack around for everyone to inspect it.

"This is more interesting," he continued, lifting up the skull, "particularly if, as I suspect, it belonged to Mr. Brandon's famous ancestor. Perhaps Chris could give us a coroner's report?" He handed the relic to Pruett, who examined it closely before answering.

"I imagine this was the cause of death," Keeks said, pointing to an area at the back of the skull. "You can see that a portion of the bone is missing. Now that could have been knocked out after death, but I don't think it was—it looks to me as though the whole area was bashed in with—"

"*A blunt instrument,*" we responded in chorus.

"Precisely. That's a contrast with the marks here," he said, turning the skull upside down and pointing to the bottom, "which are almost gouges, and look to me as though the cranium had been severed from the cervical vertebrae with some sort of a blade."

"Does it actually take some kind of tool to separate the skull from a skeleton?" Larry asked. "Wouldn't they just fall apart when they started to rot?"

"Yes, they would; but that just means that this head was separated from its body soon after death. I assume it was before burial, in fact, since this red color seems to me to be a stain of some kind that penetrates into the bone, and the gouges are the same color as the material around them."

"Can you say anything about age or sex, Keeks?" Rob asked.

I half-opened my mouth to take advantage of this straight line, but the look Danny gave me did not require telepathy to say "Don't even think about it." I pretended to clear my throat, and Chris went on unimpeded.

"Well, it's an adult, obviously. I can't say too much more than that. These two teeth that are left here are pretty well worn down, which would suggest relatively great age, or a lot of grit in the diet, or both. You could make a guess about sex by looking at the dimensions of the jaw and so forth, but I'm not that expert. It looks a little bit massive for a woman, though. It might be Brandon's grandfather, but that's about all I can say." He gave the skull back to Alfred.

"Psychometry?" Stuart asked.

The young abbot grimaced. "I'd been hoping to kick that habit," he said. "I mean, you've convinced me that it's nothing illicit, but I've begun to think it isn't entirely healthy for me, anyway."

"Nor for Jon, nor any of the rest of us, as a steady diet," Dan responded. "But it's fair enough to use your talents when you have to. Go for it."

"Very well." He stared down intently at the skull, and soon it seemed to float between his hands, the empty sockets gazing blankly at the rest of us. I had expected that Alfred would simply "read off" the psychical history of the object, as a cheap mentalist might identify a person based on a single touch

262 — John William Houghton

of the person's handkerchief. Instead, he proceeded in the same fashion as the forensic sculptors we've all seen on TV, making hundreds of measurements and adding clay a layer at a time until the outmost contours of a face appear beneath their hands. The disconcerting difference was that the Abbot's medium was light—or, rather, was our vision in itself: so that we saw, not neutral clay, but bloody flesh, white sinews, and pale yellow fat restored in sequence to the ancient skull, the staring eyes and their web of supporting muscles appearing fairly early, though the lids to close them only came with the last layer of skin. In the bright summer sun, the whole process had a faint shower of illusion, a glamour—but even the floating illusion of a dissected head was enough to make me momentarily regret the clam dip.

In a second or two, though, the thing was done, and in the same moment, Larry recognized the face: "It *is* Grandfather!"

"Are you sure, Larry?" Rob asked.

"I'm positive. I've seen him in my dreams, and when we danced together. That is him."

"Well, good," the Abbot said, releasing the illusion. "How'd the Prior get hold of his skull?"

"Maybe the grandfather was buried there at the Abbey," RJ suggested.

"Mr. Faber didn't think so," Larry said, "and this is where the lightning struck when I first used the bag."

"Maybe he could be in two places at once," said Brad.

"Or maybe he had two heads, like John the Baptist in the Middle Ages," Dan answered. "Jon, do we know anything about how he died, besides the Pakashak story? Real details, I mean?"

"Well, Larry may, and Luke Faber says there are some bits in original sources, if not in the history books. It would have been in 1839, I suppose. He was in Sumner's Tavern over at Wolf Creek when the kid got to him."

"Who was this Mr. Sumner?" the Abbot asked.

"A pioneer like the others, I guess—came up here in '35. There were a bunch of men who moved north to clear land before the main migration in the summer of '36."

"Did they all come from the same place, Chaplain?" Jeff asked.

"Well, yes, they had all been living down in Rush County."

"But they hadn't been *born* there, had they? Your own family was from England, right?"

"Right, Larry. And most of the other pioneers were, too. One fellow was from the Channel Islands, and then there was a Dutch family named Vorhees, and several from New England."

Jeff was obviously pursuing an idea: "Was Sumner one of the New Englanders?"

"I wouldn't swear to it, but I think maybe he was."

"That may be enough to explain it, Chaplain. Have you ever heard of the New England vampires?"

I hadn't, nor, apparently, had anyone else. "I didn't think there were all that many Pilgrims from Transylvania," Brad said.

"No, sir, I didn't say there were. I gather this was a local development, or else they brought it over from England with them. But there were still cases in the early part of this century where people were dug up and their bones burned beside their gravestones. Some people think the actual problem was tuberculosis—but that doesn't make any real difference. The point is that this Sumner may have believed in vampires, and when he heard the local stories about *wabeno* being a kind of undead, he went back to some local customs from his boyhood—separating the head from the body and burying it in special dirt, probably with garlic in the mouth. The head was buried some-place near the regular burial ground, on what became the Abbey property; the body was buried here."

"So maybe that's why great-grandfather never quite went away."

"Not just because his body was buried in pieces," Chris said. "The world would be haunted by everyone who ever had an appendectomy."

"Or a haircut; sure. I meant, because he wanted to see his body re-united. Native Americans did think that was very important. Maybe he fixated himself on his elemental spirit purposely, instead of accidentally—just so he could stick around."

"Wouldn't he have had to know ahead of time what was going to happen to him after he died?" Caroline asked.

"Not necessarily. I mean, it would depend on when he died, exactly: whether it was right away or not until after this that Sumner made his plans."

"Just barely possible," Chris said, "Lincoln held on all night with a mas-sive head wound."

"Well, I don't know what the details were, but I bet he'd be a lot happier if his head were buried with the rest of him. Can we do it?"

"I'd be surprised if it's covered by the lease," Rob said, "but maybe we can be careful with the turf, and get the lawn back in place the way we found it."

Jeff nodded his agreement. "At least we won't have to look all over the place; presumably that rise in the lawn is a burial mound."

"There are some gardening tools in the garage," Richard added, "but it'll be hot work in this weather." He looked at Jeff and grinned.

"Sorry," Jeff answered. "There are limits. Besides, a little perspiration builds character."

"In that case, I'll just watch," said his cousin. "I must have enough character built up to last me quite a while."

In fact, there weren't all that many tools at hand. Abbot Alfred, Brad, RJ, Dan, Caroline and I all ended up standing around and watching while the younger guys stripped off their shirts, took up shovels, and gave a reasonable imitation of the Keystone Kops on an archeological dig. Larry, I noticed, was still wearing his medicine bag.

"I hope there's nothing of historical value in the topsoil," the Abbot said.

"Not likely," Dan answered. "I suppose it's been picked over fairly thoroughly. As late as the 1970s, one of our cousins gave the county museum a collection of over a thousand stone arrowheads and axes he'd found just by walking through plowed fields over the years. Course I was a little jealous—I'd hoped he would give them to me."

"I gave you some arrowheads once," I said.

"Yeah, I remember," he answered with a smile. "And look where that got us."

Sumner had buried the *wabeno* under a single stone slab—more, I assumed, as a precaution than an honor. Jeff's opinion was confirmed by the inscription on the stone, revealed when the boys had removed all the dirt: MALEFICUS: SANCTE MICHAEL PUGNA PRO NOBIS CONTRA SATHANAM—that is, "Wizard. Holy Michael, fight for us against Satan." (Not a particularly Puritan sentiment, I reflected, but this was a 19th century New Englander: perhaps he'd been fraternizing with the Irish.) After a good deal of grunting and arguing about leverage, and just as we sidewalk superintendents were beginning to think that we'd have to get our hands dirty after all, the excavation crew managed to move the monolith. The pit beneath it had been filled with some sort of red dirt—a clay high in iron ore, I suppose—and the boys had enough sense to sift this aside carefully, a project which involved another raid on the garage for some paint brushes and trowels.

Eventually, the remains themselves were exposed—there were a fair number of beads, which seemed from their distribution to have once been attached to clothing, but no real grave goods of the sort that a family might have buried with the departed. All of these the young men left as they were; without saying anything, the others stepped out and left Larry to dust out a space above the shoulders of that red-stained skeleton, and put the crimson skull in its place. He did so carefully, and when he had himself clambered back up onto the lawn, he looked to me. "Is there something we can say?"

"Surely," I answered. "Would you take a handful of dirt and scatter it in the grave when I get to that part of the prayer? You'll know when it is."

He stooped and gathered up two handsful of the plain dark topsoil of the lawn. I paused for a moment to make sure that I recollected the whole of the familiar blessing. "In sure and certain hope of the resurrection to eternal life through our Lord Jesus Christ, we commend to Almighty God our brother, and we commit his body to the ground: earth to earth, ashes to ashes, dust to dust. The Lord bless him and keep him, and make his face to shine upon him, and give him peace. Amen."

For the first time in weeks, it began to rain—that is to say, simply to rain without being a worse than useless gully-washing thunderstorm. The slow easy downfall was not much more than a sprinkle, but it continued steadily enough that, before the mound had been reclosed, we all looked like examples of the wet-drapery style in classical sculpture.

Before they turned to their shoveling, though, there was a last act. Larry untied the medicine bag and laid it in the grave. "What does Prospero say when he breaks his wand, Father?"

"Something about rough magic, but I don't remember it, quite."

" 'To the dread rattling thunder,' " RJ quoted,

" 'Have I given fire, and rifted Jove's stout oak

With his own bolt . . . graves at my command

Have waked their sleepers, oped, and let 'em forth

By my so potent art. But this rough magic

I here abjure. . . . I'll break my staff,

Bury it certain fathoms in the earth,

And deeper than did ever plummet sound,

I'll drown my book.'

"It's from the beginning of Act Five, but he doesn't actually break the staff till the end of the act."

"That's the part I was thinking about, though: 'This rough magic I here abjure.' It's served its purpose: now let it go."

The Abbot, who had been standing behind him, put his hands on Larry's shoulders and, turning him around, looked intently, powerfully, into his eyes, as if reading what lay behind them.

"You understand there's more to it than that—you have your own talents, besides the powers of the medicine bag. You can't just reject them, any more than the Chaplain and his family or Jeff and I can." For the first time, he sounded truly abbatial, a paternal voice despite his relative youth.

Larry nodded. "I know, the bole can't refuse to blossom: but at least the dancer can choose his own step."

"But not the music," Chris said. "The morning stars sing together, but not to any human tune."

Rhys shook his head. "Music and dancing and blossoms and stars. It's all true enough," he said, "and I imagine between us Larry and I are going to have a pretty interesting first class year. But shouldn't we get on with the work before we're raided by the SPCM?"

"SPCM?" Caroline asked.

"The Society for the Prevention of Cruelty to Metaphors, my sweet. Here, take a shovel. Just because you're a girl—"

Stuart interrupted him before he had a chance to get in real trouble. "Acid rain," he said, and pointed into the grave.

There, as the misty spray of raindrops struck them, both the medicine bag and its owner's bones seemed to dissolve in a slumber into that quiet earth.

Part III: The Consul's Jewel

Introduction

As PRESIDENT of the Standing Committee of the Anglican Church in the Diocese of Michigan City, I called together the Diocesan Convention promptly after Bishop Parker's death. To my embarrassment, they equally promptly decided to elect me to fill the vacancy, and after some parliamentary maneuvering (for they had not been summoned as a special Election Convention), they did so. I prayed about it, and if I heard no actual voice of divine approval, at least I heard no heavenly objection. (And if, as it seems to me on reading back over it, that sentence appears too flippant, it is assuredly humor rooted in the real distress of not knowing, of having no seraph like Isaiah's to burn one's lips with a coal from the altar of God, as a little wake-up call.)

Ordinarily, the election of a bishop in the Anglican Church requires the consents of a majority of the sitting bishops and of a majority of the standing committees of the other dioceses. With a hundred and three dioceses, however, and some two hundred bishops, that process inevitably takes a while, and as a result, there's an alternative: if an election is held within three months of the triennial General Convention of the national Church, the Convention can vote the consent, by a majority in the House of Bishops and by a majority of the diocesan delegations in the House of Deputies. Just to make it more complicated, the three clergy and three lay deputies in each delegation are counted separately, and it takes a majority in each group of three to win the delegation. As I was elected within a few weeks of the General Convention, my name was, inevitably, introduced for consents on this fast-track process.

And thus came the second embarrassment of the whole affair. The Diocese of Delaware, having withdrawn the name of the Reverend Donald Newman from the ordinary consent process some two years before, after the episode in which I helped to draw attention to his questionable past, asked that he, too, be voted consents by the Convention. Church politicians had been sure, when his name was withdrawn and the plan to present it to Convention announced, that Delaware was hoping to match the liberal, "Broad Church" Dr. Newman with some theologically conservative candidate from one of the other two flavors of Anglicanism, the "High Church" (or "Anglo-Catholic") party and the "Low Church" (or "Evangelical") party. I myself had expected no less, but I hadn't imagined that I would be the other half of the deal, as a poster-boy for the High Church movement. Rumors of Donald Newman's not having been properly baptized, of concern to the Lows and the Highs, but not to the Broads, were played off against stories that I was so medieval as to believe in Christian magic (only the newspapers used the word "witch"). That I should think such a thing was an idea offensive to the Broads mostly because it wasn't some form of New Age Neo-paganism (though it admittedly made some of my own sponsors nervous as well).

It did look for a while as though we might actually *both* be denied consent, but Archbishop Williams managed to arrange a grand compromise that put us both into office. If I'd had somewhat less experience in such matters, I'd have called it a Devil's bargain, but Axton persuaded me it was worthwhile just to have my voice in the House of Bishops, even at the cost of having to listen to Donald Newman as well.

Chapter 1: Tuesday, October 17

"CAN YOU TAKE a call, Bishop? It's Professor Dacre."

"Of course, Mrs. Equitone. Which one is it, though—him or her?"

"It's Professor St. John Dacre, Bishop. Just a moment please. I'll put him through." I discovered early on in my new job that having a secretary provides one a few seconds to prepare oneself while calls are being transferred in. St. John Dacre, Kingery Professor of Art, Director of University Museums, and President of the Faculty Senate at our diocesan university, usually takes a bit of preparation: and not just to remind oneself to pronounce it "Sinjun." One notices immediately that he is erudite, voluble, and passionate—rather as one notices that an oncoming avalanche is heavy, cold and hard.

"Jonathan, are you still Chancellor of this madhouse?"

"That would be the 'madhouse' of Our Lady of Walsingham, I take it, St. John. So far as I know, the Charter hasn't changed lately, why? Trouble at the University Bookstore again?"

"If you want to call it a bookstore. They seem to sell more T-shirts than anything else. Do you know we're the largest outlet for insignia items in the state of Indiana?"

"It doesn't surprise me, certainly. But it does help keep up faculty salaries, after all."

"I suppose it does. Still, I could suggest a few savings on the salary line item—a certain tenured colleague in the English department, for example."

"Aha. Now you're getting to the point."

"Jonathan, I am at the point, and past it, and have been for some time now. If I hear another syllable about 'the endangered Anglican identity of Walsingham,' I shall do a good deal more than scream. There are a considerable variety of edged weapons here in the museum, and every time I leave my office for the Faculty Senate, I say to myself that that case of daggers next to the elevator is a proximate occasion of sin. Or at least it's going to be if this keeps up. Can't you just ship this woman back to Australia, or inhibit her, or something? She's a priest, you're the bishop. Take charge."

"Now, St. John, you know perfectly well I can't do any such thing. You folks on the faculty voted years ago to give Margaret Wilson tenure, and the fact that she's a priest has nothing to do with her university status. It wasn't a matter of buying a pig in a poke, either; I mean, she's always been pretty conservative."

"This isn't just conservative, Jon, it's positively revanchist. You know she's been pushing a resolution to require that a numerical majority of the faculty be Anglican. All the non-Anglicans are afraid for their jobs, and the Anglicans themselves are at each other's throats, depending on whether they agree or not. So at the Senate meeting yesterday, I said, as a sort of *reductio ad absurdum*, that since most of the undergraduate teaching is done by graduate students, logically a numerical majority of the graduate students should be Anglicans as well. Of course the Dean of the Graduate School immediately rejected any such idea, but when the student paper came out today, damned if Maggie didn't have a letter in it arguing that we need more Anglican grad students. I ask you! I mean, is there some special Anglican way of curating that I should be aware of? Some collect to J. Pierpont Morgan in an obscure section of the Prayer Book that I should say every day? Or an annual commemoration of the founding of the British Museum?"

"You *are* Anglican, St. John. Your parents were Anglican. I bet your grandparents were Anglicans."

"Yes, on both sides, and so on back for a dozen generations or so. I'm actually descended from Charles, King and Martyr, for that matter, albeit on the wrong side of the sheets. But as far as Professor Wilson is concerned, family pride counts for nothing when the current generation actually consorts openly with Dissenters and Recusants. And I'll spare you what she has to say when I suggest there's nothing wrong with having Jews or Moslems or Hindus on the faculty, even if they outnumber us. I mean, we are a minority denomination, even in England; but she just says that's all the more reason."

"Well, why not? The mere fact that you and I don't agree with her doesn't make her wrong; maybe Anglicanism would be strengthened by having a university all of its own."

"We had *two* universities all to our own in England, my Lord Bishop, from the Clarendon Code in the 1660s to Catholic Emancipation in the 1800s, and I don't think the state of religious piety at Oxford and Cambridge for that century and a half is much of a testimonial to the devotional value of enforced religious exclusivity. The Methodists and Evangelicals grew up almost in spite of it, and the Oxford movement began as an attempt to prop up its already decaying corpse."

"What a charming image you do paint, St. John. But surely you've tried all these arguments on Maggie without getting results—what more do you expect from me? Seriously, now."

"I certainly don't expect you to change *her* mind. I don't imagine anything short of direct personal revelation would. But a few well-chosen words from you could go a long way toward calming everybody else down. You will be preaching in Chapel on Sunday, won't you?"

"For the University's patronal feast? Of course: but it will be for Choral Evensong; I have a Visitation in Logansport in the morning. The daily offices aren't exactly well-attended services, though, are they? If I'm supposed to re-assure the threatened non-Anglicans, Evensong seems an unlikely venue."

"Ordinarily, it would be. But with the current atmosphere, you could preach at two in the morning and get a fair crowd if someone let your topic be known a bit ahead of time."

"Very well, then. Evensong it is. At least the agnostics will get to hear some good music that way. Are you sure the Acting Vice-chancellor won't resent this unwarranted interference?"

"She thought it a good idea this morning at breakfast. But officially, she's staying out of it altogether. As a Roman, anything she said would be in-flammatory. So I'm taking the point on this mission and she's conducting a novena to St. Jude for the Search Committee to finish its work soon and fill the vacancy so that she can return to the study of the Byzantine court. She was telling me last night about an article she's working up on the slitting of noses as a way of eliminating possible claimants to the imperial purple. She says she finds it all strangely calming after a day in the Administration Building."

"Well, tell her I unofficially said 'hi,' then. I'll see you Sunday evening."

"Surely. Now, what I really called for was to ask whether you can come by the museum on Saturday: we'll have a new item on loan I think you'd like to see."

"Something for your Alfred the Great exhibit?"

"Yes, but it hasn't been in any of the publicity yet. I didn't think I'd be able to get it—but it's being hand-delivered Thursday."

"Very good. I won't try to guess. I have to travel later on Saturday afternoon. Shall I come by about 1:00?"

"Yes, that should give us plenty of time. I'll meet you at the front door at one o'clock. And thanks again."

"No trouble, St. John. I'll see you then. Bye."

I entered the appointment in my computer's electronic date-book; the machine took the opportunity to blink out a reminder that I was about to be late for lunch. One advantage of being bishop of even a relatively small diocese like Michigan City, rather than chaplain of a relatively large prep school like Annandale Military Academy, is that the food is a good deal better. There are several excellent restaurants within walking distance of my cathedral, and of course Chicago is easily accessible by car or, amazingly at this point in history, interurban. And best of all, despite a rather generous endowment to support the episcopate, people are frequently eager to buy you a meal. Had Wimpy been a bishop, he would never have had to ask Popeye for a sandwich.

On this particular Tuesday, I was to meet Richard Davies at a little Welsh pub called Y Ddraig Goch on Third Street, not far from City Hall and the Library.

"I'm off to lunch, Mrs. Equitone. I should be back about 1:30 or so."

"Yes, Bishop. Don't forget your umbrella; it's supposed to rain." After what happened to my predecessor, they're still touchy about rainstorms around the Diocese.

"I'll be careful, Mrs. Equitone, don't worry. See you after lunch."

Y Ddraig Goch—the name is Welsh for "The Red Dragon," referring to the national symbol—is a narrow old brick building whose interior seems at first glance to be mostly a vast black bar of generally British flavo(u)r. Eventually, as one's eyes adjust to the dimness, one sees a few booths in the front room, in roughly the same proportion to the bar as Falstaff's bakery bill to his bar tab. The back bar, however, has more tables and more light, and that was where I found Richard, sipping warily at a glass of mead. Beer brew pubs are common enough these days, and quite a few wineries run their own restaurants. But Ddraig Goch is one of few places, I think—and probably the only one in Indiana—to brew its own *metheglyn*.

"*Nos da*," I said as I sat down.

"Good night to you, too, Jonathan," he replied with a smile. At rather more than six feet tall, with straw yellow hair, Richard runs toward the Saxon in outward appearance—but he has a sardonic sort of wit that seems to me an equally legitimate expression of his Celtic genes. In this case, it was evident that my occasional forays into learning Welsh with Rhys and Caroline were not having the desired effect. "I think you mean *bore da*," he added.

"Well, night or day, I hope you're having a good one. How's the local product this week?"

"Not bad at all, really. This particular one is a surprisingly dry sort of a mead, actually—sort of at the Chablis end of things. You can taste the honey flavor, but it requires you to stop and think what honey tastes like *besides* being sweet."

"I see. How about the potency? Do I dare have a glass if I'm going to go back to the office?"

"Oh, certainly. I have to drive all the way back to Annandale, and I think I'll be safe with this one sample." The server came by with my menu and place setting, and Richard somewhat ostentatiously ordered me a mug of the special in Welsh. She nodded and wrote something on her pad, but I suspect she was judging from gestures as much as from Gaelic.

"That does remind me of a story, though," Richard went on. "You know, of course, that King George VI was anything but abstemious, even during the War, and Queen Elizabeth the Queen Mother was known to have an occasional drink as well. So legend has it that one day in the sixties the Queen Mum was having a private luncheon at Buck House with her daughter, and the Queen—who drinks a good deal less than her parents ever did—said 'You know, mother, I believe I'll have a glass of wine with lunch.' To which the Queen Mother replied, 'Are you quite sure it's safe, dear? You *do* have to reign all afternoon.' "

I laughed. "You can just about picture it, can't you?" I said. "Two tweedy ladies dining alone but for slightly worn furniture, five staff and about half a dozen corgis. I don't accept the premise, though, that there's no work involved in being a bishop. You'd be surprised at how busy I've been for the last year."

"That I might, if you didn't mention it about every time I see you. But here's the waitress back to take our orders."

I hadn't actually looked at the menu, but I didn't need to. "Do you have the lamb today?" I asked, as the server set down my mead. The lamb at Ddraig Goch is exceptional—they dust it with an insane amount of ginger and black pepper, pour honey over that, and put loads of rosemary over the honey. And the whole thing is roasted, very slowly, in a pan about half-full of mead. If God had tasted this, the recipe would be in Leviticus.

"Oh, yes, Father." (We Hoosiers tend to be a bit uncertain about forms of address.) "What would you like with that?"

"Peas and potatoes, I think. And could I have the watercress salad, please?"

"Of course, Father. And you, Doctor?"

"I'll have the *cawl*, please. That comes with homemade bread, doesn't it?"

"Yes, it does. I'll bring a loaf right out, along with the salad."

As she left I said to Richard, "You know, you wouldn't have to order these ethnic specialties on my account. I mean, it's fine if you'd rather have tacos or something."

"They'd probably have to send out for Mexican. Besides, I like *cawl*. Just think of it as a way of using up all the leftover lamb from the days when you don't eat here."

"Meaning I don't leave any leftovers? I don't eat that much," I objected. "In fact, I've lost three pounds since I stopped dining in the Mess Hall—seven or eight meals a week calculated to meet the dietary needs of teenaged boys is not well-suited to a middle-aged man."

"No, hardly. Perhaps that's why we don't have more *emeritus* faculty."

"It's what got Dean Hunt, I bet. Remember back in '69—he took the steps to the Mess Hall two at a time, just as if he were a cadet, then collapsed right inside the door."

"Oh, I certainly remember. I was sitting at the faculty tables under the mezzanine, and the Commandant saw the whole thing. He took off toward the Dean, but he gave two orders in the time it took him to stand up—one for me to call the ambulance and one for the Officer-in-Charge to keep the kids under control."

"Right. Of course most of us didn't even have any idea something had happened until he came on the PA system and called us all to attention. There are some benefits to military discipline when you're trying to manage a crowd of teenagers."

"Does that mean you're not in favor of making Annandale a civilian school?"

"Was I ever?"

"There for a while in the '70s you were, as I remember. But it was in the air, I suppose."

"Well, maybe. And supporting a military system for the school is not the same as supporting the war in Vietnam, either."

My salad and the loaf of bread arrived, and after we said grace, Richard picked up a different thread of the conversation.

"You must remember Major Fletcher."

"Of course. He taught me first year Latin, back when I was a Fifth Classman."

"That would have been in '65–'66."

"Yes; exactly thirty years ago. But then he left. I had Commander Lindsley for Latin after that: he was a remarkable teacher."

"He was, indeed. I was going to ask you, though, if you knew Doug Fletcher at all."

"The Major's son? No, not really. He must have been three or four years older than I was. A big kid on the playground when I was in kindergarten, that sort of thing. He didn't go to the Academy, though—I'm almost sure he went to school downtown."

"Indeed he did. In fact, he graduated from Annandale Consolidated in 1966."

"Is that connected with his father's leaving?"

"Indirectly, yes. You see, he didn't register for the draft, but ran away to Canada. There were quite a few folks on the faculty who thought he'd had a little help from Dad to get away. Then when David Melvin was killed in July, things got a little ugly, and the Major decided to move on."

Annandale lost more graduates in the First World War than West Point—not per capita, mind you, but in absolute numbers. My fellow alumni have earned Congressional Medals of Honor in every conflict the nation has entered since the school began—the exhibit in their honor on the second floor of the old library (itself built as a memorial to the Gold Star men of the Great War, as they called it before they knew there was going to be a second one) makes a sobering version of the *carpe diem* scene from that Robin Williams film. One young graduate, extraordinary in being decorated during peacetime (it was 1933), noticed during target practice on his battleship that a spark had gotten loose in his gun turret, and threw himself on a bag of powder for a 16 inch gun to shield his mates from some of the force of the inevitable blast. Another died at Midway on December 7, 1941, holding his position against the surprise Japanese attack, even after receiving orders to retreat, until the last personnel of his headquarters were evacuated. One led his squadron back to base after taking flak over Korea, though his copilot had to land the plane when the commander had lost too much blood to survive. David Melvin was only the military advisor to an ARVN squad, but he covered their retreat. When a VC platoon had him surrounded, he refused to surrender; when he ran out of ammunition, he clubbed several more with his rifle, until they decided he wasn't worth the trouble involved in bringing him back alive. He hadn't been all that outstanding a cadet, actually, but his death inevitably made him a kind of icon—the more so when his parents sent his Medal of Honor to hang with the others in the Gold Star Room. By the time I was a First Classman in '70, the anti-war movement had permeated both the faculty and Corps of Cadets; but for a couple of years after his death, Melvin was too powerful a force to counter. It was no wonder the Major had moved on.

"What makes you ask about Fletcher?"

"I met him recently at a conference."

"Another world-religions affair?" I asked warily.

"Well, yes, it was. He was there representing Paganism."

"Do you mean 'paganism' as in indigenous cultures or 'paganism' as in a bunch of Californian screwballs pretending to be witches?"

"Neither, actually. I mean classical paganism, as in the noblest Romans. He worships Jupiter the Best and Greatest, you see."

"Surely you're not serious."

"No, really, I am. He's quite devoted to the old gods—not in a vulgar sort of way, of course, but after the fashion of the upper class."

"I wouldn't have thought the Roman upper class generally believed in their religion at all, as a religion. I always pictured Cicero and that lot as endorsing the Olympians for the sake of civic piety, but putting their real devotion into philosophy and the mystery cults. And it's hard to believe that Augustus and the Senate really thought Julius Caesar had become a god."

"Well, no, hardly. But Fletcher is interested in the last flowering of paganism— when Emperor Julian I tried to root out the corrupted parts, to make a better competitor for Christianity, or when Q. Aurelius Symmachus opposed removing the pagan altar from the Senate House in Rome."

"Julian the Apostate, as we called him in seminary. If I remember correctly, his project wasn't much of a success; though I suppose Doug Fletcher would argue that he was killed before he could make a go of it. Is he actually getting people interested in this?"

"Oh, yes, quite a number. They offer all the traditional sacrifices on the major feast days, keep the little family gods in the living room, and so on. And they are putting out a nice set of translations of Latin religious poetry and prose—mostly older versions, but nicely gotten up, and a good deal cheaper than the Loeb Library series."

"Is this a colony of some sort?"

"Apparently there is a central headquarters—someplace out in the northwest, though I've forgotten exactly where; but people can belong without living there."

"And are they building temples? I understand there's a Parthenon available down in Nashville."

"You laugh now, but I think they are planning to put up a classical building. Though if I understood him correctly, it was Augustus's *Ara Pacis* that they mean to copy."

"I can imagine that an 'Altar to Peace' would score well on the New Age front, and as I remember the sculptural program of the original is dedicated to family values, which could make the whole enterprise seem somewhat less loony."

"Isn't it rather unchristian to be so judgmental, Jonathan?"

"By your own description, they're pagans, Richard. Do you remember what happened the last time? One minute it's all Augustus and family values, and the next minute I'm a hundred and seventy-five pounds of Lion Chow in a magenta bag. Bishops have not historically dealt well with pagans."

Our meals arrived at that point, my lamb redolent of herbs and honey, and Richard's stew the instantiation of hearty. Outside, the rain had begun, with a wind coming off the lake: the coming cold front would be a reminder that autumn was well under way, and the rich brown glop in Richard's soup plate promised a homely comfort; a marigold blossom floated atop it, surrounded by an artistic arrangement of chopped leeks and parsley.

"Do you care for a flower with your lamb?" he asked.

"Of course. But I've surely convinced you by now that they're not poisonous. What have you got against them?"

"Well, if you must know, they're not Welsh. I checked a British cookbook: Putting flowers in your stew is an English custom, it said. And I see no reason to encourage Sassenach habits in a Welsh pub."

"Admirable loyalty," I said, eating the flower myself. "What's the news from AMA?"

"Not much to say, really. The public debate about going civilian is heating up, but there's not been any acknowledgment that the Board is even considering it—so all the arguments are conducted more or less *sub rosa*. No one on the faculty would want to take too extreme a position and then find out the Board had decided to go the other way."

"What, no one? I'm disappointed."

"Well, I am over-generalizing. In fact, that's partly what I wanted to talk to you about. I'm a little concerned about our Deputy Commandant."

"Captain Cicero, you mean? What's the problem?"

"I think he's overcompensating. He's the first person in that office in years not to have had a real military background, and he seems to be determined to be twice as military as anyone else, just to make up for it. As for the prospect of a civilian school, he fancies himself the defender of Annandale tradition, and the natural rallying point for concerned alumni everywhere."

"And the Board does not look with favor upon faculty who attempt to go over their heads to the alumni."

"Not even a little bit, no. Since you know him fairly well—"

"Well, I knew him as a young camper fifteen years ago, and I've worked with him in the summers."

"And he's renting your house. Don't be modest, Jonathan: You have made an impression on him, and as a prominent alum, and former faculty member, you're in a better position to tell him to cool off than most of us on the scene. I wouldn't want him to get fired from his first job."

"Well, neither would I. I'd have to find another tenant, among other things. I will have a talk with him as soon as I can. What's he been doing, besides threatening to awaken the sleeping alumnal giant?"

"He's organized two sets of weekend maneuvers already, and it's only mid-October—we haven't had maneuvers since you were a cadet, I don't believe. Of course, yours were required parts of the ROTC, but these are voluntary affairs, like those paint pellet war-games, and he's getting huge crowds of kids involved. Then he's added another drill team, for underclassmen, in addition to the Annandale Rifles, The Four Gun Drill, the Bengal Lancers and the Crimson Eagles: this group has a Highlander theme."

"That fits with the school's name, at least."

"True enough. And now he's gotten on the mailing list of a catalogue company that sells replicas of historical weapons, so he's organizing some sort of medieval wargames. I saw him in the full kit out in front of the old library the other day with a storm coming across the lake, and I swear it looked as though he were about to throw his two-handed broadsword out just to see an arm in white samite pop out of Glenarm's Bay and snatch the blade out of the air. I've actually had students ask me about tactics at Cressy and Poitiers. Before this year, I don't believe most of them had even grasped that there was a Hundred Years War, much less asked me for details of the French Order of Battle."

"All of this sounds great—he apparently has the kids actually interested in the military, instead of just tolerating it. But . . ."

"But if the Board has decided to go civilian, real interest in the military is the last thing they want to see. Exactly. Perhaps you could convince him that he should just slack off a bit. It must be exhausting, after all."

"I should think it would be; but he is very young, and the kids can be energizing when they're eager to learn what you have to teach."

"Yes, they can—energizing to the point of addiction, as we've both seen in more than one case. But I don't think Philip has come to that yet. He's certainly getting his share of hero-worship, but the whole school runs on that fuel. You just need to make sure he's more cautious about adult politics, that's all."

"I'll do my best. But here's our server back. Are you having dessert?"

"I was meditating on that before you came. We've got our choice of Lemon Cheese Pudding, Pice Ar Y Maen, or Teisen Sinamon."

"And ice cream," the waitress added. But Richard passed over the suggestion with nationalistic disdain.

"Three equally light and pleasant concoctions, if memory serves," I answered with some sarcasm. "I like the cinnamon cake, but not today; even if there weren't my diet to think of, I might want to stay awake for the afternoon."

"Yes, well, I suppose you have a point. I should get back to school myself, too, despite the allure of hot little Welsh Cakes with raisins and currants and lots of butter on top." He shook himself as if from a reverie: "Thank you, miss. I'll just have the check, please."

As I said, I rarely have to pay for lunch.

⁓

THE BISHOP'S PALACE—I always wanted to live in a palace, as a child, and I have no republican scruples about using the old-fashioned term—takes up most of a block on Washington Street near the center of Michigan City, only a couple of blocks from the Cathedral. Built by a railroad baron in the Belle Époque, it's a huge brick Tudor house with formal gardens, really almost large enough to deserve its title: though downtown redevelopment has resulted in a shopping mall on the back side of the property, I do get the compensation of flying my episcopal flag from a very respectable pole at the corner of 6th and Washington. There's far more space than one middle-aged bachelor needs (I shall soon have to stop saying that I am middle-aged, for Danny, in the cheeky way of younger brothers, invariably asks me how many ninety-year-old people I actually know: though, as far as that goes, there *have* been members of our family who passed their quincentenary). It's a somewhat more suitable place, though, for the said aging bachelor, his niece, and a distant cousin destined to be her fiancé—particularly if the younger generation are students at a local university and can save their parents a pretty penny by commuting across town instead of living in dorms. Even with three of us (each wanting a separate bed-room and study), and a live-in housekeeper with her own apartment on the first floor, the place is by no means full, but we get a reasonable amount of use out of it. The diocese is put to no particular expense, as the Smitson Fund—the endowment I mentioned before—covers my salary and the house, and the kids (or their parents) chip in for the food. I paid for the redecorating when we moved in, though there were a few do-it-yourself improvements that the four of us in the family put in during a house-blessing one night when Dan was able to come up and stay over. They're not quite like the blue protections around the old family homestead, but the palace is as well-defended as we know how to make it at the moment, and our younger generation remind me that there's always the possibility of progress: not that I have time to be doing a lot of research into the Arts Arcane.

Neither of the kids was home when I got there, but Mrs. Jameson was at work in the kitchen. I have to admit that I at first found it pretentious that I should have a domestic staff—other than perhaps someone to come in and dust, but even on that front the habits developed by a lifetime in military schools make a difference. I'd be useless in battle, but when the enemy took my headquarters, they'd find all the underclothes neatly folded. Carl Carlson, who eased the transition considerably by staying on as Archdeacon, finally convinced me that I needed help. I'd been protesting that I was a perfectly good cook, and quite capable of entertaining for a large crowd. He pointed out that whereas my guests in the past were willing to have me running back and forth from the kitchen checking on dinner while they kept each other occupied with small talk, official guests of the Bishop expect to spend time with the Bishop, and don't necessarily anticipate that their only chance to chat with the chief pastor will depend on their willingness to help peel potatoes. So it was that some of the ladies in the Cathedral parish set themselves discreetly help me find some help; and thus, in turn, came Mrs. Jameson.

Now, to begin with, Mrs. Jameson is a better cook than I am—not an insignificant qualification. Having grown up in Louisiana, she has an enviable repertoire of Southern dishes (all of them welcome to me, who still remember every detail of my first meals at Galatoire's and Commander's Palace); and of course she actually had professional training as a chef at some point. But she gets extra credit in my book for an expert knowledge of British cookery, though Danny, Rhys and Caroline all seem agreed that this is an aspect of family heritage which need not be pursued with so much diligence as I am inclined to devote to it. In any case, if I ever want Cajun Brussels Sprouts, I know that I can get them, along with a clean house, a carefully managed household budget, and discreet advice about my wardrobe that would do justice to Bunter or Jeeves. It had never occurred to me, when I was wearing plain black, how many shades of purple shirts come in.

She was working in the kitchen when I came in. I suppose I might have yelled something from the door, but it seems a bit informal, and Mrs. Jameson hasn't exactly invited informality; nor, I suppose, have I. So I walked down the hall from the garage, past the housekeeper's apartment and the back stairs and into the kitchen before I said good afternoon.

"Good afternoon, Bishop. Here's your Coca-Cola." She had it ready, in a glass with just the right amount of ice.

"Thank you very much, Mrs. Jameson. Heard the car in the driveway, eh?"

"Well, no. Actually, I usually go by the sound of the garage door opener. But you can't expect me to explain all my little tricks."

"No, of course not. I'll console myself with finding out the secret ingredient in your Sauce Béarnaise."

"If wishes were horses then bishops might ride. I'm planning to have some of those filets from Price's tonight, though, so you'll have another chance to guess. But it's no fair hanging about the kitchen to watch."

"That's just as well. I have to work on my sermon for Sunday evening, and I believe I have meetings every night but Friday, so I should get to it while I can."

"Very well. Mr. Evans and Ms. Mears said they would be home around 6:15, so I plan to serve the meal about 7:00."

"Right. Seven o'clock it is. I'll be working in the Library."

"Very good, Bishop. Have a nice nap."

Formality is one thing, but respect, apparently, is something else again. Still, I did doze off for a few minutes, and Rhys called me for Evening Prayer about half past six. I can't claim that I have always said the whole Daily Office—though I'm pretty good about Morning Prayer and Compline—but having both a family and a chapel in the house, it seems a shame not to say our prayers together when we can. And it's surprising how often I'll be sitting at a meeting of some sort and suddenly realize that something from one of the daily lessons bears directly on what we're discussing—a phenomenon which has had the edifying result of moving some of the folk of the diocese to say the office themselves, just so they'll be prepared for these episcopal outbursts.

"I understand," Caroline said when we had sat down to supper, "that you're going to talk about our Anglican identity Sunday evening."

"I heard that he was going to announce faculty hiring quotas and a new admissions policy," Rhys answered.

"On the face of it, Rhys, that suggests that you're a couple of steps farther down the rumor tree than Caroline," I said. "Still, I'm surprised that either version of the story has made it around campus this fast. St. John Dacre and I just talked about it this morning."

"Well, Rhys and I naturally hear anything about you fairly quickly: but people do seem to be awfully interested in this business."

"What do you two make of it? And could I have the green beans, please?"

"Is that litotes or zeugma?" Rhys asked, passing the dish. Both of them were studying rhetoric in a required freshman writing class.

"Linking two unrelated ideas in parallel is syllepsis, actually, which is related to zeugma, but I don't think it counts if they are in separate sentences. Litotes is understatement. Now answer my question."

"You go first, Car, since your sources are apparently better than mine."

"Well, you hear a whole bunch of arguments. There are a few people who haven't liked anything in the Anglican Church since the sixties, and what they think is that if they can make the college more Anglican, then the lib-eral—mainstream Anglicans won't want to come here, and this can be the beginning of the counter-revolution. Then there's several of the traditional parties in the Church—Anglo-Catholics, Evangelicals, and so on—who think roughly the same thing with respect to their own groups. And there are a surprising number of Evangelicals in the fundamentalist sense, who don't really care about the school being Anglican, but want to make sure that it remains Christian, instead of becoming completely secular like Harvard or Yale."

"God forbid," I said, averting my eyes from the needlepoint Harvard seal hanging over the sideboard.

"The other side," Rhys said, "argue that Anglican character is just a shell game, that it just means whatever someone wants it to mean; or that the true character of Anglicanism is comprehensiveness. They say that our churches have always been open to whoever wanted to come, and our universities should be the same."

"There's some truth to that," I interrupted. "The Archbishop was reminding us at the last meeting of the House that English parish churches were required to provide a seat for anyone in the neighborhood who wanted one, regardless of where they usually worshipped. The Church of England was meant to be the Church for every Christian in England, period."

"Exactly," he said. "Then there are people who see their own disciplines, at least, as basically secular—the 'How-do-you-do-Anglican-physics?' crowd. And there are a lot of people, of course, who actually belong to another denomination, or believe in some other religion entirely, and don't want to intervene in our family quarrel. And finally there are the agnostics and atheists, who think the whole thing is just more evidence of how ridiculous religion really is."

"Thanks; that gives me a clear picture of the territory. But what do the two of you really think?"

They glanced nervously at each other across the table, and after a couple of false starts in which they both tried to speak at once, Rhys thought a message at Caroline—*Go ahead!*—with a scowl that said as much as its psychic complement.

"Touchy subject, eh?" I said.

"Well, sort of, Uncle Jon. Rhys and I don't disagree about very much, and we haven't had a lot of fights, but this business does have sort of an edge, I guess. The best we've been able to do so far is to try to understand each other, and I guess Rhys did a fairly good job just now of summing up what I think—not the atheist part, of course, but the part about Anglicanism being a sort of generic denomination that's supposed to be open to anyone who's interested enough to follow the rules. So it seems to me that anyone who wants to study or teach at an openly Anglican university should be able to. That's not an argument for dropping our Anglican heritage, it's just saying that the heritage doesn't mean we have to shut everything else out."

I turned to Rhys: "And the Anglo-Catholic view?"

"Is that the Church is more than least-common-denominator Christianity— it's fine to say a parish church should be open to everyone willing to come, but if ninety percent of the congregation are, say, Presbyterians, you're bound to end up with either a distorted version of Anglicanism or a bunch of unhappy folks. The thing is, having you in charge and a paper commitment to the Anglican Church won't be enough to give the place its historical Anglican character when there aren't any Anglicans actually in the University."

"You're both fairly convincing. I take it from the rumors you quoted that I'm identified with the keep-it-Anglican side?"

"Not necessarily," Caroline said, "I think everyone expects, or hopes at least, that you're on their side, whatever it happens to be, and Rhys just happened to hear one form of the rumor."

"Not just happened, Caroline. After all, I'm much more likely to hear a rumor from the people I agree with than from those I don't. Not that people aren't speaking to each other, but there's still a certain built-in selection factor."

Caroline nodded. "I'm sure you're right. So basically, Uncle Jon, everyone will come to the sermon on Sunday evening expecting you to agree with them."

"Charming," I said. "It's always nice to know that you're bound to offend half the congregation regardless of what you say. Perhaps I should avoid the whole thing and just preach on our Lady of Walsingham."

They both shook their heads. "That would just provoke people to guess what you really meant," Rhys said.

"I'm afraid you'll have to bite the bullet," Caroline added.

"Well, it's several days away, and there's no sense fretting over it. I think I'm ready to bite the dessert, actually. Would anyone else like a piece of pie?"

IT WAS ABOUT two hours later, I think, that Rhys called us into his study—originally one of five bedrooms on the second floor. He was sitting at his computer desk and chuckling when Caroline and I, who had both been in the library, came to his door.

"What's so funny?" she asked.

"This bulletin board," he said. "Come look."

The screen looked fairly normal to me—several paragraphs of text separated by a few lines of the abbreviated gibberish that passes for computer addresses—and I said as much.

"Come on, sir," Rhys said. "There's no need to be pretentious with us."

"All right, I'll grant you it's apparently all in Latin, but that's not all that funny. I think there's a Latin short-wave radio station, so there might as well be Latin e-mail. How did you come across this hilarious feature?"

"I didn't say it was hilarious, I just thought it was amusing, that's all. I was looking up sources of information for my paper on Cicero for Freshman Writing, and this service was listed; but it didn't say the whole thing would be conducted in Latin. Can one of you two read it?"

"Let me try," Caroline said, pulling up a chair. "We'll see if I learned anything at University High." She had in fact gotten a very respectable 790 on the College Board Latin exam, as Rhys and I both knew, and she skimmed through the screens almost as quickly as if she were reading English. "It looks like this is more a set of texts than a discussion, actually. I mean, it doesn't seem to have a lot of original Latin composition, just mostly quotation. There's not a thing about Cicero in the last few exchanges, though; they seem to be citing big chunks of Boethius. He's late Latin, isn't he, Uncle Jon?"

"Early sixth century, yes. He was prime minister to a Gothic king in Italy, and wrote *The Consolation of Philosophy* when the king tossed him into prison for intriguing with the Eastern Emperor."

"Well, apparently these folks are interested in something called '*Quomodo substantiae.*' "

"Right. That's one of his little theological tractates; they have some interest in themselves, but I think they were more important about a hundred years ago as evidence that the old boy really was a Christian."

"Why wouldn't he be?" Rhys asked. "Wasn't Christianity the official state religion by then?"

"Well, yes, but there were still quite a few pagan holdouts. And the *Consolation* never seems to mention Christianity, which could be a sign that he was a pagan. I mean, you'd sort of expect a Christian to find his consolation in religion rather than philosophy, if you see what I mean."

"I guess that would be sensible, yes. Do you see anything useful there at all, Car?"

"Not much, no. It seems to be all later stuff, though there's a bit here about St. Jerome and Cicero that I'll translate for you if you print it out. And if you'll run get my Latin dictionary, I think I can post a message for you asking for help on Cicero."

Leaving them to the task, I went back to the library and the ticklish problem of my Sunday evening sermon.

Chapter 2: Wednesday, October 18

AT DEAN PHILIPS's request, I say the early Mass at the Cathedral on Wednesday mornings when I'm in town. The parish congregation at St. Paul's doesn't have to pay for maintenance of the ornate Gothic building, but even so, the budget doesn't stretch far enough to provide a large staff of priests, and the Archdeacon and I help out wherever we can. We don't usually open up the main church for weekday services; there are two chapels on the crypt level, which also houses the parish and diocesan offices. Since the cathedral is built on a sloping site, the north side of the crypt is at ground level, and the window of my "basement" office looks out toward the lake. The main crypt chapel, however (beneath which some of my deceased predecessors are buried), doesn't have any windows at all—a bit *too* cryptic for me; so I ordinarily exercise my episcopal prerogative by holding the Wednesday services in the small private chapel next to my office. There isn't space for a large congregation, but that's rarely a problem at 7:30 on a Wednesday morning. The eighteenth of October, however, is the feast of St. Luke the Evangelist, patron of physicians, and a group of his protégés had notified the Dean that they would be in attendance: so the service had been scheduled in the larger space. Had I had a cynical mind, I might have suspected that they'd planned to come to the early service because the twelve-thirty midday mass would have interfered with tee-off for their afternoon golf games; but the idea never occurred to me. Nobody likes a smart-aleck, even in a miter.

Now since we were to be in the crypt chapel, the Altar Guild had set up for Mass with liturgical equipment from the parish's collection, rather than with my private things; so I had to go upstairs to the parish sacristy to get a matching set of vestments. All of which explains why, having turned down the invitation to breakfast with the doctors, and having returned the parish's vestments to the sacristy closet, I was alone upstairs in the main church at about a quarter after eight. At least, if you had asked me, I would have said that was where I was; it was where I had been when I went into the sacristy, and when I began to walk down the north aisle to the stairs. But before I had taken three steps, the scene changed completely, from a line of Gothic arches, their stone gray in the light of an autumn morning, to a white marble colonnade gleaming in the full blaze of a summer sun. At the west end of the cathedral, there is a rose window above the balcony; from where I was standing, it had been just visible through the arches of the aisle. The space that suddenly opened up around me ended instead in an apse; through the colonnade, I could see that its walls and half-dome were richly covered with mosaics: above all, there was Christ, pictured just from the shoulders up, surrounded by clouds and angels, and beneath that a cross standing on some sort of hill, with the water of life running out from it. I had the impression that there were people, perhaps even a small crowd, standing about in this other space; but in the brief moment that the splendid vision lasted, I saw no one clearly—and by the time I thought to breathe again, it all was gone. I went cautiously back downstairs to my office, and was still sitting at my desk a quarter of an hour later when Carl came in for our usual morning conference.

Someone once described Carl (in terms originally applied, I think, to Heywood Broun) as looking like a large unmade bed; certainly his years at Andover and Harvard did little to inspire in him a taste for sartorial elegance, though his perma-rumpled clerical suits come from J. Press and Brooks Brothers, and his perpetually uncombed hair receives biweekly attention from a barber at the Harvard Club of Chicago.

"What's wrong, Jon?"

"Good morning to you, too. Did I say something was wrong?"

"No, but you also didn't make tea for yourself, nor coffee for the rest of us; nor do I see a Coke on your desk. And yet I know that caffeine and mornings are inseparable for you. Ergo, I suspect that something is wrong."

"I do value your penetrating intellect, Carl, honestly. It's just that I'm still not quite used to having people take such an interest in my state of mind."

"So you've said more than once. But I can't help thinking that what you mean is that you're not used to having other adults take such an interest in you: from what I've seen of young Mr. Pruett and the other members of the Annandale Alumni Association—"

"The Summer Camps have an Alumni Association. AMA itself has the Annandale Legion—it's like the Foreign Legion, we join it to forget."

"Well, judging from members of the Legion, then, your students have been looking out for you for years. But let us not digress. What's today's problem?" He settled down on the couch, prepared to listen.

I described the vision for him, and his face took on a knowing look before I had quite finished.

"When was the last time you were in Rome?" he asked.

"I've never been to Italy at all. I take it this means you recognize the building, though."

"Well, yes. The mosaic gives it away, as far as I know, but there are a couple of other signs. If I understand you correctly, this is a huge basilica, with double colonnades on each side, but the columns don't match."

"Sort of. What I meant to say was that the columns matched pair-by-pair across the nave, but none of the columns was the same color as either of the ones next to it."

"Right. That is what I thought you meant—I just spoke imprecisely. I suspect that if you had noted such details, you'd also tell me that the columns were from different architectural orders. That variety, and the double aisles, are significant. And the other thing is that your visionary church appeared to have its altar where its entrance should be. That could just be a coincidence, an accident of the way you were standing, but the fact is that there are two huge double-aisled churches built with the altar in the West rather than the East: and one of those has the mosaic you described."

"And that would be?"

"It would be St. John's Lateran."

"The Pope's cathedral? My goodness, I hope this isn't a sign I'm going over to Rome."

"I doubt it. You see, the apse-mosaic represents Christ the Savior, which was the original name of the church. The mosaic had an entirely blue background when Constantine built it—just the way you saw it; but eventually the bottom half was replaced with gold. As far as I can remember, they changed it sometime well before the Reformation, so I think you're safe on the symbolism front. It might mean you're going to become a medievalist, but that's hardly a news-bulletin."

"Not when you put it that way, no."

"Well, then. If we've established the place, let's turn to a different angle. You called this a vision: what did you mean, precisely? Where did this come from?"

"I honestly couldn't tell. That's what I've been sitting here caffeine-less trying to figure out. Given my past experience, I think I can rule out hallucinations, for the moment at least. But at the same time, I don't see how it could be magic (which would be the other immediate possibility), since I was wearing my ring the whole time, and never felt a twitch out of its defenses; nor did my cross react."

"Did any of your extra-ordinary family sense anything?"

"No, and the way we've tied the rings together, one of the kids would have contacted me instantly if they'd felt something. If it was magic, it was of some sort we've never seen before."

"What about telepathy? Would that set off your defenses?"

"No, and for that reason, I think it's the strongest possibility. I did have one other experience like that, with Abbot Alfred, as you have heard me say. Though I wasn't wearing my ring then, and I confess to being puzzled, now that you've identified the scene, as to why someone would send me a mental picture of St. John's Lateran."

"Well, the remaining possibility is that it was in fact a vision."

"It could be, I suppose. Your logic is certainly persuasive. But you've been a priest for nearly forty years—have you ever known even one real case of a vision?"

"No, I haven't; but then again, you are our Bishop, Apostle and Prophet now. Bishop Parker may have had visions, but it wasn't the sort of thing he would have discussed with me."

"Nor with anyone else, I dare say. It's not an Old Blue sort of thing, having visions."

"And not very much of a Crimson one, either, Jonathan. But we've exhausted my line of deduction. What do you propose to do?"

"Nothing—well, no, not nothing. I'll go on praying about it. But a passing and unintelligible vision can hardly be a basis for action. So I shall await understanding. Meanwhile, I suppose I should go put the water on."

"No," Carl said, "I can take care of that. You'd better boot up your computer and see what's on your schedule for today."

THE SCHEDULE in fact included a conference call with my neighboring bishops in Chicago, Kalamazoo and Indianapolis about setting up a meeting of our regional Bishops' Committee on Ministry—one of the bodies that advises us on the suitability of candidates for ordination; later in the morning, there was a meeting with the diocesan psychologist, to hear his reports on the people I'd be sending to BCOM. By then it was time for lunch, which (in keeping with the feast) I had with the Chief of Surgery from University Hospital. Then in the afternoon, I drove over to Mishawaka, where my having tea with an elderly widow gave promise of considerable reward for the Mission Establishment Fund (one of my colleagues had reminded me, at my first meeting of the House of Bishops, that fundraising is a task for the head of any charitable organization—"If you don't ask, they won't give," he said. "A president of Harvard once got 2.5 million for your alma mater by proving he could spell 'chutzpah.' ") Then I stopped at a hamburger stand for dinner (Mrs. X. was a relentless vegetarian, as it turned out) before a meeting of the board of our retreat center, over in Bristol; from there, I took the Toll Road ("Main Street of the Midwest") back to Michigan City, and by a little after midnight, I was home. Mrs. Jameson had left a plate of snickerdoodles out for me.

Chapter 3: Thursday, October 19

HAVING HAD NO NAP on Wednesday, I slept in a bit on Thursday—my appointment for the day was in Kokomo, which is quite a drive, but I didn't have to be there until about 11:30 for a luncheon and afternoon retreat with the United Churchwomen of our southern deanery. We finished earlier in the afternoon than I had expected, and as my evening meeting was with the board of the Wabana County Historical Society (to which I had been elected back in the relaxed old pre-bishop days), I decided to stop by Annandale to see for myself how Philip was doing.

The school itself was virtually unchanged, of course, though the Commandant's office had been moved, in the same year I left, to the basement of Verdun Barracks (the twin of Ypres, where we had had our day student lockers when I was a first classman—there is something distinguished about a school where most people can't even pronounce the names of the buildings). I had a moment of alumnal irritation at the move, wondering why they couldn't have left the office at Sally Port, where it had always been before; I had to admit, though, on more sober reflection, that the new location put the Commandant at the center of the campus, rather than on the periphery. I found Phil at his computer console, typing in the dispositions of the various disciplinary cases he'd heard during the day: the quarter-page yellow report slips from which he was working had not been changed in the course of the relocation.

"You know," I said, standing in his office doorway, "if you had a secretary, you'd be out of the office and ready for supper."

"Bishop Mears!" he said, looking over the top of the monitor. "It's good to see you! Excuse me for not getting up, but I have Alvarez through Delacorte alphabetized in my lap."

"Well, as I was saying . . ."

"Yes, I heard what you said: but I know what you were thinking, too—the boy never could get his paperwork done on time. But I haven't missed my meal yet—SRC isn't for twenty minutes."

"Then let me give you a chance for a bit more procrastination. Let me buy you dinner down at the Corner Tavern."

"Sounds good to me," he said, carefully transferring a pile of report slips from his lap to the desk. He stood and looked down dubiously at his army green trousers: "Do you think it's okay for me to go to a tavern in uniform?"

"It wouldn't have been twenty years ago, no—they used to have a separate door at the back for academy faculty. But I imagine if I can go in wearing scarlet, you can wear green."

"Good point, Father-in-God. Where are you parked?"

We took a booth toward the rear of the tavern, less out of Phil's concern for offense of our respective constituencies than my own sense that our conversation might prove sensitive. We made small talk till the waitress came to take our orders (like 95% of the other customers, we asked for the fried chicken), and then I tried to ease my way into the subject.

"So how's the boarding school life look after two months on the job?"

"It's pretty good, I guess. 'Course working in summer camp gave me some idea of what to expect, and in a lot of ways this job is easier. The high school kids follow directions better—when they follow them at all—and you get to live in a real house by yourself, instead of a cabin full of kids."

"That's important, really—getting some time away: particularly when you do camp and the school year together."

"I know what you mean. When you get down to it, I've been here since the middle of May, 'cause I came down right after my college grad to work on the grounds crew. This job hadn't opened up yet, and I thought I should earn some money while I could."

"Yes, I remember. Have you been able to get away at all?"

"Once, right after camp. A bunch of us went up to Chicago for the weekend. But then I had to be back to get set up for Plebe Orientation by noon on Monday."

"How was Chicago?"

"Okay, I guess. I don't remember much of the weekend."

"A couple of daiquiris too many?" (He was making good progress on a frozen strawberry drink at the time I asked.)

"No, not really. I hardly drank anything, to tell the truth. But I slept most of the weekend. Most of us did, in fact. Brian even fell asleep at dinner on Saturday—nearly did a nose-dive into the house dressing."

"Did you at least buy Frango mints?"

"Yes, I did. We were staying at the Palmer House, so it was only a couple of blocks up State Street to Field's, and I figured if you're going to be hooked on chocolate, you might as well stock up at the source. And they keep really well in the refrigerator."

"I know they do—yours isn't the first supply to have been stashed in that icebox, either. How was Plebe Orientation?"

"Okay, I guess. You can only have so much fun teaching kids how to march."

"I heard that you'd turned out to be more military than the Joint Chiefs."

"Dr. Davies must have spoken to you. Lately he's been to dropping hints what Sir Arthur Harris was to dropping high explosives."

" 'Bomber' Davies, there's an idea. Well, cut to the chase, then: can you put his hints into your own words?"

"Sure. He thinks if the Board decides to go civilian, they won't have much use for anyone who wanted to keep the school military. But there's one thing he's not allowing for," he said, holding up his Annandale summer class ring.

"You mean the alumni will force the Board to keep the school military."

"Yeah, but more than that. I mean people like us—or like me, anyway—alumni who work at the school—have an extra obligation to defend the school's traditions. We're the front line troops, the distant early warning system that lets the rest of the Association and the Legion know when the Academy's core values come under attack."

"I see the obligation . . ."

"But I'm being too idealistic."

"No, not idealistic, really, just wrong. There's no question that alumni carry a lot of weight, at this school or any other, just as parents do, and for roughly the same reason, that is, that they're the school's main sources of money. And the composition of the Board reflects that, after all—the presidents of the Alumni Association, the Legion and the Parents' Association all sit on the Board. But in fact neither the parents nor the alumni are responsible for the Academy—nor are the faculty, at this school—only the Board is. That's the legal and moral fact of the matter."

"But—"

"No, wait a second, Philip. There's more to it than that. It's not only that the Board is the sole responsible agency, but more that the Board has to be *seen* to be in charge. They would be negligent in their duty if they allowed alumni or parents or faculty to *think* they had some sort of final authority, because then some future Board might be confronted with one of those groups opposing them."

"So this is the administrative version of the old adage about beginning teachers never smiling until Christmas?"

"Sort of. But what I'm pushing toward is for you to see how this actually cashes out. The Board feels obliged to prevent any future opposition the same way the Centers for Disease Control feel obliged to prevent any outbreak of smallpox. And right now you look to them like that last little vial of variola."

"The one they're keeping in the deep freeze till they decide whether to destroy it completely."

"Precisely. And if I understand Dr. Davies correctly, you should feel very grateful if you don't feel anything worse than the early onset of a very cold winter."

"So I can chill out or be wiped out."

"That's your choice."

"So at least I'd make the point. I mean, if they fire me for trying to stir up the alumni, I may be gone, but that will stir up the alumni."

"No, Philip, I'm afraid not. In the first place, they won't fire you for contacting alumni. They'll find something much more likely to stand up in court, and if they can, they'll do other Boards the favor of making sure that no one ever hires you again. Not to be obvious, but look: You're a single man, and you've developed a whole new set of programs that put you together with the boys—programs above and beyond the requirements of your contract. Now I know you've had more girlfriends than Carter had little liver pills: but what you have to see is that if someone should decide to eliminate the virus, they'll find a way to construe something, and you'll be offered a final opportunity to resign. And since you will resign, there will be nothing to react to; and if you don't resign, the alleged reasons for your dismissal will be discreetly circulated, and not one single alumnus will raise a finger to help you. And the kids won't remember you a month after you're gone."

"They still remember you."

"Not many do, I bet. And I'd been at the school forever when I left. And I had my fifteen minutes of tabloid fame: *Anglicans Elect Witch Bishop*, and so on. Even the corps would remember something of the sort. Unfortunately, however, you're not a witch."

"Well, fortunately, I'd say, from what I've seen. But I guess that I'm persuaded not to be a martyr."

"Not over Annandale, at least. There are things worth dying for, much less being fired over, but our dear old school isn't one of them."

"Okay, fine. But isn't there some way to help the school stay military?"

"Not ultimately, no. The Board could be beyond the reach of reason, after all. But barring that, the thing to do is work on your admissions: if kids are coming here because the school is military, that will be the most persuasive argument that anyone can make."

"I can see that. I think some of the new stuff I've been doing will help admissions, as far as that goes—at least if the kids talk to their friends at home the same way they have to me. Are you going to have dessert, by the way?"

"I hadn't better, I suppose. They're bound to serve something at the meeting this evening. Don't let me stop you, though."

"No danger of that. But you may want to reconsider. They've got some fellow now who bakes the most amazing pies—I guess he's retired or something, and bakes these things in his kitchen, and lately he's been selling them."

I listened with growing amusement. "You have to remember, Phil, I haven't stopped being a native of Annandale just because I moved to Michigan City. Your mysterious pieman would be my cousin Lester. His grandfather and my mother's dad were brothers, and they used to run a dairy here in town. Then for quite a while they had a grocery store, as well, and I think Lester's dad used to bake desserts for the store. So Lester's just reviving a tradition."

"So does all that mean you'll have some after all?"

"Oh, sure, why not? My clothes don't fit me anyway." I ordered the old-fashioned cream, and Philip asked for butterscotch. "What do you do with your medieval warriors, anyway?"

"Well, recreation is the point. We try to duplicate medieval things as closely as we can. So by next spring I hope we'll get to take a trip out for the annual medieval war in Pennsylvania."

"I think I've heard of that—the loser gets Pittsburgh, isn't that the idea?"

"Yes, that's the one. But of course things here in the Midwest are so much more spread out, and there's not so much medieval simulation, and most of that is for adults. So it didn't look at first like we would have a chance to practice. But then I got to talking to Andy Clay, who's interested in Civil War recreation, and it came to us—why not have some fun by crossing periods? What if a Civil War platoon met up with a band of crusaders, for example?"

"That has some possibilities. Have you actually arranged an away game with one of Longstreet's companies, or something of the kind?"

"Well, no. The Civil War buffs aren't all as flexible as Andy. But I have found an odd school in Milwaukee with a legionary unit, and one of their advisors is going to be coming out here to look over the facilities. So we may actually set up a Romans versus medievals battle before the weather gets to be impossible."

"That sounds good, Philip. You could even have a catapult contest."

"You were on the Annandale Catapult Team when you were a cadet, weren't you?"

"For the two years that we had it, yes. In fact, I appeared on national TV at the time. They needed extra footage of kids 'talking Latin,' as the producer said, so there I was with some kid from Indianapolis, both of us in togas, and we couldn't think of anything to say to each other but 'hic, haec, hoc, huius, huius, huius.' "

"And the joke would be . . ."

"Nothing, I guess. It's just word for 'this' in the different forms. I mean, we couldn't actually carry on a conversation in Latin. The producers didn't know any better, so they put us up behind the opening titles. Latin teachers all over the country were amused."

"I'm sure they were laughing with you, not at you, Bishop. Here, let me get the check."

"No, that's okay, Philip. I remember what new teachers get paid. You just make sure you keep earning a living so you can pay the rent on that house."

"I'll do my best."

Chapter 4: Friday, October 20

TRAVEL HAS ALWAYS been a problem for bishops. Some historian from the dark ages—Bede, I suppose it must have been—complains that there are people living back in the hills who've never seen a bishop. And then there was a later character who was beloved by the people of his diocese because he occasionally took the time to get off his horse when he came to town to perform confirmations. Certainly, I wouldn't be doing my job if I weren't out on the road during the week as well as over the weekend. But there's a clear price to pay in office work whenever I get back. Mrs. Equitone and Carl keep the office running very well indeed while I'm gone (in some ways, I'm sure, it's easier for them when I'm not around to look over their shoulders) but inevitably paperwork accumulates that only I can do, or some crisis comes up that needs episcopal handling. It's like being a CEO and a traveling salesman at the same time.

Friday's crisis came in the form of a poster Carl brought to our morning meeting. "What's your feeling about traveling evangelists?" he asked.

"Oh, I don't know. We didn't see many of them come through a town as small as Annandale. They're not my cup of tea, but I suppose they're about the same mix of frauds and honest folk as anybody else."

"But you thought of frauds first."

"I guess I did. But what do you expect? If you preach in a cathedral, you're bound to be a little dubious about people who preach in a tent. I suppose I'd have had my doubts about the Wesleys if I'd lived back then."

"And vice-versa."

"Well, sure. Dissenters have always taken aim at the bishops, ever since the Reformation—not that the Wesleys were Dissenters, of course."

"Indeed. You'll be pleased to know, then, that the venerable tradition is being upheld. I saw this on a light pole Wednesday evening."

It was a poster, printed in screaming letters on a fluorescent pink and green cardstock: I include a facsimile, but a copy in black and white can hardly do it justice:

New Hope Evangelistic Center and Channel 43
present

"I WAS A SLAVE OF SATAN"

Evangelist
Br. Hudson Buchanan
FORMER WITCH & HIGH PRIEST OF SATAN
and
AUTHOR OF FANTASY NOVELS
reveals the secrets of THE NEW AGE—
LIBERALISM—and the OCCULT. *DISCOVER*
how fantasy games are corrupting our children
and rock music recruits teenagers for the legions of
HELL. *FIND OUT* how LUCIFER intends to *destroy*
American civilization. *HEAR* how babies become
sacrifices to Satan. *SEE* how witches already control
the *papers*, the *media*, *TV*, the *Government*, and
even the CHURCHES! LEARN God's plan to save a
remnant from Antichrist and the Power of the Beast.
This Friday, Saturday and Sunday
Oct. 20, 21, and 22
Ely Auditorium, New Hope College
Homer St. at Franklin Ave.
7 p.m.
Free Will Offerings Will Be Accepted.
The Buchanan Symposium's Midwestern Tour. Quad
Cities, Oct. 6-8; Milwaukee, Oct. 13-15; Michigan
City, Oct. 20-22; Detroit, Oct. 27-29; Cincinnati, Nov.
3-5; Louisville, Nov. 10-12; St. Louis, Nov. 17-19.

I put the paper down on my desk with a laugh. "Strange. I don't remember meeting Br. Buchanan at meetings of the Grand Coven."

"Chuckle if you will, Jonathan, but I phoned a couple of my colleagues in dioceses he's already visited. Most people hadn't even noticed him, but the Archdeacon of Milwaukee said she'd seen one of the posters there. And she's convinced they didn't say a thing about witches in the Church."

"So I'm going to be his special feature for the local crusade."

"That's what it looks like to me—if we're really lucky, he may even make the regular TV news. You'll note he's being sponsored by WNHE as it is: We'll be getting some free publicity."

"Oh, yes, I saw. But we've been through the publicity thing once already, after I was elected—and we survived that. This too shall pass."

"I'm sure it will, but I don't know how quickly. After the election trade-off itself, when you were about to be consecrated, the objections were from inside the Church: nobody wanted to make too much of a fuss, for fear of embarrassing the institution, and just out of a general sense that Anglicans don't make fusses. Add to that the fact that a considerable number of people didn't want to go on record as believing in magic in the first place, and the net result was a very understated sort of scandal. Br. Buchanan has few of the same restraints."

"No, I don't suppose he does. But what am I supposed to do?"

"Be forewarned, I guess. You might want to talk to Boyden Smith about what to do if someone wants to interview you."

"I'd rather not. I'm sure he's a good attorney, and I know the Chancellor values his services, but he's unctuous to a degree that makes my stomach turn. Feel free to take it up with him yourself, but I don't care to deal with him if I don't have to."

"That's fine—it's what I'm here for, after all. Now, have you thought about the vacancy at Valparaiso?"

So we moved on to other business. About halfway through a discussion of funding the diocesan newspaper, I made a mental note to say something to Caroline and Rhys at dinner.

I needn't have bothered. When I got home and walked into the kitchen, I found Mrs. Jameson working at the stove. "What," I said, "no Coke? Did someone oil the garage door opener?"

"No, Bishop. But I'm not sure you'll have time for a soda. Mr. Evans and Ms. Mears asked for an early dinner so that you could all go out for the evening, and Mr. Evans said you might want to change clothes."

"Did he indeed? Are they upstairs?"

"Yes. I believe they're watching television in the family room."

She was, as usual, correct. When I came into the room (which connects my study to the hall, on the front side of the palace), the kids were draped in ornamental postures on the couches, their attention fixed on the local news.

Caroline looked up as I came in. "Hi, Uncle Jon. We're waiting to see if we'll be on TV."

"Whatever for?"

"Haven't you heard?" Rhys said, without turning around. "There's a witch hunt on. We want to see if we're targets."

"We thought they might put our pictures in the ads," Caroline explained.

"More likely me than you, sweetheart," I answered, taking a seat in the armchair nearest the tube. "Brother Hudson seems more concerned with witches in high places than with ones in Freshman English."

Rhys muted the program with the remote. "So you know about this guy already."

"Yes, the Archdeacon brought me up to speed on his crusade this morning. Is that the family entertainment you had planned for this evening?"

"Yes, Rhys and I thought it would be fun to go and see first-hand what the old fake has to say."

"What makes you so sure he's a fake?"

"Oh, come on, Uncle Jon. 'High Priest of Satan,' he says. How can people believe it?"

"*We* can believe it," Rhys said indignantly, and I reflected that their unaccustomed disagreement over the character of the University seemed to be spilling over into other conversation. "We've seen a whole monastery full of devil-worshippers, and I'm not sure how far you could vouch for some of my branch of our own family."

"Oh, sure," Caroline said, sitting up. "But can you picture any of them becoming a traveling evangelist and bragging about it, even if one of them would have repented?"

Rhys paused as if in thought, whether considering her objection or simply trying to remember which side of the proposition he had originally defended. "Well, no, I can't."

"Nor can I," I said. "But I'm not so convinced as you two that the fellow can just be laughed off. Carl's persuaded me that he may actually have it in for me—Brother Buchanan, I mean, not Carl."

"Well, there you are then," Rhys answered. "All the more reason for the three of us to make a reconnaissance in force."

"Let's hope that force doesn't come into it," I said. "But it does sound like fun. Let me change out of clericals and I'll join you for supper—go ahead and start without me if Mrs. Jameson has it ready."

An hour later, having finished supper and dropped Mrs. Jameson off at the movieplex where she was to meet some friends, we were driving into the parking lot of Ely Auditorium. Rhys made the left turn off Homer into the gigantic parking lot (the Evangelistic Center draws in more worshippers than the mall does shoppers, a fact its Pastor mentions with some frequency in his ads), and pulled into the nearest spot, leaving us the better part of a block from the doors.

"I think there are nearer spots, my dearest," Caroline said.

"There's no need to be sarcastic, I just thought of something. Does one of you have a penknife?"

"I do," I said.

"Good. And Caroline, are you wearing your cross?"

"Sure."

"Great. And I have a convenient wooden-handled scraper here right under the seat. I think we should take a few laps around the auditorium before going in."

"And put a shield around it, you mean? What for?"

"You know me, Car. I'm just cautious. There's probably nothing to this guy, but if there is, we might as well make sure he can't call in reinforcements."

"Wouldn't he have reinforcements with him in the auditorium, if he had any at all?"

"He might, but there's no reason why he'd have to. We don't have to have your dad here with us, after all."

"That's true. What do you think, Uncle Jon?"

"I certainly see the point of being well defended, but, granted for the sake of argument that the shield could be left incomplete and thus inconspicuous until some vital moment, have you given sufficient consideration, do you think, to the question of whether, or to what degree, if we were to be subjected to some subtle magical attack, it might or might not be advisable suddenly to cover the auditorium with an eerie dome of uncreated light?"

"Oh, right," they said together. "But still," Rhys said, "he might have something planned for us."

"True enough. But whatever he has in mind for tonight can't be too violent. We'll be in public, after all."

"They burned Gryffydd Evans in public," his many-times-great-nephew muttered; but he moved to a closer parking space.

I saw no evidence, as we entered the vast auditorium, of any of the tricks and devices I've heard about in connection with the more unsavory sorts of pseudo-evangelists—there was no effort to pump us for information which might be used later in the evening, nor did anyone attempt to steer us toward particular seats. Some people were using walkers and canes, but so far as I could tell from casual observation, they all had real difficulty getting around. Then again, I reminded myself, he doesn't advertise a healing ministry.

We took places a bit less than halfway down the left side of center: the pews were arranged in an arc, with four aisles, two along the outside walls. An elaborate stage dominated the room, with risers for a large choir against the back wall, separated by a vacant sort of performing space from the pulpit, a large Plexiglas lectern standing roughly where one would have found the orchestra pit in a secular hall. The resemblance to a concert venue was reinforced by the large projection screen which hung above the whole setup like the apparatus the Opera has to show the English text for the audience during performances in foreign languages. I wondered briefly whether Brother Buchanan planned to show slides of prominent local witches during his sermon. Even before the formal part of the service began, though, we discovered the real purpose: several folks with guitars came out to lead the assembly in some warm-up singing, and the words projected on the screen took the place of printed hymnals. Inasmuch as the retirement benefits of Anglican clergy are underwritten with the profits from hymnal publication, I don't imagine we'll be adopting the system anytime soon; but I did appreciate the ingenuity of the thing.

At length, after the choir had entered and sung a hymn, the local Pastor led a prayer and introduced the evening's speaker. Stepping delicately up to the lectern—for he was a large man, shifting his bulk with some care—Brother Buchanan spoke with increasing energy, in a peculiarly penetrating baritone.

" 'Thou shalt not suffer a witch to live,' he read. "That's what it says here in the twenty-second chapter of Exodus. Leviticus 19: 26, 'Neither shall ye use enchantment, nor observe times.' And Deuteronomy 18:10-12, 'there shall not be found among you *any one* that maketh his son or his daughter to pass through the fire, *or* that useth divination, *or* an observer of times, or an enchanter, or a witch, or a charmer or a consuler with familiar spirits, or a wizard, or a necromancer. For all that do these things are an abomination unto the LORD.' That's what it says here in Scripture. 'Thou shalt not suffer a witch to live'—that was the Law that God gave to the people of Israel through Moses his chosen leader. 'Thou shalt not suffer a witch to live.' It's a crime to be a witch, and the penalty is death. That's the law. In fact, it's the law for a lot of crimes here in the front part of the Bible: all kinds of things that the Chosen People were liable to be up to in that land flowing with milk and honey. Perversions and abominations and adultery, for all those things they had a law, and according to that law, the criminals should die.

But Ezekiel 33:11, 'God desireth not the death of a sinner, but rather that he should repent and be saved.' They had a Law, and Law was good, but the most that that Law could do was say, 'Man, you are a sinner; woman, you are an abomination before the eyes of the Lord of Hosts.' That much the Law could do. But alongside the Law, the Prophets said God desireth not the death of a sinner. 'Repent and be saved,' they said. Over and over again, they said, 'Repent.' After centuries there came one greater than the prophets, living in the desert, eating locusts and honey, and dressed in camel's hair, and he said, Matthew 3, 'Repent. God's kingdom is at hand. You generation of vipers, the ax is at the root of the tree. Repent and be baptized.' And this John, a prophet and more than a prophet, when he finally saw his cousin on the river bank, on the bank of the Jordan as it runs through the Holy Land, when John saw Jesus, he said, John 1:29, 'Behold the Lamb of God, behold him that taketh away the sin of the world.'

"Now pay attention to this. The Law says, 'You are a sinner, and you ought to die.' The Prophets add, 'Repent.' But when Jesus comes, when the Savior finally appears, John the Baptist says 'He takes away the sin of the world.' You all know the story in that beautiful chapter, the eighth chapter of John, where they bring before Jesus the woman caught in adultery. And they say, 'We have a Law, and according to that Law she ought to die.' But Jesus, the savior, he sees into the hearts of men. They bring a prostitute to him—that's what the woman is, a prostitute—and they bring her in and say, 'according to the Law she ought to die.' Now Jesus knows the Law, but he knows business, too. Karl Marx didn't invent economics, after all. If this woman has been a prostitute, her customers have to come from somewhere. They aren't likely to be walking in from the next town, after all. So Jesus looks up at this crowd of men, and he says to them, 'If you're innocent, you cast the first stone.' And then when the accusers have gone away, he tells the woman, 'Neither do I accuse you: go and sin no more.' He takes away the sin of the world. They come to him and say 'According to the Law she ought to die,' but he says, 'You also are sinners. But I have come to call you all to repent. I forgive your sins. Go and sin no more.'

" 'You shall not suffer a witch to live.' That's what the Law says. But 'Go and sin no more'—that's what Jesus says. He said it to the woman taken in adultery, and he says it to you and me. Now, I don't mean just some vague idea. I mean Jesus personally says to us, 'Go and sin no more.' For I tell you, brothers and sisters, I tell you honestly, I was a witch, and Jesus suffered me to live. Jesus suffered me to live until I should accept his grace, until I should repent of my sins. Jesus told me, 'Hudson, you go and sin no more.' And thanks to him, thanks to the irresistible grace of my sweet Lord, thanks to the power of his Holy Spirit working in me, I have not sinned in that way again. Oh, my life is not perfect, brothers and sisters, it is no more without sin than yours or your neighbor's. But I have never fallen back into the sin of witchcraft. God called me out of that sin, God has, by his wonderful power, preserved me from it these twenty years. Oh yes, I joined in those dances in the woods, those rituals in suburban living rooms; you'd be surprised how cold it gets, dancing naked in a park on Halloween."

Brother Buchanan was, as I have pointed out, a corpulent man. I imagine that those members of the congregation gifted, as I am not, with strong visual imaginations, would have found the picture of him gamboling naked on the greensward more than a bit unaesthetic, even with the atmospheric addition of a harvest moon. In fact, however, they were left with little opportunity for visualization: while I had one of my odd moments of seeing entirely too much.

It was, again, a late antique scene—some sort of lecture space, perhaps even in a bath, corresponding to the auditorium in which I was seated roughly as the Lateran had corresponded to my cathedral. The room was quite full of men, most of them sitting, but a few standing, all obviously listening to someone at the center read. Unlike the former vision, however, this one included sound. It did not seem to be the sound of the reader, but rather a sort of voice-over commentator, chatting along most casually in Latin:

Adsederam ego ab eo quem maxime intueri cupiebam longius atque adeo, si situm recorderis, auersus pluribusque oppositis, ne si aegerimme quidem cuperem, uultum nutumque eius aspicere poteram ex quo mihi aliqua eius darentur signa iudicii.

Now this is not such difficult Latin that I couldn't have read it, if it had been written down like that; but I'm not quite accustomed to translating the language by ear. For the moment that the vision lasted, then, I had no idea what the narrator was saying, though it stuck in my mind with preternatural clarity.

When the modern auditorium came back into focus, it was a scene of pandemonium. Caroline was tugging on my sleeve: "Uncle Jon, come on, let's go."

Rhys had already stood, and was waiting at the end of the pew, holding a place as the people milled up and down the aisle. As I got up to go, I could see the stage more clearly. Brother Buchanan lay apparently unconscious on the floor beside the lectern, as people began to crowd around him with first aid. Caroline tugged on my sleeve again, and we left, shouldering our way up the aisle as quickly as we could.

When we were safely in the car and headed home, I asked the kids what had happened.

"Before or after the speaking in tongues?" Rhys asked.

"I don't think it was tongues, Rhys," I answered. "It sounded like Latin to me."

"I wouldn't want to disagree, Uncle Jon, but I couldn't make heads or tails of it."

"Whichever, Car. I'm sure Buchanan had no idea what he was saying."

"No, hardly. He looked as surprised as anyone, I admit."

"Could we begin at the beginning, kids? I followed everything until about two pages into the sermon, where Brother Hudson was dancing in the park."

"Right," Caroline said. "Well, right after that—I suppose it must have been at the same time you zoned out, but I wasn't watching you, so I'm not sure—right at the end of the park line, there was a kind of pause, like a splice in a sloppy video tape, and then suddenly he was talking in some other language—"

"But the lip-synch was bad."

"Right. I'm sure he was trying to go on with his sermon, but instead of what he meant to say, these other words were coming out of his mouth—"

"And he had this really wild look in his eyes—"

"And who wouldn't have, if their voice started up in business for itself."

"That's when I decided we should make tracks, before someone else noticed who he was looking at."

"Right. And that was when I noticed you were zoned out, Uncle Jon."

"And while Car was looking away was when Br. Buchanan dropped in his tracks."

"And then Rhys nudged me, and I nudged you, and you know it from there."

"Now you tell us what happened to *you*—that blackout of yours can't have been a coincidence!"

"No, no it wasn't. But I'll have to tell you another story first to put it into context."

By the time I had recounted my adventure of Wednesday morning and described in such detail as I could what had just happened to me, we were back at the palace.

"How about cookies and milk?" I asked as we walked into the kitchen.

"Sounds good," Rhys answered.

"Me, too," Caroline said. "But let's take them upstairs—I want to show you something on my computer."

"You go on up and start the machine, Car—we'll catch up."

It took us a couple of minutes to organize an evening snack—I had apparently eaten the last of the snickerdoodles, and Mrs. Jameson, in a rare failure of prescience, seemed to have thought we'd stop someplace and have a bite on our way back from the revival. Eventually, though, we put together some ice cream—well, low fat frozen yogurt, actually—and store-bought cookies, and made our way up to Caroline's study.

"Look here, you guys. Is this the same thing you heard in the vision, Uncle Jon?"

I peered over her shoulder. "Computer screens always make me feel as though I need bifocals."

"You can buy me a larger monitor for my birthday. Is this the Latin you heard?"

"As near as I can tell it is. It went by pretty fast, after all. 'I was sitting quite a ways from him whom I most desired to see, and thus, if you remember the placement of the seats, turned away from him and with many others between us; if I very much desired it, still I could not see his face and expression from which some signs of his opinion might be given to me.' Is that what you make of it?"

"Yes, that's the idea, I think. Now what will the two of you say when I tell you that's the second paragraph of one of Boethius's theological treatises?"

"Whoa, dude!" Rhys said. "Good catch."

"Very good, indeed," I added. "What's the original context of this bit?"

"So far as I can tell, Boethius is describing a public meeting where they were reading a letter on some theological topic, and he wanted to keep an eye on some elder statesman to see what the other guy's reaction to the letter was going to be."

"Right, I remember. It's his father-in-law Symmachus that he wants to watch. That would fit with what I saw, certainly, and my sense that the words were a description of the scene. The letter was an account of one of the current heresies—"

Rhys broke in on what was heading toward being another lecture. "Alrighty then. We only need to figure out why the Bishop is getting extraordinary visions of fifth-century Rome."

"That and why his soundtrack seems to overflow into Brother Buchanan."

"And, just to round things out," I added, "how these visions are getting past our defenses. We may not have put up any special shields, but I've had my ring on both times this happened, and the first time, I was wearing my cross, to boot. Yet neither of you has felt a thing, nor, presumably, has Dan. It might be worth our knowing what's up here."

"No question. Car might be able to find out something about the Roman side for us on the Internet, but for Brother Buchanan, we might want to start with something low-tech, like the ten o'clock news. It should be on channel 43 in a couple of minutes."

We trooped out to the family room, where the TV was still tuned to the evangelical station. We had to wait all the way through the local news, the weather and the sports before hearing about Brother Buchanan at the end of the show. There was, thankfully, no live video, just a publicity still of the preacher and the notice that he'd been admitted to St. Luke's University Hospital for observation after collapsing during his sermon. The revival would continue over the weekend, the news reader said, with the local pastor taking Buchanan's place.

"Well, that was disappointing," I said. "You'd think he'd have been the lead item."

"No one wants to highlight bad luck for their own side, Uncle Jon. At least he's willing to accept medical help from the tools of Satan."

"He was probably still unconscious when they took him in," Rhys observed. "After all, it's not as though they were going to haul him over to South Bend."

"Still, it is convenient that he's in our hospital," I said. "I could easily drop in and see him tomorrow."

"Are you sure that's wise, sir? It's not quite the same as sneaking into a revival meeting."

"No, it's not. But there's not much going to happen in a hospital in broad daylight, particularly when it's my turf."

"Okay. But safe isn't the same as wise, Uncle Jon. What advantage could we get by talking with Brother Buchanan? He doesn't seem to know anything but how to string together quotations from the mean parts of the Bible."

"Be fair, Car," Rhys said. "We didn't get to see whether he can dance or not." Caroline's frown hinted at disapproval.

"You're right, of course, Caroline. He may be completely nuts; but even the part of his sermon we heard did have some solid things to say about grace. I might find out we actually have something to talk about. In any case, visiting the sick is one of the corporal works of mercy."

"Yes, well," Rhys said. "There's no arguing with you when you appeal to tradition. You'd better go over there early tomorrow, though, or the HMO people will have him back on the street."

"True enough. I think I'll toddle off now, actually. If you guys are going to be up using the computer for awhile, would you make sure the house is shut up before you go to bed? Mrs. Jameson will let herself in."

"Sure thing, Uncle Jon."

"And remember to say your prayers."

"Who could forget, sir? Go to sleep."

And so I did.

Chapter 5: Saturday, October 21

I GOT UP relatively early, but Mrs. Jameson had beaten me to the punch. There was clear olfactory evidence of breakfast in the making as I came downstairs, and I headed straight for the kitchen.

"I hope you don't mind kippers, Bishop."

"I love them, as you know perfectly well. It's the kids who have trouble with fried fish for breakfast. Could I have some grapefruit, too?"

"Certainly. I'll bring it in in a moment. I've put the morning paper at your place."

The paper was open to the front page of the second section, home to the weekly gossip column: we don't accumulate enough gossip in Michigan City to feed a more frequent feature, and if it was up to me we'd get by without the one occurrence we do have. The interest this morning lay in the second paragraph, where I read the rhetorical question, "Which purple-shirted padre was seen in mufti sneaking out of a local auditorium with his young wards soon after the speaker collapsed yesterday evening—or should we say 'Witch?'" I don't imagine that my doings really count as gossip—even the eldritch ones, however sensational, come along only rarely—but I have spoken to the editor more than once about the amateur sleaze-merchant who reports the column, a man whom I hold directly responsible for the final collapse of at least two marriages in the cathedral parish in the short time since I came here. I don't, apparently, carry enough weight to get rid of the rodent, but I have managed to attract his attention. Carl tells me I should know better.

Caroline came down to breakfast as I was finishing my second kipper.

"Uncle Jon, those things stink."

"Be glad I gave up cigars. Here, we made the morning papers."

"So I see," she said, reading quickly over the item. "Where does this fellow get his information?"

"Heaven only knows. I think we're safe in assuming he doesn't spend his own Friday nights at revival meetings. I can't say I'm glad for the extra publicity, though."

"No, I suppose not. But I don't think it'll make any practical difference. Anyone who can plug directly into your head doesn't need to read the papers to find out what you've been up to, and you were planning to talk to Brother Buchanan anyway."

"Right. In fact, I'm just on my way. Did you kids find out anything interesting last night?"

"I don't think so, really. I may have something when I finish translating stuff, but mostly I don't think we know enough to know what to look for."

"The eternal problem of scholarship. I have to go over to the museum late this morning, and then maybe I'll get a chance to work on this controversial sermon for tomorrow. Are you guys going over to the university today?"

"I don't know about Rhys, but I imagine I'll go to the library. It's usually fairly empty on Saturday afternoons in the fall."

"Imagine that. Parking could be tight, though—it's a home game weekend."

"Yes, and lots of alumni around, to boot. Perhaps I'll catch the city bus. Will we see you for dinner?"

"No, I'm supposed to have dinner with the vestry at St. James's in Logansport, and they'll put me up someplace down there: the Rectory, if nothing else."

"I suppose it saves getting up early and driving down there tomorrow. We'll keep in touch."

"You bet, sweetheart. See you tomorrow afternoon."

BROTHER BUCHANAN was sitting up in bed when I got to his room, a fifth-floor single with a nice view of the lake. He looked much the same as he had when I'd first seen him on Friday: though his conversation was, thankfully, less flamboyant than his preaching.

"Bishop Mears. I'm surprised to see you, sir. Please have a seat."

"Thank you. I can understand that you would be. I have to say I'm a bit surprised myself to be recognized: but I guess you've done your research."

He bristled. "I have done a little bit, yes. I hope I don't strike you as an ignorant man, sir. I have my college degree, and I suppose you know I did earn a little money as a writer at one point in my life."

"I'm sorry. I didn't mean to suggest anything about your research skills; I was just thinking that the publicity for your revival seemed to be aimed at me, so it wasn't surprising that you'd have seen my picture."

"I don't know that I've aimed anything at you, sir," he said doggedly. "The only aim I'm taking is at Satan. I was a witch, and God saved me; they tell me you're a witch, and I know that God can save you too."

"I believe that God did save me, Brother Buchanan, nearly two thousand years ago; and you'll excuse me for seeing public discussion about my need for salvation as an attack. But we're clearly talking at cross purposes. You and I obviously understand Christianity differently, and what I heard you say last night leads me to think our definitions of witchcraft are even farther apart.

So far as I know, this dancing in the park business of yours only dates back to the 1930s; and it seems to me to be more exercise than magic."

"Surely, sir, you aren't going to suggest that Satan couldn't develop some new evil in the 1930s. Think of Germany."

"No, hardly. All I'm getting at is that there's no real connection between what you experienced and what the Bible calls witchcraft, any more than between what we call leprosy and what the Bible did."

"And so whatever it is you do can be different from both. That's clever enough, sir. But the old leprosy and the new one are still both diseases; and the Lord Jesus Christ wants to cure your disease the same as he cured mine. You just have to pray for him to come into your heart."

"I trust that he has already done so, Brother Buchanan. But we don't seem to be getting very far on this tack. Let me try being more direct. I'm trying to understand what happened last night: something similar happened to me earlier in the week, and I wonder if you could describe your sense of it."

"It wasn't you that caused it, then?" I shook my head. "One of the ushers said you were in the congregation. Still, I didn't imagine it was: there didn't seem to be any purpose in it." He shrugged. "There's not much to say about it, really. I was standing there giving my testimony, when all of a sudden someone else's words were coming out of my mouth, and then before I knew it I was on a stretcher and they were bringing me over here. That's about all there was to it."

"Was it similar to speaking in tongues, would you say?"

His round face was suddenly animated. "Oh, no, sir, not at all. When the Spirit comes upon a person, the person is moved to testify to the Lord Jesus, and the Spirit giveth utterance in other tongues. The person just sort of goes along with it. But here I wanted to keep on talking, and my mouth made the words I wanted, but the other voice came out of it anyway. It was more like being possessed than being inspired: and I don't think that it was testimony."

"In a sense, it was—at least it was theology. Did it actually seem evil to you?"

"No, sir, but I don't know that there's some 'feeling' of evil a person can rely on like that."

"Granted. But intuition can be one piece of information. Let me ask you one more question: Did you ever have any out-of-the-ordinary experiences before you got into the Neo-pagan business—anything that might suggest you had some sort of psychic ability, as opposed to magic?"

"Not that I can remember, sir, no. I've never really believed in ESP. I was never even able to be hypnotized."

"I'd been hoping that there was something illuminating in your past: but I guess I can't offer even a partial explanation of this." I stood up as I tried to summarize. "I'd have to say it's only a coincidence that you were involved—though I don't understand what the point of either one of these episodes was, I don't see what they could have to do with you."

The evangelist shook his head. "The good Lord doesn't deal in coincidences, Bishop Mears: but I'm certainly not eager to channel any more messages for you."

"Nor am I eager to receive them. Well, I guess that's all we have to say, so I'd better be going."

"Good-bye, then. I'll be praying for Jesus to open your heart."

"Thanks. I appreciate the good intentions. God bless you."

I was waiting at the nurse's station for the elevator to come when I "heard" Rhys. *Sir?*

Hi. What's up?

Your mind must be wandering: I've been trying to get your attention for twenty minutes. No emergency, but I have had a little bit of luck finding out more about Hudson Buchanan. Are you going to work at home or at the Cathedral?

At the Cathedral, I think. I have most of my things for tomorrow, but I need to go by there and pick up my vestments.

Right. In that case, I'll e-mail you the interesting bits. Try to pay more attention as you drive.

Insolent pup. See you tomorrow.

Despite Rhys's analysis, I found it a bit unsettling that he had not been able to contact me immediately when he tried: it was the first time I'd known the kids' telepathic gift to fail. It gave me another thing to puzzle over when I stopped at the Faculty Club for lunch.

I arrived early, and, as Caroline had said, the academic part of the campus seemed relatively dead: but a good number of alumni had obviously made the trip back for the annual contest with our Lady's other university, the small Roman Catholic place in South Bend. The Romans' *official* rivalry is with Wabash, Indiana's only other all-male school: but proximity and the remnants of sectarianism make our game pretty popular. I had a quiet meal, except for a certain amount of fuss from the manager, who was determined that I should try his latest dessert and accept a free lunch, to boot. I put up a token resistance.

The oldest building on campus still in regular use, the art museum's a modest neo-classical holdover from the days before the triumph of University Gothic—rather as if a mid-western county courthouse had been uncomfortably set down amidst the Oxford colleges. St. John was waiting under the portico when I arrived. Though he is rather taller than the Corsican dictator, he otherwise has an uncanny resemblance to Napoleon—if the Emperor had worn gray flannel trousers and a Corpus Christi blazer (having both a Harvard Ph.D. and an Oxford D.Phil., St. John owns a variety of academic haberdashery).

"Jonathan," he called, almost before I'd reached the top step, "It's good of you to come." We shook hands, though I think St. John had to restrain himself from genuflecting and kissing my ring. He clipped a "visitor" ID tag on my lapel, and we went inside.

"The old girl looks pretty good for almost a hundred-fifty," I said as we walked through the main hall toward the back of the building.

"Thank you, Jonathan. We think she's holding up. The building was rather heavily remodeled in the 80s, you know: as you see, the architects preserved the exterior and most of the exhibition space in what appears to be their original antebellum form. In fact, the whole thing now has structural steel reinforcements, a fire-suppression system, and the usual security devices. And the basements are entirely new, of course: we have perfectly up-to-date work spaces."

Other than its discreetly wood-paneled door, the elevator into which he led me certainly seemed modern enough: and when we came to the sub-basement, we exited into a short hallway that could just as easily have been part of a computer plant someplace in California—an impression that was only strengthened by the security camera surveying the scene and the elaborate series of electronic checks St. John had to go through to open the door. Behind it were a large room with several work tables, two or three of which seemed to reflect the current state of progress on particular restoration projects, and, opening off the main room, a pair of offices, labeled "Curator" and "Assistant."

"Pull up a stool," St. John said, gesturing toward one of the empty tables. "I have a little game for you, just to make things interesting. Is your surprise behind door number one or door number two?"

" 'Curator' being number one, I take it?" He nodded. "Well, then, as there seems to be someone moving around in the 'Assistant' office, I think I'll try that one."

"I guess I'm not cut out to be a game-show host; but we may still be able to manage a surprise. Come on out, my lord," he said toward the door.

The tall young peer to whom he spoke would have looked a bit foreign even without the form of address. There was something not quite American about the cut and pattern of his suit—Saville Row, one supposed; and there was, for that matter, something a bit odd about his person, the tiniest suggestion of a point to the ears, a slant to the eyes, an arch to the eyebrows, as if a make-up artist had tried to create the impression of a person with one elven ancestor several generations back. I stood up, duly surprised, as he came in.

"Bishop Mears," St. John said, "May I present Lord Strathspey? My lord, the Bishop of Michigan City."

"Hi, Chaplain," the young man responded as he took my hand, "it's a long time since cabin 31!"

"John-Michael Bruce-Porter—my only double-hyphenated camper in all those years of 'international students.' The last time I saw you you were only Lord Aberlour."

"A bit posh-o for an eleven-year old in short pants, I suppose," he said with a smile, "but one can't help one's inheritance. You've come up a bit in the world from the callow seminarian of twenty years hence, yourself, sir."

"Not *quite* twenty, and I think I'd graduated from seminary a few years before: though I have to plead guilty to callow. But what brings you back to Indiana, my lord?"

"Please call me Michael, and I'll try to avoid 'sir'—though it's sort of a conditioned reflex, even now. As for your question, I'd better let St. John have his surprise, now that I've had mine. Let's have a seat."

I looked at our host for the first time since his introduction. "So this wasn't it? I thought perhaps you'd arranged for Michael to give a lecture or something."

St. John appeared a bit muddled. "I have, actually, but I hadn't realized that he would be a surprise in and of himself. Perhaps if I begin at the beginning. You see, Michael here, faced with the inevitable consequences of confiscatory estate duties, prepared himself with a D.Phil. for employment in the academic world, and is now, as a result, able to maintain the hereditary ermine and velvet with his salary as curator for medieval metalwork in the Ashmolean Museum. As he did not choose to enlighten me about his youthful sojourn here behind the corn-silk curtain, I anticipated that the element of surprise would be introduced by what he was bringing with him for our exhibit." He made an elaborately deferential gesture toward Michael, who removed from his coat pocket a small purple jeweler's bag. Opening this, he carefully laid on the table an object of gold and crystal, pear-shaped in its outline; the crystal itself was tear-drop shaped, with an enamel design beneath it, like the face of an old pocket watch. The whole thing was not much bigger than one's thumb.

More precisely, the object is (I have a photo of it in the museum catalogue here in front of me) about three inches long, perhaps half that wide at its widest point, and somewhat less than an inch thick. The stem of the pear is a golden socket, about the right size to receive a pencil, in the shape of an animal's head with open mouth; the animal's throat leads to a gold plate that makes a back for the piece, while bands of gold filigree run around the outside, holding the crystal to the plate. The central band is an Old English inscription in antique capitals: "ÆLFRED MEC HEHT GEWYRCAN," "Alfred had me made." The enamel shows a seated figure in a sleeveless tunic, holding some sort of a scepter in each hand—unless perhaps they are flowers, or some sort of badly rendered cornucopia. Found in a field in the seventeenth century, the object is thought to date from the time of Alfred the Great, who was King of England—most of it, anyway—in the late ninth century.

"Either he's surprised, St. John, or he's simply stopped breathing."

"I imagine he's breathing, or he wouldn't be drooling."

"Bishops do not drool, gentlemen: they salivate discreetly. And I'm trying not even to do that. This *is* the real thing, isn't it: King Alfred's Jewel?"

"Oh, yes," St. John managed a look that was equal parts preening and false modesty. "Very much so. The Alfred Jewel doesn't ordinarily travel, but . . ."

"But Professor Dacre has some influential friends—including, um, the *legitimate* descendant of one of those Stuart ancestors of his. Since we have it here, though, wouldn't you like to take a closer look?"

"You mean it's all right to pick it up?"

"It's lasted nearly eleven hundred years," Michael answered. "I think it will hold up to even some discreet episcopal drooling. Go ahead."

I very nearly dropped it, at that, and probably would have had I not had two equally unnatural experiences in the past three days. Once again, the room around me was replaced by an alien scene: not, in this case, an image of ancient Rome, but one (as it seemed to me) from the time of the jewel itself. A man sat dictating, with a book open on his lap; he wore a blue tunic and leggings, with a red cloak fastened at the shoulder by a gold and garnet fibula. Two men stood at his shoulder, in the stereotyped pose of advisors, while two or three more sat around taking down the speaker's words on wax tablets: these scribes and advisors wore the monastic habit. I heard the man speaking—in Old English, predictably—but couldn't follow more than a word or two of it. Apparently those words were enough, however, for the vision ended, and I put down the jewel.

Immediately, Danny and the kids were present in my mind: *What hap-pened? Are you okay?*

I'm fine, I thought back. *I'll tell you more later.* My two companions were standing over me like the advisors I'd seen in the vision, though a good deal less calmly. "Great God in heaven, Jonathan!" St. John said. "That would have made camp a good deal more interesting," Michael added.

"You saw him, then?"

They glanced at each other in an unnerving, he-may-have-finally-lost-it sort of a way, and I thought it best to press on: "I'm sorry, that's reasoning in advance of the evidence. Let me begin again. What did you see just now?"

"It wasn't any *thing* in particular, sir," Michael said, "—but when you picked up the jewel, you vanished in a flash of light."

"Or, I suppose, to be precise, you were hidden by the light: it was as though you were inside a cylinder of sapphire glass, lit from within."

"It was the same blue, almost, as the windows at Chartres, wouldn't you say, St. John?"

"That shade or a bit lighter, yes. In any case, Jonathan, that was it until just now."

"Blue light, eh? That's very interesting. How long was I gone, altogether?"

"Thirty seconds or so, I'd say," St. John answered; "no more than a minute, anyway."

"But this isn't what you saw?" Michael asked.

"Well, no. But it's sort of a long story. You'll want to sit down, and I wouldn't necessarily mind a soda."

"Let's go into the Curator's office," St. John said. "The chairs are more comfortable, and I believe she has a stock of Cokes in one of those little refrigerators."

Michael grinned: "Still the Bishop's drink of choice, I take it."

"At least when it's too early for Scotch," I said. "Let's go."

I gave them as brief a summary as I could manage of the three episodes, with a smattering of background information about Dan and the kids. "So you can see," I concluded, "that the whole thing has left us with more questions than answers. Even after this experience just now, I don't see the overall point; and I'm all the more confused by Brother Buchanan and by the blue light."

"You know," Michael said, "—And I hope you'll both forgive my mentioning it—I haven't spent that much time in the Lords, but I can't *imagine* how many hours one would have to devote to eavesdropping in the library before one overheard any occupant of the Bishops' Bench tell a story remotely like this."

"I do find that I always have something to talk about when our House of Bishops breaks for lunch."

"I daresay; but there you don't have the advantage of eavesdropping curators from the Ashmolean. I have a question for you, though: do you remember any of the dictation that you heard just now?"

"More than I would have thought, for a language I only studied for a semester in college, but still just a word or two: 'se Ælmightig'—that's 'the

Almighty,' of course; and then something that sounded like 'similar' and 'settle.' It went by pretty quickly."

St. John started to say something, but Michael frowned at him, then looked at the ceiling out of the corner of his eye, with an air of concentration. "How about: 'Forþamþe ge nauht wiþ hine don ne magon, forþaem se Eca ond se Ælmightiga simle sit on þam heah setle his anwealdes, þonan he maeg eall gesion, ond gifþ ælcum be ðam ryhte æfter his gewyrhtum.'"

"Which is the passage in your paper," St. John added triumphantly.

"Exactly."

"Okay, I'll bite," I said. "That could easily have been it. I hope you'll spare me the embarrassment of trying to translate."

"Oh, of course. It means, 'For you cannot do anything against him, for the Eternal and Almighty always sits on the high throne of his power, whence he can see all and give to each justly in accordance with his works.'"

"But the translation's not the interesting part, Jonathan. I mean, it's central to Michael's argument, but it's what he's argued that's fascinating."

"More fascinating now than it was before you told us your story, sir. That little bit is from one of King Alfred's translations—"

"And he translated Boethius, if I remember correctly."

"Exactly. The *Consolation*. Which is where this passage comes from, quite near the end. So we've got Boethius again here, at second hand, so to speak. But the key point for my paper is that the king is paraphrasing here, rather than translating strictly: and what he adds that makes it a paraphrase is the reference to God sitting on a throne. In fact, the king even leaves out the two places earlier in the book where Boethius actually does refer to God enthroned—so this passage about God's eternal foresight gets a very specific linkage to the throne image. Now, if we look at the image on the enamel, we see a seated male figure: couldn't that be an illustration of this very passage?"

"I suppose; but it's a little hard for me to picture God in a short-sleeved tunic."

"That is an objection, admittedly. On the other hand, we have to consider those peculiar scepter-like objects. It's not entirely clear to me that they are scepters, but it is undoubtedly the case that the most similar image in all of Anglo-Saxon art is on a brooch illustrating the senses, where they are held by the allegorical figure of Sight."

"So," St. John said, "we have not only the seated figure, but a direct connection to the idea of God seeing the world. But the clincher is actually in a piece of work another scholar, a Professor Kornbluth, did, some years ago. She is a specialist in gemstones, and when she examined the crystal here, she found that it was not cut by an Anglo-Saxon jeweler. In fact, the enamel and the setting were apparently shaped to fit the stone."

"That's it," Michael responded. "She demonstrates, you see, that the stone was originally cut and polished by a late Roman craftsman; so for the Anglo-Saxons, it would have been a precious antique, a connection back to the imperial world—the very period in which Boethius wrote the book which the King was translating. What better artifact could the King have found to associate with this image of the climactic moment of his translation?"

"And the fact that I, with my recent Boethius-fixation, respond to the jewel by seeing the King in the very act of making the translation, makes the final proof of your hypothesis."

"Exactly, sir. Though," he went on more soberly, "I don't suppose it's the sort of evidence I could work into the paper."

"No, probably not. Still, I'm glad if it makes you feel more confident. What, by the way, do you propose that the King did with this artifact?"

"That's a debated question, of course," St. John said. "Before Michael's paper, I suppose the prevailing opinion was that the socket end held a short rod used as some sort of a pointer in reading, and that the King distributed a dozen or so of these to his bishops—though the discovery that the stone was a Roman antique made that theory a bit dubious. Even King Alfred probably didn't have a dozen Roman gemstones to hand out. The other choice is that the jewel-and-rod combination served as some sort of a rod of office; and there again, there's some difficulty with the rarity of the thing itself—who could deserve a staff of office that valuable?"

"So I'm inclined to think," Michael continued, "that it was meant for the King himself, perhaps as a staff like the ones that Roman consuls used, or perhaps as an actual scepter."

I looked dubiously at the small socket. "It wouldn't have been a very big scepter, would it?"

"Well, no," St. John said, "more like a long pencil with a valuable eraser, or a long sort of a baton: but even today there's no standard pattern for regalia."

"I suppose not. But let me make one other suggestion: you both described seeing a blue light when I picked this up. I've only seen that light once or twice, and it has never come from my own magic. My father and his grand-father used it, and we can activate what they've left behind, so to speak: but we can't cause it ourselves."

"So," St. John said, "the light we saw was caused by the same person that caused your vision. Isn't that what we've thought all along?"

Michael shook his head. "No, I don't think that's quite what you mean, is it, sir?"

"Not exactly, no. I mean, that may be true, actually, but what I was getting at is that the light is probably associated with the jewel itself. If it could be part of a pointer or a rod of office or a scepter, it could also be part of a wand."

"So Alfred had this made for a previously unheard-of court magician?"

"He wouldn't be the only famous king to have had the help of a wizard, St. John. Or for that matter, he may have used it himself."

"Now *there's* an idea I could use in a paper," Michael said with a grin.

"Only for a select audience, I imagine, my lord," I replied. "But there is a case to be made, aside from what we've seen here. You've argued that this is a Roman gemstone which the King associated with his translation of Boethius. What if the King knew the stone had actually belonged to Boethius?"

"What was your phrase a moment ago, 'Reasoning in advance of the evidence?'" Michael asked. "How could we ever know?"

"Well, do you remember what charges were brought against Boethius at his trial?"

"He was charged with treason; in fact, Alfred's preface to the translation assumes that he was really guilty."

"Treason was one charge; but the other one was necromancy. Boethius is a saint now, but his king had him put to death as a magician."

"You seem to be creating a rather distinguished group of predecessors for yourself, Jonathan."

"No more distinguished than Peter and Paul; it's just that being a bishop is more socially acceptable."

"Touché. Assuming that you're right, and that that entails the jewel being associated with your sudden interest in Boethius, is there something you propose that Michael and I should do?"

"No, I don't think so. You're obviously going to have the highest security possible in any case—" Lord Strathspey was in fact locking the jewel in the office safe as we spoke "—and I don't know what else you could do. Michael, how long are you going to be in town?"

"A fortnight, as from yesterday. I may take some side-trips, though, once the jewel's on display—I wouldn't mind going to Chicago and Kalamazoo, and I'd thought about going down to revisit Annandale, as well."

"You must do that, certainly. You'll find there are a lot of new buildings on the main campus, but it does still stir the loyal heart. Keep me posted if you need someplace to stay—they've torn down the old Inn, but I still have a house in town. One of the young faculty rents it, but he doesn't use the guest room."

"Thank you, that's very generous: I may take you up on it next week."

"Very good. And now if someone will show me how to get out of the high security area, I must get over to the Cathedral and work on my sermon."

"I'll show you out, Jonathan," St. John said. "I have a few ideas you might want to use tomorrow evening."

He had more than a few, in fact, and I thought for a minute or two that he might actually walk me all the way back to my car. Fortunately for my schedule, we tarried for only a few moments on the portico, discussing key points from Cardinal Newman's *Idea of the University*. Still, it was half past two when I got to the Cathedral.

Seated in the comfort of my office, I tried to focus my attention on my ring. *Rhys? Caroline?* I thought.

Right here, sir, Rhys responded. *Car will talk to her dad.* The fact that Dan and I can communicate with the kids but not with each other admittedly makes things a bit awkward, but it's still a lot faster than telephoning. We've learned that with one repeating Dan to me and one me to Dan, the two of them can provide simultaneous translation. *She says he says, "What was that all about?"*

I gave them a summary. *So this jewel,* Rhys said, *is a Roman magic item?*

Well, it's apparently Roman and obviously a magic item. It's not entirely clear that the two points are connected.

Caroline's dad says, "Does this mean our magic goes all the way back to King Alfred?"

I suppose it could. I always thought the Welsh side of the family brought in the magic skills, whereas Alfred was a king of Wessex, but he did have some Welsh connections, if his biography isn't a fake. But I doubt that Alfred is an ancestor, if that's what he's thinking.

He says, he won't be trying on a crown just yet.

Do we need to do anything here, Uncle Jon?

Not that I can tell, but thanks for the help. See you all later.

With this conference concluded, I decided Rhys's earlier e-mail would have to wait until I had finished the sermon for Sunday evening—and at that point it was time to be on my way to Logansport for my seven o'clock dinner appointment.

It was an easy drive—to say that US 35 runs straight from Michigan City to Logansport would be an exaggeration, but it's a more direct route than most roads in northern Indiana—and I arrived in plenty of time to put my things in Fr. Voreis's guest room and wash up before sherry was served. We had a nice, an elegant, really, dinner—more courses than I actually need to be eating, I suppose, but I wouldn't willingly have surrendered the Coquille St. Jacques, in honor of the parish's patron, the roast loin of pork, or the old-fashioned cream pie; the cherry soup and the pear, walnut and blue cheese salad, I suppose, I might have been able to live without, but duty to my hostess seemed to require that I at least try some of each.

"Edna," I said, as the youth group waiters cleared away the last of the dessert plates, "it was wonderful." There were murmurs of agreement from the ladies and gentlemen of the vestry, and more than a couple of "amens." "I can't think of when I've had such a meal."

"Sometime last February, Bishop," she said with a slight smile. "I called Mrs. Jameson to ask for suggestions. Except for the scallops, of course."

"Has a man no right to privacy anymore?"

"I'm afraid the law recognizes no cook-client privilege, Bishop," said the senior warden.

"Thank you, counselor," I replied, "I'll see that you get what's coming to you, too. But I see it's already almost ten. I take it we have some time scheduled to talk business after church tomorrow?"

"Between services, actually, Bishop," the Rector said. "But I agree it's getting late. If you'd dismiss us with your blessing . . ."

I did so, and so it was that I was in the privacy of the guest bathroom, flossing, about half an hour later when I felt such a shock that all my muscles went taut, wrenching at their ligaments, and I began to topple over. I honestly thought for a moment that something had fallen into the sink and shorted out. It took no more than that moment, however, and the sudden glare of light from my ring, to make me realize that this was the feeling of great power flowing out through me. And with that, I realized that this was the sensation, never before experienced, of the wards and defenses we had set up to give further protection to our family homes after the encounter with Rhys's undead ancestor.

All of this was, of course, the matter of an instant only, as quick as thought succeeding thought; and in the same instant Rhys and Caroline had re-established their telepathic link among us.

This is getting to be a habit! Where's the trouble? Rhys asked. *Are you okay, Caroline?*

Yes, I'm at the palace—there's nothing wrong here. Daddy?

He says he's okay, Bishop, Rhys reported. *Is there anything wrong down there in Logansport?*

No, I haven't even set up any kind of protection.

And I'm not protecting this pizza parlor, Rhys added.

It must be in Annandale, Caroline said.

Right. I'll call Philip, I said.

Dan says to be careful, Rhys thought.

Right back at him. And are you through with that pizza?

I'm on my way home now, sir.

I can take care of myself, you know, Caroline thought to all three of us.

Good, I answered. *Then when Rhys gets back to the Palace you can take care of him, too.*

Apparently Dan had much the same response, for she asked, *Have you and Daddy always thought alike?*

Just since he became a father, I answered. *Good night for now. I'll get back to you when I know something.*

Ignoring any further demands of oral hygiene, I went back to the bedroom, dug out my cell phone, and dialed home. It took Phil so long to answer that I thought I might end up talking to his recording.

"Hi, Philip. What's up?"

"Hi, Bishop. I figured you'd be calling. I think I need to get hold of Academy Security."

"Security instead of the town cops? Maybe you should start from the beginning."

"Right. You remember that I told you I was expecting a guy from Milwaukee to come down so we could plan a reenacted battle? His name was Dixon."

"Yes, you mentioned it."

"Okay. Well, he got to school this afternoon, later than I actually expected, so I started him off with the campus tour first thing—I wanted to be sure we saw the woods and the parade ground before dark—and then we went down to the old Library, because now that they've moved all the books to the new building, the old one makes a great place for a banquet, even though they've put offices in upstairs and made one of the ground floor wings into a museum; and by the time we'd gone over the place fairly thoroughly, it was past time for supper at the Mess Hall, so we went down to the pizza parlor, which was of course busy, being a Saturday night, and then we had a couple more beers afterwards, and so we just got back to the house here a couple of minutes ago."

"Might be a good place to take a breath, Philip."

"Right. Good idea. Well, we were coming into the house, and of course I unlocked the door, and then I was holding it open for Tom Dixon, so he could go in first, and when he got to the threshold there was a flash of bright blue light and he fell on his face into the living room."

"My lord! I hope he's all right!"

"I think he will be. He hasn't come around yet, but he's breathing normally and his pulse is okay."

"Good. Now where does Academy Security come into it?"

"Well, after he collapsed, of course, it didn't seem like he'd hurt his neck, so I rolled him over to check his pulse and breathing, and that's when I saw that he had something inside his coat pocket—besides his wallet, I mean, and when I fished it out, I recognized that it was that baton that Dr. Davies carries at the opening of school. He must have taken it out of the museum when we were there this afternoon—so that was why I was thinking about Security when the phone rang. What do you want me to do?"

"If he's stolen something from the Academy, I guess it makes sense to call Security—they're all sheriff's deputies, so they can make an arrest there as easily as they can on campus. I'm worried about this fellow being unconscious, though. If he doesn't come around right quick, you'll have to call the EMTs."

"But won't they want to know how he fainted in the first place?"

"I suppose. So will Security, for that matter. But most of the EMT's are cousins of mine, and they'll know the house—I suppose one more spooky scandal won't make much difference."

"Okay. Of course if he does come around, I may have to tie him up to keep him here."

"I guess, but let's try to avoid any further grounds for lawsuits if we can, though. I think harming someone by witchcraft is a felony under the common law. Do you want me to drive up? I can be there in three-quarters of an hour."

"Maybe you'd better. The guy could turn out to be some sort of magician himself, now that I think about it."

"Well, presumably, yes. But you should be safe as long as you're in the house, and I doubt if he'll try anything while he's being booked into the county jail."

"Roger that, Bishop. I'll see you about eleven."

It didn't occur to me until I had made my explanations to Ralph and Edna (an emergency at my house, I said, without going into the details) and was already on the road, relaying Philip's story to the family, that, if there were any danger from the larcenous Mister Dixon, it would likely be directed at the four of us, rather than at my tenant.

I wouldn't worry about it, Uncle Jon, Caroline thought. *None of us had any sense of a struggle in the first place.*

Right, Rhys added. *It was more like a mousetrap snapping shut than any kind of a fight.*

But Daddy says that could be just because we caught him by surprise.

I agree with your father, I thought. *Unless, of course, the guy is faking it.*

In which case we're the mice.

Possibly, Car. But if the outbound end of that spell felt as strong for everyone else as it did for me, it's hard to imagine one poor schmo being unaffected by the receiving end of it.

Fair enough, Rhys, I answered. *I just hope he is some poor schmo. I'll get back to you when I know more.*

———

THE LAST STRETCH of the trip, up road 17 and then into town on 10, is so familiar that my mind was wandering when I turned down Mears Street for home. I was startled back to reality by the simplest of things, if that is the right way to put it. There were no police cars, no security vehicles, no ambulances—nothing but Philip's car in the driveway.

I let myself in: Phil was sitting in the living room, watching a late night *Star Trek* rerun.

"Hi, Bishop. Welcome home."

"Thanks. It's good to be home, I guess." I dropped onto the couch. "What's the story?"

"Well, it's confusing. Do you want a Coke or something?"

"No, thanks; it's getting a little late in the evening, even for me. Where's the crowd?"

"Right. There was one, for a little while, but it broke up kind of quickly. I called Security right after I got off the phone with you, and of course they were here in just a couple of minutes. Dixon hadn't shown any signs of coming around, and I didn't see any reason to wake him up until they got here, as long as he was breathing and everything. But when they did come, it didn't take anything more than shaking his shoulder and calling his name, like you might anyone, and he was right back. So then they wanted to ask him a few questions about how this baton thing had ended up in his pocket."

"What did he say?"

"He didn't deny anything. He said he'd seen the baton in the museum as we were going through the Memorial Building, and just slid open the display case and took it when I wasn't looking."

"What for? Does he have a baton collection at home?"

"No, he said he recognized that it was antique ivory and figured he could sell it for a quite a bit of cash. It was all pretty simple, and he didn't say anything about the fireworks when he came into the house. It wasn't more than a couple of minutes before they had actually put handcuffs on him and were ushering him out for a trip to the county jail."

"That doesn't seem all that complicated."

"No, I guess it doesn't, but then it did become interesting, because when he went out of the house—I mean nearly at that exact moment—the prisoner escaped in the dark. At least I think that's what they're going to say when they write it up, anyway."

"Yes . . ."

"Well, it really was dark, of course, but basically he just vanished. He may have slipped out of the one guy's hands and then run away really really fast, but I'm thinking there was less to it than that, if you see what I mean."

"Teleportation of some kind."

"Some kind of beam-me-up-Mr.-Scot thing, yeah; that's my guess, anyway."

"It does seem that life is always a surprise, doesn't it? Still, if he's gone, he's gone. We're not going to find him any faster than the police will. What about the baton? I suppose Security took it with them?"

"Should have taken it, maybe; but they didn't, in fact. Neither one of them picked it up as they were taking Dixon out, and then when he disappeared they were preoccupied with finding him, not the evidence."

"So it's here."

"In that envelope there on the mantelpiece."

"Good."

"Good? That's it? Aren't you even going to look at it?"

"I've seen it before. And given the way my life has been going this week, I'm inclined to be cautious about handling any antiquities. If your hypothetical Mr. Scott could beam it out of here, it would be gone by now. So I don't think there's any great hurry to investigate."

"That makes sense, I guess. Do you want to stay the night here, or are you going to drive on back to Michigan City?"

"Oh, thanks, Phil, I'd love to stay. I'm going back down to Logan in the morning, though. I need to see the congregation, and the Vestry and I didn't actually get a chance to talk this evening."

"Are you going to take the baton with you?"

"I was thinking about that. If it's not needed as evidence, it really ought to go back to the Academy, or at least to Dr. Davies. I've certainly got no business toting it all over the northern half of the state. On the other hand, I have somebody visiting up at the University who could probably tell us in a second whether it's really antique or not."

"I could take it back over to school tomorrow, if your expert is willing to make the trip down here."

"He's an alumnus—summer school, a few years before your time—so I think he's planning to come down for a visit, anyway. Why don't we handle it that way, then—if you'll take the thing back tomorrow and fill Richard in, I'll see Michael—that's my consultant—tomorrow afternoon, and get in touch with you after that. Do you have anyplace safer than the museum to keep it, if Davies doesn't want to have it at home?"

"Oh, sure, I could lock it in the ammo safe and take the extra key. I might have to get the shells out for the Officer in Charge to fire the howitzer at Reveille and Retreat, but I have to be at school then anyway."

"That sounds like a plan. Now where do you want me to bed down?"

He rearranged several piles of clean laundry to make room for me in what was now the guest bedroom—which Dan and I had shared growing up—and, back in my old home, I was soon asleep.

Chapter 6: Sunday, October 22

THE LITTLE ALARM FUNCTION on my watch, while none too loud, managed to awaken me at what any other duty would have led me to describe as an ungodly hour. I drove back to Logansport and completed my official Visitation of St. James's with no further occult interruptions. By 2, I was back on road 35, headed for home and wishing I were better prepared for my afternoon performance at the university.

The fact was that I did not have a wave-the-magic-wand solution to the problems at Our Lady's university. Denominational colleges—at least those associated with the main-line denominations—haven't been going through a growth period, and Episcopalians have been doing rather worse than average. To the degree that Walsingham has been an exception, one might argue (indeed, many did argue) that it has prospered in inverse proportion to its emphasis on Anglican identity. On the other hand, a small university will always be searching for some niche market, and in a city about equidistant from the Roman Catholic Our Lady of the Lake to the east and the Chicago area educational megaplex to the west, it is hard to say what Walsingham has distinctively to offer other than its connection with me and my mitered and croziered predecessors.

Granted that, it remained open to question what the pedagogical content of such a distinctive connection might be: the issues actually under discussion, about the composition of the faculty and the student body, presumably depended on the answer to "What benefit do our students get from the university being Anglican—or even Christian, for that matter?" The possible responses—none of them wrong in itself—ranged from mere clannishness to recognition that Anglican Christianity is not simply a set of doctrinal statements but rather a culture best absorbed by experience.

What I eventually came around to was a point of view linked to what I call the "what religion do you think you can't believe" phenomenon. More times than I can, or care to, count, people have accosted me with some variation of "I don't see how a person with your education can believe in religion." When I pursue these conversations, it almost always turns out that the point to which the other person has objections is something I don't, in fact, believe; more often than not, it's something no educated Christian has ever believed. And frequently (this is where my name for it comes from) the person grows irate when I explain that the Christianity to which the person objects is not in fact Christianity at all.

Having spent so much time in confused skirmishes on the misconceived borders of science and religion, I think that the unique function to be served by an Anglican university is to demonstrate our understanding that those borders are peaceful. St. John had asked me if there were some Anglican way of curating an exhibit, anticipating "no" as the answer. What I had come to realize was that that "no" contained the answer to the whole problem. There is no Anglican way to curate a museum because there is not one beauty known to Anglicanism and another to art, there is not one truth known to Anglicanism and another to science, not one good for Anglicans and another for the world. Rather, as the Platonists have always said, there is one Good, one True, one Beautiful, and the University, my university—our Lady's university—at least, stands as a proclamation of that unity, that transcendent simplicity.

I suppose that sounds like sermon enough, and indeed it was; there remained only the trivial matter of connecting this with our annual celebration of what is, in all honesty, a rather trivial feast. October fifteenth commemorates not our Lady herself, not even the original founding of the medieval shrine of the Annunciation at the real Walsingham in England, but rather the moving of a statue of the Virgin from the parish church to the modern shrine in the nineteen thirties. Even that rather thin basis for a feast is subject to various mysterious dictates of athletic scheduling, term length and, for all I know, the positions of Jupiter and Mars—hence the week-late ceremony over which I was about to preside. The bottom line is that we need an early fall holiday, and this is a more-or-less convenient one. I meditated on the connection between my idea of the university and the Annunciation as I went back to the Cathedral to pick up my vestments for Evensong—a different outfit, of course, from what I'd worn for Mass at Logan in the morning.

The answer, my mental missing link, finally came to me in my office. I've always liked the Pre-Raphaelite painters, and I have a poster on the wall with a reproduction of the Dante Gabriel Rossetti *Annunciation*—scandalous in its day, with a nearly naked Gabriel and a Virgin we would classify as anorexic, or possibly a model for perfume ads. What occurred to me was that that dramatic scene, so often painted, so often pictured in the hearts of the faithful, draws our attention to the wrong thing. Remarkable, miraculous, as it is that God enabled the Virgin to consent, the real point is that at this point in human history God begins to lead a human life: here, at this moment, the Word was made flesh and dwelt among us. Without this moment in some obscure Galilean home, the home to which the original Walsingham was dedicated, the Good, the True, and the Beautiful can be dismissed as mere abstractions. But in the house at Nazareth, that transcendent simplicity becomes immanent, as undismissable as a crucified rabbi who returns from the dead.

With sermon in mind, then, and vestments in hand, I drove on to the University. I debated whether there would be time to ask St. John about contacting Lord Strathspey to solicit his opinion of the ivory rod, but decided it would be better to go straight to the Chapel.

There were not, thank heaven, picket lines outside. Once when I was an undergraduate, the Cardinal Archbishop of Boston made some decision that ended up in the firing of the Catholic chaplain. The next time the Cardinal came on campus, he was met by a flock of Roman students politely singing Luther's "A Mighty Fortress." It made the front page of the Boston *Globe.*

Saint Mary's Chapel is the largest ecclesiastical building in my diocese, outstripping the Cathedral, the Memorial Chapel at Annandale, and St. Bede's in Fort Wayne, our largest city. It is also, not all that coincidentally, a yard longer and a foot higher than the Basilica of Saint Mary at the Roman university over at South Bend: though that nineteenth century Gothic structure is in better taste than our distinctly modern chapel, a vast barn of etched glass and stainless steel that ill consorts with the rest of the campus. I wrote "barn" just now, but it occurs to me that I should have said, "barn and silo," for the east end of the building—what would be an apse in a more conventional church—is here a great round tower, also mostly of glass, that rises up to eaves trimmed with a vast crown of thorns. It does have the advantage, I have to admit, of being the one place in the diocese where I can use as much incense as I like without people complaining that the smoke has blocked their view, aggravated their asthma, or (as one Altar Guild mistress once told me, quite seriously) wilted the flowers.

As at the Cathedral, the Chapel's offices and vesting rooms are in the basement. Rhys and Caroline, already vested in cassock and surplice, met me in the reception area as I came downstairs from the parking lot.

"Hi, kids."

"Hi, Uncle Jon. Let me take your garment bag."

"Hi, Bishop. Chaplain Stewart asked us to meet you."

"That's kind of her, Rhys. Does she anticipate snipers?"

"No, sir, just a courtesy, I think."

"She's asked us to be your acolytes, too, Uncle Jon."

"Well, good. I take it that means you won't be throwing spitballs at each other during the service."

Rhys grinned as he started down the hall. *Oh, I imagine we can find other ways of being annoying.*

As if you ever had to work at it, Caroline replied.

"Speaking of esoteric communication," I said, "I still haven't read your e-mail,

Rhys, and we haven't really analyzed last night at Annandale, either. Do we have any chance of having a family dinner after the service?"

They both nodded. "Will Mrs. Jameson be expecting us, sir?"

"Oh, goodness, Rhys, I've forgotten what arrangements we did make. Would you give her a call? If she wasn't planning to cook, we can go out."

"Are you buying, Uncle Jon?"

"Don't I always?"

Not if you can help it, Rhys thought as he ducked into the office to phone. Caroline and I went on the vesting room, which was only another couple of steps down the hall. Sharon Stewart, the Chaplain, greeted me warmly; but as soon as I left her embrace, she got down to brass tacks.

"Controversy's apparently good for business, Bishop. Between that and the alumni, I've never seen such a crowd for Evensong."

"I just hope none of them brought rotten fruit."

"Does that mean you've picked a side, Uncle Jon?"

"I guess so. I mean, I have picked a side, certainly: but I'm not sure it matches up with either of the ones I've been hearing about."

"How's that?"

"I imagine that will be in the sermon, Caroline," Sharon said, "but we need to get your uncle vested if we want to hear it."

"I can still recognize orders when I hear them," I said, taking off my jacket. "How long were you in the Army, Sharon?"

Smiling, she shook her head. "It was the Marines, Bishop. I spent seven years in JAG before I went to seminary. May I leave you here while I take one last look around upstairs?"

"Absolutely. Shall we catch up with you in the narthex?"

"That'll be fine. If you'll bless incense there, we'll be ready to process—just a straight shot up the center."

"Very good. We'll be there in a minute. Semper Fi."

Rhys came in as Sharon was leaving, with a report that he'd taken Mrs. Jameson up on an offer of omelets and salad. With his help, Caroline got me vested and upstairs with time to spare. There was, certainly, a considerable crowd, though the building was by no means full. Having few duties to perform in the first part of the service, I was able to pick out a number of familiar faces in the congregation—Lord Strathspey sitting down front with the Dacres in the Vice-Chancellor's pew, an assortment of other faculty scattered in a pattern that hinted, without proving, that they had seated themselves in two parties, Margaret Wilson, as was her right, vested and sitting in the choir, and, most surprising of all, Hudson Buchanan sitting on the aisle somewhat more than halfway back.

Though Buchanan's presence put me on edge, the service was uneventful, and I got compliments on the sermon from Margaret and both the Dacres as I shook hands at the front door. I was even able to take Strathspey aside for a moment—

"Have you made any decision about going down to Annandale?"

"No, Bishop, I hadn't. Why do you ask?"

"Well, there's something down there I'd like you to have a look at."

"Happy to, of course, but I'm not much on American antiquities, you know."

"No, I think the claim is that this is European, and probably quite old, at that." His eyes glinted as if he were Sherlock Holmes on the trail of Moriarty, and I concluded, a bit hastily, "I don't want to prejudice you, though."

"Of course not, Bishop. It's always best to come to these questions with an open mind. Shall I call your office tomorrow to set up a time?"

"That would be wonderful, thank you, Michael."

As he moved away, one of the last of the congregation to leave, Caroline pulled me aside in turn, to where Rhys was speaking animatedly with Brother Buchanan.

". . . So you admit, then, that Hudson Buchanan isn't your real name."

"No, son, that's not what I said. It was originally the pen name I used in writing fantasy novels, but I've had my name legally changed since then. So it is my real name."

"Fine. Then what was your legal name before you changed it?"

The evangelist took advantage of my approach to change the subject. "Good evening, Bishop Mears. A solid sermon, sir, if a bit short."

Caroline looked at Rhys curiously, then said, "Nineteen minutes and thirty-seven seconds, sir. I just happened to be looking at my watch."

"As short as that, really, miss? It just goes to show: another ten minutes or so would have given the Bishop space to actually answer some of the 'cultured despisers of religion.' "

"That might be more than my congregations would stand for, Brother Buchanan. This is my niece Caroline, by the way: I take it you've already met my cousin Rhys."

"Pleased to meet you, Ms. Mears. Yes, Mr. Evans and I were just talking about the bad old days. But I suppose I'd better be going."

Now Rhys looked perturbed; he reached over to take Caroline's hand.

"Will we be seeing you around town, then, Brother Buchanan?" he asked.

"Only for a day or so, I'm afraid. 'Fresh fields and pastures green,' you know. I would have been gone already if the doctors had let me."

"Well, then," I said, extending my hand, "Thank you again for coming to the service, and I am sorry about last Friday."

He made an odd little bow. "Excuse me for not shaking, Bishop, but I do know about your rings. I do thank you for your good wishes, though. Good evening."

Nodding briefly to Caroline and Rhys, he made his dignified way to the door, unconscious of the stares the kids were directing at his back.

There, I heard Rhys think, *he's finally gone.*

Can you believe it? Caroline answered. *It's like having duct tape over your mouth.*

"Let's go change back into civvies," I said, adding *Maybe you can explain what you're thinking about to me on the way.*

You heard us, then, Rhys said as we walked downstairs.

Yes. Shouldn't I have?

You certainly should have, Caroline thought. *But you should have five minutes ago, too.*

And yesterday when you were at the hospital, for that matter, Rhys added. *The man's a walking jammer for telepathy.*

That should give us something to talk about over our omelets, I replied.

"Oh, let's not spoil supper, Uncle Jon. Besides, there are a few points about your sermon that I wanted to discuss."

<hr>

IN FACT, we waited until we were in the upstairs family room, where I was having a single malt and the kids some sort of hi-test coffee.

"Okay, then," Caroline began. "What do we know now that we didn't know on Friday night?"

"I think Buchanan is a fake, Car."

"He strikes me as sincere to a fault," I said.

"Well, religiously, maybe. But I thought Rhys was probing him about his name."

"Right, Car. You heard him say that it was originally a pen name, and he didn't seem anxious to reveal his secret identity."

"That did sound as though he had something to hide, I admit."

"But I don't see what, Uncle Jon. I mean, he confesses to being a Satan worshipper—and a science fiction author, for that matter."

"Which brings up another curious point," Rhys said. "The only reason I asked him about his name in the first place was that I had been doing some checking in fandom . . ."

" 'Fandom?' "

"It's a word, sir. Give me a break! The point is, even when the guy was writing, people thought he must be a pseudonym, because he never came to any of the cons—the conventions, you know."

"Surely not all the authors go to those conventions."

"No, sir, but enough do that it looks fishy for someone never to show up at even one. And besides, he never made any kind of public appearance—no book jacket signings, nor even a picture on the dust jacket."

"Even so, Rhys," Caroline said, "That explains why you asked him, but it doesn't prove anything he didn't admit."

"Granted, but it fits in somehow with what you were just saying. If no one had ever seen Hudson Buchanan, there was no reason for whatever-his-name-was to identify himself as Buchanan when he went on the evangelism circuit."

"Well, name recognition, perhaps."

"But, Uncle Jon, there can't be that much overlap between his reading public and the audience for his revivals, can there?"

"Some, presumably, or he wouldn't mention the fact in his posters."

"It could be just for shock value, bishop. But either way, he could achieve the same purpose by using his real name and just identifying himself as the author."

"The evangelist formerly known as Buchanan."

"Right, Car. So since he didn't do that, it looks as though he wanted to hide his real name. But considering what he admits to, what does he have left to hide?"

"He's keeping an awfully high profile for a former mobster."

"And he doesn't seem the mass murderer sort," I added.

"Exactly. I wouldn't put him up for anything more than a slightly fishy accountant. Even at that, I wouldn't go so far as crooked. So what I'm wondering is whether that may not be the fake part—Mr. Smith wants to be known as Br. Buchanan because Mr. Smith was a mousy little fellow who never sat on a park bench without his Bible, much less led Satanic rituals on Samhain or Beltane. And if anyone could identify Mr. Smith behind Br. Buchanan, they'd know the whole repentance thing was a sham."

"But, Rhys . . ."

"Now wait a minute . . ."

"One at a time, please. Bishop?"

"Right. I see your line of reasoning, Rhys, but as I said, he certainly does seem to be sincerely repentant."

"I think I have an answer to that, but I want to see if Car feeds me the right straight line first."

"You want me to ask about the telepathic blocking."

"Good call. And no telepathy involved, either."

"None required. It was the only loose end: but I still don't see what you're going to tie it to."

"Okay. So here's my theory. Suppose I wanted to create a Hudson Buchanan—" he put up his hand "—I know I haven't said why, but just suppose I did. I might be able to do it with plain garden-variety brainwashing, of course, like in that movie where the guy's mother wants him to kill Kennedy . . ."

Caroline grimaced and muttered, *"Manchurian Candidate."*

Rhys went on unperturbed in the wake of his great idea. "—You could do that conventionally. But with paranormal powers, you could presumably do all the usual things better, more thoroughly, so your converted person absolutely, completely believed what you implanted, and you might just be able to top it all off with some sort of a seal to make sure that no one alive could look into your agent's mind and see there what he himself couldn't see."

"I suppose with paranormal powers you could argue that anyone could do anything, Rhys. It isn't as though we know what the limits actually are."

"Right, Uncle Jon. And besides that, there's another loose end that I just thought of. We know that Buchanan blocks our telepathy, even when it's not aimed at him. But we also know that he doesn't just not block your messages from the past, he actually attracted a message that wasn't meant for him."

"But I don't think that was actually telepathy, Caroline, it was more like, I don't know, a vision. Or something."

"Okay, but look. If Rhys is arguing that this whole Manchurian candidate thing is set up with just plain psi-powers, then Buchanan, or Smith, or whatever we're going to call him would presumably still be vulnerable to magic. That wouldn't make much sense if you were sending him out into situations where he'd be attracting attention from magic-users. I mean, if that was all you could do for him, that would be one thing, but if you could make him magic-proof, that would be what you'd want to do, wouldn't it? Just being ESP-proof would be really second best. So if these visions from Boethius and so on come from some sort of magic, not ESP, we'd expect that a well-prepared Buchanan would resist both. Yet he doesn't. So he's not well-prepared. Either he's only protected against ESP, or he's not protected at all, and Rhys's theory is wrong. If we knew the right sorts of spells, we could just test his defenses and see."

"Unfortunately, being magic users without spells was part of your grandfather's plan for the family."

Rhys's face lit up, and he actually said "Aha!" "There is," he went on, "another possibility. Buchanan could be partially protected against magic. What if magic doesn't protect against itself? Car, when your grandfather and mine were fighting, the ring made a kind of hole in their defenses; they were using the same magic on both sides. So if Buchanan picks up the Bishop's messages, it could be because the person who programmed him is using the same sort of magic that we are."

"But Rhys, aren't you assuming that I'm consciously attracting these visions? Otherwise, you'd be arguing that the person who prepared Brother Buchanan and the person who's *sending* me the visions are using the same magic."

"Why couldn't they be?" Caroline asked. "After all, we don't know anything about either one; for that matter, one of them is only a theory, anyway."

"But he's my theory, and I'd hate to lose him."

"You're welcome to have him, Rhys, but it seems to me he's led us to a dead end. The closest we've gotten to an explanation is that Hudson Buchanan might be a Trojan horse prepared by a person using the same species of magic as that being used by the person or persons who keep sending me bulletins from late antiquity."

"All right then, sir, why don't we see what we can make out of your adventures over the last day and a half?"

"Only if I can be excused for a moment first."

"Sure thing, sir. I'm going to run downstairs. Do you want another Scotch?"

"No, I think I'd like a Coke, actually."

"Right. You want anything, Car?"

"No, I'm okay, thanks. While you two are busy, I'm going to print out something from my computer. Don't start till I get back."

When we reconvened, Caroline had a small sheaf of papers to distribute.

"Handouts?" Rhys said. "How quaint."

"It seemed easier than adjourning to the computer screen. What you've got here is a series of World Wide Web pages, working backwards from the Boethius material I found the other night. There are one or two academic sites about Boethius, but a lot of this stuff is put up by some group that's publishing new editions of the classics. There's a description of them on the second sheet I gave you."

"I see. Richard Davies was telling me about that the other day at lunch. But I thought he said it was a Neo-pagan group. I don't see why they'd be pushing Boethius."

"Two reasons, I think, Uncle Jon. On the one hand, I believe they claim that he really did go back to paganism before he wrote the *Consolation of Philosophy*. I know that's been disproved, but it's still their position."

"Okay, Car: what's the other shoe?"

"It's more trivial, really. One of their heroes is a senator named Q. Aurelius Symmachus, who made the last big pro-pagan speech in the Roman Senate. Apparently he was the grandfather of Boethius's father-in-law, so Boethius sort of rides on his coat-tails. Their biography of Boethius is on the third and fourth pages of your hand-out, by the way."

"But you're leading up to something else," Rhys said.

"Yes, I am. Now this site has links to other pages about Roman stuff. After you told us about this Dixon guy last night, I went back and looked for a site on Roman armies; there's a large one, and I ran off the first page of that for you, too. You'll see it's maintained for his school by the elusive Mr. Dixon. Now that's not surprising; I mean, after all, I thought he might do something of the kind—that's why I was looking in the first place. What is surprising, though, is that that isn't the only link between Dixon's school and the gang in Seattle. Apparently the school and the publishing house are run by the same folks."

"Well, Anglicans have schools and colleges, and so do Baptists, Jews and Christian Scientists, for that matter. I suppose there's no reason why pagans shouldn't do likewise."

"But this one apparently has a pretty powerful magician on its staff, sir."

"Whereas Walsingham has one less competent magician on the Board and two in its student body. It's a distinction, Rhys, but not much of a difference."

"Actually, gentlemen, what I wanted to suggest was that Dixon seems to be some sort of link himself, between the affairs in Annandale and Uncle Jon's visions of Boethius."

"It's a pretty weak link, isn't it, Car? The Neo-pagans in Seattle surely aren't sending the Bishop his dreams."

"I wouldn't think so, no; but it could be someone who opposes them who's doing it."

"You'd think they could just pick up the phone," I said. "I'm no enthusiast for a pagan comeback, but I don't see why one would have to be dealt with through para-normal channels."

"It wouldn't, sir, if they weren't using those channels in the first place. I think Car is on to something. Suppose Dixon was the one who pro-grammed Buchanan—he might serve the general purpose of distracting attention from the real pagan revival with all his garbage about demons in the park, and he'd also have the specific function of attacking you while he was in town here. Dixon himself, meanwhile, is looking for magic items to strengthen his hand, and takes an interest for some reason in this ivory wand at Annandale."

"Presumably he, or his society, thinks it goes back to classical paganism."

"Of course, Car. And if that's the kind of magic he uses, it would dovetail with Buchanan being sensitive to these visions with a classical background—they'd be coming from someone using classical magic, as well."

"Now that you've put it that way," I said, "I'm wondering about the Alfred Jewel, the piece I was looking at yesterday afternoon. Given Lord Strathspey's thesis that the stone goes back to Boethius, once the museum announces that it's here, it could be a more attractive target than any old wand, however rare the ivory."

"Maybe that's what the visions are about—not just vague messages about antiquity and Neo-paganism, but a specific request that you protect this jewel."

"That could be it, Caroline," I said, "though now our hypothetical good guys have to be in on the jewel coming to Walsingham. I thought that was a very closely held secret."

"Still and all, sir, it might be worthwhile to see if we can make the thing a little safer."

"It's already locked up like Fort Knox, Rhys. I even had to have a special ID to get in. The display areas must be equally secure."

"Would the security system stop someone from teleporting into the museum, breaking the display case, and teleporting out?"

"Well, I doubt if they specifically planned for it when they redid the building. But if Mr. Dixon could do that, why didn't he just pop into the Annandale museum and snag the baton? Or why not zap himself over to Oxford and get the jewel any old time?"

"I'll bet he can only go someplace he's already been, sir. He had never been to Annandale, so he had to go there to get the baton; but when the cops showed up and he got outside the house's defenses, he had no trouble popping back to his car, or even to Milwaukee, for that matter. Besides, *he* doesn't necessarily know he wants the stone, yet; it's the good guys who know what's up."

"The presumptive good guys, at least."

"Right, Uncle Jon. But acting on that presumption, I think we ought to try to put wards around the museum. Inconspicuous shields, as you said the other day."

"What about the ammo safe down at Annandale?" I asked.

"Has Dixon ever been there, sir?"

"Possibly, depending on how thorough Philip's campus tour was."

"Okay, that would be a possible problem. But even if he knows where the safe is, and could pick the lock, he doesn't know that's where the staff is—"

"Unless he can read Philip's mind," I added.

"Wouldn't it be easier to just ask him to keep the thing at home?" Caroline suggested.

"Okay," Rhys said, "that would be practical, I guess. What about the museum?"

"I have to admit," I said, "it couldn't hurt. But we are not going to march in circles around the museum. I'll put something together that we can do at Morning Prayer tomorrow morning. At least we know something about that sort of spell."

"Sounds like a plan, sir," Rhys said. "I think I'll go on to bed."

"It sounds good to me, too, Uncle Jon. Should I tell Daddy about all this?"

"Yes, dear, if you would, please. It wouldn't hurt to warn him about our plans for tomorrow, too."

I retired to my study and worked out a suitable ritual, and so to bed.

Chapter 7: Monday, October 23

I SET UP the altar in our chapel for the ritual the next morning by simply spreading a corporal—roughly the liturgical equivalent of a placemat—setting down a paten—a silver liturgical plate—and placing my museum pass card on it. The ritual I had used to prepare a place for Rhys's baptism and the one we had used to protect the palace were elaborate affairs based, in the first case, on the liturgy for lighting candles, and in the second on that for blessing a home. Both involved three trips around the space, with a staff, a sword, and a cross, using ashes, holy water, and incense, with a dozen prayers or more, invoking angels, evangelists, and other saints as well as the Most Holy Trinity. Though I had no real evidence to support the theory, it seemed to me likely that a similar effect could be achieved by proxy, so to speak—hence the ID card—and given the size of the proxy, small enough that one could draw circles around it, rather than staging a procession, it hardly seemed necessary to have so extensive a series of intercessions. Three prayers seemed likely to be enough for the purpose, and my index finger a reasonable substitute for staff, sword and cross. Essentially, I would hope to be protecting the jewel with the same sorts of gestures I might use to bless palms, a cross, or even a wedding ring.

We assembled for Morning Prayer at seven. I explained the plan to Rhys and Caroline, and we began with blessing the materials we would use. I said the exorcisms of salt and water, and, after combining the two, touched my hand to the liquid, saying:

"O God, you are the author of strength invincible, the King of the empire that none may overcome: you are wondrous in your triumphs, you quell the might of the dominion that opposes you, you conquer the roaring enemy and overthrow by your might the wickedness of the adversary: in fear and humility, we beseech you, O Lord, mercifully to sanctify this creature of salt and water, that wherever it may be sprinkled with the invocation of your holy Name, the assaults of the unclean spirit may be driven forth, the dread of the poisonous serpent be cast out, and the presence of your Holy Spirit established. Through Jesus Christ our Lord. Amen."

I would ordinarily have gone on to bless incense next, but in the relatively small confines of our chapel, it seemed best to put that step off to the last minute. Sprinkling the holy water on the silver bowl of ashes, I said the second blessing: "Almighty God, you have created us out the dust of the earth:

grant that these ashes may be to us a sign of our mortality and penitence, that we may remember that it is only by your gracious gift that we are given everlasting life. Through Jesus Christ our Lord. Amen."

With these preparations out of the way, we began the usual part of the service. After the psalms, lessons, canticles, creed, Lord's Prayer and suffrages, I went to the altar. At this point, Caroline did bring me the incense, and I said the traditional prayer, "At the intercession of blessed Michael the Archangel, who stands at the right hand of the altar of incense, be blessed by him in whose honor you are to be burned." Then I took the thurible from her and waved it over the ID card in the pattern of a five pointed star surrounded by a circle—a process made easier by the red lines that traced the pattern, more precisely than the spreading smoke, as I said the first collect: "Lord Christ, you are the bright and morning star, the Holy Wisdom, coeternal with the Father and the Holy Spirit: grant that we who remember before you your servant Severinus Boethius may profit from his teaching and at his intercession preserve those relics which represent him to us, as he reflects you, and you reveal the equal and eternal glory which you share with the same Father and Spirit, one God, now and forever. Amen."

I handed the thurible back to Caroline, and Rhys proffered the ashes. Dipping my finger in them, I marked the Star of David, Solomon's Seal, around the card, leaving a trail of green light to accompany the second prayer: "Blessed are you, O Lord our God, King of the universe, for you made your Son our messiah, the Son of David and the Heir of Solomon, King of Kings and Lord of Lords: grant, at the intercession of your servant Alfred King of Wessex, that those who profess your faith may be kept safe from your enemies, and protect for us the symbols of his earthly reign, that we may remember by whose power it is that all kings rule, the same your Son our savior Jesus Christ. Amen."

As Caroline was still holding the thurible, I had a little trouble switching the bowl of ashes for the bucket of holy water, which Rhys had already brought to the altar. He and I managed the transfer, however, and I went on to the third collect, sprinkling the water in the form of the cross: "Hail, Lady of Walsingham, Queen of the Saints and Mother of God: from your home in Nazareth to the foot of the cross, you nurtured and protected your son, Jesus Christ: intercede with him, we pray, for your university, and put its museum under your special protection, that its treasures may be preserved for the instruction of your students, for your own honor, and for the greater glory of your son, our savior Jesus Christ, who lives and reigns with the Father and the Holy Spirit, one God, now and for ever. Amen."

Lady blue light traced the pattern, and as I said the ordinary collect for the end of Matins, the three patterns joined to make a dome of golden light over the card.

"Let us bless the Lord," I concluded, and the kids responded, "Thanks be to God."

"I think I'll go set this outside," Caroline said, "and hope I don't pass a smoke detector along the way."

"Good luck," Rhys answered. "Bishop, you've made me nervous. Are you sure none of this is showing up over at school?"

"Hopeful, at least; I don't think I could go as far as sure. If it's working at all, something will certainly show up if the jewel is attacked—but only in the room where it's locked away. I don't know that it's doing any good, though."

"That, there's no way to know. Are you just going to leave everything set up here on the altar?"

"I imagine that would be safest. I'll just lock the chapel door and put the key upstairs in my desk."

"That sounds good to me. I'll see you at breakfast, then."

<hr/>

AFTER A PLEASANT, if perhaps slightly hurried, family meal, I took a brisk walk up the street and was sitting in my office by a few minutes after eight, ready to boot my computer and check the day's schedule. As Monday is usually my day off, I hoped to find little on the calendar.

Carl came into my office before I had a chance to sit down. "It's my day for lunch at the club, Jonathan. Do you need anything from Chicago—other than Frango mints, I mean?"

"Oh, thank you, no, Carl. I could use a candy refill, though, seriously. I could mail order it, of course, but it always seems fresher when it comes straight from the store."

"No problem at all, I'm happy to do it."

"Are you driving over?"

"No, I thought I'd take the 9:30 South Shore—you don't have to worry about parking that way, and I can go right downtown, or stop off at the university and hit the Seminary Bookstore."

"There are some books I could use, but those really don't get stale. Listen, Carl, do you have a couple of minutes to hear about my weekend?"

"Of course. Let me get my coffee and I'll be right back."

I kept my account of the whole Buchanan affair and the baton episode relatively brief, and though it nevertheless went on a bit, I finished in plenty of time for Carl to walk to the train station. Of course, it's only five blocks.

THE DAY REALLY wasn't all that crowded. I had lunch scheduled with the Mayor, who was hoping that I could still be persuaded to drop my opposition to putting floating casinos on Trail Creek, and my regular weekly meeting with Dean Philips, moved back from Tuesday because I had a conflict with a session of the Board of Trustees of the Zoological Park, at ten. I was, then, chipping away at my paperwork when Mrs. Equitone buzzed me, a few minutes after nine.

"Are you free, Bishop? It's Lord Strathspey to see you."

"Oh, yes, by all means, Mrs. Equitone. Send him in."

I got up from my desk to meet him at the door.

"Michael, you didn't have to come by. I'd expected you to phone."

"It's no trouble, Bishop. One thing seemed about as easy as the other."

"I'm glad you're here, in any case. Have a seat. Would you like a cup of coffee?"

He grinned. "Thank you, no. Don't let me stop you from having a Coke, though."

"No, that's all right; I think I'll wait until a bit later." I sat in one of the armchairs to the left of the sofa in which Michael had positioned himself.

"Now, then, you say there's a piece of antique ivory you'd like me to see?"

"Something we think is ivory that may be antique, to be precise."

"Has it a provenance?"

"Nothing useful. The piece has been in the private collection of an American for the last fifty years or so; he was fond of Roman antiquities, and might have—probably did, I guess—pick this up on a postwar trip to Europe. It probably came from Italy, or perhaps from England. The rest of the continent would be less likely, I think."

Michael began to indulge himself in a smile. "This begins to sound a good deal like Commander Lindsley."

"Nice deduction, my lord. I didn't think Commander Lindsley was still working summers when you were a camper."

"No, no, he wasn't. But you remember that they were eager to recruit us for the regular school year—so every summer for five years I saw the winter school PR movie, with a whole segment on the catapult team and Mr. Lindsley presiding over it in a Roman general's armor that had been made for Lord Olivier to wear in *Spartacus*: or at least that was what the narrator said."

"I think it was actually a copy in the commander's size, but still. You figured, then, that the person who collected Roman movie props might also be my anonymous antiquarian."

"Precisely. Now what sort of ivory is this? A diptych?"

"No, he generally brought back only things he had some use for, like the armor. A diptych he would've just had to display on the wall, like any other plaque. The thing I'd like you to look at is a little staff, which he used in his capacity as faculty marshal."

"I see. And why is the school suddenly interested in finding out about its history?"

"I'm not sure the school is interested, yet, though the realization may just now be dawning. Basically, the problem is that someone tried to steal the thing, and took it to my house in Annandale in the process. We recovered the baton, but the thief got away. So now I'm curious as to why the gizmo could be worth someone's coming all the way to Annandale to steal."

He raised one of those curiously elven eyebrows. "Really? All the way from where?"

"Oh, only Milwaukee, admittedly. But still, it shows an element of premeditation."

"I agree, it does. Well, as Holmes would say, you interest me strangely. I should certainly like to see the piece. Did you have a joint expedition in mind, or shall I hire a car and motor on down by myself?"

"Oh, I want to go along. It feels as though I've been out of the office a lot lately, but it is theoretically my day off. Are you free this afternoon?"

"I can be, certainly. This is partly a holiday for me, after all."

"Great. Why don't I pick you up, then, say about half past one, and that way we can avoid the whole which side of the road issue?"

"That will be fine. St. John has put me up at the university hotel, of course."

"Right. The Walsingham Inn it is, then. I'll see you this afternoon."

The Dean wanted to chat about the Cathedral organist, and by the time the conversation had led through the merits of guitar masses and handbell choirs—a well-traveled road for the two of us, neither of whom had much use for either of them—it was creeping on toward time for lunch, and it occurred to me that if I were going to let Capt. Cicero know we were coming, I should phone him before he went out to supervise the Mess Hall.

"Hello, Philip."

"Hi, Mom."

"I beg your pardon?"

"I'm just teasing, Bishop. You and she are the only people who use my whole name. What's up?"

"Well, I've spoken to my expert, and he'd like to come down and look at the baton this afternoon."

"That should be okay. What time were you thinking of?"

"Between two-thirty and three, I guess. I'm supposed to pick him up at the university at half-past one. Will that work?"

"Toward the end of eighth period, then. That'll be fine. I have to work with some kids during athletics, but that won't be till three-thirty, anyway."

"Great. What's the legal situation?"

"Nothing, apparently. It did occur to one of the rent-a-cops to look for Dixon's car after they left your house, and when they couldn't find it, that gave a little believability to the 'he ran away' theory. Since we have the baton and there's no sign of Dixon, the guys don't seem to be inclined to pursue things very energetically—I mean, it's just my word against his, and it would only be attempted robbery or something at worst, anyway."

"Just as well, I think. I wasn't looking forward to explanations of what knocked him out."

"You've explained worse in your day, I think. See you this afternoon."

———

ON THE ROAD SOUTH, Michael and I mostly made small talk, reminiscing about his childhood days at Annandale and reflecting, as almost anyone does who returns to the rural Midwest at this point, on how urbanized the country has become.

"Of course," he said, "the sheer scale of your American countryside is the great difference, and that hasn't changed at all."

"No, my scheme to plant hedgerows and divide all the fields up into parcels of ten acres or less has never really caught on."

"I can imagine not. The fields here must be ten times that size."

"When my immigrant ancestor came here from Hampshire, where he had been renting the manor farm in his little town, he bought six hundred and forty acres, a square mile, and he added another three hundred twenty before he died. Of course, that was only possible because the government had stolen it from the Indians, and the property had to be divided amongst the old boy's thirteen surviving children, but it was great while it lasted."

"Astounding. Now what's the explanation for these great long numbers on people's mailboxes?"

"It's for the emergency medical service. The mailman used to be able to go to rural route so-and-so, number such-and-such, but with the computers sending out ambulances, they needed an exact address for every house. That little hill we're passing on the right, by the way, is where my several-times-great-grandfather built his house. It's burned down now, of course."

"How long ago would that have been—building it, I mean?"

"The homesteaders came up here in 1834, but a lot of them lived in log cabins at first. The house that burned was built in 1863, the coldest winter on record here. Lots of local men were off at the war, but grandfather had a deferment because of his false teeth. Muzzle loading rifles, you know."

"You have a tour-guide's instinct for detail, Bishop Mears."

"Thank you, my lord. Now you should see campus ahead and to the left as we come to the crest of this hill."

"Yes, I remember . . . good heavens, what is that? A zeppelin hanger?"

"No, though it's new since your time. It's the ice-hockey arena—three separate skating areas under one roof, in fact."

"One ugly roof, as you say over here."

"Yes, quite. You'll discover that in general what's new on campus is also ugly, though there are some notable exceptions. We had good luck redecorating the meditation chapel, for example."

"Even if you do say so yourself."

"Precisely. I'm afraid they've also cut down on traffic through the center of campus, so we may not be able to park very close to Sally Port."

"That's quite all right. Why not leave the car in the park near the library, and take our tour from there?"

"I'll head that way. It'll be interesting to see what you think of the new library."

He thought no more of it than I, as it turned out, and we disparaged it cheerfully as we walked across campus. I realized in the middle of the quad that Philip and I hadn't actually agreed on a place to meet. As we were early anyway, we detoured through Verdun barracks, and found Phil in his basement office putting on the last few pieces of a suit of plate armor.

I made the introductions, and Michael said, as they shook hands, "You know, Captain, I have several of those at home, and I have never been able to get into one."

"You pretty much have to have one made, my lord, unless you're on the short side or had tall ancestors."

"Actually, the problem was more circumferential than vertical. I seem to have missed out on my share of the tubby genes. But if it isn't rude for me to ask, why?"

"Philip has a group of students who recreate medieval battles, Michael. I take it that that's the group he's meeting with later this afternoon."

"That's it," Phil agreed. "I'm hoping to have the boys ready to put on some sort of a show for homecoming this weekend, and we're into dress rehearsals, so to speak. I wasn't sure how much time I'd have to change afterwards."

"And I daresay that putting on an armor takes a certain amount of time."

"Longer than I would have thought before I tried it, my lord. There are an awful lot of little straps to fasten."

"I can imagine. And do please call me Michael. After all, we're all alumni together, I understand."

"Great, Michael. And I'm just Phil, regardless of what you hear from the Bishop. Should we head on over to Sally Port? I asked Dr. Davies to meet us there, since he's in charge of the baton."

"That makes sense," I said.

"Great. It's a little bit of a maze down here, so just follow me."

"I'm glad he didn't say, 'walk this way,'" Michael said in a stage whisper, as Philip clanked off down the hall.

Coming from the history building at the south end of the quad, Richard Davies caught up with us about halfway to Sally Port, and I introduced him to Michael.

"Jonathan has told me a bit about the background of Commander Lindsley's baton, Richard: brought over from England or Italy about fifty years ago. I wonder whether you have any other ideas about provenance?"

"No, I'm not sure there's much else to say. The Commander had a collection of these things, you know—in fact, that does bring one point to mind. He didn't just buy these items, you see—it's more like found art. One of them began as the handle on a water ski tow-rope, and another one looks suspiciously like a curtain rod with some lamp finials attached to its ends."

"So this was sort of a developmental thing, version 5.3 or whatever," Philip said.

"No, I don't even think that's true. This ivory baton was his top of the line model, but that didn't stop him from making new ones. The modified bedpost that I ordinarily carry to assemblies dates from the year he retired, I think."

"I take it then, Richard, that you think the Commander may have manipulated this piece, as well."

"I certainly wouldn't be surprised if you told me that he had. I know that he put bands of ribbon around it in the school colors, but there could easily be more to it than that."

"Well, we should know directly," I said.

Though Sally Port is no longer, despite its name, a gateway to anything in particular, the Academy having long since bought and filled in the marsh that was across the road from its original eastern border, the cadet guard is still posted just off the building's stately lobby, and the Officer of the Day called his orderlies to attention as Philip walked in.

"Good afternoon, Captain, Doctor, Chaplain, Sir."

"Afternoon, Mr. Chauviere. Have you been snacking in the Guard Room?"

"Snacking, sir? No, sir. Why, sir?"

"You looked for a moment there as though you'd swallowed something that caught in your throat—unless of course you were trying to suppress a smile."

The boy caught on at that point and drew himself into a yet more rigid posture. "Smile, sir? Of course not, sir. The Cadet cannot imagine what the Captain might be thinking about, sir. The Cadet is accustomed to seeing the Commandant's staff in tin costumes, sir."

"The Cadet had better be if he intends to borrow the Captain's mail shirt for the weekend, at least. At ease, gentlemen. How's the plan for that trebuchet going, Chauviere?"

"Pretty well, Captain. I've got the AP Physics class working on it."

"Great. Did you know that Bishop Mears was on the academy catapult team when he was a cadet?"

"Really, Bishop? That's interesting. What sort of propulsion did you use?"

"Three-quarter inch steel cable under high tension from a jack we made out of a locomotive bolt and a couple of pieces of armor plate from a tank."

"Sir?"

"We were going for distance, not authenticity. As I remember, the release mechanism was the hard part, though."

"Yes, sir. Did you find a solution?"

"We tried a stationary boot on the end of the arm, thinking we could throw a shot put that would roll out at the right angle: but eventually we went back to a sling. Even so, it's hard to get the sling to release right when you want it to."

"Um, Jonathan . . ." Richard murmured.

"Oh, right. Can't keep everyone waiting. Let me know how your project turns out, Mr. Chauviere. Captain Cicero can give you my e-mail address."

"I will, Bishop."

Removing his gauntlets, Philip led us through the faculty Officer-in-Charge's office, across the lobby from the guard, and into the back room—little more than a closet—that housed the ammo safe. After a moment of fumbling with the padlock (it was, I remembered, some sort of specialized Army issue that worked as nearly opposite as possible to civilian expectations), Phil opened the door to reveal the usual assortment of brass howitzer shells (some ready for reloading and others still sheltering a half-load of powder under their paraffin seals), sound-blocking earphones, hand cream, and paper towels. He reached down among the shells, brought out a green cardboard mailing tube, and handed it over to Richard. "I thought if I was going to carry around antique ivory, I should have it in some sort of casing," he said. "I've sat on one pair too many of sunglasses."

Richard opened the tube and looked over the rod while Philip relocked the safe. "It seems to be none the worse for wear," he said, handing it on to Strathspey.

"Great," Philip said. "We can all step out into the main office, if Michael would like to look at the thing in natural light. And that way I can sit down for awhile."

We of the laity took seats—Richard and I in chairs, Phil propping himself against the desk—while the expert took a loupe from his pocket and examined the piece in detail. He made a thorough job of it, but a smile was playing across his elfin face after only the first minute or two.

"Here you are," he said finally, handing the baton back to Richard. "Use it in good health. But I'm afraid I can't say much for the expertise of your burglar."

"What's the story?" I asked.

"Well. The carved balls on either end of the piece are plastic, and of course these colored bands are, as you saw, Richard, merely ribbon that has been stuck on. All that being said, the central section *is* ivory, but it does not appear to me to be particularly old. Now of course metalwork is my specialty, and if it were a matter of appraising a potentially valuable piece, I'd suggest having a real expert look it over. But a small rod like this one would hardly have any intrinsic value, even if it were quite old indeed."

"That's something of a relief, actually," Richard said. "Not to say that I've broken a lot of sunglasses, but I'm just as glad to know that I'm carrying about only a piece of Annandale history at graduation, and not a priceless heirloom."

"One can't help wondering, though, about Phil's thief," Michael said. "Jonathan told me he was curious as to why anyone would come from Milwaukee to steal this, and I have to say that it's difficult to believe a professional would have thought of taking it, even if the whole thing dated back to classical antiquity. Nor is it clear to me why an amateur would imagine it was valuable in the first place."

Phil glanced at me, unsure of how much Michael knew about my family history, and I picked up the conversational ball. "Yes, I should have said that that was what the thief himself said. From Philip's account, it seems more likely to me that the thief was a magic user of some sort, and took the baton thinking it was magic. Knowing where it had been for the last forty or fifty years, I figured that any interesting bits in the item's history must have come from pre-Lindsley days. Certainly, the Commander wasn't using this to draw magic circles."

"Not that we know of, at least," Richard cautioned.

"Granted. But still, it strikes me as awfully unlikely. Anyway, if the thief has been telling us the truth, that would have been one thing: you might hand down a small piece of ivory just because it *was* magic, even though it had no intrinsic value. But given what Michael's said, the charge, or whatever you call it, must have been put on this wand relatively recently."

"But, Bishop, does it make any difference? We don't even know the thing actually is magic, for that matter."

"Well, no, Philip, I don't suppose it does matter particularly, but all the weird things that have been happening to me lately have been ancient, and it would make a neater package if this fit in somehow."

"I do take Phil's point about whether the item is magic or not though, Bishop," Michael said. "I gather that you haven't touched it, thus far. What would happen if you did?"

"I'm not sure, to tell the truth. I got a big reaction the first time I handled Louie Evans's ring, but I don't go all tingly every time I open the front door of my house. After all, my father meant for us to grow up there without realizing that it had magical defenses. I suppose it all depends on the intentions of the person who made the item in the first place."

"I see," Michael replied. "Still, it's worth a try, don't you think?" He retrieved the rod from Richard and held it out temptingly toward me.

"Go ahead, Bishop," Philip said, and Richard added, "You should certainly be safe enough here."

"With a knight in shining armor?" I said. "I could hardly feel safer." Standing up, I took the rod from Michael's hand, perhaps a bit gingerly, and felt, anticlimactically, nothing at all. We all laughed at once, and I handed it back to Richard. "*Well*, then," I said. "Not conclusive, but persuasive, at least."

"Between Michael's examination and this," he replied, "It does look to me as though, if Dixon was actually hoping for a magic item, this wasn't it."

Michael and I nodded our agreement, and Phil stood up: "I have to get out to meet the kids. But I'm still puzzled. What Dixon said he came for probably isn't true, and what we thought he actually came for apparently isn't true, either. Now the guy could just plain be wrong, of course, but I wish I knew that for sure. Bishop, couldn't your friend the Abbot do one of those psychic reading things and tell us the real story of the rod?"

"He might be able to; at least he could tell us the story of the elephant it came from. But he's down at the Archabbey in St. Meinrad this week for a conference of Benedictine superiors."

"Consorting with the Pope of Rome and his detestable enormities?" Michael asked, quoting from an old Anglican litany.

"No, just being Benedictine. They think of themselves rather ecumenically, Roman, Anglican, Lutheran or whatever. In any case, we can show him the piece when he gets back. It'll be easy enough for him to drive over to campus and look through the museum."

"Great. But then just until we hear from him, it might be better for me to keep it over at the house, where it has extra protection. If that's all right with you, Richard."

He gave an expansive wave. "It's fine by me—I won't need it again until June."

"Sounds like a plan. If you wouldn't mind taking it back there then, Bishop, I'll get out to rehearsal. Michael, it was good to meet you."

"You, too, Phil. Best of luck with your reenactments."

"Thank you very much. Dr. Davies, I suppose I'll see you in the Dining Hall."

"Or at the Corner Tavern," he answered, smiling. He put the baton back in its impromptu case, Phil locked the door behind us, and with a brief farewell to Mr. Chauviere, we were on our way.

"You know, Richard," I said, as the three of us walked back toward the car, "It looks as though there's some sort of connection between our robber and those Neo-pagans of Doug Fletcher's that you were telling me about."

"How so?"

"Apparently the school where the bad guy teaches is run by the same people that are doing that new publication series."

"New pagan publications?" Michael asked, a bit amused.

"No," Richard said. "What they're coming out with is new editions and translations of the old pagan authors. Bishop Mears is pleased to take a rather condescending tone toward the whole enterprise."

"Well, bishops, pagans, what can one expect? How did you happen to hear of this project?"

"A funny kind of coincidence, really—I was at a conference on world religions, and happened to run into Doug Fletcher, whose father was on the faculty here when Jonathan was growing up. And as Jonathan said, Doug is part of the group, though I don't think he's actually involved with the publishing arm."

"Astounding. Pagans with their own evangelistic press. The colonies do offer a bit of everything."

"Some bits we could do without," I answered as we came to the lot. We made our farewells, and a few minutes later I pulled into my driveway.

"Would you like to come in?" I asked. "I'm just going to drop this off in the living room."

He shook his head. "In that case, I think I can wait here. Phil hasn't had a chance to prepare for visitors, after all."

"He's the Deputy Commandant: he ought to be ready for a surprise inspection now and then. Still, I'll just leave the car on in case you want to listen to the radio, and I'll be right back."

Entering the house without any pyrotechnics, I put the green tube carefully on the mantle, made a brief stop in the bathroom, and was soon on the road back home to supper.

—

MRS. JAMESON was apparently in her apartment when I got home. I took a Coke from the fridge and went upstairs to catch the late news on PBS. As usual, I dozed off before the end of the news summary, and awoke only when a buzz on the intercom told me that dinner was ready.

There was only one plate set at the table. "Ms. Mears and Mr. Evans are both working at the library this evening, Bishop," Mrs. Jameson said as I sat down. "I hope you won't mind pork again after Saturday evening. I saw some nice double-thick chops, and thought I remembered you saying something about liking them stuffed."

"Oh, yes, you're right. I was probably remembering a trip we took to Chicago when Dan and I were kids. I suppose we'd gone up to see the store windows at Christmas time. We had supper in the Loop and I think perhaps it was the first time we got to order grown up food. Anyway, the pork chops did make a distinct impression."

"I should say so. I can only hope you'll remember my cooking at a distance of four decades!"

"Well, three and a half, anyway. And I certainly shall if I'm preserved so long."

"Thank you, I'm sure. Would you like your salad now or after the main course?"

"Later, please. You've piqued my interest in the entree."

"Very good. I'll have it right in."

The chops were, indeed, good—better (I suspect) in fact, if not in memory, than the dinner of my childhood, which must, I think, have been in something like a drugstore dining area—certainly nothing so grand as my latter-day Chicago favorite, the Walnut Room at Marshall Field's. Before I was through with the salad, I heard the telephone ring, and thought that Mrs. Jameson would either take the message or let the machine get it: she has a justifiable concept of supper as an inviolable mystery. This time, though, she brought in the cordless handset.

"Pardon me for interrupting, Bishop. It's the Vice President. He asked if he could speak with you right away."

I hadn't actually known the Vice President when we were both at Annandale—he was a class behind me, and in one of the artillery units, so our paths never crossed. The fact that the sons of the state's Democratic senator and Republican governor were roommates at Annandale did appear now and then in the school's news releases, so I knew of the future Veep's existence; but at the time he was in the same mental category as the heirs to the two great cola fortunes who roomed together in the Troop (where the staff assigned them matching geldings named "Uncola" and "Dr. Pepper"). My acquaintance with Kevin Daniels, then, really stemmed from our adult years, when he was working his way up the political hierarchy of the Hoosier state, and serving on the AMA Board of Trustees, while I was the school chaplain. Now, as the man a heartbeat away from the leadership of the free world, he was also Annandale's Chairman of the Board, a circumstance Rhys's rhetoric text would probably have labeled "anticlimax." It was, at least, the sort of phone call for which one would lay down knife and fork.

"Good evening, Mr. Vice President."

"Right Reverend Sir, good evening. I'm sorry to interrupt your dinner, Jonathan, but I have a favor to ask of you, and I'm afraid I'm on sort of a short leash here at the moment, in case they need me to break a tie."

"That sounds exciting, at least."

"Well, you remember what one Hoosier Vice President said about the job. . . ."

" 'Not worth a bucket of warm spit,' wasn't it?"

"There's some debate about the 'spit' part here on Capitol Hill, but yes, that's pretty much it. In any case, I thought I should take advantage of free time while I had some."

"I understand. What can I do for you?"

"I doubt it made the papers out there, but George Tilden died last week."

"It may have been in the sports pages, but I didn't see it in the general news. He did still own the ball club, didn't he?"

"Oh, yes, absolutely, though his niece's been running the front office for years. The thing she has not been doing, however, is serving as an AMA Trustee, and now that George is gone, and since you have served a year on the board before as President of the summer school Alumni, we wondered if you'd be willing to take his place on the board, as a permanent member."

"I'm honored, Kevin, and I can hardly use the too-many-other-commitments line with you. But what's the hurry? It sounds as though Mr. Tilden's chair in the board room is still warm."

"I suppose it is. But the Board is to meet next Saturday—"

"Homecoming weekend."

"Exactly. And we anticipate deciding, or at least discussing, a very important issue about the future of the school. Without George, there would be an even number of Trustees—"

"And you ironically want to avoid a tie."

"It's the story of my life, but there it is."

"What if the issue is one on which I already have an opinion?"

"You'll notice I've been careful not to ask. I imagine most of the Trustees figure you'll vote their way, but we're all telling one another we respect your experience, insight, integrity and so forth."

"Were you this cynical when we were cadets?"

"The term of art is 'realistic,' and I believe that in my family we picked it up with mother's milk."

"No doubt. Let me raise another point. Did anyone note that the Bishop of Michigan City is also Chairman of the Board of the Fort Wayne Military Institute?"

"It did come up, yes. But to be frank, the schools aren't competing for the same students."

"About two dozen in the overlap group over the last ten years, all of whom ended up going to AMA. That doesn't mean things couldn't change in the future, though."

"That's a bridge we'd be willing to cross when we got to it, I think. Any other objections you care to raise?"

"No, honestly, there aren't, though I will have to check my calendar tomorrow morning to be sure I'm free on Saturday."

"Of course. And we have some room to maneuver—everyone expects to be in Annandale from Friday night on. I'll have someone at the school send you a packet with the background information. They can have it messengered to the Cathedral."

"Very well. I'll be interested to see the arguments for going civilian."

"You won't find them in this packet, Jonathan," he said, "but you might be running over your ideas about coeducation. I'll see you this weekend."

After that revelation, even Mrs. Jameson's dessert was anticlimactic.

Chapter 8: Tuesday, October 24

THE KIDS WERE still asleep when I got up, so I had a quick breakfast and said Morning Prayer in my Chapel at the Cathedral. It turned out at staff meeting that I did have commitments for Saturday, but Carl was able to rearrange my schedule, and Mrs. Equitone had the pleasure of calling Washington to confirm my attendance. Supported by such professionalism, I puttered away for an hour or so in my office and caught up on most of my work before the Zoological Trustees' meeting. I got back about eleven, and had hardly sat down before the Dacres dropped by to invite me to lunch. True to my principles, I took them up with alacrity, and by half past we'd been seated in "Come 'n' Dine," an Amish style buffet on the southeast side of town.

"So how are my reviews?" I asked.

"About what one would expect at the extremes," Bridget said. "There were respectful letters from secularists and exclusionists in yesterday's paper and this morning's. Though, of course, the editors may be trying to represent both sides of the issue. I say 'both,' but I was interested to see some letters agreeing with you right down the line. I take that to mean that you've managed to raise the *via media* to a viable alternative."

"No pun intended," St. John added.

"It certainly was intended," his wife replied, "otherwise I should have said 'middle road.' But I haven't gotten to the big news, which is that you did make one significant convert."

"Surely not—"

"Yes, indeed. I don't know whether Maggie was actually persuaded or you simply convinced her that it was a matter of godly discipline, but whichever is the case, she saw me in the humanities mail room this morning and said that she saw no reason to pursue the issue of hiring quotas at this point."

"My goodness. Do you think I should send her a note?"

"Hmmm . . ." She poked thoughtfully at a hard-boiled egg pickled in beet juice. "It's kind of you to offer, Bishop, but I'm not sure what one would say under the circumstances. Anything that might suggest she was capitulating would be likely to irritate her into changing her mind back again; and given that she is in fact capitulating, a letter that said anything else would probably strike her as hypocritical, leading to the same reaction in the end."

"Sleeping dingoes, I think, Jonathan, would be the appropriate proverb," St. John added.

353

"I shall let her lie, then. Do you think the affair will blow over without her?"

"I doubt if we'll hear much more about it in the Faculty Senate," St. John said.

"And I don't think it can sustain itself in the larger community if the Senate isn't discussing the issue. I would caution, though, that everything depends upon the new Vice-chancellor. We've joked about my being Roman Catholic, but over the long haul, I think the leader of the University has to be an Anglican, and preferably one who sees things the way you do."

"Have you passed these ideas along to the search committee?"

"I told them a long time ago that the Vice-chancellor should be Anglican. If you would arrange for me to get a copy of your sermon, I should be happy to pass it along to the committee."

"Consider it done. Is anyone ready to go back for our meat and potatoes?"

When we sat back down, St. John took the conversational reins. "I understood you've been giving Lord Strathspey the grand tour, Jonathan."

"Yes, I dragged him down to Annandale to look at a piece for me—it turned out not to be anything important, but I hope he enjoyed the trip, at least. Things have changed there since I had him as a student."

"You must have done something to impress him. He asked if you'd be willing to come over to the University tomorrow to unveil the jewel."

"I'd love to, of course. What time are you doing this?"

"About five o'clock. The hope is to be live on the evening news, I think, so Thursday will be a big opening day."

"That should be fine. I'm out of the office tomorrow morning, but I should be back in plenty of time. Am I to speak, or just give moral support?"

"I was thinking you might introduce Michael, and possibly read the collect for King Alfred at some point. But if you'll meet us down in the basement of the museum, we can work out the details before we take the jewel upstairs to the exhibit room. It's bound to be informal."

"Very good. Do you want me in a cassock or just a purple shirt?"

"Just a shirt, I think, unless you prefer the other."

"A shirt it is, then."

"Speaking of cassocks, whatever became of gaiters as an episcopal uniform?" Bridget asked.

"I don't think they lasted very long into the nineteenth century in this country," I answered, "though I've seen them mentioned in English stories up into the thirties. But that's my only knowledge of them—writing in English novels, I mean—so I'm not quite sure what they were or how you wore them."

"Gaiters," St. John said, "were a common item of eighteenth century dress that lasted amongst the higher ranks of the clergy in something of a fossilized state after the civilian fashions changed. I believe they might be described as the longest, or highest, members of the spat family, reaching so far as the knee. The concept was, I take it, to protect a gentleman's stockings, in the days of knee breeches, though farmers in a Thomas Hardy sort of world might wear leather gaiters, too, I think."

"You never cease to amaze me, my dear," Bridget replied. "What have you done with Lord Strathspey today?"

"I'm not sure, actually. We spoke on the telephone yesterday evening, but he didn't say what he had planned. He had mentioned going into Chicago to do some work at the Newberry Library, but I don't know that he meant to do it today."

"Well, I suppose he can entertain himself. It occurs to me that we should have arranged some sort of a dinner for him, though."

"Perhaps we could do something at the palace," I suggested. "I don't imagine Mrs. Jameson could manage the weekend as such short notice, but Monday would probably work. Will Michael still be here?"

"I think so," St. John said. "Though again, I don't know his plans in detail. I could inquire at the Inn to see if he's left a check-out date, if I can't get the man himself. What do you think, Bridget?"

"How could I object? It's a far more attractive proposal than having everyone into our house, even if one were to hire a caterer. On which subject, Mr. Chancellor, I think the University can meet the expenses of this entertainment."

"Thank you, Madam Pro-vice-chancellor. The Smitson fund will be relieved at the relief, I'm sure."

"I think I'd be relieved by some dessert," St. John said. "Will anyone join me?"

———

HAVING HAD an early lunch, I had time for a short nap before my first appointment of the afternoon, a committee discussion of diocesan insurance policies which left me feeling about as excited as Kevin Daniels. At four, the Senior Warden of one of our small town parishes came in to talk about the imminent retirement of their priest. Clergy deployment is one of the many things I delegate to Carl, and I ought to have referred the visitor to him; but the little congregation was actually afraid that I would take advantage of the vacancy to close them down entirely, on the grounds that they couldn't afford a full-time replacement. The suggestion *had* been raised in Diocesan

Council, in fact, but I said there, as I repeated to the Warden, that the diocese could hardly afford to close a church when the next nearer congregations were more than twenty miles away. That didn't answer the question of where to find the money, of course, and I asked the Warden to consider whether there might be someone in the parish who could be trained and ordained as a priest without giving up his or her secular job. It wasn't an easy sell—the Warden thought her congregation would want a "real priest"—and it was a little after five when we parted with the agreement that she would ask her vestry to think about it.

We usually close the offices at five, but Carl came in just as the Warden was leaving.

"Jonathan," he asked, "have you looked any further into this Hudson Buchanan person?"

"I talked with him Saturday morning and Sunday evening, and Rhys did some poking about to find out his real name, with no success. He has a theory that the fellow may not be what he seems to be."

"I think I'd be inclined to agree with your young cousin. You'll remember that I said I'd been asking around about him, and that my counterpart in Milwaukee was the only one who remembered seeing the posters. Well, I've been looking forward, too, and there's no sign of his coming in any of the other cities. Now it might arguably be too early for his publicity to have started in some of these places, but he was supposed to be in Detroit this weekend, and there's been nothing here."

"Has he given up, do you think, or did he never expect to go there in the first place?"

"That is the $64,000 question, isn't it? I was strongly inclined to think he'd never intended to go, which is what the absence of publicity most directly suggests. It occurred to me that I might be able to find out more by talking to people at the Evangelistic Center here, but they were not anxious to cooperate with someone calling from your office. So then I thought of contacting similar organizations in the Motor City. There are more to check with, of course, but I finally located an evangelical center which was still somewhat disgruntled over having to replace a revival speaker who had cancelled at the last minute."

"He called them Saturday, I suppose."

"His booking agent called them, the day after Labor Day. Apparently they plan ahead in the revival business."

"So you called the agent—"

"So I called the agent and found that Brother Buchanan had cancelled the whole tour: Des Moines, Chicago, Indianapolis, Detroit, Cincinnati, Louisville and St. Louis. End quote."

"Chicago and Indianapolis, rather than Milwaukee and Michigan City."

"Precisely. But he really had been in Milwaukee, I knew. The congregation that hosted him there said that his secretary—not his agent—had called them and asked if they'd like to be added to his schedule. He does have a reputation, and they were glad to get him. I daresay the story here in Michigan City was much the same."

"You mention that he has a reputation. Is there any chance that someone pulled off a switch?"

"Not in any straightforward way, no. The Buchanan I saw on television looks like the one all my contacts described."

"I figured that would be too easy. Do you have any suggestions for further research?"

"I'd like to know where he was in September and where he's gone; but I don't know how one would find out. When you come right down to it, we're not the FBI."

"Nor are we meant to be, I suppose. Still, I thank you for your help."

"You're more than welcome. Are you coming in to the office tomorrow morning, or going straight to Syracuse?"

"I think I'll just drive over. I like to give myself about two and a half hours, just to be on the safe side."

"I wouldn't have expected anything else. We'll see you Thursday morning, then."

"See you then."

———

ARRIVED HOME, I found Mrs. Jameson and Rhys in conference around the kitchen table, which was strewn with cookbooks and recipe cards.

"Good evening, everyone," I said. "What's cooking?"

Rhys cringed, but Mrs. Jameson was imperturbable. "Good evening, Bishop. Chancellor Dacre called this afternoon to talk about your dinner plans. I told her Monday would be fine with me, and thought I might begin my menu planning, just to be ready. That's what I was doing when Ms. Mears and Mr. Evans came home."

"I see. We had talked about hiring a caterer."

"No, that won't be necessary. We're only thinking of twelve for dinner. I might have to hire some servers, but Professor Dacre pointed out that the Students' Association has people trained for the purpose, including graduate student bartenders."

"It seems like a plan. What are you thinking about serving?"

"Let me get you your Coke and Mr. Evans can give you the background."

"It's Caroline who's done most of the background work, really, Bishop; in fact, she's upstairs on her computer now. But when we started to plan, naturally, we thought about Scots food, though we wanted something more original than haggis, and since Mrs. Jameson has these regional cookbooks for Britain, we thought we'd see exactly where Lord Strathspey grew up. And it turns out it was in England."

"Apparently," Mrs. Jameson added, putting down my soda and resuming her seat, "an Honourable Miss Bruce married an English baronet named Porter, and their son inherited the Scots title along with an English country home."

"That's Car's best guess as of a few minutes ago, at least. In any case, our young Scots lord grew up in the County of Lancaster."

"That's easy to believe," I replied. "He certainly didn't come to camp at Annandale speaking Broad Scots—but not quite a Lancastrian, either: very much the 'posh-o' accent, as he'd say."

"I'm surprised he didn't talk like a Cockney," Mrs. Jameson said. "It seems as though everyone under thirty over there tries to these days."

"Conservative parents, I think, though I never met them. Which reminds me that his end-of-the-summer reports went to some address in London."

"Oh, sure, the place in Lancaster would be a country home, and they'd live in London during the week for most of the year. But Mrs. Jameson says there's nothing particularly distinctive about London food."

"Not as compared to Lancaster, anyway," she added. "We're thinking about a mix of Hoosier and Lancastrian items for the dinner."

"That sounds very good. What comes from Lancaster besides hot pot?"

"By the time you include some of these country home recipes, there's quite a variety. But I'm not sure we should be so quick to rule out hot pot—have you even looked at the ingredients, or is it just a name?"

"Just the name, to tell the truth."

"Well, then, why don't you take this white book here and that blue one there upstairs and I'll get your dinner ready. Will a few minutes after seven be all right?"

"It's fine with me, Mrs. Jameson," Rhys said. "The Bishop can have his nap, I can watch the news, and we can squeeze in Evening Prayer before we eat."

"Cheeky lad," I said, picking up the cookbooks, "I have already had my nap." But it nonetheless worked out pretty much as he had said. I dozed off reading about a rich casserole of lamb chops, and our dinner was accompanied by a further discussion of possible menus, with some relatively calm forays into university politics and appropriately respectful comments on my conversation with the Vice President.

We made our way up to the family room after the meal.

"I couldn't help feeling that everyone but me was making small talk all through dinner," Rhys said, assuming his customary slouch on the sofa.

"A momentary lapse into good manners," Caroline replied. "I do actually have some interesting things to report about Lancaster, other than its food."

"And I should pass on some things Carl found out about Br. Buchanan."

"You could tell us what you found out yesterday, too, Uncle Jon—"

"If we'll still have time for our homework."

"Yours and mine. I have some reading to do for that Annandale trustees meeting. But there's no problem on that score. Strathspey says the Commander's baton's not even that old, much less ancient."

"And he's pretty much the last word, Uncle Jon?"

"Well, he made deferential noises about being an expert in metals and enamels, rather than ivory—but he's a good deal more qualified than anyone you'd be likely to find around here on short notice. Having you been looking up his *c.v.* along with recipes?"

"No, though I have done some poking away at his genealogy. It's like looking up thoroughbreds in the studbook, but easier."

"Mrs. Jameson said something about a cross-border marriage."

"Yes, that would be his great-grandmother and great-grandfather. He's descended from their third son, but the senior lines were killed off in the world wars. The Porters, the English side, are actually more interesting than the Bruces—"

"But—" Rhys began.

"But nothing. These Bruces aren't the royal Bruces—they're some minor offshoot or something, and God only knows how they became earls. But the Porters go right back to William the Conqueror—they actually get their name from their job in his court."

"Like the Butlers and the Marshals, both of whom did become earls, I think. The Porters seem to be underachievers."

"Well, yes, Uncle Jon. I guess that porters weren't all that important."

"Not if *Macbeth* is anything to go by . . ."

"Exactly. This family has a long history of marrying well, though. Even at the beginning, they married into an Anglo-Saxon noble family. That's where they got the land in Lancaster, where they built Preston Tower."

"You found all this in his genealogy, Car?"

"Not entirely, Rhys. It turns out their little Lancaster place is a historic landmark."

"Just because it's theirs, or does it have some architectural importance?"

"Neither one. I mean, it's probably interesting enough, architecturally, and I'm sure the family helps make the place famous—Charles Dickens wrote a short story about it, for that matter—but the place got into the history books because of the Lancashire witches."

"Okay, I'll bite. Who were the Lancashire witches?" Rhys said.

"You must have missed Uncle Jon's *Macbeth* lecture."

"Which you must have heard over the dinner table?" She nodded. "I don't think so, but maybe my attention wandered. Were these some long lost relatives of ours?"

"I doubt it," I answered. "At first they were just a pair of old women accused of witchcraft. But then a crowd of sympathizers plotted to storm the castle where they were being held. When word of that got out, the authorities decided they had a more widespread problem, and ended up hanging I don't know how many people at Lancaster Castle."

"And from what Car says, this was when Shakespeare was writing *Macbeth*?"

"Well, *Macbeth* is usually dated to 1606. The Lancashire witches were a few years later."

"1612, according to what I was reading."

"That sounds right. My point in the sophomore English class was just that Britain was on a witchcraft kick at the time."

"Right. I do remember that you told us King James wrote a book about witchcraft."

"Exactly," Caroline said. "And King James also visited Preston Tower, though that wasn't until 1616. But as long as we're talking about the guest book, they have a bigger name than King James or Dickens: the most recent theory is that Shakespeare lived there during the lost years of his boyhood."

"Along with Jesus and King Arthur, I suppose?"

"No, Uncle Jon. I'm serious. It has something to do with the Porters being Catholics, and they think Shakespeare may have been Catholic, too."

"Well, possibly, though I'm not sure that would make me move to Lancaster."

"Whichever," Rhys said. "I don't want to seem uninterested in the god of English lit, but what about Car's Lancashire witches?"

"Right. As Uncle Jon said, they were locked up in Lancaster Castle, and when the authorities heard about the plot to spring them, they sneaked them out of town and imprisoned them in Preston Tower, which was isolated and more defensible. In fact, the court met at the Tower for their trial."

"Why Preston Tower as opposed to any other stronghold in the county, Caroline?"

"The head of the family at the time was the Justice of the Peace, or something of the kind. Apparently he wanted to make sure the poor old women got what was coming to them."

"The Judge Hathorn of his day."

"More or less, Rhys: or the Brother Buchanan. What's your news about him, Uncle Jon?"

"Puzzling, mostly. But was that it about Strathspey's family?"

"Substantially, yes. I found the menu they served King James, but I doubt if Mrs. Jameson is going to roast a peacock."

"No, I suppose not. . . . Essentially, Carl found out that Buchanan had cancelled his whole fall tour in order to go to Milwaukee and come here. But we have no idea why."

"Some sort of switch?"

"That was the first thing I thought, too, Rhys. But Carl says our Buchanan at least looks like the standard model."

"Maybe that was when he was getting the psychic refitting we talked about. I mean, it was one thing when he just happened to pass through Milwaukee on his way here—it looks a lot more suspicious when we hear that Dixon's base of operations and Michigan City were the only two stops on his trip."

"That's true, Car, but whatever they did to make Mr. Smith into Br. Buchanan had to have happened long enough ago for him to build up an audience for his tours."

"Right, Rhys. But by the same token, if Smith was set up some time ago, they couldn't have been planning to aim him at us the whole time—Uncle Jon hasn't been having visions for that long."

"So the Smith-Buchanan switch was preparatory—just making the weapon, without arming it."

"Exactly, Uncle Jon. And then, contrary to what Rhys was thinking Sunday, they found out that the jewel was coming here, temptingly close but probably under your protection. Or maybe they even thought you actually wanted the jewel to use it yourself. In any case, Buchanan was called to Milwaukee to be armed, so to speak. And they sent him here in a way calculated to draw us all to the service, so they could see whether his talent would actually stand up to us. If so, you'd be no threat and they could grab the jewel and go."

"And then Boethius called, and the Bishop knocked the whole plan into a cocked hat."

"That has to be it, Rhys. Don't you think so, Uncle Jon?"

"It does hang together, but there are still a lot of hypotheses in there. We still don't know how some fellow in Milwaukee would just happen to know what the Ashmolean Museum was planning to do with one of its prize exhibits, nor why a hypothetical Neo-pagan conspiracy would be developing underground agents like Buchanan in the first place."

"That's true, sir. I mean, that those things are both hypothetical. And we haven't even dealt with how two historic owners of this jewel found out it was going to be here, or what they're trying to tell you about it."

"Which is just to say we're not making any progress," Caroline said. "But we should be able to figure some of this out. To begin with, even if we have just hypothesized about Br. Buchanan's training and deployment, I'm not sure it makes all that much difference. It may be like one of those crossword puzzle words you end up filling in because there's an 'f' in 9 across. If we get everything else straight, either we'll know that they really did train Buchanan—and maybe why—or else we'll know that it doesn't matter. But as for who knew about the jewel coming here in the first place, there's Professor Dacre, and I suppose Chancellor Dacre, and Lord Strathspey, and if I understand correctly, the Queen."

"I think we can safely eliminate Her Majesty."

"Just being thorough, Uncle Jon. I imagine we can eliminate the Dacres, too."

"Clearly, Car. Since Professor Dacre has direct access to the jewel while it's in Michigan City, he wouldn't need some elaborate scheme to take it. And unlike our hypothetical bad guys, he knew that we didn't know anything about it, so he wouldn't have to worry that we were trying to get it."

"That's persuasive, Rhys. And the same thing would be true of Lord Strathspey—he sees the jewel every morning when he comes into the office, so he has no reason to come here to steal it, or to worry about who else might want to put it to good use."

"Also persuasive, as you said, Caroline. Now the only problem is that between the two of you you've eliminated all your suspects."

"Right, Uncle Jon. But I thought we would. What I was working around to saying was that we should try to find out who *else* knew what was going on. Maybe Professor Dacre had to make some arrangement with the university insurance company. And there must be one or two steps in the Ashmolean museum administration between Strathspey and the Queen."

"I'll see them both tomorrow afternoon," I said. "I can ask."

"That leaves us back at figuring out your messages from the past, sir."

"I have nothing new on that front. Has either of you found out anything?" They both shook their heads.

"I'm not sure what there will be to find out unless you have another episode, Uncle Jon."

"Well, I'm not sure either, dear. And I know both of you want to get to your homework. So if there's nothing else for the good of the order, I think we should adjourn."

"Sounds like a plan, sir. Do *you* have plans for tomorrow evening, after your spot at the museum?"

"Not particularly. Would you like to have dinner at the faculty club?"

"You respond to cues so well, Uncle Jon. We'd love to."

━━━

THE PACKET from Annandale was nothing if not thorough—the materials ranged from financial projections to an essay (by Richard, though he'd certainly gone out of his way to avoid mentioning it to me) on the history of women at Annandale (John Marshall Glenarm, our first benefactor, had considered leaving his fortune to establish a convent school, and had only been diverted to the military academy idea by his butler, an exiled IRA activist). It was clear that simply to convert existing barracks for female occupancy—or to build new dormitories—would be an enormous expense, but on the other hand a modern-day Glenarm was reportedly waiting in the wings with an open checkbook to foot the bill. Some portion of the alumni body would presumably withdraw its financial support, but other alumni and parents had daughters whom they would be happy to see in neatly tailored cadet gray. The presumptive percentages of both groups were cited, and there was a careful cross-reference to a position paper on women's uniforms, including pros and cons on the apparently ticklish question of whether women officers would carry sabers. The most momentous decision in Annandale's history would be made with far more care than any of us cynics on the faculty would ever have imagined.

I was midway in the stack, or a bit farther, when my phone rang. It was Danny.

"Hey, big brother. What's up?"

"A preposition, usually. What's up with you?"

"Oh, not much, really. I mostly just wanted to actually *talk* to you for a change."

"Yeah, I know what you mean. The tele-teen system is fast, but it's not the same as an actual human voice."

"Right, Jon. But don't get mushy on me."

"Understood. How's life in Brown County?"

"Pretty good, to tell the truth. It's foliage season."

"Tourists?"

"Oh, sure, on my way to and from work. But no one comes down past the cabin. A half-mile of dirt road is as good as a moat."

"It does sound lovely. Not that I don't like the palace, mind you, but there's something to be said for rustic simplicity."

"Right, Marie Antoinette. And all of us here at the Petit Trianon just love your dairymaid outfit."

"It's a shepherdess outfit, silly boy. Note the crook."

"Of course. Seriously, though, if you and the kids would like to come down for the weekend, you're more than welcome. Abbot Alfred is going to stop by here for the night on his way back from St. Meinrad, but you know there's plenty of room."

"Thanks, Dan, I appreciate it. But I'm going down to the Academy."

"That's right, it is Homecoming. But your big reunion was last spring: don't tell me you're developing an interest in football."

I explained my new commitment.

"Well! Congratulations, Jon. That's certainly another feather in your miter, and I haven't got anything to compare with it. . . ."

". . . But you were thinking of some particular reason for us to come down this weekend."

"It's true, I was. You know I don't follow the papers very closely."

"Conservatively phrased, but yes, I had noticed. I wouldn't have thought you paid that much attention to TV news, for that matter."

"Fair enough, I usually don't. But I did catch the local news this evening, and I heard an interesting piece about the park rangers down here—"

"Right. Pull the other one, it's got bells on it."

"No, I'm serious. Apparently a court in Indianapolis overturned a ruling of the head ranger—whatever they actually call him—"

"I'm still not seeing the news value, Dan."

"I understand. But here's the kicker. The judge was ruling in favor of a group of Neo-pagans who wanted to book one of the park camping complexes. The rangers had tried to keep them out on what amounted to purely religious grounds."

"Hooray for the First Amendment. Are these the same Neo-pagans as our larcenous friend Mr. Dixon?"

"It was kind of hard to tell, actually. What I got out of the story was that this is supposed to be some sort of pan-pagan gathering: but the sound-bite from the pagan spokesperson did mention Jupiter, so I thought of you."

"People so often do."

"Right . . . I can't believe I've lived with that sense of humor for the last forty years."

"Nearly forty-one, in fact. And I'm told that I was a particularly humorous two-year-old. Seriously, though, the kids and I were trying to make some sense of this earlier this evening and couldn't make much more headway than to conclude that there was some sort of a conspiracy to keep me from getting my hands on the Alfred Jewel (not that I want it, mind you). Oh, and it turns out that Dixon was on a wild-goose chase: at least, Commander Lindsley's baton is a modern piece, and nothing happened when I grabbed it."

"So do you think this conspiracy extends far enough to include me, or is the pagan state fair just a coincidence?"

"It seems far-fetched, certainly. I'm developing a strong disinclination to believe in coincidence, but I don't see what they'd have to gain by pestering you."

"Neither do I. I'll keep my eyes open, just in case."

"That sounds wise. Listen, just because I'm going to Annandale doesn't mean that the kids have to go, too. Why don't I ask them if they'd like to come down?"

"Oh, I don't know, Jon. It's not as though there's anything in particular to do. I didn't even have anything specific in mind when I called you."

"No, I understand. But still, you might have a chance to visit this pagan jamboree: if there's some connection with our goings on up here, we shouldn't pass up a chance for research. And they did both work this past weekend when everyone else seemed to be goofing off."

"Fair enough. Well, tell them about it tomorrow and have them give me a call, or a thought, whichever."

"Sounds good. I have to drive over Syracuse tomorrow, but I'll be taking them to supper, if I don't see them before then. . . . Danny, if it does turn out that this has involved you, I'm sorry. I'm sorry the kids are involved in it, for that matter, though I guess I haven't told them so."

"Probably out of a sense that they'd have no more patience with that line than I do, Jon-jon. As I remember, you couldn't even put the idea across to your students at Annandale, so you needn't expect it to work with your family. We're involved with whatever this is because we're involved with you."

"Okay. I appreciate it, and I don't mean to perseverate."

"Nor to obfuscate by polysyllabification, I know. We'll take it as read. Is there anything else for the good of the order?"

"Well, if the kids do come down, and you happen to have any of that venison sausage . . ."

"I think I could even send along a roast, in fact. Particularly if they happened to carry south some Frango mints."

"Sounds like a deal."

"Tut-tut. I don't think you can deal for venison in Indiana, Jonathan. But I'll look forward to the gift exchange. We'll be just in time for Halloween."

"A family holiday for us, at least. Well, take care, little brother."

"You too, old friend. We'll be in touch."

There seemed to be no need to interrupt the kids for Dan's invitation—and perhaps his use of ordinary communication had wakened in me a coordinate idea that not everything need be done in a hurry. I read as much more of my homework as I could stomach, and went to bed at a reasonable hour.

Chapter 9: Wednesday, October 25

DEAN PHILIPS had agreed to take the early Mass at the Cathedral in order for me to go straight off to my morning meeting, and the kids were on their own morning schedules, so I said the morning office myself in the palace chapel. After my prayers, I considered whether I should dissolve the magic protections we had tried to place around the jewel, in order to retrieve my museum security pass for the afternoon. On reflection, I decided to leave things as they were. The danger of leaving the jewel open to teleporting burglars seemed to outweigh the nuisance value of whatever identification processes I might have to fool with at the university, while the public display cases at the museum would benefit at least as much as the vault from whatever further safety we might have provided.

I had an easy drive over to Syracuse, and a pleasant morning at the conference center, including a discussion of new programs we might be able to offer there by satellite linking with similar places in other dioceses. Having come over past South Bend and then south through Goshen, I decided to head back west through Nappanee and then cut north on road 35 through LaPorte. I wasn't too worried about getting back in time for my appointment at the university, but the route I'd taken in the morning went through a largish stretch on the fringes of Indiana's Amish territory, and I thought I should avoid the chance of being slowed down by horse and buggy traffic. Predictably, I suppose, there was a veritable convoy of carriages on the way to Nappanee, and road work on highway 6 west of Lapaz, to boot. I got to Michigan City about 4:30 and drove straight to Walsingham, where I found St. John and Strathspey in the basement curator's office, along with a university security officer.

"Gentlemen," I said, "good afternoon."

"Oh, hello," St. John said. "It's good to see you. Officer Crump, let me introduce you to Bishop Mears. Jonathan, I'm afraid we have some bad news."

"What's that?"

"Michael, do you want to explain?"

"Surely. We came into the office, Bishop, about half an hour ago, to get ready for the press conference. When we opened the safe and took out the jewel, I noticed immediately that there was something wrong with it."

"Wrong in what way? Had it been damaged?"

"Not precisely, no. But it felt wrong in my hand when I picked it up. I looked at it closely, and it was clear to me that this was a copy. The enameling was different, the details of the goldwork were different—and when we weighed it, sure enough, it was lighter than the original: about 35 grams versus 51.236."

"Good heavens! Do we have any idea when the switch could have been made?"

"That's an interesting question, Bishop," Officer Crump observed. "Lord Strathspey said you might be able to offer independent confirmation that the real jewel was here on Saturday."

"Well, yes. I don't know that it would be testimony that would stand up in court, necessarily, but it was certainly my impression that I was looking at the real piece."

"Perhaps you'd be willing to look at the copy for me, sir."

"Of course." St. John handed me the jewel. I pretended to look it over, for the sake of appearances, but the test was clearly completed the moment I picked the stone up and felt no reaction. "Yes, it does seem to different to me, though again, I'd defer to Lord Strathspey's opinion, in any case."

"Very good. Thank you, Bishop. If you three gentlemen will excuse me, I'm going to go pull the records of accesses to the office since last Saturday. Lord Strathspey, I suppose Professor Dacre will know how to get in touch with you?"

"Yes, officer. Thank you for your help. I'll look forward to hearing anything you turn up."

When the guard had left, we sat down around the office with the jewel on the desk between us.

"I don't even know where to start," St. John said. "We have the press conference coming up, and the actual exhibit opening, and now we can expect the police and the insurance people all over the museum."

"I don't think we should be too hasty about publicizing the switch, St. John," Michael said. "Discretion may well be the better part of valor in cases like this. Certainly, I'd give your own staff a chance for a preliminary investigation."

"Surely. What shall we say at the conference, then? We can't very well put out the fake and claim that it's real."

"No, hardly. But having said that this is a copy, I'm not sure that we are obliged to go on and explain why we're putting it on display. You haven't, after all, advertised that I would be bringing the real gem, so it isn't as though anyone were expecting it."

This was a chance to ask the question we'd been wondering about the previous evening. "Who did know the stone was coming, Michael?"

"The very thing Officer Crump asked. Not very many people, honestly. My boss, the Curator of the Ashmolean; the Vice-Chancellor; someone at the Palace, all joking aside, and that's it from the UK. More people knew the piece was being taken off display, of course, but not what was happening to it. In this country, you have the customs people, and the Dacres: I think that was the list."

"Thanks, I was just curious. But I interrupted you just as you were coming to the point."

"Right. I think that St. John can say it's a strikingly accurate copy which we're putting on display here because we have understandable security concerns about what is quite possibly the oldest piece of the English regalia. That should give me a great place from which to segue into comments on my paper."

"Wonderful. Jonathan, you look upset. I hope this doesn't strike you as dishonest."

"No, not at all. It's strictly true, and as much as anyone has a right to know. I was preoccupied with how this could have happened in the first place. It's a classic locked-room puzzle."

"Yes," Michael said, "if your mysterious baton thief had better taste in antiquities, I'd give his name to Officer Crump."

"Indeed. Though *he* showed no inclination to leave a replacement artifact behind. And, as it happens, I had taken a few precautions of my own here."

"I see. Well, I suppose the good officer will have to confine himself to more naturalistic explanations."

St. John, who presumably followed the gist of this but wasn't in on the baton question, stood and urged us toward the door. "This all sounds intriguing, gentlemen, but we should be heading upstairs. You'll bring the replica, Michael?"

"Yes, of course," he said, picking it up.

"Do you want that jeweler's bag?" I asked. "It looks like it's still in the safe, there."

"Oh no, thanks, Jonathan. It was nice touch for our thief to put his copy right into the same little velvet nest as the original, but I don't think we need take too much care of the cuckoo's egg." He dropped the copy in his coat pocket and we were off to meet the press.

All through the press conference, I kept wondering what role our attempted protection of the jewel might or might not have played in the exchange. By the time I had said goodbye to St. John and Michael, I was itching to get home and have a good look around the chapel; but it was time to meet the kids for dinner.

"You looked good on TV, Uncle Jon," Caroline said as they took their seats (student time keeping being what it is, I had had leisure not only to be seated but also to make a start on a Chivas and soda).

"Right," Rhys said, "though we did have a question—"

"I'll bet you did," I said, "but we probably shouldn't talk about it till we get back to the palace."

"Roger that, sir. So how was your day in Syracuse?"

"Pretty good, actually, though I saw a lot of the countryside. Which reminds me, Danny wants to know if you two would like to go down to Brown County for the weekend." I explained about the Pagan Festival.

"What do you think, Car?" Rhys asked. "I wouldn't mind seeing your dad again, and this Neo-pagan thing does sound kind of fishy."

"I don't know, Rhys. I mean, I'd be happy to see Daddy, but I agree with you that there's something fishy about this festival just happening to turn up in his back yard. I don't think, though, that there's anything down there to be worried about, except maybe him: where we seem to have a couple of problems on our hands up here."

"That makes sense, Car, but even if it is some sort of bait to lure us down to Bean Blossom, I don't see what harm it'd do. We were staying with your dad when the Bishop had his run-in with Abbot Trout."

"Yes, but then we didn't have any trouble keeping in touch telepathically. Now we know that Brother Buchanan, at least, can break that contact. So maybe someone is trying to isolate Uncle Jon."

"That could be, Caroline," I said, "but sometimes I think we're all becoming paranoid. If you want to go see Danny, go see him. I'll pack up some Frango mints."

The waiter came just then, and after we'd placed our orders (a fairly straightforward matter, as they offer only two entrees at supper), Rhys picked up the conversation.

"You know, Bishop, I think Car is probably right on this one. I think we should stay with you for the weekend."

"That's fine, certainly. I suppose it means we're all going down to Annandale, then."

"Great, sir. You two can stay at the house, and I'll get a bunk in the alumni dorm."

"That sounds like a plan," Caroline said. "I'll just have to make sure I get a paper written before we go."

"What are you working on?" I asked, and we spent the rest of the meal discussing freshman composition.

We'd come to the University in three separate cars, and so the kids were waiting for me in the kitchen when we got home. Rhys handed me a Coke, and Caroline said: "Okay, Uncle Jon, spill the beans. What happened to the real Jewel? No one said anything about a good copy before tonight."

"Indeed not. So far as we can tell, the original was stolen out of a safe in a locked room in a security area of the museum."

"A security area with magical protection, at that," Rhys said.

"Or so we had hoped. But I've been dying for a chance to check the chapel ever since I found out about the jewel."

"Well, what are we waiting for?" Caroline asked. "Let's go see."

Leaving my soda in the kitchen, we marched off to the chapel. I unlocked the door, and even before we turned on the lights, everything seemed to be just as we had left it: a small dome of golden light still hovered at the far end of the room. Rhys flipped the switch, and we gathered around the holy table.

"It all looks the same," Caroline said. "I suppose it's all right to dismantle it now."

"No reason not to," I answered. "The Lord be with you."

"And also with you."

"Let us pray. Almighty God, you have been our resting place from generation to generation. We give you thanks for your continued favor and goodness towards us, and, remembering your providential care for all that you have made, we pray you to end the special protection for which we have by these symbols entreated you, through Jesus Christ our Lord."

"Amen."

I stuck the ID card into my shirt pocket, and picked up the paten, intending to put it back into its cupboard. As I lifted the silver plate, I saw myself reflected in it, for a moment: but then it was as though I were looking into another room through a tiny window, or, as I realized after a moment, as though I were looking out from inside a mirror.

It was a woman's room, a dressing room, if what appeared to be antique bottles of perfume and cosmetics in front of me were anything to go by. Presumably, I was looking out from a prominent place on a make-up table. The central figure in the room—for it was occupied—confirmed my theory. She was an old woman, made up with white face and a red wig in the fashion of a circus clown. Her grandfather's aquiline nose, her carefully pleated ruff, and the fortune in jewels she casually wore made her an unmistakable character: this was the Virgin Queen herself, Elizabeth Tudor, in the last years of her long reign and extraordinary life.

She spoke in Latin, which hardly surprised me at that point in the proceedings (and after all, Henry VIII had trotted her into court to speak Latin to the Venetian ambassador when she was still a child): as I'll explain in a moment, it turned out to be an appropriate text. But at the time, I was attending instead to her actions—for as she spoke, she gestured significantly, carefully pointing amongst her strings of pearls, her diamond earrings, her ruby and sapphire brooches, her enameled miniatures, to one single gem: the Alfred Jewel. She tapped it, wagged her finger in the air, and was gone.

As I set the paten back down, Caroline grabbed my hand: "Are you okay?"

"Oh, yes, I'm fine. It's getting to be a bad habit, is all."

"Well, we'll straighten up here. You go get your Coke and we'll meet you upstairs."

I stopped in the library for a moment, found the book I thought I'd need, went on to retrieve my Coke, and headed up to the family room.

"Okay," Rhys said as the kids came in, "third time's the charm. Let's see if we can get through this without further interruptions."

"Shall I start from the beginning?"

"Yes, sir, if you think there's time enough left in the evening."

"Just barely. Make yourselves comfortable." I summarized my conversation with St. John and Michael at the museum, then described my most recent vision.

"Did you recognize the Latin, Uncle Jon?"

"Not really, but I'm sure it was Boethius. That's what I'd expect by now, at least, and it did sound like poetry, which could mean it was from the *Consolation*. It started off '*vides sedere celsos*,' which certainly has a clear rhythm."

"Is that the *Consolation of Philosophy* that you have there, Bishop?"

"Yes, in fact it is. And it has a helpful index of the first lines of all the metres, the poetic sections of the book. But I haven't peeked yet."

"Of course, the queen may not have quoted the first line, Uncle Jon, even if it is Boethius."

"Of course. But we're entitled to some luck, after all. And if this doesn't work, we can try having you identify the metrical form—I suppose the library has metrical indices to nearly every scrap of Latin verse."

"Probably, sir. Are going to look now, or shall I?"

"Sorry, Rhys. Here goes. . . . And yes, we have a winner! It's the second metre in book four.

Uides sedere celsos solii culmine regis . . .
detrahat si quis superbis uanis tegmina,
iam uidebit artas, dominos ferre catenas . . .
maeror aut fatigat aut spes lubrica torquet."

"I don't suppose it has Queen Elizabeth's own translation there, Uncle Jon?"

"No, it's a modern version, but the relevance may be in the text. It says here:

You may see kings on high upon their thrones
In shining purple robes, with weapons grim . . .
But strip these proud ones of the outward signs
Of their vain honor, and you will perceive
The secret iron chains that bind such lords:
For either grief will weary them, or hope
Will slip away, renewing all their pain."

Caroline wrinkled her nose. "You'd *think*, if they were going to translate it as poetry," she said, "that they'd at least try to duplicate the Latin meter."

"Easier said than done, my dear. Whatever the translation, it does seem to be relevant to the old girl, if a bit somber."

"Does it mean anything to us, though, sir?" Rhys asked. "Not that the other things you heard did, particularly."

"No, I can't say that they did, though we might yet see some sort of pattern. But it seems more like the texts help to authenticate the speakers than to give a message.

"I think it's fascinating, though," I went on, "to imagine that Elizabeth might have had the jewel. There's no record of it being in the crown jewels that I know of. Strathspey would certainly have mentioned it in his paper if there were."

"Why would she have had it, anyway, Uncle Jon—I mean, to what purpose?"

"The Renaissance liked things from the ancient world, didn't they, Bishop?"

"Yes, they did, Rhys, though that may not answer Caroline's question. You're assuming that Elizabeth knew the stone was Roman—which would have to mean the piece came to her with a story about its origins. She couldn't have observed the late antique polishing marks, the way the modern researcher did."

"Oh, right. But a story like that wouldn't be impossible, would it? They had stories about the True Cross in the Middle Ages."

"I'd expect that there were lots of stories that connected things with the ancient world," Caroline said, "but that most of them were fakes. But even if she didn't know about the stone being ancient, she would have known the jewel belonged to Alfred, and might have valued it just for that. Since Alfred was another Boethius translator, that would be another reason for her to point the jewel out to Uncle Jon."

"No doubt, Car. But I wonder about something else, too: she could have known the jewel was magic. Wasn't Anne Boleyn Elizabeth's mother? And didn't you tell us, sir, that she was involved in witchcraft?"

"Anne was certainly Elizabeth's mother, as far as that goes," I said. "And one theory does say that she thought she was witch, or claimed to be one, because of her extra fingers."

"And other bits, as I remember," Rhys went on. "So if Alfred thought the stone belonged to Boethius, and Alfred said Boethius was executed for practicing magic and Elizabeth knew the gem belonged to Alfred, and may have known some story about it coming from the ancient world, mightn't that story have included what Alfred thought about Boethius and the stone, so that Elizabeth would associate the stone with her mother's claim to do magic?"

"Well, yes, she might have, though it's quite a string of assumptions. For that matter, she might have known it was magic from the way it glowed when she picked it up: but whatever her mother may have claimed, there's no tradition I know of about Elizabeth being a witch—nor about Alfred, nor about Boethius, even, other than that one remark of Alfred's."

"That, Uncle Jon, and the fact that all three of them have appeared to you over the last week. So far as we know, they haven't been making a tour of all the bishops in the Anglican communion."

"She has a point, sir. We can't just ignore the fact that you're a part of this."

"Granted, but I can't say that helps me see the larger point. Even if all three of these folks were up to their distinguished necks in necromancy, I don't see what they want me to see—or what someone wants me to see about them. Remember that they've all spoken in quotations, and even Elizabeth may have just been looking at herself in the mirror, not at me."

"Right, Bishop. But either way, I agree with you that we're not seeing what they want us to see. It has to be something more than 'Wow, that rock is magic.' You suggested on Sunday that it was a request for you to keep the jewel safe, and that's what we've tried to do. But it obviously didn't work, and now here's Queen Elizabeth checking in to say we still haven't gotten the message."

"Okay, then," said Caroline, "since you mention it, is there anything we can do to figure out what's become of the magic rock?"

"It seems to me," I said, "that there are three possibilities. A, the jewel was never in the safe to begin with; B, someone penetrated the museum security system and stole the jewel, possibly by magical means; or C, the jewel is still in the safe. The problems are, A, I saw Strathspey put the jewel back in the safe after I involuntarily authenticated it; B, we at least tried to add to the museum's robust security system, and we heard nothing; and C, the only thing I saw in the safe this evening was the empty bag the jewel came in."

"Yes, but, Uncle Jon, that could just mean that, A, Lord Strathspey switched the jewels when you thought you saw him putting them away; B, our magic didn't work, which we knew was a possibility from the start; and C, the real jewel was hidden someplace in the safe all along, possibly in a secret pocket in the bag."

"You're way too devious, Car," Rhys observed.

"I'd rather think of it as perspicacity," she said.

"Whatever. But we dismissed Lord Strathspey as a suspect yesterday, when we were talking about potential thieves. He sees the jewel every day in Oxford. Why would he want to switch the jewels at all, and why would he need to come to Michigan City to do it? Even if our magic didn't work, how did someone get past the regular security system? And wouldn't security think of searching the safe and the bag to see if the stone were still in it?"

"Fair enough, Rhys," I said. "I imagine Officer Crump did search the bag, and is working right now on the security system. Obviously, there might be some magic we don't understand involved, but if so, well, we don't understand it. But as for Michael, I really don't see anything to pursue on that line. As you say, he would hardly need to come here to steal the jewel. More than that, there's no reason why he would *want* to steal it."

"He had means and opportunity," Caroline answered. "Motives are a dime a dozen."

"But so did Professor Dacre and the Bishop have motive and opportunity, Car, and you're not accusing them."

"No, but we're assuming the jewel Uncle Jon handled was real. If it was, and from the way he told us the story, only Lord Strathspey handled the jewel after that, until it was locked up. After it was locked up, you're back to the security system question. Professor Dacre must be able to get past it, and maybe others can, too, but there should be some sort of record that they did so. If it was just a flat-out switch, Lord Strathspey was the only one with the opportunity."

"That's clearly reasoned, Caroline. But when I first knew Michael, he was an honest boy, and I have no reason to think he's not an honest man now."

"If you say so, Uncle Jon. But I bet Officer Crump will have some questions for him. In any case, if we don't have anything else to discuss, I should either get to work or get to bed."

"That I can agree with," I said. "We're adjourned. Shall I see either of you at breakfast?"

"Are you going to say Mass for King Alfred tomorrow, sir?"

"I hadn't intended to, but we certainly can, if you like."

"Yes, please. Car?"

"It's fine with me, if we don't start too late."

"Seven o'clock?" I offered.

They both nodded agreement. "Great. I'll see you downstairs. God bless."

Chapter 10: Thursday, October 26

I RATHER EXPECTED the Thursday morning family mass to be the occasion for another communication from the past—we still had Chaucer to go, amongst other famous Boethius translators—but as it turned out, the whole thing went smoothly and simply, with nothing merely supernatural to mar the greater mysteries of salvation. Indeed, the whole day was preternaturally normal, compared to the way things had been going. It seemed as though I spent most it signing routine letters and documents, though I'm sure a good part of it went toward the usual office visiting, particularly as I brought Carl up to date on my adventures. I actually ate lunch by myself, grabbing a cheeseburger at the counter of Turing's Drugstore.

When I got back to the office, I started to read a report to the House of Bishops from the Standing Commission on Worship and Music. Finding myself almost unable to keep my eyes open, and feeling a little guilty about taking a nap on such an inactive day, I decided to e-mail Philip to let him know I'd be coming down for the weekend. His reply indicated that my nomination to the Board of Trustees had leaked out, but the greater secret had not:

I was *so* happy to hear that you'd agreed to serve on the Board. The school needs someone with your experience and your sense of the *TRADITION* and history. You know how important I think the military life is here, so I won't nag you, but I hope you'll vote the right way when the time comes.

I replied:

Don't worry, Phil. I don't think the military system is in any danger—certainly not from me. Looking forward to seeing you Friday. Is the Corps ready for the Veep?

To which he answered:

Yes, if we can land a helicopter on the parade ground without scaring the horses. See you then.

At least one of us was having an interesting day.

The kids were home for supper—Mrs. Jameson had teased me at breakfast with threats of burned oatcakes in Alfred's honor, but in fact served us a nice pork and apple casserole—and we worked out our plans for the trip to Annandale. Caroline expressed herself willing to miss her afternoon class in the interest of avoiding traffic, but I felt as Chancellor that I should encourage regular attendance, and we arranged to leave the palace at 3:30. Rhys, I noted in passing, had no Friday afternoon class scheduled in the first place.

"Bishop," Mrs. Jameson said as she brought in a gooseberry cobbler, "could we talk about Monday evening after dinner?"

"Of course. Do you need all three of us?"

"No, just you—I wouldn't want to interfere with anyone's schoolwork."

"You don't actually listen at doors, do you, Mrs. Jameson?" Caroline asked with a grin.

"Just all that practice from getting your uncle's Coke ready, I'll bet," Rhys said.

"I'm maintaining a dignified silence," Mrs. Jameson replied as she went back to the kitchen, though I rather thought I heard a suppressed chuckle. I joined her two helpings of cobbler later.

"I hope you don't actually object to the Lancashire hot-pot, Bishop?"

"Not at all; the recipe made it sound delicious."

"Well, then. I've checked back with the Vice-Chancellor, and we're now thinking fourteen rather than a dozen, but the student servers are confirmed. I propose that we start with potted shrimp, then the hot pot and Brussels sprouts, just to have something green—"

"How will you prepare those?" I asked.

"Undercooked, with mustard sauce. But I could do something else if you don't like sprouts."

"Oh, no, I've just always wondered. What about a sweet?"

"Assuming we can take a salad as read, I'd thought about something spectacular for a dessert, and I know that you're attached to trifle. But on second thought, it seemed to me something less heavy would be better. So I propose an orange fool, and then cheese and port or some of your single malt to follow."

"It sounds wonderful . . ." I hesitated. "You must have heard the news conference this evening."

"Yes, and I have to say that I was a bit puzzled. I'd somehow gotten the impression that part of the point of the celebration was that Lord Strathspey was bringing an actual museum piece with him, as opposed to a replica."

"That was the idea, in fact, and now there's apparently some question of a possible theft. Lord Strathspey, St. John Dacre, and I are all suspects, since we may have been the last people to see the real jewel. I don't imagine it will come to anything, but I suppose we might theoretically have a tense evening."

"Or the better part of the guest list could be in jail. I'll try to be prepared for anything, Bishop. I hope I needn't plan for magic along with the main course!"

"No more than usual. Though it's been a busy week."

"I thought perhaps it had been. Something about visions, is it?"

"More or less, yes." I gave her a thumbnail sketch of the whole affair and our various discussions of it.

"So, in the Cathedral, you had a silent picture of the Lateran; at a lecture, you heard Boethius at a lecture saying he couldn't see the face of a person whose reaction he wanted to judge; picking up the Alfred Jewel, you saw and heard the King adding something to his Boethius translation about God's inescapable vision and power; and seeing your reflection in the paten, we have Queen Elizabeth quoting Boethius on the secret burdens of purple-robed people in high places."

"And pointing to the jewel."

"And pointing to the jewel. And what have you found that all these have in common?"

"Well, three have some connection with Boethius, and two relate to the jewel, which goes back to Boethius, according to Strathspey."

"But nothing about the Lateran."

"No, that doesn't seem to fit, though I suppose Boethius must have been in it often enough."

"I suppose so, but not at the particular time you happened to see it. . . . Mightn't it be the case that you yourself are the common element?"

"How do you mean?"

"Well, each of these visions began with your situation. You've tried to see all of this as a warning about the jewel: but why couldn't it be read as a promise, instead? You have a secret burden or two, I would think, along with your purple shirts, and the message of the jewel itself is that God is in charge, God is overseeing everything. So even if you can't see his face or judge his reaction, you have the mosaic image, with the message that Christ will come in glory, that he gets the last word. Now it may not be my place to say so, but you are stubbornly independent by nature. You've adjusted to having Mrs. Equitone and Canon Carlson at the Cathedral, and me here, and Ms. Mears and Mr. Evans and the various cadets I've heard you mention before. But for all of that, you're always trying to solve things by yourself. I don't know what crisis you may be facing, and maybe it does have something to do with the jewel, but whatever may be coming, perhaps you're supposed to remember that you won't be facing it alone."

"My goodness. . . . I don't quite know what to say. You're right, of course, I'm sure. . . . I mean, I tell myself things like this (yes, I know that's ironic), but that doesn't mean I take them to heart. I'll try to do so."

She sighed. "Yes, Bishop, and I don't mean that you don't have the right intentions, but perhaps the point is that you might try to stop trying quite so much."

"Right. And if I meet the Buddha on the road, I shall kill him."

"That's the idea: Zen and the Art of Episcopacy. Now, then, I've some dishes to see to. Anything particular you'd like for breakfast?"

"Just scrambled eggs on toast, I think."

"Very good. Now scoot."

I scooted.

Upstairs, I called Danny from my study.

"Wow! Two calls in one week!"

"Sarcasm is unbecoming in one of your tender years, you know."

"Yeah, right. Seriously, though, I was about ready to call you. What's up with the kids?"

"They're going to come down to Annandale with me, unless you've changed your mind about not actually needing help."

"No, I'm fine on that score. In fact, I cruised the camp site this afternoon—lots of crystal sales people over there already, but no signs of malicious Neo-pagans plotting to steal my lawn furniture."

"It's not stealing your lawn furniture I'm worried about, Danny."

"I know, Jon-jon. And I'm not so careless about the state of my soul as it may seem. Don't think I don't appreciate your support, or haven't, every day, for all my life, big brother."

"Now who's being mushy? But since you mention it, let me ask you something. Have you ever felt I was, um, *too* independent?"

"What makes you ask?"

"Which means 'yes.' "

"It *means*, 'Judas Priest, Jonathan, how many years has it taken for *that* penny to drop.' It's like the evil twin of your pastoral instincts. You remember when we had that two-door Plymouth Scamp when we were in school, it was like a UN intervention to get you to accept a hand out of the back seat. When Mom died, you were tripping over yourself to help me—and you were a rock: but I kept wondering what being a rock was doing to you. And I know people keep telling you—I've seen it happen. But you just keep rolling along."

"Dan, I love you."

"Yeah, I know. But all joking aside, it's letting people love you that's the problem."

"You can't stop people from loving you!"

"No, but you can look remarkably uncomfortable when you realize that it's happening."

"Ouch!"

"Well, you asked for it, sort of. Besides, it's good for you."

"So everyone seems to think. Dan, is this as pathological as it sounds?"

"Oh, no, of course not. I mean, you *can* be talked into accepting help. It just takes a lot of effort, or people ganging up on you."

"Okay. Gang up anytime you think you need to. And let us know if you need help over the weekend."

"No worries, mate. See you soon."

Chapter 11: Friday, October 27

WE SAID MORNING PRAYER as a family, and I ended up having a second helping of grapefruit along with my scrambled eggs, all of which somehow made me a few minutes late for work.

"Good morning, Bishop," Mrs. Equitone said as I came in. "You just missed a call from Officer Crump at the university."

"Thank you very much, Mrs. Equitone. I'll call him right back."

"Very good. I'll get him for you, sir."

A few moments later, we were connected.

"Good morning, Bishop. Thank you for calling back."

"No problem. What can I do for you?"

"I spoke to the Vice-Chancellor and Professor Dacre late yesterday, sir, and they wanted me to give you an update on the jewel theft. We have looked over all the surveillance videos and checked the access records for the curator's office, and there's nothing at all out of the ordinary. In fact, no one seems to have opened the safe at all in the time between Saturday and Wednesday afternoons."

"I was afraid of that."

"Yes, sir. I did just want to note that there did seem to be something odd on the closed circuit TV just before the jewel was put in the safe—"

"Which is why you called me."

"Well, yes, sir."

"I have been thinking about it, actually, but I haven't been able to reach any real conclusion. I guess the best I could say is that magic might explain how the jewels were switched, but I'd be more inclined to look for almost any other explanation."

"Yes, sir. The actual point I wanted to raise, sir, had to do with that blued-out moment on the video. There is, you understand, sir, a moment there when you have the jewel and can't be seen."

"Right, I see. There is a point at which I might have pulled a switch without anyone seeing what I was doing."

"It might seem that way to the police, sir."

"I can see how it might. But I did give the jewel back to Lord Strathspey, who locked it in the safe. Presumably, if he could tell the fake was a fake as soon as he took it out of the safe on Wednesday, he could have recognized it as a fake if I'd given it to him instead of returning the real one on Saturday."

"Yes, sir. That's just what Professor Dacre said, sir. But Lord Strathspey may have been too distracted at the time to notice."

"Of course. He could have been hypnotized into thinking it was the real jewel when I in fact handed him an old overshoe, for that matter. But it's not likely. What does his lordship say?"

"No, sir, hypnosis is not likely, I agree. Like you, I prefer not to invoke magic as an explanation. Lord Strathspey was, unfortunately, out of town yesterday, but I hope to speak with him yet this morning. You should know though, sir, that if all of this were to become a police matter, there might be cause for a search warrant."

"I see. Well, thank you for the information, Officer Crump, and do please keep me informed. God bless."

Carl came through the open office door just as Mrs. Equitone buzzed in a second call. "Answer it," he said, sitting on the couch, "I can take a number."

"Good morning, Bishop. This is Steven Crotek calling, from down in Withougan."

"Doctor Crotek, good morning. How's the hospital?"

"Fine, thank you, sir. I'm glad you remember us."

"I've spent a lot of time in Riverview for one reason and another, Doctor, including being born there. What can I do for you?"

"I wanted to call and let you know that Father Mathis was admitted to the hospital about two hours ago. He's stable now, so there's no immediate worry. There were some initial signs that it might have been a heart attack, but now we're looking into some other explanations. It seems that the problem may be a sudden extremely rapid heartbeat that we call tachycardia."

"Doctor, let me put you on the speakerphone. Archdeacon Carlson, my right hand man, happens to be here in the office. Carl, it's the director of the Withougan hospital—Herb Mathis has been admitted with heart trouble of some sort. You were saying, Doctor."

"Yes. We're now thinking the diagnosis is supraventricular tachycardia. It's serious, even alarming, but it doesn't have to be life-threatening. Doctor Belger is with Father Mathis now, which is why I'm calling you—I gather that he's the senior warden of their parish."

"That's correct," Carl said. "I suppose Father Mathis will be in the ICU when he's through with the doctor?"

"For a couple of days, yes, Archdeacon. It's a manageable illness, pharmaceutically, in many patients, and we've also had good luck with surgery. Doctor Belger may want to take a while to decide on the best course of treatment."

"Would Doctor Belger do the surgery there at Riverview?"

"No, Bishop, we send patients over there to St. Luke's for this procedure—they do a lot of them, and it's the sort of thing where experience is to the patient's advantage."

"I see. And clergy can still visit your ICU pretty much any time?"

"Oh, yes, Bishop, of course."

"Very good. I'll stop by the hospital myself this afternoon, but please assure Dr. Belger and Fr. Mathis that they needn't worry about the parish—we'll make sure everything is taken care of."

"Thank you, Bishop. I know that will save them both a great deal of worry."

"No problem. I'll hope to see you this afternoon. God bless."

"So you're going to cover Christ Church on Sunday?" Carl asked as I hung up the phone.

"Mind reader!"

"I'm not even going to bother making a joke out of that one, Jonathan: it's too easy."

"Sorry. But I am going to be down there this weekend, anyway, so it's only reasonable for me to take the Masses. It's an 8 and 10:30 parish, as I remember. We can make long-term plans on Monday."

"Very good. No one can say we're not efficient. Now what I actually came to tell you was that you owe Boyden Smith an apology."

"Oh, yes?"

"Not literally, perhaps, but he has done some interesting research for me, unctuous or not. Hudson Buchanan, not surprisingly, is associated with a not-for-profit corporation."

"As are we."

"Fair enough. And it's not surprising that his corporation is called 'Hudson Buchanan Ministries.' "

"That is, in fact, how it's usually done."

"Granted. What's unusual, though, and what our friend has discovered, is that the Buchanan Ministries are affiliated, through this that and the other clever legal device and a variety of overlapping directorships of the sort that wouldn't occur to your average solicitor, to a Washington state charity whose main line is—"

"Don't tell me—they're Neo-pagans."

"Now who's playing mindreader?"

"It just confirms what we already expected about him, is all. And it ties him in institutionally to the teacher from Milwaukee who was so briefly interested in Commander Lindsley's baton down at Annandale."

"I am always happy to be the bearer of glad tidings. What was your phone call from the university about?"

"Our security man warning me that if he were a real detective he wouldn't let me leave town."

"He thinks you took the jewel?"

"He thinks I might have, but Strathspey can disabuse him of that idea. I'm not expecting search warrants to issue for the Cathedral and the Palace."

"There's a relief. Do you have time to look at a couple of new dossiers from the clergy deployment agency?"

"I do at the moment, anyway. Bring them on."

Both of the files looked fine to me, and I handed them back to Carl relatively quickly; if the parish found either of them interesting, I knew, he would conduct his own *sub rosa* inquiries to get a better picture of the candidate than any manila folder was likely to contain. In the Middle Ages, they called the archdeacon "the bishop's eyes," and Carl lived up to the title.

About ten, figuring that both of the kids should be out of class, I sent them a quick telepathic alert.

Sir, Rhys responded, *Car and I are here in the Snack Bar.*

Hi, Uncle Jon, she thought. *What's up?*

No crisis, but I wanted to ask you two a question. I have to stop in Withougan this afternoon to visit someone in the hospital and go back up there for services on Sunday morning. Do you want to come along, or shall we take separate cars?

I don't mind driving, Caroline said, *if Rhys will navigate.*

Sounds like a plan, sir. Annandale did teach us how to read maps.

Yes, and how to fold your underwear and put them neatly in your closet: I'll just hope you remember the way, I replied. *Since we're travelling separately, I may leave early if I get through here at the office. Let's touch base about five and talk about supper.*

Great, Uncle Jon. See you then.

Satisfied with my burst of organization, I slogged through the rest of the liturgy and music report, looked up the lessons for Sunday, and popped into Carl's office to see if he were free for lunch. Since it was a Friday, we went to The Moonraker, a seafood restaurant overlooking the lake. True to our collegiate backgrounds, each of us ordered a bowl of chowder, and I was just complaining about the lack of proper Bostonian pilot crackers when Strathspey walked up to our table.

"Michael," I said, "this is a surprise. Please join us. Lord Strathspey, this is Archdeacon Carlson."

"Mr. Archdeacon, it's a pleasure. Do call me Michael."

"My pleasure, Michael. And I'm Carl. 'Mr. Archdeacon' sounds like a Trollope novel. Please have a seat."

The young peer slipped, somewhat hesitantly, into a chair. "Gentlemen, I'm terribly sorry to be stalking you—I spoke to your Mrs. Equitone, who told me where you were having lunch."

"You seem quite concerned. . . . " I said, slipping into counselor mode.

He glanced at Carl. "Um, yes. . . . It involves the university museum. . . ."

"Carl is familiar with the whole situation."

He relaxed a bit. "Ah, good. Let me back up, then. I have been over in Chicago, doing some work at the Newberry Library, and came back this morning on the 10:15 interurban train. There were several messages waiting for me from Officer Crump, and when I called him back, he asked me whether I were sure that I had locked the original jewel in the safe in the first place. I told him, of course, that I certainly thought I had, and, after a bit of pushing on my part, he finally explained to me his lunatic theory that you might have switched the jewels. You can imagine my reaction! I said that even though I hadn't actually weighed the jewel after you gave it back, my not having done so was no reason to doubt the word of a bishop of the Church."

"Thank you, Michael. It's not a perfect excuse, but it should do."

"I hope so. You can see, though, why I was so concerned to speak with you right away: I couldn't actually swear with scientific certainty that you gave me the original jewel, and I wouldn't want to say something that would be used against you."

"Of course not," Carl said. "But if attention were to be drawn to the, let's say, unusual circumstances of Jonathan's examining the jewel, I suspect all bets would be off in any case. The thing to do is to recover the jewel, and I have to add that it's not entirely clear to me how energetically Officer Crump is pursuing that angle."

Michael nodded energetically. "It's not even forty-eight hours yet," I said. "I'm not sure what more he could have done, particularly without bringing the police in. And that wasn't his decision."

"No, and I'm not sure it was a wise one. In forty-eight hours, a thief could have taken the jewel anyplace in the world."

"That's true, Carl. But the fact is that in cases of art theft, especially when there's no question of breaking an object up into valuable but unrecognizable pieces, we sometimes have to wait years for the item to resurface."

"I understand: but I have no intention of having Jonathan, or for that matter the university and the diocese, under suspicion for a period of years."

"For which I, at least, am grateful. But there's nothing much we're going to do about it while our soup gets cold. Would you like to order something, Michael?"

"No, thank you, Jonathan. I got up late and had several beignets at the café in the lobby of the Palmer House. They're more filling than they look."

"Indeed," Carl said. "There's nothing quite like fried bread, whatever the culture."

"There is a favor I'd like to ask of you though, Jonathan. . . ."

"Surely, Michael. What is it?"

"One of the other messages I had waiting for me this morning was from Annandale. A young woman in the alumni office had heard that I was in the neighborhood, and wondered if I might be interested in coming down for the Homecoming weekend. Apparently, even though I'm only a summer camp alumnus, she thought a peer of the realm might make a nice bookend for the Vice President in future publicity. I called her back, and she was very persuasive. . . ."

"That would be my cousin Patty," I suggested.

"I gathered as much when we spoke. She mentioned something about cheesecake."

"An old family story, with which I need not bore you now. Do I take it that you'd like a ride?"

"That's what I was getting at, yes."

"I'd be happy to oblige, but I may be leaving fairly early, in order to make a hospital visit in Withougan. You're welcome to come along, or if you'd prefer to go later, you might be able to ride with my niece, Caroline, and my cousin Rhys. They've been looking forward to meeting you on Monday, in any case. They should be back at the Palace about 2:45—I don't imagine they'll actually leave until 3:30 or so. Here's the number," I said, jotting it on the back of a business card.

"Perhaps I shall call them, then. I do have one or two things to attend to before I go, and I do have to make sure I have some clean clothes. If we can't make some arrangement, I'll simply go ahead and hire a car. It can't be that hard to adjust to a left-hand drive."

"Not with an automatic, certainly," Carl said. "There is taxicab service to Annandale, as well—for about $75 one way, which is probably less than the car rental would be."

"Thank you, Carl, that's helpful. Now, gentlemen, if you'll excuse me, I must see to some laundry."

"Good luck, Michael. I'll look forward to seeing you in Annandale this weekend."

As soon as Michael was out of earshot, Carl leaned across the table: "Jonathan, I'm sure that young man was lying to you."

"How so?"

"When I was in Chicago on Tuesday, I stopped by the Palmer House, because I wanted to look for shoes in that little shop on the Monroe Avenue side of the building. I walked through the lobby, where they were repainting the ceiling, and I could swear that the Café du Monde was closed for remodeling."

"Well, Carl, they could simply have finished."

"Or, something could be fishy about his story. I'll phone the hotel when we get back and check out the facts of the matter."

"Good idea. In the meantime, will you have some Boston Cream Pie?"

"Thank you, no, and I doubt whether you should, either."

"Yes, drill sergeant."

"It's for your own good, Jon. Here, let me get the check."

WE STROLLED BACK to the Cathedral in a leisurely sort of way, befitting two reasonably well-fed prelates, dessert or not. Once we were back in the building, however, Carl made a beeline for his office, where, I was sure, he would soon be on the phone to the Palmer House. I sat down at my desk to check the day's e-mail. Fifteen minutes later, he was back in the doorway.

"And the verdict is?"

"Inconclusive, I'm afraid. The actual café at the east end of the lobby is still closed, but there is a makeshift area across from registration where they do serve breakfast from the café menu, including all the little square French doughnuts one might care to eat."

"So we're dealing with a technical distinction that might escape someone who's not a Palmer House regular?"

"Admittedly: but I'd still be a bit suspicious."

"That's one of the things you get paid for, after all. But honestly, Carl, even if Michael's beignets were simply an attempt to 'add an appearance of verisimilitude to an otherwise bald and unconvincing narrative,' and he spent the last couple of days in Detroit, I don't know that I should care one way or the other."

"Unless he made off with the jewel and left town to dispose of it."

"True, but he could presumably dispose of it more easily in Chicago than anyplace else near here, and still have time for breakfast in the Palmer House. All of which being said, I will try to stay on my toes."

"That's all I can ask. Is there anything you need to have done over the weekend, other than looking for a longer-term sub for Withougan?"

"Not that I can think of. I'll come in for at least part of the day on Monday so we can talk about it. If there's nothing else to be done here, I think I'll take off."

"Have a good trip. Tell Herb he'll be in our prayers."

"Will do. I'll see you Monday."

RHYS WAS IN his study when I stopped at the Palace to pick up my things for the weekend. I told him about my luncheon conversations.

"So, Bishop, do you think we should give this guy a ride or not?"

"I wouldn't if it's not convenient, but other than that I don't see anything to fret about. Even if he is a jewel thief who lies about his breakfast, and I doubt both premises, that wouldn't mean it's dangerous to have him in the back seat of one's car. I'm honestly more worried about you getting lost in the wilds of Wabana County. But check it out with Caroline, and if either of you is at all hesitant, make a polite excuse: there are plenty of other ways for Strathspey to get to Annandale."

"Very good, sir. And we'll let you know as soon as we get down there."

"That's not necessary."

"No, but you've been working so hard not to ask that it's becoming obvious."

"And Caroline says *she's* perspicacious. Okay, fine, then. I'll look forward to hearing from you when you arrive."

"Roger that, sir. Have a good trip."

I GOT TO RIVERVIEW about quarter past three, and though I didn't actually talk for all that long with Herb, who was still obviously tired from his ordeal, by the time I checked with his doctor, got the keys, and made a quick check of the church, it was going on five as I pulled into the driveway at home. I half expected to see Caroline's car there—if they'd left promptly at three, they would easily have beaten me—but on the other hand, they would probably have dropped off Caroline's things and gone straight on to the Academy.

No one answered when I rang the doorbell. Phil, having grown up in Detroit rather than Annandale, kept the doors locked, but there was still a key hidden under a stack of Reader's Digest Condensed Books on the porch, and I let myself in.

I put my luggage down on the couch, again, and glanced around the living room. There were two notes addressed to me on the mantle piece, one in a heavy cream envelope, the other scrawled on two yellow AMA report slips.

The latter was from Phil: "Met the VP (see envelope). Kewl. Cadet Chauviere and Dr. Davies suggest invite you & Michael (if here) 0000 initiation medieval grp. old library. CU there 2230 rehearsal? Phone w/ quest. @ × 1200. Help yourself to fridge. PEC"

Given the endless supply of report slips at Philip's disposal, this telegraphic style seemed to me largely affectation, though I suppose it was arguable that he was saving trees. I wasn't at all sure what the initiation of a "medieval group" might involve, but Richard's promised presence guaranteed that the proceedings would be acceptably sedate. Putting the idea on a mental back burner, I turned to Mr. Daniels' note.

"Jonathan," it read, "we're still not quite sure when everyone will get in this evening—no sense trying to gather for dinner—we'll meet officially at 8:30 tomorrow morning in the Memorial Building, but please drop by the guest house for dessert and conversation—any time after seven—Best, Kevin."

Seven o'clock for dessert left plenty of time for supper with the kids, whom I thought I could reasonably expect within the half hour. After determining that Phil did not have any Cokes in the refrigerator, I sat down with a couple of Frango mints to watch the local news on the TV.

I fell asleep, of course, and was sharply awakened by the sensation, felt for the second time in a week, of our home's defenses being triggered. After the initial shock had passed, along with the everyday disorientation that comes from suddenly waking up, I waited for the usual telepathic contact. Nothing happened, nor was I able to initiate contact myself by the means I had used so casually earlier in the day. I stepped outside, both to see whether someone were actually trying to break into the house and on the off-chance that something about the house was unexpectedly blocking our communication. Again, there was nothing.

I was standing back in the living room, scratching my head, when the phone rang.

"Jonathan."

"Hi, Dan. I just had a shocking wake-up call. What's going on?"

"I thought I knew, at first, but now I'm not quite so sure. Are the kids with you?"

"No, though they should have been here quite a while ago. Is it really ten after six?"

"Close enough, anyway. Well, I know they're not at the Palace, because I called there just a second ago."

"Okay, Dan, back up a minute. What set off the alarms in the first place? I haven't seen anyone prowling around up here."

"No, that was down here. You remember I said I cruised the Neo-pagan festival site—apparently a couple of them decided to return the favor, and didn't believe the 'no trespassing' signs I put up at the end on my drive."

"I hope you didn't cause a wreck."

"Nothing more serious than running off the road when they were knocked out, so far as I could tell with the binocs, but I'm walking down there to check. I'm on the portable phone."

"Great. I don't remember that the wards around your house went all the way down the drive."

"They didn't. But I've been experimenting lately with a couple of the nails you found from the cover of the old Book of Shadows, and with a little help from my friends, I think I may be able to show you a couple of surprises here pretty quick. Anyway, one of my experiments was to expand the perimeter a bit."

"I'm surprised that doing the magic to set that up didn't get everyone's attention."

"Me, too, but the theoretical side of it's all a bit hazy to me, still. In fact, I wasn't sure that triggering the new set-up would involve the three of you at all.

"Okay, here we are at the end of the lane. Apparently a rental car from Indianapolis, driver and passenger both unconscious. Doors unlocked, not even an airbag deployed. Let me kill the engine.

"Okay, that should hold *them* for a moment. Anyway, I didn't necessarily expect a reaction from you or the kids, but now I'm worried."

"So am I." I told him about Strathspey and the possibility that he might have asked the kids for a ride.

"He sounds like a shady character to me, Jon, but I don't see what he might have done to put the kids incommunicado. I suppose he might have knocked them both out and taken the car, but why?"

"Exactly. I suppose they might have run into Hudson Buchanan again—"

"Isn't he supposed to be in another state by now?"

"Yes, I'm just being thorough. Or they may have had an ordinary accident, which is what I'm afraid of."

"Right, me too."

"Well, you're the concerned father. Is it too soon for me to call the sheriff?"

"By police standards, yes, unless you have one who'll understand why we're particularly worried. I know Jim Box is only the Lake Patrol, but could he help?"

"The very person I was thinking of. Let me call you back after I talk to him."

"Thanks, Jon. Listen, I think I know one of these guys."

"Thomas Dixon, I bet."

"No, I've no more seen him than you have. Do you suppose I dare go through his pockets?"

"Might be a little hard to explain to the EMT's."

"They don't need anything more than a tow truck. But here's a question my new studies haven't addressed: what do you suppose I do to wake them up?"

"Just nudge them, judging by Philip's account. Or maybe move them outside your new defense perimeter. Or take away whatever magic items triggered the defense to begin with."

"Which might be anything from swords to earrings: there's a project. I bet the right magic could just move them. Or maybe I'll just drag the car out to the road with my tractor and be done with it. But then they might actually attack."

"Or, if you keep waiting, someone may come looking for them. You certainly can't keep them on hold until Abbot Alfred gets there. We're juggling too many balls at once, Dan. Let me see if I can get a search for the kids started, and I'll call you right back."

"Okay, and I'll see if I have any ideas about these two guys in the deep freeze. Should we say a prayer of some kind?"

"Right, sometimes I do forget. The Lord be with you."

"And also with you."

"Let us pray. Almighty God, hear our prayer for all those whom we love, now absent from us. Defend them from all dangers of soul and body, and grant that both they and we, drawing nearer to thee, may be bound together in the communion of thy saints and the fellowship of the Holy Spirit, through Jesus Christ our Lord."

"Amen. Now, let's get to work."

A CALL TO the Academy's Officer-in-Charge got me the direct number of the Lake Patrol. As I had hoped, Jim Box, once my sixth grade teacher, was on duty. I identified myself and said that I needed a favor.

"Sure thing, Jon. What can I do for you?"

"It's my niece, Caroline, Danny's girl, and my young cousin, Rhys Evans. They were driving over from Michigan City, supposed to leave about three, and haven't gotten here yet."

"So you're worried they might have had an accident. Have you tried any, um, unconventional means of locating them?"

"Yes, both Dan and I have, without any success at all, which was why I thought to call you. Dan says it's too early to be reporting missing persons, but on the other hand . . ."

I described Caroline's compact as best I could, didn't remember her license plate, but did at the last moment think to mention that it was registered in

Brown County, so that the "7" at the beginning of the tag might be some help. And of course I was just about hopeless for giving any physical description of the kids themselves.

"Okay, Jonathan. I'll get right on it; I can have the sheriffs and the highway patrol looking. Are you going to be at home, or are you going to the Vice President's party?"

"No secrets at all in this town, are there?"

"Come on, local law enforcement has to be kept reasonably up to date."

"Of course. The party doesn't even start until seven o'clock, so I think I can stay here at home for the better part of an hour, anyway. But if you can't get me here, do try the guest house."

With those arrangements made, I called Danny back.

"Hi, Dan. I talked to Jim, and he's going to alert everyone about the kids. How's your crisis?"

"It's being handled even as we speak. Do you known Indiana's third highest ranking cash crop?"

"After corn and soybeans? Wheat, I suppose."

"So smart and yet so naïve. You'll notice I didn't say legal crop."

"Aha. *Cannabis*, then."

"Precisely. And there's a farmer down the road whose cornfield, I think, would not stand up to close inspection."

"I know better than to ask, but are we heading anyplace with this?"

"Oh, ye of little faith. The point is, once I stopped to think, it occurred to me that here was someone with a tractor who might be willing to help out a neighbor and not ask too many questions. So I phoned him, and suggested I had reasons for wanting to seem like I wasn't at home. And he's down there now hooking a chain to the back end of the rental car. God only knows how he'll explain himself."

"So young and yet so devious. Good job, Danny. I don't want to suggest that you stay in the house for the next three days, but you might want to be on your toes, in case those guys come back with some friends."

"No question, Jon. Meanwhile, I hope our own reinforcements turn up: I think I'm really on the verge of a sudden breakthrough, if Alfred can give me some assistance."

"More power to you. What's going on with your tractor pull?"

"He's got them outside the perimeter, as you put it: I didn't ask him to drag them all the way out to the highway. In fact, he's stopped now to unhook them, and there is, as you predicted, activity inside. . . . oh, I don't believe it! They're paying him."

"Sounds like you'll have happy neighbors, at least."

"Until the fireworks start, anyway. Let's get off the phone so the police can call you back."

"Right. And if you do need me later in the evening, call the academy operator and ask for the guest house; then after 10:30, I have a gig in the old library."

"Okay. Be careful, Jon-jon."

"You, too, Danny. God bless."

———

It was, by then, about a quarter to seven. Returning to Phil's refrigerator, I made a couple of cheese sandwiches for supper, lest I seem ravenous when I did go for dessert. Forty-five minutes ticked by, accompanied by the end of the *Newshour* and a *Washington Week in Review* to which I paid precious little attention. At that point I thought I might as well go on to the party.

I was quite literally shifting into reverse to back out of the drive when another car pulled up in the street. Phil hopped out, followed closely by Strathspey. I turned off my own ignition and got out to meet them. "Michael," I said, "when did you get here?"

"My cab put me down at Sally Port at about half six, I think."

"Cab?"

"Yes, it turned out my schedule didn't mesh with your niece's, so we came separately. Didn't she tell you?"

"Actually, they haven't gotten here yet. My brother and I are rather worried."

"Jon!" Phil said. "Is there anything I can do to help?"

"No, thanks, we've contacted the state police already."

"I hope there's no question of an accident," Michael said.

"It's not impossible. We don't seem to be able to contact them through any of our family channels, and that suggests they might be unconscious. But there's nothing to be done about it from here, in any case. What have you two been up to?"

"Your cousin Patty," Michael replied, "was registering alumni in a large tent just outside Sally Port. She had made arrangements for me to stay in a room at the Annandale Inn, but couldn't leave the table to escort me across campus (not that I couldn't have found my own way). Phil happened to be passing by in a golf cart, pursuing his deputy commandant duties, and agreed to take me under his wing. So we went to my room, dropped off my things, zipped on to Phil's car, and stopped off for a quick Coney Dog at the root beer stand, an experience that brought back many childhood memories. Meanwhile, Phil has been telling me about this initiation ceremony."

"Nothing beneath the dignity of a peer of the realm, I hope."

"Indeed, not. Not only does it seem tasteful, even solemn, but Phil has also managed to dig out of the theatrical costumes a reasonable semblance of the scarlet and ermine."

"Left over from a production of *Iolanthe* for which I was the costume designer, more years ago than I care to remember."

"And that's why we were looking for you, Jon," Philip added. "To see if you had your bishop's robes with you."

"I do, as it happens, though I meant to leave them in Withougan. Is there actually a liturgical function to be performed at this ceremony?"

"An opening prayer would be good," Phil answered. "I was thinking, though, about having you and Michael and Richard in your different robes for the effect of it."

"Okay. As long as I *know* I'm playing dress-up."

"One hears that a lot around the House," Michael said. "But you must be on your way to the Vice President's reception. We mustn't keep you: the big items of business are often settled in committee, after all."

"All too true, I'm afraid. Philip, tell me again what time you want me at the old library?"

"Half past ten, Jon, if you can. I suppose compared to what you're used to there's not actually that much to rehearse, but you will want to look it all over, and the rest of us may need some practice—I want to have the place dark when the kids start showing up."

"Very good. Unless something comes up with Rhys and Caroline, I'll see you then."

We all shook hands, and I went back inside to reclaim my luggage before driving off to the party.

THE FIRST FLOOR of the guest house was not, I suppose, actually crowded, but there were certainly quite a few people there: the Superintendent and his lady, most of the Trustees (I was not, thankfully, the very last to arrive), many with persons I took to be their spouses, the VP and a couple of the usual serious-looking protectors, and the Directors of Development and Admissions. I schmoozed my way through to the dining room, where I discovered that the dessert was a selection of Cousin Lester's pies and ice cream. With a piece of rhubarb a la mode and a cup of tea, I made my way to an armchair in the den, strategically placed next to an end table. On my right there was a matching chair, still vacant, and then a sofa occupied by a couple whom I did not know, talking animatedly with each other. The older gentleman on my left, breathing from a portable oxygen tank, I recognized as Gerald Boyle, class of '39, who'd contributed both to the building of the Memorial Chapel and to its various improvements over the years. He was, I knew, agnostic on his most devout days; but he maintained an unswerving devotion to the Gold Star Men of Annandale, the classmates and friends who had died in the service of their country.

"So, Doctor Mears, good to have you back on the Board. Have you done your reading?"

"Oh, yes, sir. Wouldn't dare come 'unprepared for recitation' on my first day back."

"We used to get an hour of marching extra duty if we were reported UFR."

"It took three reports to get an hour of ED in my day, sir: I suppose it's six by now."

"No doubt. And the public schools complain about grade inflation. So, then, what do you think?"

"You're not going to let me take refuge in small talk, then, sir?"

"Once is politeness, twice is a waste of breath, a commodity with which I am no longer disposed to be prodigal. Talk to me."

"If you say so, sir. In brief, I think the change is the right way to go. As an educator, I think the only concern is that some studies say single-sex schools are better for girls. But that's not one of our options. As an alumnus, I imagine that some traditions will have to change—or will change inevitably, whether they have to or not—but Annandale's not that old. The Mearses were here on the lake before John Marshall Glenarm, after all. Radcliffe hasn't damaged Harvard's three centuries of traditions, and women clergy haven't damaged two thousand years of the Church."

"More's the pity. So there's nothing I can say to change your mind?"

"No, sir. I don't mean I won't listen to reason, but I have tried to consider all the arguments in the position papers we've seen, along with any others I could think of."

"So you *can* be logical when you want to be?"

"It comes from all that practice with Thomas Aquinas, sir. Aren't you even going to try to persuade me?"

"I told you I don't mean to waste my breath. I'll save it to persuade the people who don't agree with me. Now finish your pie before the ice cream melts."

One of the people who did not agree, it turned out, was Thad Moulson, present by virtue of his elevation, the previous July, to the presidency of the Summer School Alumni Association. Though we hadn't been classmates in the summer program, we'd graduated from our respective Ivy League rival colleges in the same year. Thad regularly expressed his surprise that in our parallel lives in Cambridge and New Haven, he'd never seen me at 'The Game.' The fact was, though I am ashamed to report it, that the chance of encountering him in the crowd would probably have kept me away even if I'd enjoyed football. On this particular evening, he homed in on me, taking the chair to my right.

"Jonathan," he said by way of greeting, "I hope you're talking some sense into Mr. Boyle." The two of them were soon re-engaged in what was apparently a long-running waste of breath, and I excused myself to take my plate back to the kitchen.

I repeated one or the other of these sorts of conversation for most of the evening, growing increasingly inattentive as time went by. It was nearly ten, and I was saying good night to the Superintendent, when I saw Jim Box come through the front door. He made his way directly across the room to me.

"Excuse me, Bishop," he said. "Could I speak to you privately for a moment?"

"Of course. Excuse me, please, General."

"Of course, Padre. We'll see you tomorrow morning."

Jim led me out onto the front porch. "This can't be good news," I said.

He shook his head. "I'm not sure whether it's good or bad. The LaPorte County Sheriff found Caroline's car over on Road 35, just north of the Starke County line, where the road crosses the Kankakee River. It was properly pulled off to the side of the road, and had the 'send help' side of a state map displayed in the back window. They spotted the car about half past five, and figured it hadn't been there for too long at that point. They said it looked at first as though the kids had sat in the car for a little while and finally decided to go get help. Once the sheriffs heard our message and made the connection, they sent someone back out to have a more careful look, and that deputy reported back that he'd found heavy tire tracks, as though a truck or an RV might have pulled off onto the berm to help them, and they had hitched a ride with the good Samaritan."

"A good Samaritan who has taken five hours to bring them the last twenty miles of their trip."

"That's what I'm worried about. Even so, though, there are any number of innocent explanations. I'm assuming that if there had been any sort of a threat or a ransom demand, you would have told me." I nodded. "And of course the police can't be checking for, um, unconventional means of abducting the two. . . ."

"No, of course not. But they were reasonably well-protected on that score; I think we would have known if something had happened."

"Fine. Now let me ask you if anyone knew the young folks' travel plans."

"Probably not, specifically. People in my office and my housekeeper knew we were coming down today, as did Dan. Lord Strathspey, who talked to them about sharing a ride down, told me they hadn't been able to agree on a time, but that doesn't mean he knew what they were actually going to do. And he apparently took a cab down here that arrived at about six, so he must have been on the road from four thirty or so. Phil Cicero knew the kids were coming down, but not when or by what route, and I suppose Rhys had registered for a bunk with the Alumni Office, but he wouldn't have told Patty when he was getting in."

"Very good. Now, look, the thing for you and Dan to do is just to go on with life as usual, as much as you can, and let us handle this. Speaking of Dan, could I have his phone number? If you don't mind, I'd like to bring him up to date myself."

"Surely. It's 555-CALL-DAN."

"Sounds like him," he said, writing it down anyway. "I suppose you're heading back to the house after the party?"

"Well, no, actually I have an activity over in the Memorial Building that I was just getting ready to go to—it sounds as though I should be home a little after one in the morning."

"Very good. I'll let you know as soon as I hear something. But try not to worry."

"Like trying not to think about elephants. Thanks for all your trouble, Jim."

He walked back to his patrol car, and I returned to the party to say good night to Kevin. In a few minutes I had recovered my vestments from my own vehicle and walked around to the lake side of the Memorial Building. Years of habit made me carry the garment bag over my left arm, leaving my right free to salute the Gold Star on the landing in front of the great oaken doors.

Phil and Richard were inside, the former in his armor, but for the helmet, the latter in a resplendent doctoral gown. They were arranging a last few decorations in the baronial great hall at the heart of the building.

"Jon," Phil said, "I'm glad you made it. Are we still a military school?"

"For the moment, my friend, for the moment. Where shall I put on my things?"

"We're using the old librarian's office for a dressing room. Richard, would you take him back? And have you seen his copy of the script? I'm going to try dimming the lights."

"Hi, Jonathan," Richard said, as we walked to the office. "You'll have to excuse him, he's a little nervous. I do have your script here—it's just standard 'here's a virtue, let's light a candle to symbolize it' material. It's all wrapped up in the shape of a vigil for a prospective knight."

"I take it you had a hand in this."

"Not much of one, actually. Phil had it fairly well thought through by the time he showed it to me."

"Let me ask you one question—is this to be taken at face value, or is it all a big game?"

"Are you here as a real bishop or a 'cleric persona,' do you mean?"

"Exactly. Could you hand me my stole, please?"

"Surely, here. It's the former, I think: certainly no worse than blessing the hounds at a fox hunt, and I've seen you do that."

"Just once, and there wasn't a real fox involved."

"Which makes it more humane, but not more authentic. Let me help with your cope."

"What's not authentic?" Phil asked, clanking into the room.

"Oh, nothing, Jonathan and I were just reminiscing about old times."

"That's the topic of the day. Did you show him that letter?"

"I was just about to. Jonathan, after your last visit, I've been poking around trying to find out more about Commander Lindsley's baton. I didn't find anything in the archives, and when we came in here earlier this evening, I looked through the museum files, such as they are. It turns out the Commander left a letter to accompany the baton, and I'm willing to bet it tells where he got it."

"What's there to bet about?"

"I'm afraid the letter is in Latin. Here, have a look. I can screw that crozier together for you."

It was a handwritten note, apparently addressed to the Commander in the typical Latin form, "Carolus Joannem S.P.D.S.V.V.," which is, "Charles sends many greetings to John. If you are well, I am well." As I glanced over the text, one or two phrases caught my eye, and I noticed that the author had signed his name at the end in the usual modern place, but still in a Latinized form, "Carolus" followed by an odd x sign: ↗.

"You're looking at the signature," Richard said.

"Indeed. What do you think the little x is for? Presumably anyone who could compose a letter in Latin would not have to make a mark instead of a signature."

"It's not an x, it's an astrological glyph, the one for Sagittarius. I have to say, though, I don't know why anyone would attach it to his name—not anyone Commander Lindsley regularly corresponded with, anyway."

"Aha. That's the answer. The Commander was about as interested in astrology as I am, but if he knew this was the sign for Sagittarius, he'd have gotten the joke."

"Which is?" Phil asked.

"Well, what does 'Sagittarius' mean in Latin?"

" 'The Archer,' does it not?" Richard asked. "It's a picture of a centaur drawing a bow."

" 'Archer' is one possible meaning, yes, but it's not the only one. 'Sagittarius' also means 'one who makes arrows.' And an arrow-maker in English is . . . ."

"A fletcher," Richard said. "As in Major Chuck Fletcher."

"Exactly. Major Fletcher, Philip, was my first Latin teacher here at Annandale, but left during the war. The Doug Fletcher we were talking about the other day is his son. He must have been the one who brought the baton back from the war, rather than the Commander."

"Cool," he said, in a tone suggesting his attention was still elsewhere. "Come out and see what you think of the lighting in the hall: I think it's going to be pretty neat. Maybe you can have a seat and translate the letter."

We followed him back out. Lit by candles, with only subdued support from bulbs in chandeliers high up in the room, it really did look majestic. Richard showed me to a seat in the center of the triple oaken throne which had once graced John Marshall Glenarm's library. It was equipped with candles in sconces, which made my translation project a bit easier. Picking the baton in question off the cushion, he took his seat on my right.

"You guys are going to look great," Phil said.

"The whole effect is stunning, Phil," Richard replied. "The boys will be more than just impressed."

I looked up from my reading. Apparently, in the half light, no one had noticed the fourth member of our party arriving. "Michael," I said, "good evening."

He stepped forward from the shadows. It seemed to me that he invested his crimson velvet and faux-ermine with dignity, looking every inch the Earl of Strathspey.

"Come have a seat," I said. "I was just thinking about you."

"My ears were burning," he replied, taking the seat on my left.

"I can see why. Richard's just given me this note to translate. It's rather school-masterish Latin, but interesting. I haven't read it to the others, so you might want to work through it aloud."

"Not my specialty," he said, "but I'll give it a go. Let's see:

Charles sends many greetings to John: if you are well, I am well. Old friend: Departing from this pleasant place, I want to leave you with a remembrance of our service together. I have told you often how war brought together an orphan boy from Kansas and the noble

Lord Aberlour as comrades in arms, and how he, dying, passed on this heirloom as a memento. So now I pass it on to you, with high hopes not only for your future but also for that of the academy we have both loved. Hail and farewell. Charles Sagittarius."

He put the note down in his lap. "So then, you've got me."

"Got you doing what?" Phil asked.

"Lord Aberlour," I answered, "is the title of the oldest sons of the Earls of Strathspey. If our Major Fletcher got the baton as a gift from a Lord Aberlour who died in World War II, it must have been Michael's uncle. And if it really was a family heirloom, then Michael would be unlikely not to have recognized it on Monday, when he told us it was a piece of modern ivory."

"And of course I did recognize it," Michael continued, "and I suppose I ought to have made a clean breast of things right then. But it's embarrassing, and there is so much at stake."

"What do you mean?" Richard asked, forestalling what I suspected might be Philip's attempt to get us back onto the subject of preparations for his ceremony.

"Well, first, the rod is antique, you see, and I would like to have it back, but the fact is that after death duties, we haven't really any money to spare. I honestly depend on my Ashmolean salary to keep body and soul together."

"And second?"

"Second is the Fletcher connection. I'm mostly certain, as certain as I can be without those DNA tests, that it was Major Fletcher who died honorably in the service of his country, and not Lord Aberlour. Indeed, I think Aberlour made a quick and cowardly retreat from the continent of Europe as soon as he, having been wounded, saw a chance to switch places with a dead American."

"I thought," Richard said, "that Chuck Fletcher—the person we thought was Chuck Fletcher—had a distinguished career in the European theater."

"Oh, he did, certainly—but that was before my Uncle David switched places with him. I have to say, just to complete this whole sordid tale, that I suspect my father eventually connived with his older brother's deception, though he would have been too young to know about it at the time it happened. Uncle David had no interest in the family inheritance—witness his casual attitude toward this baton—and in those days, there was no way to abdicate from a noble title, despite the Duke of Windsor's royal example. So my father got the inheritance, Uncle David got a new life in the Americas, and I, the late-born next generation, eventually got six pleasant summers of camping at the school Uncle David had loved."

"Well, you're certainly welcome to have your property back," Richard said. "I'm sure I speak for the Superintendent in saying that Annandale has no interest in keeping the baton away from its rightful owner." He ceremoniously handed the thing past me, and Michael took it from him with equal solemnity.

"You guys have no idea how great that looks—hey!" Philip's compliments to his own set design were interrupted by an owl which, apparently flying in through the open doors, made a line almost straight toward him, then swerved, just as he ducked, and flew upward to perch someplace in the darkling upper reaches of the hall.

"I see you have a lot of confidence in that armor, Phil," Richard laughed.

"It's a reflex," he answered. "Besides, I was worried about the bird hurting itself if it flew into me. Didn't I read about this in a history book somewhere?"

"Yes," Richard said, "it's in Bede's *Ecclesiastical History*. An English king is trying to decide whether or not to accept the Christian missionaries, and one of his noblemen says that life is like a sparrow flying into a bright warm mead hall and then back into the outer darkness. If someone can tell us about the dark parts, we should be grateful for the message."

"Right, that's it," Phil replied. "Doesn't seem like this one is in any hurry to fly out, though."

"Give it some time. You can always send some kids up to shoo it out from the balcony after the ceremony."

"Oh, sure. I guess I'm just nervous. But there really isn't anything to do until the cadets get here."

"Exactly. So relax while you can."

Michael had been fiddling with the ribbon and plastic additions to the family heirloom, presumably to see how hard it would be to restore its original appearance. I, meanwhile, had been doing some genealogical reflection.

"Speaking of rightful owners, Michael," I observed, as casually as I could, "wouldn't your theory mean that Doug Fletcher would be, well, the rightful earl, now that both of your fathers have passed away? And if Doug Fletcher is involved, as he seems to be, with the same Neo-pagan group as Thomas Dixon and Hudson Buchanan, isn't it likely that he's the one who has been trying to get the baton back? And given the methods we've seen already, doesn't it seem as though he must think the baton has some magic properties?"

"All reasonable conclusions, Jonathan," he said, glancing up for a moment. "Cousin Douglas is certainly the rightful Earl of Strathspey, assuming that his father wouldn't have been shot before he was born if the whole plot had been found out. He has, however, shown no more interest in the title than Uncle David did. And, yes, I'm sure that it has been he who has been trying to recover the baton. And finally, yes, both David and Douglas seem to share ideas about magic that run back in our family at least as far as the trial of the Lancashire witches—innocent old women, I imagine, who served as scapegoats for my less-than-innocent ancestor: and I suppose such ideas include some secret tradition about the baton. But we've all seen you handle it without any effects, and concluded that the baton is no more than it appears to be."

"Yes, but," Phil said, by now becoming interested in spite of himself, "everyone knows the old saying about appearances. Whoever said Jon's handling something was a perfect magic detector?"

"No one, I suppose, Phil," Michael answered, "though I'm afraid I may have come close to suggesting as much on Monday. But I've already admitted I was being a bit misleading then." He sighed theatrically. "We do have some time before the cadets arrive. Let me see if I can cast some light on this whole business."

He stood, and walked away from the throne. As he did so, the candles and electric lights alike grew steadily brighter and redder, till the hall blazed with the crimson of his doubly-borrowed robe. "Let me have you consider this," he said, pointing a finger toward Phil's helmet, which sat on a table with the other props for the ceremony. The helm was immediately lost within a cylinder of sapphire blue light. "Similar phenomena don't necessarily proceed from similar causes." He lowered his hand, and the light went out. "One reason, though not the only one, why we thought Jonathan's touching the baton might show its magical quality was simply that there had been a display like that one when he picked up the Alfred Jewel. I'm sorry to have to say that the effect, like the jewel, was a fake supplied by me. The vision, I hasten to add, was authentic—at least, I had nothing to do with it—but the light, I confess, was a fraud. The real Alfred Jewel, I think, would not have reacted to Jonathan's touch, any more than the baton did when he touched it on Monday afternoon."

"I think I see," Richard said, "but let me ask just to be sure: why not?"

"Because the jewel is broken; or, conversely, the rod is broken. In either case, they belong together, like this." He took what was, I supposed, the real jewel out of his pocket and fitted it easily on top of the ivory wand. He gestured tentatively with it. "There, you see, it holds together all on its own, without rivets, solder, or superglue."

"Neat," said Phil. "What does it actually do?"

"It was meant, I think, to ensure victory. I believe that the stone was consecrated as an offering at the senatorial Altar of Victory, probably by Quintus Aurelius Symmachus. The ivory rod itself was a consul's staff of office, and either belonged to Symmachus or is part of the magical project that Boethius was working on when he was locked away—both of them were consuls. The goldwork suggests that either the piece was never completed in antiquity, or that it came to King Alfred in need of refurbishment. Originally, of course, 'victory' would have meant preserving the unity of the Empire and, most likely, driving those pesky Christians out of power. I imagine it also worked, though, to drive off the Spanish Armada and to hold the Vikings at bay."

"It doesn't seem to have been much help at the Battle of Hastings," Phil observed.

"I doubt whether King Harold had it, and, if he did, whether Edward taught him to use it. It's an established fact that some of the Anglo-Saxon regalia were buried with King Edward and only recovered much later."

"True enough," Richard said. "But I'm like Phil, Michael—what does the little gizmo actually do?"

"That depends, my cousin would say, on what one is able to dare. Consider Mr. Dixon, for example, who isn't really a very big cog in the machine. Everyone seems to have agreed with the conclusion that he was able to teleport himself away from Jonathan's house, ignoring the simpler explanation that, having slipped away from the deputies for only a moment, he made himself invisible. That's a relatively easy piece of magic. *Actually* moving from one place to another—" there was a flash, and he stood on the balcony "—requires far more skill, or the help of an object like this." He leapt over the low stone balustrade and floated gently back down to the floor. "One doesn't even require a broom," he grinned.

"Awesome," Phil said, and I couldn't disagree. These were not, perhaps, useful magical skills, but they were things Danny, Rhys, Caroline and I had never managed to learn.

"The next logical question, then," I said, "is, What is your cousin able to dare?"

"You think I'm joking," Michael answered, "but he really does aim at the extermination of Christianity and the revival of classical paganism. It's been a hundred years since Nietzsche exposed Christianity to the world as a slave morality, suited only to pathetic sheep, but Nietzsche could only argue for an abstract philosophy in its place. And none of the magics and Neo-paganisms that have come along since than have really been able to do more than burn incense and dance around in the nude. The person who has this artifact will be able to show that paganism is not only a noble philosophy, it actually works. People want power, and Douglas talks about a religion that will put it into their hands."

"How can you tell religion from magic?" Phil asked.

"Some say that you cannot; Douglas would say that it makes no difference."

"What I'm wondering is, who gets the toys?" Richard said, standing to pace around a bit as he spoke. "Surely he doesn't imagine more than one person using that baton at a time."

"No, there would still have to be a priesthood—a Pontifex Maximus and all. But the Popes have kept that title warm over the course of the centuries."

"Admittedly," I said. "Yet you wouldn't expect me to agree with your cousin that religion doesn't work and magic does. There's a place in *Huckleberry Finn* where Huck gives up on religion when God doesn't answer his prayers for a fishhook. If magic could give him a fishhook, so could a passing fisherman. Religion is supposed to be about giving him something else."

"Like what, Jon?" Phil asked.

"Hope. Peace. The courage to be. The answer to the feeling of absolute dependence. The knowledge of God, according to the extent of his capacity for knowledge. Self-sacrificing love, on my understanding of it."

"But didn't Jesus actually give people fish and bread and wine?"

"I suppose so, yes, Philip, but those actions are all consciously symbolic." By now, I was growing animated, and stood up to pace around myself. "If Jesus wasn't pointing to something more than food, he should've done something to eliminate hunger, rather than just cater a meal or two."

"But, my dear Bishop," Michael said, "you, of all people, have religion *and* magic at your disposal. What about your flock who have to get by with that hope that you mentioned? Douglas might claim that they were better off with his offering than yours, if they could have only one."

"Except," Richard objected, "that, as you've already said, he isn't proposing to give them either one. He keeps all the power to himself."

"Which brings me to the point," I said. "I'm as willing as anyone else to discuss theology—more so, for that matter. But what do we do to prevent your cousin from making himself the first pagan Pontifex Maximus since 381?"

"That's not exactly the plan. Douglas has, for some reason, a curious attachment to Jupiter the Best and Greatest, who had his own particular priest."

"The *flamen dialis*," Richard added.

"Exactly. It's an obscure office, but I have to say I don't see any reason to keep it from him."

At this point, finally, suspicion gained the upper hand in some part of my internal debate, and I extended my ring's defenses over Richard and Philip, letting its golden light play against the red. Michael acknowledged this with a slight nod of the head. "Locking the proverbial barn door, I'm afraid," he said.

"I don't get it, Jon," Phil said. "What's with the extra fireworks?"

"I'm afraid Jonathan has realized my last little bit of misdirection. He's been hearing me prattle on about Douglas and his ideas, and if I may play mind reader for a moment, I imagine he has been thinking, 'Well, yes, fine, we don't want that fellow to have the baton, but what's the alternative?' After all, one could simply take the whole piece back to the Ashmolean, though in that case there would have been little reason to bring the jewel here in the first place. But if Cousin Douglas isn't going to be top dog in the new pagan order, who is?"

"I see," Phil answered. "Modesty forbids you to say."

"Just so. Douglas and I have in fact been cooperating on this project for some little while."

"I don't see any reason for this to be melodramatic," Richard said. "If you and Doug Fletcher want to revive paganism and use magic to do it, go ahead and try; and if Jonathan and his family want to defend Christianity and keep their magic out of it, good for them. Time will tell."

Michael smiled wryly. "The free market applied to religion. You do make it sound attractive. But I'm conscious of the time, and I'm afraid that we have other arrangements under way: undercutting the competition, so to speak. My cousin, with appropriate help, should be dropping in on the Bishop's brother at any moment to invite him to join our party in the park, and Jonathan and I will be joining them. Sadly, as there are one or two felonies involved in the process, I shall have to arrange for you and Phil to forget this whole conversation—replacing it with some idea or another that the Bishop and I were called away on important business. Douglas, you see, is fascinated with the perfect sacrifice to Jupiter Feretrius, the so-called *spolia opima*—a phrase that means literally 'the nourishing plunder.' It's a sacrifice to give thanks for victory, on the one hand, and, at the same time, to insure the future growth of the state."

"A human sacrifice," I said.

"Well, yes, Bishop, but one reserved for the highest enemies of the Roman state. The four of you will be in the best of company." He gestured, and immediately Rhys and Caroline were standing with us, their hands caught back with plastic twist ties and their mouths covered with duct tape. Above the tape, they glared out with almost identical looks of fury. Behind them, closer to Phil, and holding nothing more magical than a pistol, was Hudson Buchanan, looking somewhat glassy-eyed. All three were cloaked in crimson light.

"Despite his pathetic career in witchcraft," Michael observed to no one in particular, "he has no skill for magic at all—but a real affinity for hypnosis. Brother Buchanan is, however woozy, perfectly capable of using that weapon, gentlemen. I don't think yellow light will protect you against bullets. Just a little precaution against mundane interference, and a reminder to you two youngsters not to try anything."

I had tried, even before he had a chance to make this little speech, to extend my own shield, but pushing the golden dome against the red was the psychic equivalent of pushing against a stone wall—or, rather, a locomotive: for while he was speaking, he thrust back my defense, to the point where it covered only me where I stood near the triple throne. Obviously, he could have eliminated it entirely, if he'd chosen to.

Just then, however, Michael faced mundane interference of a sort he'd probably not imagined, as the owl we'd seen earlier stooped down on him, falling straight toward his face. The bird represented no real threat, I suppose, but the instinct to cover one's face is a powerful one, and distracting, while it lasts. In this case, it was enough to preoccupy Michael for a moment, enough for him to lose his grip on the wand. Richard dove to grab it, and as the red shield faltered, I pushed back against it. Even without the wand, however, Michael put up a strong resistance, and he succeeded in recovering the object before Richard could take it.

In the meantime, however, Philip had taken advantage of the moment. Brother Buchanan was not standing particularly close to him—certainly well beyond arm's reach. He was an easy target, though, for a two-handed sword, and Philip spun around with his like a glittering disk, catching Buchanan squarely above the ear with the flat of the blade, and knocking him down and out.

Free of Buchanan's numbing influence, the kids immediately established our telepathic connection. *Let's do it*, Rhys thought, and with the three of us, we were able to put up a more credible effort, pushing against the ruby shield from two sides, as it were. *Where's Dan?* I thought.

"Right here, big brother," he said, suddenly appearing beside me. "I'd been doing some fairly intense studying, but I was interrupted by the real Lord Strathspey. Allow me to introduce you." He gestured, and Doug Fletcher was standing near Philip. Like Rhys and Caroline, he was bound and gagged, but his restraints were made of pale blue light. With another twitch of Dan's finger, Rhys and Caroline were free. A third, and Abbot Alfred appeared, the owl flying to perch on his shoulder.

"Now," Dan said, "John-Michael Aubrey Bruce-Porter, wit thou well, that thou art here overmatched. Thou seest thy cousin already my prisoner, awaiting his just doom. For that thou hast with him in privy conspiracy compassed mine own death, and the deaths of those most near to me in blood and affection, and that by black treachery, thou knowest that I owe thee no quarter, nor any measure of respite. Thou knowest the law of this high art, 'Do what thou wilt, an thou harm none,' and thou knowest, too, that evil returneth on its sender three-fold. And yet, saving the reverence of this my brother and our Holy Mother the Church, I would not handle thee

406 — John William Houghton

here according to thy deserts, but rather by the precepts of mercy. Do thou now, therefore, abjure thy power and all the arts arcane, and submit thee to me: or else abide not my judgment alone."

It was a speech our ancestors might have made in verse, but I assumed the archaic English would be equally effective to solemnize Dan's language, as ritual magic required. Michael, however, affected to greet it with contempt. "Are you trying to condescend to me, Daniel Mears? I'm afraid you really don't understand the power of the jewel." He pointed over his head, and a chunk of the banister tore loose.

"Look out, Dr. Davies," Rhys shouted, but he needn't have bothered—Danny stopped it in midair and, without even a hint of a lapse of concentration on our defense or Doug's restraints, lowered it to the floor at Richard's feet. He was, I could tell, drawing strength from the rest of us, but using it more effectively than we had ever imagined. *Neat trick*, I thought, and Caroline replied, *He says, "Just wait."*

Aloud, he said, "Nay, rather, thou little wittest its power or its nature. But as thou hast chosen, so mote it be. I arrest thee of sorcery by the name of Michael, pretended Lord Strathspey." He clenched his fist, and coils of sapphire blue tightened around the red. Michael seemed to draw on some deep reserve of strength, as his defense was about to collapse altogether, and poured it all into a fiery tongue of power.

But Danny had anticipated him—or, indeed, provoked him: for, rather than resist this onslaught, Dan directed it, instead, turning it toward the triple throne. There it flattened and flowed around every surface of the ancient wood, until the whole piece glowed; and then, suddenly, throned on the light itself, the three guardians of the jewel whom I had seen over the previous weeks appeared. I glanced at Richard and Phil and could tell from their expressions that this time it was not just I who saw the ancient visitors. Dan turned his hand to force Michael around, but he need hardly have bothered, for the king, queen and consul commanded all of our attention.

It was Elizabeth who spoke for the three of them. "You know us, prisoner at the bar, and you cannot doubt that we know you and your deeds, seeing them as they were and as they might have been, in the Highest Cause. What will you say, then, lest the treble vengeance of the arts arcane be imposed upon you?"

"I say defiance of you all and of your pretended highest cause. My power is my cause and highest law, beneath the judgments of the elder gods."

"They are pretended gods, the rebel angels whom the Emperor on high holds ever in despite. You err if you imagine they will honor you."

"My honor is my own; it does not need increase from any man or god."

"So be it, then: To those in whom you put your trust we do commit you."

Across the room, Abbot Alfred caught my eye and silently held up his hands, as if to show his palms. It was, he knew, a gesture that would remind me of Christ showing his wounded hands to the disciples after his Resurrection, a sign of God's mercy, extended even to friends who had deserted him.

"An it please Your Majesty," I said. "This man is young, and even his cousin, of whom Your Majesty has not spoken here, has many years before him. Ought they now to be cut off from all hope, when mercy now might lead to repentance in the end?"

"Right Reverend Father, this one, at least, is a declared enemy of God and his Christ."

"But even so, Madam, as the illustrious ex-consul has taught us, if the evil are suffered to persist in evil, they work only their own condemnation."

"He also teaches that to punish the evil is to do them good."

"None the less, that the evil should repent is better, for 'the Lord God desireth not the death of sinners, but that we should repent and be saved.' "

"Then what would you have us do, Bishop?"

"Can you not deprive them of the power that my brother demanded that they yield, and take away from them as well their knowledge of magic?"

She raised one painted eyebrow. "You would leave them the desire for power, with no way of obtaining it?"

"Without knowing the desire for power, madam, we may never understand our true powerlessness, nor hope in the power supreme."

"Very well. Here you are apostle, prophet and chief pastor, Christ's overseer for his holy church, and we will yield to your wisdom. Douglas Stewart Bruce-Porter, falsely named Fletcher, we shall return to the worship of his false gods along with Thomas Dixon, who knew nothing of the true purpose of this conspiracy. John-Michael Aubrey Bruce-Porter, falsely Lord Strathspey, shall know only that he brought the true jewel here, hoping that the ivory rod was its proper mate, and that the learned doctor freely returned it to him. Inasmuch as either his uncle or his cousin could in time have renounced the title, we will not deprive him of it, and he will not remember the letter you have read. Hudson Buchanan we deem their victim rather than an accomplice, and as he truly believes the Gospel, we will release him to preach it without their domination.

"Hear us, then, you sorcerers both: your power is forfeit, though your lives be spared, and from henceforth you shall remember nothing of what you have plotted. Neither shall you remember or learn anew true magic, either small or great. So mote it be."

Dan released the shackles from the two, and they slumped to the floor, unconscious. Richard hurried to Strathspey to pick up the rod, while Philip belatedly collected Buchanan's pistol.

"What about this?" Richard asked.

"I understand what the Queen said about Lord Strathspey, but can't you just take it apart, Dr. Davies?" Rhys asked.

"We could, Rhys," Danny answered, "but someone might put it together again."

"And we can't just destroy the jewel," Caroline observed.

"Not without getting a good deal more insurance for the University," I said.

"So then we should destroy the rod, after all," Richard said. "It will be a shame to lose it, but better that than someone abuse the power."

"It need not be destroyed," the Queen said. "The power placed within it can be transferred."

"But ma'am," said Rhys, "then we would face some other object of equal power."

"Unless the power were divided," Caroline said. "Not into two pieces that fit together like this, but into several independent items that would be less dangerous."

"Until someone gathered them up again," her father said.

"Forgive me if I'm interfering," Philip said, "but doesn't this power come from people in the first place?"

"Yes, Captain," Elizabeth answered, "from many people over the centuries, beginning with the lord Consul's great ancestor."

"Then, Your Majesty, couldn't the power be given back to a person—to the Bishop, or Mr. Mears, or Rhys or Caroline?"

We all shook our heads at once. "We have power enough, and to spare," Dan said.

"I wonder, though," said Caroline, "what about Brother Buchanan? Even if he had the power, it sounds as though he'd be unable to use it, and unwilling even if he were able."

"I'm not so sure," I said. "Michael did say he was unskilled, but it's telepathy that he seems to block. He certainly hasn't prevented people from using magic promiscuously here this evening."

"With all due respect," Abbot Alfred interjected, "I believe Her Majesty spoke imprecisely. The power in these magic items must surely have come from God originally, even though people made the things themselves."

"Surely, Father Abbot, for everything that has being must have it from God. But what use would you make of this commonplace?"

"If it please Your Majesty, could not the power of this thing be returned to God in the Holy Sacrament?"

For the first time, Elizabeth looked at the companions, as if in silent consultation. I remembered that she had been notoriously unwilling to insist on an opinion as to whether God is truly present in the Eucharistic bread and wine.

"It could be done," she replied, eventually. "Are there bread and wine at hand, and will the Bishop read the service?"

"I would, Madam, but in this diocese, the Sacrament is reserved. Perhaps my brother's newly found talents would extend to transporting Abbot Alfred to and from his chapel?"

"In an instant," Dan said, though it took a minute or two in fact. Presumably Alfred had to spend some time actually retrieving the Sacrament from its safekeeping in the chapel of All Angels. He returned with a monstrance, a glass chamber mounted in a gilded bronze sunburst on a stand, designed for the display of a single consecrated host, particularly at the service of Benediction. He set the object down on the table next to Philip's helmet, and Richard, genuflecting to the Sacrament, placed the wand next to it. They turned to the Queen, who said, "The Bishop can do what is required," and Alfred brought me the humeral veil, the vestment worn when carrying the monstrance (essentially a long strip of cloth draped over the shoulders and around the hands, its original purpose was nothing more sophisticated than protecting the gilding from priests' sweaty palms).

"The Lord be with you," I said.

"And also with you."

"Let us pray.

"God of all power and might, from whom descends every good and perfect gift, accept now the return of this gift of great power, and as your beloved Son has left us in this wonderful sacrament a memorial of his passion, grant us so to venerate the sacred mysteries of his body and blood, that we may ever perceive within ourselves the fruit of his redemption: who lives and reigns with you and the Holy Spirit, one God, forever and ever. Amen."

An arc of red light leapt from the jewel to the Host, like a welling fountain of bright blood that grew in brilliance until, for the moment it endured, it blinded us.

When our vision returned, the three guardians of the jewel were gone, and with them Doug Fletcher and Hudson Buchanan, each, I supposed, with appropriate adjustments to his memory. Michael was standing, apparently unsurprised to see the jewel and the rod reunited on the table in front of him.

I went forward to kneel before the monstrance and began to say the hymn St. Thomas Aquinas had written in honor of the Body of Christ:

> Therefore we before him bending
> This great sacrament revere:
> Types and shadows have their ending,
> For the newer rite is here:
> Faith, the outward sense befriending,
> Makes our inward vision clear.

Then, as I had done so often before, I stood to take the mystery of the world's redemption in my hands, to proclaim God's blessing on these friends and relatives, and even on this enemy, all kneeling around me on the gray stone floor of the high Gothic hall. On Michael, in the robes of his nobility, who might yet trust in something outside himself; on Richard in his gown and Philip in his armor, as if a medieval painter had set out to illustrate the idea of this military school, which had done so much to shape my life, and which I would, in the morning, reshape; on Alfred, after so short a time as Abbot, a strong tower of prayer, an abba, a father, to more than just his monastic family; on Caroline and Rhys, holding hands as in one of my earliest memories of them, still for a moment undetermined, still open to all the potential of the future; and on Dan, now in full possession of our heritage, a master mage like all our fathers before him. I lifted up the Word made flesh and blessed them all.

Baton Rouge, 23 September, 2000

Author's Note

THE COUNTY OF WABANA, the town of Annandale and its eccentric early citizen, John Marshall Glenarm, were the inventions of the Hoosier author Meredith Nicholson, in his 1905 novel *The House of a Thousand Candles*, though I have taken the liberty of replacing Nicholson's girls school (St. Agatha's) with a military academy.

Titchfield, Halesowen, Welbeck and Talyllychau were real houses of the Premonstratensian Order.

The original legend of Pau-koo-shuck can be found in Daniel McDonald, *A Twentieth Century History of Marshall County, Indiana* (Chicago: Lewis Publishing, 1908) I, 41-42. For the New England Vampires, see now Michael E. Bell, *Food for the Dead: On the Trail of New England's Vampires* (New York: Carroll & Graf, 2001).

The real Diocese of Northern Indiana in the Episcopal Church originally had its cathedral in Michigan City, but the resemblance between that judicature and the Anglican Diocese of Michigan City ends there; so, too, with the Barker Mansion in Michigan City and Jonathan Mears's Palace, and Hoghton Tower (really visited by King James and perhaps Shakespeare's hide-out as a young man) and Preston Tower.

The Ashmolean Museum contains, as it happens, both the original Alfred Jewel and a facsimile (displayed for comparison purposes next to the Minster Lovell Jewel). The details of Lord Strathspey's argument are my own, but Professor Kornbluth's paper is quite real: I don't know whether she or I was the more surprised when I realized that we were sharing an elevator at the International Medieval Congress in Kalamazoo and inflicted on her the story of Bishop Mears's dealings with the Jewel.

MY THANKS ARE DUE to The Rev'd Eileen Shanley-Roberts, Neal K. Keesee, Ph.D., Prof. T. A. Shippey, and Messrs. Louis Epstein and Ian Frederick, for their detailed comments on earlier versions of this story; to Charles King for his meticulous design; and to Robert Esther, M.D., Christopher Pruett, M.D., Richard Davies, Ph.D., J. M. B. Porter, Ph.D., the late Rev'd Leigh Axton Williams, J.D., the late John A. Acker, Jr., and Messrs. Austin Barrett, Kurt Chauviere, Philip Cicero, Robert English, Jefferson Mills, Richard Platt, and Bradley Peniston for permission to name persons in this story after them. I need hardly add that the characters themselves are entirely fictional, and neither their personalities, sentiments nor actions reflect those of their namesakes. This is all the more true of my Mears ancestors, who were, so far as I know, all peaceful farmers in the Meon Valley of Hampshire.

Printed in the United States
200319BV00010B/46-51/A

9 781588 321244